Sill

is

The

Collection

Three very different,
complete love stories.
Something for every mood…

Ryder's Wife—Sharon Sala
Sensation: *passionate, dramatic and thrilling*

The Littlest Marine—Maureen Child
Desire: *intense, provocative and sensual*

Wife in the Mail—Marie Ferrarella
Special Edition: *vivid, satisfying, full of family, life and love*

SHARON SALA

is a child of the country. As a farmer's daughter, she found that her vivid imagination made solitude a thing to cherish. During her adult life, she learned to survive by taking things one day at a time. An inveterate dreamer, she yearned to share the stories her imagination created. For Sharon, her dreams have come true, and she claims one of her greatest joys is when her stories become tools for healing.

MAUREEN CHILD

was born and raised in Southern California, USA and is the only person she knows who longs for an occasional change of season. She is delighted to be writing for Silhouette Books, and is especially excited to be a part of the Desire line.

An avid reader, she looks forward to those rare rainy California days when she can curl up and sink into a good book. Or two. When she isn't busy writing, she and her husband of twenty-five years like to travel, leaving their two grown children in charge of the neurotic golden retriever who is the *real* head of the household.

MARIE FERRARELLA

lives in southern California. She describes herself as the tired mother of two over-energetic children and the contented wife of one wonderful man. This Romance Writers of America RITA award-winning author is thrilled to be following her dream of writing full-time.

The Romance Collection

Ryder's Wife

Sharon Sala

The Littlest Marine

Maureen Child

Wife in the Mail

Marie Ferrarella

First published in Great Britain 2003
Silhouette Books, Eton House, 18-24 Paradise Road, Richmond, Surrey TW9 1SR

ISBN 0 373 04932 3

55-0103

Printed and bound in Spain
by Litografia Rosés S.A., Barcelona

Contents

Dear Reader,

We're very proud and excited to be able to offer you three lovely books by three very popular and successful Silhouette authors, brought together in this wonderful three-in-one collection.

These three books represent the kind of stories that you would find in our Scnsation, Desire and Special Edition series, and offer the perfect opportunity to sample lines you might not have tried before.

Look out for more from all of these authors—Sharon Sala features in Sensation in March, Maureen Child has stories coming up in Desire in March and April, and keep an eye open for Marie Ferrarella in next month's Special Edition selection.

So as you can see, there are plenty of chances to pick up something new from one of these writers over the next few months now that you've discovered them!

All the best,

The Editors

Ryder's Wife

Sharon Sala

Magic comes to us in myriad forms. There is magic in the beauty of a sunrise, in the reflection on a dewdrop hanging from the petals of a rose. A mother's touch is magic when it soothes a crying child. And laughter is magic that no medicine can match.

There have been many magic moments in my life that are mine alone to keep. But I would like to acknowledge the two people who have made their own kind of magic in helping me create this world in which I write.

To Meredith Bernstein—an agent extraordinaire who stands behind me faithfully and does not know the meaning of the word 'no'.

To Jan Goldstoff—a publicist with a golden touch, whose visions are exceeded only by her persistence.

Prologue

December—on the plains near Abilene, Texas

Heat penetrated the black void of unconsciousness in which Ryder Justice was drifting. Even in the depths from which he was trying to escape, he smelled the hair burning on the backs of his arms and knew another level of fear. He moaned, and the movement of air through his lungs yanked him rudely into the now. Gritting his teeth against the pain racking his every breath, he struggled to sit upright. Acrid smoke drifted up his nose, mingling with the coppery taste of fresh blood as he fumbled with the latch to his seat belt. That which had most probably saved his life was now holding him hostage.

A sheet of rain blew in the broken window to his left and into his eyes. It was as effective as a slap in the face. Cognizance returned full force.

Just beyond the crumpled cockpit, he could see flames licking at the metal and eating their way toward him, and he remembered being up in the sky, and getting caught in the storm. A stroke of lightning lit up the night sky and he flinched as he remembered another bolt of lightning and how the plane had shuddered, then rocked. And afterward, the sensation of an electric free fall.

An instinct for survival pushed past the misery of broken ribs and bleeding cuts, past the bone-jarring ache that came with every movement, every breath. He'd survived being struck by lightning. The plane had crashed and he was still alive to tell the tale. By God, he would not sit here and burn to death when he still had legs to crawl.

And at that moment, he remembered he was not alone. He turned.

"Dad?"

Another streak of lightning snaked across the sky, momentarily illuminating what was left of the cabin. After that, Ryder had only the encroaching fire by which to see, but it was more than enough. Stunned by the horror of what the crash had done to Micah Justice, he refused to believe what his mind already knew.

The straps holding him in place suddenly came free and Ryder struggled to get out of his seat. Ignoring wave after wave of pain-filled nausea, he freed his father from the seat and managed to get them both out of the wreckage and into the falling rain.

Sometimes crawling, sometimes pushing, he dragged himself and his father's lifeless body until he found himself beneath some sort of overhang.

Shivering from pain, shock, and the chill of rain-soaked clothing, he scooted as far back as he could get beneath the outcropping of rocks, pulling Micah's body with him, then cradling his father's head against his chest as he would have a sleeping child.

A gust of wind cornered the overhang, blowing rain and a peppering of hail on Ryder's outstretched legs, and at that moment the fuselage blew, erupting into the night in an orange ball of fire. Ryder closed his eyes against the blast, and held his father that much tighter, refusing to accept the motion as wasted effort.

"Dad?"

Again, Micah Justice did not answer. There was no familiar, sarcastic chuckle, no awkward pat from a strong man's hands for comfort. Ryder buried his face against the back of his father's shirt and took a long, aching breath. He knew, but his heart wasn't ready to face the truth.

"Dad...come on, Dad. You can do this. You've told me time and time again that it takes a hell of a lot to put a Justice man down."

Thunder rumbled across the sky, and the deep angry rumble sounded like his heart felt as grief began to settle. His arms tightened around his father's body, and for the first time since the accident had happened, tears began to fall, mingling with the raindrops clinging to Ryder's scorched and battered face.

Holding his father close, he began to rock, muttering beneath his breath and in his father's ear, although Micah Justice had already moved beyond the sound of his second son's voice.

"Please, Dad, talk to me." Ryder's voice broke. "Dad... Daddy, don't do this," he pleaded. "Don't leave us. We need you. All of us need you. Roman will go to hell without you on his case...and Royal, think of Royal. What will happen to the ranch and Royal if you don't wake up?"

A second explosion followed on the tail of the first—smaller, but still powerful in intensity. Bits of burning metal shot up into the sky and then fell down upon the ground nearby. Another flash of lightning, this time closer, revealed more of the truth Ryder Justice had been trying to deny. Micah was dead. Probably upon impact. And he was left with an inescapable fact. His father was dead, and he'd been piloting the plane. This time, when thunder rumbled overhead, it drowned out the sounds of Ryder Justice's grief.

Chapter 1

July—Ruban Crossing, Mississippi

"Casey, darling, you should never wear black. It makes you look like a crow."

Before Casey could take offense at what her half brother, Miles Dunn just said, he took a seat with the rest of the Ruban family, who were gathering for the reading of Delaney Ruban's will.

She picked a piece of lint from the skirt of her black silk dress and tilted her chin, reminding herself that she wasn't going to cry. Not now, and especially not in front of Lash Marlow, her grandfather's lawyer. Although he was sitting behind his desk and watching each arrival with a focused, predatory gaze, Casey was aware that he was also watching her every move. And it had been that way with them for more years than she cared to remember.

In spite of her love for her grandfather, Delaney Ruban, and in spite of Delaney's hopes that she and Lash might someday marry, Casey had been unable to bring herself to comply.

She'd been a willing student of Delaney's tutorial with regards to the Ruban empire, but she refused to give up what passed as the personal portion of her life. It didn't amount to much, but it was all she had that she could honestly call her own. Even more important, she didn't love Lash Marlow and had no intention of spending the rest of her life with a man who measured the value of a person by monetary worth.

She shifted nervously in her seat, wishing this day to be over. As Delaney's closest living relative and the heir who had been groomed to take over the vast Ruban holdings, she knew the task that lay ahead of her, right down to how many family members would be looking to her for sustenance.

Not for the first time since her grandfather's stroke six weeks ago did she wish her father and mother were still alive. And, if Chip Ruban hadn't taken his wife, Alysa, to Hawaii for their tenth wedding anniversary, they might still be. But he had, and they'd drowned in a boating accident off the coast of Oahu, leaving their only child, six-year-old Casey, as well as Alysa's ten-year-old twins from a previous marriage, to be raised by an absent and overbearing grandfather who quickly pawned off those duties to someone else.

Alysa's mother, Eudora Deathridge, was moved into the mansion and given full authority and responsibility of her daughter's children. And although she was Casey's grandmother as well, Casey found herself grasping for space in a lap already too full for one more small, six-year-old girl.

With the instinct of a child who knows where she is loved, she turned to Joshua Bass and his wife, Matilda. The butler and the cook. The kitchen became the center of her universe. In Tilly Bass's loving arms, she learned to trust and love again. On Joshua's shoulders, she saw the world in which she lived from a new and different angle, and in doing so, learned not to be afraid of reaching for the stars. They became the surrogate parents she had needed, and now, twenty years later, they were the anchors that kept her life on a straight and honorable path.

And while Tilly and Joshua nurtured and loved her, at thirteen years old, Casey suddenly became the focus of Delaney Ruban's world. He had looked up one day and realized that he wasn't getting any younger, and since Casey was his son's only child, she was, of course, to be his heir.

He looked for the child he'd all but ignored and found a girl on the brink of womanhood. Elated that she'd grown up so well without much of his effort, he decided that it was time she branched out past the familiarity of her school, her friends and Tilly Bass's kitchen.

And so it began. The treat of accompanying him on business trips became the first step in a lifelong education. Before long, Casey was spending all of her summers with him at his office. At first, she blossomed under his tutoring. Her grandfather had never given her anything but presents, and now he was sharing his time with her. It took the better part of Casey's teenage years before she realized Delaney's reasons for spending time with her were selfish. Someone must step into his shoes when he was gone. He'd decided it would be Casey.

And now, at twenty-six, Casey was about to become CEO of a multimillion-dollar corporation with holdings in everything from cotton mills to racehorses. Thanks to the last ten years of Delaney's coaching, she was more than up to the task.

A low murmur of indistinguishable voices hummed behind her like a worn-out motor, rising and falling with the advent of each new person to enter the room. She closed her eyes and took a deep breath. It wasn't the job that daunted her. It was those who were gathering. They were the ones who would be waiting for her to fail.

Someone else touched her on the shoulder. She looked up. It was her sister, Erica.

"Nice dress, Casey darling." Erica's eyes glittered sharply as she fingered the fabric. "I suppose it has a silver lining, too. Just like your life."

"Erica, really," Eudora Deathridge said, and gave her eldest granddaughter a none-too-gentle nudge as they moved past Casey to take their seats.

Casey let the comment roll off her shoulders, and as the women passed by her Eudora squeezed Casey's arm. It was nothing new. Miles and Erica had begrudged Casey everything from the day she was born—from being a Ruban, to being the one Delaney had chosen to follow in his footsteps. In all their lives, they had shared a mother, but little else.

Lash Marlow cleared his throat, well aware that the sound added to the building tension. ''I believe we are all here now. Shall we begin?''

Casey's pulse accelerated. She gripped the arms of the chair, focusing on the man behind the desk and was struck by an odd, almost satisfied smile on Lash's face. Reluctantly, she accepted the fact that he was privy to secrets about their lives she wished he did not know. It made her feel vulnerable, and vulnerability was a weakness Rubans were not allowed to feel. She watched as Marlow shifted in his seat and straightened the papers in front of him. It was the will. Delaney's will.

Fresh tears spiked her lashes as she struggled with composure, trying to come to terms with the fact that Delaney was dead. He'd been such a large and vital man that overlooking his age had been simple. But nature had not been as kind. Despite his ebullient personality and lust for life, the past eighty-two years had taken their toll. And no matter how hard he had tried to ignore the inevitable, he had failed.

Ultimately, Lash began to read and Casey's mind wandered, only now and then tuning in on his voice as it droned into the ominous quiet of the room. Once in a while a low murmur of voices became noticeable behind her, and she supposed Miles and Erica were voicing their opinions of the bequeathals being read.

''And to my beloved granddaughter, Casey Dee Ruban...''

Casey shook off the fugue in which she'd been hanging and focused.

''...the bulk of my estate and the home in which she's been residing since her parents' death, as well as the controlling reins of Ruban Enterprises. But to inherit...''

Startled, her gaze slid from the papers in Lash's hands to his face. What did he mean...to inherit? Have mercy, what has Delaney done?

''To qualify for the entire aforementioned inheritance, my granddaughter, Casey Dee Ruban, must marry within forty-eight hours of the reading of my will, and must live with her husband, in his residence and under his protection, for the duration of at least one year, or she will forfeit her birthright. If she chooses not to adhere to my last request, then the bulk of my estate will be deeded to my step-grandchildren, Miles and Erica Dunn.''

Casey stood. Rage, coupled with a shock she couldn't deny made her shake, but the tremor never reached her voice. She looked at Lash: at his cool, handsome face, his blond, wavy hair, his pale green eyes. Her eyes darkened as she leaned forward, bracing herself against his desk.

''Surely I cannot be held to this!''

To his credit, Lash's gaze never wavered. ''I'm sorry, Casey. I know this must come as a shock, but I can assure you it's legal. Your grandfather was of sound mind and body when this was written. I tried to talk him out of such an unreasonable clause, but...''

When Lash shrugged, as if to say it was out of his hands, she looked away.

Someone choked in the back of the room. Casey didn't have to look to know that it was probably Miles, reveling in his unexpected windfall.

A red haze swam before her eyes and she willed herself not to faint. Marry? She hadn't seriously dated a man in over five years. The only man who persisted in being a part of her life was...

She looked up. The expression on Lash's face was too calm, almost expectant. How long had he known about this? Even worse, what had he and Delaney planned?

She swayed, staggered by the idea of being bound to Lash Marlow by law, as well as in the eyes of God, even for so much as a year.

Lash stood. His voice was low, his touch solicitous as he tried to take her in his arms.

''Casey, I'm here. Let me help you—''

She stepped back. The selfish glitter in Lash's eyes was too obvious to ignore.

Damn you, Delaney, damn you to hell.

She walked out of the room, leaving those behind to wonder what the outcome might be.

Hours later, the sun was about to set on the day as a low-slung black sports car rounded the corner of an unpaved road down in the flatlands. The trailing rooster tail of dust was evidence of how fast the car was traveling. The skid the car took as it cornered was proof of Casey Ruban's desperate state of mind. She'd been driving for hours, trying to think of a way out of her dilemma without having to acquiesce to the terms of her grandfather's will.

By naming Miles and Erica as the recipients of his estate should she default, Delaney had been certain Casey would comply. He'd been well aware of her disdain for the sycophantic life-style her half brother and half sister had chosen to live. They were thirty years old. Both had college degrees. Neither saw fit to use them.

Therefore, he had surmised that Casey would ultimately agree to his conditions. And he also knew Casey had no special man in her life, which would most certainly make Lash the prime candidate to fulfill the terms of the will. But he hadn't counted on Casey's total defiance, or the wild streak of rebellion that had driven her deep into the Mississippi Delta.

A short while later, the sun was gone and it was the time of evening when the world existed in shades of gray, faded by distance or muted by overlying shadows. Ahead, Casey could just make out the blinking lights on what appeared to be a roadhouse.

The fact that Sonny's Place was in the middle of nowhere was of no consequence to her. What mattered were the number of cars and pickup trucks parked outside the building. It stood to reason there would be a large number of men inside.

Blinking back a fresh set of angry tears, she gritted her teeth, focusing on the decision she'd made. As she accelerated, her fingers gripped the steering wheel until her knuckles turned white.

She turned into the parking lot in a skid, slamming on her brakes and barely missing a truck parked beneath the wide-spread limbs of an ancient oak. Gravel spewed, spit out from beneath the wheels of her sports car like a bad taste.

Casey killed the engine and was out of the car before the dust had time to settle. There was a defiant tilt to her chin and determination in her stride as she started toward the entrance, yet when she stepped inside, a moment of unrefined terror swamped her. Dank air, thick smoke and the scent of stale beer hit her in the face like a slap. And then Lash's smirk flashed in her mind and she let the door swing shut behind her.

Ryder Justice sat with his back to the wall, nursing the same beer he'd bought over an hour earlier. He hadn't really wanted the drink, he'd just wanted a place to sit down.

The months and the miles since he'd walked out on his family and his business had long ago run together. He didn't know what day it was and didn't really care. All that mattered was staying on the move. It was the only way he knew to stay ahead of the memories that had nearly driven him insane.

A few words with the man at the next table had assured him he'd be sleeping on the ground again tonight. He was too far from a town to rent a room, and too nearly broke to consider wasting the money.

A grimy ceiling fan spun overhead, stirring the hot, muggy air without actually cooling it. He lifted the long-neck bottle, intent on draining what was left in one swallow when the door flew open and the woman walked into the room. Her appearance was sudden, as was the swift jolt of interest he felt when she lifted her hand to her face, pushing at the black tangle of her windblown hair that had fallen across her forehead.

She was taller than average, and the kind of woman who, at first glance, seemed on the verge of skinny. Except for the voluptuous curves of her breasts beneath the black, clinging fabric of her dress, she appeared shapeless. And then she turned suddenly, startled by the man who came in behind her, and as she did, the dress she was wearing flared, cupping slim, shapely hips before falling back into loose, generic folds.

Ryder's interest grew. It was fairly obvious that she wasn't the kind of woman who frequented places like this. Her movements were short, almost jerky, as if she were as surprised to find herself here as the men were to see her. And although he was some distance away, he thought she looked as if she'd been crying.

Who hurt you, pretty girl? What drove you into the flatlands?

The beer forgotten, he leaned forward, studying her face as one might study a map, wondering what—or who—had backed her into a corner. And he was certain she'd been backed into a corner or she wouldn't be here. He knew the look of desperation. It stared back at him every time he looked in a mirror. And like every other man in the place, he sat with anticipation, waiting for her to make the first move.

A half dozen dirty yellow lightbulbs dangled from a sagging fixture in the middle of the room. Only four of the bulbs were burning, cloaking the fog of cigarette smoke and dust with a sickly amber glow.

Heads turned and the understated rumble of voices trickled to a halt as Casey's eyes slowly adjusted to the lack of light. When she was certain she'd seen the location of every man in the place, she took a deep breath and sauntered into the middle of the room, well aware that each man was mentally stripping her—from the black silk dress flaring just above her knees to the opaque black stockings on her legs.

Behind her, she heard the bartender gasp then mutter the name Ruban. She'd been recognized! Her lips firmed. It would seem that even down here in the Delta she was unable to escape the power of Delaney Ruban's name.

Smoke drifted, burning her eyes and searing her nostrils with the acrid odor, yet she refused to move away. She turned slowly, judging the faces before her, looking for a man who might have the guts to consider what she was about to ask.

The bartender interrupted her train of thought.

''Miss, is there something I can do? Are you having car trouble? If you are, I'd be more than glad to call a tow truck for you.''

There was nervous fear on the bartender's face. Casey knew just how he felt. Her own stomach was doing a few flops of its own. She shivered anxiously, and at that point, almost walked out of the room. But as she turned to go, the image of Lash Marlow's face slid into her mind. It was all the impetus she needed. She turned again, this time putting herself between the men and the door.

''I need something all right,'' Casey said, and when she heard her voice break, she cleared her throat and took a deep breath. This time when she spoke, her words came out loud and clear. ''I don't need a tow truck. I need a man.''

The bartender grabbed a shotgun from beneath the bar and jacked a shell into the chamber as the room erupted.

Wide-eyed, Casey spun toward the sound.

The appearance of the gun was enough to quiet the ruckus she'd started, but only momentarily. When the bartender began to speak, she knew her chances of succeeding were swiftly fading.

"Hold your seats, men. That there is Casey Ruban. Old Delaney Ruban's granddaughter, so unless you're real tired of living, I suggest you suck it up and stay where you're at. This shotgun won't do nearly as much harm to you as the Rubans can."

"I heard he's dead," someone muttered from the back of the room.

"But the rest of them aren't," the bartender said.

Casey spun toward the men in sudden anger. "Let me finish."

At that point, they were so caught up in what she'd said, they would have let her do anything she asked.

"I need a husband."

Someone cursed, another laughed a little nervously.

Casey chose to ignore it all. "I'm willing to marry the first unattached man who's got the guts to stand with me against my family."

When no one moved or spoke, hope began to die. This was a crazy idea, as crazy as what Delaney had done to her, but she couldn't bring herself to quit. Not yet.

With an overwhelming sense of hopelessness and a shame unlike anything she'd ever known, she lifted her head, selling herself in the only way she knew how. She started walking, moving between the tables, staying just out of reach of the daring men's grasp.

"I'll live with you. Cook your food. I'll even share your bed."

Total silence reigned and Casey could hear their harsh, rasping breaths as they considered taking her to bed and suffering the consequences. If this hadn't been so pitiful, she would have smiled. It would seem that Delaney was going to win after all.

A sound came out of the shadows. The sound of chair legs scraping against the grit and dirt on the old wooden floor, and the unmistakable rap of boot heels marking off the distance between Casey and the back of the room. She squinted against the smoke and the harsh, overhead glare, trying to see, and then when she did, felt an overwhelming urge to run.

The man had *don't care* in his walk and the coldest eyes she'd ever seen. Their deep gray-blue cast was the color of a Mississippi sky running before a storm front. An old, olive drab duffel bag hung awkwardly on the breadth of his shoulders, as if it had to find a place of its own somewhere between the chip and the weight of the world.

He was tall, his clothing worn and ragged. But it was the still expression on his tanned, handsome face that gave her pause.

Before she had time to consider the odds of winding up face-down and dead in a ditch at some murderer's hands, he was standing before her.

Casey took a deep breath. Murderer be damned. Her grandfather had already signed her fate. At least she was going to be the one who controlled the strings to which it was attached.

"Well?" she asked, and surprised herself by not flinching when he reached out and brushed at a wild strand of hair that had been stuck to her cheek.

Ryder Justice was surprised by the vehemence in her voice. He'd been around long enough to know when someone was afraid. From the moment she'd walked into the room, her fear had been palpable, yet just now when he'd touched her, she hadn't blinked. And the power in her voice told him there was more to her backbone than the soft, silky skin obviously covering it. He also knew what it felt like to be backed into a corner, and for some reason this woman was as far in a hole as a person could get and not be buried. And, he was tired of running. So damned tired he couldn't think.

"Well, what?" he asked.

Casey's breath caught on a gasp. His voice was low and deep and an image of him whispering in her ear shattered what was left of her composure. Hang in there, she warned herself, then lifted her chin.

"I asked a question. Do you have an answer?"

Ryder touched the side of her cheek and felt an odd sense of pride when, once again, she stood without flinching.

"About the only thing I have to my name is guts. If that's all you need, then I'm your man."

"Hey, man, you don't know what you're getting yourself into," the bartender warned.

Ryder's gaze never wavered from Casey Ruban's face. Once again, his voice broke the quiet, wrapping around Casey's senses and making her shake from within.

"I know enough," he said.

"My name is Casey Ruban," she said. "What's yours?"

"Ryder Justice."

Justice! Casey took it as a sign. Justice was exactly what she'd been searching for.

"You swear you are free to marry?"

He nodded.

"My grandfather always said his handshake was as good as his word," Casey said, and offered her hand.

Without pause, Ryder enfolded it within the breadth of his own and once again, Casey felt herself being swallowed whole. Her gaze centered on their hands entwined and she had a sudden image of their bodies in similar positions. She bit her lip and stifled a shudder. Now was not the time to get queasy. She had an empire to save.

"Come with me," she said shortly. "We have a little over twenty-four hours to get blood tests, apply for a license, and find a justice of the peace."

At the mention of haste, his gaze instinctively drifted toward her belly partially concealed beneath the loose-fitting dress.

Once, being an unwed mother might have horrified Casey. Now she wished that was all she was facing.

"Wrong guess, Mr. Justice. It's just that I've got myself in a race with the devil, and I don't like to lose."

Ryder followed without comment. He'd been on a first-name basis with the old hound himself for some time now. He never thought to consider the fact that the devil was giving someone else a hard time as well.

The room erupted into a roar as they stepped outside, and Casey found herself all but running toward her car. Only after she slid behind the wheel and locked them in did she feel safe. And then she glanced toward the man beside her and knew she was fooling herself.

His presence dwarfed the sports car's interior. He scooted the seat as far back as it would go and still his knees were up against the dash. The duffel bag he'd had on his shoulders was now between his feet, and Casey imagined she could hear the rhythmic thud of his heartbeat as he turned a cool, calculating gaze her way.

"Buckle up, Mr. Justice."

He reached for the seat belt out of reflex, then gave Casey another longer, calculating look.

"I have a question," he said.

Casey's heart dropped. Please stranger, don't back out on me now.

"I have one for you, too," she said quickly.

"Ladies first."

She almost smiled. "Do you have a home? Do you have a job?"

His expression blanked, and Casey would have sworn she saw pain on his face before he answered.

"I don't have an address or a job. Does it matter?"

She thought fast, remembering the conditions of the will. She had to live in her husband's residence and under his protection. This was good news. It was something she could control.

"Do you have a driver's license?" she asked.

He nodded.

"Good, then you're hired."

He cocked an eyebrow as Casey started the car.

"Exactly what have I been hired to do?"

"You're going to be the new chauffeur for the Ruban family. You... I mean...we...will live in the apartment over the garage on Delaney's...I mean, on my estate."

Ryder frowned. "Lady, I have to ask. Why marry a stranger?"

She backed out of the parking lot, the tires spinning on loose gravel as she drove onto the road, heading back the same way she'd come.

"Because I will be damned before I let myself be forced into marriage with a man I can't abide."

He wondered about the man she'd obviously left behind. "You don't know me. What if you can't abide me, either?"

Her gaze was fixed on the patch of road visible in the twin beams of her headlights.

"Living a year with a total stranger is better than living one night under Lash Marlow's roof. Besides, I don't like to be told what to do."

So, his name is Lash Marlow. This time Ryder did smile, but only a little.

"Casey."

Startled by the sound of her name on his lips, she turned her gaze from the road to his face.

"What?"

"I think you should try calling me Ryder. I've never gone to bed with a woman who called me Mister, and I don't intend to start now."

Gone to bed with...!

Almost too late she remembered what she was doing and swerved to avoid the ditch at which she was heading. By the time she had the car and herself under control, she was too desperate to argue the point.

First things first. Marriage. Then rules. After that, take it one day at a time. It was the only way she knew.

Chapter 2

There was something to be said for the power of the Ruban name. It had gotten Casey and Ryder through blood tests without an appointment, gotten a court clerk out of bed and down to the county courthouse in the middle of the night to issue a marriage license, then dragged an old family friend out of bed before sunrise to perform the impromptu ceremony. The waiting period most people would have experienced was waived for Delaney Ruban's granddaughter.

"You all take yourselves a seat now," Sudie Harris said, and pulled her housecoat a little tighter across her chest. "Judge will be here directly."

Casey dropped into the nearest chair, well aware that Harmon Harris's wife had taken one look at Ryder Justice and found him lacking in both worth and substance. When Ryder refused a seat and walked to the window instead, something about the way he was standing made her nervous. What if he was already sorry he'd gotten into this mess? What if he was thinking about leaving? Nervously, she got up.

"Mr. Justice, I—"

He turned and she choked on her words. He was so big. So

menacing. So much a stranger. What in God's name had she done?

"What did you call me?" he asked.

She swallowed and the lump in her throat seemed to be getting larger by the minute. Oh, Lord. "Ryder. I meant to say, Ryder."

His eyes narrowed thoughtfully. Casey Ruban was on the verge of a breakdown. She might not know it, but he recognized the signs. Her eyes were feverishly bright and the knuckles on her fingers had gone from red to white from the fists that she'd made. Add to that, a breathing pattern that was little more than a series of short, quick gasps, and he figured it wouldn't take much for her to fall apart.

"That's better," he said shortly. "Now sit down before you fall down."

Casey did as she was told and then tried not to look at his backside as he turned away. It was impossible. In a few short minutes she would be tied to this man as she'd never been bound before, not only by law, but in the closest of proximity. Wife! Dear God, she was going to be that man's wife.

She watched as he shrugged his shoulders in a quiet, almost weary gesture, rubbing at his neck and massaging the muscles with long, brown fingers. She couldn't quit staring at his hands. Out of nowhere a random thought came barreling into her sleep-starved mind. *I wonder if he's a gentle lover.*

Startled, she shuddered and looked away, wishing Judge Harris would hurry. She doubted there was little about Ryder Justice that was gentle, and the tension between them was making her crazy.

Torn between the fear that she was jumping into a worse mess than the one she was already in, and fear that at the last minute he wouldn't go through with the ceremony, she wanted to cry. Instead, she closed her eyes. All I want to do is go to bed and sleep for a month, then wake up and find out this was all a bad dream, she thought.

Somewhere in another part of the house a clock chimed five times. Startled, she glanced at her watch. Five o'clock! In a little over an hour the sun would be up. Footsteps sounded on the stairwell behind them. She stood and turned to face the man who was entering the room.

From Harmon Harris's expression, he was none too pleased to see who awaited him. ''Casey Dee, what on earth are you doin' here in the middle of the night?''

''Getting married, and it's not the middle of the night, it's almost dawn.''

Regardless of whether it was night or day, Ruban women did not sneak around to get married, and Harmon knew it. He stared at the man near his living room window, then glared at Casey.

''Not to him?''

She gritted her teeth, preparing herself for a fight.

''Yes sir, to him. We have blood tests and the license right here.'' She thrust the papers into the judge's hands.

When he noted the dates he frowned, staring at her hard and long, from her head to the middle of her belly. Like Ryder before him, Harmon was assuming the only reason a woman would rush into marriage was to give a bastard child a name.

''Hell, girl, the ink is hardly dry on this stuff. What's the big rush?''

''You can get that look off your face,'' Casey muttered. ''I'm not pregnant. I haven't even been exposed.''

Bushy eyebrows lowered over his prominent nose as Harmon Harris laid the papers to one side and took Casey by the arm.

''I've known you a long time, Honey, and this isn't like you. Before I perform any ceremony, I want an explanation.''

Casey's gaze never wavered. ''If Delaney were alive, you could ask him yourself. All I know is, I had forty-eight hours to find myself a husband or forfeit my inheritance to Miles and Erica.''

The judge's eyebrows rose perceptibly. ''You're joking!''

Her shoulders slumped. ''I wish I were.''

He glanced over her shoulder to Ryder. ''I don't understand.''

Then his voice lowered. ''Why not marry Lash Marlow? You've known him nearly all your life. Why this man?''

''Because he's not Lash.''

The judge didn't comment. He didn't have to. Casey's answer pretty much said it all.

''Who is he?''

''His name is Ryder Justice.''

"I know that," the judge said. "It says so on the papers. What I'm asking is *who* are his people?"

Casey shrugged. "I haven't the faintest idea, and quite frankly I don't care. What I do know is I will not be coerced, especially by a dead man, into marrying someone I do not even like, never mind the fact that I don't love him. Do you understand that?"

Suddenly Casey and Harmon realized they were no longer alone.

"Is there a problem?" Ryder asked.

There was something about the look on the big man's face that made Harmon Harris release his grasp on Casey's arms.

Harmon sighed. "No, I don't suppose there is. Casey is of age and enough of her own woman to do as she chooses." He turned. "Sudie, go next door and wake up Millard Shreves. We're gonna need ourselves another witness."

Casey relaxed as Judge Harris's wife hurried to do his bidding. It was going to be all right.

"It will take Millard a bit to get out of bed," the judge explained. "If you two want to freshen up before the ceremony, the guest bath is down the hall on your right. However, you're going to have to excuse me for a bit. I'm going to be needing some coffee."

Having put the wheels in motion, he left Casey and Ryder alone in the Harris parlor with Sudie's crocheted doilies and silk flower bouquets.

Casey put a hand to her hair, feeling the disarray. She started to the bathroom for a quick wash then remembered Ryder. Was it safe to leave him alone, or would he bolt at the first chance he got? She glanced back at him, and to her dismay realized he was watching her. It was almost as if he'd read her mind.

"Go on," he said. "I'll be here when you get back."

There was something compelling about this man, something she couldn't quite name. There was a strength within him that a couple of days' worth of whiskers and a faded T-shirt and jeans could not hide. Right now his eyes seemed blue, although at first they'd seemed gray. Their color was as changeable as the weather. She hoped his disposition did not seesaw as well and knew she was staring, but she couldn't help it. Although she was afraid of what he might tell her, there was something she needed to know.

"Why did you agree to go along with this madness?"

His expression hardened. "Don't dig too deep, Casey. You might find worms in the dirt you're taking out of the hole."

Startled, she pivoted and headed for the bathroom, telling herself it was exhaustion that was making her shake, and not the implied warning in his words.

"...pronounce you man and wife. What God has joined together, let no man put asunder."

Judge Harris's clock began to chime.

Once. Twice. Three times it sounded.

Casey exhaled slowly.

Four times. Five times. Six times the gong echoed within the silence of the room.

She went limp, and were it not for the firm grip Ryder had on her arm, she wouldn't have been able to stand. But she'd done it. It was over! The Ruban empire was safe, but dear God, could she say the same about herself?

"Congratulations. You may kiss your bride," Harmon added, although he doubted, considering the reasons for the ceremony, there was much to celebrate.

Both Ryder and Casey stared, first at Judge Harris who'd just granted permission for something neither had been prepared to act upon, then at each other as they contemplated the deed.

To Casey's dismay, her vision blurred.

Ryder had intended on holding his ground until he saw her tears. It was her weakness, rather than the bulldog determination with which she'd gotten them this far, that made him do what he did next. He'd entered into this farce without giving a thought for consequences, much the same way he used to go through life. But that was before he'd killed his father and lost his nerve to fly.

Intending only to assure her, he cupped her cheek with the palm of one hand, gentling her much in the same way his brother, Royal, tended the horses on his ranch, giving them time to adjust to his presence.

"Easy, now," he said softly, and when he felt her pulse beginning to slow, he lowered his head.

Casey saw him coming. Her lips parted. Whether it was to voice an objection or to ease his way, Ryder didn't know and didn't care. His focus was on her mouth and the woman who now bore his name.

Casey's breath caught at the back of her throat and this time, had Ryder not been holding her up, her legs would have given way. Whatever her intent had been, it stopped along with her heart when Ryder Justice kissed his wife.

It should have been awkward—their first joining—but it wasn't. The ease with which they touched, then the gentleness with which the kiss deepened felt right, even familiar. At the point of embracing, the judge's voice broke their connection.

"Well, now," he said, and made no attempt to hide a yawn. "I suppose you two are as hitched as a couple can be."

When Ryder moved away, Casey felt a sudden sense of loss, and then reality intruded and she felt nothing but dismay. She had no intentions of pursuing the intimate part of a marriage and the sooner Ryder Justice realized that, the better off they would be. She stepped back, then turned away, unwilling to let him see how deeply she'd been affected by what he'd done.

"It served its purpose," she said shortly, and started looking for her purse. "What do I owe you?"

While she was fumbling for cash, Ryder was dealing with uneasiness of his own. The kiss was supposed to have been nothing but a formality. He hadn't expected to feel anything because it had been months since he'd allowed himself the luxury. But something had happened to him between the time her breath had brushed his cheek and their point of contact. Left with nothing but a lingering dissatisfaction he couldn't identify, he, too, turned away. It was almost as if he'd left something undone. He hadn't been prepared for what the kiss had evoked—what it felt like to hold someone close, the pleasure that comes from lying in a willing woman's arms.

He inhaled slowly and considered the woman who was now his wife, if in name only. He had agreed to marry her and no matter what, he was a man of his word. But he didn't want to like her. There was already a time limit on their relationship. God forbid his feelings should ever go deeper.

Casey said something that made the judge laugh and Ryder turned to see what was funny. Instead of an answer, he found himself watching as Casey peeled five twenty-dollar bills from a wad of cash in her handbag and handed them to the judge. He frowned, then looked away, uncomfortable with the fact that a woman was paying his way for anything, and more than a little bit anxious as to how he was supposed to fit into her life. He had already suspected she came from money. Her car and her clothes had given her away, and the money she stuffed back in her purse only confirmed his suspicions.

For the first time since he'd run away, he thought about what he'd left behind, yet not once did he consider confessing his true background and identity to Casey.

She thought she'd married a bum, a no-account drifter without a penny to his name. His eyes narrowed as he stared out into the burgeoning dawn. Part of it was true. He didn't have two quarters with him that he could rub together. At this point, the fact that he owned four airplanes and a helicopter, and that his charter service had been in the black for nearly eleven years didn't matter. Nor did the fact that the deed to nearly fourteen hundred acres of prime real estate on the outskirts of San Antonio was in his name.

Sick at heart from an accident he couldn't forget, he'd walked away from it all. Things of monetary value had become unimportant to Ryder. If he could have, he would have given up everything just to have his father back alive and well.

But there would be no trading with God...or the devil. Micah Justice was dead and buried, and no matter how far Ryder went, he couldn't outrun his guilt.

Someone cleared their throat. He looked up. It would seem that Sudie was patiently waiting to lock them out. Casey held the front door ajar. Her posture and the tone of her voice gave away her impatience.

"Are you ready to go?" she asked.

Something inside him snapped. The quiet in which he'd encompassed himself over the past few months suddenly seemed too confining. Sarcasm colored his answer.

"I don't know, Mrs. Justice, are you?"

Her bossy, managerial attitude disappeared like air out of a punctured balloon. He had the satisfaction of seeing her pale as he walked past her and out the door.

The air was muggy, a promise of another long, hot July day. Sweat was already rolling down the middle of Casey's back and there was a snag in her stockings. Since yesterday when she'd made her exit from Lash's office, her hairdo had been windblown and finger-combed a dozen times. The last time she remembered putting on makeup was right before she'd gotten out of the car to go into the office for the reading of the will. She felt like hell and figured she looked a shade or two worse. She was exhausted and couldn't wait to get home and into a bed.

But thirty minutes outside of Ruban Crossing, Casey's plans were about to change. The flashing red-and-blue lights of a Mississippi highway patrol were an unwelcome addition to the events of the day. She had expected complications, but not quite so soon, or from the state police. She looked at Ryder, then began pulling over to the side of the road.

"I wasn't speeding," she said.

Ryder glanced over his shoulder, then started unbuckling his seat belt. The highway patrolman was already out of his vehicle with his gun drawn, and although the air conditioner was on and Casey's car windows were up, they could hear him shouting for them to get out of the car.

"I don't think that's the problem."

"What do you mean?" Casey asked, and turned. There was a gun pointed straight at her head.

"Get out of the car!" the patrolman shouted again. "Do it! Do it now!"

Stunned by the order, Casey began fumbling with her seat belt, but couldn't seem to find the catch. The harder she tried, the worse her fingers shook, and the longer she delayed, the louder and more insistent the officer became.

"Let me," Ryder said, and to her relief, the latch gave way, freeing her from the straps.

She opened the door. "Look, Officer, I don't know what..."

"Get out and put your hands on the hood of the car! You!" he shouted, pointing the gun at Ryder. "On the passenger side! Come around the front of the car with your hands in the air!"

Ryder didn't argue. He'd learned years ago never to argue with an armed man, especially one wearing a badge.

By now, Casey was out of the car and furious. "What's the meaning of this?"

Handcuffs snapped. First one on her right wrist, then the remaining cuff on her other.

"Sit down," the officer ordered, pushing Casey none too gently to a seat beside the rear wheel of her car before proceeding to cuff Ryder in the same smooth manner. He hauled Ryder off to the back seat of his patrol car and shut him inside while Casey watched in disbelief.

"This better be good," Casey said, as the officer returned and helped her to her feet.

"You're driving a stolen car and the woman who owns it has been reported missing."

Casey couldn't believe what she was hearing. "*I* am not missing, and *this* is my car."

The officer took a long, slow look at the disheveled woman in black and didn't bother to hide a smirk.

"That car belongs to Casey Ruban. Her family reported her missing when she didn't come home last night."

"I repeat, this is my car, and I didn't go home because I was out getting myself married," she said.

"Excuse me?" the officer asked.

She closed her eyes, counted to ten, then glared at the patrolman, derisively enunciating each syllable.

"Married. Capital *m*—little *a*—double *r—i—e—d*...Married. Last night...no, actually it was early this morning that we got married. You might say I've been on my honeymoon and you..." she frowned against the glare of early morning sun, peering at the name tag on the front of his uniform "...Officer Howard, have just stuffed my groom in the back of your patrol car. I want him out, and I want the handcuffs taken off both of us now, or I swear to God I will have your badge and all that goes with it."

Her adamancy startled the cop, and for the first time since he'd pulled them over, he began to consider the possibility of having been wrong in his first assumption. But he'd been so focused on being the one to get a lead on the missing heir that he hadn't followed protocol by asking for their identification first.

"I'll need to see some identification," he said.

"It's in my purse in the front seat, along with a copy of my marriage license. Want to see that, too?"

He unlocked her cuffs and opened the door. "No funny business," he said shortly, as Casey leaned inside.

She handed him the marriage license, her driver's license, as well as the title to her car. "There's nothing funny about any of this, and when I get home, I'm going to have someone's hide for this."

The officer looked long and hard at the picture on the driver's license and then at Casey. There was little resemblance between the cool, composed woman in the picture and the fiery-eyed hellion standing before him.

Casey could see he still wasn't buying her explanation, but she wasn't about to explain the mess she was in, thanks to her grandfather's will. She opted for something he would probably believe.

"Oh, for God's sake," Casey snapped. "I've been on my honeymoon, okay? You try a wedding night in the back seat of a car and see how good you look!"

The patrolman flushed with embarrassment as he began to realize the seriousness of his situation. Unless he made peace with this woman now, he could be in big trouble. The Ruban name carried a lot of clout.

"Sorry, Miss Ruban...I mean uh..."

"Justice," Casey said. "The name is Justice." She pointed toward the cruiser. "About my husband..."

Moments later, Ryder found himself standing by the side of the road, watching as an officer of the law did everything but crawl as an excuse for his overzealous behavior.

"Thank you for being so understanding," the officer said, as Casey brushed at the dirt on the back of her dress.

"We'll call it even if you just don't notify my family," she said. "I want to surprise them on my own."

"Yes, ma'am. I'll just call this in to headquarters so you won't be stopped again."

"Fine," she said, and didn't bother to watch as he drove away. When she glanced up at Ryder, he was grinning.

"What's so funny?" she asked.

"You're hell on wheels, aren't you, wife?"

"Don't call me that," she said, and slammed herself bodily into the seat behind the wheel.

Ryder was still grinning when he took the seat beside her. "Want me to drive?" he asked. "After all, I'm going to be your chauffeur."

Her bottom lip slid slightly forward as she started the car, leaving the side of the road in a flurry of flying dust and gravel.

"I guess not," Ryder drawled, and then settled back into the passenger seat. The longer he was around this woman, the more he liked her. She reminded him a little bit of his brother, Roman, who chose to believe that laws and rules were made by men with too much time on their hands.

There was a pasty white sheen on Lash Marlow's face as he hung up the phone. He glanced at the clock over the mantel and swiped a shaky hand through his hair. It was almost noon. Time was running out.

His thoughts were jumbled as he considered the possibilities of where Casey might be. Damn Delaney for insisting on that forty-eight hour time frame. He'd told him from the start it wasn't a good idea, but Delaney had insisted, claiming he knew his granddaughter better than anyone. He'd sworn she would never adhere to the terms of the will unless pushed.

Lash felt sick. It seemed obvious that he and Delaney Ruban had pushed too much.

"Any news?" Eudora asked, and not for the first time wished she'd sat beside her youngest granddaughter during the reading of the will. She was still convinced she might have been able to soften the blow Casey had received. If she had, maybe they wouldn't have spent a sleepless night expecting the worst.

Lash shook his head and reached for another antacid. Instead, his fingers closed around the rabbit's foot in his pocket, and he rubbed it lightly, making a bet with himself that everything would be all right.

Taking comfort from his superstitious gesture, he decided to forego the antacid. It probably wouldn't help anyway. He was long past worry and far past panic. From the way his gut was burning, he was either starting a new ulcer or about to have a heart attack. He'd expected Casey to be difficult, but he hadn't expected this. If she didn't show up soon, it would be too late.

Miles lounged near the window overlooking the tennis courts, contemplating the party he would throw when he got his hands on the money. He was sick and tired of pretending to be worried about Casey. As far as he was concerned, she could stay gone. For the past six years, even if she was his sister, she'd been nothing but a judgmental little bitch, always harping at him and Erica to get jobs of their own.

Eudora paced back and forth, fanning herself with a dampened handkerchief. "I just can't bear this suspense. Oh dear. Oh dear."

Miles rolled his eyes. "Oh, let it rest, Grandmother. She'll come home when it suits her."

Eudora frowned as she fanned, although the small square of fabric did little to stir the air. "I'm just sick about this. What if something awful has happened?" When no one echoed her concern, she sank into a nearby chair, dabbing at her eyes. "Poor, dear Casey."

"Poor, dear Casey, my ass." Erica muttered, and sloshed a liberal helping of Jack Daniel's into her iced tea and sat down near her twin. Ice clinked against crystal as she swirled the liquid before lifting the glass to her mouth.

Lash glanced at his watch and dug his own handkerchief from his pocket, mopping at a fine line of perspiration that kept breaking out across his brow. Time was running out. If she didn't show soon, his worst fears would be realized. Miles and Erica would be in control of the Ruban fortune and Lash's dreams to resurrect the Marlow estate to its former glory would be dashed. At this moment he didn't know whom he hated worse—Delaney for causing the fuss, or Miles for the possum-eating grin he'd been wearing all day.

Never one to let a good silence extend itself, Eudora tucked her handkerchief into her cleavage and rang a small bell near her chair.

Moments later a tall, dark-skinned man dressed in virgin whites entered the room. Still straight and handsome at sixty, the only evidence of Joshua Bass's age was the liberal dusting of gray in his hair.

"Yes, ma'am?"

Eudora pointed toward a nearby table. "Joshua, we're all out of tea."

"Yes, ma'am."

He picked up the tray and started out of the room when Eudora remembered.

"Oh, Joshua!"

He paused. "Yes, ma'am?"

"Have Tilly put some lemon in the tea this time. I do believe lemon helps cut the miasma of July."

Casey entered on the tail of Eudora's order, countermanding it with one of her own. She took the tray out of Joshua's hands and set it down, then to the continuing dismay of her family, gave him a huge, breathless hug, which he gladly returned.

Casey smiled up at Joshua, taking comfort in the love she saw there in his eyes. "Forget the tea, Joshie. Bring a bottle of Delaney's best champagne instead. We're going to toast my marriage."

Joshua looked startled, and his first thought was what his Tilly was going to say. Casey was as close to their hearts as if she'd been born of their blood and here she was about to drink to a marriage they knew she didn't want.

Miles's face turned an angry red. Erica choked on a piece of ice, and Eudora clasped her hands to her throat and started to cry.

As for Lash he went weak with relief. Not only was Casey back, but she seemed willing to celebrate their upcoming union with no remorse. He went toward her with outstretched hands.

"Casey, darling, I'm so glad you..."

And that was the moment they realized Casey had not come alone. The unexpected face of a stranger at Casey's back, never mind his trail-weary appearance, startled them all into sudden silence.

''Everyone...this is Ryder Justice.'' She glanced at Ryder. To her surprise, he seemed calm, almost disinterested. ''Ryder—my family.'' She pointed them out, one by one, starting with Eudora. ''This is my Gran.'' She glanced at Miles and Erica and the expressions on their faces said it all. She sighed. Some things never change. ''The two beautiful blondes with the fabulous scowls are my brother and sister, Miles and Erica.''

As she smiled at Joshua, her voice softened. ''And this is Joshua Bass. He and his wife, Tilly, helped raise me.''

Ryder nodded. ''It's a pleasure, sir,'' he said quietly. ''And, I'd say you and your wife have done a fine job. Casey is quite a woman.''

She gave Ryder a quick look of surprise. The praise was unexpected.

Joshua grinned, pleased to have been recognized as part of the family.

''Casey, really! He's one of the help,'' Eudora said, and then flushed, embarrassed that she'd been put in the position of having to remark upon the differences in their stations in life.

Casey's chin jutted. ''Unlike the majority of this family, Joshua has a job. I have a job as well. I fail to see the difference.'' Then she softened her rebuke by winking at Joshua. ''Joshie, hurry and bring that champagne. We have some celebrating to do.''

Lash had more on his mind than sipping champagne and social niceties. He glanced at his watch. There were a million things to do and so little time.

''Casey, dearest, we've been so worried. When you didn't come home last night I even called the state police. We all realize the will came as a terrible shock to you, but if you'd just waited a bit, I could have saved you from all this turmoil. You know how I feel about you. It was only a matter of time before you came to your senses and did what was best for everyone.''

When he reached for her hand, Casey took an instinctive step back, right into Ryder's arms.

''Easy,'' Ryder said softly, and Casey shivered. That was what he'd said earlier, right before he'd kissed her.

''I don't need saving,'' she told Lash. ''And I've already come to my senses. I saved myself.''

A nerve jerked at the side of Lash's eye, causing it to twitch. "What do you mean?"

Although Ryder was no longer touching Casey, she knew he was still behind her, and, oddly enough, it was his solid presence that gave her the courage to say what had to be said. She pulled the copy of their marriage license from her purse and handed it to Lash without batting an eye.

"Ryder and I were married this morning. I suppose you'll need this to confirm the legalities and finalize the edicts of the will."

"Married?"

The shriek came from across the room. Casey wasn't sure whether it was Miles or Erica who'd come undone, and she didn't much care.

The paper fell from Lash's fingers and onto the floor as shock spread across his face. Speech was impossible. All he could do was stare at the woman who'd dashed his last hopes. She seemed calm, even smug about what she'd done, and as he looked, he began to hate.

At this point, Joshua came back into the room with an uncorked bottle of champagne and a tray full of glasses. Casey took it from his hands.

"I'll pour while you go get Tilly. This won't be official until you two are in on my news. Also, will you please tell Bea to get the apartment over the garage ready. When it's cleaned, have someone move my things out there, okay?"

Joshua left with an anxious glance.

"Why on earth would you be doing such a thing?" Eudora asked.

Before Casey could respond, Ryder stepped to her side. For a moment, Casey had the sensation of what it would be like to never stand alone against this family again.

His voice was cool, his manner calm and assured. "Because a wife lives with her husband, and as of yesterday, I'm your new chauffeur, that's why."

Miles's snort of disbelief was echoed by his sister. "My God, Casey, marrying some ne'er-do-well is bad enough, but a chauffeur? Have you no shame?"

Ryder's expression underwent a remarkable change, from calm

to quiet fury. He never took his eyes from Miles. "I don't care if he is your brother—do not expect me to like that little pig."

Casey almost laughed. The look of shock on her brother's face was priceless.

"You don't have to," she said, and then felt obligated to add, "but you can't hurt him."

Ryder gave Miles another cool stare, then took the champagne Casey handed him. "There's more than one way to skin a cat," he drawled, and gave Miles a cool, studied look. Then he lifted the glass toward her in a silent toast, pinning Casey with a stormy gaze that left her stunned.

"To justice," he said, letting them decide for themselves what he'd meant.

Chapter 3

After the family accepted the shock of Casey's news, there was one more person Casey needed to see. While Ryder was prowling through the garage and the cars that were to be under his control, she slipped into the kitchen in search of Matilda Bass. The need to lay her head on Tilly's shoulder was overwhelming. She hoped when she did, that she would manage not to cry.

And Tilly wasn't all that hard to find.

"Come here to me, girl," Tilly said, and opened her arms.

Casey walked into them without hesitation. "You didn't come drink champagne with me."

Tilly ignored the rebuke. She had her own idea of her place in this world and in spite of the money the Rubans had, she wouldn't have traded places with them for any of it. She had more self-esteem than to socialize with people who chose to look down on her because she cooked the food that they ate.

"Well now, what have you gone and done?" Tilly asked.

Her sympathy was almost Casey's undoing. "Saved us all, I hope," Casey replied.

Tilly frowned. She'd already heard through the family grapevine what a burden the old man Ruban had heaped on her baby's head.

"If you ask me, that old man needed his head examined," Tilly mumbled, stroking her hand gently up and down the middle of Casey's back.

Casey sighed. "Well, it's over and done with," she said.

Tilly stepped back, her dark eyes boring into Casey's gaze. "Nothing is ever over and done with, girl. Not while people draw breath. You be careful. I don't know why, but I don't like the feel of all this."

Casey managed a laugh. "Don't go all witchy on me, now. You know what Joshie says about you messin' with that kind of stuff."

Tilly sniffed. The reference to her mother's and grandmother's predilection for voodoo did not apply to her. "I do not indulge myself in the black arts and you know it," Tilly huffed.

Casey grinned and then gave Tilly a last, quick hug. "I know. I was only teasing." Then her laughter faded. "Say a prayer for me, Mammo."

Casey hadn't used that childhood name in years. It brought quick tears to Tilly's eyes, and because it was an emotion in which she rarely indulged, she was all the more brusque with her answer. "Knowing you, I'd better say two," she said, and gave Casey a swift swat on the rear. "Now you run on along. I've got dinner to fix before Joshua and I go on home."

Casey paused on her way out the door. "Tilly?"

"What, baby girl?"

"Have you ever regretted staying on here as cook? You and Joshua are so smart, you could have done a lot of other things besides wait on a small, selfish family."

Tilly turned, and the serious tone of her voice was proof of her sincerity. "Maybe I could have, but not my Josh. You've got to remember, he only hears good in one ear. That handicap lost him a whole lot of jobs early on in our marriage. By the time we landed here with your grandfather, he was glad to have the work. And Mr. Ruban was more than fair. Our pay is good. We have health insurance, something a lot of our friends do not. And, because your grandfather did not like change in his household, the incentive he gave us to stay on was to set up trusts for our retirement. Actually, we're better off than some other members of our family who have college degrees.'' And then she smiled. ''Besides, I like to cook, and who else would have raised my baby if Josh and I hadn't been here?''

This time, Casey didn't bother to hide her tears. She wrapped her arms around Tilly's neck. ''I love you, Mammo.''

''I love you, too, girl. Now run on home. You've got yourself a man to tend.''

Startled, Casey did as she was told, and after that, the day went surprisingly well.

Although Miles and Erica no longer had any hopes of attaining control of the Ruban fortune, their circumstances were still the same. Before, they had come and gone as they pleased, spent and slept at Delaney Ruban's expense. For them, nothing had changed.

As for Eudora, she'd sacrificed much for her dead daughter's children. Years ago she'd given up a suitor who could have made her golden years something to remember. She'd left her home on Long Island and came to Mississippi with the best of intentions. She refused to consider that she'd contributed to the ruination of her eldest grandchildren by coercing Delaney to leave their upbringing in her care when he'd begun to focus his attention on Casey.

She hadn't meant to make them so dependent on others, but it had happened anyway. And now that their life-styles were pretty much set in stone, she felt it her moral obligation to see that their comfort level stayed the same.

Yet when it came to sacrifices, it was Casey who'd sacrificed the most. Whatever dreams she might have harbored with regard to her personal life were gone. She was married to a stranger, and for the next twelve months, had resigned herself to the fact.

At her demand, Ryder had been sent into Ruban Crossing with a handful of money and orders as to what to buy, while she went in to the office. There was a merger pending and an entire factory of workers in Jackson, Mississippi who were waiting to learn if they still had their jobs. She didn't want another day to pass without assuring them. In fact, everything was running so smoothly it should have been the warning Casey needed, because when the sun went down, tempers began to rise.

Casey climbed the stairs leading to the garage apartment and tried not to think of her spacious bedroom across the courtyard; of her sunken bathtub and the cool, marble floor, or of her queen-size bed and the down-filled pillows of which she was so fond. Her stomach growled and she wondered what feast Tilly was concocting across the way for the evening meal. At this point, she began to consider the benefits she was losing by having to live under Ryder Justice's roof. Who would cook? Where did she put her dirty clothes?

Caution forbade her to use any of the services available across the way. From the expression on Lash Marlow's face when he'd left the house this morning, she knew his anger would not easily disappear. It would be just like him to try and catch her cheating on the terms of the will.

Oh, well, she thought. I can always order takeout and take my clothes to the cleaners.

She took out her key to open the door then found it already unlocked. Her pulse skipped a beat. That meant *he* was home. Quietly, so as not to alert the ''tiger'' who lurked within, she shut the door behind her and then stood, absorbing the sight of what was to be her home for the next twelve months.

The entire apartment consisted of three small rooms, the accumulation of which were still not the size of her bedroom inside the mansion. But it was clean, and blessedly quiet. For today, it was enough.

Just when she was beginning to relax, she noticed a man's shirt draped over an easy chair and a pair of dusty, black boots on the floor nearby. Reality set in.

Never one to put off what had to be done, she reminded herself that the sooner the confrontation began, the sooner it would be over. She sat her briefcase by the door and looked toward the bedroom. Since he wasn't in here, he had to be in there.

She walked inside. Several pairs of blue jeans lay on the bed, along with a half dozen white long-sleeved shirts, a new sport coat and a broad-brimmed black Stetson. A pile of her best lingerie was on the floor next to the dresser. She frowned, wondering why her things were on the floor.

She stared at the clothes. Where were the uniforms she'd told him to get? She'd given him the address of the place where they'd rented them before. Ruban Crossing was a fair-size city, but he'd had all afternoon to find one simple address.

She opened the closet. It was full of her clothing and nothing else. She looked back at the bed. That explained why he hadn't hung his up. Obviously, there was no place left for them to hang.

She turned around, eyeing the small room with distaste, then shrugged. Tomorrow, she'd go through her things and have Bea take part of them back to the main house. It was the least she could do.

A door creaked behind her. She spun and then froze. Ryder had obviously just had a bath. Steam enveloped him as he stepped out of the doorway and into the room with her, giving him the appearance of emerging from a cloud. His hair was spiky and still dripping water as he began to towel it dry.

Her thoughts tangled. Most men would appear smaller without benefit of clothing. But not him. He enveloped the space in which he moved, almost as if he took it with him as he went.

Casey frowned again, biting at the inside of her lip and wondering why she hadn't had the foresight to wait outside. How would she ever get past the memory of this much man covered with such a small, insignificant towel?

''Sorry,'' Ryder said, and gave his hair a last, halfhearted rub before tossing the wet towel back into the bathroom floor. ''Didn't know you were here.''

Casey tilted her chin, determined he not know how shaken she was.

''Obviously,'' she said shortly, and then pointed toward the clothes on the bed. ''I gave you money to get uniforms, not all this.''

Ryder's eyes narrowed, and Casey knew the moment the words were out of her mouth that she'd ticked him off. He walked to a bedside table and withdrew a handful of money, then stuffed it in her hand.

''What's this?'' Casey asked.

''Your money.''

''But how did you pay for all this?''

He didn't answer, and she glared. But when he spun and started toward her, she took an instinctive step backward. When he bypassed her for the dresser beyond, she caught herself breathing a small sigh of relief. Determined to get to the bottom of his behavior, she struck again, only this time with more venom.

''I asked you a question,'' she snapped.

Her relief was short-lived. When he turned, the anger on his face almost stopped her heart.

''Don't go there,'' he said quietly.

''Go where? I don't know what you mean.''

''There's one thing we'd better get straight right now. I don't take orders from you, and I don't take your money. I pay my own way.''

She couldn't imagine how he'd obtained the clothes. For all she knew he might have stolen the stuff. She would have been shocked to know he had a gold credit card with an unlimited line. And, if she'd known, would have been even more surprised to learn he hadn't used it in months.

''But the uniforms...why didn't you do as you were told?''

As far as Ryder was concerned, what was in his past was none of her business. Suddenly he was right in front of her. His breath was hot, his words angry.

''Because you're not my boss, you're my wife. I gave you my name, and I'll drive you and yours anywhere they please for the next twelve months, but I'm not wearing a damned monkey suit to do it.''

Casey's mouth dropped. Never in her entire life had anyone had the gall to defy her in such a manner. Before she could think of a comeback, he turned away, opened the top drawer of the dresser, withdrew a brand-new pair of white cotton briefs and dropped his towel.

She bolted, taking with her the image of a long-limbed body that was hard and fit and brown all over.

A few minutes later he emerged from the bedroom in his bare feet, wearing an old and faded pair of jeans and no shirt. The casual are-you-still-here glance he gave her made her furious.

Disgusted with herself for not standing her ground, she watched from across the room as he sauntered into the kitchen and opened the refrigerator. When he bent down to look inside, the urge to hit him was so strong it startled her. She was not the type of woman to resort to violence. Then she rescinded her own opinion of herself. At least she *hadn't* been. But that was before she'd driven into the flatlands and brought out a husband.

He set a package of raw hamburger meat on the counter then went back to the refrigerator. She didn't know what angered her most, the fact that he was being deliberately mutinous, or that she was being ignored.

Smoothing her hands down the front of her blue summer suit, she tossed back her hair and slipped into the sarcastic mode she used to keep Miles and Erica at bay.

"Are you finished?" she drawled, wanting the bathroom all to herself.

Ryder straightened, looking at her from across the open refrigerator door. He stared at her, from the top of her hair to the open toes of her sling-back pumps. A slight grin tilted the corner of his mouth as he stepped back and closed the door.

His thoughts went to the year stretching out before them, considering which one of them would be the first to break. "Finished?" he muttered. "We haven't even started."

With that, he moved toward her.

Panic came swiftly and Casey wondered if the family would be able to hear her scream from here. She held up her hand in a warning gesture.

"Don't you dare!" she said, and winced at the squeak in her voice.

She was scared! The fact surprised him. She'd walked into a bar with a roomful of strange men and offered herself up as a golden goat without batting an eye. She'd roused a doctor, a county clerk and a judge out of bed to do her bidding. She'd stared down a roomful of antagonistic relatives and kept a lawyer out of her pants who seemed to have had his own hidden agenda, and she was suddenly scared? And of him? It didn't make sense. He hadn't done anything to warrant this. Yet when he might have eased her fears, he found himself letting them grow.

When he got within inches of her stark, white face, he realized why. This woman, who was his wife, was damned pretty. In fact, if a man didn't get picky about that little bitty mole at the left corner of her lips, she was beautiful.

Sexually, he was a starving man and this woman was legally his wife. Although he'd cut himself off from everyone he cared for, he'd been unable to cut off the emotions of a normal, red-blooded man. Keeping her slightly afraid was a safe way of keeping her at arms' length. Yet when her eyes widened fearfully and her color rose, he relented.

"Easy," he said. "All I need to know is how you like it and do you want more than one?"

She would have sworn that her heart shot straight up her throat and she had to swallow several times to work up enough spit to be able to speak. *More than one? Oh my God!* "I don't think you understand the situation here," she stuttered.

"What? Don't tell me you don't eat meat."

Her face flushed as she thought of his lean, bare body. "Eat? Meat?"

"Do you like hot and red, slightly pink, or hard as a rock?"

Her eyes widened even more and her voice began to quiver. "I don't do things like that," she whispered, and put her hand to her throat, unconsciously stifling that scream she'd been considering.

He frowned. Things like what? All he needed to know was if she wanted... And then it dawned on him what interpretation she'd put on their conversation. He stifled a grin and pointed back to the counter.

"Are you telling me you don't do hamburgers?"

"Hamburgers?"

He went straight past her and out a small side door onto the attached deck above the driveway, opened the lid to a smoking barbecue grill, checked the coals, then let the lid drop back down with a clank.

"The charcoal is ready." He headed back toward the kitchen, pausing at the package of hamburger. "One last chance. Do you want one hamburger or two, and how do you want it cooked?"

There was a silly grin on her face as she slumped to the floor in a dead faint.

Ryder sat in the room's only chair, watching as Casey began to regain consciousness. The sofa he'd laid her on was a small, two-cushion affair, and he'd been forced to make the decision as to whether her head would be down and her feet up, or vice versa.

He'd opted to lay her head on the cushions and let her legs dangle. No sooner had he done so than one of her legs slipped from the arm of the sofa and onto the floor, leaving her in an indelicate, spread-eagled faint.

Ryder stifled a grin. Waking in such a compromising position would embarrass anyone. For Casey, a woman obviously used to nothing but the best, it would be the height of humiliation. In a considerate move, he removed her shoes, then lifted her leg back in alignment with the other. But when it slipped off again, he decided to leave it, and her, alone.

As he watched, he couldn't help but stare at the woman who was now his wife. He was still a little shocked at himself for going along with such a hare-brained scheme. The Justice men were not impulsive. They had always considered the consequences and then lived with their decisions without regrets. Until now. While it was too late to consider anything, it remained to be seen if there would be regrets.

He kept looking at her, separating her features in his mind. It wasn't just that she was pretty, though he couldn't keep his eyes off her thick black hair and those big green eyes. And her skin—it looked like silk, ivory silk.

And Ryder remembered that when she smiled, her mouth had a tendency to curl at one corner first before the other decided to follow. It gave her an impish expression, which he knew was deceiving. If this woman had an ounce of playfulness in her, he hadn't seen it. The devil maybe, but nothing so frivolous as an imp.

While he was watching, she blinked. And when she groaned and reached for the back of her head, he grimaced. It had been thumped pretty good when she'd fainted. He felt bad about that.

She might be touchy as hell, and they might not agree on anything, but he didn't want her hurt.

Casey opened her eyes. The ceiling didn't look familiar, and for a moment, she wondered where she was. A whiff of charcoal smoke drifted past her nose and, all too swiftly, her memory returned.

Seconds later, she became aware of the implications of her less than ladylike sprawl. What had that man done to her while she'd been unconscious? Better yet, where was he?

She turned her head and caught him staring at her from a chair on the other side of the coffee table. When he grinned and winked, she swiveled to an upright position, grabbing at her skirt and smoothing at her hair. When she could think without the room spinning beneath her, she glared at him.

''What did you do to me?''

He arched an eyebrow. ''Not nearly as much as I wanted,'' he replied, and knew he'd scored a hit when she doubled up her fists. He stifled a laugh. ''Easy, now. I was just kidding. I've been the picture of decorum. I picked you up from the floor, laid you on the sofa, and have been waiting for you to come to.''

Her southern manners forced her to thank him. ''I appreciate your consideration.''

His grin widened. ''Honesty won't permit me to accept your compliment. I have to admit it was hunger that kept me waiting for you. I was taught that it's bad manners to eat in front of people without offering them some, too. And, you never did answer my question. How do you want your hamburger?''

If she'd had a shoe, she would have thrown it. As it was, she had to satisfy herself with a regal, albeit shaky, exit from the room, slamming the door shut between them with a solid thud.

''Does that mean you don't want one?'' Ryder yelled.

She yanked the door open long enough to give him what was left of her mind.

''You're a swine. A gentleman would have covered my legs and bathed my head with a cold compress.''

''If you wanted a gentleman, you shouldn't have gone shopping for a husband down in the Delta.''

She glared and slammed the door again, this time louder and firmer.

"I suppose this means no to the hamburgers?"

The door opened again, but the only thing to come out was the sound of Casey's voice at its most dignified. The shriek in her tone was gone and she was enunciating each word, as if speaking to someone lacking in mental capacity.

"No, it does not. I will have a hamburger, well-done, light on the salt, heavy on the pepper."

This time when she closed the door, it was with a ladylike click. The glitter in Ryder's eyes was sharp, the grin on his face sardonic.

"So you like it hot, do you, wife? That's interesting. Very interesting indeed."

He reentered the tiny kitchen and began making patties from the hamburger meat before carrying them out to the grill. As he slapped them on the grate, smoke began to rise and the fire began to pop and sizzle as fat dripped onto the burning charcoal.

Oddly, it reminded him of Casey in the midst of her family, putting up a smoke screen to keep them from knowing how scared she was, and popping wisecracks and issuing orders before anyone could tell her what to do.

He closed the lid and sighed. He had married a total stranger for the hell of it, but he hadn't counted on the family that came with her. In fact, they reminded him of snakes, writhing and coiling and biting out at each other in some crazy sort of frenzy.

He thought of his own family, of how loud and rambunctious—of how close and loving they'd been—of how empty and scattered they now were. And how the world as he'd known it had ended because of something he'd done.

He went back inside, leaving the hamburgers and his memories behind.

"Want another one?" Ryder asked, indicating the two remaining well-done patties congealing in their own grease on a pea green plate.

Casey eyed the plate. Besides being an atrocious shade of green, the plate was chipped. She'd never eaten from a chipped plate before. She suspected this night was the beginning of many firsts. Dabbing at the corner of her mouth with a paper towel, she shook her head.

"No, thank you, I'm quite full." Grudgingly she added, "It was very good."

Ryder nodded and continued to stare at a ketchup stain near his fork. What now? Conversation with this woman had been nearly impossible. Every time he opened his mouth to speak, she jumped. And she watched his every move with those big green eyes, as if she expected to be pounced upon at any moment. Hell, she was beginning to make him antsy, too.

He glanced at his watch. "It's almost nine."

She paled.

He sighed.

"Easy now, lady."

"Casey," she said. "My name is Casey."

His expression darkened. "Yes, and my name is Ryder. Unfortunately, that's all we know about each other." When she looked away, his frustration rose.

"Casey, look at me."

She did, but with trepidation.

"There's something I think needs to be said. This is going to be a long haul for both of us. I suppose we each had an agenda for even considering this situation, but it's done, and for your sake, it has to work, right?"

She thought of Miles and Erica, and then of Lash. "Yes."

"Okay, then there's something I think you should know about me."

Her head jerked up and she was suddenly staring at him in a still, waiting manner. Oh dear, what was he about to reveal?

Again, he sensed her fear. "Dammit, don't look at me like that. I am not a dangerous man. I do not taunt women. I do not hurt women. I do not force women to do anything they do not want, and that includes the issue of sex."

Startled by his bluntness, Casey blushed. "I've been meaning to talk to you about that," she said.

"I'm listening."

"There won't be any."

Her announcement came as no surprise, but Ryder was unprepared for the sense of disappointment he felt. He chalked it up to several months of denial and let it go at that.

He shrugged. "I will abide by whatever rules you feel comfortable in setting, but I have a couple of my own. I am not your servant. I don't take orders...but I will listen to suggestions."

He watched her swallow a couple of times, but she remained silent.

"Well, do you have any?"

Casey blinked. "Any what?"

"Suggestions."

"Uh...no, I don't suppose so."

"Okay, then that's settled. Why don't you start the dishes? I want to make sure the fire is out in the grill."

He got up before he had time to see her panic again.

"Ryder?"

He turned.

She waved helplessly over the table and the dirty dishes. "I've never done dishes before."

"You've never...!" Then he muttered beneath his breath. "Good grief."

"What's wrong?"

"You've never done dishes."

She hated him for that dumbfounded look he was wearing.

"That's what I said. I also don't do windows," she snapped.

"And I don't suppose you can cook, either."

She had the grace to flush. "No."

He groaned.

Casey was surprised at her feelings of inadequacy. She hired and fired with the best of them, bought and sold corporations without batting an eye. How dare he consider her lacking in capabilities?

"It's not my fault," she argued.

"Then whose is it?"

She had no answer.

"If you ask me, it's high time you learned. Soap is under the sink, the dishcloth is in it. You're a smart lady. Figure the rest out for yourself."

"Where are you going?" Casey asked, as he started out the door.

"To put out a fire then take a shower."

"But you already had a shower," she said, remembering the steam...and the towel..and the bare-naked body.

"Yeah, so maybe I have more than one fire that needs quenching, okay?"

It took exactly five seconds for the implication of what he'd suggested to sink in, and another few for her to be able to move. After that, she was glad to have something to do besides think about what he'd said...and why he'd said it.

The air was thick and muggy from the lingering heat of the day. It was that time of the evening just before dusk and right after the sun has passed beyond the horizon. A family of martens swooped grass-high in daring flight then soared heavenward, constantly feeding on the mosquitos in the air.

Graystone, the home that had been in the Marlow family since before the War of Northern Aggression, loomed large upon the landscape. It was a three-story monolith which had seen better days. Its regal structure and the land upon which it sat was sadly in need of repair, yet at a distance, the charm of the pillared edifice was still imposing.

Lash reclined in an old wicker chair on the veranda of his family home, nursing his third bourbon and water and surveying all that was his. This was his favorite time of the day. It wasn't because the workday was over and he was taking a well-earned rest. It was because Graystone looked better at half-light.

He tossed back the last of his drink, trying to pinpoint exactly where his plans for glory had gone wrong. The liquor burned and he silently cursed the fact that he could no longer afford the best. He was drinking cheap bourbon, living in the servant's wing while the rest of the mansion was closed off, and down to doing for himself. He didn't even have the funds to hire a housekeeper and made only enough at his law practice to keep the taxes paid on his home and himself afloat.

His belly growled. Without conscious thought, he pushed himself up from the chair and entered the house, taking care to lock the door behind him. Just for a moment, he stood in the great hall, staring up at the spiral staircase gracing the entryway, remembering another time when the house had been alive with laughter and people.

Something moved in the far corner of the hall. He winced as the sound of scurrying feet scratched on the marble flooring, then disappeared behind a breakfront. It wasn't the first rodent of that size he'd seen inside these walls, but tonight, it would be one too many.

He started to shake, first with rage, then from despair. It was over! There would be no more dreams of bringing Graystone back to her former beauty, or of returning dignity to the Marlow name. And it was all because of Casey.

A red haze blurred his vision. He drew back and threw his glass toward the place where he'd last seen the rat. It shattered against the wall, splintering into minute crystal shards. Only afterward did he remember that it had been part of a set, but regret swiftly faded. What did it matter? His only guests wore long tails and came on four feet...in the dark...in the middle of the night.

Startled by the sound of breaking glass, the rat that had taken refuge behind the breakfront made a run down the hallway for the deeper shadows beyond. As it did, something inside of Lash snapped. He grabbed at his grandfather's ivory-handled walking stick that had been standing in the hall tree for more than forty years, and ran, catching the rat just as it neared safety. He swung down with deadly force and the sound shattered the silence within the old walls as well as what was left of Lash's reason. Glass splintered on the wall behind him as he drew back the cane, but he didn't notice.

Even after the rat was dead, Lash continued to hail it with a barrage of blows until gore began to splatter on his shoes and the cuffs of his pants.

But in his mind, the rat had been dispatched from the first blow he'd struck. He was oblivious to the overkill, or that he might have lost more than his control. He kept venting his rage on a woman who'd dashed his dreams. And it wasn't the rodent who was coming apart on the cool marble floor. It was the beautiful and complacent surface of Casey Ruban's face.

When he finally stopped, his body was shaking from exertion and the muscles in his arms were burning from the energy he'd spent. He stared in disbelief at what he'd done, then tossed the cane down on the floor, disgusted by its condition.

Weary in both body and spirit, he turned and then stared at the wall in disbelief. The mirror! The glass in the ornate, gold-rimmed mirror that had hung in this hall for as long as he could remember, was shattered. His heart began to pound as he looked at the broken and refracted image of himself—a true reflection of his life.

He stepped back in horror and reached for the rabbit's foot in the pocket of his pants. All he could think as he backed away was, Seven long years of bad luck.

Chapter 4

Casey roused from a restless sleep. Disoriented by unfamiliar surroundings, it took a few moments for reality to return. Someone moaned. Her first thought was that Ryder could be sick. Quietly, she crawled out of bed and tiptoed to the door, aware that he'd made his bed in the middle of the living room floor. The moan came again, only this time, louder.

When she'd seen him last, he'd been unfolding a sleeping bag. But this was frightening. She didn't know what to make of it. What if he was hurt, or sick?

Just as she turned the doorknob something crashed to the floor. An image of intruders made her hesitate, but only for a moment.

The door opened inward on well-oiled hinges. She peered into the living room, searching the shadows to make certain she and Ryder were still alone. The outer door was shut, as were the windows. As she listened, the hum of the central air-conditioning unit kicked on, changing the texture of the night. She took a step forward, then another, then another until she was behind the sofa and peering over it.

Ryder was stretched out in his sleeping bag there on the floor.

Lying half in and half out of the faint glow from the security lights outside, he seemed more shadow than substance.

And while she was watching, he jerked and then moaned, throwing one arm over his eyes, as if warding off some unseen blow.

This explained the sounds that had wakened her. Ryder appeared to be dreaming. She moved closer, leaning over the sofa for a better view. And as she did, accidentally scooted it with the force of her body. The wooden legs screeched across the vinyl flooring like chalk on a blackboard. The sound was enough to wake the dead...and Ryder.

He came up and out of his sleeping bag and before Casey could react, he had grabbed her by the throat, and pinned her to the wall. His face and body were in darkness, but there was enough light for her to know to be afraid. The look in his eyes was grim, and the grip he had around her throat was all but deadly. She grabbed at his wrists before his grip tightened further.

"Ryder...Ryder, it's me."

"Oh, my God!" He jerked, moving his hand from her throat to the side of her face in a quick gesture of assurance. "Dammit, Casey, I'm sorry, but you startled me."

Casey closed her eyes as her legs went weak.

She rubbed at the tightness in her throat where his fingers had been. "It's okay. It was partly my fault for sneaking up on you like that."

Remorse shafted through him as he saw her fingering her throat. Dammit, he'd hurt her. He caught her hand, and then the moment they touched, wished that he'd kept his hands to himself. She was too close and too tempting.

Her focus suddenly shifted from her throat to him. They were face-to-face—body to body, and only inches from each other's lips.

Breath caught. Hearts stopped. First hers, then his.

She swallowed. "You were having a bad dream."

He inhaled slowly then spoke. "I'm sorry I frightened you."

Once again, she was struck by the size of him, of the breadth of his shoulders blocking out the light coming through the windows behind him.

"It's okay. It was partly my fault," she said.

She moved her hand and accidentally brushed the surface of his chest. His skin felt combustible. Muscles tensed beneath her fingertips and she jerked back her hand.

When he took a deep breath, she looked up. His eyes were glittering and there was a faint sheen of perspiration on his body. At that moment, she remembered what she was wearing, and realized what he was not.

He slept in the buff.

Her gown was short and sheer.

Seduction had been the last thing on her mind when she'd bought it, but from the way Ryder was staring at her now, it wasn't far from his. She could almost hear what he was thinking. He *was* her husband. This *was* their first night alone. But from her standpoint, what he was so obviously thinking could not—must not—happen.

Ryder was in shock. To wake up from the horror of reliving the crash that had killed his father to find a beautiful, half-dressed woman within reach made him want. He wanted to make love. He wanted to feel the softness of a woman's body—a woman's lips. To get lost in that certain rapture. To celebrate life because he couldn't forget death. That's what he wanted. But it wasn't going to happen, and because he knew it, his voice was harsh and angry.

"Go back to bed."

She tried to explain. "Look, I didn't mean to—"

He pinned her against the wall with a hand on either side of her head and leaned down, so close to her that his whisper was as loud as a shout.

"Either get the hell out of my sight or take off your clothes."

Casey bolted for the bedroom, slamming the door behind her and then leaning against it, as if the weight of her body might add strength to the flimsy barrier that stood between them.

For several interminable seconds she stood without moving, listening for the sound of footsteps. When all she heard were a few muffled curses and then the sound of a slamming door, she relaxed and then panicked. What if he was leaving for good?

She opened the door with a jerk, but when she realized all of his things were still inside, she shut it again. She crawled into bed and pulled up the covers, again, erecting another puny barrier between them.

In spite of the cool air circulating throughout the room, it seemed stifling. And while she waited anxiously for him to return, she considered their temporary bonds.

Ryder Justice had promised to love and honor her, to take care of her in sickness and in health. She didn't know about the loving, but some part of her trusted that he wouldn't lie. He'd said he would stay the year and she believed him. It was that fact alone that gave her ease enough to go back to sleep.

When she woke again, the alarm on the bedside table was going off, and water was running in the shower.

Casey's first impulse was fear. He'd come into her room and she'd never known. Her second was picturing what he was doing. Remembering the condition in which he'd emerged last night, she jumped out of bed, grabbing for her robe and slippers as she ran a hasty brush through the tangles in her hair. This time when he came out of the shower, she had no intention of being anywhere in sight.

When she exited the apartment, she stood for a moment on the landing, savoring the Mississippi morning. It was going to be another hot one, she could tell. The thought of freshly brewed coffee and some of Tilly's hot biscuits and jelly drew her down the stairs with haste, across the courtyard, in the back door of the mansion, and into the kitchen.

"Something smells good," she said.

The woman standing at the stove turned in quick surprise. There was a faint flush from the hcat of the oven staining her face and a warning in her eyes.

"Casey Dee, you scared me half to death."

"I'm sorry," Casey said, and went for her good-morning hug.

Tilly smoothed and fussed at the long hair hanging down Casey's back, then hugged her tightly to soften the accusation in her words. "Well now, girl, what are you doing over here without your man?"

She sighed. If only things were as simple now as they'd been back when she was a child.

"He's in the shower." Casey slumped in a chair with a pout. "Oh, Tilly, Delaney has made such a mess out of my life."

"No, ma'am. Delaney didn't do it, you did. He just went and made some silly rule, and as always, you're still running along behind him, trying to make everything right."

Casey was speechless. This wasn't the sympathy she'd been wanting. She tried to glare, but it just wasn't possible. Not at Tilly. And then she sighed. Tilly always gave her sympathy, but where Casey wanted it or not, it also came with the truth.

"So, he started it," Casey said, and managed to grin.

"And you sure did finish it, didn't you, girl? The very idea! Going down to the flatlands to find yourself a man."

Casey's eyebrows rose. "How did you know?"

Tilly snorted delicately and returned to stirring the eggs she'd been cooking. "I know, 'cause you're my baby," she said softly. "I know 'cause I make it my business to know."

The air in Casey's throat became too thick to breathe. She stood and slipped her arms around Tilly's waist, then laid her cheek in the middle of her back, relishing the familiarity of freshly ironed fabric and a steady heartbeat.

"And I thank God that you care," Casey said softly. "You and Joshua are all the family I have left."

Tilly set the skillet off the fire and turned until she and Casey were eye to eye. "No, girl, you're wrong. You've got yourself a husband now."

Casey's laugh was brittle. "I don't have a husband. I have a stranger for a year."

Tilly took her by the shoulders and shook her. "What you have is a chance. Now make the most of it." Before Casey could argue further, Tilly waved her away. "Go tell your man my biscuits are about ready to come out of the oven. By the time you two get back, bacon and eggs will be ready, too."

"But I don't know if he likes..."

Tilly's stare never wavered. "Then don't you think it's about time you found out?"

Casey exited the kitchen with as much grace as she could muster. After her and Ryder's encounter last night, she was almost afraid to face him. The tail of her robe was dragging as she walked up the stairs. When she stumbled and came close to falling, she picked it up and walked the rest of the way with the hem held above her ankles.

Ryder met her at the door. She knew that she was staring, but she hadn't been prepared for the change in his appearance. Clean-shaven, smelling like soap and something light and musky, he seemed taller than ever. She tried not to gawk, but the new blue jeans he was wearing suited him all too well, and he'd left the top three buttons on his long-sleeved white shirt undone, revealing far too much of that broad, brown chest for her peace of mind. The only thing she recognized from before were his old black boots, and even they were shining. Still damp from his shower, his hair gleamed black in the early morning sunshine.

"Mornin'," he said softly, and stepped aside to let her in. "Someone from the house just called. Said they wanted a ride into the city."

Casey blinked, telling herself to concentrate on what he was saying instead of how he looked, but it was difficult. Today, those grey eyes of his almost looked blue.

"It isn't even eight o'clock," she muttered. "You haven't had breakfast, and they can wait."

A slight grin cornered one edge of his mouth and then slid out of sight. "I don't know what we'll eat. Yesterday I forgot to buy milk."

"It doesn't matter. This morning we're having breakfast in the kitchen with Tilly. She said to hurry."

"Who's Tilly?"

"The woman who raised me after Mother and Father were killed. She's Joshua's wife. You remember him from yesterday?"

He nodded, then reached for the broad-brimmed, black Stetson hanging by the door. "Someone else's cooking sounds good to me." When Casey moved toward their bedroom, he paused. "Aren't you coming, or don't you eat with the hired help?"

She spun, and there was no mistaking the anger in her voice. "Don't *ever,* and I mean, *ever,* refer to Tilly or Joshua as servants again. Do you understand?"

Surprised by her vehemence, his estimation of her went up a notch. ''Yes, ma'am, I believe that I do.''

Again, Casey realized she'd overreacted. He must be as off-center as she felt. ''Sorry. I didn't mean...''

''Easy now.''

Her stomach tied itself into a little knot. If only he'd quit saying those words in those tones.

''I am easy,'' she said, and then groaned beneath her breath as a grin spread across his face. ''Don't say it,'' she muttered. ''You know what I meant.''

''Casey.''

A little nervous about what he would say next, she couldn't have been more surprised by what came out.

''Don't ever apologize for having a good heart.''

After witnessing the dangerous side of him last night, his gentleness was the last thing she would have expected.

''Was that a compliment?'' she asked.

He ignored her. ''Hurry up and get dressed. I'm starving.''

''Feel free to go on ahead. Tilly will be glad to...''

''No.''

''No?''

''I'll wait for you,'' he said.

She inhaled sharply, and then shut the bedroom door behind her as she went inside. Her hands were shaking as she sorted through the closet for something to wear.

I'll wait for you.

His promise was echoing inside her head as she brushed and zipped and buttoned. Putting on makeup was even more difficult because she found herself looking through tears, but she refused to let them fall. She wasn't going to let that man get to her, not in any way.

Erica sauntered into the downstairs kitchen just as Tilly was dishing up the eggs.

''What's taking so long this morning?'' Erica grumbled, picking a strip of hot, crisp bacon from the platter and crunching it between her teeth.

"Get on out of my kitchen," Tilly said. "Everything is right on time and you know it."

Erica hated this woman's uppity manner, and at the same time, respected her authority just enough not to argue.

"It's not your kitchen," Erica grumbled, taking one last piece of bacon with her as she started out of the room.

"It's not yours, either," Tilly said sharply, and banged a spoon on the side of the pan to punctuate her remark.

Erica glared. And then the back door opened and she forgot what she'd been about to say. She forgot she was chewing, or that she was holding her next bite in her hand. All she could do was stare—right past her sister to the man behind her. Almost choking, she managed to swallow, then dropped the other piece of bacon back onto the platter.

Casey didn't see Erica. Her focus was on the woman at the stove. Until Matilda Bass passed judgment on what she'd done, she wouldn't feel right.

"Tilly, this is my, uh...this is Ryder Justice. Ryder, this is Matilda Bass. I consider her my second mother, as well as the best cook in the whole state of Mississippi."

Upon entering the kitchen, he'd taken off his hat. He extended his hand in a gesture of friendship, which Tilly accepted with obvious reticence. But Ryder behaved as if he'd known her all of his life.

"Mrs. Bass, it's a pleasure. If everything tastes as good as it smells, I'd warrant Casey is right."

Tilly's gaze wavered. She hadn't been prepared for someone like him, and he *was* someone, that she could tell. She frowned slightly. This man didn't look like any drifter out of the flatlands. He didn't sound like one, either. His words were sweet, his appearance sweeter. All she could think was, He'd better be good to my girl.

She nodded regally, accepting the praise as just. "Call me Tilly, and I'm pleased to meet you, sir. You aren't from these parts, are you?"

He grinned. "I don't answer to anything but Ryder, and no, ma'am, I'm not."

Tilly nodded in satisfaction. ''I knew as much. I'd be guessing you're from Oklahoma...or Texas. Am I right?''

Startled by her perception, he didn't have it in him to lie. ''Yes, ma'am... Texas.''

Casey felt strange. Here she was married to the man and she'd been so caught up in her own agenda, she hadn't had enough curiosity about him to wonder where he was from, or how he'd gotten from there to here.

''Then sit,'' Tilly said. ''Food's ready.''

Only after they'd taken their seats did Casey realize Erica was in the room. She looked up at her and smiled, but when her sister sauntered over to Ryder and ran her fingertips lightly across his back, measuring their breadth from shoulder to shoulder, the urge to slap her away from him was almost overwhelming.

There was a cold, mirthless smile on Erica's face as she finally glanced in Casey's direction.

''Well, well, princess. Even when you fall, you land on your feet, don't you?''

Casey's hackles rose even further. ''Let it go, Erica.''

Erica's expression was bland, but her eyes glittered with envy. ''Oh my, I guess that didn't come out quite right, did it?''

The antagonism between the two sisters was palpable. Ryder suspected it probably had more to do with old wounds than with his arrival into their midst. Nevertheless, whatever its roots, he seemed to be the latest weed to cause dissent. He took it upon himself to change the subject.

''Someone called me earlier for a ride into town. Do you know who it was?''

Erica's smile broadened. ''It wasn't me, but that's not such a bad idea. I'll bet you give really good rides.''

Ryder's expression blanked, and if Erica had been as astute as she believed herself to be, she would have backed off then, before it was too late. But she didn't.

''I'm even better at giving a hard time to people who tick me off,'' he said.

Erica's expression froze. A slap in the face couldn't have stunned her more.

If Casey had been the impulsive type, she would have thrown

her arms around his neck and hugged him. But she wasn't, and the moment passed.

"Tell whoever it is that Ryder is unavailable until we've finished our breakfast," she said. "This morning, my husband and I just want a little peace and quiet and a meal to ourselves."

Ryder's eyebrows rose. Husband! Now she was admitting he was her husband?

Suddenly Ryder's mouth was only inches from Casey's ear. She could feel his breath—almost hear the laughter in his voice as he whispered.

"I thought we weren't using *that* word."

Casey glared.

Erica was left with nowhere to go but out. She walked away, leaving Ryder with a contemplative stare that Casey chose to ignore.

"I guess if a person is observant, they can learn something new every day," he muttered.

Casey looked up. "Like what?"

"Never knew there were any barracudas in Mississippi."

"Excuse me?"

"Nothing," Ryder said. "I was just thinking out loud."

Tilly's back was to the pair, but her smile was wide as she added the finishing touch to her eggs before setting them on the table. She wasn't the type of woman to make snap judgments, but after the way Ryder had cut Erica Dunn off at the mouth, she was pretty sure he was going to do just fine.

She set the plates before them. "Now eat up before my eggs get cold." She set a full pan of steaming hot biscuits in front of them as well. "Fresh out of the oven, Casey Dee, just the way you like them."

Casey rolled her eyes in appreciation of the golden brown tops and reached for one to butter.

"Since you're a married lady now and have your own place, I guess you'll be needing to learn how to make these," Tilly said. "When you get time, I'll be needing to teach you."

Casey looked stunned. Ryder hid his grin behind a bite of scrambled eggs. Poor Casey. It would seem that her life had taken more changes than she was ready to accept.

''Making biscuits seems a bit of a leap for a woman who can't boil water,'' Ryder said.

Ignoring Casey's gasp, he scooped a spoonful of strawberry preserves onto his biscuit and then bit into the hot bread, chewing with relish.

''Well, I never,'' she muttered.

Ryder swallowed, took a slow sip of coffee, then fixed Casey with a sultry gaze. ''I know that, wife. But one of these days you will.''

The implications of what he'd just said were impossible to misinterpret. He hadn't been talking about biscuits, and they both knew it. Furious that he kept catching her off guard, she stabbed at the food on her plate with undue force, scraping the tines of the fork across the china and earning her a cool I-taught-you-better-than-that look from Tilly.

The rest of the meal passed in relative silence, broken only by the coming and going of Tilly and Joshua as they carried food into the breakfast room for the family who would now be living off the fruit of Casey's labors. It was Ryder who finally broke the silence.

''That does it for me,'' he said. ''I guess I'd better go earn my keep.'' He winked at Casey, taking small delight in the fact that she didn't welcome it, and tweaked her ear for the hell of it as he passed.

''Do you know where you're going?'' Casey asked, as he sauntered out of the room.

He paused, then turned, and once again, she was struck by the fact that his answer had nothing to do with the question she'd asked.

''No. But then it hasn't really mattered for months now. Why should today be any different?''

When he disappeared, she was forced to accept the fact that not only had she married a stranger, but it would seem one with more secrets than he cared to tell.

She took a last gulp of her coffee and tossed down her napkin. If he had her troubles, he'd have something to complain about. She glanced at her watch. It was a quarter to nine. Past time for the boss to be at work. But, since she *was* the boss, she was going to finish her coffee.

Meanwhile, Ryder was making his way through the maze of rooms and getting a firsthand impression of the atmosphere in which Casey had grown up.

The mansion itself was grand—with three stories of granite blocks that came far too close to resembling a castle rather than a home. The only thing Ryder felt was missing was a moat. The snakes and crocodiles were already in place, but they walked on two legs, rather than four, and hid their sharp teeth behind fake smiles.

His footsteps echoed on the cold marble floors as he made his way toward the muted sound of voices coming from a room up the hallway and to the right. The breakfast room, he presumed.

As he entered the doorway, he paused, staring at the bright morning sun beaming in through spotless windows, through which an arbor of hot pink bougainvillea could be seen.

The crystal on the table was elegant. The china was a plain, classic white with a delicate gold rim, and the silverware gleamed with a high, polished gloss as the people in residence lifted it to their mouths. Flowers were everywhere. Cut and in vases. Growing from pots. In one-dimensional form, painted on canvas and framed, then hung at just the right level for the eye to see.

In spite of the heat of the day, Ryder shuddered. Such elegance. Such cold, cold elegance. He thought of the woman who'd come storming into that bar with her long hair down and windblown, wearing that bit of a black dress, and tried to picture her being raised in a place like this. For some reason, the little he knew of Casey didn't jibe with these surroundings. How could a woman with so much passion survive in a house with no joy—no life?

And Casey Ruban Justice had passion, of that he had no doubt. Most of the time she seemed to keep it channeled toward the business end of her world, but every so often her guard slipped, and had she known it, in those moments, Ryder saw more of her soul than she would have liked.

He settled his Stetson a little tighter on his head, as if bracing himself for a gale wind, and sauntered into the breakfast room as if he owned the place.

"Who wanted the ride?"

Three sets of equally startled expressions turned in his direction. Erica was still seething from his earlier put-down and chose to ignore him.

Miles stared, holding his cup of coffee suspended halfway between table and lips, trying to picture this clean-cut, larger-than-life cowboy as the same ragged derelict who'd come trailing in behind Casey yesterday morning.

Eudora gasped and set her cup down in its saucer with a sharp, unladylike clink.

"Why, it was me," she said. "But I'm not quite ready."

Ryder smiled. "I've got all day. Don't hurry on my account."

"For future reference, you need not come into the family area," Miles drawled. "Simply wait out front."

Ryder shifted his stance. It wasn't much. Only an inch or so. But to Miles, it seemed to make the man that much taller. And it made Miles distinctly uncomfortable looking up at so much man.

"Look," Ryder growled. "Let's get one thing straight. Like it or not, and I can't say that I care much for it myself, for the time being, I *am* part of your family. Therefore, do not expect me to scuttle around outside the back door like some damned stray dog looking for a handout. Do I make myself clear?"

Miles' face turned a bloody shade of red. All he could do was splutter and look toward Erica, who was usually the more verbal of the pair, for support. Unaware that Ryder had already put her in her place, he was unprepared for his sister's silence. He tried again.

"But Casey said..."

"Casey can say whatever she chooses," Ryder said. "However, you might want to remember that she's my wife, not my boss. And, you might also want to remember that while I mind my own business, I expect others to do the same." Then he touched the brim of his hat and winked at Eudora. "I'll be outside when you're ready."

He walked out.

When he was halfway down the hall, the breakfast room

seemed to erupt into a cacophony of sound. Three separate voices, all talking at once in various tones of disbelief. Unable to remember the last time he'd felt this alive, he grinned all the way out the door.

Chapter 5

"Stop there!" Eudora ordered, pointing toward a boutique on the upcoming street corner.

Ryder aimed the gleaming white Lincoln toward a horizontal parking space and slid into it with nothing to spare. Before Eudora could object to the fact that he'd parked several doors down and she was going to have to walk, he had opened the door and was reaching in to help her out.

Smoothing at her hair and clothes, she began to issue her standard orders. "I don't know how long I'll be, but..."

"No problem," he said. "I'm coming with you," he said, and offered her his arm.

Ignoring the shocked expression on her face, he escorted her up the street and into the store. Eudora was so stunned by his actions that she let herself be led into The Pink Boutique.

The saleslady all but fawned as she met her at the door. "Mrs. Deathridge, please accept our condolences on your recent loss. Delaney Ruban will be missed."

"Yes, well, I thank you on behalf of the family," Eudora muttered, casting a sidelong glance at Ryder who was still standing at her side. He was too big to ignore and seemed too determined to dissuade from accompanying her. She waved toward an overstuffed chair near the alcove where the dressing rooms were situated. "You may wait over there."

Ryder took his seat without comment. Eudora watched as he carefully lifted the Stetson from his head. Placing it crown-side down in his lap, he seemed to settle.

After that she relaxed, but only slightly. There was something about that man that unnerved her. Even though he was now across the room from her and sitting still, his presence was overpowering. Frowning, she turned away and began sorting through the garments on the racks, still conscious of his eyes boring into her back. He took up space. That's what he did. He took up entirely too much space.

Half an hour came and went, along with the saleslady's patience. Eudora had picked through and complained about everything the store carried in her size. It made no difference to her that Gladys was nearly in tears, or that the manager had made several pointed trips through the room, each time giving Gladys a sharp, condemning look for not being able to placate a customer, especially one from Ruban Crossing's foremost family.

Eudora was so caught up with the seriousness of her shopping spree that she'd completely forgotten Ryder's existence, so when he spoke, he had Eudora's...and the saleslady's...immediate and undivided attention.

"Take the blue one."

Eudora spun, still holding the dress in question. "Were you speaking to me?"

Ryder tilted his head. "It matches your eyes. Always did like blue-eyed women."

Having said his piece, he stretched, giving himself permission to take up even more of the floor space by unfolding his long legs out before him. While she watched, he locked his hands across his belly as if he didn't have a care in the world.

Eudora wasn't accustomed to having anyone, especially a chauffeur, give her advice on her choices of clothing, yet this man's entrance into their world had already changed their lives.

She heard herself repeating his suggestion as if it had true merit and wondered if she was finally losing her mind.

"The blue?"

He nodded, then shrugged. "Yes, ma'am, but it was just a suggestion. My father always said it never paid to rush a woman."

"Oh, do quit calling me ma'am," Eudora said. "It sounds too elderly."

Ryder looked up and almost grinned. "Well, now, Dora, didn't anyone ever tell you that age is in the mind of the beholder?"

Eudora's mouth dropped. This man was positively impossible. Of course he should have known she meant for him to call her Mrs. Deathridge, not Dora! The very idea, shortening her name like that.

But the deed had already been done, and the name rang in her ears. Dora. That was what her husband, Henry, had called her, and Henry had been dead for all these many years. She gave Ryder a sidelong glance and disappeared into the dressing room with the blue dress in her hand. Dora. Dora. What would Erica and Miles have to say about this?

She shut the door behind her then looked up. Her reflection looked back. For a moment, she almost didn't recognize herself. Her eyes were bright—from shock, of course. But the glimmer did give life to her expression. Dora. She held the blue dress up beneath her chin. He was right. It brought out the true color of her eyes. She smiled. Maybe he wasn't so bad after all.

Only after he was alone did Ryder realize what he'd said. He'd actually thought of his father without coming unglued. In fact, just for a moment, it had felt damned good to remember him at all.

He jammed his Stetson on his head then pulled the brim down low across his forehead and closed his eyes. Ah God, but he missed that old man. So much that it hurt.

Lash stood on the veranda, staring at the brake lights on the plumber's van as it slowed to take a corner. A soft, early morning breeze lifted the hair from his forehead, cooling the sweat that had beaded minutes earlier when the plumber had handed him his bill.

Despair settled a little closer upon his shoulders.

Impulsively, he walked down the steps and out into the yard, heading for the gazebo. As a child, it had been his favorite place. As an adult, it was where he went to hide.

Ivy clung to the latticed walls, crocheted by nature into heavy loops of variegated green. Inside, the air rarely moved and only the most persistent rays of sunshine were able to pick and poke their way through the dense growth.

He dropped onto the bench in a slump, then wadded the bill and tossed it into the gathering pile on the floor. Why bother to keep track if they couldn't be paid?

Minutes passed. He looked down at his watch. It was past time to open the office. With a sigh, he shoved himself off the bench, giving the pile of unpaid bills a final glance. Poor Graystone. She was so sick—in need of too many repairs for his meager pocket to accommodate.

His eyes misted as he walked across the yard. As he entered the house in search of his suit coat and briefcase, a continuing thought kept running through his mind.

It was Casey's fault. Casey had ruined it all. Beautiful, willful Casey who had so much, while he had nothing at all. He yanked his coat from a hook, thinking of the parties that would be given in her honor, coveting the priceless wedding gifts she would certainly be receiving as her due.

Despair fed anger. Anger fed hate. And something fell to the floor behind him with a clank. He spun in time to see a long, hairless tail disappearing beneath the cupboard. A rat. Another damned rat.

He grabbed a can of corn from the cabinet, firing it toward the place where he'd seen it last. "What the hell are you still doing here? I thought rats abandoned sinking ships."

Several items had fallen off a low shelf and onto the floor as the door to the cupboard flew open. The sight of spilled salt sent Lash to his knees. Scrambling to regain his sense of balance in his superstitious world, he grabbed a pinch of the salt and tossed it over his shoulder. Even though one part of his brain told him that spilled salt did not bad luck make, he was too much a product of his upbringing to ignore it all now.

Still down on his knees, he set to retrieving the few family heirlooms he hadn't sold. It wasn't until he was setting his grandfather's sorghum pewter pitcher back on the shelf that he noticed a small, flat box at the back of the cupboard. Frowning, he pulled it out. When he opened the lid, his eyes widened and a delighted smile lit up his somber expression. Grandfather's letter opener! He'd completely forgotten its existence.

He ran a tentative finger down the thin, double-edged blade, remembering the hours he'd spent in Aaron Marlow's lap, remembering the first time his grandfather had let him use it without help. For all its beauty, it was still a small and deadly thing.

A brown shadow moved to the right of Lash's hand. He reacted without thinking. Seconds later, he rocked back on his heels in shock, staring at the carcass of the rat and the small silver dagger embedded in its body.

Bile rose, burning his throat and choking him as he scrambled to his feet and ran for the sink just in time to keep from puking on himself. When he was able to look back without gagging, all he could see was his family honor embedded in the belly of the rat.

In Lash's mind, it was the last and ultimate disgrace. Wild-eyed and looking for someone else to blame, he stared at the salt. Bad luck. Bad luck. It was all a matter of bad luck.

In a daze, he yanked the dagger out of the rat, wiping off the bloody blade on the kitchen curtain. His hands were shaking as he laid it back in the box. So, he'd come to this, and thanks to Casey Justice, this is where he would stay.

He shuddered then sighed as he closed the lid to the box. Casey. He'd lost everything because of her. The box felt warm in his hands as he slipped it into his pocket before picking up his briefcase.

A muscle jerked in his jaw as he walked out of the house. Once again, he glanced at his watch. There was something he needed to do before he went to the office. He didn't know where his manners had gone. He should have thought of it before.

* * *

Casey tossed her pen down on the desk and swiveled her chair to face the window overlooking the business district of Ruban Crossing. As she did, a flash of white caught her eye and she stood abruptly, searching for a glimpse of the family's white Lincoln.

Was that Ryder? She looked until her eyes began to burn and the muscles in the backs of her legs began to knot. Disgusted with herself, she turned away from the window to return to her chair.

The high gloss on her desk was obliterated by a mountain of paperwork to her left, which was only increments smaller than the mountain of paperwork to her right. She closed her eyes and tried to relax, playing her favorite what-if game. The one that went...what if she walked out of the office and never came back? In her mind, she was halfway out of town when her secretary, Nola Sue, buzzed.

"Mrs. Justice, you have a delivery."

The mention of her name change alone was enough to yank Casey back to reality.

"Just sign for it. I'll pick it up later."

"I'm sorry, Mrs. Justice, but the man insists on your signature only."

Casey sighed. "Then send him in."

Moments later, the door opened and a uniformed messenger came into the room. Brief and to the point, he handed her a clipboard and a pen.

"Sign here, please."

Casey did as she was told, casually eyeing the flat, oblong package the man laid on her desk.

"Good day, Mrs. Justice."

And then he was gone.

My, how word does get around in this town, Casey thought, as she slipped a letter opener between the folds of paper. A glimmer of color began to emerge from beneath the plain, brown wrapping. The second layer of paper was a thick, pure white embossed with silver doves. An obvious allusion to the wedding that hardly was. Curious now, she abandoned the letter opener for her fingers and tore through that layer to a flat black box.

It was a little over a foot in length and no more than three or four inches in width. The lid was hinged by two delicate foil butterflies. Casey gasped at the contents as a card fell out and into her lap.

Inside lay a miniature rapier on thick, black velvet. She lifted it from the case, hefting it lightly. It felt heavy, even warm in her hand, and she knew before she turned it over to view the silversmith's mark that it was probably solid silver. It was the most elaborate letter opener she'd ever seen.

Curious, she laid it aside and picked up the card, all the while wondering who would send her such a thing. She read, "Casey, On your nuptials: You deserve this...and so much more. Lash."

She frowned at the oddity of the phrasing, then laid the card aside and picked the small rapier up again, eyeing the double-edged blade with caution. Something near the tip caught her eye. At first, she thought it was rust, and that the letter opener must not be silver after all, because silver did not rust. Even after she ran the tip of her finger across the spot, it didn't come off. But when she lifted it for a closer look, she suddenly shifted in her seat, making room for the unexpected sense of foreboding that swept over her.

She swiveled her chair toward the window and full light, tilting the blade for a closer look still, then tested the spot with the tip of a fingernail. It came away on her nail. Startled, she grabbed for a tissue and wiped at her finger, unprepared for the small, red stain that suddenly appeared against stark white.

She couldn't quit staring. The spot wasn't rust, it was blood—dried blood. But in such a small amount that it might have gone unnoticed.

Now her delight in such a gift was replaced with dismay. It seemed a travesty of something pure to receive a wedding gift with blood on it. The urge to put it out of sight was strong. She laid it back in the box, closing the lid with care, but the words on the card had now taken on a sinister meaning.

You deserve this...and so much more.

Deserve what? What did she deserve? The silver...the knife...or the blood?

The phone rang. It was the private line that only family ever used. She grabbed for it like a lifeline.

"Hello."

"Casey, darling, it's Erica. Have you seen Grandmother?"

For once, she was almost thankful for the whine in her half sister's voice. It gave her something else on which to focus besides Lash's gift.

"No, I'm sorry, but I haven't."

Erica sighed. "It's nearly one o'clock. She was going to meet me for lunch, and she's thirty minutes late. She's never late, you know."

Casey frowned. That much was true. Gran had a thing about being tardy.

"It's probably all his fault," Erica said.

"All whose fault?" Casey asked.

"Your husband...the family chauffeur...however you choose to define him. He took Grandmother shopping hours ago and no one's seen a sign of them since." The tone of Erica's voice rose an octave. "We don't know a thing about him. I can't believe you actually brought a stranger into this household, shoved him down our throats and then expected us to accept his presence as status quo."

Casey stifled a sigh. This was all she needed.

"Look, Erica. Nothing has happened to Gran. If it had, Ryder would have called. He is not a fiend. Besides, why didn't you call her instead of me? There's a phone in the Lincoln."

"I know that," Erica snapped. "But no one's answering."

Casey looked at the stacks of files on her desk and wondered how her grandfather had gone so wrong. She was beating her head against a thousand brick walls and all Erica had to worry about was a late luncheon date.

"I don't know what to tell you," Casey said. "I'm sure she's fine. I'm sorry she's late."

The connection between them was broken when Erica slammed the receiver back into the cradle. For a few wonderful moments, all Casey could hear were muffled voices from the outer office. With a dogged determination of which Delaney Ruban would have been proud, Casey dropped the gift into a drawer and buzzed Nola Sue.

"Cancel my lunch with Rosewell and Associates. Reschedule for sometime next week."

"Yes, ma'am," Nola Sue said, making notations as she listened to Casey's orders. "Do you want me to order you something to eat?"

"I suppose," she said. "And call home. Tell them I'll be working late and not to hold dinner."

Within seconds, she'd forgotten about Lash Marlow's present and Erica's phone call. Her entire focus was on the figures before her and the study she would need before she could make an offer for the acquisition of the Harmon Canneries near Tupelo.

A short while later, Nola Sue set a small, plastic tub of chicken salad, a cold roll, and a melting cup of iced tea on the corner of Casey's desk and tiptoed out without uttering a word.

It was sometime later before Casey even noticed that lunch had been served.

"Want some ketchup on those fries?" Ryder asked. Eudora poked the lingering end of a fast-food French fry into her mouth and then shook her head. Seconds later, Ryder handed her a fistful of paper napkins.

"Thank you," she said.

When she was certain Ryder's attention was otherwise occupied, she licked the salt from her fingers before drying them on the paper napkins he'd tossed in her lap, then leaned back against the seat, sighing with satisfaction.

She couldn't remember the last time food had tasted this good. Stifling a small belch, she lifted her cup to her lips and latched onto the straw poking through the plastic lid, sucking with all her might. A couple of swallows later, she began to suck air.

"How about another cherry limeade?"

"No, but thank you," Eudora said, and tossed a used napkin on the floor next to the wrapper that had been around her cheeseburger.

The food had been delicious. She wasn't going to think about the fact that it had all been served in recycled paper. There was something about reusing paper—in any form or fashion—that smacked of poverty. Eudora Deathridge had not suffered a day of want in her entire life, and had no intentions of starting now. She belched again, then sighed. This had been worth her impending heartburn.

Ryder hid a grin. He'd given her hell this morning and knew it. From the time they'd entered the first store, to the last one they'd exited just before lunch, he'd been on her heels at every turn.

He had been nothing but respectful. It wasn't in him to be anything else. But he figured the "family" needed to know right off that while he didn't mind driving them all over kingdom come, he was going to do it his way. And if that meant making himself a slight nuisance, then so be it. He was the best when it came to being a pain in the ass. If they didn't believe him, then they could just ask his...

Oh, God. He'd done it again. Micah's name kept hovering at the edge of his mind, popping out when least expected. He hated being weak, but guilt was eating him alive. No longer hungry, he began stuffing his leftovers back into the sack they'd come in.

"Here you go, Dora." He handed the half-filled sack over the seat.

Surprised by the gesture, she took it before she thought, letting it dangle between her fingers like something foul.

"What am I to do with this?"

"Trash. Put your trash in it."

She stared at the papers she'd tossed on the floorboard in disbelief. He was asking her to pick up trash? This time he'd overstepped his bounds.

"Now see here," she complained. "I don't think you..."

Ryder turned. Their gazes met. His eyes were dark and filled with a pain she hadn't expected.

"Need some help?"

"I don't believe so," she said quietly. "But thank you just the same."

She opened the sack and leaned down. A few moments later, she handed it back, watching as he tossed it in a barrel on the way out of the parking lot.

"Ryder."

He glanced up. Again, their gazes met briefly, this time in the rearview mirror.

"Yes, ma'am?"

"I'm ready to go home now."

He took the next turn, wishing he could say the same.

It was after eight o'clock. Ryder paced the small apartment like a caged bear—back and forth, from window to chair, unable to concentrate on the story on television, or eat the food congealing on his plate. Stifled by the presence of walls, he refused to admit that he was worried about Casey's absence.

Another half hour passed. By this time, he was steaming. He knew for a fact that Miles had packed up and left for a three-day trip to New Orleans to play. Erica and her grandmother had had a fight and Erica was sulking in her room because Dora had refused to grovel for forgetting their lunch date. Even Joshua and Tilly had finished up for the night and gone home. But Casey was still on the job. Something about that just didn't sit right with him, and his patience was gone.

He grabbed his hat on the way out the door. In a shorter time than one might have imagined, he had parked outside the Ruban Building and was on his way inside. A guard stopped him at the door.

"Sorry sir, but the offices are closed for the night."

Ryder shocked himself by announcing, "I'm here to pick up my wife."

"And who might that be?" the guard asked.

"Her name is—was—Casey Ruban."

The man took a quick step back, eyeing Ryder with new attention.

"You'd be the fellow Miss Ruban married."

Ryder nodded.

"Well, now, I might need to see some identification...just for the first time, you understand."

Ryder opened his wallet.

"Justice...yep, that would be you, all right," the guard said. "We heard Miss Ruban had married a man named Justice." He reached for the phone. "Just a minute, sir, and I'll let her know you're here."

"No," Ryder said, and then softened the tone of his voice with a halfhearted grin. "I was sort of planning to surprise her."

The guard smiled. "Yes, sir, I understand. Take the elevator to the top floor. Her office is the first one on your right."

"Thanks," Ryder said.

"You're welcome, sir," the guard said. "And congratulations on your marriage. Miss Ruban is a fine lady."

Ryder nodded. Even though she was a little hardheaded, he was beginning to have the same opinion of her himself.

By the time he got to her office, his sense of injustice was in high form. He walked inside and past the empty secretary's desk without pausing; his gaze fixed on the thin line of light showing from beneath the door on the far side of the room.

Casey's head hurt, her shoulders ached, and she was so far past hungry it didn't count. What was worse, she didn't even know it. Realization of her condition came only after the door to her office swung open and Ryder stalked into the room.

Startled, she stood too swiftly. The room began to tilt.

Ryder saw her sway and grabbed her arm before she staggered.

All she could think to say was, "What are you doing here?" before he took the pen from her hand, and turned out the desk lamp.

"I came to take you home. Your day is over. It's night. It's time to rest. It's time to slow the hell down. Do you understand me?"

He was mad. That was what surprised her most. Why should he be angry? It took a bit to realize that he wasn't angry at her. He was angry on her behalf. At that point, lack of food and exhaustion kicked in. Damn him, he wasn't supposed to be nice...at least, not like this.

She shrugged out of his grasp and reached for her purse. "I don't need you telling me what to do."

He stood between her and the doorway and once again, Casey caught a glimpse of the same man who'd come out of the shadows of Sonny's Place and taken a dare no other man had had the guts to take.

"Then consider it a suggestion," he said quietly, and reached for her arm.

This time she didn't pull away. They walked all the way to the elevator without talking, then past the night guard who grinned and winked. Silence was maintained all the way out to the car. It was only after Casey felt the seat at the back of her legs that she began to relax.

Ryder slid behind the wheel, then looked at her. It didn't take him long to make the decision. "Buckle up. You choose, but you're not going home until you eat."

Casey wrinkled her nose. "The car smells like French fries."

"Dora spilled a few. I'll clean it out tomorrow."

It took Casey a moment for the answer to connect. Dora? French fries? In the car? She turned where she sat, staring at Ryder in sudden confusion.

"Who's Dora?"

"You are bad off," he said, as he put the car in gear and backed out of the parking space. "She's your grandmother, isn't she?"

"You called her Dora?"

He shrugged as he pulled into traffic. "Said she didn't want me calling her ma'am."

"Why was Dora...I mean Gran...eating French fries in the car?"

"Because they went with her cheeseburger and cherry limeade."

Casey's mouth dropped. "She ate fast food?"

He grinned. "Ate it real fast, too. Never saw a woman so hungry."

Casey still didn't believe she was getting the story straight. "She ate her meal in the back seat of a car?"

Ryder gave her a sidelong glance. "Are you still faint?"

She covered her face with her hands and groaned. "My God, why did you take Gran to a fast-food restaurant?"

"Because she was hungry, that's why."

"But..."

He took the corner in a delicate skid, the likes of which the Lincoln had never seen. "You know what?"

Casey clutched at her seat belt, almost afraid to ask. "What?"

"You people are too uptight. You need to loosen up a little. If you did, you might find out you like it. Better yet, you might even live long enough to spend all that money you're so dead set on making."

There wasn't a civil thought in her head as Ryder turned off the highway and into another parking lot. But when he opened the door to help her out, the odor of charbroiled meat made her forget her anger. A few moments later, she realized where he'd brought her, and if she hadn't been so hungry, she would have laughed.

As he led her in the restaurant, she would have been willing to bet the last dollar she had in her pocket that, by tomorrow, it would be all over Ruban Crossing that Eudora Deathridge had eaten French fries in the back seat of a car. What was going to ice this piece of gossip was the fact that Casey and her honky-tonk husband had also shared a late-night dinner at Smoky Joe's. As restaurants go, it wasn't bad. It was Smoky Joe's sideline that gave him, and his restaurant, such a bad reputation.

Casey lifted her chin as they walked inside. She could tell by the sounds coming from the back room that the floor show was in full swing.

"Wonder what's going on back there?" Ryder asked, as he guided Casey to an empty booth.

"Mud wrestling," she said. One eyebrow arched as she waited for his reaction.

His interest sparked, he had to ask. "Women or 'gators?"

"Women," she replied.

She watched as the light in his eyes faded. She sighed. She should have known it would take more than naked women in a hot tub's worth of red clay to get him excited.

"I think he saves the 'gators for Saturday nights."

He handed her a menu. "Good. It'll give us a reason to come back."

Chapter 6

"I'm coming out. Are you decent?" Ryder yelled.

Casey pulled the sheet up past her breasts and tried to look relaxed as the bathroom door opened. He emerged, but she'd closed her eyes too late. My God! Doesn't he own a bathrobe? she wondered.

"I'll be through in a second," he said.

Casey could hear drawers opening and closing and clenched her eyelids even tighter. That damp towel around his waist was far too brief for her piece of mind.

Footsteps moved toward the doorway.

She opened her eyes. Too soon. She'd looked too soon. He was still there, standing in the doorway in a pair of white briefs. Lamplight spilled into the bedroom from behind him.

This time, his presence did more than unnerve her. Even though his face was in shadow, she knew he was watching her.

She held her breath.

He didn't speak.

In the bathroom next door, water dripped from the showerhead and into the tub. Then dripped again. Then again. Then again.

He started toward her, one slow step at a time. Casey stifled a moan, clutching at the sheet until her fingers went numb. Once she started to speak, and couldn't remember enough words to string together in one sentence. She went from panic to dismay to a calm she didn't expect. But when he walked past her and into the bathroom without saying a word, her calm moved to disbelief.

This time when he emerged, he didn't look back. The door swung shut between them with a firm thud and Casey was left with nothing but the sound of a racing heart. The drip no longer dripped. The man was no longer a threat. She was safe and sound and alone in her bed—and she didn't remember ever feeling as lonely as she did right now.

"What's wrong with me?"

She rolled onto her stomach, punching her pillow and yanking at her nightgown until she heard ribbons tearing. Finally, she closed her eyes, willing herself to sleep, and blamed her restless spirit on the barbecue she'd eaten at Smoky Joe's.

A chair scooted in the other room. He was obviously making his bed out on the floor. The comfort of hers as opposed to the one he was about to take made her feel guilty. She thumped her pillow and shifted her position. She just couldn't help it. He'd known from the start this wasn't going to be a normal marriage.

But no one told him he'd be sleeping on the floor for the next twelve months.

The long, unmistakable rasp of a large metal zipper being undone plucked at her conscience. The sleeping bag.

She rolled over on her back and opened her eyes. Although the king-size bed took up a lot of space in the bedroom, there was still ample room in which to move about. Their sleeping arrangements could do with an overhaul. Maybe if she traded the king-size bed for two twin-size ones—

Her nerves shifted into higher gear. That would be fair, but it would also increase the intimacy of their sleeping arrangements. She trusted herself to cope with it, but could she trust the man who was now her husband to stay in his own bed and on his own side of the room?

Well, why not? They were adults. Hopefully, two responsible

adults. Nothing was going to happen. Having satisfied herself with what seemed a plausible solution, she sighed with exhaustion.

Lord, but it felt good to lie down. At the same time, she realized that she was here in bed, fed, bathed and resting because Ryder Justice had seen to it. She rolled back over on her stomach and burrowed her nose a little deeper into her pillow, savoring the knowledge that someone cared enough about her to make a scene. What she couldn't do was make a big deal out of it. Ryder Justice was simply passing through her life, not becoming a part of it.

Ryder couldn't sleep. The floor was hard. The covers hot. He kicked them back, leaving his body bare to the night, and still the cool flow of air blowing across his arms and legs could not ease the tension coiling within him.

Images kept popping into his mind. Casey alone at her desk. Casey in the other room, alone in that bed. He sat up with a jerk and reached for his jeans. Get out. Get out now before you make a mistake you can't fix.

Ryder didn't hesitate. He didn't need to know whether it was conscience or gut instinct warning him off. All he knew was he had to put some distance between himself and the woman who was his wife.

Grabbing his boots, he exited the apartment, then sat down at the top of the landing to put them on. The air outside felt thick, almost too warm and too stifling to breathe. Perspiration instantly broke the surface of his skin. He stood, then started down the stairs with no goal in mind other than to move.

Security lights dotted the grounds of the vast estate, highlighting the driveways, the doors to the house, and the area just inside the rim of trees circling the lawns. Down on the highway outside the city, he heard an eighteen-wheeler shifting gears as the driver maneuvered around a curve in the road.

Crickets rasped. A night bird called. A stringy cloud floated past the surface of a pale half-moon. Ryder lifted his head, inhaling the scents, absorbing the sounds. Ordinary sounds. But there was nothing ordinary about his situation, and there hadn't been since he'd walked out on his life six months earlier.

For lack of a better destination, he aimed for the trees at the far edge of the estate. It felt good to move, to be doing something besides lying in the dark and wishing for something he couldn't have. He glanced up at the mansion as he passed, trying to imagine what it would be like to grow up in such an austere environment. He'd had wide open spaces and brothers. Horses to ride and endless days of childhood where nothing ever changed and the status quo was your security blanket with which to sleep each night.

Music drifted to him from somewhere out beyond the ring of lights, probably from a passing car. It reminded him of the nights at home when he and Roman and Royal had been kids; of watching his mother and father dancing cheek to cheek out on the front porch while an old portable radio played nearby. He wiped a shaky hand across his face, remembering the night Barbara Justice had died leaving Micah to raise their three young sons alone.

Ryder paused, blindly reaching for the nearest tree as his composure crumpled.

You were the strong one, Daddy. You survived everything...except what I did to you.

Long, silent moments passed while Ryder stood in judgment of himself. Moments in which his heart broke and bled countless times over. And finally, it was the sound of laughter from another passing car that brought him to his senses.

Laughter. Proof that life does go on.

Angry that he was still part of that life, he moved deeper into the trees and away from temptation, unaware that he was being watched from the upper windows of the family home.

When Ryder moved out of sight, Erica stepped away from the window and flopped down on her bed, but the intensity of her conversation with Miles was still going strong. Although it was not necessary, she caught herself whispering into the phone.

"I said, I don't know what he's doing, but he's not sleeping in our dear sister's bed, that's for sure."

New Orleans at midnight was lively. More than once, Miles had given serious thought to never going home. He downed the last of the bourbon in his glass and then waved to a passing waitress for a refill before shifting his cell phone to his other ear.

"Look, sister darling, I already told you. It doesn't matter if he and Casey never get it on. The terms of the will have been met. She got married. She's living under his roof—under his protection. If it lasts a year, she's done her part."

Erica pouted. "It isn't fair."

Miles lifted his glass in a silent toast to a woman across the room before answering. "Who ever said life was fair?"

Erica kicked off her slippers and stretched out on her bed, absently admiring the color of polish on her fingers and toes. Practicing a pout she hadn't used in years, Erica's voice rose an octave.

"I can certainly vouch for the fact that life around here is deadly dull. When are you coming home?"

The woman in the bar lifted her own glass in a long-distance toast to Miles and smiled. His pulse reacted by skipping an anticipatory beat.

"Soon. Maybe tomorrow. The day after for sure."

Erica frowned. "Well, all I can say is you'd better hurry. Grandmother is beginning to waffle. In fact, if I didn't know better, I'd think she was quite smitten with Casey's honky-tonk man."

That wasn't something Miles wanted to hear. "You're kidding!"

"No, I'm not. She missed a lunch date with me and has been closemouthed about the reason why. All I know is, she scolded me for a comment I made about the chauffeur and then took herself off to her room."

The woman across the room was smiling openly now. Miles knew an invitation when it was being sent, and listening to his sister whine about an old woman's bad attitude was ruining the moment.

"Look, Sis, I've got to go. When I know my flight, I'll call. Someone will have to pick me up at the airport."

He disconnected in Erica's ear. She tossed her phone aside and picked up the television remote, but there was nothing on the tube that was as interesting as the man who was wandering through their woods. Curiosity won out over caution as she rolled out of bed in search of her shoes. She wouldn't go far. Certainly no farther than the back lawn. Definitely not into the trees. But she was going. She couldn't stand the suspense any longer.

Ryder walked until the darkness lifted from his spirit. When he came to himself enough to stop, he realized he could no longer see the house. In fact, he wasn't even sure which way it was and right now he didn't much care. Out here there were no walls to hold him back. He could run as far and as fast as his legs would take him, just as he'd been doing before he'd walked into that bar down in the flatlands. Casey had changed everything. And he'd let her.

Now his running days were over. Maybe he had no purpose on which to focus, but she certainly did. He'd never seen a woman so driven, so determined to succeed at all costs. He'd given her his word—and the Justice men did not go back on their word.

In the distance, a hound bayed and another answered. He recognized the sounds. They had keyed on a prey. At that moment, in the dark, alone in the woods, he could almost empathize with whatever creature was on the run. He knew what it felt like to be lost with nowhere to go. To run and run and then wind up at a dead end and facing destruction. That's where he'd been going when Casey Ruban walked into his life. In a way, he'd come to look upon her as his anchor, because without her, he had nowhere to go.

He turned back the way he'd come. A short while later he emerged from the woods to find himself within yards of the place at which he'd entered. Instinct and the need to get back to her had led him home.

He started across the lawn when a shadow moved between him and the bush to his right. Instinctively he doubled his fists, preparing to do battle when Erica stepped into the light.

"Sorry," she said. "Did I frighten you?"

He combed a shaky hand through his hair as adrenaline began to subside.

"No."

She giggled nervously and took a step closer, then another, then another, until she could feel the heat emanating from his body.

Her eyes widened as a single bead of sweat pooled at the base of his neck, then spilled over onto the broad surface of his chest. When the sweat split the middle of Ryder's belly, she moved another step closer, tilting her chin until their gazes met. The invitation was in her eyes...in her voice...in the thrust of her breasts beneath pale yellow silk.

"Ummm, I didn't know little sister liked them this rough-cut. Poor Lash. He never stood a chance against a stud like you."

Like a moth drawn to a flame, she reached out, her intentions painfully clear, and found her arm suddenly locked in a painful grip.

Their gazes met. His dark and wary, warning her away; hers wild and frightened by what she perceived as an imminent threat.

"Let me go!" she gasped.

"Then back off," Ryder said, his voice just above a whisper.

She gasped, stung by the outrage of such an obvious refusal of her company, and yanked herself free.

"How dare you?" she said.

"No, sister dear, how dare you?"

Heat suffused her face. "I don't know what you mean," she cried.

His voice lowered, his words wrapping around her conscience, burning deeper and deeper with each angry syllable.

"Like hell. Don't tell me you only came out here to see if your sister's new husband would play hide-and-seek."

A sense of shame she didn't expect kept her momentarily silent. He was right, and she hated him for that and so much more. Unfortunately, Erica had never learned the wisdom of silence.

"I came out here because I thought I saw a prowler."

Ryder raked her with a gaze that left her feeling as if she'd been stripped and branded. If she hadn't been so afraid to turn her back on him, she would have dashed into the house.

"The only thing on the prowl out here is you," he said, and then walked away.

Her fear subsided as the distance between them grew, but it was obvious to Erica that Ryder wasn't afraid of the dark—or of anything else on this earth.

Erica clenched her fists and thought about screaming—actually thought about tearing her own nightgown, scratching her own face and arms and crying rape just to get the son of a bitch in trouble. But she was too vain to deal with marring her skin and too angry to fake being scared.

"Damn you," she muttered, and spun on one heel before stalking back into the house. "Damn you and that stupid wife of yours all to hell!"

She slammed the door shut behind her, her breasts heaving, her face flushed with a rage she hadn't felt in years, and suddenly found herself standing in a wash of white light.

She shrieked. "Tilly! My God! You scared me to death! What do you mean by sneaking around down here in the middle of the night?"

Tilly loomed over her like a dark, avenging angel. "Well, now, Miss Erica, I was just about to ask you the same thing."

At a loss for words, Erica pushed past her. She didn't have to explain herself to the help. She was halfway down the hallway when Tilly spoke, and her voice carried all too clearly in the quiet of the house.

"I saw what you did."

Erica stumbled, then picked up the tail of her gown, and started running toward the stairs. When she reached the safety of her room, she turned the lock and then threw herself on the bed and burst into tears. Somehow, she was going to have to find a way to make this right. It wouldn't do to make her baby sister angry. Not now. Not when she controlled the purse strings and everything else that mattered in Erica's world.

Ryder shut the door behind him, then stood in the darkness, listening. Casey was asleep. Even though the bedroom door was closed, he imagined he could hear the soft, even sounds of her breathing. The air-conditioning unit kicked on and the hum quickly drowned out all but the angry thunder of his own heart.

He looked down at himself, at the sweat running down his body, at the grass stains on the legs of his jeans, and took off his boots. He dropped his jeans by the bedroom door and kept on walking. Careful not to wake Casey, he closed the door to the bathroom before turning on the light.

Completely nude, he stepped beneath the showerhead before turning on the water, uncaring that the first surge came out fast and cold. He reached for the soap and began to scrub himself clean. This time when he was through, he knew he'd be able to sleep. His mind was as weary as his body.

He wrapped another towel around his waist before turning off the light, then opened the door, standing for a moment and letting his eyes adjust to the shadows. When he could see without stumbling, he started across the room.

Later, he would tell himself if he hadn't looked down...if he hadn't seen all that long dark hair strewn across her pillow and thought about what it would feel like to sleep wrapped up in its length, he might have made it out of the room.

But, he had looked, and the thought had crossed his mind, and now he stood without moving at the foot of her bed, studying the face of the woman to whom he'd given his name.

She slept on her back with one arm flung over her head and the other resting on her belly. His first impression of her hadn't changed. She was truly a beautiful woman. But he'd learned since that first meeting in Sonny's Bar that the essence of Casey Ruban Justice did not lie in the strength of her features, but in the strength of the woman who wore them.

There in the quiet intimacy of a bedroom they had yet to share, Ryder realized he might not know the woman who was his wife, but he respected the hell out of what she stood for, and for tonight, that was enough on which to sleep.

He walked out, taking great care not to let the door bang shut behind him. The sleeping bag was right where he'd left it. He dropped his towel and crawled into it as bare as the day he'd been born, then closed his eyes, waiting for sleep to overtake his weary mind.

In the room next door and in the bathroom beyond, water dripped from the showerhead at a slow, methodic rate. And they slept, and finally, morning came back to start a new day.

Erica was playing it cool. In her mind, the incident with Casey's husband had never happened. She strode down the hall with purpose, heading for the kitchen, fully aware that was where Ryder would be eating his meal.

"There you are," she said, as if he'd been in hiding. "Miles called. You need to go to the airport and pick him up."

Tilly set a stack of dishes in the sink and wiped her hands on her apron as Ryder stood up from the table. "Oh, set yourself down and finish your food," she told him. "That boy won't be here any earlier than noon. He doesn't like to get up in the morning, so I dare say he won't be on any of the morning flights."

Erica refused to rise to Tilly's bait. "Here's his flight number and the time of his arrival. Don't be late. Miles doesn't like to be kept waiting."

Ryder slipped the note in his pocket without comment.

Erica pivoted, her duty done, and got all the way to the hallway before she got the guts to turn and ask, "Has anyone seen Casey this morning? I needed to talk to her about something."

"Board of directors meeting this morning. Been gone since seven," Ryder replied.

"Pooh," Erica said. "Business, always business."

"And that business keeps you off the streets, missy," Tilly told her sharply, banging a lid on a pan for good measure.

"And you in the kitchen where you belong," Erica retorted, and walked out, wishing she'd made a more ladylike exit by keeping her mouth shut. It seemed so common to argue with the help. Next time she wouldn't give the old biddy the satisfaction of a response.

"That woman makes my teeth ache," Tilly muttered.

Ryder kept silent, but he knew what she meant. A woman who would willingly seduce her sister's man wasn't the kind of woman who could ever be trusted. He took a long sip of coffee. Even if the sister wasn't sleeping with the man herself, it was still crossing a line no family member should ever cross.

Tilly topped off Ryder's coffee, then did something she'd promised herself years ago never to do. She meddled in family business.

"You watch out for that woman," Tilly warned.

Ryder glanced up, more than a little surprised.

"I know more than you think I know," she said softly. "I saw what she tried to do the other night."

Ryder's eyes narrowed as he braced himself for a retribution that never came.

"And I heard what you said."

He shifted uncomfortably in his chair and busied himself with adding sugar to coffee he didn't want.

Tilly put her hand on Ryder's shoulder and kept it there until he looked up.

"I have my notions about things," she told him.

"I'll just bet that you do."

Tilly refused to be swayed by the engaging grin he gave her.

"First time I laid eyes on you, I knew you were a good man. After what I saw the other night, I know you're going to be good for my Casey, too."

This time, Ryder was more than uncomfortable.

"Look, what's between Casey and me is strictly business," he said. "She asked for help. I offered. It's as simple as that."

Tilly lifted her chin and turned away, refusing to listen to what he had to say. "You're wrong, you know. Nothing is ever simple between a man and a woman."

Ryder set his cup down with a thump, sloshing the freshly sweetened brew out onto the white-tiled tabletop.

"I better be going," he stated. "The Lincoln needs gas, and I've got to find out where the airport is before noon."

Tilly turned. "You go on and get your gas. You find that airport and do your job and bring Mr. Miles on home. But you just remember this. It doesn't matter how long and how hard you work during the day, come nighttime, you and Casey Dee are going to be all alone."

Ryder reached for his hat. He damn sure didn't need anyone reminding him of that.

"Find yourselves some common ground," Tilly called out as he left the room. "You hear me? You have to start somewhere. Forget the gap and look for the bridge."

He was still thinking about that bridge Tilly had been talking about when he took the highway exit leading to the airport. A small, twin-engine Cessna lifted off directly in front of his view and he found himself stopping in the middle of the road to watch its ascent.

Even though the plane was a good half mile away and already several hundred feet in the air, his toes curled in his boots and he caught himself holding his breath until the plane leveled off. He lost sight of it when it turned toward the sun.

A car honked behind him, and he slipped his foot off the brake and drove on. But the damage had already been done. The hunger to fly was mixed up in his mind with the fear of repeating a deadly mistake all over again.

Get it in gear, he reminded himself, and began looking for a place to park. He didn't have to fly. He was only here to give a man a ride home. No big deal. But his hands were shaking when he got out of the car, and the closer he got to the terminal, the slower his stride became. It was all he could do to make himself walk inside, but he did it.

Cool air hit him in the face, and he inhaled deeply, welcoming the change in temperature as his nerves began to settle. He paused while he got his bearings, then started toward the arrival gate of the flight on which Miles Dunn would arrive.

His nerves were strung so tight, he caught himself holding his breath. Twice he had to remind himself to ease up. And he should have known this would happen. Just because he wasn't piloting the planes didn't make this experience any easier.

He settled the Stetson firmly upon his head and gave the announcement boards a closer look. Being here brought back too many bad memories. That was all. Just too many memories. And no man ever died from memories.

"Flight 1272 from Atlanta and New Orleans is now arriving at Gate Three."

Buoyed by the announcement, Ryder took his bearings then started walking. Erica had claimed that Miles didn't like to be kept waiting and God knows he didn't have any desire to linger in the place himself.

Miles was hung over. His head throbbed and his belly kept lurching from one side of his rib cage to the other as he filed out of the plane along with the other passengers. Bile rose as he stared at the drooping diaper of the toddler in front of him. An all too pungent odor drifted upward, adding to the nausea he already had. That kid was carrying a load and badly in need of a change. When a sickly sweat broke out on his upper lip, he mumbled an excuse and shoved his way past them, desperately searching the waiting crowd for Erica.

He saw the Stetson first, then the man beneath it and groaned. Damn her, why didn't she come herself?

''Here are my claim stubs,'' he said shortly, slapping them into Ryder's hand. ''I'll meet you in baggage.''

Ryder took the stubs without comment and waited beside the men's room until Miles came out.

''I thought I told you I'd meet you in baggage,'' Miles muttered.

Ryder gave him a pointed look. ''Wasn't sure you'd make it that far.''

Miles's face turned red.

''Lead the way,'' Ryder said, and Miles did.

Luggage was just beginning to come through the roundabout as Miles dropped onto a nearby bench.

''Rough flight?'' Ryder asked.

Miles looked up from where he was sitting and belched.

Ryder cocked an eyebrow and stifled a grin. ''Tell me which ones are yours,'' he said, pointing toward the varied assortment of circling suitcases.

''Four pieces. Brown-and-green alligator. Can't miss them.''

Ryder nodded and a short while later, pulled the last one from the rack. Miles watched with a bleary eye, unwilling to move until he had to.

''That's it,'' Ryder announced, and lifted a bag in each hand. ''I'll get these. You bring the rest,'' and started toward the exit without looking back.

Miles sat with his mouth agape while blood thundered wildly through every minuscule vein in his head. He stared at the remaining two bags in disbelief. The nerve of the man! Expecting him to carry his own luggage!

Miles staggered to his feet and hefted a bag in each hand before following Ryder's retreat.

"This just figures," he mumbled, as he staggered out of the door. "You can't get good help these days no matter how hard you try."

When they started home, Miles began to relax, reveling in the cool, quiet ambience of the Lincoln's spacious back seat. But that was before the car phone rang. After that, Miles's homecoming took an unexpected turn.

Chapter 7

The car phone rang as Ryder was leaving the airport and turning onto the highway. He answered on the second ring.

"This is Ryder."

When that slow, deep voice settled in her ear, Casey breathed a sigh of relief.

"Ryder, where are you?"

He frowned. "Casey, is that you?"

She turned away from the noise behind her, trying to block out the paramedics' voices, as well as the police officer on the scene. "Yes, it's me."

"I already picked him up. Just a minute and I'll hand him the phone."

"Picked up who?" she asked.

"Your brother, Miles."

"I don't want to talk to Miles. I want to talk to you."

Ryder's frown deepened as her voice suddenly shattered.

"I have a problem. Can you come help me?"

Before he could answer her, the ambulance that had been parked behind her took off for the hospital with sirens running. Startled by the unexpected noises in the background of their conversation, it began to dawn on him that there was more behind her request for help than the obvious.

"Casey, what's wrong?"

He heard her inhale, and then she spoke, and her voice was so soft he had to strain to hear her answer.

"I had a wreck."

The car swerved beneath him and Miles began to curse from the back seat. Even though it was broad daylight and Ryder was driving down the highway leading into Ruban Crossing, in his mind, he saw light flash across a dark, storm-filled sky, heard the sharp crack of lightning as it struck the fuselage of his plane, and smelled smoke, even though the air inside the car was cool and clean.

His fingers curled around the steering wheel in reflex, and it took him several seconds to realize what he was experiencing was a flashback, and that everything was safe and under control. He took a deep breath and started over, asking what mattered most.

"Are you hurt?"

"No...at least not much."

An odd tension settled inside his belly. Her voice was shaking. If she wasn't hurt, then she'd at least scared herself to death.

"Are you at the hospital?"

He thought he heard a sob in her voice as she answered. "No, I'm still at the scene."

"Easy, honey. Just tell me where you are and how to get there."

She told him, and only afterward realized what he'd called her, but by then it didn't matter. He was already sliding to a stop at the intersection where the accident had occurred, and it would seem from the way the back door was flung open, he'd stopped just in time.

Miles leaned out and threw up on the right rear tire as Ryder jumped out of the front seat. After that, Casey didn't see anything but the look on her husband's face. She took a deep breath and started toward him.

Ryder felt sick. He could see a bump on her forehead that was already turning blue, and there was a small trickle of blood at the edge of her lip.

Wrecks. Damn, damn, damn, but he hated the sight of spilled fuel and crumpled metal. It reminded him of things he'd spent months trying to forget.

"Come here," he said softly, and pulled her close against his chest while he surveyed what was left of her car. The front half had been shifted all the way to the right, compliments of a one-ton truck that had run a red light. "Thank God for air bags," he said, eyeing the one that had inflated inside her car.

Her voice was shaking as she reached up, tentatively testing the size of the bump on her forehead. "It wasn't my fault."

Ryder caught her fingers, then lifted them to his lips in a quiet, easy gesture before cupping her face with his hand.

"It wouldn't matter if it was. What matters is getting you to a doctor. Why didn't they send an ambulance for you?"

"I told them I wanted to wait for you. Besides, I didn't think I needed..."

He missed whatever it was she said next. He kept hearing her say she'd been waiting for him. That did it. Whatever hesitation he'd had about holding her close was gone. He tilted her chin, carefully surveying the burgeoning bruises and angry red scrapes on the tender surface of her skin.

"I don't care what you think. You're going and that's that."

Casey rested her forehead against his chest. How long had it been since she'd had someone upon whom she could lean? When his grip around her firmed, for the first time in as long as she could remember, she felt safe...really safe. As she ran her tongue along the lower edge of her lip, tears began to well in her eyes.

She looked up at him for confirmation. "My lip is bleeding, isn't it?"

He wanted to kiss away the shock and the pain and the stunned expression in her eyes. He thought better of the urge and hugged her instead.

"Easy now. Let's get you in out of this sun. You can wait in the car with Miles while I tell that officer where I'm taking you."

"It's probably okay for me to leave," Casey said. "He already took my statement."

But she did as she was told, grateful for the fact that someone was taking over. It seemed her good sense and practicality was lost somewhere in the wreckage of her car and she couldn't think what to do next.

When she got inside, Miles was ominously silent. Casey glanced over her shoulder, wincing slightly as a strained muscle rejected the motion.

His condition would have been funny if it hadn't been too painful to laugh. He lay stretched out in the back seat with his arm thrown over his eyes, shielding them from the sun. He looked worse than she felt.

"Rough flight?"

He groaned and mumbled something she didn't understand. She turned around and closed her eyes, wishing that the world would stop spinning so she could get off.

Seconds later Ryder slid behind the wheel. He leaned over and fastened Casey's seat belt without giving her a chance to respond, then glanced in the back seat at his other passenger.

"Buckle up."

A brief, quick click broke the silence. It would seem that Ryder had made a believer out of Miles.

The trip to the emergency room was faultless, and it didn't take the doctor long to address Casey's bumps and bruises. They were minor. The injury that would take the longest to heal was to her peace of mind.

"While you're at it, you may as well give this one a going over," Ryder said, pointing at Miles who was slumped in a chair near the emergency room door.

Doctor Hitchcock frowned. "Was he in the accident, too?"

Ryder shook his head. "No. I had just picked him up at the airport when Casey called. He's a little the worse for wear. Guess his stomach's had a longer ride than it could tolerate."

Hitchcock gave Miles a judgmental look. He'd been doctoring the Ruban family for years, and it wasn't the first time he'd seen this one in a condition of his own making.

"Looks to me like he just needs a little of the hair of the dog that bit him."

It was the word *hair* that did it. Miles's stomach was too queasy for anything, including metaphors. He bolted for the bathroom seconds ahead of another surge.

Hitchcock snorted beneath his breath, but his eyes were twinkling as he glanced at Ryder.

"Casey will be ready to go by the time you bring the car around. Meanwhile, I suppose I can give the party animal something to help his nausea."

Casey tried a smile, but her lip was too swollen to do much about it, and her head was beginning to throb. "Thank you, Doctor Joe."

He patted her on the arm. "Don't thank me. Thank the good Lord for sparing you worse injury."

"Amen to that," Ryder said quietly, and went to get the car.

The doctor stared after him, then turned, giving Casey a long, intent look. "So, that's the new husband, is it?"

She sighed. "You heard."

He shook his head. "Lord, honey, who hasn't? Your sudden marriage has set the biggest piece of gossip in motion that Ruban Crossing has ever known. I don't know what Delaney was thinking when he pulled that stunt, but I can guarantee it wasn't these results."

Casey's eyes darkened in frustration. "I know what he wanted. He'd been after me for years to...let's see, how did he put it...marry well."

Hitchcock frowned. He'd known Delaney Ruban all of his life. In fact, they'd grown up together, and while Delaney had acquired more money in his lifetime than a man had a right to expect, he'd been obsessed about overcoming his upbringing as the son of a flatlands sharecropper.

"By that, I suppose you're referring to a socially acceptable marriage, such as to a fellow like Lash Marlow?"

Her shoulders slumped. "I couldn't do it, Doctor Joe. I couldn't marry a man I didn't love."

An odd smile broke the wrinkles in the old doctor's face. He looked toward the cowboy who was pulling that big white car to a stop outside the door.

"So, it must have been love at first sight for you two, then."

Casey looked startled. "Oh no! It was nothing like that. Ryder is a good man...at least I think he is. But we have an understanding. I'm just fulfilling the terms of Delaney's will. Nothing less. Nothing more. In a year, this will all be over."

Unaware that he'd been the topic of their conversation, Ryder came up the hallway, shook the doctor's hand, and all but carried Casey out to the waiting car.

Hitchcock had his own ideas about understandings. *That's what you say now, Casey Dee, but a year is a long, long time.*

As Miles Dunn staggered out of the bathroom with a wet paper towel pressed to his forehead, Hitchcock reminded himself of the vows he'd taken to administer to *all* who were sick or in need of healing and took him by the arm.

"Come with me, boy."

Miles looked out the door toward the car. He could see Casey was already seated inside. "But they're about to—"

"They'll wait." Hitchcock said. "Besides, this will make you feel better."

The doctor had said the magic words. Miles followed without further comment.

"Lord have mercy!"

If Tilly had said it once, she'd said it a dozen times since Ryder's arrival at the Ruban estate. And she was saying it again as Joshua passed through the kitchen on his way upstairs with an ice bag for Miles's head. The soup bubbling on the stove was for Casey. The tears running down her face were those of relief after she'd seen for herself that her girl was all right.

The house phone rang just as Ryder came in the back door.

Startled by the sound, Tilly jumped and the soup she was stirring sloshed over the side of the pot and splattered with a hiss onto the hot cooktop.

"Lord have mercy!" she muttered again.

"I'll get it," Ryder offered, and answered the phone before Tilly burst into a fresh set of tears.

Well aware that the call had to be from someone in the family, Ryder's answer was less than formal.

"This is Ryder, what's up?"

Erica's complaint was left hanging on the edge of her tongue.

Somehow she didn't have the guts to say what she'd intended to say, at least not in the same tone of voice.

"Umm...I was wondering if someone was bringing up the ice bag for Miles's poor head."

Miles's poor head be damned, Ryder thought, but kept his opinion to himself. He glanced at Tilly.

"Erica wants to know about some ice bag."

"Tell her it's on the way up."

"It's on the way—"

"I heard her," Erica said. "Thank you."

"No problem," Ryder said, and started to hang up.

"Wait!" Erica shouted.

Ryder waited. It was her call. Her question. Her move.

"Is Casey all right? I mean, Miles said she'd had an accident."

"Come see for yourself," he offered. "She's at the apartment lying down, and I think she'd appreciate her sister's presence."

The thought of being in close proximity with Ryder gave Erica a chill. "Oh, I couldn't possibly leave Miles on his own. Grandmother isn't here and when she comes in, she's going to be beside herself that all of this happened while she was having her hair done."

A quiet anger he'd been trying to stifle suddenly bubbled over. "There's not a damned thing wrong with Miles. He's hung over, not hurt. Casey is the one who could have died today." He slammed the phone sharply onto the cradle and hoped that the disconnect popped in her ear.

Tilly hid her reaction, but she was secretly pleased. It was comforting to see someone else willing to champion her girl, especially a man who wasn't afraid to speak his mind.

Ryder turned, anger still evident in his voice. "Did Casey grow up in the same house with Miles and Erica?"

Tilly nodded.

"Then tell me something—how in blazes did she turn out so right and them so wrong? That pair must have been raised on ice water, not milk."

"They had each other," Tilly said. "After Casey's parents died, she didn't have much of anyone to baby her. Delaney loved her, but his intentions were focused on giving her the skills to run his empire, and truth be told, Mrs. Deathridge played favorites with the twins.''

''Casey had you,'' Ryder said.

Tilly nodded. ''Yes, that she did.'' She handed him a pot filled with the soup she'd just made. ''It's vegetable beef, her favorite.''

Ryder accepted the offering. ''Thanks. Considering the blow Casey took to her mouth, that's about all she's going to feel like eating.''

Tilly let him out the door, then watched as he crossed the courtyard, went up the stairs and into the garage apartment, carrying the hot pot of soup as if it were the crown jewels. When he was safely inside, she stepped back and closed the door. For the first time in weeks, she felt confident that things in this household were about to change for the better.

Not only did Ryder seem to respect Casey, but it looked as if he were willing to become her protector. However, just to be on the safe side, she might concoct a little potion. It wouldn't amount to much. Just a few herbs for good luck that she could sprinkle on their doorstep. Not a real spell.

Reclining in a nest of pillows, Casey winced as she reached for the phone, then had to shift the stack of papers in her lap to allow room for the smaller pillows beneath each of her elbows. Even though the accident had caused her to miss a stockholder's luncheon, it hadn't taken her long to regroup and bring the business to her.

At her request, her secretary had sent files on the most pressing issues and left the others that were pending back at the office. With a bowl of Tilly's soup for sustenance and the knowledge that Ryder was no farther away than the sound of her voice, she set up office in the middle of her bed and began going over the reports in question.

She read until the pain between her eyebrows grew too sharp to ignore and changed her tactics to returning the phone calls that had come to her office during her absence. It wasn't any easier. By late afternoon, it felt as if her lip was swollen to twice its normal size and the left side of her jaw was becoming increasingly sore. The last time she'd gotten up to go to the bathroom, she'd groaned at the sight of her face. The abrasion on her cheek was starting to scab, and by tomorrow, she was going to have one heck of a black eye.

Twice during this time, Ryder had appeared in the doorway. Once he'd frowned at the stack of work in her lap before disappearing without comment. The second time he'd come, the glare on his face was impossible to ignore, yet he'd still maintained a stoic silence about her behavior.

But the shock of the wreck was beginning to take its toll. Casey was near tears and wishing she could sweep everything off her bed, curl up in a ball beneath the covers and maybe cry herself to sleep. She heard footsteps coming up the outside stairs, then again inside the apartment. It was Ryder. She recognized the rhythm with which he walked.

He entered her bedroom without knocking just as the phone rang near her elbow. Before she could answer, he had it in his hands.

"Ruban Enterprises. No, I'm sorry, she is out for the rest of the day. Call 555-4000 and make an appointment with her secretary."

He tossed the portable phone completely out of her reach.

Casey frowned. "Hey! I wasn't through...."

"Yes, you are. Besides, I brought you a surprise."

Casey sputtered in useless dismay as Ryder swept aside the files on which she'd been working. When he held out his hand, she sighed and took what he offered, using his strength to lever herself to an upright position on the side of the bed, then groaned when her muscles protested.

"Oh! I feel like I've been run over by a truck."

"That's not funny," Ryder said, and scooped her into his arms before she had time to argue. "Besides, if you think you hurt now, just wait until tomorrow."

If it hadn't been so painful, she might have smiled. "Thank you for such inspiring words of wisdom," she said, and slid her arm around his neck for balance as he carried her into the living room.

When he settled her down on the couch, she put her feet up on the footstool and eased herself into a comfortable position.

"Trust me, I know what I'm talking about," he said. "By morning, every muscle you have is going to protest. At any rate, you should have been in bed hours ago."

"I was in bed," Casey argued.

"I meant, alone. Not with a half-ton of papers and that damned phone. If you'd wanted company, you should have let me know. I would have been glad to oblige."

When she blushed, Ryder knew he'd gotten his point across.

Refusing to give him the benefit of seeing how much his words had bothered her, she folded her hands in her lap and looked around the room.

"So, where's my surprise?"

He went to the kitchen, returning moments later with a handful of paper towels and a box he'd taken out of the freezer.

"What's this?" Casey asked, as he plopped it in her lap.

"Popsicles. Assorted flavors. Pick which one you want and I'll put the others back for later."

Her delight was only slightly more than her surprise. "Popsicles? You brought me Popsicles?"

"They won't hurt your mouth, I swear. In fact, it's going to feel pretty darn good on that swollen lip." He took the box out of her lap and tore open the top like an impatient child who couldn't wait for permission. "Which one do you want first? The red ones are cherry. The green ones are lime. The orange ones speak for themselves."

"I like grape. Are there any grape ones?"

"Grape it is," Ryder said, as he peeled the paper from a length of frozen purple ice.

Casey wrapped a paper towel around the wooden stick and took a lick, then another, then carefully eased her mouth around the end of the Popsicle and sucked gently. Cold, grape-flavored juice ran over her lips, into her mouth and onto her tongue. She closed her eyes, savoring the uniqueness of a childhood treat she hadn't had in years.

"Ummm, you were right. It tastes wonderful and doesn't hurt a bit."

Ryder caught himself holding his breath and squeezing the box of Popsicles until one broke inside the box under pressure. If someone had ever tried to tell him that women with black eyes and fat lips were sexy, he would have laughed in their face.

Unaware of the war waging inside her husband's conscience, Casey looked up. "Aren't you having any?"

Ryder shuddered then blinked. "I've had more than enough already," he muttered, and when someone knocked on the door, was saved from having to explain. "I'll get it. Sit still and eat your Popsicle before it melts."

Surprised by the unexpectedness of company, whoever it might be, Casey lifted a hand to her face. "I look so terrible."

Ryder's expression went flat. "I think your priorities got a little confused. Be glad you're alive to tell the tale."

The chill in his voice was only less intimidating than the look he was wearing. At that moment, Casey realized how little she really knew about the man who'd given her his name.

The knock sounded again and Ryder turned with the Popsicles still in hand and strode to the door, yanking it open with an abrupt, angry motion.

Outside heat swept inside, causing moisture to condense on the outside of the Popsicle box. Ryder was speechless. It was Eudora and she was clutching at the tail of her skirt with one hand and holding down her freshly done hair with the other as a hot, hasty wind blasted against the wall of the building.

"Are you going to ask me in, or am I to blow away?" Eudora asked.

He quickly regained his manners and stepped aside. "Sorry."

Eudora stepped over the threshold and into the apartment as if it were an everyday occurrence for her to be visiting the servants' quarters, when in actuality, she was quite curious as to the accommodations in which Casey had chosen to live.

The furnishings inside the garage apartment were simple compared to the elegance of the mansion, but to her surprise, the small rooms seemed comfortable...even homey. In fact it reminded her a bit of the first place she and Henry had shared.

Casey waved from where she was sitting. "Gran! Come in! I'm so glad you..."

Eudora gasped and clutched a hand to her throat as she walked toward Casey in disbelief.

"Oh my! Erica said you'd had an accident, but she led me to believe it wasn't..."

Eudora stopped talking, aware that whatever else she said was going to make Erica out to be thoughtless and uncaring. And while she silently acknowledged that fact from time to time, she wasn't willing to admit it aloud. Tears welled as she reached out to touch the side of Casey's cheek.

"Sweetheart, your face. Your poor little face. I'm so sorry. Is there anything I can do?"

Casey shook her head and then winced at the motion. "I'm fine, Gran. Actually, I look worse than I feel."

"I doubt that," Ryder said, and then extended the box toward Eudora. "What's your pleasure? We have orange, cherry or lime. We're saving the grape for Casey. They're her favorite."

Casey tried not to grin, but the shock on her grandmother's face was impossible to miss.

"Excuse me?" Eudora asked, eyeing the box Ryder had thrust beneath her nose.

"Popsicles. Want one?"

Casey held hers up to demonstrate, then realized it was melting and stuck it back in her mouth and sucked, rescuing the juice that would have dripped into the paper around the stick.

"Well, I don't think..."

Ryder dangled it under her nose. "Oh, come on, Dora. Have one."

When she almost grinned, Ryder knew she was hooked. "You're real fond of cherry limeade, so I'll bet you'd like a cherry one, wouldn't you?"

Without waiting for her to answer, he took one out of the box, unwrapped it as he'd done for Casey, and handed it to her with a paper towel around the stick to catch the drips.

"If anyone wants seconds, they'll be in the freezer."

Eudora stared at the icy treat he'd thrust in her hands and then straightened her shoulders, as if bracing herself for the worst. But when she lifted it to her mouth, the taste brought back sweet memories that made her heart ache. By the time she'd regained her sense of self, Ryder had made himself scarce.

"Well, now," Eudora said, and leaned back against the sofa cushions. "He's something, isn't he?"

There wasn't much she could add to what Gran had already said. "Yes, I suppose that he is."

"The question then remains, what are you going to do with him for the next twelve months? Somehow, I can't see him playing chauffeur forever."

Eudora ran the Popsicle in her mouth like a straw and sucked up what was melting with a delicate slurp while Casey thought about what Gran had said. What *was* Ryder going to do for the next twelve months? Even more important, what did she want him to do?

The clock on the bedside table stared back at Casey with an unblinking response. No matter how many times she looked, it seemed that time was standing still. It was midnight, and she'd been in bed for over two hours and had yet to relax enough to sleep. But it wasn't because she wasn't tired. She was. In fact, so tired that her bones ached.

She couldn't rest because every time she closed her eyes she kept seeing that truck coming out of nowhere—feeling the jarring impact of metal against metal—hearing her own scream cut off by the air bag that inflated in her face.

She rolled over on her side, then out of frustration, kept scooting until she was out of bed. If she could just get her mind into another channel, maybe she would be able to relax.

The bedroom door was slightly ajar, and she eased into the narrow opening like a shadow moving through space. Her body felt like one giant bruise, and every step she took was a lesson in endurance. As she started toward the kitchen, the room was suddenly bathed in light. She stifled a sigh. I should have known, she thought.

"What's wrong?"

She turned and then stammered on the apology she'd been about to make. Legs. He had the longest, strongest looking legs she'd ever seen on a man, and they were moving toward her. Casey made herself focus on his face.

"Uh...I couldn't sleep."

His touch was gentle on her forehead as he felt for a rising temperature.

"You don't have a fever," he said, and cupped her face, peering intently into her eyes and checking for dilated pupils or anything else that would alert him to complications from her head injury.

But that could change at any minute, Casey told herself, and took a step back.

"I thought I'd get a drink of water," she said.

"I'll get it for you." He moved past her and into the small kitchen, sucking up the space and what was left of Casey's breath.

Moments later, he thrust a glass into her hands. Ice clinked against the sides as she lifted it to her lips and drank.

"Better?" he asked, as she handed it back.

She nodded and turned away. Ryder set the glass down and followed her awkward movements through the room with a thoughtful gaze. This was about more than a restless night. The tension in her posture and on her face was impossible to miss.

"You're afraid, aren't you?"

Startled by his perception, Casey turned and then couldn't hold the intensity of his gaze.

"It's okay," Ryder said. "Anyone would feel the same."

"How do you know so much about what I feel?" she asked.

"Let's just say, I've been there."

"You mean you've been in a—"

He interrupted, and Casey got the impression that it was because he didn't want to talk about it.

"Want me to sit with you for a while?" When she hesitated, he felt obligated to add, "No strings attached. Just one friend to another, okay?"

Her legs ached, her head was throbbing, and her eyelids were burning from lack of sleep. Maybe some company *would* help her to relax.

"Are you sure you don't mind?" she asked.

His eyes darkened and his mouth quirked, just enough to make her wonder what he was really thinking.

"No, ma'am, I don't mind a bit."

"Then, yes, I would like some company. But just for a while, okay?"

He nodded. "Okay." He followed her into the bedroom, leaving the door wide open between the two rooms.

A muscle pulled at the side of her neck and she winced as she started to crawl into bed.

"Easy," he said, as he helped her slide into a more comfortable position. "Want me to rub something on those stiff muscles? It might help you relax."

"Yes, please," Casey answered.

He disappeared into the bathroom and came out moments later with a tube of ointment. Casey's eyes widened as the bed gave beneath his weight and she rolled over on her side, her heart racing as she bared her shoulder at his request.

She was stiff and nervous and he felt her resistance to his touch as if he'd invaded her space.

"Easy...just take it easy," he coaxed, and laid his palm on the curve of her arm.

Casey flinched, and then when he began to move, she closed her eyes and let herself go. Gentle. His touch was so gentle. The ointment was a lubricant between his skin and hers, smoothing the way for the pressure of his fingers as he began to knead at the offending muscle.

"Oooh, that feels good," she said with a sigh, settling into the rhythm of his touch.

Ryder clinched his jaw and tried not to think of what else could be good between them.

The room became quiet and there was nothing to hear but the slide of skin against skin and the uneven breathing of strangers who just happened to be husband and wife. Several minutes passed and Casey had been lulled into letting down her guard when Ryder spoke.

"Casey."

Her pulse jerked, a little startled by the sound of his voice.

"What?"

His fingers curled around her shoulder, his thumb resting at the base of her neck beneath her hair.

"I'm very glad you're okay."

Breath caught at the back of her throat and she squeezed her eyes shut as tears suddenly seeped out from beneath her lashes.

"Thank you, Ryder. So am I."

"Does your shoulder feel better?"

Her voice was just above a whisper. "Yes."

She heard him putting the lid back on the tube of ointment and felt the bed giving beneath the movement of his body. And then she thought of the loneliness of the night and the fear that kept coming when she closed her eyes, and asked the unforgivable.

"Ryder?"

Half on and half off of the bed, he paused. "What?"

"Would you mind—" She never finished the question.

"Would I mind what?" he finally asked.

"Would you mind staying with me? Just until I fall asleep?"

She couldn't see it, but a small smile tilted the corner of his mouth as he turned to her in the dark.

"No, honey, I wouldn't mind at all."

Casey held her breath as the mattress yielded to the greater pressure of his body.

"Easy does it," he whispered, and lightly rubbed her arm to let her know that he was there.

She closed her eyes and so did he, but not for the same reason. Ryder didn't want to think about the slender indentation of her waist so near his hand, or the gentle flare of hip just below it. He didn't want to remember the silky feel of her skin beneath his touch, or the way she sounded when she sighed. She had suffered much this day, and didn't deserve what he was thinking. But as time wore on, he couldn't get past wishing they were lying in bed for something other than rest.

Chapter 8

Sometime during the night it started to rain. It was a slow, heavy downpour that rolled like thick molasses off of the roof above where Casey and Ryder were sleeping, encompassing them within a dark, wet cocoon of sound.

Ryder woke with a start, the dream in which he'd been lost still so fresh in his mind that he came close to believing it was real. He looked down at Casey who lay sleeping with her head upon his chest and her hand splayed across the beat of his heart. Any man would consider himself fortunate to be in Ryder's place. The only problem was, she wasn't as awake and willing as she'd been in his dream.

The air felt close. The room seemed smaller. He ached. He wanted. He couldn't have. He moved, but only enough to brush the thick length of her hair that had fallen across her face. Her eyelashes fluttered against his chest. Her breasts had flattened against his side and she'd thrown her leg across the lower half of his body, pinning him in place. He swallowed a groan and made himself lie still when all he wanted was to be so far inside her warmth that nothing else mattered.

But lying still didn't help his misery, and finally, he slipped out of her arms and rolled out of bed, then stood in the dark looking down at her as she slept.

She trusts you.

Rain hammered against the roof as need hammered through him.

She's been hurt.

Hard. Constant. Insistent.

Justice men do not use women.

He turned and walked out of the room, grabbing his jeans from a chair as he headed for the door. He needed some air.

Some distance. Something else on which to focus besides the thrust of her breast and the juncture of her thighs. He kept telling himself that this overwhelming feeling was nothing more than a result of proximity, that reason would return with daylight and distance, but his heart wasn't listening. He'd spent time with plenty of other women in his life and had been able to separate fact from fiction.

When he opened the door and stepped out on the landing, all he could see was a sheet of black rain falling directly before him. The security light was off. He reached back inside and flipped the light switch, clicking it on and then off again. The power was out.

The porch was damp beneath his bare feet, but it felt good to be concentrating on something besides sex. He combed his fingers through his hair and took a deep breath. The lack of electricity explained the sultry temperature inside the apartment, but it didn't excuse the sluggish flow of blood through his veins. That blame lay with the woman who'd interfered in his dream.

A soft mist blowing off the rain drifted into his face. He looked up. The small overhang under which he was standing offered little shelter, yet it was enough for him to get by. Right now, he couldn't have walked back in the apartment and minded his own business if his life depended on it. The dream was too real. She'd been too willing and so soft and he'd been halfway inside her and going for broke when something...call it conscience, call it reality, had yanked him rudely awake. Now he was left with nothing but a sexual hangover, an ache with no way of release. The muscles in his belly knotted and he drew a deep breath.

"Ryder?"

He groaned. She was right behind him.

"What's wrong?" she asked. "Is something wrong?"

"Go back to bed," he said harshly, unwilling to turn around.

A hand crossed the bare surface of his back on its way to his shoulder. He pivoted, and she was right before him.

Humidity draped the fabric of her gown to every plane, angle and curve, delineating a fullness of breasts and a slim, flat belly. Sticking to places on her body it had no business, taunting Ryder by the reminder of what lay beneath.

His fingers curled into fists and he took a deep breath as he reminded himself that she was bruised and battered and didn't deserve this from him. "Are you all right?"

"I just woke up and you were gone and I thought..." Her voice trailed off into nothing as she waited for an explanation that didn't come.

Silence grew and the rain continued to fall.

Casey sensed his uneasiness but did not immediately attribute it to herself. They were still strangers. There was so much they didn't know about each other. This mood he seemed to be in could have come from a number of reasons. And then suddenly the security light on the pole beyond the apartment came on. Although it was instantly diffused by the downpour, it was more than enough by which to see.

Dear God. It was all she could think as she shrank from the wild, hungry need on his face.

The moment she moved, he knew that he'd given himself away. Because he couldn't go forward, he took a reluctant step back and walked out into the rain before one of them made a mistake that couldn't be fixed.

Shocked by his sudden departure, Casey cried out, but it was too late. He was already gone—lost in the downpour, beyond the sound of her voice.

Ryder didn't remember getting down the stairs. It was the rain that brought back his reason and calmed a wild, racing heart. Warm and heavy, it enveloped him—falling on his face, on his chest, down his body.

He began to walk, his bare feet sometimes ankle-deep in the

runoff. He walked until a tree appeared in his path, then another, then another, and he realized he'd walked into the forest at the back of the estate. He paused at the edge, aware that he could go no farther in the state he was in, and found himself a place beneath the outspread limbs of an old magnolia.

Rain sounded like bullets as it peppered down on the large, waxy leaves above his head. But the longer he stood, the more the sound reminded him of hail. He drew a deep, shuddering breath and then cursed. It had hailed on them the night of the crash.

He closed his eyes, remembering the dead weight of holding his father's lifeless body in his arms. Someone moaned and as he went to his knees, he knew it was himself that he had heard. Pain shafted through him, leaving him smothered beneath a familiar cover of guilt.

"Ah, God, make this stop," he cried and then buried his face in his hands.

Back at the apartment, Casey stood on the landing, staring out at the night, anxiously watching for Ryder's return. The urge to go after him was strong, yet she stayed her ground, well aware that it was her presence that had driven him away.

Mist dampened her hair and her gown, plastering both to her face and her body and still she waited. Finally, she bowed her head and closed her eyes. "Dear Lord, help me find a way to make this right."

And the rain continued to fall.

Some time later, it stopped as suddenly as it had started—turned off at the tap with nothing but a leak now and then from a low-hanging cloud.

Ryder came up the stairs in a bone-weary daze, weary from lack of sleep and from wrestling with the demons inside himself. His bare feet split the puddle at the top of the landing and he walked inside without care for the fact that he would be dripping every inch of the way to the bath.

When he closed the door behind him, the cool waft of air that encircled his face told him the air-conditioning was back on inside. That was good. He'd had enough of close quarters to last him a lifetime and the night wasn't even over.

He walked quietly, so as not to disturb Casey's slumber in the other room, and was halfway across the floor when her voice stopped him in his tracks.

"I'm sorry," Casey said quietly. "Very, very sorry. I asked too much of you and you were too much the gentleman to tell me so." He heard her shudder on a breath. "I humbly beg your forgiveness."

A puddle was forming where he stood and yet the despair in her voice kept him pinned to the spot.

"There's nothing to forgive."

"Only me. I was selfish...thoughtless. I promise it won't happen again."

Why did that not make him happy? "Just let it go."

"I laid out some fresh towels. The bed is turned back. From this night on, we'll take turns sleeping in the bed."

The thought of her, bruised and aching and waiting up for him to come back from trying to outrun his devils made him angry, more with himself than with her; however, she caught the force of his guilt.

"Like hell. Go to bed and close your eyes. I didn't get mowed down by a truck. I don't have a busted lip or a black eye, and if I hurt, it's of my own making, not yours."

"But this arrangement isn't fair to you."

He almost laughed. "Hell, honey, there hasn't been two minutes of fair in my life in so long I wouldn't know it if it stood up and slapped my face." His voice softened. "Go to bed...please."

It was the please that did it. She stood, moving past him in the dark like a pale ghost. Only after she was safe in bed with the sheets up to her chin did she sense him coming through the room. He paused at the bathroom door.

"If I'm gone when you wake up, call Tilly. She'll bring you some breakfast."

"I'll need a ride to work," she reminded him.

"No, you won't. I think you need another day of rest. Tomorrow is Friday. That will give you a long weekend to recuperate."

She totally ignored the fact that he'd just told her what to do, but at this point, it made no sense to argue with a sensible suggestion. "Where will you be?" Casey asked.

"Checking on your car that was towed. Contacting your insurance company." This time he managed a chuckle. "You know, doing stuff."

"Thank you," she said.

"For what?"

"For doing my *stuff.*"

This time, he really did laugh, and the sound carried Casey off into a deep, dreamless sleep.

Miles fought the covers beneath which he was sleeping as his dreams jumped from one crazy scenario to another. One minute he was flying high above the ground without a plane, flapping his arms like a gut-shot crow and trying to find a safe place to land, and the next moment he was standing in the middle of the intersection where Casey had had her wreck, watching in mute horror as her black sports car and the one-ton truck with which she had collided kept coming at him over and over from different angles. Each time he would escape being crushed between their vehicles, the scene would rewind and replay. On a nearby street corner, his grandmother kept pointing her finger and shouting. "I told you so! I told you so!"

He awoke bathed in sweat, only then aware that it was pouring down rain and the electricity was off. He cursed the bad taste in his mouth and got up with a thump just as the power returned. He could tell because his digital clock started blinking and the security lights outside came on all at once, returning a familiar pale glow to the curtains at his window.

He shoved them aside, looking down through the rain to the lawn below, and knew that the weather tomorrow would be miserable. The air would feel like a sauna and the bar ditches would be filled and overflowing.

"What the hell?"

There, through the rain, he thought he saw movement! He watched, staring harder, trying to focus on the shape. Just as he was about to reach for the phone to call the police, the figure moved within a pale ring of a security light and Miles froze, his hand in midair.

"Him." He stepped forward, all but pressing his nose against the glass for a better look. There was no mistaking who it was below. It was Ryder, half-dressed and moving at what seemed a desperate pace. He watched until the man disappeared from view before settling back down in his bed, his drink of water forgotten.

Long after it had stopped raining and he was back in bed, he kept wondering what would drive a man out of his bed and into a night like this? Had he and Casey fought? A twinge of guilt pushed at the edge of his conscience. She had gone through some hell of her own today. Tomorrow he'd send her some flowers. Having settled that, he turned over and quickly fell back asleep. It didn't occur to Miles that Casey would ultimately wind up paying for her own flowers, and if it had, he wouldn't have cared. To Miles, it was the thought that would count.

Lash awoke with a curse. Water was dripping from the ceiling and onto his left cheek. He got up to push his bed to a new location and stubbed his toe in the dark. The roof leaked. What else was new? The real problem lay in the fact that he was sleeping on the ground floor and it was still coming in through the ceiling. He didn't even want to think how the upper two stories of Graystone would be suffering tonight. Cursing his wet bed and sore toe, he crawled back between the sheets, turned his damp pillow to the other side, and lay down.

Only sleep wouldn't come. No matter how hard he tried, his mind refused to relax. He thought of the phone call he'd had this afternoon from the police. Just for a moment before they'd completely explained, he'd thought they'd been calling to inform him of Casey's death, and then he realized that because he was the family lawyer, they'd called to tell him where they'd towed her car.

What bothered him most about the incident was the lack of emotion he'd felt at the news. He loved her. At least he thought he had. Wasn't a man supposed to cry at such a loss?

He closed his eyes, trying to imagine Casey dead, picturing the hordes of people that would come to her funeral, of the eulogy he would have delivered expounding her life. He saw her lying in the casket, beautiful even in death, and felt guilt that he was letting himself play so lightly with something as serious as her life.

He rolled over, taking the sheets with him as he turned on his side, still haunted by the sight of her face. As he tried to sleep, his thoughts began to unfurl like jumbled up scenes in an unedited movie.

In one scene, she stared at him, cool and patient, and he realized that he was remembering the way she'd looked the day of the reading of the will. He tossed, rolling himself and the covers to the other side of the bed where Casey lay in wait for his arrival. There she stood again, her face a study in shock that slowly turned to a cold, white rage. He remembered that well. It was the way she'd looked when he'd announced the terms of Delaney Ruban's will.

He groaned. He could have talked Delaney out of the foolishness. *Oh God, if only I had.* But it was too late. Lash had presumed too much and he knew it. Who could have known? The Casey he thought he knew would never have gone into the flatlands and come out married to some hitchhiker, to some stranger she found in a bar.

And therein lay part of Lash's dilemma. He'd bet his life and the restoration of his family's honor on a woman who had never existed outside the realm of his imagination. In other words, he'd bet the farm on a woman who didn't exist.

"Casey."

The sound of her name on his lips made him crazy. He rolled onto his back, staring up at the ceiling. If things had gone the way they should have, she would be here, right now, in bed beside him. He closed his eyes and saw her smile, imagined he could feel the touch of her hand on his face, the breath of her laughter against his neck. He reached out, tracing the shape of her body with his fingertips, watching her eyes as they grew heavy with passion. He grew hot, then hard and aching, and when there was no one around to take care of the need, he reached down and dealt with it on his own, calling her name aloud as his body betrayed him.

"More flowers for little sister," Joshua announced, carrying another vase of cut flowers into the library and setting them on a table just out of the sunlight.

Casey smiled, more at the use of her childhood name than for the flowers he carried into the room. She started to get up when he waved her back.

"You stay where you're put," he ordered. "I'll be bringin' those cards to you."

Casey laughed. "You sure are bossy today."

Joshua lifted the card from the flowers and dropped it in her lap.

"No more than usual, I'd say."

He straightened the edge of the blue afghan covering her legs then patted her knee as he'd done so often when she was a child. His dark eyes searched the marks on her face. Her lip was no longer swollen, but the bruises were spreading and the scratches had scabbed over. The sights deepened the frown on his brow. He couldn't have cared for her more if she'd been born of his blood.

"You be needin' anything, you just give me a ring, you hear?"

Casey reached out and caught his hand, pulling it to her cheek. "Thank you, Joshie...for everything."

He shook his head, embarrassed at emotion he couldn't hide. "Don't need to thank me for doing my job," he muttered, and stalked out of the room as fast as his legs would take him.

Casey glanced at the card, then back at the flowers. These were from Libertine Delacroix and they were pulling double duty: get-well sympathies and congratulations on Casey's recent wedding. She smiled. If Delaney were here he would be eating this up. Libertine was at the top of the county's social echelon. She had a summer home in Ruban Crossing and the family home on the river outside of Jackson.

The doorbell rang at the same time that the telephone pealed. Aware that Joshua couldn't be in two places at once, she picked up the phone.

"Ruban residence."

"Casey? Is that you?"

It was Lash. At that moment, she wished with all her heart that she'd let the darned thing ring.

"Yes, it's me. What can I do for you?"

She heard him clear his throat and could imagine the papers he would be shuffling as he gathered his thoughts. However, he surprised her with a quick retort.

"I heard about your accident and am so very glad that you're all right."

"Thank you."

"Yes, well...I know this may be an inconvenient time, but I was wondering if I might come by. There are some papers you need to sign."

She frowned. The last person she wanted to see was Lash and the last thing she wanted to do was think about her grandfather's death. But if there were more papers to sign regarding Delaney's will, she would have to do both.

"Well, I was just about to—"

"It won't take long."

She was honest enough to know that what she'd done by marrying Ryder had probably ended a lifetime of plans Lash must have had. Everyone knew that Lash's father had gone through the Marlow money as if it had been water and that his mother had run off with a trucker soon afterward. Everyone also knew what while Lash was a lawyer of the courts, his only ambitions leaned toward the restoration of his family name and the family home. And, if she'd married him as Delaney had planned, it could have happened. He would have had unlimited money at his disposal.

She shuddered. It was a wonder he didn't hate her guts. She thought of the wedding gift he'd sent that was still in her desk drawer at the office. In spite of his own disappointment, Lash had found it within himself to do the right thing and wish her well. She sighed. Guilty conscience won out.

"I suppose so," she said. "If it won't take long."

"Certainly not, my dear. I can promise that what I need won't take long at all."

"Then I'll be waiting."

She hung up the phone as Ryder walked in the room carrying

a bright yellow, happy face balloon. The frown on her face disappeared.

"Oh, how sweet! Who sent me the balloon? I haven't had a balloon since I was little."

He leaned over and kissed the top of her head, then handed it to her.

"It's kind of pitiful compared to all these elegant flowers, but it seemed like a good idea at the time."

Although the kiss was as harmless as if it had come from a child, Casey felt her face flush. After last night, the word *harmless* did not mesh with the man who'd walked out of the apartment and into the rain.

"Is this from you?"

He stood at the end of the couch, absorbing the aftermath of yesterday's wreck on her face. Finally, he nodded, and then he grinned and Casey thought she would forever remember the way he looked, smiling down at her with the sunlight coming through the window behind him.

"With no strings attached." Then he laughed aloud when she dangled the one tied to the balloon. "Except the obvious, of course."

Casey grinned and handed him the balloon. "Will you tie it on the back of that chair for me?"

He did as she asked, then gave the balloon a final thump and set it to bobbing as he moved away. The big yellow happy face smiled down at her from across the room. Casey smiled back, then noticed that Ryder was leaving.

"Can't you sit down and talk to me?"

Ryder stopped at the doorway. When he turned, there was an odd, almost childlike hurt on his face.

"You don't need to pretend with me, Casey."

Suddenly, last night was out in the open. All the tension that had sent him out in the rain was back between them and there was nothing to say that would change what had happened.

Angry, she threw off the afghan and stood, unwilling to say this lying down. "The last time I played pretend, I was six years old. I pretended my mother and father weren't dead. When it didn't come true, I never tried again."

Ryder absorbed her anger as well as the passion with which she spoke, letting it flow over and then around him. Just when he thought she was finished, she came at him again. It would seem she wasn't through.

"There are things that need to be said between us. I would think that saying them in the bright light of day would be a hell of a lot smarter than waiting for dark. The world closes in when the sun goes down. Even with the absence of light, I've found it a difficult place in which to hide."

Stunned by the truth in her words, he couldn't find it in himself to walk away.

"So...is this our first fight?" he asked, and was rewarded by the red flush he saw staining her cheeks.

"Can't you be serious?" she muttered.

"Well, yes, ma'am, I can be serious as hell. However, I don't think you're one bit ready for that."

Casey paled. Just when she told herself he was a comfortable man to be around, that stranger came back.

"I thought you'd like to know that carpenters will be arriving tomorrow. I'm adding on a room to the garage apartment. Since we won't be sharing a... I mean we can't... We aren't going to..." She took a deep breath and started over, ignoring the heat on her face and neck. "You won't have to sleep on the floor much longer."

He thought about waking to find her wrapped in his arms. "That's real thoughtful of you, Casey."

"It is only fair."

His voice softened. "And you're always fair, aren't you, girl?"

Before she could answer, Joshua entered the room with Lash Marlow at his heels.

"Mr. Marlow is here. Says he has an appointment."

Willing herself not to flinch at what she perceived as accusation in Lash Marlow's expression, Casey eased herself back to the couch.

"Lash, it's good to see you. Ryder and I were just about to have coffee. Won't you join us?"

Lash pivoted, surprised that he and Casey would not be alone.

"That's all right," Ryder said. "I'll just leave you two alone to—"

"No!" Casey took a deep breath and made herself relax when she really wanted to scream. "There's no need," she said, softening her words with a smile. "It's nothing confidential. Only some papers to sign."

"She's right. Please don't leave on my account," Lash said and then smiled, and the sight made Casey shudder. It was the least happy expression she'd ever seen on anyone's face.

"Besides, I believe there should be no secrets between a man and his wife," he added.

Casey couldn't look Ryder in the face, and Ryder refused to sit down. Even after Joshua returned with the tray of coffee and Ryder had accepted his cup, the words kept ringing in his ears. *No secrets. No secrets.* Hell, there hadn't been more than ten minutes of honesty between them since he'd said "I do."

She thought he was a footloose drifter who'd wasted his life on the road. He didn't have it in him to tell her the truth because he was still trying to come to terms with some truths of his own.

There was a little matter of being responsible for his father's death and still finding the courage to live with it.

Every breath Ryder took was a reminder to him that Micah could no longer do the same. Every sunset he saw, every morning that came, came with the knowledge that, for his father, those simple pleasures had ceased. He carried his guilt with the ease of a man who's lived long with the shroud. Close to his heart. Selfish with the pain that shoved at him day after day.

Casey handed back the last of the papers. Lash took them from her, letting his fingertips accidentally brush the palm of her hand.

When she flinched, he had an urge to lean over and slap her face. How dare she have judged him and found him lacking? His family could trace their lineage back to the *Mayflower.*

Then he glanced at Ryder, careful to hide his thoughts. He would bet a lot—if he had it to bet—that this one didn't have two nickels to call his own. *At least I have my education—and several generations of a fine and noble name.* In Lash's opinion, Ryder Justice was nothing more than a stray, an alley cat of a man who'd been in the right place at the right time. That's what he was. That and nothing more.

Lash slid the papers into his briefcase and stood. "I'd better be going—let you get some rest and let your husband get on with his work."

The sarcasm was there. It wasn't obvious, but that wasn't Lash Marlow's way. Casey chose to ignore the dig, and then she remembered the gift that he'd sent.

"Lash. I haven't had time to send a card, but I want to thank you in person for the lovely wedding gift you had sent to the office. It's stunning, truly stunning."

Lash turned, and there was an odd, satisfied smile on his face. "It's an heirloom, you know. It belonged to my grandfather, Aaron Marlow."

Casey looked startled. She'd had no idea. "Why, Lash, that's generous of you, but you really shouldn't have."

His gaze turned flat, almost expressionless. "Oh, it was nothing," he said. "After all, if things had been different, it would have been yours anyway. I thought you should have something to remember me by." He ventured a look at Ryder who had remained silent throughout their entire conversation. "I don't want you to think I'm treading on your territory," he said. "It's just that Casey and I have known each other for years."

Ryder set down his cup and then glanced at Casey before looking back at Lash. "I'm not worried. Casey is a woman of her word. Besides, I'm not a man who believes in boundaries."

Lash was more than mildly interested in the concept of what Ryder had to say. "So by that are you hinting at the fact that you believe in open marriages?"

Ryder took one step forward, but it was enough to back Lash up two.

"Not only no, but hell, no," Ryder said. "A man and woman stay together out of a commitment, not because there's a fence they can't climb."

Feeling slightly threatened by something he didn't quite understand, Lash started for the door. "At any rate, I hope you both get what you deserve."

Ryder thought about what the lawyer had said long after he was gone. There was something about him that didn't quite mesh.

Chapter 9

A month to the day from their wedding, the extra room over the garage was finished, and it was none too soon. There had been far too many times when Casey had seen Ryder's brown, bare body, and Ryder had spent way too many nights alone on a floor when he had a wife who slept alone in their bed. After thirty days of marriage, they were no longer strangers, but the strangeness of their situation was about to make them enemies.

''Just put the bed over here,'' Casey said, pointing at the wall opposite the sliding glass doors. ''And the dresser here, the easy chair there... No, there I think, nearer the corner lamp. Yes, that's perfect.''

A small, birdlike woman wearing a stiff blue uniform and high-top tennis shoes scurried into the room with an armload of Ryder's clothes, bypassing the deliverymen from the furniture store.

Her graying blond hair was pulled up in a ponytail reminiscent of the sixties. Her eyebrows were thick and black with a permanent arch, compliments of a number seven jet eyebrow pencil. The look was topped off with sky blue eyeshadow and frosted pink lipstick. Bea Bonnaducci's appearance hadn't changed since

1961, the year she'd graduated high school. The way Bea had it figured, if it had worked for her then, it should work for her now.

"Where would you be wantin' me to put the mister's things?" she asked.

"Put that stuff in the dresser and hang those in the closet. At last he has plenty of space."

Bea did as Casey directed and then scooted out of the room for a second load, leaving her to deal with the last of the furniture being carried in.

And in the midst of it all, Ryder strode into the bedroom, his nostrils flaring with indignation. He glared at the men who were setting the last pieces of the furniture in place, and when they left, he exploded.

"Damn it to hell, Casey! You waited until Dora sent me on some wild-goose chase and then you set Bea to digging in my stuff. I know you want me out of your hair, but you could have waited for me to get back."

Stunned, Casey stood mute beneath his attack, unable to find a single thing to say that would calm the fire in Ryder's eyes. She watched as he paced from one side of the room to the other. When he stepped inside the brand-new bathroom, he gave it no more than ten seconds of consideration before coming back out again.

"I thought you would be glad to have your own space," she finally said.

He spun, his posture stiff, looking for a fight that just wasn't there. "I didn't say I wasn't," he muttered. "What I said was..." He sighed, then thrust his hand through his hair in a gesture of frustration. "Oh hell, forget what I said." He stomped out of the room as suddenly as he'd appeared.

Casey plopped down on the side of the bed and knew she was going to cry. It wasn't so much the fact that he had yelled at her. It was the disappointment that did her in. He'd done so much for her over the past four weeks. All she had wanted to do was return the favor.

She doubled her fists in her lap, staring intently at a pattern on the carpet and telling herself that if she concentrated enough, the tears wouldn't come. In the midst of memorizing the number of paisley swirls in a square, a teardrop rolled down her cheek and into her lap. She drew a shuddering breath and closed her eyes. It didn't stop the pain or the tears. They rolled in silent succession.

Ryder walked back into the room carrying the last of his clothes that were on hangers and jammed them onto the rod.

"I sent Bea back to the house," he said, and then the bottom fell out of his world. Casey was crying, and it was all his fault.

"Oh, hell, Casey, please don't cry."

"I am not crying," she said, and hiccuped on a sob.

He stood, frozen to the spot by the pain in her voice and wondered when it had happened. When had she gotten under his skin? And there was no mistaking the fact that she was there. Why else did he feel as if he were about to explode?

"I am a total bastard."

It wasn't what she'd expected him to say. She looked up.

He groaned beneath his breath. Those big green eyes, the ones he'd come to know so well, were swimming in tears.

"I am the lowest form of a heel."

She sniffed and he dug a handkerchief out of his pocket and laid it in her hands.

"I do not deserve to see another day."

She blew her nose and then handed the handkerchief back. "Oh, don't be so dramatic," she said. "I suspect you were just being a man."

He stuffed the handkerchief, snot, tears, and all into his pocket and tried not to be offended by what she said. "Exactly what does that mean?"

Casey shrugged. "Tilly says when men don't want to show their emotions, they either curse or yell. You did both, which leads me to believe you were severely upset in a way I did not expect."

He frowned. Damn, but that woman knew way too much about men for his peace of mind. "At any rate, I am truly sorry. I'm sorry I yelled. I'm sorry I cursed. I will try not to let it happen again."

She tried to glare. When angry, he was a force to behold, but when penitent, there was something about him that made her want to throw her arms around him and...

Her face turned red as she jumped up from the bed. ''Don't make promises you can't keep,'' she said, and stomped from the room.

Ryder groaned and followed her into the living room. She was fiddling with a stack of magazines. It made him nervous. He had a hunch she wasn't through yanking his chain, and when she spoke, he knew he'd been right.

''Ryder?''

If he was smart, he'd walk out right now before she dug in her heels, but where Casey was concerned, he wasn't smart, he was caught, and had been since that day in the bar down in the flatlands.

''What?''

''I don't understand. Why did you get so angry?''

''I wasn't really...''

''Truth.''

He sighed. Damn. Delaney Ruban had done a real good job on her. When she got a notion, she stuck to it with fierce intensity, and it wasn't in him to lie.

''I don't know. I walked in the apartment. Bea was going through my stuff. Too much was changing too fast.'' His voice lowered and Casey had to concentrate to hear what he said. ''I guess I'm uncomfortable with change.''

''But nothing has changed,'' she said.

''No, Casey, you're wrong. We're married.'' He held up his hand. ''And before you tie yourself into a little knot, I know it's not a *real* marriage, but dammit, I was just getting used to, to...things.''

He took a deep breath. What he was about to say was going to reveal more than he wanted, but she'd asked for the truth, and truth she was going to get.

''Even if we don't share anything but a name, there is a certain rhythm to our relationship that I was learning to accept.'' Then he thrust a hand through his hair and lifted his chin. She didn't have to like this, but it had to be said. ''Dammit, I guess I wasn't ready to lose what little of you that I had.''

Casey knew she was standing on solid ground, but for the life of her she couldn't feel it. Something inside of her kept getting lighter and lighter and she wondered if she was going to pass out...or fly.

"I didn't throw you away, Ryder. I only bought you a bed."

He took the magazines out of her hands and tossed them on the table, then pulled her into his arms. His chin rested at the crown of her head. His arms locked easily across her shoulders, holding her in place.

"I'm sorry I made you cry. I like my room. I promise to like the bed."

Casey closed her eyes and tried not to think of trying it out together just to test it for bounce. "And I'm sorry I keep bulldozing my way through your life."

His fingers itched to take down her hair, lay her across that bed and show her what bulldozing was all about. Instead, he counted to ten, pasted a smile on his face, and kissed the top of her head before letting her go.

"I suppose we should celebrate tonight," he said.

"Celebrate how?"

"You know, a room-warming. Maybe I should take you back to Smoky Joe's for some more barbecue." He grinned. "It's Saturday. That means it's alligator night, remember?"

She rolled her eyes.

"Well, then, maybe we could make it a christen-the-bed party, so to speak."

Casey's voice rose an octave. "Christen the bed?"

"Yeah, I always heard it was bad luck to sleep in a bed without breaking it in."

"Breaking?" She winced. She'd never heard herself squeak before.

"Yeah, come here, honey. I'll show you."

He dragged her across the room before she could argue and all the while she was moving she kept telling herself to do something—say something—anything except follow him across the room! But she didn't. She went where she was led as if she didn't have a brain in her head. When he leaned over the bed and picked up a pillow, adrenaline shot through her body like a bullet out of a gun.

Oh God, oh God, this is happening. It's really happening.

And then the pillow hit her square in the face.

She staggered, tasting fabric and feathers and reeling from shock. "Why on earth did you—?"

He sidestepped her and the question with a grin on his face and swung again. The blow landed on her backside, sending her sprawling facedown on the mattress. She grabbed the other pillow out of reflex, but it was instinct that made her swing and roll at the same time, crowing with delight as it caught Ryder up by the side of his head.

"That's nothing," he warned. "You're no match for me." He began to circle the foot of the bed.

"I'll make you eat those words," Casey cried, and leaped up on the mattress, using it as a bridge to get to the other side and away from Ryder's intent.

She was turning around as he drew back his arm and let fly.

The pillow shot through the air like a padded cannonball and stifled the jeer she'd been about to make. Within seconds, she found herself eating more feathers. But there was an upside to his latest attack. She now had both pillows.

"Aha!" she shouted, waving a pillow in each hand. The glee on his face made her nervous. When he started toward her, she began to retreat.

"Aha? What the hell is *aha?* I've never been hit with an *aha* before. Do they hurt?"

Casey panicked, threw both pillows at once and then ran. "No fair," she screamed.

He caught her in a flying tackle in the middle of the bed, at once mashing her face into the mattress and himself onto her. The weight of him was so great that breathing was almost impossible, and then just when she thought her lungs would burst, she found herself flat on her back and gasping for air. When she could talk and breathe at the same time, she looked up. Ryder was sitting on her legs with his arms above his head in a triumphant gesture.

"I hereby declare this bed has been thoroughly christened."

Casey doubled up her fist and thumped him in the middle of his belly.

"You cheated," she said, and tried to hit him again.

"Easy," he warned, and caught her fist before it could do any more damage. ''Justice men never cheat. We just rearrange the odds.''

Casey tried to stay mad, but the grin wouldn't stay off her face. ''That's priceless.''

''What's priceless?'' he asked.

''Rearranging the odds. Delaney Ruban would have loved you.''

Ryder's expression stilled. He couldn't quit looking at the woman beneath him. At the joy in her eyes. The smile on her face. Her hand on his leg.

He touched her. First her hair, then her face. And when she bit her lower lip and looked away, he heard himself asking, ''What about his granddaughter? How does she feel?''

Casey felt as if all the breath had been knocked from her lungs. She was all too aware of his weight on her legs, his hand on her face, the need in his eyes.

''I...''

''Never mind,'' he whispered, and braced himself above her with an arm on either side of her face. ''I think I'd rather find out for myself.''

She knew what the shape of his mouth felt like. They'd kissed before. Once, and just before dawn, in Judge Harris's front parlor on the day of the wedding. She thought she was prepared for what was about to happen. She couldn't have been more wrong. The man she'd kissed before had been a stranger. This time it was different. She'd seen this man wearing nothing but a towel—walked into his embrace on the day of her wreck—slept in his arms—laughed with him—cried with him—fought with him. She closed her eyes and tensed as his breath swept her cheek.

The gentle brush of mouth-to-mouth contact was familiar, even comfortable, and all of that changed when Casey's arms automatically wrapped around his neck. Ryder groaned and then rolled, taking her with him until she was the one on top and he was pinned beneath. She heard him whisper her name. Felt his hands in her hair—down her back—cupping her hips. Urgency sparked between them as their lips met again, then again, and then again.

Her pulse was racing, his body was betraying him. It was all there—from the wild glitter in his eyes, to the need coiling deep in her belly. She lowered her forehead until it was touching the space just above his heart. In spite of the heat between them she started to shake.

Ryder groaned. They'd gone too fast. But, dear Lord, who could have known they would go up in flames? They'd blindsided each other with nothing more than a kiss. He was almost afraid to guess at what might happen if they ever made love.

"Easy, Casey. Easy, honey," he said softly, rubbing his hands up and down her back in a slow, soothing motion. "That just got out of hand. I didn't mean to scare you, okay?"

She rolled off him and got as far as the side of the bed before covering her face with her hands. "Oh, my God. Oh, my God."

Ryder silently cursed himself for starting something they hadn't been ready to finish. But he'd gotten his answer. Delaney Ruban's granddaughter might not love him, but she wasn't immune to him either. There was something there. He just wasn't sure what it was. He rolled over on his side and reached out, touching her back with the palm of his hand.

"Casey, look at me."

When she flinched, he got up with a curse and walked out of the room.

She couldn't think, couldn't move, couldn't speak. All she could do was remember his weight pressing her down and never wanting the connection to stop. Of feeling his mouth cover hers, of mingling breaths and racing hearts and resenting the clothing that separated her skin from his.

The phone rang, and the timing couldn't have been worse. Moments later, Ryder walked back in the room and tossed the portable phone near her leg.

"It's for you."

Casey looked up, but he was already gone. She picked up the phone with shaking hands and cleared her throat.

"Hello?"

"Mrs. Justice, this is Charles Byner, down at the bank. I just need your authorization to clear a check. It's quite a large sum above what's in the account and I need your approval to authorize the draw.''

Casey swept a hand through her hair, trying to come to terms with reality. ''I'm sorry,'' she said, trying to focus. ''What did you say?''

''No problem,'' he said. ''I'm really sorry to bother you at home, but Mr. Ruban had specific orders with regards to these particular accounts and since you're now the one in charge, I need authorization from you to clear the check, although it is more than a thousand dollars over the balance.''

Casey sat up straight, her mind immediately jumping gears as she realized what he meant.

''Which account? Miles's or Erica's?''

The clerk lowered his voice. ''It's the one in Mr. Dunn's name. The check is for twenty-six hundred dollars. That's about eleven hundred dollars above the balance.''

Casey stood. ''What is the balance, exactly?''

His voice lowered even more. ''Let me just pull that up on the screen. Yes...here it is. The balance as of today is exactly $1,400.17.''

Casey gritted her teeth. ''And was the usual amount of five thousand dollars deposited into that account at the first of this month?''

''Ummm, yes, ma'am, it was.''

By now, Casey was livid. Delaney had set a precedent years ago that was about to come to a screeching halt. ''Honor the check, Mr. Byner. I'll have enough money transferred into the account to cover it, but I'll be at the bank first thing Monday morning to make some new arrangements.''

''Yes, ma'am,'' the clerk said, and hung up.

Casey disconnected, then immediately rang the bank back through another department and dealt with the transfer in a no-nonsense voice. When she was finished, she headed for the house phone on the kitchen wall.

''Tilly, is Miles at home?''

''He's in the pool,'' Tilly answered.

''Would you please ask him to meet me in the library? There's something we need to discuss.''

She hung up to find Ryder watching her.

"You okay?"

Casey's nerves were just beginning to settle. She hadn't expected it, but knowing that in spite of what had just happened between them, Ryder was still able to ask about her welfare, made her feel safe.

"No," Casey said. "But I will be."

"Need any backup?"

"Are you offering?"

The smile on his face was slight. "Are you asking?"

"It might get ugly," she said.

He dropped the clothes he was carrying onto the back of a chair.

"Honey girl, the last few months of my life haven't been anything but."

Surprised by the revelation, she would have given a lot to continue this conversation. Ryder was closemouthed with regards to anything about his past, and hearing him admit even this much was a definite surprise. But the confrontation with Miles was long overdue, and this latest stunt was, for Casey, the last straw.

"Then come if you want. For better or worse, you are part of this family."

"Unless I think it matters, you won't even know I'm around."

She nodded and started down the stairs, and it wasn't until they'd entered the house and were on their way to the library that she had fully accepted the impact of Ryder's presence in her life. The problems within her world were no longer just hers. They were theirs.

She entered the room wearing an expression the board members of Ruban Enterprises would have recognized. It was her no-holds-barred-don't-mess-with-me look. Ryder had disappeared somewhere between the library and the hall, yet she sensed he wouldn't be far away. Unlike Miles, he wasn't the kind of man who went back on his word.

And Miles wasn't far behind. She could hear the splat of bare feet on marble flooring as he made his way in from the pool. The careless smile on his face was no more than she expected as he sauntered into the library with a beach towel draped across his neck and water dripping onto the floor.

"I'm here. What's up?" he asked.

Casey schooled herself to a calm she didn't feel. "I just had a call from the bank."

If she hadn't known him so well, she might have missed the nervous flicker in his eyes.

He strolled over to the bar and poured himself a drink, even taking a sip before asking, "And what does that have to do with me?"

"Everything. It seems you wrote a check you couldn't cover."

He shrugged. "Oh, that. Delaney never used to mind when—"

"Delaney is dead, remember?"

Miles blinked. It was his only reaction to the cold, even tone of his half sister's voice.

"And in the grand scheme of things, exactly what does that mean?" he drawled.

"It means your glory days are over, Miles. I don't know what the hell you're doing with your money. I don't even want to know. What I will tell you is that your world is slightly out of sync, and as your loving sister, I intend to do all that I can to bring it back in order."

He set the glass down with a thump. "What are you getting at?"

"It's more a case of what are you trying to pull? Any unemployed, thirty-year-old man should not be spending in excess of five thousand dollars a month. Therefore, I am going to do you a favor. As of Monday, you will report to Princeton Hamilton in the legal department of Ruban Enterprises. You have a law degree. You're going to put it to work."

Miles froze. An angry flush began to spread from his neck, upward. "You bitch! You can't run my life."

Casey shrugged. "You're right. But I'm running Ruban Enterprises, aren't I? I covered this hot check, but I won't do it again. Also, there will be no more instant deposits into your account, because as of the end of this month, it will be closed. No more free rides, Miles."

Miles was so angry he couldn't form a complete sentence. His hands were shaking as he yanked the towel from around his neck and started toward her.

The urge to run was overwhelming, but Casey stood her ground as he shoved his way into her space and thrust a finger up against her nose.

"Don't let your power go to your head, sister dear. Someone might just have to knock you off that pedestal for your own damned good."

The anger on Miles's face was impossible to ignore and the knowledge that their relationship had come to this made her sick to her stomach. It hurt to know she was still the outcast when it came to family love. She reached out to him.

"I'm not trying to play God, Miles. You're my brother. I care for you very much, but don't you see? You're wasting the best years of your life."

He slapped her hand away and then grabbed her by the arm, yanking her sharply until she came close to crying aloud.

"You're going to be sorry for this," he said softly. "You're going to be very, very sorry."

He turned and walked out of the room, leaving Casey reeling from the venom in his voice. But his triumphant exit ended four steps outside the library door. Ryder had him by the arm and shoved up against the wall before he had time to call out for help. Miles had seen plenty of angry men in his life, but he'd never been afraid until now.

Ryder slammed his hand in the middle of Miles's chest, pinning him in place. "You son of a bitch. If I ever hear you talk to your sister again like that, you'll wish you'd never been born."

"It's none of your business," Miles said, and felt shame that his voice was shaking.

"That's where you're wrong. Whether any of you like it or not, she's my wife. What happens to her *is* my business. And I'm telling you now, so you'll be forewarned, if anything *ever* happens to Casey, I'm coming after you first."

So great was his fear that if Ryder hadn't been holding him up, Miles would have been on the floor.

"What the hell do you mean by that?"

"Exactly what I said," Ryder replied softly. "You better hope to God she doesn't have any enemies, because from this day forward, I hold you responsible for her welfare.''

Miles's eyes bulged. ''I would never wish Casey any real harm. I was just mad, that's all. Hell's fire, man, she's my sister.''

''Then start acting like her brother.''

Miles went limp as all the anger slid out of his heart. Truth hurt. ''Let me go.''

Ryder didn't move—didn't speak—and didn't turn him loose.

Miles saw himself mirrored in Ryder's eyes and didn't like what he saw.

''I didn't mean what I said to her. And I suppose in a way she's right.''

Ryder turned him loose, but refused to move back. ''Remember what I said. She hurts—you bleed.''

Miles took off down the hall as if the devil were at his heels. By the time he got back to the pool, he'd convinced himself that putting his education to work was not only going to happen, but that it could have its benefits.

Ryder watched Miles until he was out of the house, and then stepped inside the library. Casey was at the window, staring out onto the lawn overlooking the back of the estate.

''Casey?''

She spun, and Ryder wished he'd given in to the urge and punched Miles right in the face before they'd had their little talk. She looked so hurt. So lost. So alone.

''I heard some of what you said to Miles.''

Ryder could tell there was something serious on her mind. He waited for her to continue.

''I don't know how I got so lucky, but I am forever grateful for your presence in my life.''

He wanted to hold her. He settled for a brief smile instead. ''Oh, I don't know about that,'' he drawled. ''I'd come near saying that I'm the lucky one. Besides, we Justice men don't take kindly to anyone messing with our women.''

Casey swallowed a sigh. If only she was his woman in the ways that counted. ''So, are you telling me that there's more than one of you that's been turned loose on the world out there?''

The smile slid off his face and she knew she'd said the wrong thing. "I'm not who matters," he said shortly. "I don't think Miles will give you any more trouble, but if he does, you know where I'll be."

He walked out and she had the strangest sensation that he'd just walked out of her life, rather than out of the room. In fact, the thought was so strong that she actually followed him through the house, then stood in the doorway and watched until he entered their apartment.

What did I say? What was it that turned him off and sent him running?

But there were no answers for Casey, at least not today.

However, when the mailman drove away from the Justice ranch outside of Dallas, he gave Royal Justice a clue to solving a mystery that had been worrying him and his brother, Roman, for months.

"Daddy, Daddy, I bwought you da mail."

Ignoring the trail of letters and papers she was stringing as she ran, Royal Justice swung his three-year-old daughter, Madeline, up in his arms and kissed her soundly.

"You sure did, honey. You're getting to be such a big girl."

"Gwinny helped," Maddie said, pointing at the baby-sitter who was coming behind at a fast clip, picking up the pieces that Maddie had lost.

"Good for Gwinny," Royal said. Gwinneth Anderson grinned, handed Royal Justice the rest of his mail, and took Maddie by the hand. "Come on, Scooter, it's time to feed the pups."

Maddie bolted, leaving Royal with a handful of letters and a smile on his face. He dropped into the nearest chair and began going through the mail with a practiced eye, discarding the junk and setting aside the bills to be paid. Every now and then one would be addressed to his brother, Ryder, and that one was tossed into a box with an accumulating stack that threatened to overflow. It was all he knew to do. It was Roman who'd saved Ryder's business from ruin.

Roman had taken over the charter service without batting an eye, claiming he could run his private investigation service and Ryder's charter business in the same location. He hired two pilots, an accountant, and then dug in for the long haul, convinced that Ryder would be back when he was ready.

Privately, Royal was a lot less optimistic, but that was just the difference in their personalities, not a lesser belief in the brother who was missing. He loved Ryder as much as Roman did and worried daily about his whereabouts, sometimes even wondering if he was still alive. It had been so long and they hadn't had a word.

He was down to the next-to-the-last letter in the lot, and he started to toss it in Ryder's box when he looked at the return address. MasterCard. No big deal. Everyone has credit cards.

And then he realized what he was looking at and took a deep breath as he tore into the flap. When he pulled out the itemized bill, he started to shake. Someone had used Ryder's card! Over the period of three weeks, someone had charged several hundred dollars' worth of men's clothing in Ryder's name.

Royal was as scared as he'd ever been in his life. Either Ryder was alive and well and buying up a storm, or someone was using his card. The implications of how anyone might come by Ryder's belongings was more than he could handle alone. He bolted up from the chair and headed for the phone. Moments later, a familiar voice growled in his ear.

''This is Justice Air and The Justice Way. State your business and we'll get back to you as soon as possible.''

Royal groaned. That damned answering machine. When it beeped, he started talking.

''Roman, this is Royal. I just got a letter from—''

''It's me,'' Roman said.

''Well, hell,'' Royal said. ''Why didn't you pick up the first time?''

''Wasn't in the mood to chitchat,'' he said shortly.

Royal cursed beneath his breath. That was so typically Roman. ''The mail just came.''

Roman snorted indelicately. ''Don't tell me. You just won the Publisher's Clearing House Sweepstakes.''

''Oh, shut the hell up,'' Royal muttered. ''I'm serious.''

''And I'm busy,'' Roman said. ''Unless my favorite niece has done something utterly charming that I need to know about, I don't have time to—''

''Someone charged nearly a thousand dollars on Ryder's MasterCard. The bill came today.''

Sarcasm was noticeably missing as Roman snapped, ''Give me the dates. The store codes, anything that—no, wait! I've got a better idea. Fax me a copy of the bill.''

''Oh, hell,'' Royal said. ''You know I'm not good at making that damned thing work.''

''Then get Maddie to help. She knows how,'' Roman said. ''And do it now. If Ryder's alive, I'll find out soon enough. If someone is using his ID, they're going to wish they'd never been born.''

''It's on its way,'' Royal said, and hung up the phone.

He turned, staring at the fax machine on the desk near the window, facing the fact that while he knew just about everything there was to know about ranching, the age of computers had him hanging in air. It was humiliating to know that a three-year-old could do what he had yet to accomplish, but this concerned Ryder, and it was no time to get macho about a damned old machine.

He headed for the back door at a fast clip. ''Hey, Maddie,'' he yelled. ''Come help me fax something to Uncle Roman.''

Chapter 10

By Labor Day, Miles had become Eudora's fair-haired boy. Somehow, the fact that he was gainfully employed had become his idea and Casey's ultimatum had never happened. She couldn't have cared less who took the credit. His streak of ambition had even rubbed off on Erica. She kept making noises about pursuing a career of her own and spent hours each day pouring over *Fortune 500* magazines in search of ideas.

At night when it was time to go to bed, Ryder no longer wandered in and out of the bedroom in various stages of undress. Casey had her bathroom all to herself and began to realize why Ryder had become so upset when she'd moved him out of her life. The routine they'd been in had become normal, even comforting, and it was over. Because of the new bedroom, whatever connection they'd made between themselves was gone. In an odd sort of way, it was like being divorced.

But the awareness between them kept growing. It was there in the way Ryder watched her when he thought she wasn't looking—and the way his hand lingered on her arm long after the need for keeping her balance had come and gone—even the brief, sibling-like kisses they left on each other's cheek before saying good-night. They were wanna-be lovers, playing at being friends. And always, in the back of their minds, was the knowledge that the marriage they shared was a farce and the lie they were living was the very wedge that kept them apart.

It was just past noon when Casey turned off the highway and accelerated up the driveway into the Ruban estate, gunning the engine of her new car and taking the curve in a near skid. She pulled up to the garage and stopped just as Ryder slid out from beneath the Lincoln. His black hair was wind-blown and the grin on his face was too devil-may-care to ignore. His jeans were oil-slicked, his chest brown and bare. He was wiping his hands on a rag as he headed her way.

"Where's the fire?"

She wanted to throw her arms around his neck and beg him to crawl back under that car and take her with him, but she couldn't. At least, not today.

She bolted for the stairs. "I know, I was driving a little too fast, but I'm in a hurry." She hiked up her skirt and began to run up the steps, two at a time.

"Take off those damned high heels if you're going to run like that," Ryder yelled. When she didn't oblige, he threw down the grease rag. "Hardheaded woman," he muttered, and followed her inside.

She was in the bedroom. A suitcase was open and she was yanking clothes from a hanger and tossing them on the bed with abandon. Anxiety seized him. She was packing to travel.

"What's the rush?"

"I've got to be in Chicago by morning. I have less than an hour and a half to get packed and get to the airport." She turned in a helpless circle, then dived back into the bottom of her closet, muttering as shoes came flying out behind her. "I can't find my black heels."

Ryder bent down and picked up a pair from the pile in the floor. "Like these?"

She straightened. A smile creased her face as she yanked them from his hands. "Yes! You're a magician. Thanks a bunch."

His belly was starting to turn. He kept telling himself it was going to be okay, that the only reason this was bothering him was because the news was so sudden.

"So, what's in Chicago?"

"Digidyne Industries. We've been after them for years. Once before, Delaney had the deal all but done and they backed out. I just got a call that the CEO had a heart attack and died. The heirs are going to put it on the auction block and I want first dibs."

Ryder started to pace, sidestepping her trips from the closet and back as she packed what she needed to wear. "So, it's a big deal, huh?"

"Very! I'm lucky that Delaney's old contact even thought to make the call and let me know. Otherwise, we would have been out in the cold."

"Yeah, that was lucky all right." He sat down on the edge of the bed, staring at the toes of his boots.

Casey glanced up. "You need to hurry and clean up. We're going to have to drive like mad to make my plane." Then she grinned. "However, that should pose no problem for you." It was a joke within the household that the family chauffeur drove, as Eudora had put it, "Like a bat coming out of hell with its wings on fire."

"Yeah, no problem," Ryder said, and walked out.

A few minutes later, Casey burst into his room, her face flushed with energy, her eyes alight with excitement. "I'm ready."

Ryder walked out of the bathroom, buttoning a clean shirt. He didn't stop to analyze the wisdom of what he was about to do, he just knew that if he let her get on that damned plane without a piece of his heart, he wouldn't make it until she got back.

Casey went willingly as he took her in his arms and crushed her against his chest in a smothering embrace.

"Just be careful, okay?"

She laughed. "Tell that to the pilot. I'm afraid it's out of my hands."

He groaned and threaded his fingers through her hair, crushing the curls and dragging her closer. "Don't make light of fate, Casey Dee. Sometimes when you're not looking, it'll kick you right in the teeth."

The first thought in Casey's mind was that he wasn't kidding. Even more, he seemed panicked about the upcoming flight.

"I'll be fine," she said. "This happens to me all the time. Year before last, Delaney and I logged over seven thousand miles in the air. Of course we were in Europe three times, but that was an unusual year."

God, keep her safe, Ryder thought, then he lowered his mouth and drew her close. Casey closed her eyes, yielding, bending to his will and embrace, swept away by the unexpected demands of a kiss that left her breathless and more than a little bit stunned.

When he whispered against her cheek, she opened her eyes. His panic had become contagious.

"I want you back in one piece."

She shivered. She'd never seen him like this. It was almost as if he were in some kind of pain.

"I'll certainly do my best," she said, trying to lighten the moment. She grabbed at the undone buttons on his shirt and started buttoning them up. "I'm sorry to repeat myself, but we've got to hurry."

He tucked in his shirt and picked up her bags. His heart was pounding.

"Go get in the car," he grumbled. "I'll make sure you catch that damned plane. But when you get back, we need to talk."

Casey looked startled. An ultimatum?

She got in the car, watching as he dumped her bags in the trunk and then slid behind the wheel. Something was wrong, terribly wrong. If only they had time to talk now. She looked at her watch. They would be lucky if they made the plane, never mind finishing a conversation.

He only glanced at her once. "Buckle up."

She'd ridden with him too many times before to doubt the necessity of doing as he'd asked. She did as she was told.

Casey was the last passenger to get on. She stood in the boarding area with her ticket in hand, waiting for the attendant to give her a boarding pass. Ryder stood beside her, pale-faced and stoic, yet his eyes never left her face. She reached out and touched his hand, wishing their circumstances were different, wishing she could throw herself in his arms and tell him he meant more to her than she could say.

"I'll call as soon as we land and let you know where I'll be staying."

Ryder nodded, trying to maintain his equilibrium, but he felt sick. The high-pitched whine of the jet's engines vibrated the windows overlooking the runway. In seconds, Casey was going to be up in that sky, and he knew only too well it was a hell of a long way down. He wanted to grab her and shake her until she listened to sense. Ruban Enterprises didn't need another Fortune 500 business. It was already a gargantuan conglomerate of its own accord. Why acquire more?

But he couldn't find a way to say what was in his heart. He couldn't say, I'm afraid I'll lose you like I lost my father. He couldn't say, I'm afraid I'll lose you before we ever make love. He couldn't say, I love you—because that wasn't part of the deal.

And then waiting was no longer an option.

"Take care!" Casey shouted, and started running down the gate toward the plane.

Ryder took several steps forward when the attendant grabbed his arm. "Sorry, sir, this is as far as you can go."

He groaned. God help him, but he'd missed his chance. Just when he'd found a way to say the words without coming apart, she was gone.

He went to the observation deck, watching as the big silver plane started backing out of its slot. His fingers knotted around the rail as it rolled onto the runway. And when liftoff came, sweat was running down the middle of his back and he was praying with every breath. When the plane was no longer in sight, Ryder leaned his forehead against the vast expanse of glass, unaware of the heat against his brow. He closed his eyes, trying to picture her face.

"I love you, Casey." But when all was said and done, he was a case of too little, too late.

It was almost sundown when Ryder walked into the apartment. His heart sank as a red blinking light winked at him from across the room. He tossed the car keys on the kitchen counter and pressed the button, waiting for the sound of Casey's voice.

"Hi, there. Sorry I missed you. I'm staying at the Ritz Carlton. Here is the number." Ryder jotted it down as she spoke, then settled back to listen to the rest of the message. "The flight was fine, just a little bumpy. I'll be in meetings all day tomorrow, but I'll try to call you tomorrow night. Take care." She paused, and Ryder would have sworn he heard her take a deep breath. "Well...anyway...I'll miss you."

The machine beeped. The message was over. Casey was gone. He played it over once more just to listen to the sound of her voice, and wished to hell that Dora hadn't broken a nail. She'd had a fit the size of Dallas and nothing had satisfied her but to make an emergency run to her manicurist to get it fixed. He'd missed Casey's call because of a broken nail.

The house phone rang. "Now what?" he muttered, and shoved himself out of the chair. Tilly was on the line.

"I'm making pot roast. You come on over here and get yourself some food."

The last thing he wanted was to eat or to talk. Casey hadn't been gone four hours and already there was a hole inside of him that food couldn't fill.

"Thanks, but I think I'll just stick around here for the evening."

"If you change your mind, you know how to get here."

"Yes, ma'am, I do."

He hung up and then headed for the shower. After he cleaned up, maybe he'd watch a little TV, have an early night. After all, he had the whole place to himself. And it was the loneliest feeling he could ever remember.

By morning, it had started to rain. By the next day, and then the next, it alternated between gray skies and drizzle, with a downpour now and then in between. And as if the rain wasn't bad enough, a line of heavy thunderstorms was pushing its way into the state and today was the day that Casey was due to come home.

He sat at the window looking out at the rain, ignoring the fact that today he'd already angered Erica and caused Eudora to have to change her plans.

He didn't give a damn that Erica had a lunch date with a banker to discuss buying a business. He couldn't have cared less whether or not Dora was going to miss her bridge luncheon. Erica knew how to drive and Dora could take a cab.

Erica argued, then whined, then begged. When she realized that nothing was working, she started in with what she considered simple reasoning. If she drove herself, then there was no way she could keep from having to walk in the rain. At this point, Ryder had heard enough.

"Where are you meeting the banker for lunch?" he asked.

She sniffed. "The Tea Room."

"Take an umbrella, and use their valet parking."

Erica knew when she'd been had. She rolled her eyes and flounced out of the library, muttering beneath her breath about hardheaded men who did not know their place.

Eudora patted her hair and straightened her belt. She was certain that the rapport she'd developed with this man would bring him around.

"Ryder, dear, it's Evadine Nelson's turn to play hostess for the bridge club. She lives right at the edge of town, remember? Hers is that big white house with the portico that I so admire."

"Yes, ma'am, I remember the house," Ryder said.

Eudora beamed. "Then you won't mind just dropping me off. It won't take more than half an hour either way. If Delaney hadn't insisted on building this place out in the middle of nowhere, we wouldn't be so isolated."

Ryder shook his head. "Dora, you weren't listening to me. I'm not budging until Casey calls. Dammit, look outside. There's a storm due in within hours. Chances are, her plane will be delayed, or the pilot will wind up trying to outrun it. Either way, I want to know what the hell is going on. I'll call a cab for you, but I'm not playing chauffeur today and that's that."

She rolled her eyes. "You know, things have been upside down ever since Casey brought you into this family. You're supposed to be the chauffeur. Chauffeurs are supposed to do as they're told." She tried to glare.

"So fire me," he said, and kissed her cheek, which brought a smile to her eyes that she just couldn't hide. "Go on with you then," she spluttered. "Go sit and wait for that phone call." She walked away, mumbling beneath her breath. "Land sakes, what will Evadine say? Me coming to her door in a cab, like some commoner."

Ryder followed her out the door. "Dora, you are a fine lady, but you are not the Queen Mother. Taking a cab now and then is good for the soul."

Eudora pivoted, giving him a cool, pointed stare. "I declare," she said, about to give him a piece of her mind, but Ryder didn't wait around to listen.

He ran from the main house all the way across the courtyard, then up the stairs just ahead of a cool gust of wind. Pausing at the landing, he looked up at the sky, judging the dark, angry swirl of clouds overhead. Today was not a good day to fly.

As soon as he entered the apartment, he turned on the television and flipped to a local station he knew would be broadcasting weather bulletins all day. With the phone at his side, he sat down to wait for her call.

A half hour went by. By this time he was pacing the floor. She'd promised to call before she left. She wasn't the kind of person who'd break a promise.

"A line of severe thunderstorms is blanketing the state," the TV announcer stated.

He turned toward the television, picked up the remote and upped the volume.

"Wind velocities have been measured at fifty to sixty miles per hour with gusts up to seventy and eighty. Authorities advise staying off of the roads and avoiding low-lying areas that are prone to flooding."

He glanced toward his bedroom. A sheet of rain splattered itself against the sliding glass doors that led onto the deck. His belly tied itself in a knot and he frowned, trying once again to focus on the weather man's report.

"The line runs from..."

Ryder groaned. On the map, the line of storms was virtually from the top to bottom of the state and moving eastward at a very fast pace. What was even more disturbing, the front extended across a large portion of the northern states, including Illinois. Maybe that's why he hadn't heard anything. Maybe her flight had been delayed and she was waiting for new information before she called.

No sooner had he thought it than the phone rang right near his hand. He jumped and then grabbed it before it had time to ring again.''

''Hello?''

''Ryder! It's me! I'm in a cab on the way to the airport. Traffic is a mess, but I'll make my flight. I should get into Ruban Crossing around three. Can you pick me up?''

''What's the weather like up there?''

''Ummm, it's raining a little, but no big deal.''

No big deal. ''It's raining like crazy here. Why don't you just take a later flight, or better yet, take the first one out tomorrow?''

She laughed. ''Now I know I've been gone too long. You are already making excuses as to why I shouldn't come back.''

He got up and walked to the sliding glass doors and then jumped when a stroke of lightning tore across the sky right above his head.

''Did you hear that?'' he asked, as the phone cracked in his ear. ''A storm front is moving through. Today is not a good day to fly.''

There was laughter in her voice. ''It will be fine. You know they won't take off if there's any danger. Besides, the pilots usually just fly above the storms and land behind them.''

He felt sick. Something inside kept telling him this was wrong—so wrong. ''Casey, don't. I know what I'm talking about. Please, for God's sake, don't get on that plane.''

The underlying fear in his voice was about to make her nervous. She decided to change the subject. ''You didn't even ask me if the deal went through!''

He sighed and shifted the phone to the other ear. ''Okay, I'll bite. How did the meetings go?''

She hugged herself, resisting the urge to giggle. She was pretty sure that CEOs did not giggle. ''We got it!'' she crowed.

"It's a done deal. I swear, Delaney is probably rolling over in his grave as we speak."

"Don't be talking about graves."

She laughed. "Just be at the airport. I can't wait to get home."

Their connection began to break up. "Remember," Casey said. "Flight 209. Three o'clock."

"Dammit, Casey, I don't want you to—"

The line was dead. Ryder hung up with a curse and sat back down, staring at the television as if it were the lifeline between himself and sanity.

Ryder heard someone groan. That's when he looked up at the airport monitor, watching as the On Time notice of Flight 209 from Chicago was changed to Delayed.

His gut hitched itself into a knot. It figured. While it wasn't raining at the moment, the sky was black and the intermittent flashes of cloud-to-ground lightning could be seen for miles. It was an all too familiar scene. One right out of his nightmares.

He stood and walked to the observation point overlooking the runway. A couple of planes were waiting to take off, another was off-loading. Except for the weather, nothing seemed out of sync.

I'm just borrowing trouble.

Fifteen minutes passed, and then Flight 209 was a half hour late and before he knew it, an hour overdue. And, the information on the monitor hadn't changed.

He'd been up and down the terminal a dozen times, walking, trying to pass the time and ease the nervous tension that kept growing within him. Now he was back at the arrival gate, standing at the windows and watching the skies.

Suddenly, the skin crawled on the back of his neck and he turned. Nearby, a child was crying. A teenager was on a cell phone. A weary traveler had given in to exhaustion and was sound asleep, his head lolling, his mouth slack as every now and then a slight snore escaped. The attendant at the check-in desk was on the phone. Nothing out of the ordinary. Nothing to warrant the gut-wrenching instinct he'd had that he was about to be attacked.

He glanced up at the monitor and sighed, then out of curiosity, back at the attendant. But when her expression suddenly froze and he saw her look up in fright, the same sensation came over him again, this time pulling a kink in the knot already present in his belly.

Easy. It doesn't mean a thing.

Down the broad walkway, a small horn honked three times in succession. "Coming through. Coming through."

His focus shifted to the electric cart coming down the terminal. It stopped in front of the attendant's desk as she ran out from behind the counter. When she handed the driver a computer printout, the other man grimaced and wiped a hand across his face. Ryder stared as they scanned the list together. When the driver lifted his head and began to scan the waiting area, Ryder knew. He didn't know how, but he knew.

He started walking—past the crying child, past the teenager on the cell phone, past the sleeping traveler. He came to a halt directly in front of the cart and didn't wait for permission to interrupt.

"What happened?"

Both men looked up at him at once. But it was the glance they shared before one of them spoke that nearly sent Ryder to his knees. He'd been right. Something was worse than wrong.

"I'm sorry, sir? Were you speaking to us?" the driver asked.

Ryder leaned forward and pointed to the readout. "Don't play games."

Before either one of them could answer, an announcement came over the loudspeaker.

"All those waiting for information regarding the arrival of Flight 209 out of Chicago, please go to the VIP lounge in the west wing."

Ryder stared into the eyes of the man behind the wheel and felt the ground coming up to hit him in the face. He leaned forward, steadying himself on the cart.

"Are you all right?" the man asked.

Ryder took a deep breath and lifted his head. "Should I be?"

The man looked away.

Ryder's voice died on a prayer. "Oh, God...no."

"Sir, you need to go to the VIP lounge in—"

"I heard," he said shortly, and walked away, following the

small crowd of people who were making their way down the terminal. A few looked nervous, aware that the request was unorthodox. Some merely followed directions—like cattle on their way to a slaughter.

An official from the airline was waiting for them inside the door. And Ryder stood with the crowd, listening to the end of his world and wondering how a man was supposed to live with so damned much regret.

"We're sorry to inform you that Flight 209 has crashed in a cornfield just outside the Illinois border."

A few started to cry. Others stood, like Ryder, waiting for the miracle that would pronounce their loved ones okay.

"At this point, we don't know why this has happened, but there have been eyewitness reports that lead us to believe the plane might have been struck by lightning. We do know it was on fire when it went down."

Someone's perfume was too strong. The cloying scent drifted up Ryder's nostrils. From this day on, he would hate the smell of musk. A woman shrieked and sank to the floor while a man somewhere behind Ryder started to curse.

"On behalf of our airline, I am very sorry to have to tell you..."

Ryder tilted his chin and closed his eyes, waiting for the blow.

"...there were no survivors."

The wail that spread across the room began as a joint groan of disbelief. Ryder covered his face and then wished he'd covered his ears, instead. Maybe if he hadn't heard it, it wouldn't be true.

They were saying something about a passenger list and a verification of names, but he couldn't stand still. He knew if he didn't get out, he was going to come undone. He burst out of the lounge, even as someone was calling him back, and started the long walk back down the terminal.

One step at a time. That's how he would get out of the airport. But how would he get home? How could he face that apartment without Casey?

But as far as he walked, he knew he couldn't run away from the truth. He'd spent the last seven months trying to forget what he'd done to his father and now this? How far, he wondered, would he have to run to get away from Casey's ghost? And with every step that he took, the thing that hurt worst was knowing he'd never said, I love you.

Casey kept glancing at her watch, then out the window of the plane. Neither hastened the arrival time of her flight. She was going to be at least an hour late getting home. Poor Ryder. He would no sooner get back to the apartment and hear her message on the machine than he'd have to come right back to the airport again.

She leaned her head against the seat and closed her eyes, weary from the grueling three-day set of negotiations. But it was done! She'd proven her mettle in more ways than one. She'd been thrust into Delaney Ruban's shoes far earlier than she'd ever envisioned, and while she'd known *what* to do, it was the *doing* she'd accomplished that made her feel proud. Delaney had worked all his life to create his empire. She couldn't have lived with herself if she'd been the cause of its ruin.

Yet the glow she had expected to feel from her success was dim in comparison to the anticipation she felt in just getting home to the man who was her husband. She kept remembering their first meeting in Sonny's Bar, of how he'd come out of the shadows and into her life. Now she couldn't imagine what her life would be like without him.

Half an hour into the flight, the plane lurched, and she grabbed at her seat belt, testing the lock that was firmly in place. A few seconds later, it leveled back off and she relaxed. Ryder had been right. This wasn't a good day to fly. Intermittent turbulence had been nonstop since takeoff, and she told herself she should have seen it coming.

Right after she'd talked to Ryder, her cab had come to a complete halt on the freeway. Traffic had snarled itself into a knot that only time had been unable to unravel. She'd known then that unless a miracle occurred, she was going to miss her flight.

For Casey, the miracle did occur, but not in the way she'd envisioned. She arrived at the airport forty-five minutes late. Not only had she missed her flight, she'd missed her lunch and her mood was not getting better. Just when she thought she was going to have to spend another night in Chicago after all, an airline with a later flight into Ruban Crossing had a cancellation. At last she was on her way home.

''Ladies and gentlemen, we will be arriving in Ruban Crossing in about five minutes. Please turn off all electronic and computer devices and prepare for landing.''

Casey did so with anticipation. If Ryder hadn't already received her call about the change in flights, she would call home as soon as she got to a phone. By the time she collected her luggage, he would be picking her up.

And then the plane touched down and taxied down the runway, then up to the gate to unload. It was one of the few times in her life she wasn't flying first class, but she didn't even mind having to sit toward the back of the plane, or being one of the last to get off. She was home.

Ryder moved aside out of instinct as a fresh swarm of passengers began to come out of the hallway to his right. His hands started to shake as he watched a man laugh and wave to a woman and child who were just arriving.

It isn't fair. That damned plane got here in one piece. Why not hers?

Twice he tried to move through the crowd and was unsuccessful each time, so he stood against the wall, waiting as face after smiling face moved past. Finally the flow was down to single file and he stepped away from the wall.

''Ryder!''

The hair stood up on the back of his neck and he stopped, but couldn't bring himself to turn. He had to be hearing things. Just for a moment, he thought he'd heard Casey calling his name.

He took a deep breath, clenched his teeth, and started moving again.

''Ryder! Wait!''

He groaned. God! He hadn't even been this bad after Micah was killed.

Someone grabbed his arm and he turned.

Casey dropped her briefcase and threw her arms around his

neck. ''I can't believe you're still here! This is fabulous luck! I thought I would have to—''

When her arms went around his neck, he started to shake. And when he felt her breath on his face, and her laughter rumble across his senses, he lifted her off her feet.

''My God...my God.'' It was all he could say as he buried his face against her neck, turning them both in a small, tight circle in the middle of the crowd.

His grip was almost painful, but Casey laughed as her feet dangled off the floor. This was definitely the way to be welcomed home.

''Maybe I should have stayed that extra day after all,'' she said. ''If absence makes the—''

''You're alive.''

The laugh died in her voice. ''Of course I'm alive.''

He set her down on the floor, then cupped her face in his hands, and the tears in his eyes were impossible to miss.

''You missed your plane, didn't you?''

She nodded. ''You wouldn't believe the traffic jam my cab got in. I missed my flight, my lunch, my—''

''The plane crashed. There were no survivors. I thought you were dead.''

She paled and then clutched at his arm, fixing her gaze on the shape of his mouth and the words coming out. She shook her head, finding it difficult to believe what he was telling her, but he was too distraught to ignore. Goose bumps broke out on her skin as the impact began to sink in.

''When my cab got stuck in traffic, the first thing I thought was if I missed my plane, I wouldn't get to go home, and if I didn't get home, I would have to spend another night away from you.''

Ryder's heart skipped a beat. ''I missed you, too,'' he said softly.

''No, you don't quite understand,'' Casey said. ''I did something selfish, very selfish, as I sat in that cab. I prayed for a miracle so I could get home. When I missed my plane, I was certain my prayer had not been answered.'' Tears filled her eyes.

"Oh Ryder, why me? Why was I spared when so many others had to die?"

He crushed her to him. "I don't know, and I don't care. All I know is, five minutes ago I was trying to find a reason to take another damned breath and now..." Unable to finish, he held her close as a shudder swept through his body.

Suddenly, Casey felt like crying. "Ryder?"

He eased up, but was unable to quit touching her and began brushing the hair from her face. "What is it, honey?"

"Will you take me home?"

He held out his hand.

Chapter 11

Casey kept trying to focus on the familiarity of the countryside through which they were driving, but all she kept seeing was the look on Ryder's face when he'd turned around at the airport and seen her. It hadn't been filled with concern, it had been torn by devastation. To her, that meant only one thing. He cared for her as much as she had learned to care for him. Oh God, please don't let me be setting myself up for a fall, she thought.

"I'm going to let you out at the big house," Ryder said. "You need to let your family know that you're safe—just in case they've heard broadcasts about the crash."

Casey couldn't quit trembling. For some reason, her life had been spared and she didn't understand why. Ryder's presence was solid, unwavering; she felt a need to stay within the sound of his voice. "Where will you be?"

Just for a second he took his eyes off the road. "Right where I've been for the last three days. Waiting for you to come home."

She looked out the window and started to cry. "Oh Ryder, why? All those people. They'll never come home."

He saw Micah's face in his mind and as he did, suddenly realized that the pain of the last few months wasn't as sharp as it had been. Ever conscious of the woman in the seat beside him, he had to face the fact that if it hadn't been for a tragedy, he and Casey would never have met. He tried to imagine his life without her and couldn't. Something inside him clicked.

"I don't know, but I'm beginning to accept that everything that happens to us in life happens for a reason."

Her voice was shaking. "What could possibly be the reason for so many deaths?"

His voice was gruff as he turned off the highway. "Damned if I know. Maybe it was just their time to go."

Moments later, the gray slate roof of the main house appeared over the tops of the trees, and soon afterward, the house itself was visible.

"You're home," Ryder said.

Casey's gaze moved from the mansion to the small, unobtrusive apartment over the garage. "Yes, so I am."

It was the red blinking light on the answering machine that drew him into the apartment. He knew what it said, but he played it anyway, reliving his joy as he waited for the sound of Casey's voice to fill the room.

"Ryder, it's me, again. This day couldn't get much worse. I missed my flight."

He closed his eyes, listening to the rest of the message and feeling awed by the twist fate had taken on their behalf. When it was over he put her suitcase on her bed, then looked around. Some changes had taken place since he'd left to pick her up.

The apartment was clean. Bea had probably seen to that. A fresh bouquet of flowers was on her bedside table, more than likely thanks to Eudora. She was big on flowers. He walked out of the room and into the kitchen. There was a note on the refrigerator door. Thanks to Tilly, there was food inside, ready to be eaten.

He turned on the faucet and let the water run until it was cool, then filled a glass and drank it dry; filled it again, and did the same. When he put it down empty, his hand was shaking. He walked into his bedroom and sat down on the edge of the bed.

The intense quiet assailed him and for the first time since Casey had grabbed his arm in the airport and turned the light back on in his world, he let himself think of the brief period of time when he'd thought she was dead. Uppermost had been the overwhelming sense of pain and loss, but there'd also been regret. Regret that their lives had been so screwed up when they met. Regret that he'd never said aloud what he knew in his heart to be true.

A shuddering breath slid up and out of his throat. He'd been given a second chance, and he wasn't going to waste precious time again. Footsteps sounded on the stairs outside. He tensed. It was Casey. The front door opened and he heard her call out.

"Ryder?"

He stood. For him, there was no turning back.

"Oh, there you are! It was so quiet I didn't think you were here."

He paused in the doorway, staring at her and memorizing the way she looked and the way she moved. Her long, black hair was pinned up off her neck and slightly tousled from travel. Her eyes were wide and still a little shocked, her lips looked tender, almost bruised, as if she'd bitten them to keep from crying, which he supposed she had. He watched as she absently brushed at a speck on her suit. Red was a power color, she'd told him. He could definitely agree. She held a power over him he couldn't ignore.

When she stepped out of her shoes and bent down to pick them up, the hem of her skirt slid even higher up her legs, accentuating their length. His heart filled. That woman was his wife.

"Casey."

She glanced up, her shoes still in her hand.

"I need to tell you something."

That's right! He'd told her the day she left that when she got back they needed to talk. Her heart skipped a beat as she waited for him to continue. Instead, he started toward her.

"Today, when I thought I'd lost you, do you know what I regretted most?"

She shook her head, her eyes widening as he cupped her cheek.

"That I hadn't told you the truth about how I felt." His gaze bored into hers. "I know what I'm going to say wasn't part of our bargain, but dammit, sometimes things change. I am sick and tired of pretending I'm satisfied with being your husband in name only. I love you, lady. I want to lie with you, make love with you. I don't want another night to pass without holding you in my arms. If you can't handle this, then say so, because in about three seconds, it'll be too late.''

Casey's eyes were full of tears as she dropped her shoes and put her arms around his neck. ''Why waste three seconds when the answer is yes...a thousand times yes?''

Ryder reached behind her and locked the door, then her feet left the floor. ''Your place or mine?''

''Anywhere, Ryder, as long as you're there.''

He headed for his bedroom with her in his arms. When he put her down, his hands went straight to the buttons on her suit. His voice was shaking. ''God give me strength,'' he whispered, fumbling as he tried to push buttons through holes.

''Let me,'' Casey said, and finished what he'd been trying to do.

She walked toward the sliding glass doors, pulling shut the drapes as she dropped the jacket of her suit on a nearby chair. On her way back to Ryder she stepped out of her skirt.

He wasn't prepared for the woman beneath the suit; not the wisp of red bra, the matching bikini panties, the long, silk stockings or the black lace garter belt holding them up. And this time, when he swept her off her feet, he wrapped her legs around his waist and sank down onto the bed with her still in his arms.

He nuzzled the curve of her neck, savoring the joy of being able to hold her, inhaling the faint but lingering scent of her perfume, testing the soft crush of her breasts against his chest, and knowing that the tight draw of his own muscles next to that wisp of red silk between her legs was becoming difficult to ignore. He held her close, savoring the joy of knowing she was still alive.

''Today I rode a roller coaster into hell and came out with an angel in my arms. I don't know why we were given a second chance, but I don't intend to waste it.''

Her arms tightened around his neck as she rained brief, tiny kisses along the side of his cheek and his chin. He grabbed her face, gazing into her eyes and watching them fill with tears until he thought he could see all the way to her soul.

''I feel like I'm about to make love to a ghost. I can't believe

I'm holding you, feeling your breath on my cheek, your arms around my neck. I must be the luckiest man in the world."

Casey's breath snagged on a sob. "I'm the one who got lucky. The day I got lost in the flatlands and found you in Sonny's Bar was the day my life began to change. You've stood with me. You've stood by me. I will never be able to repay you for what you've already done in my name."

"Hell, darlin', I don't want your money. I want your love."

"Then take it, Ryder. It's yours."

He rolled until she was lying beneath him in those bits of red-and-black lace. With an impatient snap, he undid the clasps on her garter belt and rolled down her stockings, silken inch at a time.

Longing to be one with this man was driving Casey to the brink of making a fool of herself. She struggled to help as he undid her bra. But when he hooked his thumbs in the waistband of her bikini briefs and started pulling them down, she moaned and closed her eyes.

Ryder leaned down and kissed the valley between her breasts.

His breath was soft against her face as he moved to her lips. "Are you okay?"

"No," she gasped, and tunneled her fingers through his hair. "Unless you hurry, I may never be okay again."

After that, he came out of his clothes with no regard to order, and when he threaded his fingers through hers and stretched out beside her, he closed his eyes and said a last small prayer of thanksgiving that he'd been given this chance.

Then Ryder Justice made love to his wife.

Casey propped herself on one elbow, looking at Ryder as he slept. She knew the shape of his face, the nearly square, stubborn jaw. Her gaze moved to his hands—broad and strong with long, supple fingers. She shivered, remembering what they'd done to her body in the name of love. Dear Lord, but he knew the buttons to push to make a strong woman weak with longing.

His chest rose and fell with each even breath that he drew, yet a short while ago, she'd felt the thunder of his pulse as he'd lain down upon her and driven himself into her, over and over, in mindless repetition.

Her body quickened in response to the memory and she glanced down to the bulge of him covered just below the waist with a sheet. Hers. He was hers. Before, they'd traded vows and made empty promises in front of Judge Harmon Harris. Today, they'd pledged their love in a way that would endure.

She reached out, gently laying her hand in the middle of his chest just so she could feel the steady rhythm of his heart, and as she did, he sighed and shifted in his sleep. She watched the thick brush of his eyelashes fluttering as some nameless dream pulled him further away from her. From his thick, black hair to those stormy gray eyes, she knew her man well. But she knew nothing of what made him tick.

Astute businesswoman that she was, she knew that in business, the swiftest way to achieve success was to know all there was to know about an enemy...or a competitor. And while Ryder was neither of those, he still had too many secrets for her peace of mind. He wasn't the type of man one would expect to find wandering the highways and byways of the Mississippi Delta. His education was obvious, his breeding even more so. Delaney would have called him a thoroughbred. Casey had an overpowering need to know this man who called her wife. There had to be more to him than a man who knew how to love and make love with a fine-burning passion.

She laid her head down on his chest and closed her eyes, smiling to herself as he pulled her to him. Even in sleep, his claim on her was strong.

Tomorrow. She would start the wheels of an investigation rolling tomorrow. But quiet. She'd keep it low-key and quiet. And it wouldn't be like she was snooping. She had a right to know all there was to know about the man she had married. Didn't she?

Royal Justice raced his daughter, Maddie, for the phone. He lost. Her tiny fingers curled around the receiver as she lifted it to her ear, speaking fast in order to get it all out before her daddy could snatch it out of her hands.

"Hello. This is Maddie. Is this you?"

Roman Justice kicked back in his chair and propped his feet on the top of his desk, absorbing the sweet sound of his only niece's voice.

"Well, hello, little bit. Yes, it's me. Is this you?"

Maddie giggled just as Royal got to the phone.

"Let me talk! Let me talk!" she shrieked, as Royal lifted it out of her hands. "It's Unca Roman. He called to talk to me!"

Royal shushed her with a finger to his lips and then lifted the receiver to his ear. "Roman?"

Roman flipped open a folder on the desk before him. "Brother, you're gonna have to get yourself some skates. If you can't beat a three-year-old to the phone, you're already in hot water. Just think what it'll be like when she's a teenager."

"Bite your damned lip," Royal muttered as Maddie danced around his legs, begging to be put back on the phone. "I assume you have a reason for calling."

As always, Roman Justice did not waste words. "Ryder's alive."

Royal turned and sank into a nearby chair with a sigh of relief. "Thank the good Lord. What have you learned? Why hasn't he called? Is he all right?"

"Hell, you're just like Maddie. One thing at a time. Your guess is as good as mine as to why he hasn't called, but if I had to bet on a reason, I'd say he hasn't turned loose of the guilt."

"But it wasn't his fault. The FAA told him that. We told him that. Lord have mercy, even the preacher who preached Dad's funeral told him that."

"Yeah, well you know Ryder. The only person he ever listened to was Dad and he's—"

"Yeah, right," Royal said, and pulled Maddie onto his lap, whispering a promise that she could talk when he was through.

"So, what's the story?"

"Hang on to your hat, brother. He's married and living in some place in Mississippi called Ruban Crossing."

"He's what?"

"You heard me."

Royal shook his head. "Married! Ryder, of all people. His wife must be something to have talked a maverick like him into settling down. Do you think we ought to give him a call? You know—to wish him well and all that?''

A fly buzzed past Roman's ear. He never moved, but his gaze followed the flight of the fly as it sailed past his nose. Somewhere between one breath and the next, he snatched the fly in midflight, holding it captive in his fist while he finished his conversation.

''Hell, no. You know better than that. Ryder is the one who ran away from home. If we call him, it would be like that time Mama came after the three of us for sneaking off to the pond to go fishing when we were supposed to be in school, remember?''

Royal laughed. ''Remember? Lord, I had nightmares for years afterward. And you're right. If Mama had just given us time, we would have been home for supper and everything would have been all right. As it was, we were dragged home with our tails between our legs. It took weeks before I could look Dad in the face without feeling shame.''

''Just be glad we know where Ryder is.''

Royal sighed. ''Right, and thanks for calling.''

''No problem.''

Maddie tugged at Royal's arm. ''Your niece needs to tell you something, okay?''

A rare smile shifted the sternness on Roman's face. ''If it's Maddie, it's always okay.''

''Unca Roman?''

''What is it, little bit?''

''You pwomised to take me to the zoo.''

''I know.''

''So when is you gonna do it?''

The smile on his face widened. ''Whenever you want.''

''Now!'' she crowed. ''I want to do it wight now.''

The fly buzzed frantically against the palm of his hand as he glanced up at the clock. ''Put your daddy back on the phone and let me ask,'' he said.

Maddie handed her father the phone. ''It's for you. And you gots to say yes.''

Royal pretended to frown, but it was all a big fake. He nearly always said yes to his very best girl.

''What?''

"Your daughter and I have a date with the zoo. She wants to go now."

"Fine with me," Royal said. "Just remember, she can't have everything she wants to eat, even if she begs. The last time she threw up on your boots."

"They were my boots. My problem. I'll be there within the hour." He hung up the phone and then smashed his hand flat on the top of his desk, ending the fly's last bid for freedom.

Royal hung up. At least there was one uncle left upon whom Maddie could depend. He didn't know what he thought about Ryder getting married, and truth be told, didn't have time to worry about it. Ryder was alive and well. That was all that could matter.

Not even in Lash Marlow's worst nightmares had he envisioned the day that something this degrading would happen to him. But it was here, in his hands, on plain white bond, typed all in capitals in clear, black ink. He stuck his hand in his pocket, rubbing at the rabbit's foot over and over and the words still didn't change.

Foreclosure.

He'd slept with the knowledge all night, and when he'd awakened this morning, had almost convinced himself that it was all a bad dream. Until he'd come into the kitchen to make coffee.

The letter was there where he'd left it last night. He'd picked it up again, rereading it over and over until his stomach rolled and his heart was thundering in his ears.

One powerful word and it was enough to bring what was left of his world to an end. He tossed the letter back onto the kitchen table, forgot about the coffee, and went to the breakfront to pour himself a drink. The decanter was empty—just like his life. He stared around the room, trying to find some sense of reason for drawing his next breath when something hit the front door.

That would be the morning paper.

He waited until he was certain the paperboy was gone. Even the eleven-year-old boy who delivered the papers had quit believing the check was in the mail.

The rubber band broke as he was rolling it off the paper, snapping the palm of his hand and bringing a quick set of tears to his eyes.

''Ow! Dammit, that hurt,'' he muttered, and tossed the paper on the kitchen table next to the letter.

He'd make that coffee after all. At least he could have coffee with the morning paper. That was a civilized thing to do.

When the coffee began to brew, he sat down and began to unroll it, but the edges kept curling back toward the way they'd been rolled and he cursed beneath his breath. It should be against the law to roll up a paper. He remembered the days when his father had insisted on having the help iron his morning paper flat before bringing it to him to read. He grinned, also remembering the occasional times when it would arrive with one of the pages scorched. Such a commotion over paper and ink.

In the middle of pouring himself a cup of freshly brewed coffee, the phone rang. Still lost in memories of grander days, he answered without thinking.

''Mr. Marlow, this is Denzel Cusper, down at the bank. I wanted to call you early, before you left for the office. We had several checks of yours come in yesterday and I'm afraid your account is a little short of funds. You know, we value your business. Your grandfather banked with us. Your father banked with us. We value the Marlow name, and that's why I knew you'd want to take care of this right away.''

There was a sick smile on Lash's face, although Denzel Cusper could not see it. He bit his lip and pretended he wasn't lying through his teeth. ''Why, you're right of course! I don't know how I let that oversight occur, but I'll take care of it on my way in to the office.'' He could hear the Denzel Cusper's sigh of relief.

''That's just fine,'' Denzel said. ''I'll just be holding these checks until your deposit clears.''

''Thank you for calling,'' Lash said.

''No problem. Always glad to give a valued customer a helping hand.''

Lash hung up the phone and poured his coffee down the sink. He didn't need caffeine. He needed money. He'd already spent his monthly retainer from the Ruban family, and the other clients he often represented were worse off than he was.

The foreclosure letter was still on the table right where he'd left it. Now this. Checks were going to bounce. He didn't even want to know how many. He had represented people who'd written hot checks, and he couldn't remember a one who'd gotten off without serving their time. The law was swift with regards to stealing, in any form.

Shame filled him. Thank God his grandfather hadn't lived to see this day. What his father hadn't lost, Lash had wound up selling to stay afloat. And now it was gone and Lash Marlow was sinking fast. In days gone by, there would have been only one honorable way with which to deal with this shame. Lash thought of the handgun in the drawer beneath the phone. He glanced at the paper he had yet to read. He could just picture the headlines.

"Local Lawyer—DOA."

Dead on arrival. He shuddered. There would be a scandal, but he wouldn't be around to face it. And while he was contemplating the virtue of an easy way out, his gaze fell on the corner of a familiar face pictured on the front page of the paper. He pressed the page flat.

"Ruban Heir Saved by Traffic Jam"

His eyes widened and he began to read, and when he was through, he stared down at Casey's picture in disbelief. Why? Why did someone like her keep getting all the breaks while everything he did threw him further and further off course?

"You bitch."

Startled, he looked up, expecting to see someone standing in the doorway of the kitchen. When he realized it was himself that he had heard, he looked back down and started to shake.

"You selfish, worthless, little bitch. I'd give my life to find a way to make you sorry for what you've done."

Casey's face smiled back up at him from the page, taunting him in a way he could not accept. He let go of his rage, giving hate full rein, and began to consider the wisdom of what he'd just said.

He knew people who would do very dirty deeds for very little money, which was exactly what Lash Marlow had. But if his scheme worked, when he was through, he would be the one in the dough, and that sharecropper's granddaughter would be sorry she'd thumbed her nose in a Marlow's face.

* * *

"Oh, my."

Casey's quiet remark got Ryder's attention. In the act of dressing for the day, he came out of the bedroom in nothing but his blue jeans. Casey was standing by the kitchen table, her morning cup of coffee forgotten as she stared at the headlines in disbelief.

"Ruban Heir Saved by Traffic Jam"

"How do they find these things out so fast?"

Ryder put his arms around her, reading over her shoulder as he cuddled her. When he saw the headlines, he sighed. Because of who she was, she would always be news.

"It doesn't matter. As long as they leave you alone, they can print your favorite recipe for toast for all I care."

She dropped the paper on the table and leaned against him. "I don't have a recipe for toast. I can't cook. Remember?"

He grinned. "Then you have nothing to worry about, right?"

She laughed and turned in his arms. "So it would seem."

His eyes darkened as he cupped her hips and pulled her close, letting her feel what was on his mind.

Her robe slipped open, revealing the clean bare lines of her body beneath. Ryder groaned and lowered his head, razing the tender skin on her neck with a series of nips and kisses that left her trembling for more than this sensual tease.

Casey shivered. "Make love to me."

With a flip of his wrist, her robe fell to the floor at his feet. He reached out, tracing the shape of her breast with the tip of his finger, then encircling her waist with his hands, holding her fast—wishing he could hold on forever.

"You are so beautiful, Casey Dee."

Her head lolled as his hands began to work their magic.

Skin tingled. Nerves tensed. Muscles coiled.

He lowered his mouth, trapping her lips and swallowing her sigh.

Heat built.

When his hand dipped between her thighs, she groaned.

Honey flowed.

She reached for his zipper, then for him, needing him—guiding him—to her—in her.

It happened fast. One minute she was standing, the next she

was on the cabinet with Ryder between her legs. ''Buckle up,'' he whispered.

Casey wrapped her arms around his neck and her legs around his waist. It felt as if everything inside of her was fighting to get out. Her heart was pounding against her chest. Her blood was racing through her veins. That sweet, sweet heat was building in her belly and she wanted the release. Clutching at him as hard as she could, she buried her face against his shoulder.

''Oh, Ryder, please now.''

He began to surge against her in a hard, even rhythm. Over and over. Minute upon minute. Rocking. Hammering. Driving toward pleasure. Too close to hold back.

Casey's senses were swimming. There was nothing upon which she could focus except him inside her. And suddenly gravity shifted and she lost her sense of balance. Grabbing him tighter, she arched toward a thrust, crying aloud. ''Ryder...Ryder...I'm coming undone.''

Sweat ran down the middle of his back as she held him, encompassed him, pulling him deeper and deeper toward total release. He shifted his hands from her back to her hips—pulling her forward—moving faster. His voice was harsh, his words low and thick with oncoming passion.

''Then let it happen. I'm coming with you.''

One cry broke the silence, then another, deeper and more prolonged, followed by soft, shaken sobs and gentle words of praise.

A short time later, Ryder picked up his wife and carried her out of the room. The newspaper that had sparked the mood lay forgotten on the floor. Had Casey seen it again, she would not have disputed the claim. The traffic jam wasn't the first thing to save her life. It was the man she'd found in the flatlands down at Sonny's Bar.

Chapter 12

"This is all I have to go on. See what you can come up with. Oh, and I want this kept confidential, understand?"

"Yes, Mrs. Justice. Of course."

Casey hung up the phone then swiveled her chair until she was gazing out the office windows. Outside, sunshine beamed down on Ruban Crossing, sweltering the inhabitants with a humidity that left everyone limp and weary. A flock of seagulls swooped past her vision, then disappeared around the corner of the building. On their way to the river—on their way to someplace cool.

She told herself what she'd done was for the best, and that no matter what her investigator found out about Ryder, she would love him just the same. But in the following weeks since they'd first made love, she sensed he was holding something back and it made her nervous. What if the revelation of his secrets brought an end to their relationship? She closed her eyes and said a small, quiet prayer. That just couldn't happen. She couldn't give him up. Not when he'd become the most important thing in her life.

The intercom buzzed. She turned back to her desk.

"Yes?"

"Libertine Delacroix on line two for you."

Casey picked up the phone. ''Libby, it's been a long time!''

''Yes, darlin', way too long,'' Libertine said. ''I would have called about this sooner, but I thought that with Delaney goin' an' dyin' on us like he did, and then you gettin' married and all, well—I just thought I'd give everythin' time to settle.''

Casey grinned. Libertine Delacroix's southern drawl was too thick to be believed, especially when Casey knew for certain that Libertine had been born and raised in Utah. The only thing south about her upbringing had been the window over her bed. However, after marrying Winston Delacroix and moving to their family home outside of Jackson, Mississippi, Libertine's speech had become as rich as southern fried chicken.

''How is that darlin' husband of yours, anyway?'' Libertine asked.

An image of Ryder's face above hers as he slid into her body flashed through Casey's mind. She closed her eyes and leaned back in her chair, suddenly weak with longing.

''Why, he's just fine. Thank you for asking,'' Casey said.

''Good. I'm havin' a little party Saturday night. I want you two to come. You'll be the guests of honor, of course.''

Casey opened her eyes and sat up straight. Libertine had never had a *little* party in her life.

''That sounds wonderful,'' she said. ''But what do you mean by little?''

''Oh, no more than forty or fifty. It'll be fun! Come in costume of course and be prepared to be showered with belated wedding gifts as well.''

Casey rolled her eyes. Good grief. A sit-down, costume party, wedding shower dinner? Only Libertine would attempt to pull off such a stunt.

''Thank you, Libby, Ryder and I will be looking forward to it.''

Libertine giggled. ''I do declare. I hear he's just the handsomest thing. Leave it up to you to pull the coup of the decade. I wouldn't have had the nerve, you know—goin' down in the Delta like that and callin' Delaney's bluff. Oh well, see you Saturday night, sugar. Eightish—costumes—prepare to have fun!''

Casey winced as Libertine disconnected. Lord have mercy!

Costumes. She hadn't been able to get him in a chauffeur's uniform. What was he going to say about this?

A dragonfly darted past Casey's nose as she leaned on the fender of the Lincoln, watching while Ryder poured oil into the engine. Still in her work clothes, she was careful not to get grime on her suit. It was an original and one of her favorites.

Ryder didn't seem to have the same set of worries. He was minus a shirt, minus his hat, and as of moments ago when she'd unloaded the news about Libertine's call, minus his good humor.

"So, you're going to put me on parade. I was wondering when this might happen."

Casey winced. "That's not fair. I'm not the one hosting this party, therefore I am not the one putting you anywhere. Libertine Delacroix is famous for her parties. She was also one of my mother's closest friends—at least, that's what Tilly says."

Ryder tossed the empty oil can into the trash and wiped his hands. "Step back," he ordered, and slammed the hood shut with a resounding thump.

Casey followed him into the garage. "Her food is always fabulous. She has the best chef in the county, you know."

"Can't be better than Tilly's," he said shortly.

"They're giving us a belated wedding shower. I didn't know how to say no."

Ryder turned, and there was a light in his eyes she recognized all too well. "Oh, I don't know about that. You pretty much said a big loud no to the terms of your grandfather's will."

She glared. "That's different."

He grinned.

"We're to go in costume."

The grin slid off his face. "Like hell."

Casey groaned. "Ryder, please. Don't be difficult about this. I love you madly. You can't blame me for wanting all of my acquaintances to meet you."

"Yeah, right, and I'm supposed to remember these people the next time I see them when I've been introduced to them in costumes? Let's see, what would I say? Oh, I know. You were the pirate, right? And you—weren't you that Playboy Bunny?"

She grinned. "I can heartily assure you that there will not be a single Playboy Bunny present."

He yanked his shirt from a hook and pulled it on with a jerk. "Well hell, you know that refusing you is impossible. However...just remember you're going to owe me, big time."

Casey threw her arms around his neck and kissed him full on the lips. "Thank you, thank you, thank you."

The corner of his mouth tilted as he nuzzled the spot just below her right ear. "You're very welcome."

Before their play went beyond a point of no return, Tilly stepped out the back door. "Casey, honey, telephone call for you."

Casey waved to let Tilly know that she'd heard, then turned back to Ryder. "So, what kind of costume do you want to wear?"

He cursed beneath his breath.

"Ryder, you promised."

"You don't worry about what I'll wear," he muttered. "I said I'd go, so I'll dress the part."

It wasn't what she wanted to hear, but knowing Ryder, it was the best she was going to get.

"Want to go out to dinner?" she asked.

"Want to go to Smoky Joe's?"

Casey groaned. She knew when she'd been had. "It's not alligator night."

He grinned. "I don't care. I have a hankering to see someone else's tail get slapped in the mud besides mine."

She made a face and then ran for the phone.

"Don't run in those damned heels," he yelled, but it was too late. She'd already done it. He frowned. One of these days she was going to break her leg pulling a stunt like that.

Casey leaned over the deck and waved at Miles and Erica as they came out of the main house. Erica's white antebellum dress floated just above the ground, billowing out around her and swaying with every step that she took. Miles looked dashing in black and quite reminiscent of a riverboat gambler. Eudora was sick with a cold and had declined the invitation with no small amount of regret. But she couldn't show up at a party with a box of tissues beneath her arm, no matter what costume she might wear. It just wasn't done.

"Hurry up!" Miles shouted, pointing toward a long white limousine pulling up in the driveway. "The limo's here."

"I'll be right down!" she called, and ran back into the apartment, closing and locking the patio door behind her.

Without Ryder, the apartment seemed too large and empty. He'd been gone for more than two hours, and although he called over an hour ago, claiming his costume had been undergoing alterations, he still wasn't back.

"Oh, Ryder, if you let me down at this late date, I'll never forgive you," she muttered, as she made a last-minute check through the apartment, making sure she had everything she'd intended to take.

She paused before the mirror then turned, glancing over her shoulder, making sure her own costume was in place, then smiling in satisfaction at the fluffy, white bunny tail right in the middle of her backside. She turned, ignoring the plunge of fabric barely covering her breasts and readjusted her long white ears. The black fishnet stockings made her legs look sexy, and her three-inch heels completed the picture. Yes, she made a darn good Playboy Bunny, even if she did think so herself.

As she started down the stairs to the waiting limo, she made a bet with herself. *By the time I get to the bottom of the stairs, Ryder will be driving up.* When her foot hit the last one she looked up. The Lincoln was nowhere in sight.

"Damn and double damn," she mumbled, and started across the courtyard. *Okay, by the time I get to the limo, he'll be home.*

When she drew even with the limousine's black bumper, she lifted her head to gaze down the long empty driveway. Her expression fell. She couldn't believe it. He'd actually let her down. What was she going to say to Libertine when they arrived?

The driver hurried around the car to where she was standing, then opened the door.

"Watch your ears—and your tail, darlin'. Wouldn't want either one of them to fall off before you got the chance to shine."

She looked up, then gasped. "Ryder!"

"Your ride awaits. Now don't tell me you're about to change your mind after I went to all this trouble."

She blinked. It was him. Resplendent in a dark, double-breasted chauffeur's uniform with more gold braid and buttons than an admiral might wear.

He tipped his cap and held the door ajar. "Ma'am?"

She threw her arms around his neck. "You are going to steal the show."

He held her close, patting at the fluff of her tail. "I'd a whole lot rather steal me a rabbit."

"Oh, for Pete's sake," Miles grumbled from inside the car. "Let's get a move on or we're going to be late."

Casey quickly took her seat, quite out of place beside a riverboat gambler and an old-fashioned southern belle.

Erica glared. Leave it up to Casey. "I swear, little sister, whatever you do tonight, don't bend over. You'll positively *spill* out of that disreputable thing you are wearing."

Miles grinned, for once taking Casey's side instead of his twin's. "Oh, I don't know about that, Erica. Even if she is our sister, she looks rather stunning."

Erica sniffed. "You would say that. After all, you're just a man."

The glass door slid open behind Casey's head. Ryder's voice drifted out into the uneasy silence. "Buckle up."

"Have mercy," Erica shrieked, and grabbed for a seat belt as the limo took off, leaving a black streak of rubber to show where it had been.

Miles needed no warning. He was already strapped and waiting for takeoff when the limo accelerated. He'd ridden with this man before.

Casey laughed aloud, then blew Ryder a kiss as he turned onto the highway. Tonight was just about perfect.

Of the guests who'd come in full costume to Libertine's party, nine were in Rebel gray. Of those nine, only Lash Marlow wore the uniform of a southern general, and he wore it with pride. His great-great-grandfather Marlow had been a general during the

War of Northern Aggression. It seemed fitting that he carry out the tradition, if only for the night.

But his pride in the past died a humiliating death when the Ruban party arrived. His gaze went past Miles and Erica Dunn. They were Rubans by marriage only. In the grand scheme of things, and blood being thicker than water, it was Casey who counted. But when he saw her and then the man at her side, it was all he could do to stay quiet. How dare she flaunt what she'd done to him?

Libertine Delacroix, who for tonight had dressed as Lady Liberty, was speechless for all of twenty seconds when she saw them, and then broke into peals of laughter.

''Casey, darlin', I should have known you'd outshine us all. And just look at this man on your arm! Introduce me this instant, you hear?''

Casey grinned. ''Libby, this is my husband, Ryder Justice. Ryder, my very dear friend, Libertine Delacroix.''

Libertine held out her hand. Ryder took it, then lifted it to his lips. ''I'm real partial to liberated women, Mrs. Delacroix. It's a pleasure to meet you.''

Libertine giggled at his play of words on her costume and name. ''The pleasure is all mine, I'm sure,'' she drawled, then slipped her hand beneath his elbow. ''Come along, you two. There's a ton of people who are just dyin' to meet you.''

''I'll just bet,'' he muttered beneath his breath.

Casey pinched his arm. He looked down and winked at her.

''You promised to be nice,'' she warned.

''No, I didn't. I just promised to come.''

She laughed at the sparkle in his eyes. Dear Lord, but she loved this man, so much that sometimes it scared her. She threaded her fingers through his, content for tonight to follow his lead.

An oblong silver tray glittered beneath the lights of the chandelier in the great hall as the wedding gifts were unwrapped before the guests. Crystal sparkled, fine china gleamed. Lash stood among the crowd, oohing and aahing along with them as each new piece was put up on display, and all the while, the idea he'd been fostering took deeper root in his mind.

Damn her—and him. He stared at the tall man in the chauffeur's uniform and resented him for not being ashamed. How can he hold his head high? By wearing that ridiculous costume, he'd all but announced to the world that he was nothing but hired help. Yet when Ryder casually tucked a wayward curl on Casey's forehead back beneath the rabbit ears she was wearing, Lash's stomach rolled. The look she gave him made gorge rise in his throat. *Damn her to hell. She never looked at me like that.* And that hurt, more than he was able to admit.

Out on the patio behind him, the band Libertine had hired was setting up to play. The thought of making small talk and pretending for another two or three hours seemed impossible to Lash, but he couldn't bring himself to leave.

Unaware of Lash's growing antagonism, Casey undid the bow on the very last gift and then lifted the box lid, pulling out a crystal-and-silver ice bucket and tongs.

"It won't hold a six-pack, but it sure is pretty," Ryder drawled.

Casey grinned at him as everyone laughed. By now, the guests had figured out that Casey Ruban's husband had been one jump ahead of them all night. Instead of trying to be something he wasn't, he dared them to dislike who he was. They had tried and failed miserably. Ryder Justice was too intriguing to dislike and too handsome to ignore.

"This has been wonderful," Casey said. "Ryder and I thank you for your kindness and generosity."

Ryder took Casey by the hand and stood. "All kidding aside, it's been a pleasure meeting my wife's friends. Maybe one day we can return the favor."

Casey was surprised at his initiative, and more than a little bit pleased. He kept coming through for her, again and again.

Libertine waved her hand above the crowd. "This way, this way, my dears. We've dined. We've showered. The evening can't end without dancing."

The crowd followed her through open French doors and out onto a massive flagstone patio. People broke off into couples and soon the impromptu dance floor was crowded.

Inside, Casey wound her arms around Ryder's neck and leaned her head on his shoulder.

"What's the matter, Hoppy, are you tired?"

She tried not to laugh, but his jest was entirely too charming to ignore.

"Yes, but deliciously so." His hands were stroking at the small of her back, right where it ached the most. She wondered how he knew.

"Think you might have one good dance in you? I just realized I've never danced with my wife."

"If you don't mind dancing with a barefoot bunny, I'd be delighted."

He cocked an eyebrow. "It can happen. I like bare."

She ran a finger down the middle of his chest, stopping just above the spot where his belly button would be. "Yes, I know."

He waited. She kicked off her shoes. He took her in his arms just as the next song began. Drums hammered out a rollicking beat and a guitarist joined in, running his fingers up and down the frets as the strings vibrated beneath his touch.

"Oh darn," Casey said. "It's too fast."

Ryder took her hand and placed it in the center of his chest. "You're listening to the wrong rhythm," he said softly. "Feel the one in here. It's the one to follow."

He glanced down at her feet. "I'd sure hate to mash one of those poor little toes. Better hitch a ride on my boots, honey, then all you'll have to worry about is hanging on."

A lump came to Casey's throat as she stepped up on his toes. Sure enough, when Ryder started to move, she could almost hear the slow, steady beat of a loving man's heart. The ache in her feet disappeared. She laid her cheek on his shoulder and followed his lead as he circled them slowly up and down the marbled floors of Libertine Delacroix's great hall.

Out on the patio, Lash Marlow stood in the shadows, staring back into the house. The intimacy of the lady bunny standing on the chauffeur's feet was not lost on him, nor were the tender kisses he saw Ryder giving his wife.

Lash's hand slid to the long sword hanging from the belt around his waist. It would be all too easy to draw it now while everyone was otherwise occupied and slash those stupid smiles off of both their faces, but that wouldn't get him what he deserved. No, he had other plans for Casey, and it wouldn't be long before he set them in motion.

Bunny ears hung on one corner of the bedpost, a chauffeur's cap on the other. Clothing was strewn across the floor and the chairs. In the bed, Ryder and Casey slept as bare as the day they'd been born, entwined within each other's arms.

Outside, a wind began to blow. A cool front was moving in. Something clattered against the patio door leading onto the deck. Ryder shifted in his sleep and rolled onto his back as he fell deeper and deeper into the dream playing out in his head.

Lightning flashed and the plane bucked. Seconds afterward, smoke began filling the cabin. There was a whine to the engines as the plane began to lose altitude. Ryder pulled back on the stick, fighting the pull of gravity with all of his strength.

"God help us both," Micah said.

Ryder jerked, his head tossing on the pillow from side to side. He hadn't remembered hearing his father's voice—until now.

Lightning flashed again, illuminating the horizon and the tops of a stand of trees, but Ryder was hardly aware. It was all he could do to see the instrument panel through the thick veil of smoke. Muscles in his arms began to jerk from the stress of trying to control the plane's rapid descent, and still he would not let go. Yet no matter how hard he fought, it would not respond.

"I love you, boy."

Tears seeped from beneath Ryder's lashes and out onto the surface of his cheeks.

I love you, too, Dad.

One of the windows in the cockpit shattered. Smoke dissipated at an alarming rate. Visibility cleared, and then Ryder wished it had not. There was at least half a second's worth of time to see that they were going to die.

He sat up with a jerk, gasping for air, unaware that his cheeks were wet with tears.

"Oh, God."

He rolled out of the bed and reached for his jeans. He had to get out. He had to move. He couldn't breathe.

Casey felt the bed give. Suddenly she was no longer lying on

Ryder's chest. She blinked, then opened her eyes. The sight of him jerking on pants and stomping out of the room was enough to yank her rudely awake. She didn't have to turn on a light to know something was dreadfully wrong. It was there in the shadowy movements of his body as he fled from the room. Seconds later, the front door banged, and Casey knew he was gone.

She crawled out of bed on all fours, searching for something to wear as she hurried through the house. One of his T-shirts was hanging on the doorknob. She grabbed it, pulling it over her head as she ran. It hung to a point just above her knees, but when she opened the front door, the fierce wind quickly plastered it to her body, leaving her feeling naked all over again.

She stood at the top of the landing, searching the grounds for a sign of where Ryder had gone. And then she saw him moving toward the trees at the back of the estate, and she bolted down the stairs after him.

Ryder moved without thought, trying to escape the dream clinging fast to his mind. It was just like before. No matter how fast he ran, he couldn't escape the truth. Micah had died, but he hadn't.

Wind whistled through the trees just ahead. It was an eerie wail, not unlike that of a woman's shriek. Without looking to the sky, he knew a storm was brewing. He stopped, then lifted his arms out on either side of his body like a bird in flight, and faced the force of nature for what it was. Unpredictable.

Unstoppable. Uncontrollable.

The first drops of rain were beginning to fall when Casey caught him. She didn't stop to ask him why. She didn't care that she was getting wet. She just threw herself into his arms, becoming his anchor against the storm.

Ryder groaned and wrapped his arms around her, and although the wind still blew and the rain still fell, he knew a sudden sense of peace. He dug his hands through the wind-whipped tangle of her hair and shuddered as she bent to his will.

Rain was falling harder now and he couldn't find the words to explain the horror and guilt that he lived with every day.

Casey clutched at him in desperation. His gaze became fixed

upon her face, and she could see his eyes. They were as wild and as stormy as the night. His fingers coiled in her hair. His body was trembling against her. A chill began to seep into her bones, and she knew she had to get them out of the weather. The gardener's shed was nearby. She pushed out of his arms, then grabbed him by the hand and started running. To her everlasting relief, he followed.

When she slammed the door shut behind them, the sound of the rain upon the metal roof was almost deafening, but at least they were no longer standing in the midst of it all.

"Lord have mercy," she said, and shivered as she lifted her hair from her neck and twisted it. Water ran out, then down her shoulder and onto her feet. She reached for the light switch.

It didn't work. It figured. In Ruban Crossing, if the wind blew or rain fell, inevitably, the power went out.

She turned, and knew Ryder was right before her, although she could barely see his face.

"Ryder?"

His hand cupped her shoulder, then her cheek. He stepped closer until their foreheads were touching and she could hear the ragged sounds of his breath. She lifted a hand to his face, and even though they'd just come out of a storm, she had the strangest sensation that what she felt were tears, not rain.

"Sweetheart?"

His lips found hers, stifling whatever else she might have said. They were cool and wet and softened upon impact, molding themselves to her mouth with tender persistence.

Casey sighed and when his arms encircled her, she leaned into his embrace. His hands were moving up and down her arms, across her shoulders, upon her hips. When he discovered she wore nothing beneath his shirt but herself, she felt him pause. His voice came out of the silence, little more than a whisper, but what he said made her blush in the dark.

Her hesitation was brief. There was nothing he could ask that would shame her. There was nothing she wouldn't do with or for this man who called her wife. She pulled the wet T-shirt over her head and dropped it on the floor. Her hands moved to his waist, then beneath the wet denim covering the straining thrust of his manhood.

When she took him in her hands, he groaned. When she knelt, she heard him take a deep breath. And she knew for the rest of her life, the sound of rain on a roof would bring back the memory of what she had done in the dark to bring Ryder Justice to his knees.

Joshua came into the kitchen. "Found this in the gardener's shed this morning."

Casey looked up from the kitchen table. Pink tinged her cheeks, but her expression remained calm.

Ryder glanced at Casey, then looked away. Even after the onslaught of emotions they'd shared last night, he'd been unable to explain what had sent him into the storm.

"It looks like one of my T-shirts," Ryder said. "I know I left one in the garage, but *I* didn't leave one in the shed."

Casey sighed. He hadn't lied. Not really. She was the one who left the shirt. Not him.

Joshua shrugged. "I think it will clean up all right. It's not torn, just wet and muddy."

"Thanks," Ryder said, and returned to the paper he'd been reading.

Tilly stared at the couple sitting side by side at her kitchen table. Everything seemed the same—except her instincts told her it wasn't.

"Is there something you'd be wanting to talk about?" she asked.

Ryder and Casey looked up, first at her, then at each other, before shaking their heads. Casey smiled. "No, ma'am."

Tilly glared. "I didn't get to be fifty-nine years old by being a fool." She banged a pot on the stove to accentuate her claim. "I know when something's not right. Did you two have a fight? 'Cause if you did, I'm telling you now, the best way to end it is talk it all out." She pointed a spoon at Joshua. "Tell them Josh! Tell them I know what I'm talking about."

Joshua rolled his eyes, thankful he was on the far side of the room from that spoon. "My Tilly knows what she's talking about. She always does. If you don't believe me, then ask her."

Ryder grinned behind his paper as Tilly lit into Joshua for making jest of her claims. It was just as well. It changed the subject, which was fine with him.

He glanced at Casey. Worry was there on her face. He'd have to be a fool not to see it. But he'd give her credit. She hadn't asked a single question. She'd just been there, giving herself to soothe his pain.

He glanced at her face—at her mouth—at her hands. Dear Lord, but she had soothed much more than his pain. Impulsively, he leaned over, slid his hand at the back of her head and pulled her forward. Their mouths met. More than slightly surprised, she parted her lips. His were hard and unyielding, demanding that she remember what they were, what they shared.

She gave herself up to the kiss and felt more pain than passion behind the embrace. One day. One day he would talk. Until then, she would have to be satisfied with waiting for his answers—or with what she learned on her own. The private investigator she'd hired was due back on Monday with a final report. Surely she would have some sort of answer by then. Even if it didn't come from Ryder, she had a right to know.

Chapter 13

Last night's rain had washed everything clean. Lash took his morning cup of coffee out onto the veranda and gazed across the yard into the trees beyond. Although it wasn't visible from where he stood, he could hear the water rushing through the creek below. He smiled to himself and took a slow, careful sip of the hot brew, careful not to burn his lips.

It was all falling into place. The kidnapping of Delaney Ruban's heir was a brilliant plan. He knew exactly how it was going to happen—who was going to do the deed—even the amount of ransom he was going to ask for the safe return of Ryder Justice's wife.

The ideal location in which she would be hidden had all but fallen into his lap. An aging client had been admitted to a nursing home via letter and phone by a distant cousin. The law offices of Marlow Incorporated had been given power of attorney to see to her monetary needs, as well as prepare for the impending funeral that was bound to occur.

Lash had done as the family had asked. Fostoria Biggers was now residing in the second room on the right at the Natchez Home for the Aged. Fostoria's money was in the bank, but Lash Marlow's name was on the signature card of her account. Her home out in the country was to be put on the market, and it would be—as soon as he no longer had need of it, which would be right after the Rubans coughed up three million dollars for Casey's safe return.

Friday he'd closed his office and gone to Natchez. The two men he'd hired with five hundred dollars he'd borrowed from Fostoria Biggers's account had come into town last night and were in a motel waiting for his call. The five hundred dollars was just a down payment on what he'd promised them when Casey's abduction was completed.

He took another sip of his coffee as he came down from the steps. He laughed to himself, and the sound caused a pair of white egrets roosting in an overhead tree to take flight. Fifty thousand dollars. Last month he couldn't have come up with fifty dollars, and now he had promised Bernie Pike and Skeet Wilson fifty thousand. And, compared to what he would have in his pocket before the week was over, it was a pittance.

The air was rich with the scent of bougainvillea that grew wild within the skeletal arms of a long-dead oak. The grass was still wet from last night's rain and by the time he reached the ivy-covered gazebo, the hems of his slacks were damp.

He stepped inside, then set down his cup and looked around. For the first time in more years than he cared to count, he could see light at the end of his tunnel of financial woes. It wouldn't be long before he could begin the repairs on Graystone and he could hardly wait. Even the gazebo was long overdue for a face-lift. And while it would have to wait just a little bit longer, there was one thing he could do.

He began gathering up the unpaid bills he'd been tossing on the gazebo floor, making a pile of them in the middle of the yard. Since the grass was damp, he had no qualms about what he did next.

He struck a match and gave it a toss. The papers were damp as well, but finally one caught—then another—then another, and while he watched, the ugly reminders of his past went up in smoke.

* * *

The folder from Childers Investigations lay on Casey's desk unopened. The private investigator was gone—had been for over twenty minutes, and Casey hadn't been able to bring herself to read the report. Fear overlayed curiosity as she stared at the name beneath the Childers logo.

Ryder Justice—Confidential.

Right now her world was just about perfect. But when she opened this up, it could reveal a Pandora's box of despair that no amount of money could buy, sell or fix.

She walked to the window overlooking the downtown area of Ruban Crossing and stared out onto the street without seeing the traffic or the flow of people coming and going into the Ruban Building itself. And because she was so lost in thought, she didn't see Ryder drive up and park, nor did she see him getting out of the Lincoln with her briefcase—the one she'd left in the kitchen chair during breakfast.

She glanced back at her desk, then walked to the far side of the room to refill her coffee cup. Another cup couldn't hurt. And it was as good an excuse as any to put off reading the report.

Her intercom buzzed, then Nola Sue's voice lisped into the silence.

"Mrs. Justice, your husband is here with your briefcase. He's on his way in."

A smile of delight broke the somberness of Casey's features as Ryder came through the doorway, dangling her briefcase from the ends of his fingers.

"Hi, darlin', sorry to interrupt, but I thought you might be needing this. I'll just lay it on your desk and get out of your hair."

Casey gasped. The report! It was on her desk! Before she could think to move, Ryder was halfway there.

Hot coffee sloshed on her fingers as she shoved the cup on the counter and made a run for the desk. "Ryder, wait!"

Startled by the urgency of her shout, the briefcase slid across the desk and then onto the floor, taking everything with it as it fell.

"Sorry about that," he said quickly, and knelt, intent on gathering up what he had spilled. But he froze in the act, unable to ignore the fact that his name was on every sheet of paper he picked up.

"It's not what you think," Casey said quickly, as she grabbed at the papers he was holding.

The look on Ryder's face had undergone a frightening transformation. The sexy smile he'd worn into the room had been replaced by a grim expression of disbelief. He stood, his words thick with anger.

"What does this mean?"

"I...uh—"

"You had me investigated?"

"You don't understand."

"So—you're telling me you *didn't* have me investigated."

Casey couldn't look him in the face. "I didn't say that."

"Then...what you're trying to say is that file is not a dossier of my life story."

Because she was so afraid, she took the defensive. "What I did was—"

"What you just did was stand there and tell me a lie."

She paled. The cold, hard glitter in his eyes was scaring her to death. Dear God, what had she done?"

"I did it for you," she said. "For us."

He pivoted, then picked up a cup full of pencils from her desk and flung them against the wall. They shattered and scattered like so much buckshot against a tin barn. Moments later, Casey's secretary burst into the room.

Ryder spun. "Get out."

Nola Sue gave Casey a wild, helpless glance and left at Casey's quick nod.

Ryder was so hurt, so betrayed by what she had done that he didn't trust himself to touch her. When she reached for him, he shoved her hand aside. "Well? Did you find what you were looking for?"

Panic-stricken, she wanted to throw herself into his arms and beg his forgiveness. But she couldn't weaken now, not when their future was at stake.

"I didn't read it."

The curse he flung into the air between them was short and to the point. Casey took it as her just due.

"But it's true. I was afraid to read it."

He grabbed at the scattered sheets he'd tossed on her desk and waved them in her face. "Why, Casey? Don't you know enough about me by now? Couldn't you trust that there was nothing in my past that could hurt you?" He groaned, and threw the papers on the floor. "Damn you. I would die before I let anyone hurt you—even myself."

This time she couldn't stop the tears. They spilled in silent misery.

He kicked at the papers on which he was standing, sending them scooting across the floor. "Then if you haven't read them, I'll save you the trouble. Depending on the depth of the report the investigator did, you will see that I'm the middle child of three sons born to Micah and Barbara Justice. They were ranchers. My older brother, Royal, still lives on the family ranch south of Dallas. My younger brother, Roman, is ex-military and is now a private investigator. I am a pilot. I own and run a charter service out of a private airport on the outskirts of Fort Worth. I also own a little under fourteen hundred acres of prime real estate on the outskirts of San Antonio, Texas, and unlike what you believed about me when we met, I am comfortably solvent. Before you, I had never been married, but last winter, I did something I'd never done before in my entire life."

Casey tensed.

"I ran away from home."

It wasn't what she'd expected him to say. Truth be told, she didn't know what she'd expected, but that certainly hadn't been it.

"I don't understand. What happened to make you turn your back on family and friends? Has it anything to do with the nightmares you have? The ones that drive you out of our bed? The ones you won't talk about?"

He started to shake, and Casey wished to God she'd never meddled.

"I was piloting a plane that crashed. I walked away. My father did not. He's dead because of me."

The look that passed between them was full of painful memories. For Casey, they were of the panic she'd seen on his face when he'd taken her to the airport. Of the plea in his voice not to fly in the storm. Of the desperation in his touch when he'd seen she was alive.

For Ryder, it was the death of a myth he'd been living. Of pretending that everything between them was perfect. Of hiding behind a marriage of convenience instead of facing the truth.

''You know, wife—I don't think you should be so judgmental about the terms your grandfather put in his will. From where I'm standing, you've picked up his manipulating ways all too well.''

With that, he turned and walked out of the office, ignoring the sound of her voice crying out his name—calling him back.

It was all Casey could do not to cry. ''Are you sure you haven't seen him all day?''

Joshua shook his head. ''No, sugar, I'm sorry. The last time I saw him he was on his way to your office with your briefcase.''

She groaned, folded her arms on Tilly's kitchen table and hid her face from the truth. *Please don't let him be gone.*

Tilly sat down beside her. ''I knew something was wrong between you two the other day. I told Joshua so, didn't I?''

Joshua nodded.

Casey slammed her fist down on the table. ''The other day was nothing.'' She stood, unable to sit still any longer. ''If only I could turn the clock back to that morning, none of this would have happened.''

Eudora came hurrying into the kitchen. ''What on earth is wrong? I could hear shouting all the way down the hall.''

''Mr. Ryder is gone,'' Tilly said, and then started to cry.

Eudora looked startled, then glanced at Casey for confirmation. ''Is this true?''

Casey threw up her hands. ''I don't know. He isn't in the habit of telling me anything important in his life,'' and slammed the door behind her as she left.

''Well, I declare,'' Eudora said, and dabbed at her eyes with a tissue as Erica came into the kitchen.

''What's going on?'' Erica asked.

''Ryder is missing,'' Eudora said.

Erica looked startled and turned as her brother, Miles, sauntered into the kitchen with his hands in his pockets, as if he didn't have a care in the world. ''What's everyone doing in the kitchen?''

''Ryder ran off,'' Erica said.

His expression changed from one of boredom to intrigue. ''Really?''

Eudora frowned. ''I don't believe it. I've seen the way he looks at Casey. I suspect they've just had an argument.''

Miles scratched his head, as if a thought just occurred.

''If he's gone, I wonder what that does to the terms of Delaney's will?''

It was one of the few times in his life that his grandmother chose to slap his face.

Sometime toward morning, Casey cried herself to sleep. She would have been happy to know Ryder hadn't gone too far. But she didn't know, and because of the press it would cause, she hadn't called the police. If she had, though, it wouldn't have taken them long to locate that familiar white Lincoln. It was parked at the airport in very plain sight. And it wouldn't have taken all that much longer to locate the driver. He was standing outside of the fences that separated the highway from runway, watching as planes took off and landed, trying to exorcise the demon that had driven the wedge between him and the woman he loved. It had taken hours before his conscience would let him admit that while she'd gone about it all wrong, she'd had the right to know.

As he watched, a small private plane was taxiing for takeoff, and he curled his fingers through the holes in the chain links, forcing himself to stand as the plane belied the laws of gravity. Since his arrival, over fifty planes had moved past his location, and not a one had crashed on takeoff or landing.

Then why spare me?

The question haunted him as much, if not more, than the fact that his father was dead. Weary in body and soul, he finally moved from the fence toward the car. He didn't know how, but he and Casey had to find a way to make things right. Living life without her wasn't worth the breath it would take.

But when he reached the car, it wouldn't start. The battery was so dead that jumper cables wouldn't even work, and because the battery was dead, the car phone was also inoperable. Ryder cursed luck and fate and everything in between, knowing that all he had to do was go inside the terminal and call home, but the idea of getting Casey out at four in the morning didn't seem all that wise, especially after the fight they'd had.

Forced to wait until daybreak when a mobile repairman could be called, he crawled into the back seat of the car, locked himself inside, and lay down and went to sleep. When he awoke, sun was beaming in the window on his face and it was long past nine. He groaned. Casey would be at the office. It would be tonight before they could talk.

"So," Miles said. "You're saying if Casey doesn't fulfill the terms of Delaney's will by staying with her husband for the entire year, it could still mean default?"

Lash leaned back in his chair and nodded, while his heart skipped a beat. This was his chance. This was the opportunity he'd been waiting for. Adrenaline surged as he contemplated the call he would make. Suddenly, he wanted Miles Dunn out of his face and he wanted it now.

"Look, Miles, it's simply a matter of wait and see. All married couples argue and they usually make up. I don't advise you to put too much hope in what you're thinking."

Miles looked slightly embarrassed as he stood. "Of course you're right. And I hope you don't think I was looking to gain anything by Casey's misfortune."

"Of course not," Lash said, as he ushered him out of his office.

When Miles was finally gone, Lash told his secretary to hold all his calls, then he slipped out the back door. He intended to make certain that the call he was about to make could not be traced back to him.

Casey was trying to concentrate on a stockholders' report when the phone by her elbow suddenly rang. It was the private line that only family used. She grabbed at the receiver, answering on the first ring. It had to be Ryder. Please God, let it be him.

"Hello?"

"Is this Miz Justice? Miz Ryder Justice?"

She frowned. The voice was crude and unfamiliar. "Yes, to whom am I speaking?"

"This here is Taft Glass. There's a fellow out here by my place who done went and had hisself a bad wreck. I found him myself when I went out this mornin' to check my trot lines. Looks like he'd been there all night. He's pinned in this big white car and all, and they're workin' to get him out, but he keeps callin' out your name. I told them medics I'd come up here to the bait and tackle shop and give you a call."

All the blood drained from Casey's face. She gripped the phone in desperation. Oh my God, she thought. I lay in bed and slept last night while Ryder was alone and hurt and crying out for help. Her hand started to shake and she gripped the phone tighter. This was why he hadn't come home.

She reached for paper and pen. "Give me the directions to the scene of the accident," she demanded, and wrote at a furious pace as Taft Glass continued to speak.

She grabbed for her purse at the same time she disconnected. Her legs were shaking and she wanted to cry, but this was no time for her to be weak. Ryder's well-being was all that counted.

Halfway to the door, she thought of the wallet she'd tossed in the desk drawer this morning and raced back to get it. She reached in and grabbed, getting a handful of pens along with the small leather case. Without taking time to sift through the mess, she tossed it all in her handbag and dashed out the door.

"Nola Sue, cancel all of my appointments. I don't know when I'll be back, but I'll call. My husband has been injured in a wreck."

Nola Sue was still registering shock as the door slammed shut behind Casey's exit.

"It's got to be here somewhere," Casey muttered, glancing down again at her hastily written map, as she had more than once during the last half hour.

This part of the countryside was one she'd never been in. She was deep in the Mississippi marshlands and hadn't seen a house since she'd turned off the last gravel road.

She took the upcoming curve at a high rate of speed, skidding slightly as the road suddenly straightened. Suddenly, her nerves went on alert. A few hundred yards up ahead she could see a cluster of parked vehicles. She'd found them!

It didn't occur to her to wonder why there were no police cars in sight, and no medical units trying to get Ryder free. All she saw was the front half of a white car buried in a bayou and the back half sticking up in the air, like an awkward straw in a giant cup of thick, soupy mud.

Fear for Ryder made her miss the fact that the buried car was a '59 Ford and that it had certainly been in the water longer than overnight. Fact was, it had been there closer to a year, and it was still there because the owner had moved away soon after, leaving it stuck the same way he'd left owing rent.

But to Casey, the sight was appalling. Her heart nearly stopped. Dear Lord, the man hadn't told her the car had gone off into water. She couldn't bring herself to think about Ryder not being alive. She had to explain to him about the investigation. He had to understand that she'd done it because she loved him, not because she didn't trust him. In a panic, she braked to a skidding halt, unable to contemplate the idea of growing old without him.

A heavyset man separated himself from the cluster of vehicles and started toward her, while another man, tall and skinny with long, graying hair, watched from the tailgate of his truck. The man coming toward her was short and his T-shirted belly had a tendency to laze over the waistband of his faded blue jeans. The baseball cap he wore scrunched over his ears accentuated the fact that he was in dire need of a haircut. Unruly blond wisps stuck out from beneath the rim of the cap like greasy duck feathers.

A niggle of warning ticked off in Casey's head. This wasn't what she'd been expecting. When he leaned in the window and leered, she knew something wasn't right.

"Miz Justice?"

"Yes, I'm Casey Justice."

Bernie Pike grinned and yanked her out of the car. "Damn, lady. It took you long enough to get here."

Panic shafted through her as she struggled to pull herself free. "Where's Ryder? Where's my husband?"

He laughed. "Now, that's probably about what he's going to be asking himself when you don't show up tonight."

"What do you mean?"

He slapped a rag on her face. It smelled of hospital corridors and science classes she thought she'd forgotten.

"Consider yourself kidnapped, honey, and hope that someone in your family thinks you're worth the price it's gonna take to get you back home."

She screamed and fought, tearing the cloth from her eyes and kicking off her shoes as she tried to run. Something sharp pierced her arm, then the world opened up and swallowed her whole.

Ryder got as far as the edge of town and knew he couldn't wait any longer to see his wife. Night was too far away. In spite of the fact that he looked as if he'd slept in his clothes, which he had, he needed to see Casey now. He parked in front of the Ruban Building and told himself they would find a way to make things right.

Nola Sue gasped as Ryder walked into the office. "Mr. Justice, thank goodness you're all right!"

Casey's secretary wasn't making much sense. "What do you mean?"

"You know. With your wreck and all, we had no way of knowing how serious your injuries might be."

He frowned. "I wasn't in any wreck."

Her hands fluttered around her throat as his words sank in. "But Mrs. Justice said you'd had a wreck. She raced out of here in a terrible state."

Suddenly there was a knot in the pit of his stomach. He didn't want to think about what this might mean. "When?"

Nola Sue glanced at the clock. "Oh, at least an hour ago, maybe longer."

A muscle jerked in Ryder's jaw. "Who told her something like that?"

She shrugged. "I don't know. I just know that someone called her on the private line. You know, the one the family uses.'' She blushed. ''I heard it ring. The walls aren't all that thick.''

Damn, this doesn't feel right. ''I want to look inside her office. Would you come with me? You'll know better than I would if something important is missing.''

Nola Sue followed Ryder inside, and together they made a thorough search of the place.

''No, I'm sorry, sir, but everything looks the same.''

Ryder tried a smile. ''I'm sure we're just borrowing trouble. She's probably at home, cursing the fact that someone sent her on a wild-goose chase.''

Nola Sue nodded. ''I'll bet you're right.''

Even though he suspected it was useless, Ryder continued to stand in the middle of the room. He kept thinking that they'd missed something. He could almost feel it.

When they'd started their search, her top desk drawer had been half-open, but Nola Sue had said nothing was missing. There was a pad of paper and a pen right by the phone, just like—

He froze. The pad. Maybe she'd written something on there that would give him a clue. He raced to the desk, then dug a pencil out of the drawer. Carefully, he rubbed the side of the lead on the blank piece of paper, going from side to side as he moved down the page. Inch by inch, a set of directions was slowly revealed.

Nola Sue leaned over his shoulder. ''Oh my goodness. That's way out of town. In fact, if I remember correctly, that's out in the marsh.''

His gut kicked, reminding him that fate was not kind. ''Call the house. See if she's home.''

Nola Sue did as she was told and, moments later, gave him the bad news. No one had seen her since early this morning.

Ryder looked down at the pad, afraid to consider where his thoughts were leading, and picked up the phone.

''What are you doing?'' she asked.

''Calling the police. Something's not right. Someone has played a pretty sick joke on Casey, or her life could be in danger. Either way, I'm not waiting to find out.''

* * *

Casey woke up with a start. Several things became obvious to her all at once. She couldn't see. She couldn't move. Her arm was sore and there was a bitter taste in her mouth. And, she remembered why. She took a deep breath and heard herself sob.

"So, girlie, girlie, I see you're comin' around."

She froze. *Oh God, I am not alone.*

"Please, let me go."

He laughed, and Casey felt like a fool. It had been a stupid thing to ask, but she'd had to, just the same.

"Now, we can't be doin' that. Not until your people come up with the dough. We went to a lot of trouble to set this all up, you know. Don't you think we ought to be paid for our time?"

Dear God, I've been kidnapped! "They'll pay," she said, and then choked on a sob.

He laughed again. "And why the hell not? It ain't like you're short on dough, now, is it?"

Something skittered across her leg and she kicked and screamed in sudden fright.

"Hey! Ain't no need for all that screamin'. If you can't keep your mouth shut, I'll just have to gag you, too—you hear?"

Her voice was still shaking, but there was just enough indignation to get the man's attention. "Something ran across my leg."

"Probably just a lizard. They's all kinds of water critters down here. Be glad it wasn't no snake."

She shuddered and thought of Ryder. Obviously, he hadn't been in any wreck. They'd used that excuse to sucker her right into their hands. If she'd had a foot free, she would have kicked herself. And along with that knowledge, came a question she was afraid to have answered. If Ryder wasn't in a wreck, then where was he? The thought of never seeing him again, of dying and not being able to explain to him why she'd done what she'd done was devastating.

"I need to go to the bathroom."

The man cursed. "I told 'em not to leave me out here. I told 'em somethin' like this was bound to happen. But hell no, did anyone listen?"

"Please."

He yanked at the cord binding her wrists to get her attention, then untied her ankles, dragging her up from the bed and standing her on her bare feet. A few steps later, he gave her a push.

"You got a couple of minutes, no more. And don't try nothin', either." His hand cupped her breast, and Casey could feel his breath on her face. "You'll be sorry if you do."

Casey wouldn't move, wouldn't let him know how scared she was, or how repulsed she was by his touch.

"Well, what the hell are you waitin' for?" he yelled.

She held out her hands. "For you to untie me."

He cursed, but moments later, she felt the rope come loose around her wrists and heard the door slam shut between them.

"No funny business," he yelled. "And remember, I'm right outside this door."

Her hands were shaking as she tore at the rag covering her eyes. When it fell free to the floor, she staggered from the unexpected glare of light. Quick to take advantage of the privilege she'd been granted, she did what she had to do, aware that it could be hours before he might let her get up again.

As she washed her hands, she searched her surroundings for something—anything, that might help her escape. But there was nothing in sight. Not even a window in the tiny, airless room.

The only remarkable thing she could see was a varied assortment of crocheted knickknacks sitting on floors, on shelves, even hanging from the walls. It explained nothing.

"Get out here, now!" the man yelled, and Casey jumped. "And put that blindfold back on your face or you'll be sorry."

She did as she was told, although she was already as sorry as a woman could be and still be breathing. If only she could start this day over.

Her hand was on the doorknob when the man suddenly yanked it open. He grabbed her by the hand, retied her wrists and ankles, and shoved her back down on a bed.

Loath to recline in a room with a man she could not see, Casey sat with her back against the bedstead, her knees pulled toward her chin. It wasn't much, but it was as good a defensive position as she could manage. The urge to come undone was almost overwhelming, but she refused to give way. She was going to need all of her wits to survive.

Chapter 14

Just as Ryder had feared, Casey's car was found at the location she'd written on the notepad. What broke his heart was learning they'd also found her shoes. For once, she must have heeded his warning and kicked off her shoes before trying to run.

Unfortunately, it had done her no good. There wasn't a clue as to where she'd been taken.

Now, just like before when she'd gone to Chicago, Ryder sat by the phone, again waiting for word. Only this time, the phone had been tapped, and when they heard—if they heard—he knew the request wouldn't be for a ride home. If Ryder's fears were correct, it would be for money in return for his wife.

Eudora had been given a sedative and was in her room asleep.

Erica was curled in a chair in the corner with her head on her knees, trying to come to terms with the fact that a member of their family was a possible kidnap victim and trying not to let herself think that if Casey didn't ever come home, everything that had been Delaney Ruban's would then belong to her and Miles. It shamed her to realize that she'd already envisioned what she would wear to her sister's funeral. She didn't want Casey to be dead. Not really. Right now, she would be perfectly satisfied if

Casey were back and being the constant source of discord in their lives.

Before Mason Gant had become a detective on the police force in Ruban Crossing, he had been a star running back on his college football team. He'd planned on a career in the NFL, not one behind a badge. But a single tackle had changed his plans and the rest of his life. Before he knew it, fifteen years had come and gone and he was now Detective Gant, and carried a notebook and pen, not a pigskin.

Because of the identity of the missing person, he knew that this could very well be one of the most important investigations of his career and was not giving an inch as to protocol. He'd interviewed all of the hired help and the immediate family, except one. Miles Dunn had been the last to come home and the last to be apprised of his sister's situation. And as Miles slumped in a chair, it was Gant's opinion that Dunn wasn't nearly as bereaved as he would have liked.

"And where were you?" Gant asked, pinning Miles in place with a casual stare.

Miles raised his eyebrows in disbelief. "Why on earth should it matter where I was at? My sister is missing. Why aren't you out trying to find her?" Taking heart in the fact that several of Ruban Crossing's finest were present, he glanced at Ryder, confident that he could say what was on his mind without coming to harm. "Better yet, why aren't you questioning her husband? We don't really know a thing about him."

"Oh, but we do, and his story checks out clean. Besides, he has nothing to gain from her demise. On the other hand, you and your sister have several hundred million dollars at stake. Am I right?"

Erica stood up with a gasp of indignation as Miles shifted nervously in his seat. "Of course not. Casey inherited."

The detective persisted. "But what happens if she dies?"

Miles shrugged. "I wouldn't really know."

As the family lawyer, Lash was in attendance. At this point he interrupted, but seemed hesitant to do so. "That's not exactly true, Miles. You did come to my office this morning and ask what would happen if Casey defaulted on the terms of Delaney's will."

Ryder came to his feet, and if there hadn't been a desk and a chair between them, he would have put his fist in Miles's face.

Miles spun, his face livid with anger. "You're twisting everything. You knew I was asking because we all thought Ryder had flown the coop."

Lash looked repentant. "I'm sorry, Miles, but I felt obligated to tell the truth. If anyone needs me, you know where I can be reached." He picked up his briefcase and made a quick exit.

Ryder was shaking with anger. "You son of a bitch. Do you remember what I told you? If Casey hurts—you bleed."

The low, even tone in Ryder's voice frightened Miles far more than any shout of rage could have done. He scrambled to his feet and backed toward the door, looking frantically toward the police for protection.

"Sit down!" Gant said, and then glanced at Ryder. "While I can understand your indignation, this isn't getting us anywhere. A woman is missing and all you people seem able to do is fight among yourselves."

Ryder hunched his shoulders and stalked to the windows overlooking the courtyard, looking up at the small apartment over the garage. Precious minutes passed as pain twisted within him, drawing and pulling like a dull knife. The night before last, he'd slept in Casey's arms. They'd made love with an abandon that had surprised even him. And less than thirty-six hours later, someone had lied to Casey and stolen from Ryder the thing he cared for most—his wife.

And then suddenly the phone rang, and everyone jumped as if they'd been shot.

"You answer it," Gant directed, pointing at Ryder.

Ryder said a prayer and picked up the phone. "Hello."

"This is a recording. I will not repeat myself, so pay attention. Casey Justice is with me. At the moment, she is alive. If you choose to ignore my conditions, she will not stay that way long. For her release, I want three million dollars in small, unmarked bills, none of them larger in denomination than a fifty, none of them smaller than a five. I will call you at five o'clock, day after tomorrow, and tell you where and when to make the drop."

The line went dead, with the computerized sound of an altered voice still grinding in his ear. ''Did you get that?'' Ryder asked.

Gant nodded. ''All we can do now is wait.''

Ryder slammed the phone down. ''Like hell. That's three days. In three days, anything could happen to Casey. Don't you have any leads? Didn't anything turn up when forensics went over her car?''

Gant was a man who believed in telling it like it was. ''Forensics is still going over her car, and you know as well as I do that we don't have any other leads. However, we will actively be pursuing the investigation.''

Ryder covered his face with his hands and turned away. He felt sick to his stomach and couldn't quit shaking. He kept thinking about Casey. Of how afraid she must be. ''Dear Lord. Why is this happening?''

Gant briefly touched Ryder's arm. ''Because someone got greedy, Mr. Justice. Now I suggest you try to get some rest. The next forty-eight hours will be crucial. The FBI should be here by morning.'' He grinned wryly. ''You'll probably have to repeat everything you've told me to them. They're kind of partial to taking their own statements.'' His smile faded. ''I think you should be prepared for the possibility that the kidnappers are going to want you, or another member of the family, to make the drop.''

''I'll do whatever they ask, but I'm not very good at waiting.'' He exhaled slowly, as if the action pained him. ''There will be time to rest after Casey gets home.''

Gant looked away. He was too aware that the odds of that happening weren't all that good.

''If anyone needs me, I'll be at the apartment,'' Ryder said, and started down the hall when Erica caught up with him.

''Ryder.''

He stopped and turned.

Looking him straight in the face was the hardest thing she'd ever done. From start to finish, she was ashamed of the way she'd behaved, but she didn't know how to say it without admitting she'd been in the wrong.

''What do you want?'' he asked.

"If you don't want to be by yourself, I know Casey would want you to stay here in the main house. You could have her room."

"I don't think so, but thanks." He turned away.

"Ryder, wait, please!"

He took a deep breath and turned around again. "Yeah?"

"I'm sorry."

He didn't respond.

"I have never regretted anything as much as I have regretted the stunt I pulled with you. All I can say is, I have envied Casey her place in this family all of her life, and it's not even her fault. She was born a Ruban. Our mother became one by marriage. Miles and I have been on the outside looking in ever since the day Mother said, 'I do.'" Her chin quivered as she continued. "However, not even in my ugliest moment have I ever wished Casey to come to harm. I ask your forgiveness, and when Casey comes home, I will ask hers, too."

Ryder knew truth when he heard it, and in his opinion, it was probably the first time in her life that Erica Dunn had been completely honest, with herself, and with someone else. And because she was Casey's sister, he held out his hand.

"Truce."

She smiled. "Truce." And she accepted the offer of friendship. "Sure I can't change your mind?"

He shook his head and then hurried out the door. Erica watched as he ran up the stairs to the apartment, and although she couldn't hear it, imagined the thud as he slammed the door shut behind him.

Ryder grabbed the phone as soon as he came in the door, then sat down with it in his lap. Within seconds, he was punching in numbers, then waiting as it began to ring. Four rings later, the answering machine kicked on.

He closed his eyes as he listened to the message. It had been so long—too long since he'd heard the sound of his brother's voice.

"This is Justice Air and The Justice Way. State your name, your business, and if you want a call back, leave your number. Wait for the beep."

It didn't register to be surprised that Roman was now in charge of his business as well. Casey was foremost on his mind.

"Roman, it's Ryder. For once, pick up the damned phone."

A distinct click sounded in Ryder's ear, and he closed his eyes with relief.

"It's about damned time," Roman growled.

"Give me grief later," Ryder said. "Right now, I need you, brother, as I have never needed you before."

Roman sat up. Ryder was thirty-three years old and to Roman's knowledge, he had never asked a soul for help before in his life. "What's wrong?"

"My wife has been kidnapped. I want her back, Roman." His voice broke. "Dammit, I need her back. If anything happens to her, I won't—"

"Where are you?"

"Ruban Crossing, Mississippi."

"Hell, I knew that," Roman muttered. "I mean physical directions to your home."

Startled, it took Ryder a moment to reconnect his thoughts. Then he sighed. He should have known. After all, his brother *was* a private investigator.

"Got a pen and paper?" he asked.

"Does a bear—"

Ryder laughed aloud, drowning out the rest of Roman's remark. It made him feel good, almost normal, to hear Roman's ever present sarcasm. Some things never change.

He gave Roman directions to the Ruban estate, and when he hung up, for the first time since this nightmare had started to unfold, he knew a small sense of relief.

In a small, unused room in a forgotten part of Delaney Ruban's house, candles were burning, on pedestals, in cups, on plates, even on the floor. Candlelight flickered upon the walls and on the bare, lithe body of Matilda Bass, giving the cafe au lait colour of her skin a rich, golden glow.

Her hair was undone and hanging well below her waist and she moved as one in a trance, methodically unrolling a cloth she'd brought into the room. A handful of small, white bones fell out of the folds, arranging themselves in a crude sort of circle as they rolled to a stop.

She leaned forward, her bare breasts shifting, and she was barely aware of the thick, silken length of her hair against the skin on her back, blind to the candlelight surrounding her as she sat.

At her side lay a knife, the shaft, old and yellowed. The blade was long and thin, the kind that pierces and kills and leaves nothing behind but a tiny, red mark. The carvings on the handle were old and held a power all of their own.

When Joshua entered, Tilly sensed the air in the room stirring, and somewhere within her mind, she sifted through the change and knew that nothing threatened what she was about to do. Her focus shifted again as she went to her knees before the circle of bones, whispering in a language that she'd learned at her grandmother's knee.

Lash downshifted Fostoria Biggers's small white compact and turned into the overgrown driveway leading up to her house. It was nearly dark, and he knew that coming out here was risky, but he wanted to see for himself that the mighty Casey Ruban had been brought to her knees. Using Fostoria's car was just another way of blurring his trail.

The house was small and nearing total dilapidation. In fact, if possible, it was in worse condition than his beloved Graystone. Fostoria's porch had sagged some years ago, and was nearly rotted through from the wetlands upon which it had been built. Paint had peeled off all the siding except in a few sheltered places, and the curtains that hung at the windows were faded and limp. The grass in the yard was ankle high and Lash winced as he thought of walking through it. There was no telling what kind of reptiles were lying in wait.

He made it through the yard and onto the porch. Sidestepping the worst of the sag in the planks, he walked into the house as if he owned it. Bernie Pike spun toward the sound, his gun pointed directly at Lash's chest.

"Dammit, Marlow, you scared the hell out of me."

Lash frowned. "Point that thing somewhere else."

Bernie did as he was told.

''Where is she?'' Lash asked.

Bernie pointed toward the first door on the right down the hall. ''I put her in there. It was the only room that had a bed.''

Lash nodded.

''When's Skeet comin' to relieve me?''

Lash frowned. ''I told you two to guard her. I didn't think I would have to set up a work schedule for you as well. Call him and find out for yourself.''

Bernie shivered and glanced nervously out the open door. ''I'm ready to get my money and get the hell out of this swamp. There's snakes and lizards and all matter of critters out here. When is it all goin' down?''

''Day after tomorrow.''

Bernie frowned and then cursed. ''What's the holdup? I thought them people had plenty of money.''

Lash glanced down the hall at the closed door and then grinned. ''Oh, they do, but I intend to delay the inevitable as long as possible. Why put her out of her misery—until she knows what real misery is like?''

There was an expression on Lash Marlow's face that made Bernie Pike shudder. He shifted his gun to his other hand, thankful that he was working for this man, not running from him.

''So, what do you want me to do?'' Bernie asked.

Lash took a deep breath, his pulse quickening as he glanced at the closed door. ''Get out. Get out and don't come back inside until I tell you to.''

Bernie looked startled and then a slow grin spread across his face as he did what he was told.

When the house was quiet, and Lash could hear nothing but the sound of his own heartbeat in his ears, he gave his rabbit's foot a last quick rub, and started down the hall.

Casey's hands were numb and her throat was dry. She needed a drink in the very worst way, but calling attention to herself was the last thing she wanted to do. As long as her abductor thought she was asleep, he pretty much left her alone.

Something was crawling on the floor beside the bed and she

prayed it stayed there. But the scritch-scratch of toenails on hardwood flooring was impossible to ignore. She kept telling herself that as long as she couldn't see what was making the noise, then she couldn't be afraid.

And then the air shifted, and another sound blended with those in her head and she tensed. That was the door! Someone was inside the room. Casey had learned a trick from Delaney early on in her life to take control of a situation by being the first to speak. She saw no reason to change her strategy now.

"I would like a drink of water."

A low, ugly chuckle centered itself within the waiting silence and Casey gasped. That didn't sound like her abductor. Someone else had entered the picture.

"Casey, Casey, ever the prima donna, aren't you? Tied up like a sow going to market and still giving orders. Now what do you suppose it would take to bring you to your knees?"

"Lash?"

The blindfold was yanked from her face.

Casey blinked rapidly, trying to clear her vision as her eyes adjusted to the change in light. Lash leaned down and pinched the sides of her cheeks with his thumbs and fingers, squeezing and squeezing until speech was impossible and tears sprang to her eyes.

"That's it. Cry for me, honey. Show me you care."

Casey jerked, trying to free herself from his grasp, and then to her surprise, he turned her loose and shoved her, sending her sprawling. Before she could think, he had untied her ankles and straddled her legs.

Panic shafted through Casey's mind. Lash's intentions were all too plain. And when he leaned forward, pressing the palms of his hands against the swell of her breasts, she groaned and wrestled with the ties still binding her wrists. They wouldn't give.

"Lash, for God's sake, don't."

His slap ricocheted off the side of her jaw. "You don't tell me what to do. I'm the one in control. I'm the one who calls the plays, princess, and right now, I'm going to take a little of what was rightfully mine."

His fingers curled in the top of her blouse, and when he yanked, buttons flew, hitting the wall and scattering across the floor. Something scurried out from under the bed and Casey knew that one good thing had come from Lash's arrival. At least that creature was gone. If she only knew how to get rid of this one for good, she would never ask for anything again.

He laughed, and then grabbed at the hem of her skirt as adrenaline surged through him. This was power. He wished he'd thought of it sooner. At last he felt like a man.

Casey kicked and bit and screamed until her throat was hoarse. It served no purpose other than to arouse him more. His hands were at the juncture of her legs when the room began to grow dark before her eyes. A fresh sheen of perspiration broke out on Casey's skin as the sensation of fainting became imminent. Horrified at what he would do if she was unconscious and helpless, Casey thought of a prayer that didn't make it aloud. The darkness in the room was growing, and it was beginning to pull her in.

Her submission was so unexpected that Lash also paused, wondering what trick she was trying to pull. But she was far too limp and far too still for a joke. Frustrated that she would not be awake to suffer his touch, he thrust a knee between her legs, readying to shove himself in as well. And then Casey began to speak.

Surprised, he looked down. Her eyes were still closed. She was still limp—almost lifeless. And he would have sworn the voice that he heard was not her own.

Her breathing had slowed, and at first glance, she seemed to be asleep. But the words pouring out of her mouth were fluent in cadence, foreign in sound and speech, universal in intent. One brief, staccato sentence after another, she was invoking a curse of such magnitude upon Lash Marlow's head that he couldn't do anything but stare. Word after word, the curse continued, pouring upon every living person hereafter who might carry an ounce of his blood in their veins. Spoken in the old patois of French-speaking slaves, the threat became even more insidious as the promises continued.

Lash jerked his hand back from her legs as if he'd been burned. Pale and sickening, a cold sweat suddenly beaded upon his face. Lash was a true son of the south. He'd been born and bred in the ways of the past. He, too, spoke French like a native, and although he was a well-read, highly educated man, there was that part of him that had grown up believing in curses and superstitions and extremely bad luck.

"Shut up! Shut up!" His scream rent the air as he drew back and slapped her in the face.

It was after Casey tasted her own blood that she took a deep breath and opened her eyes.

Horror crawled up the back of Lash's spine. The woman looking out at him from Casey's face wasn't the green-eyed woman he'd known and coveted. This woman's eyes were black, and she was staring at him from hell.

He grabbed at his clothes, scrambling to get off of her legs and away from her body like a man gone crazy. When he was on the other side of the room, he pointed a finger toward where she lay and told himself it didn't matter. Words were just words. She couldn't stop the success of what he'd set in place. But everywhere he moved, her eyes followed him, staring—blaming—reminding him of what she'd just said.

"Say what you will, you stupid bitch," he growled. Then he laughed. But it was a nervous, jerky sort of bark. "Day after tomorrow it will all be over. I'll be rich, and you'll be dead."

And then he was gone, and while she lay on the bed, she came to an acceptance she didn't understand. Even though she was locked in this room and helpless in the face of her abductors, for a while, she had not been alone. Instead of being afraid, she took comfort in the knowledge. All she could remember was feeling sick and then falling into a deep, black hole. What had transpired after that, she could only guess, but she knew she had not been raped. And in the face of all that, it still wasn't the biggest horror of all.

Lash Marlow had purposefully let her see his face. She closed her eyes. She would never see Ryder again.

It was 3:00 a.m. when the knock sounded on Ryder's front door. Half in and half out of a weary doze, he staggered to his feet and made his way through the darkened rooms, turning on lights as he went. He grabbed the doorknob and jerked.

Roman walked inside, tossed a suitcase on the sofa and kicked the door shut behind him. Brother to brother, the two men looked at each other, judging the changes in each that the last few months had made. Finally, it was Roman who broke the silence.

"You look like hell."

Ryder walked into his brother's outstretched arms. Their embrace was brief, but it served its purpose. It was proof to Ryder that the connection he'd tried to sever with his family was still as strong as it had ever been.

"You got here fast," he said.

Roman glanced around the room. "I figured I'd better."

Ryder hadn't expected to be so overwhelmed by the sight of his brother's face. It was all he could do to speak without breaking down. "Help me, Roman. Help me find her and get her back."

Roman's grasp was strong on Ryder's arm. "That's why I came, brother. That's why I came."

Like the sleuth that he was, Roman began to move about the room, picking up things and laying them down again, feeling, judging, absorbing the world in which his brother had been living. A photograph sat on a nearby table. Roman picked it up.

"Is this her?"

Ryder nodded. It had been taken the night of Libertine Delacroix's party. It hurt to look at it and remember how happy they'd been. "Yeah, minus the ears and tail," Ryder said.

One of Roman's rare grins slid into place. "Leave it up to you to run away from home and come out smelling like a rose."

"Well, I do declare!"

Eudora's ladylike gasp that accompanied her remark was in reaction to seeing the Justice brothers coming through the front door of the main house.

From the cold, handsome faces to the dark straight hair and those square, stubborn chins, they were alike as two peas in a pod. Their blue jeans were pressed and starched and their long-sleeved white shirts were a perfect contrast to the tan of their skin. The tilt of their Stetsons rode at the same cocky slant, and their steps synchronized as they stepped off space on the pale, marble floor.

''Dora, this is my brother, Roman Justice. Roman—Casey's grandmother, Eudora Deathridge.''

Roman's expression never changed as he tilted his hat. ''Ma'am.''

A shiver moved through her as she looked into Roman's eyes. They were dark, and the expression seemed hard and flat. And she knew if he hadn't looked so much like Ryder, she would have been afraid of this man.

Ryder touched her arm. ''We're going to use the library for a while, okay?''

''Why, yes, dear. Whatever you need,'' she said, and then made as graceful an exit as she could manage.

''There it is,'' Ryder said, pointing to the computer system in the far corner of the room.

Roman headed for it with unerring intent. Within moments, he was into the system and had it on-line.

''How did you do that?'' Ryder asked. ''I can never make those things do what I want them to do.''

Roman looked up. ''You just don't use the right kind of persuasion,'' he replied, then moved his eyes back to the screen.

Ryder found himself a chair and sat down. This morning, Roman had asked him for a list of names of people with whom Casey most closely associated. The question had surprised him. All this time he'd been thinking in terms of faceless strangers, not a betrayal from family or friend.

He'd asked why and was still shaken by his brother's cold answer. ''Because trust will betray you every time.''

It hurt him to know the depth of Roman's bitterness toward the human race. But his own life was in such a mess, he couldn't argue the point. All he could do was trust the fact that Roman had been in this business long enough to know what he was doing.

''Well, now, this is interesting.''

Ryder came out of his chair like a shot. They were the first words that Roman had spoken since he'd sat down at the computer over an hour ago.

''What?'' Ryder asked.

Roman leaned back in his chair. "Besides being the family lawyer, what is Lash Marlow to Casey?"

Ryder frowned. "Nothing, although I think her grandfather would have wished it otherwise. Remember what I told you about the will, and how we met?"

Roman nodded.

"Casey once mentioned that when Lash Marlow read that clause in the will, he was almost gloating. You know, like an I've-got-you-now look."

Roman stared at the screen. "He's broke."

Startled, Ryder moved to look over Roman's shoulder. "You must be mistaken. His family is old money. That's what everyone says."

"He has been served with a foreclosure notice, and up until two weeks ago, his accounts were all overdrawn."

Ryder frowned. "How the hell did you get that computer to do that?"

"That's privileged info, brother."

"Did you hack into the bank's computers?"

Roman spun his chair around as one of his rare smiles slowly broke across his face. "Now, Ryder, why would I do a thing like that? It's illegal."

Ryder started to pace. "Okay, so Lash Marlow is hard up for money. I'd venture to say at least half the people in Ruban Crossing could say the same."

He paused to look out the window overlooking the grounds. His gaze fell on the gardener's shed. Despair surfaced as he thought of holding Casey in his arms, and what they'd done that night in the name of love. It was all he could do to focus on what had to be done.

"Look Roman, there's no guarantee that whoever has Casey is even a local. In the business world, the Ruban name is known worldwide. Their holdings are vast. Casey's inheritance has recently been in all the papers...twice. Once when Delaney died. Again when that plane she was supposed to be on crashed and burned with all aboard."

Roman listened without comment, but when he turned back to the computer, his gaze was fixed, his thoughts whirling. He kept thinking of what his C.O. used to say just before they'd go out on a mission. *Never overlook the obvious. It will get you killed every time.* In Roman's opinion, Lash Marlow had an obvious axe to grind. What remained to be seen was if he was the kind of man who could betray a client...or a friend.

The family was gathering in the main salon, and while they whispered among themselves as to the possible reason Detective Gant might have for calling them all together again, Ryder's thoughts were on something else. A few moments ago, he'd glanced up at the clock. Forty-eight hours ago to the minute, he'd walked into Casey's office a happy man. Within the space of time it took to spill papers from a desk, his world had come to an end. All last night he'd kept hearing the sound of her voice as she'd begged him to come back inside her office. If only he had.

A few moments later, the doorbell chimed and they heard Joshua directing Mason Gant into the room.

"Thanks for being so prompt," Gant said, waving away Joshua's offer of coffee. He glanced around the room. "I have some news," he announced, and when Ryder took a step forward, he held up his hand. "Sorry, I phrased that wrong. It is news, but not of Casey."

The doorbell pealed again and Joshua hurried from the room. Moments later, Lash Marlow followed him back.

"Sorry I'm late," Lash said, smoothing his hand over his windblown hair. "Had to be in court first thing this morning."

Gant nodded. "I just got here myself." He looked around. "Is everyone here?"

"Everyone but Bea. Today's her day off," Tilly said.

Gant pulled out his notebook. "I have her address. I'll catch up with her later."

"Detective Gant, before you start, there's someone I want you to meet."

Gant looked up, surprised by Ryder's remark. He thought he'd met everyone when he was here before. Suddenly a man walked into his line of vision and he realized that the fellow had been standing in plain sight all along, but had been so quiet and so still that he'd completely overlooked his presence.

His first impression was that the man was military. His second was special forces. And then he focused on his face and Gant knew before he spoke that this man was Ryder's brother...if not his twin.

"I'd wager your last name is Justice," Gant said.

Roman held out his hand. "Roman Justice, private investigator out of Dallas. I won't get in your way if you don't get in mine."

Gant grinned as they shook hands. He liked a man who said what he thought.

A coffee cup shattered, breaking the brief silence as everyone turned toward the sound. Lash was against the wall. He was pale and shaking and staring down at the floor.

"It slipped out of my hands."

Joshua ran to get a broom as Tilly fussed with the splatters that dappled the edge of a soft, moss-green rug.

Ryder stared at Lash, as if seeing him for the very first time. He couldn't bring himself to believe that anyone who knew Casey would want to cause her harm. And Marlow was, as usual, every inch the gentleman—from the cut of his clothes to the style of his hair. But why was Lash so upset over a spilled cup of coffee? Ryder kept staring and staring, remembering his brother's words and trying to see past the obvious to the man beneath. Suddenly, something about Lash's appearance struck a sour note.

"Hey, Marlow."

At the sound of Ryder's voice, Lash jerked as if he'd been slapped. He looked up. "Yes?"

"What the hell happened to your hand?"

He didn't have to look down to know they were referring to the row of skinned knuckles on his right hand and the long red gash that ran from one edge of his wrist to the other. Gorge rose in his throat as he struggled with an answer they all might believe. He could hardly tell them it was the remnants of his bout with Casey.

He managed a laugh. "I locked myself out of the house last night. Graystone may be past her prime, but like the lady she is, she does not easily part with her virtue. I broke a window trying to get inside. Lucky for me I didn't cut my own wrist, right?"

The answer was plausible enough. Ryder shrugged. If the man

had cut his own throat, he couldn't have cared less. If there was news that pertained to Casey, he wanted to know now.

"Look Gant, let's get down to business. Why did you call us all together?"

Lash was counting his blessings that the subject of his wounds had been changed. But his relief was short-lived when Gant started to talk.

"Forensics came up with a print on Casey's car that doesn't match anyone else in the family."

Ryder stiffened. Was this their first break? "Do you have an ID?"

Gant nodded. "Belongs to a low-life hood out of Natchez named Bernie Pike."

Lash felt his legs going out from under him and slid into a chair before he made another social faux pas. By the time everyone present had assured the detective they knew nothing about the name, he had himself under control.

Although Gant's meeting with the family had been necessary, he hadn't really expected anything to come from this lead. At least, not from this quarter. He was gathering his things and readying to leave when he suddenly remembered another fact he needed to verify.

Lash Marlow was on his way out the door when Gant called him back.

"Marlow! Wait!"

Lash spun, his nerves tightening with every breath that he took. "Yes?"

"About the ransom. Will you be able to get it all together by tomorrow?"

He went weak with relief. "Yes, sir. The bank has been most helpful in this case. Some of it arrived today by armored car. The rest should be here before noon tomorrow."

Gant nodded. "Good. I don't want any last minute hitches. When that call comes in, I want to be ready to roll."

Lash stifled a smile. "I couldn't agree with you more."

Chapter 15

Now that Casey was no longer blindfolded, the thick layer of dust covering the floor in the room where she was being held was obvious. The footprints marring the gray-white surface were evidence of the degree of traffic that had come into Fostoria Biggers's home since she'd been gone. The absence of glass in two of the three windows of her temporary cell did little to offer an avenue for her to escape. They had all been boarded up from the outside. She couldn't get out and fresh air couldn't get in.

Last night when they thought she'd been sleeping, she'd dug and pulled and pushed at the boards until her fingers were raw and her nails were gone. Only after she heard one of the men stirring around had she ceased her futile bid for freedom.

Now, she thought it was some time after daybreak. The smell of morning coffee had drifted into the room. On the one hand, she felt justified in celebrating the arrival of a new day, but if Lash was to be believed, she would not celebrate another.

She stood at the door, holding her breath and desperately trying to hear what the two men in the other room were saying. It was impossible. Their voices were too low and the door was too thick to hear anything other than an occasional murmur.

A plate lay on the floor near her feet. Remnants of the sandwich they'd given her yesterday to eat. She'd taken the food and a good look at the filth on their hands and decided she would rather go to her grave hungry.

Whatever it was that kept coming and going through a hole in the floor had made a meal of it last night. By now she didn't much care what she shared the room with, as long as it came on four feet instead of two.

In deference to her constant requests for drinks of water and bathroom privileges, her feet and hands were no longer tied. And, since Lash's departure yesterday, the blindfold had also been discarded. But while she now had an odd sort of freedom within the small, boarded-up room, the implications behind it were frightening. They no longer cared if she saw their faces because she would not be alive to tell the tale.

The sound of a chair being scooted across the floor made Casey bolt for the other side of the room. Ever since the arrival of Skeet Wilson, Pike's cohort, Casey had been afraid to sleep. Bernie had threatened her, but it was Skeet Wilson whom she knew would willingly do the deed. He was tall and skinny and walked with a limp. His hair was long and gray and tied at the back of his neck with a piece of shoestring. Some sort of blanket fuzz was caught in the knot and it was Casey's opinion that the shoestring had been there for a very long time. Skeet bore more scars on his face than teeth in his head, and he carried them all with a wild sort of pride. He had a face straight out of a nightmare with the disposition to match.

She stood with her back against the wall, holding her breath and praying that it would be Bernie who came in the door. If she'd been betting on the odds of that happening, she would have lost.

Skeet Wilson stepped inside then paused, carefully eyeing the tall, slender woman with her back against the wall. Even though the blue suit she was wearing was filthy and torn and her legs and feet were bare and scratched, there was an odd sort of dignity to the way she was braced. In a way, he admired her. But it didn't matter what he thought. Skeet was a man who could be bought.

And right now, Casey Justice wasn't a woman to him, she was fifty thousand dollars on the hoof.

"What?" Casey asked, as always, choosing to be the first one to speak.

Skeet grinned and smoothed his hand down the front of his fly, just to remind her who was boss. "Bed check."

Unless a miracle occurred, today was the last day of her life, but she refused to go out screaming and crying and begging for mercy they weren't capable of giving. She lifted her chin and squarely met his gaze.

"It's certainly obvious where you spent your last vacation."

It crossed his mind to be pissed, but her reference to the fact this his speech was peppered with penitentiary lingo was too good to ignore. He grinned, revealing his lack of a full set of teeth. And she was right. His world did revolve around the legal system. Just not on the side of law and order.

"Don't get too prissy, lady. You're real close to meetin' your maker."

Don't let him see your fear.

The thought came out of nowhere, and somehow Casey knew that at that moment, Ryder was with her in the only way he could be. Her hands fisted as she stared him down.

"That's what the mugger said before he snatched the old lady's purse and ran into the street."

Skeet's smirk froze on his face. Either she was losing her mind or it was already gone. He'd never known a woman with the balls to try to tell a joke to someone who was holding her captive. "That don't make much sense."

"It does if you know that, seconds later, the mugger was run over by a car. The old lady then walked into the street, lifted her purse out of the dead mugger's hands and bent over and whispered something in his ear."

Skeet knew he shouldn't ask, but he was too intrigued to let the subject lie.

"So, what did she say?"

Casey grinned. "To tell her maker hello."

Skeet cursed and slammed the door shut between them. He

wasn't all that smart, but it didn't take a genius to figure out what she'd been getting at and he didn't like it.

He and Bernie had gone through a lot these last two days. Marlow had threatened them with everything from murder to reneging on the last of their money if they so much as touched a hair on Casey Justice's head. Marlow had all but frothed at the mouth, claiming that right was to be his. Sick of his ranting, they'd finally complied. But Skeet wouldn't be sorry to see the last of her. She was too damned mouthy for her own good.

He kicked at an empty bean can in the middle of the floor and flopped back down in his chair. There wasn't any way this plan could fail. By tonight, he and Bernie would be rolling in dough. After that, he didn't give a damn what Marlow did with the bitch. Whatever it was, it was still less than she deserved.

''What are those?'' Ryder asked, as Roman sorted through a small case in his lap.

''Tracking devices, something like the ones the FBI will probably put in with the ransom money.''

Ryder nodded, although his opinion of the FBI left a lot to be desired. In his opinion, they asked too many questions and didn't give enough answers. They acted as if what was going on was none of his business.

''Won't the kidnappers be expecting something like that?''

Roman looked up. ''That's why I've got these. The Feds can do their thing. I'm going to do mine.''

''They're not going to like it,'' Ryder warned. ''You already ticked Wyandott off yesterday.''

Roman leaned back in his chair, remembering the confrontation he'd had with the special agent in charge. ''No one dies from being ticked.''

''You are a hard man, Roman Justice.''

''Tell it to Uncle Sam. He took credit for making me this way. He can take the blame, as well.''

If the situation had been anything else, Ryder could have laughed. As it was, he almost felt sorry for the man who got in his brother's way.

He glanced at the clock. It was almost noon. Where the hell

was Lash Marlow with the money? He kept remembering what Roman had told him about Marlow's financial situation. It seemed to him that there was a fault in the theory that Lash should be responsible for its deliverance. It was like giving a starving man the keys to the cupboard.

The doorbell rang. Ryder jumped, then started down the hall, unwilling to wait for Joshua to let whoever it was in. Maybe there was news of Casey. But the Feds beat him to it. Lash was admitted carrying two large duffel bags.

"I've got it!" he crowed.

Two men in dark suits relieved him of the bags, leaving him standing in the hall with a jubilant smile on his face. Lash could hardly contain his joy. It was almost over.

"The armored car was late," Lash said, by way of an explanation for his tardiness.

Ryder listened without comment.

Lash smoothed a hand over his hair. "Any news?"

Ryder shook his head. "No."

What seemed to be a genuine grimace of dismay spread across his face. "You know, sometimes this all seems like a dream."

"More like a nightmare, if you ask me."

Lash nodded. "Of course, that's what I meant."

A man Ryder had never seen before came out into the hall from the main salon. Another Fed.

"Mr. Marlow, Detective Gant wants to speak with you."

Lash straightened his suit coat and followed the man into the room. Ryder was right behind.

Gant waved his hand toward the open bags. "It's all here, I presume?"

Lash nodded. "Three million dollars in unmarked bills. None of them larger in denomination than a fifty, none of them smaller than a five."

Gant nodded and turned back to the desk while Ryder struggled with a notion that wouldn't come. Something Lash had just said rang a chord of memory, but he couldn't figure out why.

Lash started toward the door. "If you have no further need of me, court awaits."

Gant paused and looked to Wyandott, who was officially in

charge of the investigation. Wyandott didn't bother to look up. Gant shrugged. "I guess not. But if something comes up, I'll know where to find you, right?"

Lash chuckled. "One can only hope."

Ryder's hands were itching. The urge to grab Lash was overwhelming. It was all he could do to stay put as Marlow left. But at this point, Ryder couldn't pinpoint what it was that was bugging him.

The front door slammed behind Lash as Roman walked in the room.

"Who was here?" Roman asked.

"Marlow. He brought the ransom money."

Ryder pointed toward the bags on the desk and the men who were working on securing tracking devices within the bags.

It was when Roman started toward the desk that the notion hovering in the back of Ryder's mind started to take shape.

"Hey, Gant."

Gant looked up. "Yeah?"

"Marlow was gone when the kidnapper called, remember?"

Gant nodded.

"Then who told him how the money was to be paid?"

"I did," Gant said, then glanced at Wyandott, who had already expressed some displeasure in the way Gant had handled things thus far. "I knew it wouldn't be easy to accumulate that much money in small bills. Thought he needed as much time as possible."

But that wasn't what Ryder needed to know. "No...exactly what did you tell him?"

"I don't follow you," Gant said. "What are you getting at?"

Ryder's nerves were on edge. The more he thought about Lash, the more certain he became. "I want to know what you told him to bring."

"I said something to the effect that we needed three million dollars in small, unmarked bills by noon today."

"Did you tell him what denominations?"

"I told him no hundred-dollar bills. Everything had to be smaller than one-hundred dollar bills."

Oh, my God. What if Roman was right on target about Lash

Marlow's involvement all along? "Then did you or any of your men ever play that tape for Marlow?"

"What tape?" Gant asked.

"The one you made when the ransom call came in."

Gant shrugged. "I don't know. I know I didn't." He looked at Wyandott. "Did you or any of your men?" All answers were negative.

The flesh crawled on the back of Ryder's neck. "Then can any of you explain to me why Marlow just quoted the kidnapper's exact terminology of the request he made for ransom?"

Roman pivoted, already following the line of his brother's thoughts. "I wasn't in here. What did Marlow say?"

Ryder stared around the room, daring the men to disagree. "You all heard him. He said, 'Three million dollars in unmarked bills. None of them larger in denomination than a fifty, none of them smaller than a five.'"

"Son of a bitch." Gant's epitaph was echoed in more than one man's thoughts. "If memory serves, that's just about word for word."

Wyandott looked surprised, then began issuing new orders as Ryder turned and started running. Roman caught him at the door.

"You can't do what you're thinking."

Ryder yanked himself free. His words came out a cold, even tone. "You don't know what I'm thinking."

Roman tightened his hold. "That's where you're wrong. I know exactly what you're thinking, and I don't blame you one bit. But you've got to think of Casey. If Marlow is involved and he's alerted before the drop even goes down, what's going to happen to her? Better yet, how the hell would we know where to find her?"

Ryder hit the wall with the flat of his palm and then wiped a hand across his face. Every time he took a step he wanted to run, but to where? What had they done with his wife?

"My God," he said. "What the hell do you expect me to do? Wait until someone brings her back to me in a body bag?"

Roman got up in his face, and this time, he was the one on the defensive. "No, I expect you to let me do my job."

Ryder doubled his fists and refused to give an inch, even to his brother. Helpless in the face of so much logic, the urge to lash out was overwhelming.

Roman sighed. He didn't understand this kind of commitment between a man and a woman, but he'd seen enough of it to know it went beyond any blood ties. And as he gazed into his brother's face, he had a flashback of a little boy with mud in his hair and fire in his eyes. He remembered that same little boy had not only whipped the boy who'd beaten him up to take away his baseball, but he'd gotten the ball back, too. Even then, Ryder Justice had been a force with which to reckon.

"So, what's it going to be?" Roman asked.

Even though the urge to argue was overwhelming, Ryder relented, slumping against the wall. "Then do it. Just know that every step you take I'm going to be on your heels."

"Wouldn't have it any other way, brother, but that will come later. Right now, there's one little thing I need to do before the day gets any older, and I don't want help in getting it done."

It felt wrong, and it hurt like hell to watch Roman going out the door without him, but Ryder stood his ground. Roman was right. He'd asked for his help. The least he could do was give him the leeway to do it.

"Give 'em hell, Roman."

Roman looked back, just as he started out the door. "Is there any other way?"

Lash was making himself a ham and cheese sandwich. He'd even gotten out his mother's good china on which to eat it. He slathered mustard on one slice of bread and mayonnaise on the other. *And why not? It's about time things started going my way.*

The sandwich was thick with meat, cheese, and lettuce. He pushed a toothpick into an olive, then topped his sandwich by stabbing the toothpick into the bread with a flourish. Now there was only one thing left. He opened the refrigerator and took out a bottle of wine. Chilled to perfection.

He walked out of the kitchen toward the old dining hall with china, wine and food in hand. When he stepped inside, there was a feeling of relief unlike any he'd ever known.

Spiderwebs draped the dust-covered chandelier above the table like torn and tattered lace. One of the panes was out at the top of a floor-to-ceiling window overlooking the back of the property and there was a bird's nest in the corner of the room. But Lash didn't see the ruin and decay. His jubilation was focused on former glory and future renovation.

The cork popped on the wine and he smiled to himself as he filled his glass. As he sipped, the chill of the grape and the dry, vintage taste of fine wine tingled on his tongue. He set the half-empty glass down in a patch of sunlight, admiring the way a sunbeam pierced the liquid.

He pulled the toothpick out of his food, popped the olive into his mouth, and chewed down. There was an instant awareness of an odd, unfamiliar taste as he gasped and spit the olive out into his hand.

And the moment he saw it, his flesh crawled. Somewhere within his mind, a drumbeat sounded. Then it began to hammer, faster and faster until he couldn't move—couldn't speak. He heard a cry, and then the faint, but unmistakable, sounds of a woman's soft voice. The language was French, spoken in the patois of the slaves his great-great-grandfather had once owned.

He jumped up from his chair and flung what was left of the olive onto the dust-covered table before running out of the room. The celebration and his meal were forgotten in the horror of what he'd just seen. And as the sounds of his footsteps faded away, the carcass of a small, white worm fell out of the olive and into the patch of sunlight beaming down through the wine.

Lash ran out of the house and into the woods, searching for a solace his mind couldn't find. To any other person, it would have been an unfortunate choice of an olive from a nearly full jar, but to Lash, it was the first step in a curse that had started to come true.

Decay. Everything around you will fall to decay. Flesh will fall off of your bones and be consumed by the worms.

Raised in a superstition as old as the land itself, in Lash Marlow's mind, the curse Casey invoked had begun. He thought about what would happen if he just called the whole thing off. If he could, he would have turned back the clock, stopped what he'd started before it was too late. As always, Lash's instinct for good was too little, too late.

Roman crouched beneath the low-hanging branches of a weeping willow, watching as Marlow came out of his house and ran into the woods bordering the backyard. He frowned. Whatever it was that had sent him running couldn't have come at a better time. And still he waited, ever cautious, searching the grounds around the house for signs of other life. Except for the leaves in the trees, nothing moved.

Like a shadow, he came out from hiding, heading straight toward the dark blue sedan parked in front of the house. Within seconds of reaching it, he had secured a tracking device under the frame and was on his way back when he saw something that gave him pause. The fender of a small white car was just visible through the partially opened door of a nearby shed.

He frowned. According to the information he'd pulled from the Department of Motor Vehicles, Lash Marlow owned one car—a midnight blue, four-door sedan. He swerved in midstep and bolted for the shed, constantly searching the area for signs of Marlow's arrival.

The car was a small, white compact—at least eight, maybe ten years old. He glanced in at the gauges and whistled softly beneath his breath as he saw the odometer. Less than thirty thousand miles on a ten-year-old car?

What the hell, he thought. So, maybe Marlow just bought himself a second car and the change of ownership had yet to be registered. The mileage alone would make the car worthwhile. But he couldn't let go of the notion that he was wrong. This was a little old lady's car, not the type a man like Marlow would want to be seen driving.

And then it hit him. Little old lady! As in a woman named Fostoria Biggers? Her name had come up in conjunction with Marlow's when he'd been into the bank records and he'd thought little of a lawyer being an executor of an estate. It was done every day. But what if...?

He dropped to his knees. Regardless of why it was here, it was another vehicle that would be at Lash Marlow's disposal. Without wasting any more time, he affixed a bug to this car as well, and while he was on his knees, his attention was drawn from the car itself to the condition of the tires. He crawled closer. The treads were packed with mud and grass. He picked at the grass. To his surprise, it still bent to the touch. He frowned. Someone had recently been driving this car. But where?

A door slammed. Roman's nerves went on alert. It was time to get out. He'd done what he'd come to do.

The call came in at exactly one minute to five. Every man in the room went on alert as Ryder reached for the phone.

"Ryder Justice speaking."

Like before, the voice had been altered. A mechanical whir was audible in the background.

"This is a recording. In fifteen minutes, Ryder Justice is to bring the money to the corner of Delaney and Fourth. There is a newsstand nearby. It will be closed. Set the bags inside the stand and drive away. If anyone attempts to follow the man who picks them up, Delaney Ruban's granddaughter will be meat for the 'gators. If you do as you're told, Casey Justice will be released."

The recording ended long before a trace could be made. Ryder cursed beneath his breath as he hung up the phone. He felt sick to his stomach. 'Gator meat? God help them all.

He started toward the front door. "Put the bags in the car."

"Wait!" Wyandott shouted.

Ryder turned. "Do what I said," he ordered. "Delaney and Fourth is halfway across town. I'll be lucky to get there in fifteen minutes as it is."

"I want one of my men in the back seat of your car."

Ryder grabbed him by the arm and pushed him up against a nearby desk. His voice was shaking. "I don't give a tinker's damn what you want. That's not your wife someone threatened to feed to the 'gators, it's mine. Now put the damned bags in the car or I'll do it myself."

Roman peeled Ryder's hands off of the agent's jacket. "Easy, brother. He's just doing his job."

Ryder spun, his eyes blazing with anger. "Don't push me, Roman. I've been hanging on the edge of reason for so damned long it hardly matters.'' His voice broke. ''If I lose Casey—''

''Put the bags in the car,'' Wyandott said. ''We won't be far behind.''

Ryder pointed at Wyandott. ''I don't know who will pick up these bags after I'm gone, but if one of your men even sneezes in his direction and my wife dies as a direct result, I will kill him...and then you for giving the order.''

Wyandott's face reddened, but he stepped aside.

Within seconds, Ryder was in the car and out of the driveway, leaving a cloud of dust and a group of men running for their cars to keep up. Roman watched from the step until they had all disappeared, and then he jumped in his car and drove out of the driveway in the opposite direction. He had his own agenda to follow.

Eudora watched from an upstairs window and then returned to her bed in tears. Downstairs in the library, Miles and Erica sat in uneasy silence, now and then venturing a glance at the other without voicing their thoughts.

Out in the kitchen, Tilly sat in a chair near a window overlooking the drive. Her posture was straight, her expression fixed. Only her eyes revealed her pain. They were wide and tear-filled as she watched for someone to bring her sweet baby home.

Everyone was waiting for a miracle.

Bernie Pike opened the door to Casey's room as his partner, Skeet, entered carrying another plate of food and a can of some sort of cola.

''Last meal,'' Skeet said, waving the plate in Casey's direction.

The urge to cry was almost more than she could bear. If only she was somewhere else and lying in Ryder's arms. But she didn't cry, and she wasn't in Ryder's arms, and she crawled off of the bed with undue haste. She wouldn't put herself in the position of giving Bernie and Skeet any more ideas than they already had. She didn't know that Lash had threatened everything but death to them if they so much as touched a hair on her head. She didn't know he'd saved that joy for himself.

"I thought prisoners were given a choice as to what they wanted to eat."

Skeet chuckled and dropped the plate at the foot of the bed and tossed the unopened can of soda beside it.

"Sorry, sweet thing. You get beans and weiners."

Casey glanced at the plate. The only thing good about it was that the small, lunch-size can of beans and weiners was still unopened. "And I was so hoping for your head on a platter."

Skeet slapped his leg and laughed, then elbowed Bernie and laughed again. "She's a hoot, ain't she Bernie? It's a damned shame Marlow is gonna 'do' her." Before Casey could think to react, Skeet reached for her breast. "I still think I'd like a little taste of what she has to offer. What Marlow won't know won't hurt him, right?"

Casey grabbed the can of beans from the plate and bounced it off of his head.

Skeet ducked, but it was too late. He yelped in pain when the can hit the corner of his temple. Seconds later, she was flat on her back on the bed with Skeet on top of her.

"You bitch! I'll make you..."

Bernie cursed and grabbed, pulling his partner off the woman and the bed. "Get away from her, dammit. You heard Marlow. You might want to part with your dillydally, but I don't. Besides, you asked for it."

Skeet's rage was slow to subside as he considered whether or not Lash Marlow was capable of castrating anyone. Finally, he decided he didn't want to test the theory enough to try again.

"You got about two more hours to play hell on this earth, then you can die on an empty stomach," he yelled, and out of spite, took the can of beans and weiners and stomped out of the room.

Bernie looked at Casey and shrugged, as if to say it was all her fault, then shut the door behind him. The lock turned with a sharp, distinct *click* and when they were gone, Casey dropped to the floor and pulled her knees up close to her chest.

For the first time since the ordeal had begun, she was losing all hope. And the worst was in knowing Ryder would never know how sorry she was for betraying him by the investigation. They'd parted in anger and she would die with that on her conscience.

Despair shattered the last of her resolve. She slumped onto the floor, her legs drawn up against her chest in a fetal position, and she started to cry—slow, aching tears that welled and spilled in a continuous flow of pain.

Casey cried until she lost all track of time. Had it been two hours or two minutes since Skeet's warning that her time to die was close at hand? Was Lash already on his way? She remembered the wild expression on his face when last she'd seen him.

"God help me," she prayed, and then choked on a sob as she realized she was lying in a position to see directly beneath her bed.

The elongated neck and small, unblinking eyes of the creature beneath her bed were startling, but for Casey, who'd lived in imminent fear for the last three days of being eaten alive, it was a large relief.

"Well, my word," she said, and reached under the bed, pulling out a small, brown terrapin that had taken her move as threatening and disappeared into its shell. "So it was you I heard all the time."

Sympathetic to the fear that had caused it to retreat, Casey quickly set it free, and as she did, saw something else under the bed that made her heart leap. There, in the corner beneath her bed! It looked like—

She crawled to her feet and pulled the bed away from the wall just enough to reach behind. When her fingers curled around the butter soft leather, she pulled. She was right! It was her purse.

She clutched it to her chest as she crawled onto the bed, then held her breath, listening to make sure that Bernie and Skeet were not about to come in.

Three days ago seemed like a lifetime. Casey couldn't remember what she'd been carrying in her purse, or even what she'd been doing when she'd gotten the call about Ryder's wreck. Her fingers were shaking as she undid the clasp. But when she opened it up, her hopes fell. Her shoulders slumped as she dumped the meager contents onto the bed.

Her wallet was gone, as was the compact cell phone she usually carried. She should have known this would be too good to be true. There wasn't anything left but a handful of tissues, some pencils and pens, her lipstick and small, plastic bottle of lotion.

Frustrated by the letdown, she slammed the purse down on the bed beside her and then winced when something within the purse itself hurt her hand.

"What in the...?"

She opened it back up. There was nothing inside but the black satin lining. She tilted it, then thrust in her hand, feeling within the bag itself. Something was there...but not inside...it was beneath...no, between. She pulled at the lining like turning a sock inside out, and saw the rent in the fabric near the clasp.

Curious now as to what was inside, she stuck her finger in the fragile lining and pulled. It ripped and then parted. Carefully, Casey thrust a finger inside, then another, and searched until she felt something cool and hard and sharp. And as she traced the object's length, realization dawned. Her hands were shaking as she pulled it out. She tried to think of how the letter opener Lash had given her as a gift had gotten out of her desk drawer and into her purse.

And then she remembered running back to grab her wallet on the day of the call, and of grabbing a handful of pens along with it as she dropped it inside her purse. That must have been it. She'd gotten the letter opener with everything else. And because it had been so sharp, it had gone straight through the lining and lodged in between.

She looked toward the door as her fingers curled around the miniature rapier's silver shaft. It wasn't much, but it was the first means she'd had of self-defense and she had no intention of letting it go to waste.

A laugh boomed out in a nearby room. Casey flinched, then shoved the dagger beneath her pillow. Not now, she told herself. Only when it was time. When it was time.

Chapter 16

Ryder pulled up to the newsstand with less than a minute to spare. He double-parked in the street and grabbed the two bags, moving in an all-out sprint. The stand was closed, just as the kidnapper had promised, but a small, side door stood ajar, and he shouldered his way inside.

It was little more than three walls and a roof. The half wall that opened up to the public could be propped overhead like a porch, shading the counter beneath. The concrete sidewalk served as its floor, and Ryder dropped both bags on it with a thump and walked out.

All the way back to the car, he had the impression that he was being watched. He didn't know whether that came from the Feds who had followed him here, or from the kidnapper waiting for him to leave. When he slid into the driver's seat and started the car, his instincts kept telling him not to leave—not to leave Casey's welfare up to kidnappers. But he ignored the urge and drove away, and had never been this afraid in his life—not even the night his plane had crashed—not even when he'd known that Micah was dead. He left with the knowledge that he'd done all he could do. The ransom had been delivered. Hopefully, his next point of contact would be the phone call telling him where to pick up his wife.

As Ryder drove away, Wyandott and his men began to slip into place around the area. A couple of blocks away, Gant watched from his car with binoculars trained on the door through which Ryder had come and gone.

And the wait began.

Five minutes passed, then ten, then twenty. In spite of the coolness of the evening breeze blowing through his window, Gant was starting to sweat. He could just imagine what was going through Wyandott's mind. The Feds must have been made. If the kidnappers got spooked and didn't pick up the ransom, he wouldn't give a plug nickel for Casey Justice's chance of survival.

Just when he thought it was over, an old man turned the corner and headed down the street, pulling a little red wagon behind him as he made toward the stand. Gant thought nothing of his presence until the man paused at the door, opened it up and then stepped in, leaving his wagon just outside.

Gant sat straight up in the seat, adjusting his binoculars for a clearer view as the man emerged. But it wasn't the bags Ryder had put inside that he was carrying out. It was a large black garbage bag. He tossed it into the wagon and started down the street when Wyandott's men suddenly converged upon him.

Gant threw down his binoculars in disbelief and started his car. In spite of the kidnapper's instructions, Wyandott was pulling him in. God help them all if this stunt got Casey Justice killed.

"You're under arrest!" Wyandott shouted, as two of his agents wrestled the old man to the ground.

The terror on the old fellow's face seemed sincere. "What did I do? What did I do?"

An agent slapped handcuffs around his wrists while another tore into the bag. But they all stared in disbelief as a cascade of crushed aluminum cans fell onto the street.

"What the hell?" Wyandott muttered.

"They're mine, fair and square," the old man cried, as they pulled him to his feet. "Anthony gave them to me."

Wyandott turned. "Who the hell is Anthony?"

"The man who owns the newsstand. I pick them up once a week, regular as clockwork. Everyone knows. Anthony doesn't care. He saves them for me."

A knot was beginning to form in the pit of Wyandott's belly. He pivoted and pointed toward the stand. "Check it out!" Two of the agents were already running as Gant's car slid to a halt near the curb.

Gant strode toward Wyandott with murder in his eyes. "Have you lost your mind?"

Wyandott hunched his shoulders and thrust out his jaw. "Mind your own damned business."

"This is my city. That makes it my business," Gant yelled.

One of the agents came running. "Sir! You'd better come take a look."

Everyone converged on the stand, leaving the old man handcuffed and alone in the street near his cans.

The bags were gone!

"This is impossible," Wyandott muttered. "We didn't take our eyes off of this stand for a second. Not a damned second."

Gant stepped inside, and, as he did, caught his toe. He staggered, then looked down. A certainty came over him that they'd been lying in wait for nothing. Chances were that the bags had disappeared seconds after Ryder had left.

"He didn't take them out, he took them down," Gant said, pointing toward the slightly raised edge of a lid covering the opening that led down to the sewers.

Wyandott paled. "Hell." He grabbed his two-way. "Ambrewster...is that bug sending?"

The radio crackled, and then the man's voice came over the air loud and clear. "No sir. Everything is status quo."

Gant was on his knees and pulling at the lid when several of the agents followed his lead and began to help. A flashlight was produced, and even though they were yards above them, and it was black as a devil's heart down below, there was enough light to see two empty bags lying at the foot of the ladder.

And they had their answer. The signal wasn't sending because the bags were more or less right where Ryder had left them...minus the three million dollars that had been inside.

The radio crackled again. Wyandott jerked.

''Captain...this is Tucker...come in, sir.''

''Go ahead.''

''Sir, we've been following Marlow as you ordered. He parked his car and went into the courthouse at fourteen hundred hours. We have men stationed at every exit and he has yet to come out.''

Wyandott was starting to worry. He kept thinking of the threat Justice had made to his face. This wasn't going down as he'd planned.

''I want to know if he's inside. Look for him, dammit, and don't stop until you do. He's mixed up in this somehow, I know it.''

Ryder turned off of the highway without slowing down and skidded to a halt in front of the mansion. He was out of the car before the dust had time to settle.

But when Roman came around the house on the run, Ryder paused at the front door with his hand on the knob. He could tell by the look on his brother's face that something had happened.

''What?''

Roman grabbed him by the arm. ''Gant just called me. The drop went sour. The kidnapper went underground into the sewers. He's got the money and all they've got left are those damned bags.''

Disbelief, coupled with a pain Ryder couldn't name, nearly sent him to his knees. It was coming undone.

Roman grabbed him by the arm. ''Don't give out on me now. We're going to plan B. Come with me. We don't have much time.''

For the first time since Ryder had exited the car, he became aware of a loud, popping sound, but he was too focused on Roman to consider the source. ''Where are we going?''

''Marlow is on the move,'' Roman said. ''I've been tracking him, but he's moving out of range. You're going to have to help me, brother, or we're going to lose our best chance to find your wife.''

They had just cleared the corner of the house in full stride, when Ryder stopped in his tracks.

"Son of a bitch."

Roman grabbed him by the arm, almost yelling in his face to be heard above the noise. "It's a Bell Jet Ranger, just like the one you have at home."

"I know what it is," Ryder said, staring at the helicopter's spinning rotors. "Where the hell did you get it?"

Roman almost grinned. "I borrowed it, so don't wreck the damned thing. I have to take it back when we're through."

Ryder started to sweat. Wreck? Hell, that meant making it fly first.

Roman grabbed him by the shoulder and jerked. "Are you going to stand there, or are we going to try to save your wife?"

Ryder started to run. "If you stole this, I'll break your neck."

"Just shut up and get in," Roman yelled, as he leaped into the passenger seat and grabbed at a laptop computer he'd laid on the floor.

A strange sensation swept through Ryder's body as he climbed into the seat. The sounds were familiar, even the feel of the seat at his back and the scent of fuel mixing with the dust and debris flying through the air caused by the rotor's massive pull.

Then he glanced at his brother and the moving blip on the computer screen in front of him. The tracking devices! Roman had bugged Marlow's car after all. His pulse surged. "Is that him?"

Roman nodded. "Yes, but I'm losing him. Take her up!"

Ryder stared. That blip kept blinking—blinking—blinking—like a pulse. Like Casey's pulse. He grabbed the seat belt. It snapped shut with a click he felt rather than heard. He took a deep breath and pushed in on the throttle and it felt as if the helicopter took a deep breath. Ryder glanced at the blip one last time and the guilt he'd been living with for the better part of a year simply disappeared.

"Roman."

Roman glanced at his brother.

"Buckle up."

Seconds later, the chopper went straight up in the air, then flew into the setting sun like a hawk flying out of a storm.

* * *

Lash was ecstatic. It had all been too easy. Just this afternoon, he'd driven Fostoria Biggers's little car to an abandoned garage near the downtown courthouse, then taken a cab back home. A short time later, he got in his own sedan, drove to his office, picked up some legal briefs, then drove to the courthouse and parked in his usual place.

Only when he got into the elevator, he didn't go up, he went down. Down into the basement. Down through a maze of heating pipes and furnaces, past the janitor's quarters where he picked up two large bags he'd hidden earlier, as well as a pair of gloves which he immediately put on. He was smarter than Pike. He wasn't leaving traces of himself anywhere to be found.

Down he went into a shaft leading straight to the sewers beneath the city. Counting tunnels and watching for numbers written on the walls beside the ladders with something akin to delight, Lash knew when he reached number seventy-nine that he was directly beneath the newsstand.

He waited, and minutes later, he heard the echo of boots against metal as Ryder Justice walked across the sewer lid and dropped the bags full of money...his money. A smile broke the concentration on his face. So far, so good.

He knew the bags were bugged. He'd watched the Feds planting the bugs himself. So he transferred the money from their bags into the ones he'd brought, and left the original bags and their bugs right where he knew they would eventually be found.

Once again, he was using the underground sewers of Ruban Crossing as a means by which to travel. With the narrow beam of a small flashlight for guidance, he began to count tunnels and ladders again until he came to ladder number sixty-five. This time he went up, coming out in the alley just outside the abandoned garage where he'd parked Fostoria Biggers's car.

When he drove out of the city, he was three million dollars to the good. As for the fifty thousand he was supposed to pay Bernie and Skeet, it was unfortunate, but he was going to have to renege.

It wasn't his fault Bernie had left fingerprints behind when they'd yanked Casey out of her car. Eventually the police would find Bernie Pike. And if they found Bernie, Skeet Wilson would not be far behind. Lash didn't trust them to keep quiet about his part in the crime. He couldn't leave witnesses. Not after he'd gone this far.

As he drove, he reached down and felt the outside of his pocket, reassuring himself that his gun was still there. Once or twice, as he pictured pulling the trigger and ending two men's lives, he came close to rethinking his decision. And then he would remind himself that, for three million dollars, he could live with a little bit of guilt.

All he had to do was walk in the house, pull the trigger two times and they would be out of the picture. At this point, his imagination began to wane. He kept picturing himself opening the door to the room in which Casey was being kept and pointing his gun at her as well. After that, the image faded. Would she beg? Would she cry? Would he be able to kill the woman he once thought he loved?

Fostoria Biggers's little car fishtailed in loose dirt as Lash sailed down the road toward her home. Only a few more miles.

"He's turning south," Roman said, and held on to his laptop as, moments later, the helicopter took the same turn, yielding to Ryder's skill.

Roman's gaze was completely focused on the screen before him. And the farther they flew, the more certain he was of where Lash Marlow was going.

"There's nothing out here but swamp grass and trees," Ryder muttered, as he banked the chopper sharp to the right, sometimes skimming so close to the treetops that the skids tore the leaves as they flew by.

Roman frowned, grabbing at the computer and leaning into another sharp turn. "If you were partial to driving there, you should have said so—I'd have gotten one of these things with wheels."

"Am I still on course?" Ryder asked.

Roman looked down at the screen. "Yes. We can't be more than a half a mile behind."

Half a mile. Would that be the difference between Casey's life—or Casey's death?

"I don't like this," Ryder said, glancing down at the blur of terrain beneath them. "There's nothing out here but snakes, alligators and wildcats."

"And the house where Fostoria Biggers was born and raised."

The helicopter dipped. Not much, but enough to let Roman know Ryder had been startled by what he'd said.

"Who is Fostoria Biggers?"

"One of Marlow's clients. I thought it was a little too convenient that Marlow has her car and her power of attorney. I checked land records at the courthouse. Would you believe that her house is just a little farther south...in the direction in which Marlow has been driving?"

Ryder looked startled. "How long have you known about this?"

Roman shrugged. "Bits and pieces of it since the first day. But it didn't all start falling into place until you caught Marlow repeating the kidnapper's demands, word for word. After that, we didn't exactly have time to talk. I figured you wouldn't mind if I took the initiative."

Ryder's expression was grim. "I don't care what you do. But when we get where we're going, Marlow is mine."

Roman nodded. That much he understood. He glanced back at the screen. "Read 'em and weep, brother. It looks like our runner is about to stop."

Ryder's heart skipped a beat as he looked down at the screen. For the first time since they'd gone airborne, the blip was stationary. He glanced out the windows, searching for a sign of the car and a place to set down.

It was Roman who saw it first. "There!" he shouted. "I see the top of a roof up ahead in that clearing." He leaned farther forward and pointed across Ryder's line of vision. "There's the road, just to your left."

"I see it," Ryder drawled. He gave his brother one last glance, and there was a wealth of understanding between them in that single look. "Hang on. We're going down."

It was getting late. Casey could tell by the temperature of the bare wooden floors beneath her feet. Every nerve she had was on alert. She'd said her prayers, and such as it was, her little game plan was already in place. The contents of the bottle of lotion she'd found in her purse was in a puddle on the floor just inside her door. Her letter opener was in one hand, held fast at the hilt, and an unopened can of beans was in the other.

Oddly enough, Bernie had had a change of heart, and sneaked them back in to her when Skeet wasn't looking. From the size of his belly hanging over his belt, she supposed he didn't think a person should die on an empty stomach. And, she was as ready to die as she would ever be, but not without a fight.

Just as she was about to get herself a drink of water from the bathroom sink, she heard a shout of jubilation outside her door. Her thirst forgotten, she stifled a moan. That could only mean one thing. Lash had arrived. Bernie and Skeet were about to get paid.

Lash pulled up to the house and put the car into Park, but left it running. This trip was going to be a real hit-and-run. He had to get back into the city and pick up his car at the courthouse. It was the final stage of his plan, and one that would tie up the last loose ends.

He was halfway up the steps when Bernie Pike met him at the door. "Did you get it?" Bernie asked.

Lash grinned and nodded as he put his hand in his pocket. "Where's Skeet?" Lash asked. "I want to pay you both at the same time."

"I'm right here," Skeet said.

"Hot damn," Bernie said. "My horoscope said this was my lucky day."

The gun was in Lash's hand before either man thought to react. Bernie went down still wearing his smile. Skeet had started to run and then stumbled and fell when Lash's second shot caught him square in the back. The echo of the gunshots beneath the roof of the old porch were still ringing in Lash's ears as he nudged each man with the toe of his shoe. Neither moved, nor would they ever again.

While Lash was staring down at their bodies, something fell on his sleeve. He looked down and then shrieked in sudden panic. Frantic, he brushed it off with the butt of the gun, then stomped it flat. What was left of a caterpillar lay squashed on the floor of the porch.

Another worm. A rapid staccato of drumbeats began again, ricocheting through Lash's mind as he backed away from the worm and into the house with his gun drawn. He was all the way inside and halfway across the floor before he realized he had his back to the door of the room in which Casey was being kept. He crouched and spun. Heart pounding and slightly breathless, he aimed the gun at the middle of the door.

It took a bit for him to calm down. And when he did, he went to the door, rattling the knob just enough to let her know he was coming.

The tone of his voice took on a high, singsong pitch. "Here I come, ready or not."

He opened the door, saw her standing across the room, and stepped inside, right into the puddle of lotion.

One second Lash was looking at Casey and the next he was staring at the ceiling and struggling to breathe. He clutched his chest with a groan and rolled as air began to fill his deflated lungs.

"Damn you," he gasped, crawling to his feet just in time to duck an object that came flying through the air. Although he knew it wasn't Casey, he pulled the trigger in self-defense, then gasped as something splattered all over his face. He looked down at himself in disbelief. Beans? He'd shot a can of beans?

For Casey, the two shots outside the door were unexpected. But when total silence followed, Casey suspected her worst fears were about to come true. Not only was Lash capable of killing her, but she'd bet her last dollar he'd just done away with Bernie and Skeet. It figured. He wasn't the kind of man to leave loose ends untied. Lash was nothing if not neat.

She backed against the far wall, and when his voice taunted at her through the door, she traded the dagger in her right hand for the can of beans, then held her breath and waited.

The door opened, and to her undying relief, Lash hit the oil slick of lotion and fell flat on his back. While he was struggling for breath, she hauled back and sent the beans sailing, then ducked when his shot went wild.

While he was still brushing at the thick sauce and beans splattering his coat, she came at him. It was only through an inborn sense of self-preservation that he looked up in time to see her coming, but he didn't move in time to save himself from the dagger's sharp thrust.

He swung at her head with the butt of his gun just as the pain began to burn through his chest. Casey went limp, slumping to the floor at his feet as Lash stared at the familiar silver shaft sticking out of his chest.

The drumbeat got louder. He kept thinking of the dagger sticking out of that fat rat's body, and now it was in him. The analogy was as sickening as the nausea rolling in his belly.

By now, the drumbeat was so loud in his head that he couldn't hear himself scream. And yet the soft patois of the French-speaking slave, warning—predicting—promising, could still be heard above the drum.

Sharp like a serpent's tooth, it will spill your blood and your flesh will be eaten by the worms of the earth.

In a wild kind of panic, he yanked at the handle, ignoring the pain, losing sight of the fact that, with Casey Justice unconscious and helpless at his feet, his goal was well within reach. Blood welled then poured out of the wound, and Lash staggered from the shock of seeing his life spilling on Casey's legs.

And then he heard her groan, and a certainty came upon him. *Kill her now, before it's too late.*

He wiped at the sweat beading on his brow and aimed the gun. He had to do it now while she was unconscious. He no longer had the guts to let her witness her own death. Not anymore.

He leaned down, jabbing the barrel of the gun at her head as the room began to spin around him. And then footsteps sounded on the porch outside and he turned and froze. A gourd rattled, like a rattlesnake's warning, and the drumbeat grew louder, hammering—hammering—in what was left of his mind.

Crazed with pain and the impending vision of his own mortality, he lifted his gun, his wild gaze drawn to the shadow crossing the floor ahead of the man coming in.

When the first two shots came within seconds of each other, Ryder panicked. He tightened his grip on the gun Roman had given him and picked up his pace as he moved through the marsh beyond the old house. Brush caught on his blue jeans and tore at his shirt. Limbs slapped at his face and stung his eyelids and eyes. Water splashed up his legs to the tops of his knees and he kept on running, assuming that whatever was in his path would have to move of its own accord. His focus was on the house just visible in the distance, and the small white car parked nearby.

A hundred yards from the house, he saw the bodies of two men sprawled upon the porch and fear lent fresh speed to his steps. That explained the two shots. Water splashed a bit to his right and he knew that Roman was there on his heels as they ran out of the marsh and into the clearing.

Another shot rang out and Ryder almost stumbled. Dear God, it wasn't possible that they'd come this far just to be too late. He couldn't let himself believe that God would do that to him...not twice.

Two seconds, then ten seconds, and Ryder was up on the porch. He cleared Bernie Pike's body in a smooth, single leap and came in the front door on the run.

"Dammit, Ryder, look out."

Roman's warning came late, but it would not have slowed his intent. He kept thinking of that blip on the computer screen.

Had his wife's heart stopped when it had, too?

He saw them both at the same time. Marlow was straddling Casey's body with his gun aimed at Ryder's heart. And the knowledge that he'd come too late filled his soul. Despair shattered his focus. Rage clouded any caution he might have used. His mind was screaming out her name as he pointed the gun at Marlow's chest.

"You lying son of a bitch."

They were the last words Lash Marlow would hear as Ryder pulled the trigger.

Lash's shot went wild as Ryder's bullet struck Marlow in the chest. He bucked upon impact, and Ryder fired again, then emptied his gun in him just to see him dance.

Roman was only seconds behind. He came through the door with his gun ready, the echo of Ryder's last shot roaring in his ears. But hope died as he saw the woman on the floor and Marlow lying nearby. It looked as if Ryder would have his revenge, but little else.

Ryder's gun was clicking on empty chambers when Roman took it out of his hand. Ryder jerked, then groaned and let it go. The pain in his chest was spilling out into his legs and into his mind. He couldn't think past the sight of her battered and broken body lying still upon the floor.

Roman started toward the two bodies but Ryder stopped him. With tears streaming down his face, he grabbed his brother's arm. "No. Let me."

Roman ached for his brother's pain as he stepped aside, and Ryder walked into the room, absorbing the filth and degradation of the place in which she'd been kept. Dropping to his knees, he lifted her from the filth on the floor and into his arms.

Blood ran down her legs as her head lolled against his shoulder, and then he couldn't see her face for his tears. His heart broke as he cradled her against his chest.

His voice broke along with his heart. "No more! No more!" Laying his head near her cheek, he choked on a cry. "Ah God, I can't take anymore!"

His shoulders hunched as he bent from the burden of living when those he loved kept dying around him.

Roman knelt at his side, sharing his brother's pain. He glanced at the woman in Ryder's arms. Even through the bruises and dirt, her beauty was plain to see. Years ago, he'd shut himself off from this kind of loss. He'd seen so much death and too much misery to let himself be hurt by it anymore, but this was too close to home. This woman, Ryder's wife, was gone too soon. He reached out, lifted her hair from the blood on her face, and as he did, his finger brushed the curve of her neck.

His eyes widened as he tensed and shoved Ryder's hand aside. When he felt the pulse beating strong and sure, he rocked back on his heels. A miracle! That's what it was. A heaven-sent miracle.

Ryder choked on a sob. "Don't Roman. Just leave us alone."

Roman grabbed his brother's hand, his voice shaking as he

pressed it at the pulse point on Casey's neck. "She's alive, Ryder. I swear to God, your wife is alive!"

At that same moment in the Ruban household many miles away, Matilda Bass heard a whisper. She froze, and then tilted her head, straining to hear. As suddenly as the whisper had come, it was gone, and Tilly's body went limp. She leaned against the cabinet as the bowl she was holding slipped out of her hands and onto the floor, shattering into a thousand tiny pieces, just like the weight that had been on her heart.

Joshua spun, wide-eyed and startled. And then he saw her face.

"Tilly?"

"They found her, they found her. My baby girl is alive."

Epilogue

From below, the shiny black helicopter flying high above the earth resembled an oversize dragonfly charging through the air. From up above, the earth resembled a vast crazy quilt in varying shades of greens and browns that covered the landscape over which they were flying.

As if at some unseen signpost up in the sky, the pilot suddenly shifted course and soon, a long black rooftop became visible in the distance, along with the roofs of several outbuildings, connected together with a chain stitch of holding pens and corrals.

Casey leaned forward, grabbing at Ryder's leg as her eyes lit with excitement. "Is that it? Is that the Justice ranch?"

Ryder grinned at her. "That's it, darlin'. All seven thousand acres."

Her smile was nervous as she glanced at him. "I'm a little anxious about meeting your family."

"Easy now, you know they're going to love you."

She sighed. "I wish I could have promised you the same thing when I took you home to mine."

Ryder laughed. "At least they like me now."

''Like! Oh, Ryder, in their eyes, you are the next best thing to sliced bread and you know it.''

His grin widened. ''Only because Miles's new girlfriend keeps him too busy to meddle in our affairs.''

Casey nodded in agreement. ''And who would have thought that Erica would go on vacation and come home with a husband?''

''Yeah, and he has a job, which was more than you could say for me when you dumped me in their laps. Dora is walking in tall cotton over the fact that they are moving to Atlanta and taking her with them.''

Casey laughed aloud. ''Gran will miss you. You were the best chauffeur we ever had.''

''Dora and I understand each other,'' he said. ''But let's be honest, I was the worst chauffeur, and you know it. However, now that I have moved my planes and the charter service to Ruban Crossing, I have become a bona fide, acceptable businessman.''

She patted his leg in a tender gesture. ''Tilly was right all along. Somehow she knew you belonged. You are the best thing that ever happened to my family.'' Her voice broke. ''And to me.''

Ryder gave her a quick, nervous glance. A few months ago he'd cradled her body on the floor of Fostoria Biggers's bedroom, certain that his world had just come to an end. Sometimes at night he still lay awake just to watch her sleep. What she had endured was beyond his understanding; that she had endured it at all was a miracle in itself.

Now, most of the time she was fine. But once in a while, when things got too quiet, he saw her soul slip into a shadow and he knew she was fighting a dark demon of her own. He knew from experience that it would take time, and a whole lot of love, for the memories of what she'd endured to recede.

''I love you,'' he said softly.

Casey shivered, as if struck by an unexplained chill, and then she lifted her head and smiled and Ryder relaxed. For now, Casey was back in the light.

"I love you, too, wild man. Now take me home. I have a need to feel Texas under my feet."

Relieved that the moment had passed, he grinned. "Royal is going to love hearing you say that. He's a real homebody. He lives for his daughter and the ranch, and I can tell you right now that, except for a remarkable resemblance which we all share, Royal is nothing like Roman."

A small shudder rippled through Casey's body, but she refused to deny it access. Remembering Roman also meant remembering when they'd first met. Of waking up and seeing Ryder—of being lifted into the helicopter and looking up at an echo of her husband's face as Ryder laid her in Roman's arms—of helicopters and hospitals—of police and FBI. Of fearing the dark and doctors and needles. Of Tilly's hand on her cheek and Joshie's kiss on her brow. And always, overshadowing everything and everyone, was Ryder. Ever present, ever faithful, everlasting.

She turned to look out the other side of the helicopter, marveling at the size of the cattle herds in the far distance. From up here, the cattle looked like so many ants. Finally, she was able to say what she thought.

"Roman will always have a special place in my heart. I like him a lot."

Ryder's grin slid a little off center as his emotions betrayed him. "Oh, hell, honey, I like him, too. He's my brother. And I owe him more than I will ever be able to repay."

The look they shared was brief, but it was enough to remember they had a lot for which to be thankful.

Moments later, Ryder shoved the controls of the helicopter forward and it started to descend, aiming for a wide, flat area behind some barns like a horsefly heading for the rump of a steer.

That night, and long after Royal and Maddie had gone to bed, Ryder walked the halls of the house in which he'd been raised, visiting the ghosts that had driven him away. Unable to sleep, he'd checked on Casey one last time and then gone outside to the wide front porch to listen to the night.

It was spring, and the air was sweet and cool. The scent of flowers in the nearby flower bed reminded him of Casey. To him, she would always be a fresh breath of spring. She'd been his savior in so many ways that he couldn't begin to take count, and they'd come too close to losing that which made life worth living. That day in Fostoria Biggers's house, when he'd touched her skin and felt the pulse of her life beating beneath his fingertips, he'd known then that they'd been given a second chance.

A night owl hooted from a nearby tree and Ryder paused, listening to the familiar sound. A cow lowed in a nearby pasture, calling for her baby. Moments later, a plaintive bawl announced the baby's location, and all was well. Ryder took a deep breath, absorbing the peace of home and the assurance that he'd done the right thing by bringing Casey here to visit.

A quick breeze came up, lifting the hair away from his forehead and brushing against his chest like a lover's fingers. He glanced up at the sky and then to the faint wisps of clouds overhead, judging the possibility of a rain before morning.

And while he was looking at stars, the breeze seemed to shift, and the skin on his flesh tightened in warning. A sound came out of the night, like a whisper, or a memory, but it was there in his mind. And he knew who it was that his heart finally heard.

Welcome home, son.

He turned toward the house. But it wasn't Micah who came out of the door.

Casey came off of the porch and out into the dew-damp grass to stand beside him. She lifted her hand to his cheek, feeling, rather than seeing the tears that had started to fall.

''Sweetheart, are you all right?''

Ryder wrapped his arms around her, holding her close until he could feel the even beat of her heart. He buried his face in the curve of her neck and took a deep breath. Flowers. She always smelled like flowers.

''Now that you're here, I'm more than all right.''

Casey sighed, and held him even closer. ''Come to bed, Ryder. I can't sleep without you.''

He lifted her into his arms. ''Then buckle up, darlin', and I'll take you to dreamland.''

* * * * *

Look out for Sharon Sala's next book
The Way To Yesterday *in March.*

The Littlest Marine

Maureen Child

To Amy J Fetzer,
friend and fellow writer—thanks for walking me through life in the corps, and for a friendship that means a lot to me.

Also, my thanks to Sergeant Major Robert Fetzer, USMC, for allowing me to borrow his rank—and for answering all of the questions I pestered Amy with.
Be happy in your new home, Amy.
You'll be missed

One

The maid of honor and the best man were barely speaking. Other than that, the rehearsal of the rehearsal dinner seemed to be a success.

Still, Elizabeth Stone thought, nowhere was it written that as maid of honor she *had* to like the best man.

"So—" her sister, Terry, leaned in close to her and whispered beneath the hum of conversation around them "—what do you think of him? Wasn't I right? Isn't he perfect for you?"

The "he" being Harding Casey, best man, career Marine and the source of the jitters rattling around in the pit of Elizabeth's stomach.

She reached for her wineglass, took a slow sip of white Zinfandel, then answered in as low pitched a voice as possible. “I’m trying *not* to think about him.”

“Ooooh,” the younger woman said as her eyebrows arched high on her forehead. “Sounds promising.”

Frowning slightly, Elizabeth set her wineglass down
and told herself that it was useless to argue with her sister over this. For almost a year, Terry had been trying to set her up with Harding Casey, her fiancé Mike’s best friend. This little gathering was as close as she had come to succeeding.

“Look,” Terry said quietly, “you two are going to be together practically every day for the next week. Wouldn’t it make more sense if you at least *tried* to like him?”

“Now that you bring it up,” Elizabeth said, half turning in her seat to face her sister squarely. “I still don’t understand why I have to spend all week with the man. *You’re* the one getting married.”

“Yeah....” Terry’s expression went soft and dreamy, and despite the fact that Elizabeth had no real desire of her own to get married, a small sliver of envy pierced her heart. What would it be like, she wondered, to feel what Terry so obviously felt for Mike?

In the next instant, though, she remembered that she wasn’t interested in finding a man. She had her own life. A successful one, thanks very much, and she was already happy. Why should she go out looking for someone who would only require her to make all kinds of changes in what she considered a darn near perfect existence?

With that thought firmly in mind, she prodded her sister. ‘‘Terry, you know I’m delighted to be your maid of honor, but—’’

‘‘No *buts,*’’ she interrupted. ‘‘You promised that you would help out, Lizzie.’’

‘‘Sure, but why—’’

‘‘There’s no way I can do all of the little things that have to be done this week.’’ Terry leaned forward and clutched her sister’s hand. ‘‘Come on, Lizzie. You can handle Harding for one little week, can’t you?’’

There was a challenge if ever she’d heard one. Grimly Elizabeth shot a covert glance at the man across from her. Black hair, cut into a military, ‘‘high and tight’’ haircut, strong jaw, straight nose, well-shaped mouth, and eyes blue enough to make Paul Newman’s look a dingy gray. Standing up, he was six-feet-five inches of solid muscle, had a voice deep enough to cause earthquakes and made her stomach pitch with nerves and expectation with a single glance. Sure. She could handle him. No problem.

Lordy, she was in trouble. The only thing that kept her from having some serious fantasies about the man was the uniform he wore so proudly.

Muffling a sigh, she said softly, ‘‘Little sister, you should understand better than anyone else why I don’t want anything to do with a military type.’’

Terry did nothing to hide her grumble of frustration. ‘‘Honestly, Lizzie, you would think you grew up manacled to a wall.’’

‘‘Yeah. A wall that was reassigned every two or three years.’’

Elizabeth, known as ''Lizzie'' only to her family, had hated growing up as a Marine brat. Shifting from place to place, moving wherever their father's orders had taken them. Never really at home. Making new friends only to leave them behind. The one constant in her life...the one friend she had always been able to count on was Terry. Her sister. Who had grown up to fall in love with a Marine. But at least Terry's soon-to-be husband had left the Corps.

Harding Casey—Hard Case to his friends, looked like a lifer to her.

''You just hate the military.''

''No, I don't,'' Elizabeth said. ''I've just served my time, that's all. You've got to be relieved that Mike left the Corps. Admit it.''

''I told him he didn't have to. It was his decision.''

''A good one, too.'' Elizabeth reached for her wineglass, then rethought it and settled her hand in her lap. ''At least you won't be stumping all around the world like Mom did, trying to make homes out of impersonal barracks buildings.''

''Jeez, Lizzie—'' Terry's voice dropped as she shot a quick look at the other diners to make sure no one could hear them ''—you make it all sound so ugly. We had a great family. A terrific life. We've seen places most people only dream about.''

True, Elizabeth thought. All true. But while they had been traveling around the world like modern-day gypsies, all Elizabeth had ever wanted was a home. A real home. One where she could stay put for more than three years. One where she could paint the walls any color she liked and not even consider who might be moving in after she'd gone.

Apparently, whatever gypsy gene Terry had inherited from their parents had bypassed Elizabeth altogether.

"Yeah," Elizabeth said quietly. "It was terrific."

Terry grinned, obviously not hearing the sarcasm. "Okay, now tell me how right I was about Harding. He *is* a babe, isn't he?"

Babe? Oh, he was more than a babe. But there was no way she would admit as much to Terry. She shot Harding Casey a covert glance only to find him watching her through those incredible eyes of his. Goose bumps raced up her arms. Her heartbeat quickened, and her palms were suddenly damp. This was no ordinary attraction to a handsome man. It was almost as if something inside her...*recognized* him. As if he was someone she had been waiting for.

Get a grip, she told herself as the ridiculous thought took root.

Grab her, Harding thought. Grab her, kiss her, caress her...he shook his head slightly in a vain attempt to rid himself of the almost-overpowering impulses throbbing inside him. Impulses that had been haunting him since meeting Elizabeth Stone three hours ago.

Her chin length, curly brown hair seemed to tempt him to spear his fingers through it. Those even darker brown eyes of hers mesmerized him, and he wanted to lose himself in their depths, discover her secrets. He called on years of strict military training to hide his reaction to her figure. A body made for lounging beside a fire and quiet, private picnics on moonlit beaches. His gaze slipped lower, and Harding felt something in his chest stagger. The deep vee neckline of her red silk blouse gaped a bit as she leaned in toward her sister. He caught a fleeting glimpse of pale ivory flesh and felt his mouth go dry.

He was in big trouble.

Harding shifted his gaze from Elizabeth's face to the bottle of beer in front of him. He *had* to quit staring at her. Curling his fingers around the still-cold bottle, he lifted it and took a long drink.

''So, you old Devil Dog,'' Mike Hall whispered as he leaned in close. ''What do you think of our Lizzie?''

A brief smile touched Harding's lips, then faded. Devil Dog. The traditional greeting between Marines. Even though Mike had left the Corps a year ago, after meeting and falling in love with Terry, clearly the Corps hadn't left him.

But, *Lizzie?*

He risked another quick look at the woman opposite him, reminding himself not to eat her alive with his eyes. No, she was no *Lizzie.* Definitely an *Elizabeth.*

Perhaps, he mused, *Beth.*

''C'mon Hard Case,'' Mike prodded. ''What's the verdict?''

He forced a casual shrug. ''She seems…nice.''

''Nice?'' Mike looked at him, astonished. ''A solid year I've been telling you about her, and all you can say when you finally meet her is that she seems *nice?*''

"Yeah, you told me about her." Harding snorted a smothered laugh. "You also told me about how she hated growing up in the Corps. And about all the grief she gave you when she was trying to get Terry to dump you."

Mike frowned. "She was trying to protect her sister."

"Sure, by taking shots at you and the Corps."

"She's changed. She likes me now." Mike shook his head slowly. "Finally figured out that I really do love Terry."

Fine. He could understand defending and protecting a sister. But Elizabeth Stone had made his friend miserable for almost six months. The fact that she was gorgeous didn't make up for that. He took a long swig of his beer. "Great, she likes you," he said slowly. "But she still hates the Corps."

Mike shrugged. "Terry says that Lizzie never liked all of the moving around their folks did while they were growing up. Even I don't think that's an easy way to raise kids...which is why I got out."

"I still can't believe you left."

"Twenty years was long enough for me."

"Not me," Harding said flatly. Why any man would give up the Corps for a woman was simply beyond him. The Marines had given him everything. A home. A family that included every Marine stationed anywhere in the world. A sense of belonging...of doing something for his country.

Nope. He would *never* give up all that to please a woman who would probably just end up leaving him, anyway.

''You and she would be great together.''

Harding scowled. ''Butt out, buddy.''

''Hell, Hard Case.'' Mike sat back, shaking his head. ''You're in worse shape than I thought.''

He snapped his friend an irritated look.

Mike ignored it. ''If you don't know a gorgeous, successful woman when you see her, the Corps ought to drum you out on the grounds of failing eyesight.''

''Very funny.''

''I'm serious.''

''Will you let it go?''

''Probably not,'' Mike admitted.

''What is it with you and your kind?''

Mike laughed easily. He was still the only person Harding had ever known who was unimpressed with the patented Hard Case glare.

''What do you mean, my kind?''

Harding took another swallow of beer, deliberately kept his gaze from sliding toward Elizabeth and concentrated instead on getting his best friend off his back. ''You Noah's Ark people.''

Mike laughed again, but Harding went right on, warming to his theme.

''The minute you find somebody, you're just not happy until everyone around you is traveling in pairs.'' He kept his voice low so that only Mike would be able to hear him above the hum of other conversations taking place in the crowded, oceanfront restaurant. As he talked, he saw that Mike's smile faded. ''You try every which way to drag the rest of us off, kicking and screaming toward some fairy-tale ending. Some of us are meant to be alone, you know.

Not everybody finds happily ever after. Hell, not everyone is *looking* for it.''

Leaning forward, resting his forearms on his thighs, Mike held his beer bottle cupped in both hands and stared at it thoughtfully before saying quietly, ''You need more than the Corps, Hard Case.''

He snorted. ''Look who's talking. You joined up the same time I did. For twenty years, the Corps was enough for you.''

''I retired when I found out different.''

''Yeah.'' Harding shook his head. He still couldn't understand how a man walked away from his whole life without a backward glance. As for himself, he was in the Corps for the long haul. He already had twenty years in, and he planned on staying until they threw him out. Bodily.

How did Mike stand it, going from gunnery sergeant of a batallion to head of security for some civilian computer firm?

''There *is* life off the base,'' his friend commented as if reading his mind.

''Not so I've noticed.''

''You know,'' Mike said, and this time his voice held a tinge of the old impatience, ''they should have named you Hard *Head,* instead of Hard Case.''

Harding swallowed a smile along with the last of his beer, then set the empty bottle down on the table.

''That's it for me,'' Mike said and stood up. ''I know when to quit.''

''Never have before,'' Harding pointed out.

''For tonight, Hard Case. Only for tonight.'' Mike grinned again and patted his friend's shoulder as he moved around the table. ‘‘But for right now, I think I’ll steal a dance with your date. I’ll even let you borrow my gorgeous, almost bride for a quick spin around the floor.’’

Mike took Elizabeth’s hand and led her onto the shining wooden dance floor. And even when the rest of the wedding party left the table to join the dancers, Harding’s gaze never left them.

Two

The recorded easy-rock music swelled softly, drowning conversation.

Harding looked at Terry and found her watching him with a knowing smile.

"Pretty, isn't she?"

Just what he needed—another prospective matchmaker. He shook his head and stood up. Walking to her side, he said, "Don't you start on me, too."

Terry was a good dancer, but short enough that Harding felt as though he was doubled over on the dance floor. He nodded as she talked, and hoped he wasn't agreeing to anything he would regret later. But dammit, he just couldn't seem to keep his mind on what she was saying. Instead, his gaze continued to dart around the floor, following Elizabeth and Mike's progress. She smiled at his friend, and Harding's insides tightened.

One song led into the next and he hardly noticed, until Mike and Elizabeth stopped alongside them.

"Okay, pal," Mike said. "You've had enough time with that gorgeous woman, and this one—" he jerked his head to indicate Elizabeth "—keeps begging me to get you to dance with her."

"Mike!"

Her future brother-in-law ignored her as he deftly pulled Terry into his arms and gently shoved Elizabeth at Harding. "Have fun!" he said as they danced away.

Someone bumped into her, nudging her closer to Harding.

"Nice music," she commented, and glanced around the floor at the dancing couples.

"Yes, ma'am," he said.

She winced and tilted her head back to meet his gaze. "If we're going to be together all week, Mr. Casey, I think you should know, I *hate* being called 'ma'am.'"

"Yes, ma'am," he said deliberately. "Probably as much as I hate being called, 'Mr. Casey.'"

"What should I call you," she asked, "Sergeant?"

"It's Sergeant Major, actually."

"I know."

"That's right," he said with a short nod. "Your father is a Marine."

"Was," she corrected, loudly enough to be heard over the music. "He's retired."

"Impossible," he retorted. "Once a Marine, always a Marine."

"Yeah," she admitted on a sigh. "I know."

He decided to ignore her obvious dislike for the military. "How about you call me Harding, and I'll call you Elizabeth?"

She pulled in a long, slow, deep breath, and he fought to keep his gaze from dropping to the swell of her breasts.

"Deal," she said. "'Harding.' It's an unusual name."

He shrugged. "Old English. It means 'son of the warrior.'"

She nodded. "Naturally."

An exuberant dancer bumped against her, sending her crashing into Harding's chest. She put her hands up to stop her fall, then backed away from him quickly, as if burned.

Silence again. Two people, standing in the middle of the dance floor, surrounded by whirling couples. Stupid for the two of them to simply stand there and get trampled.

He didn't have the slightest doubt that Mike and Terry were covertly watching...hoping for *something* to happen between the two of them. In fact, that was the main reason he hadn't already asked Elizabeth to dance. He knew it was just what his old pal wanted—no, expected. Mike probably figured at the same time, though, that Harding would refuse to dance just to spite him.

With that thought firmly in mind, Harding smiled

to himself. He had always believed in keeping the enemy guessing.

''Would you like to dance?'' They both said at the same time.

Harding looked at her, catching the amusement twinkling in her eyes, and found himself smiling in acknowledgment.

''There's no reason we shouldn't enjoy ourselves, is there?'' Elizabeth asked.

''Not a single one,'' he agreed, and extended one hand toward her. As her palm brushed across his, that same sense of electricity shot up the length of his arm. He gritted his teeth and muttered, ''Ooo-rah!''

''Oh, Lord,'' she groaned quietly.

He pulled her into his arms.

It felt as though she had been made just for him. Her head nestled beneath his chin, her breasts pressed to his chest, her hand resting lightly in his. Harding closed his eyes briefly and prayed for strength.

He felt solid, Elizabeth told herself. Right. Her left hand stole across his shoulder to the back of his neck. Miles of muscles, she thought, and briefly entertained the notion of seeing those muscles in their bare naked glory. Her breath caught in her throat, and her stomach did a series of somersaults. She stumbled slightly, then stepped quickly to get back into the rhythm of the dance.

Nope, she told herself firmly. She would *not* let him get to her. She had spent a whole year avoiding this man and, darn it, she wasn't about to cave in to hormones in one night.

Elizabeth's three-inch heels wobbled beneath her,

and Harding's arm around her waist tightened in response. Glancing up at him, she met his smile with one of her own.

"Did I step on your toes?" he asked.

Good-looking, great body *and* polite, she thought. He knew very well he hadn't stepped on her toes. He was simply covering for her misstep.

"No," she said. "My mind must have drifted." Now that had to be the biggest understatement since Custer said, "I think I see an Indian." Of course, nowadays, it would be "Native American."

"It's been a while since I've been dancing," he said.

"Me, too." Brilliant, she thought. Nothing better than some scintillating after-dinner conversation.

"So," she said, trying to say *something* intelligent, "how long have you and Mike known each other?" She already knew the answer to that one. Hadn't she been hearing Mike sing this man's praises for the past year?

"We met in boot camp."

"Long time ago?"

"Twenty years."

Oh my, yes, this conversation was getting better and better.

He executed a smooth turn that lifted the hem of her skirt to swirl around her legs. "So what made you stay in the Marines?" she asked, needing to talk to keep her mind off other, more distracting thoughts.

"What made you decide to be a cook?"

She bristled slightly. "Chef," she said. "Pastry chef, to be specific."

His eyebrows lifted. ''I stand corrected.'' He held her tightly to him, did a series of turns that left her breathless, then led her back into a standard waltz.

When she could speak again, she tilted her head back to look into those blue eyes of his. ''I enjoy cooking. I'm good at it.''

''Ditto.''

''Huh?''

''I enjoy being a Marine,'' he explained further. ''I'm good at it.''

''Oh.'' Yep, she thought. Her father would *love* this guy. Two men cut from the same cloth, so to speak. ''Where are you stationed?'' she asked next.

''Camp Pendleton.''

She bit her tongue to stop herself from admitting that she had already known that, too. Terry and Mike talked about him all the time. She would even be willing to bet that she knew what he had for breakfast every morning. The bridal couple had not been exactly subtle in their matchmaking efforts.

''Isn't that sort of a long drive from here?''

''With traffic, about an hour.''

She nodded as his thighs moved against hers. Her brain slipped into neutral. They moved through the dancing couples with an almost magical ease. Gliding, swaying around the floor, it was as if they had been dancing together for years.

The song ended, giving way to another, and they went on, oblivious to anyone else in the room.

His legs brushed hers. He threaded his thick, callused fingers through hers, and their palms met. His hand on her waist dipped a bit, coming to rest on the curve of her behind. Everywhere he touched her, Elizabeth felt as though she was on fire.

Raw, primitive heat coursed through her body, making her heart pound and her blood race. Her breasts rubbed against his chest and her nipples tightened expectantly. A damp ache settled in her center, making her thighs tremble.

How was she supposed to ignore him if her own body was working against her?

"So," he asked suddenly, "what made you change your mind about Mike and Terry?"

She squeezed her eyes shut briefly before looking up at him. "They told you I was against their marriage?"

"Yes, ma'am."

"I was afraid of that."

"Don't worry about it," Harding told her. "Mike admired you for it even while he was complaining to me about you trying to split them up."

"He did?"

"Yeah. Said you were just trying to protect your sister." His gaze settled on her. "Loyalty's something we admire in the Corps."

She nodded, understanding completely. "*Semper fi,*" she whispered.

"You got it."

Elizabeth was a little ashamed now of the hard time she had given Mike when he and Terry had started dating. And she had to give her sister's fiancé points. He hadn't given up and he hadn't held her opposition against her. "He's a nice man."

"The best." His tone changed when he added,

"I'm not so nice. You made Mike pretty miserable for a long time."

"I guess I'm not so nice, either." She stiffened in his arms. It was one thing for her to regret her own behavior privately, but she wasn't about to stand still for a lecture. "Terry's always been too romantic for her own good. I had to look out for her."

After a long moment he nodded, then asked, "And who looks out for you?"

Her stomach flip-flopped as she stared into his eyes. Ignoring it, she answered, "I do."

As another song ended, he looked down at her, his gaze clashing with hers in a silent tumult of emotion. Elizabeth drew one long, shuddering breath. What was it about this man? She wasn't a stranger to men in uniform, so that old cliché didn't hold true. Clearly then, it was something about Harding Casey himself that was getting to her. She wasn't willing to risk that. Desperately unsettled, she whispered, "I think I'd better get back home."

"Already?" That voice of his rumbled along her spine and sent every one of her nerve endings into overdrive.

Deliberately she took a step back, pulling her hand from his grasp. "Yeah. Terry wants me to run a couple of errands for her in the morning, and who knows what she and Mike will have planned for us later in the day."

"They are trying to keep us together, aren't they?"

"Terry's always been stubborn."

"Mike, too."

She nodded, telling herself to move. Get away.

Walk fast, no, *run* to a car. Any car that promised her a ride home. Why hadn't she driven herself?

Because she had listened to Terry, that's why.

"Anyway," she said, starting off the dance floor toward their table. "Thanks for the dances, and I guess I'll see you tomorrow."

"Just a minute," he said, and she glanced back to see him wind his way through the swaying couples to speak with Mike. In moments he was back again. Taking her elbow, he said, "All right, let's go."

"*Let's?* You're leaving, too?"

He shot her a quick look. "I'm taking you home."

"Oh, that's not necessary," she babbled. "I'll just grab a cab."

"Look," he said, "you came with Terry. You need a ride. I'm available. Why wait for a cab when you're ready to leave now?"

Terrific, she thought. Not just a Marine. The Sir Galahad of Marines.

"Really, Harding," she started to say.

The sentence trailed off into silence as soon as she met his gaze. There was no way this man was going to put her in a cab.

Inhaling deeply, she blew the air out in a rush and accepted the inevitable. "Okay then, let's go."

Windows down, the cold, sea-kissed air rushed in at them as Harding steered his late-model Mustang north, up Pacific Coast Highway.

"Nice car," she said after several moments of tense silence.

"Rented," he muttered.

''Where's yours?'' Elizabeth asked, more out of politeness than actual curiosity.

''Don't have one.''

Conversation would be a lot simpler, she told herself, if she didn't have to practically use a bayonet to force him to contribute. He'd been a heck of a lot chattier on the dance floor, she thought. Why the change? Was it because now it was just the two of them? Well, whatever the reason, Elizabeth wasn't going to sit in stony silence the whole way home.

''You live in Huntington Beach, California and don't own a car?'' she asked.

He shot her a sidelong glance. ''Too much trouble to own one when you're never in one place more than a few years. All that hassle with changing license plates and registration...''

A veritable *flood* of information. And with it, memories. Her father, too, had never owned a car until he and Elizabeth's mother had retired to Florida several years before.

Harding lapsed into silence again, and she bit her tongue to keep from being the one to speak first this time. But maybe she shouldn't be so hard on him, she thought. She had seen the look on his face while they danced. She knew that he had been feeling the same overpowering attraction that she had experienced. All things considered, she thought, they were doing well indeed, having *any* sort of conversation.

Although, she told herself as miles of beach road disappeared behind them, perhaps it would be better all the way around if they each simply owned up to the truth of what was happening between them. She looked at his stoic profile and knew that if they were going to get this out into the open, it would be up to her to start the ball rolling.

Before she could change her mind, she said, ''This won't work, you know.''

His breath left him in a rush. He gave her a brief, half smile before turning his gaze back to the road. ''I'm glad you see that, too.''

''Of course I do,'' Elizabeth told him.

Shaking his head, he went on as if she hadn't spoken. ''The last thing I need in my life is a woman.''

''I feel the same way,'' she tossed in and was rewarded with a quizzical look. Correcting herself, she said quickly, ''About a man, I mean. Particularly, a Marine.''

He frowned at the distinction, then nodded and started talking again, as if her words had broken a dam that had stood as long as it was able. ''I tried marriage once, you know.''

''No, I didn't.'' Strange, that with all the information Terry had given her about Harding Casey, the woman had never added the fairly pertinent point concerning a wife.

''Yeah,'' he said, almost to himself. ''Only lasted a few months.''

''What happened?''

He shrugged those massive shoulders. ''She left me. Better in the end, I suppose. She couldn't handle being a Marine wife.''

Unwillingly, she felt a stab of empathy for the woman. She remembered all too clearly how hard her mother had worked, trying to give her children a sense of permanence even while traipsing around the world. "It's not an easy job," she said.

He grinned, and her stomach flipped. She sincerely hoped he wouldn't do that often, during the next week they were to spend together.

"That's right. You *would* know. Your father is career Marine."

"Yeah, and you could say my mother was, too. Lord knows she should have gotten a medal or two."

He bowed his head slightly in acknowledgment. "It takes a special woman to handle it. My ex didn't like the idea of long absences, for one thing."

"Ah, deployment," she said softly, remembering all of the times her father had been gone in her life.

"Six months every eighteen months," he said.

Christmases, she thought. Summers, school plays...

"And," he went on, oblivious to her silence, "she wasn't real keen on the notion of packing up and moving every three years or so, never quite sure which base she'd end up on."

It was a hassle, she remembered, though her mother had always looked on it as another adventure. Terry, too, for that matter. Just because she herself didn't care for the life didn't mean that there weren't plenty of women who did. To be completely honest, her own mother had thrived on it.

Finally she said slowly, "You know, Harding, any woman who really loves a man can put up with just about anything. I think you just picked a lemon in the garden of love."

He came to a stop at a traffic signal and swiveled

his head to look at her in the reflected yellow glow of a fog lamp streetlight.

"You're probably right," he conceded. "But either way, once was enough for me. I won't try it again. A mistake like that is hard to correct and almost impossible to forget."

The light turned green, and he stepped on the gas.

"I agree completely." Elizabeth settled back into her seat, more comfortable than she had been all night. What a relief it was to get this all into the open. "That's why I have no intention of marrying. *Especially* a military man. Growing up with one was enough. Besides, I've yet to meet any man I would be interested in enough to even *think* about marriage." She turned her head to watch the black waves roll in toward shore. "And I like having my time to myself. I need it. To think. To work."

"I know just what you mean," he said. As they neared the Huntington Beach pier, he pulled the car close to the curb, threw it into Park and shut off the engine.

She looked at him. "What are you up to?"

"Not a thing, ma'am. Just thought you might like to take a little stroll on the beach before heading back to your place."

Odd, that once they had started talking openly about how neither of them was interested in the other, they were getting along great.

"You know something?" she said. "That sounds like a wonderful idea."

He got out, came around to her side and opened the door for her. Once he'd helped her out of the low-slung car, he released her hand and walked beside her as they crossed the street to the steps leading down to the sand.

''I'm really glad we had that little talk, Harding.''

''I am, too, Elizabeth,'' he said. ''We'll be spending a lot of time together this coming week, and there's no reason why we can't relax and enjoy each other's company. As friends.''

Friends. Sure. Why not? They could do it. They were both grown-ups. Uncontrollable lust was for teenagers or for those who had no self-control.

''Friends,'' she agreed firmly. At the bottom of the steps, she paused to step out of her high heels.

''You should maybe keep those on at least until we're clear of the pier. There's probably broken glass all over the place.''

She looked up at him briefly. ''High heels and sand do not mix, Harding.''

He nodded slowly, then before she could say another word, he bent down, scooped her up in his arms and cradled her against his chest.

Her heartbeat thundered in her ears. Her breathing shortened, became more difficult.

''What are you doing?'' she managed to ask.

Grinning at her, he said, ''Helping a *friend.*''

''Oh.'' She swallowed with difficulty and ordered her pulse rate to slow down. ''Okay.''

Friend, she thought silently. Repeatedly. Maybe if she said it often enough, her body would start to believe it.

Three

Harding set his new ''friend'' down gently and took a step back from her. His body was on full alert. Hard. Ready. Eager. Too much more of this ''friendship'' and he would be a dead man.

Or maybe a live-and-in-pain one who wished he were dead.

But what was he thinking? He was a Marine. He had been in battle. Survived whizzing bullets and stupid recruits. Surely he could last out a week in the company of Elizabeth Stone.

He shot her a look from the corner of his eye and had to admit that a week with Elizabeth Stone was going to be much tougher on him than any enemy soldier with a puny little machine gun could be.

In silence they started walking along the shoreline. The tide was out, and the slow ripples of water surged sluggishly toward the beach, occasionally sneaking up close enough to them that the two people did a quick step to one side to stay dry.

Sea-air-scented wind ruffled across the surface of the ocean, and a full moon lent a silvery, almost bright, light to the darkness.

"What was Mike saying to you at the restaurant earlier?"

"Hmm?" He looked at her, thought for a minute, then said, "Oh."

"You don't have to say," she said with a gentle laugh. "I'll bet I could guess."

"Yes, you probably could." Chances were very good that Terry had been saying approximately the same things to her.

"Why do you suppose they're trying so hard to bring us together?"

He shrugged again. "They mean well."

"So did the Crusaders."

Harding laughed aloud at her gloomy tone as much as at her words.

She looked up at him and grinned. "I guess there really isn't anything we can do to stop them, is there?"

"Short of getting married?" he asked. "No."

"Well, as much as I love Terry," Elizabeth said, and bent down to pick up a piece of driftwood, "I'm not willing to marry somebody just to make her happy."

"Amen."

She tossed the stick into the receding tide and stared at it for several long moments as it rocked on the rippling surface before being pulled back out to sea. "I haven't been down here in far too long," she said wistfully.

Smiling, he echoed her earlier astonishment that he hadn't owned a car. "What? You live in California and don't go to the beach?"

She caught on to what he was doing and said, "Touché."

They started strolling again in a companionable silence. An older couple, walking a tiny dog on a long leash, passed them with a muttered greeting. From far off down the beach they saw the wavering, indistinct glow of small fires burning in the cement fire rings. On the clear, still air, laughter and snatches of campfire songs drifted to them.

But Harding paid no attention to any of it. Instead, his concentration was focused on the woman walking alongside him, carrying her high heels in one hand. He watched the soft breeze lift her dark brown curls off her neck and thought he caught the scent of her perfume. Something light and feminine and alluring, it sent daggers of need digging into his guts.

Damn, what if he had listened to Mike a year ago when his friend had first suggested he meet Elizabeth Stone? What might his life have been like these past twelve months? Torture? Or bliss?

Torture, most definitely.

Because no matter how much he wanted her...no matter how powerful the attraction was between them...he wouldn't allow anything to come of it.

In fact, he couldn't imagine why Mike and Terry had thought to pair the two of them up, anyway. They couldn't be more different. He snorted a choked laugh and shook his head.

"What's so funny?" she asked. Reaching up, she plucked at a long strand of windblown hair that had attached itself to her eyelashes.

"Just thinking," he answered. "Mike and Terry must have been nuts to believe you and I—"

"Nuts," she agreed.

"Me, a career Marine, and—" he stopped, cocked his head at her and wondered aloud "—what is it you're called? The Princess of Party Cooking?"

Now Elizabeth laughed. "Some reviewer gave me that tag a couple of years ago." She shrugged. "My publisher loved it and ran with it. The name stuck. But all I really am is a pastry chef."

"Who writes bestselling cookbooks."

"*Co*writes," she countered, holding up one finger to admonish him. "Which means, I supply the recipes and a few humorous stories about some of my more memorable disasters and Vicki, the writer I work with, puts it all together and makes me sound brilliant."

Harding looked at her, surprise gleaming in his eyes. "Not many people would admit that they don't actually write their own books."

She smiled at him. "No point in denying it. Vicki's name is right there on the cover."

"And whose idea was that?"

Elizabeth's gaze shifted to the darkness of the sea. "Mine," she admitted. "I can cook, but I can't write, and I don't want to take bows for something I didn't do."

He knew lots of people who wouldn't have been bothered by that in the least. There was more to Elizabeth Stone than just the way she kicked his hormones into high gear.

Moving away from those ideas, he instead focused on what he had been thinking before. "Still, what could a Marine and a 'princess' possibly have in common?"

"Not much, besides knowing two people with way too much time on their hands."

"True."

She swiveled her head to look at him, and one glance from those dark, fathomless eyes of hers and he felt as keyed up and tightly strung as he did the night before a battle.

He sucked in a quick, deep breath and saw her do the same before she turned away abruptly.

Elizabeth bent down, picked up another, longer stick and turned her back on the ocean.

"What are you doing?" he asked, silently grateful that she had broken eye contact.

"Something I haven't done in years," she said, and started writing her name in the water-soaked sand at the edge of the tide.

He stood to one side and watched her.

When she had finished with her own name, she went on, inscribing his name, using the last *H* in Elizabeth as the first *H* in Harding. Her task complete, she tossed the stick aside and stood back, admiring her handiwork. Then she looked up at him expectantly.

"Very nice," he said. "Until the tide shifts." Then

the ocean would run in, obliterating their names like an eraser moving over a chalkboard.

"Nothing is forever," she told him, and as she spoke a rogue surge of water rushed across her ankles and sluiced past her feet. The seawater rippled across their names in a haphazard pattern, and in a moment most of the script was gone.

"See?" she said with a lightness that didn't quite cover the note of disappointment in her voice. Then, glancing down at her soaking wet nylons, she grimaced and walked away from the ocean's edge, closer to him. "Hold these for a minute, will you?" she asked, and handed him her heels.

As she lifted the hem of her already short skirt, he tensed and asked, "What are you doing?"

Bent at the waist, she looked up at him briefly. "I'm just going to take off these nylons."

"Out here?" Did his voice sound as strained to her as it did to him?

"There's nobody around but you and me."

That only made things worse.

Harding took in another deep gulp of cold air and hoped it would do something to stop the flames erupting inside him. As a gentleman should, he half turned, to give her some privacy. Besides, there was no point in torturing himself.

She saw the movement and chuckled. "Don't worry about it, Harding. They're not panty hose."

Oh, God, he thought, closing his eyes on a quiet groan. *Garters?*

"They're just thigh-highs," she went on, when he still didn't turn back toward her.

Thigh-highs. *Black* thigh-highs. His body tightened at the mental image of lace and sheer black fabric hugging and caressing those long legs of hers.

"For heaven's sake, Harding," she said. "Look at me. You would see more flesh if I was wearing shorts!"

He turned around, then, and bit back another, deeper groan. It was worse than he had thought. Thigh-highs indeed. Apparently Elizabeth Stone was completely unaware of just how seductive she looked.

The wide, black lace elastic band hugged the creamy white flesh of her upper thigh and gave way to sheer, black silk covering the rest of her leg. Slowly she smoothed her palms along the stocking, rolling the fragile material beneath her fingertips, exposing her pale white skin, inch by tantalizing inch.

Mouth dry, throat tight, he watched her, unable and unwilling to look away. Her hands moved down her leg, and his palms itched to help her.

By the time she had removed the first stocking, his breathing was strangled. When she started in on the second, bending over slowly to complete the task, his gaze shifted to the curve of her behind beneath the short, tight black skirt.

His fingers tightened around the shoes he held in one hand until he felt the tips of the high heels dig into his palm. He deliberately concentrated on that small discomfort in order to take his mind off the nearly overwhelming pain of his aching groin.

Finally she straightened up and tossed her hair back out of her eyes. "That feels better," she said, balling her wet nylons up in her hands. "Nothing worse than soggy stockings."

"Uh-huh." He could think of a few things worse.

"Harding?"

He swallowed heavily. "Yes, ma'am?"

"You okay?"

"Yeah," he ground out. "I'm fine." Or he would be as soon as he could get back to the base and stand under a cold shower for two or three hours. Or days.

"You don't *look* fine."

"Forget it."

She blinked, surprised at his gruff tone. "Okay."

"Look," he said, more hotly than he had planned, "we talked about this. How whatever it was we're feeling for each other won't work."

"So?"

"So, I'd appreciate you not making this any harder than it already is."

"I made it harder by taking off my stockings?"

Rock hard, he thought.

"Jeez, Harding, relax." She shook her head and turned her face into the wind. "We're both adults. We can handle this…attraction without acting on it."

"I didn't say I was going to act on it. I *said* you were making things more difficult than they had to be."

"Aren't you overreacting just a little?"

"I don't think so."

"Maybe," she said with a long look at his obviously uncomfortable expression, "you'd better take me back home, then."

Now *that* sounded like a plan. Get out from under

the damn full moon, away from the soft, sea-scented breezes and the lulling, hypnotic rush of the ocean. Once distanced from this romantic setting, it would be easier to stick to the friendship they had so recently agreed upon.

"That's probably a good idea," he said abruptly.

"I'll take those," she muttered, and reached for her shoes.

She moved in close, destroying his good intentions. Her scent surrounded him. Her warmth called to him, and he couldn't withstand it. His resolve disappeared. Instead of giving her the shoes, he dropped them to the sand and grabbed her hand. Harding felt it again immediately. That sudden jolt of awareness. Of heat. Electricity. And she felt it, too. He could see it in her eyes.

Instinctively he pulled her closer. Without a word she moved into the circle of his arms and tilted her head back for his kiss. Moonlight dusted her features, and even as he bent to claim her mouth, he knew he shouldn't. Knew that once the line was crossed it would be impossible to go back.

The wind picked up, and the roar of the ocean sounded all around them.

He brushed his lips across hers gently, once. Twice. Then his mouth came down on hers with a hard, steady pressure, and a crashing wave of sensation fell on him. As if the night sky were lit up with fireworks, he felt himself come to life. He felt an intense connection with this woman, and when she suddenly broke away and took a staggering step back from him, it was as if he'd been dunked in a pool of ice water.

Breathless and stunned at her reaction to a simple kiss, Elizabeth took a step away from the man who had just touched her so deeply. It was small consolation to see her own shocked feelings etched into the Marine's stoic features.

"All right," she whispered, and started walking backward, keeping a wary eye on him. "Maybe you weren't overreacting." She shook her head and added, "We can't do this, Harding. *I* can't do this." Then she turned and ran across the sand. She raced toward the pier and the street beyond where there were lights, people and a car that could carry her back to her house.

To safety.

She heard him running after her and knew that she would never be able to beat him. He had years of training behind him while all she had to show for exercise was a folded-up treadmill that made an excellent silent butler.

Before she got close to the steps leading back to the street, Harding caught up with her. Grabbing her upper arm, he turned her around to face him.

"Why did you run?"

Why was he pretending he didn't know the answer to that?

"You know why."

He reached up and ran one hand across his severe military haircut. "You don't have to run from me," he growled. "I wouldn't hurt you."

"I know that," she snapped, irritated with herself more than him. Good Lord, she was thirty-two years old. She had been kissed before. Often. Why was she reacting like a giddy teenager on her first date?

Because, a voice in the back of her mind answered, she had never been kissed like *that* before.

"Look, Harding," she said, trying to explain something that just might prove to be unexplainable. "I wasn't scared. Exactly. Just...surprised." Stunned would have been a better word. "I guess I wasn't really running away from you—it was more like running from whatever it is that happens between us whenever we get too close."

He nodded abruptly, his mouth thinning into a grim line. "I know the feeling."

"You were right when you said we shouldn't make this more difficult than it already is." Elizabeth forced a deep breath of cold air into her lungs. "Why start something that neither one of us has any intention of finishing?"

He looked at her for a long, slow minute. "The only reason I can think of, is that Marines don't run."

She choked out a laugh. "I'm not a Marine."

"No," he said and pulled her close to him. "But I am."

This time, when their lips met, Elizabeth was prepared for the incredible sensations skittering inside her. At least she thought she was. She gasped as the opening ripples of excitement coursed through her, then she gave herself up to the inevitable. She had known from the moment she had first looked into his blue eyes that this kiss was coming, and instead of worrying about the repercussions, gave herself up to the wonder of it.

He parted her lips with the tip of his tongue, and when she opened for him, he plundered her mouth like an invading army. Daggers of desire pricked at her insides, and when he held her tighter, closer, she pressed herself into him, flattening her breasts against his chest.

He cupped the back of her head, his fingers combing through her hair and she reached up, wrapped her arms around his neck and held on as if afraid she was about to slip off the edge of the world. His right hand moved across her back, down her spine to the curve of her bottom. He followed that curve and held her against his hardness. An answering need blossomed inside her, and she moaned gently.

Tearing his mouth from hers, Harding dipped his head to lavish damp kisses along the length of her neck. His arms tightened around her like twin bands of twisted steel. Desire screamed inside her. The feeling was more, so much more than she had expected. Elizabeth had the wild, insane desire to rip off her clothes and offer herself to him there. In the sand.

She craved his touch more than her next breath.

"Harding," she whispered, "I want—"

"Way to go, soldier boy!" A loud voice, filled with laughter, splintered the moment.

Harding straightened abruptly, pulled her close to him protectively and shielded her while she pulled herself together.

Laughter floated down to them from the pier above, and after a moment or two, shuffling footsteps told them that their audience had moved on.

She buried her face against Harding's chest.

''Damn teenagers,'' he muttered. ''They're everywhere. What I wouldn't give to get that kid in boot camp.''

''Good God,'' Elizabeth groaned, her voice muffled. ''What were we doing…thinking?''

''Thinking didn't have much to do with what we were doing,'' he told her and stood stock-still for a long moment, keeping his arms firmly around her. Finally though, he said, ''C'mon. I'll take you back to your place.''

Elizabeth drew in a long, shuddering breath as he lifted her into his arms again to carry her across the glass-littered sand. Ridiculous, but she almost enjoyed being carried around like some modern-day Jane to his Tarzan. She had never known a man strong enough to lift her not-so-small form as easily as he would have a child.

Her arm around his shoulders, she tried not to think about the hard, corded muscles lying just beneath his uniform. Or about how much she would love to feel his naked strength beneath her fingertips.

When she thought she could speak without her voice shaking, she tried to lighten the incredibly tension-filled moment. ''I thought you said Marines don't run?''

He glanced at her, then shifted his gaze to a point above her head. ''They don't. But they have been known to make a strategic retreat now and again…when absolutely necessary.''

''Like now?''

''Princess, *exactly* like now.''

Four

"Look, Harding," she said and stared up into those lake blue eyes of his. "I don't think this friendship thing is going to work."

"Probably not," he conceded as he set her down on the sidewalk.

Surprised, she nodded at him thoughtfully and pushed the button for the Walk signal. "Somehow, I had the feeling you were going to prove to be one of those die-hard Marines."

"Meaning what, exactly?" The light changed. He took her elbow and guided her across Pacific Coast Highway.

"Meaning," she said, forcing herself to keep up with his much-longer stride, "not knowing when to give up. Surrender."

He stopped alongside the car and looked down at

her. One corner of his mouth quirked, and her insides jumped. Ignoring the sudden rush of adrenaline to the pit of her stomach, Elizabeth went on. "I mean, since we both know that friendship has already been blown out of the water, we can simply call Mike and Terry and tell them that the deal's off. We can each help out...we're just not going to be doing it together."

"Nope."

It took a moment for that one word to sink in.

"What do you mean, 'nope'?"

"I mean," he said, opening the car door for her, "I have no intention of telling Mike that I can't handle being around you for a week."

"But—"

"Princess," he said, "I've been in battle. I've been stranded in jungles with nothing to eat but my own shoes." His voice deepened as he loomed over her, and Elizabeth's head fell back on her neck as she struggled to maintain eye contact. "I've taken lazy, unmotivated teenagers and made them into first-class Marines. I've been in charge of *hundreds* of men and tons of equipment."

"So?" she managed to ask.

"So, I'm damn sure *not* running up the white flag because of a couple of kisses." That said, he jerked his head toward the car. "Now, get in and I'll take you home."

Bristling at the command, Elizabeth pitched her wet shoes and stockings into the car, planted her fists on her hips and gave him a glare guaranteed to melt stone. "We're not leaving yet, Marine."

His black eyebrows lifted.

Who the hell did he think he was? Did he really think that *he* could ignore her better than *she* could ignore him? This was precisely why she had always steered clear of the military type. Giving orders was second nature to them. Well, if he thought he could tell *her* to do *anything,* he had a big surprise coming.

Poking him in the chest with the tip of her index finger, she went on. ''I've never been in battle or a jungle. But I have faced down a hungry crowd with nothing to feed them but a ruined soufflé and over-done bread. I've met deadlines, done book tours that left me so tired, death looked like a vacation, and, mister, there isn't a Marine *alive* who can outlast *me.*''

He opened his mouth to speak, but she cut him off.

''And as for those kisses, don't flatter yourself. I've been kissed before, buster—and if that's the best you've got, believe me, I'll be able to keep from hurling myself at your manly chest.''

A glimmer of a smile raced across his features, then disappeared.

''Manly chest, eh?''

''A figure of speech,'' she said. A *true* figure of speech, but that was beside the point. Also beside the point was the fact that she had lied about the potency of his kisses. Sure she had been kissed before. But never like that.

''You finished?'' he asked.

''For now.''

He nodded slowly. ''Fine, I just want to say one thing.''

''What?''

"You may be tougher than you look, princess. But *this* Marine can outlast *you* anytime."

"Humph!" She'd lost track of exactly what they were talking about here, so she figured that answer was her only safe one.

"Then we're agreed?" he asked.

"Agreed," she snapped, then added, "Agreed on what?"

"That a couple of kisses are no reason to admit defeat."

"Oh. Sure."

"Fine, then, it's settled." He set one hand on the top of the car door and ushered her inside with the other. "We can't be friends, but we can last out the week in each other's company."

"No problem," she said firmly, and settled back in the seat as he closed the car door and walked around to the other side. He slid into the driver's seat, jammed the key into the ignition, then looked at her before firing up the engine.

Blue eyes locked with brown. Elizabeth's heartbeat jumped into high gear. The palms of her hands were sweaty, and deep within her a core of heat burst into flame.

"No problem," she whispered.

"Right," he said, with as little conviction as she felt.

The South Coast Plaza mall was packed. Saturday-morning crowds teemed through the cavernous place. Moms pushing strollers, crying babies, lounging teenagers, professional types with cell phones glued to their ears all competed for walking room.

Elizabeth came to an abrupt stop beside the escalator. A stroller clipped her heel and rolled on past without even slowing down. She winced, shot the oblivious mother a glare, then turned back to the man on her right.

Harding looked hopelessly out of place. That spit-and-polish Marine exterior stood out like several sore thumbs, in the midst of suburbia. She shook her head as she looked up—*way* up at him. Without the benefit of her three-inch heels, Elizabeth felt short for the first time in her life.

Mercy, he was gorgeous. Just for a moment she allowed herself to remember how it had felt to be cradled against that massive chest of his. Memories rushed into her brain. The strength of his arms. The warmth of his kiss.

The abrupt way he'd left her at her front door the night before.

She drew one deep, shaky breath. This was going to be a long week.

"So what's first?" Harding asked, startling Elizabeth out of her reverie.

"Oh!" She glanced down at the list in her hand. Her sister, Terry, was nothing if not efficient. On the small memo pad, there was a different list for every day during this last hectic week before the wedding. Looking under Saturday, Elizabeth read out loud, "Pick up going-away dress at the Flim Flam."

"Flim Flam?" Harding echoed.

"A new dress shop here in the mall."

He nodded. "Anything else?"

"Yeah, she wants us to pick up Mike's wedding present at Macy's."

"Where's that?" Harding asked, staring into the distance.

"At the other end of the mall." Elizabeth checked her watch. They had plenty of time, actually, but it gave her something to do. "Why don't you go to Macy's, I'll pick up her dress then meet you at the coffee bar."

"All right," he said. "What am I picking up?"

She laughed shortly. "Sorry. Go to the jewelry counter. Terry bought him a watch last week, and the engraving is finally done. They'll be holding it for her there." She dug into her shoulder bag and came up with a receipt. Handing it to him, she said, "Show them this. You shouldn't have a problem. It's already paid for."

He glanced at the paper, folded it neatly into fours, then tucked it into his pants pocket.

"Macy's is right at the end of that concourse," she told him, pointing off to the left.

He smirked at her. "I think I'll be able to find it."

She shrugged. "Okay then, see you at the coffee bar in one hour."

Elizabeth turned to go, but he grabbed her hand, pulling her back to his side. Carefully he checked the time on her wristwatch, then adjusted hers to match his exactly.

"Synchronizing our watches?" she said on a muffled laugh.

"Yep." He gave her a brief nod, then said, "Coffee bar, eleven hundred thirty hours."

She stifled the groan building in her chest. Memories of all the years she had spent living according to military time flashed through her brain and left again just as quickly. It didn't matter. She was through with all of that. She and Harding were only going to be around each other for a week—there was no point in arguing with him all the time.

"Fine. Eleven-thirty. The coffee bar's on the second level," she said, "right next to—"

"I'll find it."

"But this mall is really big, Harding. It can be very confusing." Elizabeth shopped there all the time, and even she had been known to lose her bearings a time or two.

He gave her a slow, patronizing, infuriating smile as he shook his head. "Elizabeth, in the Corps, I am what is known as a pathfinder."

That was a new one to her. One eyebrow rose as she asked, "As in *Last of the Mohicans?*"

He frowned briefly. "As in I am trained to be able to survive in a jungle with nothing but a piece of string and a knife. I *think* I'll be able to find my way around a shopping center."

She felt she should point out that very few jungles are equipped with banks of elevators, hundreds of people, strolling musicians, a double-decker carousel and dozens of corridors, each of them just like the last. But…who was she to argue with a pathfinder?

"Okay, Hawkeye," Elizabeth said with a half smile. "Go to it! On my mark, I'll meet you in one hour.'' She looked down at her watch, snapped out ''Mark!'' then turned on her heel and disappeared into the crowds.

Amazing. One minute she was there and the next she wasn't. In the constantly shifting crowd of people, he couldn't even catch a glimpse of her. He didn't even want to *think* about what this place must be like during the Christmas shopping rush.

Minutes ticked by before he told himself to get moving. He wanted to be sitting at that blasted coffee bar having a nice, leisurely snack by the time she arrived. Mumbling ''Excuse me'' to the elderly woman who crashed right into him, Harding stepped onto the escalator and descended into Suburban Hell.

Fifty-five minutes later, Harding tightened his grip on the small Macy's package in his hand and started down yet another corridor. He glanced from storefront to storefront, sure he'd been that way before. Frowning, he came to a dead stop in front of a kitchenware shop. Dammit, he recognized that three-foot-tall chicken in the display window. Either he was walking in circles or there was more than *one* chicken wearing a chef's hat decorated with big red hearts somewhere in this blasted mall.

Scowling furiously, he glanced at his wristwatch. Nearly time. So much for having a leisurely snack while waiting for Elizabeth. At this rate he'd be lucky to find the damned coffee bar before the wedding.

A logical voice in his head told him he should just find a directory kiosk. He seemed to recall seeing one...somewhere. But that went sorely against the grain. Of course, he could simply ask someone for directions. He shook his head at the thought. No. He'd made his brag. He'd told Elizabeth that he could find his way through this overpriced maze, and blast it, that's just what he was going to do.

He still had five full minutes. Plenty of time. He would not be beaten by a shopping mall!

"Excuse me, private," a soft voice said from behind him.

Private? He stiffened at the insult, turned around and looked down into the sharp green eyes of a woman at least seventy years old. Her silvery hair was permed and sprayed into submission, and her bright pink sweatshirt had the words Mall Walker emblazoned across the front. He assumed the term had nothing in common with another well-known phrase... *street walker.*

"Yes, ma'am?" he asked.

"Don't you look handsome?" she said softly, with a slow shake of her head. "My, I always *did* love a Marine uniform better than just about anything...."

"Thank you, ma'am," he started, already looking for a chance to get away. He had only five minutes to find that coffee shop. Harding glanced at the short woman planted firmly in front of him. What was it about a uniform that got people talking?

"You know, my dear late husband, Edgar, was a Marine."

"Yes, ma'am?" He gave a mental sigh and wondered how he would be able to escape without hurting the woman's feelings. He didn't want to be rude, but he simply didn't have the time to listen to a stream of memories from a military admirer.

"Oh my, yes. He was a private, too."

He winced inwardly at the slap at his rank. It couldn't hurt to straighten her out a little. "Actually ma'am, I'm a Sergeant Major."

"No matter." She waved one hand at him and gave him a small smile. "My Edgar was a part of D Day, you know."

"Really?" People streamed past him like a swiftly moving river rushing past a rock. A rock buried deep in the mud and moving nowhere. Fast. He resisted looking at his watch again.

"Oh, yes. Why, if it hadn't been for my Edgar, who knows what might have happened on that horrible day." She paused, and when he didn't prompt her, she added, "World War II? D Day? The Normandy Invasion? Surely they teach privates about World War II these days."

"Yes, ma'am," he said, and bit down on the inside of his cheek to keep from smiling wryly. "I believe it's been mentioned a time or two."

"Well, thank heavens. I'd hate to think Edgar's sacrifice was in vain, you know."

Sacrifice? Immediately contrite that he hadn't given her his complete attention, he told himself that the widow of a fellow Marine deserved better. Quietly Harding said, "I'm sorry ma'am. He died at Normandy, then?"

She jerked her head back and stared at him, horrified. "I should say not! Why he's at the Golf Pro shop this very minute."

Now he really *was* lost. "But you said 'his sacrifice'?"

She frowned at him. ''My Edgar was deathly ill at the time...his sinuses have always been a source of travail for the dear man...yet he put his own misery aside in order to drive the men to the harbor where they boarded the ships to mount the invasion. If not for my Edgar—'' she shook her head slowly ''—why, everything might have turned out differently.''

Oh, for— Giving her a polite nod, he sent his best to Edgar and made his escape as quickly as possible. Pick a direction. Any direction. Some pathfinder, he told himself. Yet in his own defense, he had to admit that the people now rushing through familiar territory would be completely lost in a jungle. He, on the other hand, would shine in such a situation.

He glanced at his watch and grumbled in irritation. Eleven thirty-five. Shifting his gaze to sweep across the crowded mall, he was almost ready to cry defeat and look for a directory when he had a better idea.

Casually he strolled toward a group of four teenage girls and stopped just a foot or two short of them. Then he wondered aloud, ''Now where was that coffee bar?''

One of the girls giggled and elbowed her friend who was staring at Harding in wide-eyed appreciation. ''Are you looking for Lola's Latte?'' the giggler asked.

Lola? Latte? ''Would that be the coffee bar on the second level?'' he asked, just to make sure.

''That's the one,'' another girl piped up.

''Then, yes,'' Harding told them. ''I am looking for Lola's.'' He swallowed what was left of his pride and asked, ''Do you know where it is?''

"Sure," the giggler spoke up again, pushed past her friends and sidled up close to Harding.

She couldn't have been more than seventeen, so he took a hasty step back. Quite a day. First Grandma, then a kid.

"Go right along here," the girl said, "turn right at the Pokey Puppy, go past the Discovery store and Lola's is right next to Potato Pete's."

Potato, Pokey, Discovery, he had to get out of this place. "Thanks, ladies," he said, and started moving, ignoring the giggler's heavy sigh as he brushed past her. He was already late, but if he hurried, maybe he'd get lucky. Maybe Elizabeth had gotten held up at the dress shop. Maybe he would still beat her to their appointment.

Then again, maybe not.

He slowed down purposely when he saw her sitting at a small round table outside Lola's, leisurely sipping from an oversize yellow coffee cup. Bad enough that he was late. No sense in looking like he was running.

In the instant before she saw him, Harding took a long minute to appreciate the picture she made.

No one should be able to look as good in jeans as she did in black silk. But somehow, Elizabeth managed it. Those worn, faded Levi's of hers hugged her long, slender legs like the hands of a familiar lover. Her tight blue T-shirt clung to her full breasts, defining a figure made to drive a man crazy. She shook her soft brown hair back from her face, and her gold hoop earrings glinted in the sunshine spilling in from the overhead skylight.

Harding gritted his teeth. He'd already had one

long, sleepless night, thanks to memories of her and the kisses they'd shared on a moonlit beach. Studying her in such close detail wasn't helping any.

She spotted him and raised a hand to wave at him. He swallowed the groan rising in his chest as his gaze locked on the smooth expanse of lightly tanned skin exposed between the hem of her shirt and the waistband of her jeans.

He walked to the coffee bar as quickly as he could, ignoring the ache in his groin caused by just the sight of her. He had the distinct feeling that as long as he was around Elizabeth Stone, he wouldn't be walking in comfort.

A smile curved one corner of her mouth as he dropped into the chair opposite her. Glancing first at her watch, she looked at him through amused brown eyes. "Eleven forty-five, Sergeant Major."

"I know." He shifted in the chair, set the Macy's bag on the table and tried to ignore the tantalizing temptation of her luscious mouth.

She grinned, and something inside him tightened.

"Lost?" she asked.

"No," he corrected. "Just...delayed."

"Uh-huh," Elizabeth nodded, set her cup down and signaled for the waiter. Looking back at Harding, she asked, "Would you like a cup of coffee? A compass? Or perhaps just a knife and a piece of string?"

The glimmer of amusement in her eyes couldn't be ignored. Neither could the knot of need centering low in his belly. Humiliating as it was to admit, he wanted her more than anything. Even her laughter at his ineptness wasn't enough to quash the desire building within him.

Determined to ignore the direction his thoughts were taking, he forced a smile and admitted, "Coffee would be great. And if you're going to leave me alone in this place again...a compass wouldn't be out of line."

Elizabeth looked surprised, then a short chuckle rippled past her throat and settled over him. Reaching across the table, she lightly laid her hand atop his.

"Congratulations, Harding. You're the first man I've ever known to admit to being lost."

He looked down at their joined hands. Jagged streaks of heat stabbed at him. Lifting his gaze, he met hers and saw the same staggering sense of awareness reflected in her eyes.

Immediately she pulled her hand back and buried it in her lap.

A waiter silently came up to the table.

And the moment was lost.

But Harding had a feeling that during the next week with Elizabeth, there would be plenty of such moments.

Five

That was a mistake.

Under cover of the tabletop, Elizabeth rubbed the fingers of her right hand together. It did no good, though. Her flesh still tingled as if she'd received a small electrical shock.

She should have known better than to touch him. Hadn't the memory of his kisses kept her up half the night? Yes, but by the time dawn had streaked across the sky, she had managed to convince herself that she had imagined her strange, overpowering reaction to Harding Casey. So much for that theory.

''Elizabeth?'' he asked. ''Are you all right?''

No. Definitely not. ''Sure,'' she said, forcing a lightness she didn't feel into her tone. ''I'm fine.''

''Then, you don't want another cup of coffee?'' he

asked, nodding his head toward the impatient-looking waiter standing alongside their table.

Lord. Apparently a simple touch of Harding's hand could send her into a zombielike state where she didn't even hear conversations going on around her. How long had the two of them been waiting for her attention?

"Actually," she said, pushing her nearly empty cup to one side. "I'd love another, thanks."

Harding nodded at the young man, who shook his head in exasperation before picking up her cup and moving off.

"So where were you?" he asked when they were alone again.

"What do you mean?" Dumb. She knew exactly what he meant.

He smiled knowingly. "Your body was here, but your mind was someplace else entirely. Thinking up new recipes?"

"All right. I mean, yes." It was better than anything she could come up with at the moment.

He nodded slowly. "I guess your ideas must come to you all the time."

"Oh, yes," she answered honestly. "My imagination is always active." Way *too* active at times, but she didn't need to tell him that.

"Mike tells me that you're making the wedding cake."

With the conversation moving to safe ground, Elizabeth smiled and breathed a sigh of relief. "I couldn't let my own sister get married with just any old cake, could I?"

''No, I suppose not.'' He folded his large, callused hands together on the bright yellow tabletop. ''Still, it's a lot of work, isn't it?''

Elizabeth, despite her best intentions, was staring at those hands of his, imagining what it would be like to feel them moving over her flesh. Stroking. Caressing. Exploring.

''Elizabeth?''

''Hmm?'' She snapped out of her dangerous daydream and caught his wary stare.

''Are you *sure* everything's all right?''

''I'm fine, Sergeant Major,'' she said firmly, determined to get past this ridiculous fascination she had for him. ''As to the cake—'' she sincerely *hoped* they had still been talking about the cake when she zoned out ''—it will take some time, but it will be worth it.''

''I can hardly wait to taste it,'' he said softly.

Unwillingly her gaze shifted to his mouth. A slow chill slithered up her spine, and she shivered. Thankfully, the waiter chose just that moment to appear, drinks in hand.

Setting them down in front of her and Harding, the young man gave her another glance, then moved away quickly.

Terrific. Even strangers were noticing her odd behavior. What had happened to all of the strong words she'd thrown at him the night before? Wasn't she the one who had said that she could outlast any Marine? Wasn't she the one who had said that spending a week with him wouldn't bother her in the slightest?

Well, it had only been two days, and not only was she bothered, she was *hot* and bothered.

"So," Harding asked, picking up the fire-engine red cup, "what am I having?"

"I beg your pardon?"

"I told him to bring me one of whatever you were drinking. It seemed easier than trying to decipher that menu."

She smiled. True, there were far too many different types of drinks listed on the chalkboard over the counter. Being a creature of habit, Elizabeth always ordered the tried and true. "It's café mocha."

He raised his cup to his lips, sniffed, smiled and tasted. "It's good."

"Darn right," she said, taking a sip herself. "It's chocolate. Hard not to be good."

"Mike told me you were a fanatic about chocolate."

"*Fanatic* is a hard word."

"But appropriate?"

She smiled. "Definitely."

"And is the wedding cake chocolate?"

"On the inside, you bet. The outside will be traditional white...with a few surprising elements."

"A lot like the chef, then. Traditional, but with surprises."

"What do you mean?"

He reached across the table and captured one of her hands. Instantly a jolt of electricity skittered up the length of her arm. Judging by the flash of awareness in his eyes, Harding had felt it, too.

"That's what I'm talking about," he said softly.

''Every time I touch you, I feel it. Something out of the ordinary. Something surprising. Startling.''

She pulled her hand free, not because she wanted to, but because it was the only prudent move. ''I thought we decided last night, that this...*thing* between us wasn't going to go anywhere.''

''I know what we said.'' He spoke softly, keeping his already-deep voice pitched to a level that made her think of moonlight. Firelight. Naked passion. ''But this is damned hard to ignore.''

''We have to try.'' She held her coffee cup in both hands and took a long sip before continuing. ''Look, Harding,'' she said, ''we're not kids. We don't have to give in to what is basically just a hormonal urge.'' Just the thought of surrender, though, brought another chill to her spine.

''Is that all it is?'' he whispered.

''It's all it can be.'' She pulled a deep breath into her lungs and prayed that her voice would be steady when she spoke again. ''Neither one of us is interested in a relationship. You're a career Marine—and though there's nothing *wrong* with that—''

''Gee, thanks.''

''I grew up in the military. I've had enough.''

''I didn't ask you to marry me.''

She blushed. Dammit, she could feel heat and color race up her neck and blossom in her cheeks. Served her right. He *hadn't* suggested any long-term relationship. All he had talked about was their obvious attraction for each other. Hardly a declaration of undying love, for goodness' sake.

What was wrong with her, anyway? She hadn't felt

so clumsy and nervous around a man since she was seventeen. And this was no time to lose her sense of balance.

"You're right." Elizabeth forced a choked laugh past the knot in her throat. "You didn't. And if you had, I would have said no."

Something flickered in his eyes, but was gone before she could identify it. He nodded slowly, his mouth grim. "So, what's the problem with talking about whatever this is that's going on between us?"

"It's pointless, Harding," she said. "And dangerous."

"How do you figure?" His index finger curled through the handle of the coffee cup. He lifted it, took a drink and waited for her answer.

"Neither one of us wants this relationship to last beyond Mike and Terry's wedding, right?"

"Yeah, but—" he shrugged again and set the cup down "—we'll probably be seeing each other off and on for years as we visit them."

Years. Years of torture. Years of watching him. Wanting him. Swell.

"All the more reason to stop this before it starts," she told him briskly. "If we were to give in to this...*thing,* imagine how awkward the situation would be every time we met."

One corner of his mouth turned up in a half smile. Damn. Why did he have to be so good-looking? Why couldn't Mike's best friend have been a one-eyed troll with a bad leg?

"You don't think this is awkward already?"

''Difficult, not awkward. Awkward is making polite conversation with someone you've seen naked.''

Now she couldn't mistake the emotion flaring up in his eyes. Desire. Instantaneous, combustible desire. She recognized it immediately, because she was feeling the same thing. Just the thought of Harding Casey, naked, invading her body with his own, was enough to start small tingles of expectation thrumming in her center. She shifted uncomfortably in the seat.

A long, tension-filled minute passed before Harding tore his gaze from hers. ''You're right,'' he said.

''I am?'' She cleared her throat. ''About what in particular?''

''About this. Talking about it. Thinking about it. It's pointless. Not to mention frustrating as hell.'' He stood up abruptly. Checking the total on their check, he pulled a bill from his pants pocket, tossed it onto the table and said, ''We'd better get going, Elizabeth.'' Picking up their packages, he held his free hand out to her, to help her up.

She stared at it for a long moment, then lifted her gaze to his. If she put her hand in his, the flames would ignite, and they would be right back where they started.

''Oh,'' he said, finally understanding her hesitation. ''Yeah. Okay.'' His hand fell to his side, and he stepped back, giving her plenty of room to walk past him into the milling crowds.

Safety in numbers, Elizabeth told herself. As long as they surrounded themselves with people, neither of them would be tempted to give in to what they both really wanted.

A long, hot, incredibly satisfying night of lovemaking.

Mentally grasping for a change in subject, she blurted, "What else has Mike told you about me?"

Anaheim Stadium was crowded. Too early in the season for the Angels' die-hard fans to be disgusted at yet another lost chance at the Pennant, the stands were filled with people telling each other that this year would be *the* year.

Harding looked to his right briefly. Mike and Terry were so wrapped up in each other, they probably hadn't noticed that the game was half-over. Shifting his gaze, he looked at the woman sitting on his left. Three days. He'd only known her for three days...and yet, it felt like forever. He hardly remembered a time when he hadn't had the image of her soft brown eyes in his mind. Her scent haunted him and every moment spent with her was a strange combination of pleasure and torture.

No woman had ever affected him like this.

Elizabeth made a notation on the score book page of the program laying across her lap, then shouted at the home plate umpire.

"If you can't see any better than that, I'll give you a ride home. You shouldn't be driving!"

Harding suppressed a chuckle and only half heard the man sitting behind them mutter, "You tell 'im, lady!"

Who would have guessed that Elizabeth Stone, the Princess of Party Cooking, was such a rabid baseball fan? Sure, Mike had told him that she enjoyed the game…but she actually kept score. Not just listing home runs, but pitcher substitutions, pinch runners…everything.

He smiled to himself as she reached up to push her hair behind her ears. Her gold hoop earrings winked in the glare of the overhead stadium lights. Harding curled his fingers into his palms to keep himself from touching her. All day, every day, he had been quelling that impulse. And it wasn't getting any easier.

His body tightened. He clenched his jaw at the discomfort. A discomfort he was becoming all too accustomed to.

He stood up abruptly, and Elizabeth looked at him.

"I'm going for something to eat," he said, more gruffly than he had intended. "You want anything?"

She glanced at Mike and Terry. Her sister was leaning in to accept her fiancé's kiss. Muttering under her breath, Elizabeth stood, laid her program on her seat and said, "I'll come with you."

So much for getting a little distance, he told himself. Glancing over his shoulder, he asked, "Mike. You two want anything?"

Mike didn't even look up. He just shook his head and kissed Terry again. Grumbling softly, Harding stepped out onto the stepped aisle and followed Elizabeth to the upper level. He tried to keep his gaze from locking onto the seductive sway of her bottom in those worn jeans. But he failed.

The line at the snack bar was ten people deep. They joined the crowd silently, Harding standing directly in back of her. An inch or so of space separated them, and still he could feel the heat emanating from her and taunting him with her nearness.

Where had all of his resistance gone? What had happened to the man who had insisted that he could spend a week in this woman's company without giving in to desire? Humph. The answer was easy. Three days into the week, that fool of a man was discovering that he was feeling something *more* than desire. Something that wouldn't be ignored and apparently had no intention of going away.

''Enjoying the game?'' she asked over the noisy hum of the crowd.

''Not as much as you are,'' he said. Conversation was good. Maybe talking would help keep his mind too occupied for dangerous daydreams.

She glanced at him over her shoulder and smiled. ''Baseball was the one thing my father and I shared. We never stayed in one place long enough to call any team 'ours,' so we always cheered for the Yankees. Since I moved to California, I've finally got a home team to root for. The Angels beak my heart annually, but I won't give up on them.''

''Never surrender?''

''Exactly.''

The crowd moved as one, inching closer to the snack counter. Mingled scents of popcorn, roasting hot dogs and beer floated in the air.

Someone jostled Elizabeth, pushing her backward, into Harding. Her bottom brushed against his already aching groin, and he sucked in a gulp of air in response. He grabbed her upper arms and held her still. If she moved again, he was a dead man.

''Harding,'' she muttered, pressing herself closer against him. ''This isn't working.''

''Tell me about it.'' His teeth ground together when she leaned into him.

''I'll never last out the week.''

He dipped his head to whisper in her ear. ''Me, either.''

She shivered slightly as his breath brushed across her skin. He dropped one hand to her waist. Sliding his arm around her front, he held her tightly to him.

Elizabeth let her head fall back onto his chest. Her eyes closed as she concentrated on the feel of his hard readiness pressed against her bottom. She shifted her hips slightly and felt his quick intake of breath.

''How hungry are you?'' he whispered, once more tickling her flesh with his breath.

She licked suddenly dry lips. It didn't matter that they were standing in the middle of a rowdy crowd. If anything, that fact only made their private dance more exciting. Dangerous.

During the last few moments, she had forgotten all about the baseball game, the snack bar, even her sister and Mike, still sitting in the stands. For now, all she knew or cared about was the man holding her. The man whose touch electrified her. The man she wanted more than she wanted her next breath.

It was pointless to deny this attraction. This desire. Even now the flames of passion were licking at her center, stirring her senses into a whirlwind of need that threatened to choke off her air.

''I'm not hungry, Harding,'' she answered softly. ''Not for a hot dog, anyway.''

"Then let's get out of here," he muttered thickly. Keeping one arm around her waist, he guided her through the crowd until they were clear. He kept walking until they were half-hidden behind a concrete pillar.

Every breath strained her lungs to the bursting point. Elizabeth looked up into his eyes, then lifted one hand to cup his cheek. "This is crazy, Harding. We've only known each other three days."

He turned his face into her hand, kissing the palm. Lifting one hand, he captured hers and squeezed it before saying, "We *met* three days ago. But we've heard about each other for a year now."

"Still..." She shook her head, some rational corner of her mind trying to deny what was happening.

"I know your favorite color is blue," he whispered. "You hate cats, love dogs and always wanted three children—two boys and a girl."

She swallowed heavily before speaking. "I know you have no family beyond the Corps. You kill plants by overwatering them, and you like your coffee black with two sugars."

He gave her a slow, lopsided smile. "We're not strangers, Elizabeth. From the moment we met, I knew this was where we were headed."

Her heartbeat skittered, then accelerated, slamming against her rib cage. Every inch of her body felt as though it was on fire. She ran the pad of her thumb across his lips, and when his tongue darted out to taste her flesh, she gasped, feeling the intimate caress down to the soles of her feet.

"I knew it, too, Harding," she managed to say. "And I don't want to fight it anymore."

He groaned slightly and moved in even closer to her, until they were both hidden in the shadows. "Fighting's not what I have in mind," he whispered. Then he dipped his head and claimed her mouth for the kiss they'd both been waiting for.

She sagged against him, offering herself up to the flames of desire raging through her. His tongue parted her lips and swept inside her mouth, stealing what was left of her breath and charging her with a hum of energy that lit up her insides like a fireworks display.

Time stopped. His fingers speared through her hair at the sides of her head and held her still for his gentle assault on her senses. Every stroke of his tongue brought new sensations, sharper pangs of need. She met him, touch for touch, caress for caress, their tongues twining together in an ancient dance of desire.

A distant roar of applause and cheers from the stadium crowd finally broke them apart, reminding them both where they were. Harding took a half step backward, clearly reluctant to leave her.

"I'll go back to our seats," he said softly. "Tell Mike and Terry that you're not feeling well. I'm going to take you home."

She nodded, her throat too full to speak, her emotions too near the surface. She could still taste him. Running her tongue lightly over her lips, Elizabeth shivered as his gaze followed the sultry motion. There was no way she would be able to simply sit and watch a baseball game. Not now. Not when her body was alive with expectation.

"Wait here," he told her. "I'll be back in a minute."

He turned, took a step, then stopped. Looking back at her, Harding stared directly into her eyes for a long, slow minute. Finally he asked, "Are you sure this is what you want, Elizabeth?"

There it was. Her chance to call a halt to this insanity that had overtaken them. With the word *No* she knew Harding would escort her back to her seat, and they could go on as they had been…each pretending that this magic between them didn't exist. Each trying to forget what had happened in the past few stolen moments.

"Hurry back, Harding," she whispered brokenly, making the only decision she could.

Six

The twenty-five-minute drive from the stadium to her condo had never seemed so long before. Freeway miles flew past, but once on the side streets, they were caught by every red light.

Elizabeth shifted in the Mustang's bucket seat and shot a glance at the man beside her. Immediately, her stomach began to pitch and turn. She wasn't regretting her decision—but the strained silence arching between them made the whole situation a bit...strange. She'd never known such passionate urgings before she'd met Harding Casey. But then, she'd never known a man like him before, either.

Spirals of need curled within her, prompting another uncomfortable shift in her seat. Her favorite jeans felt too tight. Too constraining. The seat belt slashing across her front pressed against her breasts, increasing the ache already planted by want. She bit her lip and groaned her frustration when yet another red light stopped them only a few blocks from her condo.

"Think somebody's trying to tell us something?" Harding asked tightly.

She looked at him sharply. Was *he* regretting their hasty decision to leave the ballpark for her house?

"Changing your mind, Harding?" Somehow, she squeezed those words past the knot in her throat, then held her breath as she waited for his answer.

He turned his head to look at her, and she knew immediately that nothing had changed. Even in the darkness his eyes seemed to burn with the same fires streaking through her. His right hand dropped from the steering wheel. He reached across the automatic gearshift, laying his palm on her left leg. Slowly, firmly, he stroked her thigh. She felt the heat of his touch slip through the worn denim fabric and sink down into her bones. She held her breath as his hand moved to her inner thigh.

"What do you think, Elizabeth?" he asked quietly, shifting his hand until his fingers cupped her aching center.

Breath rushed from her lungs. She stared into his eyes and saw her own need and hunger reflected back at her. His fingers smoothed up and down over the denim stretched across the joining of her thighs. His gaze held hers, refusing to let her look away. The lake blue of his eyes darkened with every ragged breath she drew, and when she parted her legs farther, she watched his features tighten.

The driver behind them honked his horn, demanding they notice that the light had turned green. Elizabeth squelched a groan threatening to erupt from her chest. She didn't want him to stop touching her. She suddenly couldn't bear the thought of not having his hands on her.

Harding scowled into his rearview mirror and stepped on the gas. He guided the responsive car with one hand on the wheel. Though he kept his eyes on the road, his right hand continued to torture Elizabeth. As if responding to a need as deep as her own, he didn't break the contact between them.

She let her head loll against the seat back, and she closed her eyes to the streetlights whizzing past. In the enclosed shelter of his car, it was as though the entire world had disappeared, leaving only the two of them.

As the Mustang slowed down again, she thought she heard him mutter a curse, but she wasn't sure. She wasn't sure of anything beyond the incredible sensation of his fingers moving on her body.

The Mustang's engine hummed as they waited out another red light. Elizabeth turned her head and opened her eyes to look at him. Their gazes locked and held as she felt his nimble fingers undoing the button fly of her jeans.

"Harding," she whispered, suddenly all too aware of the cars behind and alongside them. True, it was dark, but what if someone saw them anyway? "You can't—"

"I already have," he countered, and slid his fingertips down over her abdomen and beneath the band of her panties.

"Oh, my," she gasped and lifted her hips, unconsciously helping him toward his goal.

"Oh, Elizabeth," he said softly. His fingertips slowly caressed her damp heat—without the barrier of her jeans.

Embarrassed, excited and tortured almost to the breaking point, she looked away from him, directing a blank stare toward the traffic streaming across the intersection in front of them. Dangerous, her mind screamed. Scandalous.

She was allowing a man to make love to her while they sat at a red light on Beach Boulevard. What was worse, she had no intention of stopping him.

What was happening to her? Where was the safe, sane woman she had always been? She grabbed the armrest, curling her fingers into the padded black vinyl. The stream of traffic in front of her blurred. Half closing her eyes, she bit down hard on her bottom lip to keep from crying out at his tender, intimate touch.

"Not much farther," he said as the light turned green and they were able to go again.

She nodded, swallowed, then heard herself say, "Hurry, Harding. Hurry."

His fingertips found her most sensitive spot. Unable to help herself, she moaned softly and spread her legs wider in response. She lifted her hips off the seat slightly, instinctively trying to draw him in farther. But the strong denim fabric would only give so far.

Frustration and expectation warred within her. She glanced at him again and noted the taut lines of strain etched into his face. Shifting for a quick look at her surroundings, Elizabeth saw that they were only a block or two from her house now.

So close.

And still so far.

She leaned toward him as far as her seat belt would allow. Harding shot her a look from the corner of his eye as she came nearer.

"Elizabeth?"

The deep rumble of his voice filled the car, but she didn't answer him. Instead, she laid one hand on his powerfully muscled thigh and felt it tighten reflexively. His fingers clenched around the steering wheel. Running her palm lightly up and down the inside of his thigh, she tried to share the incredible sensations he was showering on her. Her fingers brushed across his groin as he made the left turn into her condominium complex.

He muttered something unintelligible as he reluctantly pulled his hand free of her jeans and maneuvered the car into a parking slot in front of her condo. Yanking on the emergency brake, he turned off the engine, snatched the keys out of the ignition, then got out of the car. She fumbled with the buttons on her jeans and still had her own door open before he arrived.

Reaching into the car, he helped her out, kept a tight hold on her hand and marched up the flower-lined walkway to her front door, Elizabeth stepping quickly to keep up with him.

She tried to get the key into the dead-bolt lock three times before Harding took it from her, slid it home and turned it, opening the door in a rush. They stepped inside, he slammed the door, set the lock again and grabbed for her.

Elizabeth clutched at his shoulders in the dimly lit foyer. His hands were everywhere. Touching, caressing. He lifted the hem of her shirt and dragged it up and over her head. She shook her hair back from her face and reached for the buttons on his uniform.

''This is crazy,'' she whispered as the last button was freed.

''Completely nuts,'' he agreed, shrugging out of his shirt, then pulling his white undershirt off as well.

''We're not thinking,'' she muttered, and gasped as his knuckles brushed her skin. He undid the front clasp of her bra, then pushed it off her shoulders so he could admire her breasts unhampered. ''We should be thinking.''

''Probably,'' he said, lifting one of her breasts and rubbing his thumb across the distended nipple.

''Ohh....'' She moaned helplessly, took his free hand and placed it on her other breast. Shudders wracked her body as ribbons of pleasure swirled through her. ''What if we regret this tomorrow, Harding?''

He bent his head, drew one nipple into his mouth and slowly, lovingly, circled it with his tongue. After too brief a time, he straightened again. ''It'd still be worth it,'' he whispered.

Lifting her hands to his broad, naked chest, her fingers entwined themselves in the dark hair sprinkled across his flesh. His shining, silver dog tags tinkled musically as she stroked his skin. Her thumbs dusted over his flat nipples, and he groaned, grabbing her to him tightly.

Sliding his fingers into her hair, he tipped her head back and held her for his kiss. His mouth came down on hers like a dying man who'd been offered a last drink of water. His tongue plundered her mouth, taking all she had to offer and silently demanding more.

Everything in her was on fire. She felt the rush of passion building into an inferno and gave herself over to the flames. Clutching at him, she dug her fingernails into his shoulders and hung on as if he was the only steady point in her universe. Whatever it was that lay between them, it was more powerful than anything she had ever known. Though her mind still worried about what she was doing, her body knew it was right.

She twisted slightly in his arms, rubbing her breasts against his chest, loving the feel of her own soft flesh brushing over his hard muscles. She luxuriated in the feel of his strong arms wrapped around her bare back. Then one of his hands dropped to her behind, pulling her tightly to his hard readiness, and she groaned again, louder this time.

She needed him now.

She had to feel him entering her body, becoming one with her.

"Harding," she gasped as she broke their kiss.

"Now," he muttered, and buried his face in the curve of her neck and shoulder.

"Yes," she whispered. "Upstairs. First door."

He lifted her easily, and she didn't even have time to enjoy the sensation of being carried before he set her on her feet beside the queen-size bed. He took a step back and tore at his belt buckle.

Frantic now, Elizabeth unbuttoned her jeans and pushed them and her panties down her legs, only to be stopped by her running shoes. Hurriedly she toed her shoes off, then kicked off her pants. She turned to face him and stared silently. He was more amazing than she had expected. Tall and muscular, his body was a testament to the rigorous training of the Marine Corps.

Her gaze dropped to his groin, and she felt a momentary pang of worry when she realized how large and ready he was.

But then he came to her, sweeping her into the circle of his arms and laying her down onto the mattress. And at once, the inferno between them leaped into life again. She parted her legs as he moved over her and positioned himself between her thighs. She felt the featherlight touch of his hands smoothing up and down the insides of her legs. The tips of his fingers explored her most tender flesh, dipping in and out of the moist heat of her body until Elizabeth was ready to shatter into a million tiny pieces.

''Harding,'' she gasped, looking up into his darkened blue eyes. ''Harding, I need...''

''Just what I need, Elizabeth,'' he finished for her, and came up on his knees. Slipping his hands beneath her, he lifted her hips slightly and drove himself home.

She arched into him, her head digging into the mattress, her arms up, blindly reaching for him. He shifted, moving his hands to the mattress on either side of her head. Bracing himself, he leaned over her, stared down into her wide eyes and moved within her.

Over and over, he retreated and advanced, hurtling them both ever closer to the mindless explosion of sensation awaiting them. She felt it building, humming along her nerve endings, toying with her. Teasing her with its nearness. Her fingers clenched tightly behind his neck, she rocked her hips in time with his, their dance racing to its conclusion.

When the first tremor shook her, she held him tighter, closer. Taking a deep breath, she threw herself over the edge of caution and into the whirlpool of release. Each rippling explosion of satisfaction rocked her harder than the one before. She cried out as her pleasure crested, and held him tighter still when he stiffened, moaned her name and emptied himself inside her.

Harding had never known anything like it. His groin ached with satisfaction, and already, a new, stronger need was rising up within him. The blood rushed through his veins and his own heartbeat thundered in his ears.

She moved beneath him, and he immediately levered himself up onto his elbows.

"Don't," she said quickly.

"Don't what?"

"Don't pull away yet."

His body hardened and thickened inside her. Her damp, tight warmth surrounded him, and he felt as though he would never leave the sanctuary he had found. Instinctively he rocked his hips against her, showing her without words that he had no intention of pulling away from her.

Her hands slid up and down his back, and everywhere she touched came alive. Her palms dusted his flesh and he groaned quietly. "I want you again," he whispered, and bent to take one of her nipples into his mouth.

She arched against him, and he grazed the distended bud with the edges of his teeth. His tongue worked her nipple, circling, flicking at the tender flesh with short strokes.

"This can't be happening again," she said on a half sigh. "So soon..."

"Again," he whispered as he lifted his head and looked down into her eyes. "And again and again. I can't get enough of you, Elizabeth. The taste of you, the feel of you." He pushed his body deeper inside her, enjoying the sparkle of pleasure he saw flickering in her eyes. She wanted him as badly as he did her. That knowledge fed the flames of his own passion.

Harding wrapped his arms around her, and when he eased himself up onto his haunches, he kept her with him, his body buried within her. She straddled him, her legs on either side of his thighs. Wiggling her hips slightly, she took him even deeper inside as his hands dropped to her hips.

Her head fell back, and Harding looked his fill of her. In the moonlight streaming through the second-story window, her brown hair glimmered and shone. Curls fell in a tangled mass around her head, and her gold hoops swung in abandon, making her look like some ancient, pagan goddess—naked but for the gold at her ears.

His hands encompassed her narrow waist briefly before he allowed one of his hands to slide down her abdomen to the nest of pale brown curls at the juncture of her thighs. She tensed, waiting. He smiled to himself and stroked her most sensitive spot.

She straightened up on his lap, shifting her hips from side to side, cradling his body with hers. Her hands at his shoulders, she bent to claim his mouth, and this time he let her be the aggressor. She branded him with strokes of her tongue, stealing his breath and giving him hers.

Unable to wait another moment, Harding placed both hands on her hips. Then, guiding her, he helped her move on him. Each time she took him inside her, he felt his world shift. When completion roared toward them, he clamped his mouth to hers, devouring her sighs and muffling his own shout of satisfaction.

She didn't remember moving, but when she opened her eyes again, she was lying on fresh, cool sheets, the quilt pulled neatly over her.

And Harding.

She glanced down at her waist and laid one hand on the arm he had wrapped around her. Her body still humming with the lingering effects of their lovemaking, she was embarrassed to admit—even to herself—that she wanted more. Needed more.

"Awake?" he asked quietly.

"Uh-huh," she said on a sigh. "What time is it?"

"Around midnight."

Nodding, she turned in his arms until she could see him.

Bracing himself on one elbow, Harding looked down at her steadily. Somberly.

A warning sounded somewhere deep inside her. Whatever afterglow she was experiencing, Harding apparently wasn't.

''What is it?'' she managed to ask.

He frowned slightly, released her long enough to rub one hand across his face, then said, ''We have to talk.''

Something cold slithered along her spine. She pulled the sheet up higher over her breasts, scooted a couple of inches away from him. ''If you're thinking about apologizing to me, don't.''

''Elizabeth...''

''I mean it, Harding.'' Strange how quickly a glow could disappear. Stranger still how much colder she felt now that it was gone. ''We're both grown-ups. We knew what we were doing.''

''Not entirely.''

She pulled a bit farther away from him, pushed her hair out of her eyes and asked, ''What's that supposed to mean?''

''We didn't take any precautions,'' he said flatly.

''Precau—'' Good heavens. Her stomach dropped, and she thought she even felt her heartbeat skitter a bit as the implications of what he was saying sunk in.

Sitting up, she crossed her legs Indian style and clutched the quilt to her like a frightened virgin. Despite the situation, she almost laughed. A bit late for trying to protect her virtue.

"I don't see a damn thing funny in this," he pointed out.

"Not funny," she corrected. "Ridiculous. Embarrassing."

"Embarrassing?"

"Of course. These days, any teenager knows better than to do what we just did!"

He pushed himself off the mattress and began to pace. "I don't suppose you take the Pill?" he asked on one of his trips around the room.

"No," she said, shaking her head. "There didn't seem to be any point." Flopping back against the headboard, she frowned and admitted wryly, "I don't exactly have what you would call a busy love life."

He stopped dead and looked at her, one eyebrow lifted into a high arch.

"Sure, tonight," she shot at him. "But before you there was only—" She broke off and stared at him.

"What?"

"Is that what your concern is for? Trying to find out if I've got anything *contagious?*"

"Dammit, Elizabeth."

"Rest easy, Harding." She clumsily got out of bed, still dragging that quilt with her. Wrapping it around her, she tossed the tail end of the blanket over one shoulder, lifted her chin and said, "I'm completely safe. I've only been with one other man and—"

"One?"

A flush of heat stormed up her neck and stained her cheeks. "Apparently I've given you the wrong impression, here. Believe me, the way I acted with you tonight is not my normal behavior. I don't ordinarily hop into the sack with someone I've known for three days.''

''That's not what I meant—''

''I can understand why you might not want to believe me, what with the evidence all to the contrary...''

''Elizabeth,'' he said, and took a step toward her.

She jumped backward. As insulting as his comment had been, she didn't trust herself if he was to touch her. Damn his eyes, anyway, she would probably melt into him and find herself flat on her back again.

He took a deep breath before speaking in a slow, too calm voice, ''I didn't mean that. I was only surprised that a woman like you—''

''Fast and loose?''

''Dammit, stop putting words in my mouth!''

Her bottom lip trembled, and she bit down on it, hard. She wasn't going to cry, blast it. Not now. Not in front of him.

Harding saw the sheen of unshed tears swimming in her eyes and cringed inwardly. Damn, he'd made a mess of this. When he'd awakened with her in his arms, he had experienced an inner peace that he had never known before. Staring down at her features while she slept, his mind had taken an incredibly wild turn.

His imagination had leaped from this one night of passion to a lifetime of promises and children. Just the thought of it had terrified him—and yet, somehow intrigued him almost as much. *That* was the moment he had realized that he'd been a careless idiot.

Children? A baby?

Hell, how could he *not* have used a damn condom? Fine, he had the excuse of being somewhat out of practice. He'd been living a practically celibate life since his divorce. One-night stands didn't interest him—and anything more might have led to a relationship. Definitely something he didn't want.

Even the threat of which he'd managed to avoid neatly.

Until Elizabeth Stone.

Gritting his teeth, he started toward her again, determined to say his piece. She backed up, her feet tangling in the quilt she clutched to her chest as if it was Superman's cape. Her balance dissolved, and she swung one arm wide, searching for a handhold. Before she could fall, Harding caught her, dragging her up tight against him.

"Let me go."

"Not yet," he said, and lifted her chin with his thumb and forefinger until she was looking at him. Those eyes of hers mesmerized him. The deep brown color shimmered beneath a teary film. He wanted to hold her, kiss her, make love to her again until they rekindled the fire between them. Instead, though, he said, "All I meant was that I couldn't believe there were so many stupid men in the world." Not that he was complaining. He much preferred the fact that there hadn't been many men in her life.

She stopped twisting and wriggling to get free.

"A woman as beautiful and warm as you should be fighting them off with a stick."

"I have," she said pointedly.

"Until me." He smiled sadly. It wasn't an easy

thing, knowing that he had allowed his hormones to rage so out of control that he'd put her at risk.

She stiffened in his arms. "Harding, let me go."

"Not until I say what I started to say before."

"Which is *what* exactly?"

The watery film in her eyes had dissipated some, to be replaced by a flash of anger. Anger, he knew, was much easier to deal with.

"Elizabeth, I wasn't worrying about diseases." Hadn't it occurred to her yet? Apparently not. He paused, still holding her gaze with his own. "I was thinking more along the lines of a *baby.*"

Her jaw dropped.

"Oh, my God," she whispered.

"Is there a chance?" he asked.

"Of course there's a *chance,*" she muttered, moving away from him as his hold eased up. Sitting down on the edge of the bed, she continued to talk. "Not much of one, probably. It was only the one time."

"Two times."

She flushed again. "Two."

He hadn't known that there were still women who blushed. "I'm sorry, Elizabeth, this is all my fault."

"Stop saying you're sorry," she snapped.

"What?"

"I mean it, Harding." Glaring up at him, she went on. "Tonight happened because we *both* wanted it. You're in the clear, Sergeant Major."

The clear? Did she expect him to disappear? Leave her to pay whatever consequences might arise because of tonight? A strong surge of anger shot through him. "What the hell does that mean?"

''That means that if I hear another apology from you, I'll scream.'' She scooted back onto the bed, wrapped in the cocoon of her quilt. ''Will you please leave, now?''

He inhaled sharply and blew the air out of his lungs in an exasperated rush. Staring at her, he saw that she had closed herself off from him as effectively as if she had slammed a door in his face. There wouldn't be any talking to her tonight. Not if he expected her to listen. *Really* listen.

Fine then. They could talk tomorrow. When she would hopefully be reasonable. Bending down, he snatched at his clothes and hurriedly pulled them on. Glancing at her, he noted that she kept her gaze averted.

In a matter of minutes he was standing beside the bed, waiting for her to acknowledge him. Finally she shot him a look from the corner of her eye.

''We'll talk about this tomorrow. I'll call you in the morning.''

''I'll call you,'' she countered firmly, ''when I'm ready to talk about it.''

Harding bent down, picked her up by the shoulders and planted a hard, quick kiss on her lips. Briefly he thought he felt her kiss him back, but then her defenses went up and she turned into a block of wood. Disappointed, he dropped her back onto the bed, turned and marched to the door. There he stopped, pointed at her and ordered, ''Zero nine thirty hours, Elizabeth. You pick up the damned phone.''

Seven

She pulled up to the main gate at Camp Pendleton just as dawn was streaking the sky. Sparing a quick glance for the deep rose-colored clouds, she turned her complete attention on the young Marine guard standing beside her car. She must be getting old, she thought. The kid didn't look more than nineteen. She rolled down the window.

"Can I help you, ma'am?" he asked.

Boy, she hated being called ma'am. Dismissing the distraction, she got straight to the business that had brought her to the Marine base.

"I'd like to see Sergeant Major Harding Casey, please."

"Yes, ma'am," the Marine said, his gaze drifting over a paper attached to the clipboard he carried. "Is he expecting you?"

''No,'' she confessed. ''He's not.''

''Which battalion is he with, ma'am? I'll have to call the Sergeant Major before letting you in.''

Battalion. Dammit. Of course they would have to know which battalion. And which regiment. Why hadn't she thought of that? She'd been raised on Marine bases. She knew firsthand the thoroughness of the gate guards.

And she didn't have the slightest idea which battalion Harding was assigned to.

Lifting one hand, she rubbed her forehead right between her eyes. Her head was pounding, and her eyes felt gritty from lack of sleep. All night, she'd lain awake, remembering everything that had passed between Harding Casey and her. Everything from the incredible passion and closeness they'd shared, to the moment when he'd destroyed the magic by apologizing and then capping that off with an order to answer her telephone.

Just who the hell did Hard Case Casey think he was, anyway? One night of lovemaking...no matter how mind-shattering...did *not* give him authority over her.

But it *might* have given her a baby.

No, no, no. Don't even think it. The chances had to be astronomically slim. Surely the odds were with her. And yet, something inside her turned over. She had always wanted a child. Three, actually. And lately she had begun to think it would never happen. What if it *had,* now? What if she was pregnant this very moment? She glanced down at her flat belly, covered by the jeans Harding had manipulated so nicely the night before, and cautiously laid her palm protectively over it.

"Ma'am?" The young Marine cleared his throat meaningfully. "His battalion and regiment?"

"I don't know," she admitted, not sure what to do now.

He must have seen the indecision in her face because he almost smiled. "If you'll pull your car off to the side there, ma'am, I'll see what I can find out."

She did as she was told, turned the engine off and waited. Watching the Marine, she saw him step into the small cubicle inside the gate and reach for a phone. Before he could use it, though, another guard appeared from behind the building. The two men spoke in tones she couldn't quite hear, until the second Marine said loudly, with a glance in her direction, "A *woman* to see Hard Case?"

She didn't know whether to be relieved or insulted. But there was definitely a part of her delighted to hear that women weren't streaming in and out of this gate visiting Harding. Elizabeth watched the second guard grab the phone, speak to someone for a moment, then hang up. He walked to her car, briefly gave her directions to Harding's quarters, then smiled and stepped back out of her way.

As she steered her Toyota along the streets of the base, an eerie feeling began to creep over her. Though her father had never been stationed at Pendleton, the base was so much like all of the others she'd lived on, she felt almost as if she were coming home.

Memories rushed into her brain, and even the air seemed almost too thick to breathe. The drive to Harding's quarters became a short, personal tour of her past. She noticed tricycles and skateboards that had been left out on front lawns, and immediately remembered bravely pedaling her first two-wheeler down a sidewalk while her father ran along behind, tightly gripping the back of the bike to keep her safe.

She saw basketball hoops and chalk-marked sidewalks, which released the memory of her, Terry and her mother playing hopscotch on hot summer afternoons. Shadow pictures raced through her brain as she passed a tidy church, the PX, restaurants and the parade grounds. All of it so familiar.

Strange, but for years, whenever she thought about her childhood, all she remembered was the pain of always moving around—never belonging anywhere—constant uncertainty. Now, though, other images reared up and demanded to be noticed. The good times. And there had been many of them. Life on a military base wasn't always easy. But almost in compensation for the trials, came the joy of feeling as though you were part of a huge family. A family where each member looked out for the other. A family where arguments and old injuries were put aside in times of need.

An unexpected sheen of tears filled her eyes, and she was nearly blinded by the past. But she blinked them back as she pulled up in front of the senior staff NCO billeting barracks. Determinedly, she put her past where it belonged. She would need all of her wits about her during this little confrontation with Harding.

Especially since she wasn't at all sure what it was she'd come to say.

As if the thought of his name had conjured him up, a door in the barracks building opened and there he was. Standing on the threshold of his quarters with a frown on his face and his silver dog tags gleaming against his tanned flesh, he had one bare shoulder propped against the doorjamb, his arms folded across his chest. He had pulled on a pair of uniform trousers, but otherwise he was naked.

Instantly memories of the night before flitted through her already-tired brain. Elizabeth's mouth went dry, and she had to force herself to move suddenly shaky legs. Once out of the car, though, she walked directly to him without stumbling once.

She stepped past him, entering the apartment. He followed her in and silently closed the door. Taking a deep breath, she turned around slowly and her gaze collided with his.

''Good morning,'' he said. ''Zero nine thirty already?''

''No,'' she snapped, refusing to rise to the sarcasm. ''I had to talk to you and couldn't wait for my 'assigned time.'''

He looked mildly surprised, but he nodded and started for the kitchen. ''Come on. I think we're both going to need coffee.'' Over his shoulder, he added, ''Sorry, but I'm fresh out of café mocha.''

''I'll suffer,'' she countered and wanted to bite her tongue. If she expected to have a civilized conversation with the man, she shouldn't start by firing a warning shot.

The kitchen was small, barely big enough for two people. Faded green curtains graced the only window and on the tiny, two-seater table, was a plastic basket filled with apples and bananas.

While he started the coffee, she walked a slow circle around that table. "Look, Harding, I think there are a few things we have to get straight."

"I agree."

"Good." That was a start, wasn't it?

Finished, he turned, propped himself against the countertop and crossed his arms over his chest again. Above the gurgle and hiss of the coffeemaker, he asked, "So who goes first? You or me?"

"Me," she said quickly. "I've been thinking about this all night."

He gave her a slow nod, but his expression was unreadable.

She stopped behind one of two ladder-back wooden chairs. Curling her fingers over the top slat, she said firmly, "What you did last night was way out of line."

He smiled wryly. "I think we established *that* much before I left."

"I'm not talking about the sex," she snapped. "I'm talking about the way you apologized, took all responsibility, then walked out."

"You asked me to leave."

She waved that comment aside for the moment. "I'm a big girl, Harding. I make my own choices, and I take responsibility for those choices myself."

"Fine."

''And,'' she added, ''nobody *orders* me to be waiting at a telephone at a certain time and place.''

''All right.'' He half straightened and reached up to rub one hand across his hair. ''We're both to blame. Happy?''

''Yes, thanks.'' She sat down on the chair and waited while he poured them each a cup of coffee. When he was seated in the chair opposite her, he started talking before she could say another word.

''Look, Elizabeth,'' he said, and she knew she wasn't going to like whatever was coming next. ''I did some thinking last night, too. And whoever is to blame, what happened last night was a mistake. A big one.''

Even though she'd thought the same thing herself earlier, hearing him say it out loud sent an aching emptiness ricocheting around inside her.

''And,'' he went on, staring into his coffee cup as if looking for the right words, ''once this wedding is over, I think it's best if we don't see each other again.''

''You do?''

''Yeah.'' Leaving his drink untouched, he jumped up from the chair, walked the short distance to the sink, then turned around to face her. In the dish drainer behind him, there were one plate, one glass, one cup and one set of silverware left overnight to dry.

Rubbing a hand across his naked chest, he added, ''There's no point. Neither one of us wants a relationship, Elizabeth. If we keep seeing each other, it'll only cause a lot of pain.''

Speechless, she stared at him. Well, what had she expected? Hadn't she come to the base to tell him the same thing? Wasn't this the only reasonable solution to a situation that was already getting out of hand? Why, then, did it hurt to have him say it to her?

She took hold of her coffee cup with both hands and scrambled for something to say. "I thought Marines were supposed to be able to take pain." Did her voice really sound so soft and injured? Or was it only her imagination?

Harding crossed to her and squatted alongside her chair. Looking directly into her eyes, he said, "Yeah, we can take it. We just don't like *causing* it." Trying for a smile, he added, "Except of course, to the enemy."

How strange this all was. A week ago she had never met this man. Now she was sitting in his kitchen, talking about dissolving a relationship that didn't really exist, not knowing if she was or wasn't carrying his child.

"It's better this way, Elizabeth," he said softly and reached for one of her hands. He paused for a long moment before saying, "I deploy in less than a month."

Her gaze shot to his. Deployment. More memories rose up to kick her in the stomach. Memories of her father, gone for six months at a time. Summers missed, lonely Christmases, cards and letters and posing for pictures that Mom could send to Dad, so far away. She remembered occasional phone calls and listening to the sound of his voice, so faint and distant.

Visions of her mother, trying to be both mom and dad to Terry and her. Echoes of her mother's lonely tears when she thought her daughters were asleep. So many absences. So many missed birthdays and kisses and hugs. So many missed chances.

She swallowed back the images and forced herself to ask, "Where?"

Grimly he said, "Okinawa."

The other side of the world. In less than a month he would be thousands of miles away from her. Elizabeth nodded and pulled her hand free of his, missing the electrifying warmth of his touch even as she told herself to get used to missing it.

Unable to sit still a moment longer, she stood up and walked back into the small, neat living room. For the first time she noticed the military beige walls and carpets. So familiar and yet…so different.

Her mother had always prided herself on making all of the different quarters they'd lived in home. Photos, framed postcards, hers and Terry's artwork splashed across the refrigerator, rag rugs and always, fresh flowers. Things to let people know that a family lived there. People. Not just Marines.

Small personal touches that were sadly lacking in Harding's place.

A handful of framed photographs lined the mantel over an empty fireplace, and one lone plant stood limply in the corner. Otherwise the place might have been vacant.

Noting her observation, Harding said softly, "I don't keep a lot of *things.*" She turned to look at him. "And a man alone can't have pets." He half shrugged. ''When I'm deployed, who would I get to take care of a dog?''

Loneliness tinged his voice, and the sharp edge of it slashed at her. She wondered if he even knew it was there. ''At least you've got a plant. Mike told me you couldn't be trusted with one.''

One corner of his mouth lifted slightly. ''It's on loan from First Sergeant McCoy's wife. She said the apartment needed something alive in it. She'll nurse it back to health when I ship out.''

Elizabeth nodded, but her thoughts were already spinning. How different their homes were. His was empty. Hers was crammed full of things. *Things.* Not people. For years, she'd been concentrating on building the secure home she'd always longed for. She had gathered up furnishings and knickknacks as if they would be enough to anchor her. But except for Terry and an occasional visit with her parents, her life was empty of people.

A chill raced along her spine, and she shivered. Was she any better than Harding? Had she really made herself a home? Or had she only stacked her possessions high enough to hide the emptiness surrounding her?

Harding watched the play of emotions darting across her features and would have given anything to know what she was thinking. Having her arrive at the base, so unexpectedly, had been like a gift. He'd lain awake all night, thinking about her, worrying about what they might be starting, knowing he should distance himself from her and wondering how in the hell he would be able to do that without dying a little every day for the rest of his life.

How had the world managed to change so completely in so little time? And how could he ever go back to living without her?

She took a breath and it caught in her throat. A tiny, choking sound issued from her, and it was like a bayonet in his back, urging him to her. He crossed the few feet of worn carpet separating them and pulled her into his arms. She buried her face in his chest, and for several long moments Harding simply stood there, holding her. He inhaled her soft, flowery scent, drawing it deep into his lungs, as if he could keep it with him always. He stroked her short, curly hair and listened until her breathing settled into a steady rhythm again.

Looking down, he let go of her only long enough to cup her face in his hands. Smoothing his thumbs across her cheekbones, he was relieved to see she hadn't been crying. But there was something in her eyes—some change that he couldn't quite identify.

"Harding," she said softly, hesitantly, "what are we going to do?"

His gaze drifted over her features slowly, like the most loving of caresses. He would remember this moment, this woman for the rest of his life. Again, the pads of his thumbs brushed over her cheeks. His fingers brushed her hair at her temples. Soft. So soft. "I don't know, Elizabeth. I don't have any answers."

"Then let's not ask each other any more questions," she said thickly. Her palms slid up his chest, her fingertips outlining his flat nipples.

He squeezed his eyes shut at the featherlight strokes of her flesh on his. His groin tightened and he ached to be with her. Inside her.

No questions? No answers? Was that enough?

"Elizabeth," he ground out, "I'm still leaving in a month. Six months I'll be away."

She reached up and laid one hand across his mouth. "We have now, Harding. For whatever reasons, we have now."

"This will only make the leaving harder," he said, feeling that he should remind her that pain was the only possible outcome of their being together.

"But it will make the now so much easier," she said, and went up on her toes to kiss him.

Even a saint couldn't have resisted her kiss—and Harding Casey was no saint. He groaned in the back of his throat, and his arms closed around her, tightening until he felt the buttons of her jeans pressing into his belly. Slipping one hand down lower, he cupped her behind and pulled her hard against him. Another groan escaped from his throat, and he lowered his mouth to take hers.

Her lips parted for him, and his tongue swept into her warmth, claiming her, branding her with each stroke. She wrapped her arms around him, running her palms up and down his back, creating a friction of heat that shot through him with the force of a sustained artillery attack.

In seconds he was more hungry for her than he had been the night before. Now he knew what awaited him in her warmth. He had experienced the wonder of her and couldn't wait to find it again. Gasping for air, he broke their kiss, tossed her up and over his shoulder and headed for the bedroom.

As he walked, Elizabeth lavished kisses over his broad back. Then, sliding her hands down beneath the waistband of his trousers, she smoothed her palms over his behind, dragging her nails across his skin until he thought he might explode from want before he was even deep within her.

In his bedroom, Harding dipped to one side, flipped her onto his mattress and quickly helped her out of her clothes. As he stepped out of his pants, he yanked open the drawer in the bedside table and fumbled in its depths for a long minute. When he finally found one of the condoms he'd had stashed there for two years, he straightened up and slammed the drawer shut again.

This time they would do things right. This time there would be no chances taken. This time, he would care for her the way she should be cared for. He glanced at her and saw her watching him. Raking his gaze over her body, he felt his own stir and ache in readiness. He tore the foil slightly before her hand on his stopped him.

"Let me," she said and took the packet from him.

His groin tightened even further at the mental image of her hands on him, but he gritted his teeth and stood very still, waiting. She opened the packet, removed the condom and slowly positioned it over the sensitive tip of him. Harding sucked in air through clenched teeth and kept his gaze locked on her and what she was doing to him. Inch by glorious inch, she slid the fragile material down his length, smoothing and caressing as she went. When she was finished, she cupped him tenderly, her fingers stroking, exploring him. Harding's blood pounded in his veins, and his heartbeat sounded like the bass drums in the Marine Corps band.

"Enough," he growled and eased her down onto the bed. Parting her thighs, he looked his fill of her. His fingertips explored her opening, gently readying her for his entry. But her body was as tensely strung as his. She was molten heat, calling to him, urging him closer. A moment later he leaned over her and drove himself home. Her tight warmth surrounded him, and when he was buried deep within her, he allowed himself a groan of satisfaction at having found the wonder again.

Then need hammered at him as desperately as her fingernails raked across his back. Her hips lifted and fell, and her breath came hot on his neck.

Taking a handful of her hair, he pulled her head back gently, and stared down into the eyes that had been haunting him since his first sight of them.

"Whatever happens, Elizabeth, we will always have this between us. This...*magic.*"

He withdrew and plunged even deeper inside her. She gasped, shuddered, met his gaze and echoed, *"Magic."*

Desire and the flames of an all-consuming passion licked at them, driving them both to the conclusion that brought them each, however briefly, peace.

Eight

"We have *got* to stop meeting like this," Elizabeth said, her body still humming with the aftershocks of their lovemaking. She hadn't intended for this to happen again. All she had wanted to do was *talk* to him.

Harding rolled to one side, stifling a deep-throated groan as he moved. Grabbing a pillow, he jammed it beneath his head. Then, glancing at her, he agreed, "Too many more of these 'talks' and I'll be a dead man."

Pushing one hand through her hair, Elizabeth scooted backward until her back was propped against the headboard. She tugged one of the rumpled sheets up over her breasts and looked at the man lying beside her.

"This is nuts, Harding," she said with a quiet laugh.

"Don't I know it." Ruefully he shook his head, stood up and walked into the bathroom. A few seconds later he joined her on the bed again. Drawing her up close to his side, he kissed the top of her head. "So much for all of our fine notions about self-control."

"I don't know what it is about you, Marine," she said, and tucked her head underneath his chin. "But every time you touch me, I tend to burst into flames."

"I'm getting a little singed myself."

"What are we supposed to do about this, Harding?"

"Enjoy it while it lasts?"

She pushed back a bit and cocked her head to look at him. "Isn't that asking for trouble?"

"Not if we remember to be more careful than we were last night."

Elizabeth settled back against him and nodded slowly. Enjoy each other. Somehow it sounded so… empty. Ridiculous, she knew. After all, they were both adults.

"Regrets?" he asked quietly.

"Not really," she answered, and knew she sounded unconvincing.

"Elizabeth," he said, "just because we can't see a future together…that doesn't mean we can't have a present."

"I know that." She shook her head gently, then pushed her hair back behind her ears. "It's only that I've never—"

"Had a lover?" he finished for her.

She smiled wryly. ''You make it sound so reasonable.''

''Isn't it?''

''I suppose so,'' she said thoughtfully. ''I guess I never considered myself the take-a-lover kind of woman.''

''More of a white-picket-fence type of girl?''

''No.'' She laughed again at the notion. ''I was always too concentrated on my career to think about husbands and cute little houses and station wagons.''

''Ah...'' He ran one hand up and down her arm in long, soothing strokes. ''Well, all of your concentration worked. You *are* the Princess of Party Cooking.''

She gave his hand a playful smack.

''Isn't it what you thought it would be?'' he asked. ''Your career, I mean?''

''Oh, I love it,'' she admitted softly. ''There is nothing more fun than being in a well-stocked kitchen, dreaming up some new and tantalizing dessert.''

''Nothing?'' he asked, letting his fingertips trail along the edge of her breast.

She sucked in a breath. ''Well, *almost* nothing.''

''Thank you.''

''You're welcome.''

''So,'' he said, ''if your career is all you wanted it to be, and you don't particularly *want* a husband, what's wrong with having a lover?''

There was a long pause while she thought that one over. Nothing wrong with it, she supposed. But, if that were true, why did she suddenly feel so... debauched? Her traditional upbringing must be rearing its ugly head, she decided. Well, if that was all it was, she would just have to get over it. As she had when she'd first decided to have a career instead of a husband. Either that or live the life of a well-fed nun.

Making up her mind, she nodded against his chest. "You're right. There's nothing wrong with having a man in my life occasionally."

His hand on her arm stilled, then continued its gentle stroking.

Of course, she would have to give up the one little corner of her dream that she hadn't allowed herself to think of for years. Children. Lovers do not necessarily make good fathers. And 1990s or not, she didn't know if she could be a good enough single parent to risk having a child alone.

Oh, she knew lots of women were doing it these days. Most of them doing it quite well, too. But the staggering responsibility of being both mother and father was one she wasn't sure she was strong enough to carry.

Immediately she remembered the night before, the first time they'd made love and the fact that there had been no protection. Was it possible that one slip had already resulted in a child? Was she, even now, pregnant with Harding's baby?

She closed her eyes, telling herself firmly not to think about that yet. It was too early to worry. Especially since she wasn't sure if she had anything to worry about. Yet.

Imagine, all of this had come about because her sister had fallen in love.

Her mind racing, Elizabeth suddenly wondered what Mike and Terry would have to say if they could see her and Harding right now. She chuckled gently at the envisioned expression on her sister's face.

"What's so funny?"

"I was just thinking about Mike and Terry and how they worked at trying to get us together for a solid year with no success."

He laughed shortly, and the sound rumbled beneath her ear. "Yeah, all I heard about was how great we would be together."

"Me, too." She tipped her head back again to look up at him. "Can you imagine the 'I told you so's' we'd have to listen to if they found out about this?"

He pushed one hand through his short hair. "Mike would never let me forget it."

"Terry, either. She lives for this sort of thing."

"So, then," he said, cupping her cheek with one big palm, "we don't tell them?"

"My lips are sealed," she said.

"Not permanently, I hope." He smiled wickedly and wiggled both of his eyebrows.

Shaking her head, she grinned at him. "It's better if they don't know, anyway. After all, they were hoping for marriage, not—"

"A red-hot, fire-breathing affair?" he finished for her.

"Exactly." She ran the flat of her hand across his chest.

He caught her hand, holding it tightly. "But just because we don't want to get married, that doesn't mean we can't enjoy what we have for as long as we have it, right?''

''Right,'' she said, despite the pang of regret echoing deep inside her. Less than a month, he'd said. He was leaving in less than four weeks and would be gone for six long months. And when he returned, there was no guarantee that they would reconnect. Maybe he wouldn't even want to see her. Regret slithered through her again. Already she missed him.

She could admit, if only to herself, that she was dreading his leaving. How terrible could it be for her to have these moments with him to remember when he was gone?

''What's making you frown?'' he asked.

''Nothing,'' she lied, and forced a smile she didn't quite feel.

''You're thinking about last night, aren't you?''

''No, I wasn't.''

''We have to talk about that, Elizabeth.''

''Yeah, I know,'' she said, and thought, Not now. Not this minute.

He sighed and held her closer. ''Whatever happens, we'll work it out together.''

''Harding, you don't have to worry about it, all right?'' she said. ''Like I told you, I'm a big girl. I can take care of myself.''

''I know you can,'' he countered, staring down into her eyes. ''But if you are pregnant, there would be someone else to consider besides yourself.''

''Oh, my, a baby.'' Mixed emotions blended together in the depths of her soul. One minute she saw herself cuddling a newborn to her breast. She blocked the next image, refusing to entertain the notion at all. Banishing both mental pictures, she shook her head firmly. "No, it won't happen."

"When will we know for sure?"

"*I'll* know in about two weeks."

"Good. I don't ship out for three weeks yet, so we'll have time to decide what to do."

"Harding," she tried to ease away from him, but he held her tighter. "I won't try to keep you out of this, and of course you'll get a chance to give me your opinion on what I should do, but the final decision will be mine."

He was quiet for several long minutes, and Elizabeth held her breath, wondering what he would have to say. She hadn't known him long, of course. But through Mike and Terry she knew what kind of man he was. She couldn't imagine him *not* having an opinion.

Finally he inhaled sharply and blew it out in a rush. "We have two weeks. Two weeks before we know if a decision will be necessary. I suggest we wait to discuss it until we know if we have something to talk about."

She sighed her relief. Now that she was here, with him, she didn't want to ruin what time she had with him by fighting over what was still a *theoretical* baby.

Slipping one of his hands beneath the sheet she'd pulled up over her breasts, he found one of her nipples and gently teased it until she was curling into him, nearly purring with pleasure.

"Elizabeth," he whispered in her ear.

"Hmm?"

''Are we going to be spending the entire day in my bed?'' He dipped his head to nibble at the base of her throat.

''Have you got some official Marine business to take care of?'' she asked, tilting her head back to give him easier access.

''Nope,'' his tongue flicked against her pulse point. ''I took this whole week off as leave time. I'm officially a free man.''

''Did Terry give us chores for today?'' she mumbled, and bit his shoulder gently.

''Finished the last ones yesterday.'' He shifted, moving down the length of her body, trailing hot, damp kisses along her flesh. ''All that's left is you making the cake.''

''Then, Sergeant Major, I suggest we spend the day in bed, resting up for the rest of the week.''

He looked up from her abdomen and gave her a quick, wicked smile. ''We stay in this bed, princess, there'll be no resting.''

Elizabeth shifted on the sheets, parting her legs when he moved to kneel between them. His fingers dusted along the insides of her thighs, and she felt herself jump in response. ''Princess, huh?'' she murmured as his hands slid beneath her bottom. ''Well, Hard Case—'' she broke off and looked at him quizzically. ''Why do they call you Hard Case, anyway?''

''Do you really need to know that *now?*'' he asked quietly, and lifted her hips high, easing her legs into place over his shoulders.

Suddenly aware of what he was about to do, Elizabeth gasped, ''Harding!''

''Just lie back, princess,'' he said with a knowing smile.

Then his mouth covered her, and all of her thoughts dissolved into a hazy mist of delicious sensations.

At 10:00 p.m. the night before the wedding, Elizabeth sat at her kitchen table, listening to her mother and Terry as she decorated the cake.

''I just don't understand why the bachelor party *has* to be held the night before the wedding.''

''Tradition,'' Sally Stone told her younger daughter for the third time.

Terry stuck her index finger into the small, stainless steel bowl containing lilac-tinted frosting and winced when Elizabeth smacked her hand.

''Hey, I just wanted a taste.''

Elizabeth shook her head, filled the pastry bag with the lilac confection and prepared to create rosettes. ''Taste it tomorrow.''

''Your sister's right,'' Sally said.

''Naturally.'' Terry gave her mother a sly grin. ''Lizzie was always your favorite.''

Elizabeth laughed.

''Let's not start that again,'' their mom said and stood up. ''Anyone like a cup of tea before I send Terry to bed to get some sleep?''

The woman in question frowned. ''The men are out drinking beer, and I get hot tea and an early bedtime?''

''I think we can do better than that,'' Elizabeth told her sister. She nodded toward the slate blue side-by-side refrigerator in the corner. ''There's wine in the fridge.''

Terry smiled and jumped to her feet. ''How about it, Mom? Feel like giving me a grand send-off?''

The older woman looked at first one daughter, then the other. Eyes twinkling, she said, ''Sure. We'll have a toast. But then, the bride goes to bed. I don't want my beautiful daughter posing for her wedding pictures with bags under her eyes.''

''Okay, okay,'' Terry agreed, and reached into the refrigerator. She grabbed a bottle of white Zinfandel, set it on the table and crossed the wide, well-appointed kitchen. ''Glasses in the same place?''

''Of course.'' Elizabeth kept her eyes on her job. She still had two layers to pipe rosettes on, before she could add the final flourishes to what she hoped would be a masterpiece. Naturally the job would go a lot faster if she was working as she preferred to work. Alone, with Beethoven on the CD player. But with her parents spending the weekend at her condo and Terry opting to join them for one last night of family togetherness, that wasn't an option.

''Okay, Lizzie,'' Terry said as she filled the third glass, ''take a break. That's an order.''

''Hey, if you don't want a cake at the wedding,'' she teased, ''just say so. It's all right with me.''

''One minute, master chef. One minute to give your baby sister a toast.''

Elizabeth sighed, set the pastry bag down onto the table and picked up her glass. Standing, she looked at the other women, each in turn. Terry looked wonderful, eager and happy. Their mother was still beautiful, even though there was more gray in her hair than blond these days. Those blue eyes of hers shone with pride, and Elizabeth was suddenly struck with an almost overpowering surge of love for the family she had sometimes taken for granted.

In the next instant the three of them lifted their Waterford crystal glasses and brought them together, less than an inch apart.

"Here's to—" Terry hesitated, then grinned "—Mike getting to the church on time."

"He'll be there," Elizabeth told her. "Harding will watch out for him."

Sally Stone shot a long, thoughtful look at her older daughter before saying, "Don't worry, Terry. Your father promised me that your groom would be at the church on time and clearheaded." Tapping her glass to the other two, she said, "Here's to my baby. May she always be as happy as she is tonight."

"Here, here," Elizabeth echoed.

"I will be," Terry whispered.

"Now go to bed," Sally said after a sip of wine.

"Mother," Terry answered with a laugh. "Ten is a little early, don't you think?"

In response, Sally took her daughter's glass and set it on the table. "I've seen the way you and Mike look at each other," she said with a knowing smile. "No doubt you'll be up all night tomorrow night. Wouldn't you like to be well rested and um...*energetic?*"

"*Mother!*" Terry laughed outright.

"What?" Sally looked at each of them. "We're all grown-ups, aren't we?"

"Apparently," Elizabeth said ruefully. It was the

first time their mother had ever talked about sex and one of her girls in the same sentence.

Terry hugged her mother tightly, gave her a resounding kiss on the forehead, then said, ''You're absolutely right, Mom. I'm going to bed.'' She walked to the doorway, then stopped and turned around. '''Night, Lizzie,'' she said. ''And thanks for everything.''

Elizabeth took another sip of wine, letting the chilled, fruity drink slide down her throat slowly before answering. ''You're welcome. I'll see you in the morning.''

Terry nodded brightly and disappeared down the hallway. They heard her run up the stairs and the soft echo of a door closing.

Taking her seat beside Elizabeth again, Sally turned her wineglass between her hands. ''Is everything all right, dear?''

She glanced at her mother. ''Sure. Why wouldn't it be?''

''No reason,'' Sally said with a shrug. ''It was good of you to offer to make Terry's cake.''

Elizabeth smiled to herself and moved on to the next frosted layer. ''I couldn't very well let her order some ordinary-looking, dry-tasting cake from a bakery, could I?''

''No, I suppose you couldn't have.''

Shooting a sidelong glance at her mother, Elizabeth wondered what the woman was working up to. Her mom had never had trouble saying what was on her mind.

''I do wonder, dear,'' Sally said softly.

"About what?"

"Well, how you feel about your younger sister getting married before you."

"Mom," Elizabeth paused in her decorating, smoothing the pastry bag and forcing the frosting down closer to the tip. "You can't be serious."

Sally kept her gaze fixed on the wineglass between her palms. "It might bother some women, you know. Make them feel like...old maids."

Elizabeth laughed, ignoring the tiny stab of pain deep inside her. "Come on, Mom. These are the 1990s not the 1890s."

"I know that, but still, some women might have tender feelings about such a thing."

"Some women maybe. Not me."

"I hope not."

Elizabeth laid the pastry bag down and reached over to cover her mother's hand with one of hers. "Remember me, Mom? I'm the daughter who didn't *want* to get married?"

"People change."

"Not always."

"I'm not blind, Lizzie," her mother said softly.

"What's that supposed to mean?"

"I've seen the way you look at Harding Casey."

Uncomfortable with the turn the conversation had taken, Elizabeth picked up the pastry bag and went to work. It gave her a good excuse to keep from looking into her mother's eyes. Eyes that had always been able to tell truth from lies.

"Your father and I like him very much."

"Of course Dad likes him. Harding's a career Marine. What's not to like?"

"It's not just that," Sally said quickly, "though for your father, I admit it *is* a positive sign. But I think Harding is a nice man. He's polite, charming, witty and looks at you as though you're one of those desserts you're so famous for."

Heat stained her cheeks. She felt the color race up her neck, blossoming on her face like wild roses. Dipping her head closer to her work, she said, "Don't look for things that aren't there, Mom."

"I don't think I am," Sally answered quietly. Reaching for her daughter, she tipped Elizabeth's chin up with her fingertips until their gazes met and locked. "And at the same time, sweetie, don't you try to hide from something that might be the gift of a lifetime."

Tears suddenly blinded her. She didn't know whether it was her mother's gentle touch or her soft voice or the fact that those same words had been whispering around inside her own head for days. But whatever the reason, she blinked them back stubbornly.

"Harding and I are...*friends.*" Somehow she just couldn't call him her lover to her mother's face. Thirty-two or not, some things one just didn't say to one's mom.

"Friends," Sally echoed sadly. "Is that all you want from him?"

"That's all there is," she said firmly.

"Lizzie honey, the sparks that fly when you two are near each other are bright enough to light up a city.'' She smiled tenderly. ''Friends don't usually have that effect on each other.''

''We're very *close* friends.''

''Ahh...'' Sally nodded, patted Elizabeth's cheek, then let her hand fall away. ''I thought as much. It's in your eyes, honey, how much you care for him.''

''Mom...''

''Does he feel the same? Yes,'' she answered herself in the next breath. ''Of course he does. Even your dad noticed.''

''Don't make this into something it isn't, Mom,'' Elizabeth warned her. ''In three weeks Harding's being deployed to Okinawa for six months, and that will be that.''

''Will it?'' Sally mumbled. ''I wonder.''

Nine

The groomsmen, all Marines, were wearing their dress blues uniforms. Only the groom himself wore a tuxedo, and Harding was the only person who seemed to notice Mike looking at the uniforms surrounding him just a bit wistfully.

But once he had gotten a look at his bride, that expression in his eyes faded to be replaced by a joy that was so strong, Harding had had to look away from it. It was either that, or be eaten by jealousy for his best friend's good fortune.

All through the short ceremony, Harding's gaze had continually shifted to Elizabeth standing just opposite him at the small altar. Beautiful in a silvery, lilac-colored, off-the-shoulder dress, all he could think was that it should have been the two of them standing in front of the preacher. It should have been *them* repeating those ancient words about love and loyalty and commitment.

He would never have believed it of himself. But the truth was hard to ignore—especially while staring into Elizabeth's eyes.

Lifting his bottle of beer to his lips, Harding looked around the reception hall, trying to find her without seeming obvious. He took a long drink as he casually noted the other Marines in the room, each of them surrounded by a cluster of women. Smiling to himself, he remembered plenty of times when he, too, had used the effect of dress blues on civilians to his best advantage.

Odd that only a week after meeting one particular woman he had no interest in any other. Odd, or fate? he wondered. Was it really fate taking a hand in things? Had he and Elizabeth been brought together by some karmic force?

He whistled low and soft, looked at his beer bottle suspiciously, then set it down on the table beside him. Apparently two beers was enough to kick his imagination into high gear.

Fate?

Karma?

No, what had happened between them was simple science. *Chemistry.*

Across the wide, crowded hall from him, he finally caught a glimpse of the woman who had turned his brain into slush.

Busying herself around the cake table, she was making last-minute adjustments to the most-gorgeous-looking cake he had ever seen. Five layers, divided by white plastic columns, the wedding dessert had been lovingly decorated with lilac frosting flowers, silver stars and studded with real, live roses. Sterling silver rosebuds, fully bloomed lavender roses and white baby's breath, each blossom tucked into a tiny plastic bud vase then attached to the cake. Tendrils of ribbons streamed from the icing and lay in curled abandon at the base of the cake.

Elizabeth really *was* the Princess of Party Cooking.

Everyone who had seen the cake had paused to admire it. He had listened to their praise for the chef and taken great pride in every word.

"Beautiful, isn't she?" a voice from nearby asked him.

Startled out of his thoughts, Harding half turned to meet the steady gaze of Elizabeth's father. Marine Captain Harry Stone, retired, still looked as if he was ready to report to the parade ground.

At six foot one, Captain Stone stood tall and straight. A receding hairline, more gray than dark brown, and fine lines around his eyes and mouth were the only marks of age on the man.

Instinctively Harding straightened almost to attention. "Yes, sir," he said. "She is."

The captain's gaze shifted to his daughter, unaware of their regard. "You know, Lizzie always was the more hardheaded of my daughters. The one most like me, I guess."

"Sir?" Was he supposed to agree? Wouldn't that be insulting the man? Although he had to admit, Elizabeth was definitely a strong woman. One who knew her own mind and wasn't afraid to voice her opinion. It was one of the things he liked best about her.

"She's not fond of change, you know," her father was saying. "Never has been. Guess that's why she didn't like being raised in the Corps. Hated the moving. The deploying."

Harding nodded and wished for another beer. "My ex-wife felt the same way. Military marriages aren't the easiest thing in the world to maintain."

Captain Stone chuckled, shaking his head. "Never thought I'd hear a career Devil Dog complain about hard work."

Harding shot him a look. Hard work was a part of his life. He had never backed away from a challenge.

"Ease up, Sergeant Major," Elizabeth's father said softly, to avoid being overheard by the wandering guests. "I'm not trying to insult you—"

Harding nodded.

"I'm only trying to point out to you that the seemingly impossible is, most often, something we're afraid to try. Once tried, impossible becomes possible."

"Not always, Captain," Harding muttered, remembering the sense of failure he had experienced when his ex-wife left him, decrying the hard life of being married to the Corps.

"Call me Harry," the older man offered. "And no, Sergeant Major. There are no guarantees. But I can tell you from experience that a good marriage is a blessing." Unconsciously his gaze drifted from his daughter to his wife, chatting and laughing with several other women. His eyes softened, and his features gentled. "The right woman is more than a wife. She's a partner. A friend."

Harding shifted uncomfortably. What was this all about? Was the man actually trying to bring Elizabeth and him together? Hell, as her father, the captain should know better than anyone that his daughter was dead set against any kind of relationship with a career soldier.

Running one finger around the inside collar of his tunic, Harding had to wonder what this man would say if he knew that Elizabeth and he were lovers. Would he still be getting this speech about honor and commitment? Or would the captain be holding a noose?

Feeling distinctly uncomfortable with the conversation, Harding blurted, "If you'll excuse me, sir, I believe I'll go find your younger daughter and give her my condolences on marrying Mike."

The older man smiled. "Certainly, Marine. Go ahead."

Harding escaped immediately, blending into the crowd, losing himself amidst the mingle of voices, the snatches of laughter.

He didn't see the thoughtful expression on Captain Stone's face. Nor did he witness the meaningful glance the captain sent his smiling wife.

There was nothing left to do.

Elizabeth had managed to keep herself busy from the end of the ceremony until now. But she had worked herself out of a job. The buffet-style meal was being catered by a company entirely capable of managing their own help, and her masterpiece of a wedding cake was set up, awaiting its moment.

Clutching a glass of champagne, she wandered aimlessly at the edges of the crowd, smiling to friends and nodding pleasantly to strangers. Always, though, she kept one eye out for Harding.

Standing across the altar from him during the wedding, she had hardly heard the words of the ceremony. Instead, she had indulged silly daydreams—visions of Harding and her standing before a minister. Harding and her holding hands, exchanging rings and promises. Harding and her kissing before a gathering of friends and families, then listening to the applause erupt from the pews.

Silly, she told herself, and took another sip of champagne. No, more than silly. Ludicrous. She didn't even *want* to be married. Let alone to a Marine.

''Oh, Lizzie!''

She turned around in time to see her younger sister sweep down on her, veil flying, eyes sparkling. Terry enveloped her in a hug, then pulled back and grinned happily.

''Isn't this fabulous?''

''Yeah,'' Elizabeth said, unable to keep from returning Terry's smile. ''It's wonderful.''

''I actually cried at my own wedding,'' Terry said with a half laugh. ''But it was so beautiful, I just couldn't help it.''

''*You're* beautiful, kiddo.''

She glanced down at her full-skirted, ivory lace wedding dress and nodded before looking back up at her sister. ''You know, I think I am, today.'' She reached for one of Elizabeth's hands and gave it a squeeze. "The cake turned out so gorgeous. Thank you, Lizzie."

"You're welcome." Winking, she added, "And it tastes even better than it looks."

"Naturally," Terry huffed with pride.

Linking her arm through her sister's, Terry started walking slowly. "Doesn't Harding look handsome in his uniform?"

Elizabeth narrowed her gaze and looked at her sister suspiciously. Her mother had already pointed out how well Harding filled out a set of dress blues. As if she hadn't noticed without any help from her family.

Deliberately she shrugged. "I never said he wasn't handsome."

Terry's lips twitched. "Has he told you how he got his nickname? Hard Case?"

Intrigued, Elizabeth said, "No." Of course, the only time she had actually *asked* for the information, he had been otherwise occupied. A ribbon of heat swirled through her body as she recalled exactly *what* he had been doing at the time.

"Well," Terry said, apparently not noticing her sister's momentary lapse of attention. "Mike told me. It started in boot camp. Mike says Harding refused to accept less than the best from himself. He pushed himself higher and harder than any of the others—which only earned his squad mates extra duty—because he would show them up so badly."

Elizabeth nodded. That sounded like what she would have expected from Harding Casey.

"When the guys called him on it, he only challenged them to improve." Terry shook her head and smiled. "Anyway, his stubbornness started the nickname there. But when he was sent to Grenada, some of his men were pinned down by enemy fire with no way out."

Immediately Elizabeth, the daughter of a soldier, envisioned the scene in her mind. She saw a small group of Marines, trapped, with bullets biting into the dust at their feet, zinging off rocks by their heads.

Terry continued. "Apparently, when no one else could think of what to do, Harding went in, under fire, and risked his own life to pull his men out—one by one. He went back time and again until they were all safe." She shrugged, stopped and faced her sister squarely. "He simply refused to give up. Refused to accept failure."

Her eyes teared at the mental picture of Harding risking his life repeatedly for the lives of his men. It was so clear to her, she could almost hear the bullets flying.

"Lizzie," Terry whispered urgently. "There's something between you two, isn't there?"

So much for keeping it a secret, Elizabeth thought as she nodded miserably.

"I knew it," Terry crowed. "I knew you two would be good together."

"Don't book the church," Elizabeth said, before her little sister could get up a full head of steam. "Whatever Harding and I have, it's not going to end in marriage."

"Lizzie..."

''Let it go, Terry.'' She looked directly into her sister's eyes. ''Please. You know I never planned on getting married. And Harding is shipping out in less than three weeks.''

''He'll be back, though.''

Yes, he would be back. But would he be coming back to her? Or would the heat of the fire between them burn itself out while he was gone?

She didn't voice her thoughts, merely shook her head sadly.

Grabbing both of her hands, Terry bent in close and whispered fiercely. ''Lizzie, don't blow this. Don't blow a chance to be happy.''

''Stop, Terry. You don't know—''

''I know, I know. You hate the military.''

''Not the military itself,'' she corrected. ''It's the constant moving, never belonging I don't like. And the absences. Don't you remember all of those times when Dad was gone? All of the birthdays he missed? The Christmases?''

''Sure I do,'' Terry said. ''But I remember everything else, too. I remember his homecomings and having him there, at home every night. I remember the love.''

''So do I, Terry,'' Elizabeth said softly, ''but—''

''No buts,'' her sister said. ''I told you how stubborn Hard Case is, right?''

Elizabeth nodded.

''If he loves you, Lizzie, he won't stop. Just like in Grenada, he'll keep coming back. He'll slip under any bullets you throw at him and keep coming back until you're convinced. As for the travel and deployment,'' she shrugged. ''It wouldn't be hard, Lizzie. Not if you really love him.''

She wanted to believe, which surprised her. A week ago she wouldn't have even entertained the notion of marriage at all. Now, here she was having a heart-to-heart with her baby sister about a Marine of all people.

Taking a deep breath, she gave her weary mind permission to shut down for a while. There was simply too much to think about. And now wasn't the time for it.

''I appreciate it, Terry,'' she said, leaning into her sister for a quick hug. ''But Harding and I don't love each other.'' Not a lie, was it?

The blushing bride didn't look convinced.

''Look,'' Elizabeth said, ''just enjoy your own wedding day, all right? Quit worrying about planning mine?''

''Okay,'' she finally answered. ''But we'll talk about this again. When Mike and I get back from Jamaica?''

Elizabeth nodded, grateful for the respite. Hopefully, by the time the honeymooners were back, this firestorm with Harding would have fizzled out, and there would be nothing to talk about.

''There you are,'' Mike announced, coming up behind his new wife and swinging her in a wide circle. ''No one will dance with me.''

''Well,'' Terry retorted, ''we can't have that, can we?''

As the newlyweds started for the dance floor, arm

in arm, Terry looked back over her shoulder. ''Later?''

Elizabeth nodded, relieved to be alone again.

''Dance with me?'' A familiar, deep voice rumbled from behind her and she slowly turned around. Her heartbeat thundered in her ears, her blood raced through her veins and her knees wobbled unsteadily.

Would she always react like this to him? she wondered. Would his voice always sink to the base of her spine and send chills coursing up and down her back?

His clear blue eyes locked with hers, and Elizabeth felt herself drowning in their depths. She couldn't have looked away if her life had hung in the balance.

''Dance with me,'' he repeated, this time making it a command, not a request.

She nodded slightly and took the hand he offered her. Sizzles of heat snaked up her arm from their joined hands as she followed him to the dance floor. There, he turned, pulled her into his arms and began to lead her around the floor. Swaying, their bodies touching, she let her mind wander, giving herself over to the sensation of being held by him.

Remembering that in less than three weeks he would be gone from her life.

Harding clenched his jaw tight and somehow managed to keep his grasp on her gentle. ''Nice wedding,'' he said.

''It was, wasn't it?''

''They look happy.''

She turned her head and looked at the happy couple. He did too. Mike and Terry were lost in each other. Joy radiated from them like warmth from the sun.

"What were you and your sister talking about?" he asked quietly. He had come up on them too late to overhear anything, but from the expression on Elizabeth's features, she hadn't been any too pleased with the conversation.

Elizabeth shifted her gaze to meet his. He studied those soft brown eyes for a long moment, but whatever she was thinking, she was managing to conceal it from him.

"Nothing, really," she said, and he knew she was lying.

The only reason she would have to lie was if she had been talking about him. Damn, he wondered what she had said.

"You've made quite an impression on my parents," Elizabeth said and moved with him through a slow turn.

"They're nice people." Lord, it was as if they were strangers. This polite conversation was tearing at him.

"I saw you and Dad talking together earlier," she commented.

He stiffened slightly. He wasn't about to let her know that he and his father were discussing her. She would immediately want to know what had been said—and the truth was, he wasn't very sure of that himself.

"Anything you want to tell me about?" she asked.

"No," he said, avoiding her gaze. Just like her, he was lying. Now he was convinced she and Terry had been talking about him. "Just two old Marines exchanging war stories."

She looked up at him, her eyes delving deeply into his. He would never get tired of staring into her eyes.

"My parents will be leaving tomorrow."

"So soon?" he asked, despite the fact that this seemed like the longest weekend of his life. Not being able to be with her was harder on him than boot camp had ever been.

She smiled wryly as if reading his mind. "Yes. Dad's anxious to get back to his cronies and the golf course, and Mom's sure that the volunteer staff at the local hospital can't get along without her."

Her smile didn't falter, but he could see that the thought of her parents leaving made her sad. "You'll miss them."

"Yeah, I will." Elizabeth inhaled sharply. "We don't get together often enough. But, ever since Dad retired, they're almost never home. Always off on some little trip or other."

"So even though he left the Corps, they still travel a lot."

She nodded. "I hadn't thought of it like that, but yes. Sometimes," she added wistfully, "compared to them I feel like a stick-in-the-mud."

He frowned slightly and pulled her closer against him. He inhaled the soft, sweet scent of the fresh lavender and sterling rosebuds that made up the wreath encircling her head. Harding concentrated on that scent, trying to memorize it, so that when he was alone, in Okinawa, thousands of miles from her, he would be able to draw on that memory and bring her close.

She laid her head down on his shoulder, apparently deciding to ignore whoever might be watching them. His right hand smoothed up and down her back, caressing the silk covering her flesh.

Silent now, they danced together with controlled, yet fluid movements. The intimacy of their dance announcing that they were more than polite strangers. He felt her soft sigh, and all he wanted to do was pick her up, carry her to the Mustang outside and drive like a shot to her condo.

But he couldn't. Not with her parents in residence.

Memories of the past few days filled him, making his body tight and hard and filling his mind with erotic images of Elizabeth.

He saw her as he made love to her, looking into her eyes as a climax took her. He saw her smile and reach for him. He saw her naked in her kitchen, scrambling eggs for the two of them at one in the morning.

His right hand slipped lower on her back, riding just above the swell of her behind. His fingers itched to touch her. The crowd of dancers swirled around them, but for him, it was as if they were alone in the room. All he saw was her. All he felt was her.

All he wanted was her.

A warning jolt shot through him. For all of his care, all of his noble intentions of keeping his distance, he wanted Elizabeth. Not just for the few short weeks he had remaining stateside, but for a lifetime.

But a lifetime of Elizabeth meant marriage.

The truth shocked him.

The depths of his feelings rattled around inside him like a sword in a scabbard.

He loved her. More than he had ever imagined it possible to love a woman, he loved Elizabeth Stone.

Yet that simple fact was met and challenged by another.

She didn't want a husband. And even if she did, he had already tried marriage…and failed miserably.

Ten

Two weeks slipped by with almost eerie speed.

Elizabeth tried not to notice the calendar. She made every effort to not think beyond the moment. Daily, while working in her kitchen, testing new recipes, she had to focus to keep her mind on the work at hand. And still her gaze drifted to the clock on the wall, slowly counting down the hours until Harding would arrive.

She turned the water on, sending clouds of steam rushing up into her face. Squirting liquid soap into the sink, she absently watched bubbles froth and blossom on the surface of the wash water. Somewhere in the back of her mind, she noticed that the Beethoven CD had ended, but she didn't move to replace it. Instead, as she picked up a dishcloth and began to work, she indulged herself in thoughts of Harding.

They had eased into a familiar routine over the past two weeks. He reported for duty at the base every morning, then as soon as his shift was finished, he drove to her condo. They had dinner, rented movies and sometimes went for walks on the beach.

And they loved.

Elizabeth shivered as she washed a cherished ceramic bowl and set it in the dish drainer. She rarely used the dishwasher, since most of her equipment was too treasured to trust to machinery. Besides, washing dishes freed her mind, and she had thought up some of her best recipes while her hands were buried in soapsuds.

As she turned off the water, she reached for a fresh towel and began drying the mountain of mixing bowls and utensils. While she worked, her mind wandered back to the subject that seemed to fascinate it most.

Harding Casey.

Images raced through her brain. Erotic images. Loving images. Together they had christened nearly every room in her condo. There wasn't a place in her home where she could go and not be reminded of him. His touch. His kisses. His deep voice and the whispered words of passion that had been ingrained in her memory.

All night, every night, they lay in each other's arms, talking of their pasts, because any mention of a future would only destroy their present. And every morning at dawn he rose from her bed, showered and dressed. Then he left her to return to the base.

And every morning when he was gone, she moved over on her queen-size mattress to lie where he had lain. The still-warm sheets comforted her, his pillow rested beneath her head, and she dreamed of that night, when he would come again.

But the few short days they had left were quickly passing. In no time she would be alone again.

What would she do when he was gone?

Mechanically she walked around the kitchen, returning her equipment to its proper places. Soon, he would be leaving. Six long months when she wouldn't see him...be held by him.

And there was no guarantee that she would see him again when he returned, either. She stopped short, caught by that thought. Did she *want* a guarantee? Wasn't she the one who had insisted from the start that she wasn't looking for a long-term relationship? Hadn't she insisted that marriage wasn't in her plans?

Marriage? Where had that come from?

She almost laughed aloud at the pitiful attempt at self-delusion. Thoughts of marriage had been lurking near the edge of her consciousness for days. So far she hadn't let them get any further.

Tossing the damp towel down onto the butcher-block counter, Elizabeth stared around at the world she'd created for herself so painstakingly. Up-to-the-minute appliances. Plenty of workspace. Homey, yet modern. Everything she had wanted her home to be.

And yet...until meeting Harding Casey, she had never noticed just how *empty* it was. How the wind blowing across the shutters sounded like a soft sigh. Folding her arms over her chest, she leaned against the countertop, feeling the edge of the butcher block bite into the base of her spine.

Had the place *always* been this quiet? she wondered. Was that the reason she was constantly feeding the CD player or flipping on the TV? Or had she noticed the quiet now merely because the past three weeks she had rarely been alone?

Rubbing her face briskly with both hands, she then reached up and yanked her tortoiseshell headband off. Instantly a budding headache eased. She combed her fingers through her hair and tugged at the hem of her pale pink tank top.

Glancing down at herself, she wondered vaguely if she should change clothes before Harding arrived. A white splotch of flour and water had crusted over, in the center of her shirt between her breasts, and there was a grease stain on the right leg of her cutoff denim shorts.

Then she heard the front door open.

''Elizabeth?''

''In here,'' she called out, a familiar excitement already flooding her system. Her stomach muscles tightened, and every inch of her body went on red alert. Would she always feel this incredible surge of elation just at the sound of his voice?

He stepped through the kitchen doorway, a white paper bag resting in the curve of one arm. A familiar, somehow cloying, aroma filled the kitchen and Elizabeth swallowed heavily.

''Chinese?'' she asked.

He shrugged and set the bag on the table. ''I figured you might like takeout for a change.''

Thoughtful. She loved Chinese food. Her stomach jumped again, but this time it wasn't as pleasant a sensation. Licking suddenly dry lips, she tried to ignore the flutter of unease rippling through her.

"Getting tired of my cooking?" she teased as she took a step closer to him.

"Nope," he assured her with a wink. "But I've got plans for you lady...and they don't include cooking."

Oh, Lord. Her knees turned to jelly, and damp heat rushed to her center. "What kind of plans?" she asked, after clearing her throat.

He pulled her up tight against him and wrapped his arms around her. Elizabeth closed her eyes tight, wanting to always remember what it felt like to be held this close to him. There were six months of lonely nights ahead of her, and she would need every one of her memories to survive them.

She bent her head and buried her nose in his shoulder, hoping to avoid the almost overpowering odor of sweet-and-sour sauce.

Harding threaded his fingers through her hair, cupping the back of her head in his palm.

The need didn't ease. The hunger he felt for her only strengthened with each passing day. He kept telling himself that a passion as hot as theirs couldn't last. Couldn't sustain itself. But not only did it continue to burn, it continued to surpass itself.

She shuddered in his arms, and he told himself he was a lucky man. There weren't many men, he would wager, who had a woman as eager for him as he was for her. Smiling to himself, he looked down and eased her head back until he could see her clearly.

Eyes closed, her lips clamped tightly, she looked a

bit paler than she had when he had walked in. As he watched her, she swallowed heavily, inhaled, then grimaced.

"Elizabeth?" he asked, sudden concern overriding his desire. "Are you all right?"

"I'm fine," she said through clenched teeth.

"Well, you don't *look* fine," he told her. As he spoke he saw tiny beads of sweat break out on her forehead. Alarmed, he laid the back of his hand against her clammy skin to check for a fever.

She pushed back out of his arms. "I'm not sick, Harding," she said, her voice ringing with determination. "It's just that smell."

Frowning, he studied her. "What smell?"

Elizabeth waved one hand at the sack on the table. "That." She inhaled sharply again, scowled and took a few steps away from the food. "Can't you smell it?"

He sniffed the air appreciatively. "Yeah. It smells great."

She shook her head, lifting one hand to cover her mouth. "What did you get, anyway?"

"Your favorites," he said, really confused now. "Egg rolls, fried rice, cashew chicken and sweet-and-sour pork."

"That's the smell." Her lips pulled back from her teeth, and she nearly snarled at the cartoned food.

"What?" He reached into the sack, pulling out one of the small white cartons. "The pork?" he asked, opening the top and taking a step toward her. "It's the same stuff we had last week. You loved it."

She backed up like a vampire from a cross. "No.

It's different. The sweet-and-sour sauce. Must be bad.''

He inhaled deeply, letting the mingle of spices and seasonings rush into his lungs. Nothing wrong there, he told himself, and glanced at the woman still back-pedaling out of the kitchen. If he wasn't mistaken, Elizabeth's features had taken on a decidedly green cast.

''Are you all right?''

''Yes,'' she said quickly, then shook her head. Her eyes wide, she mumbled, ''No,'' just before she turned and ran out of the room.

Hot on her heels, Harding rounded the corner to the bathroom in time to hold her head as she was thoroughly sick. Several minutes later he offered her a damp washcloth and led her to the living room. There, he sat her on the couch and eased down onto the coffee table directly opposite her.

''How long have you been sick?'' he asked. He didn't want to think about her lying around the house all day, miserable and alone.

''I wasn't sick,'' she said. ''Not until I got a whiff of that...'' she shuddered and pointed at the kitchen.

''You mean the—''

She held one hand up. ''Please. Don't even say it.''

Reaching out, he touched her forehead again, pleased to note that she didn't seem quite so chilled and clammy anymore. ''No fever.''

Letting her head fall against the overstuffed sofa back, she muttered thickly, ''I told you. I'm not sick.''

''Then why else would you—'' He stopped dead.

As far as he knew there was only one reason—other than the flu or food poisoning—for a woman to be sick to her stomach.

The same thought had apparently occurred to her. She lifted her head gingerly and looked at him. ''This doesn't necessarily mean a thing.''

''Yeah, right.'' He stood up, keeping his gaze locked with hers. ''When were you due?''

''Excuse me?''

''Stow it, princess,'' he said softly. ''When?''

''A few days ago.'' When he jerked her a nod and started for the front door, she added quickly, ''But I've been late before.''

''I'll be right back,'' he told her as he grabbed the doorknob and turned.

''Where are you going?'' she asked.

''To the drugstore,'' he said simply. ''It's time to find out one way or the other.''

He actually purchased two different pregnancy test kits. Elizabeth stared at Harding as he paced aimlessly around her bedroom. When he returned from the pharmacy with the kits, he had told her that they shouldn't trust such a major test to one kit. She couldn't help wondering though if the real reason was he was hoping for two different responses so they could have another bit of breathing space.

Elizabeth didn't know *what* she was hoping for.

She'd gone over and over the options in her mind, but none of the other choices were valid ones for *her*. She couldn't give away her own child, only to perhaps have to one day face an eighteen-year-old adult angry about being abandoned. As for the other choice, she couldn't reconcile herself to that idea at all.

"Isn't it time, yet?" Harding asked.

She glanced over at him and sympathized. His solemn, almost-grim features echoed her own.

"No," she said. "The timer's set. It'll ring when the tests are finished."

He nodded, rubbed one hand over the back of his neck and stared down at the rose-colored carpet. "Five minutes never seemed so long before."

"I know." She wished time could stand still. She wished she could think of something brilliant—or comforting—to say.

A digital timer screeched suddenly, sending both of them into a dash for the doorway. Elizabeth beat him since she was a good three feet closer. Shutting off the ringing alarm, she took a deep breath, picked up the two plastic wands and looked down into the test squares.

"Well?" Harding asked from behind her. "What's the verdict?"

Her hands trembling, she inhaled sharply and forced a smile as she turned around to face him. "The verdict is mixed," she said.

"What do you mean?" He took a step closer. "One says yes, the other no?"

"Not quite," she told him as a wave of uneasiness washed over her. "According to these, I'm definitely pregnant."

Not a flicker of emotion showed on his face. "Then what's this 'mixed verdict' business about?"

"Well." She choked on a laugh. "One's pink, the

other's blue. So I'm pregnant, we just don't know what it is, a boy or a girl."

"That's not very funny." If anything, his features had become even more solemn.

"Give me a minute, I'm new at this." She was babbling. She could feel it. She just couldn't stop it. "I know, it's twins. A boy *and* a girl."

"Elizabeth..."

"Or, no." She waved both wands in the air like a drunken conductor. "I know—with our luck, it's quadruplets!"

Harding stepped up close to her. Taking the test sticks from her hands, he glanced at the results, then laid them both down on the counter behind her.

Elizabeth shivered, suddenly cold right down to her bones. She was talking a mile a minute and he was too damned quiet.

A baby.

At thirty-two years old, she was going to have a baby.

A sheen of tears filled her eyes, and her vision blurred. Dropping one hand to her flat abdomen, she laid her palm gently atop her nesting child as if to apologize for ever wishing it away.

Harding saw the movement and immediately covered her hand with his. She looked up at him, and he was struck to the core by the unexpected film of tears shimmering in her eyes.

"Good heavens, Harding," she whispered, her voice catching on a strangled sob. "We actually made a baby."

His throat too tight to speak, he simply pulled her

into the circle of his arms. Nestling her head beneath his chin, he gently stroked her back with long, caressing movements in an attempt to calm and comfort her.

A baby.

At thirty-eight he was going to be a father.

Something inside his chest tightened around his heart until he thought that organ might burst. Most of his life, he'd been alone. He hadn't had a family since he was a kid. And except for his one glaring failure at marriage, he had never *tried* to create a family of his own.

The Corps had always been enough.

Until now.

"I suppose," she said, her voice muffled against his chest, "you want to talk about it right this minute."

He smiled briefly. She knew him well. "Yeah," he said, dropping a kiss onto the top of her head. "I do."

She pulled in one long, shuddering breath and nodded before stepping away from him. "Okay, but let's go into the kitchen, huh? I could use some coffee."

He frowned as she stepped past him and made her way down the hall. "Do you think you should be drinking caffeine?"

"Oh." Elizabeth's steps faltered slightly. "I don't know. I guess not, though. Okay, I'll settle for herbal tea."

Following after her, he took a seat at the kitchen table and waited for her to settle herself. Strange, how well he had gotten to know her in the past three weeks. He knew that she needed to be moving when her mind was busy. He also knew that until she sat down with her cup of tea in hand, she wasn't going to be listening to him.

As she moved around the room, he let his mind drift. In less than a week, he would be shipping out for Okinawa. He wouldn't be here to help her through the next several months. He wouldn't be able to hold her head for her when she was sick or to comfort her when she was worried.

Harding leaned back in his chair and reached up to undo his collar button and yank his tie off. She sat down on the opposite side of the table, cupped her mug between her palms and took a long, slow sip of tea. Only then did she look at him.

"You haven't said much," she accused gently.

That was only one of the differences between them, he thought. When her emotions ran high, so did her tongue. He, on the other hand, had a tendency to keep quiet until he had his thoughts together.

"I want to make sure I say what I have to say right."

Her gaze flicked away from his, then back again. She looked to be steeling herself. "What do you have to say, Harding? Just spit it out. Lord knows, I did."

"All right," he said. Reaching across the table separating them, he took her mug and set it aside. Then he covered both of her hands with his. There was really only one thing to say, and he had to get it right. Everything depended on it. Inhaling sharply, deeply, he said on a rush, "I want you to marry me before I ship out, Elizabeth."

She drew her hands out from under his. Staring

straight into his eyes, she said softly, ''Somehow, I knew that's what you were going to say.''

''That's not an answer,'' he reminded her.

''You're right,'' she agreed and nodded absently. ''But this is. My answer is no, Harding. I *won't* marry you. I can't.''

Eleven

"Why the hell not?"

She winced inwardly. That short, sharp question came out in a voice rough with undisguised frustration. Elizabeth could understand how he felt, and she really didn't enjoy turning down a marriage proposal from the father of her newly discovered child. But she wasn't about to sacrifice the lives of three people on the altar of *propriety.*

Preparing herself for what she knew would be a fierce battle, she deliberately kept her voice even and calm as she said, "Because you don't love me, Harding. You're proposing for the wrong reason."

He jumped to his feet, sending his chair clattering to the floor. Stopping, he bent, righted the chair again, then strode to the sink where he turned around to look at her again. "How do you know I *don't* love you?

Maybe I've loved you all along and was too stupid—or too wary to say so.''

Something inside her leaped at that notion, and she deliberately quashed the budding eagerness. She knew Harding Casey well. He was an honorable man to whom doing the right thing came as second nature. Of course he would lie and proclaim his love. He didn't want to ship out on deployment leaving behind his pregnant lover without *trying* to help.

''No, Harding,'' she said firmly. ''You never would have asked me to marry you if I weren't pregnant.''

''We'll never know that for sure, will we?''

No, they wouldn't. A small spear of regret shivered through her. How strange life was, she told herself. A month ago she would have sworn that she wasn't the slightest bit interested in marriage. She had long since buried her old dreams of children and resigned herself to the knowledge that she would never be a mother.

Now, four weeks later, she was pregnant and refusing the proposal of a man she loved.

Love. She breathed slowly, deeply as the acknowledgment settled into her bones. She loved Harding Casey. Career Marine. That elusive emotion had sneaked up on her when she wasn't looking, and now things were too complicated for her to surrender to a love that might be all one-sided.

''You wouldn't have proposed, Harding,'' she insisted. He'd made it perfectly clear from the beginning of their relationship that he wasn't looking for a wife, any more than she wanted a husband.

''Oh,'' he said, slipping into sarcasm, ''so now you're the *Psychic* Princess of Party Cooking?''

''You said yourself that you had already tried marriage once and weren't interested in trying again.''

''That was then. Things are different now.''

She nodded sadly. ''I know. The baby.''

He inhaled sharply and curled his fingers tightly around the edge of the countertop. ''Yes, the baby. This changes things. But dammit, Elizabeth, I cared about you before the baby, and you know it.''

''Caring and wanting to marry someone are two entirely different things.'' Elizabeth folded her hands in her lap and tried to rein in her rising temper. ''There's no reason for us to fight about this, Harding.''

''There's plenty of reason, princess,'' he countered and crossed her kitchen floor in a few long, angry strides. Glaring down at her, he went on. ''In less than a week, I'm out of here. I'll be thousands of miles away for six damn months.''

''Harding,'' she tried to interrupt.

''And you'll be here, pregnant with *my* baby. Alone.''

She stood up, folded her arms across her chest and met his glare with one of her own. ''I've lived alone for quite a while now, you know. I've managed to take care of myself quite nicely so far without the help of a certain Sergeant Major.''

''Yeah, well up to now you haven't been pregnant, have you?''

No, she hadn't. A momentary thread of worry unwound within her. Oh, she didn't doubt that she could handle the pregnancy on her own. But once the baby was here, then what?

She paused mentally and almost sighed in relief. Apparently she had already made the most important decision. There would *definitely* be a baby.

Already Elizabeth felt the first stirrings of a long-denied maternal urge. She could no more rid herself of this baby than she could stop breathing. But answering one question only posed more.

What would her fairly liberal parents have to say about their unmarried, oldest daughter giving birth to their first grandchild? Could she handle the incredible responsibility of raising a child? And most important, was she capable of giving a child enough love so that it wouldn't miss having a live-in father? Or would she louse things up so badly her child would one day tell a doctor that "it's all my mother's fault"?

"Elizabeth?"

She dismissed her wandering thoughts and focused her attention on the man standing so close to her. "I'm sorry, Harding."

He grabbed her upper arms and pulled her closer. Staring into her eyes, looking for reassurance, he asked, "Are you going to—"

"No," she said. "I'm not going to end the pregnancy."

He exhaled heavily, clearly relieved.

"In fact," she said and forced a half smile. "I want to thank you."

"For what?"

"For the baby."

Harding shook his head briskly as if he couldn't believe what he was hearing. "Thank me?"

"Yes. I had given up on the hope of having children. So thank you."

"Oh." He released her and took a long step back. "You're welcome. Anytime."

She stiffened slightly, and Harding was sure his sarcastic comment had struck home. Dammit, she was shutting him out as completely as if he had already left the country. He felt like a sperm donor. Thanks so much, goodbye now. Have a nice life. Well, she wasn't going to get rid of him so easily.

Reaching up, he smoothed both hands along the sides of his head. How was he supposed to convince her to marry him if he couldn't convince her that he loved her?

Blast it, he should have said something at the wedding. Or any time during the past two weeks. Why hadn't he asked her to marry him sooner? Before the baby. Hell, he knew why. Because he'd been a husband once before...and done a poor job of it, too. He hadn't wanted to risk hurting Elizabeth *or* himself with another failure.

Even now the thought of marriage terrified him. But the thought of living without her paralyzed him. And now there was his child to consider, too. His child. A well of emotion rose up in his chest. He wanted to be a part of his kid's life. Not a part-time parent every other weekend and three weeks in the summer.

He wanted it all. A home. Elizabeth. The baby. But even if she believed he loved her, would she marry him? Or would his being in the Corps stand in their way? What would he do then? Was he willing to give up his career? The only life he'd ever known? The Corps was more than a job to him. It was his life. It was a matter of pride. And honor. And duty. Could he stop being a Marine? Even if it meant having Elizabeth?

"You want me to resign, Elizabeth?" he asked suddenly, steeling himself for her answer.

She took a step toward him. "I would never ask you to give up who you are for me."

"You hate the military."

"I hate the absences. The moving around."

"That's part of it."

"I know," she said. "But, Harding, your leaving the Corps wouldn't change the fact that you proposed for the sake of your child."

"I didn't, though," he retorted, and reached for her again. He felt her tremble beneath his hands and lowered his voice. "I love you. Dammit, I never thought I'd be saying those words, Elizabeth. But I am, and I mean them."

"Harding," she started.

"No." He pulled her tightly to him, wrapping his arms around her and holding on for dear life. "I *love* you." Staring down into her soft brown eyes, he willed her to read the truth in his. But all he saw shining up at him was a deep sadness. "You're a hardheaded woman, Elizabeth, but I don't give up easily."

"You should, Harding," she said. "For both our sakes."

"I can't," he told her solemnly. "For that very reason."

She laid her palms against his chest and pushed out of his arms. The ache inside him blossomed as she tried to distance herself from him. He saw her close herself off as effectively as if she had stepped into a tiny room and shut the door behind her.

"Elizabeth," he said softly, already feeling her loss. "I won't be pushed away. Not from you and not from my child."

She threw a quick glance at him. "I would never try to keep you from your child."

"You are. Now."

"No, I'm just refusing to marry you."

"It's the same thing."

"No, it isn't," she replied hotly. "Lots of people share custody of their children. The kids grow up fine."

"Most do," he admitted. It was all slipping away from him. He felt it go and was powerless to stop it. "But if those kids had a choice, I figure most of them would want their mom and dad living in the same house. They'd rather be together."

"Sometimes we don't get a choice."

"And sometimes we do—we just make the wrong one," he countered quickly. "Don't do that, Elizabeth. Don't make a choice we'll all be sorry for. I don't want to be a visitor in my kid's life." He paused a moment, then added, "Or yours."

Her bottom lip trembled slightly, but she lifted her chin and fought through whatever she was feeling. "This will all work out, Harding. You'll see."

"All I see is that you're willing to turn your back on me and what we've found together."

She crossed her arms over her chest and rubbed her hands up and down her arms. "What we found was just what we both wanted, Harding. A few weeks together. A temporary affair enjoyed by two adults."

And they called *him* Hard Case. Stepping up close to her, he cupped her face in his hands and held her still when she would have moved away. "That's how it started, princess. I don't deny that we weren't *looking* for love. But whether we wanted it or not, it's here."

She shook her head and closed her eyes against his piercing gaze.

"It's here, princess. And it's the real thing. I think it always was, despite what we told ourselves. Trust me on this. I know." He smiled sadly, remembering the one other time in his life when he had thought himself in love. That puny emotion wasn't a tenth of what he had found with Elizabeth. Damn, why hadn't he had the courage to face that one simple fact before now? When he might have had a chance. "If we throw it away, not only will we miss an opportunity to be happy…our baby will be cheated out of a family."

"Stop, Harding," she whispered, still keeping her eyes closed. "Please stop."

"I'll never stop, Elizabeth." He stroked her cheekbones with the pads of his thumbs, wiping away a solitary tear that had seeped from the corner of her eye. "I don't quit. Even when it might be less painful to walk away, I don't." He bent his head and planted a series of soft, gentle kisses along her brow. ‘‘You can’t get rid of me, and the only way you can convince me to stop asking you to marry me is to tell me you don’t love me.’’

She opened her mouth to speak, and he had to smile at her stubbornness. Covering her lips with his fingertips, he added, ‘‘Say it and *mean* it.’’

She closed her mouth and opened her eyes. He was heartened to see a sheen of tears filming over their deep brown color. She loved him. She was simply too afraid to take a chance. He understood fear. But cowering in a corner trying to avoid it only made fear a stronger, more terrifying opponent. He had to make her see that the only way to defeat the fear was to stand against it.

Together. ‘‘This isn’t over,’’ he whispered. ‘‘Not by a long shot.’’

Two days later Elizabeth stared at her most recent culinary disaster.

‘‘Why did no one ever tell me that pregnant women can’t bake?’’ she muttered. Grabbing her cow-shaped hot pads, she picked up the torte pan and carried it to the trash can. There she dumped the charred pastry and glared in disgust at the mess.

It wasn’t being pregnant that was ruining her ability to cook. It was thoughts of Harding. Blast him, she hadn’t been able to think about anything but him since he’d left her house two nights before.

And the situation wasn’t being helped by the fact that she hadn’t heard so much as a word from him in that time, either. What happened to all of his talk about not quitting? Not giving up on her? Was this some bizarre backward way of asking a woman to marry you? By ignoring her until she lost her mind, then sweeping in and overpowering her?

Setting the still-hot pan onto a folded-up, blue-checked towel, she plopped down into a chair. Resting her elbow on the tabletop, she propped her chin on her knuckles and glanced at the clock on the opposite wall.

Only one in the afternoon. She still had way too much daylight left before she could go to bed. Not that she could even look forward to sleep these days. Her dreams were filled with Harding, and memories of the past few weeks. The images tore at her, preventing sleep. Last night she had even dreamed about her child—only her unborn baby had been about six in her dream. Six and angry. Angry that his daddy wasn't around and furious that she wasn't doing anything about it.

Elizabeth yawned, then frowned when the phone rang, interrupting her perfectly good self-pity party.

Pushing herself to her feet, she walked across the room, leaned her back against the wall and snatched the receiver from its cradle.

"Yes?"

"Elizabeth Stone?" a deep voice asked.

A ridiculous flutter of excitement rippled through her body before she realized that the voice was unfamiliar.

"Yes? Who is this?" She straightened up from the wall.

"This is Captain Haynes at Camp Pendleton."

Dread settled in her chest. Her stomach took a nosedive, and she had to swallow past a hard knot in her throat. Danger to a soldier didn't solely exist on a battlefield. There were training accidents all the time. Her heartbeat unsteady, she forced herself to ask, "What is it? Is Harding all right? Was he hurt?"

"No, ma'am, the Sergeant Major is fine," the voice said. "In fact, I'm actually calling on his behalf."

Relief rushed in to replace the dread. "What do you mean?"

"I'd like to offer myself as a character witness for Sergeant Major Casey," the captain said.

"I'm sorry?" She frowned at the phone in her hand.

"I've known Sergeant Major Casey for several years now. I find him to be an exemplary Marine and an honorable man."

Elizabeth crossed the room to the sink, stretching out the phone cord to its limits. Turning on the tap, she poured herself a glass of cold water, took a quick sip and said, "That's very nice to hear, Captain. But I don't understand why you would call me to—"

"I owe Harding Casey," the man said, effectively cutting her off. "If I can help him straighten things out with his fiancée, I'm happy to help."

She inhaled sharply, set the glass down and walked back to the phone cradle. Fiancée. Varied emotions scattered through her like fallen leaves caught in a whirlwind. Amusement, anger, frustration, sympathy and love all warred within her, battling for supremacy. Finally she gathered her wits and told him very politely, "I appreciate your thoughtfulness, Captain."

She wasn't going to tell the man that she wasn't engaged to Harding. It would be the same as calling him a liar, and that she wasn't prepared to do. Especially to his commanding officer.

"Not a problem at all, Ms. Stone," he said, and his voice sounded as though he was pleased with the results of his call. "If there's anything else I can do, please feel free to contact me here at the base."

"Thank you," she managed to say, "but I think you've done enough."

After he hung up, Elizabeth slammed the phone back into its base and glared at it. What was Harding up to now? Was he going to have every officer he knew call her to vouch for him? Did he really think that other people's opinions would be enough to sway her decision?

She shook her head and wished there were more time. More time for Harding and her to know each other. To get used to the idea of a baby. But she was out of time and she knew it. In just a few more days he would be leaving.

The doorbell rang and she jumped, startled. Tossing a glance from the now-silent phone to the front door, she wondered briefly if she should even answer the thing. For all she knew, the Marine Corps marching band might be standing in her front yard.

She laughed at her own exaggeration, determinedly went to the front door and threw it open wide. On her porch stood two women about her age, a blonde and a brunette, each of them with a toddler by the hand. "Can I help you?" she asked hesitantly.

''Are you Elizabeth Stone?'' one of the women asked.

Wary now, she answered slowly. ''Yeesss...''

They smiled at her. ''Thank goodness,'' the blonde said. ''We've been driving around this condominium complex for twenty minutes. They all look alike!''

Foolishly Elizabeth felt she should apologize for their troubles. She didn't. ''Do I know you?''

''Nope,'' the brunette assured her as she picked up her little girl who'd begun to whine and slung her on one hip. ''We're here because of Hard Case.''

A sinking sensation started in the middle of her chest and slowly drifted down her body until it came to rest in the pit of her stomach. Apparently Harding wasn't finished ''convincing'' her yet.

''Let me guess,'' she said wryly. ''Character witnesses?''

''Heck, no,'' the blonde replied. ''Harding doesn't need a character witness. Anyone who knows him will tell you that.''

The brunette spoke up, her voice drowning out her friend's defensive, squeaky tone. ''Harding told us you were engaged, but that you were a little leery about marrying into the Corps.''

Perfect. She swallowed back a groan of frustration. These women weren't at fault. This was all Harding's doing.

''He thought it might help if we talked to you,'' the brunette finished.

Trapped, Elizabeth's good manners kicked in. Her mother would have been proud. ''Would you like to come in?''

"No, thanks," the blonde said as she bent to scoop up her son. "Tony's tired and we want to get back home for nap time. We only stopped by because we were up here shopping and—"

"It doesn't matter why we stopped," the brunette cut in again. "We only wanted to tell you that we can understand how you feel." She glanced at her friend. "Neither one of us was real crazy about marrying a Marine, either."

"Yeah," the blonde said. "I never figured me to be the military type." She shrugged and smiled. "But you can't plan who you'll fall in love with. Besides, it worked out fine." She grinned at her friend, then looked back at Elizabeth. "For both of us."

"Marines aren't always the easiest men to live with," the brunette continued as she gently pressed her daughter's head into her shoulder where the child promptly fell asleep. "But they are definitely the best."

Elizabeth felt she should say *something* in her own defense, so she blurted, "My father is a retired captain. I know about life in the Corps."

Rather than getting approval from one Marine family to another, she received a frosty glare from the brunette.

"If you're Marine, what's the problem? You should already know what life in the Corps is like."

"I *do* know. That's the problem." She couldn't believe she was having such a conversation with strangers! Just wait until she saw Harding Casey again. "Look, I've done my share of suitcase living.

It's not something I enjoy. Surely you can understand that.''

The blonde shook her head slowly as if sorry for Elizabeth. The brunette was a tad more direct. ''My husband risks his *life* for his country,'' she said solemnly, yet with a spark of defiance. ''All he asks of me is that I risk moving to a new neighborhood every few years.''

Elizabeth hadn't really thought of it like that, and she felt slightly ashamed of herself. Her lifelong complaint sounded suddenly petty and childish. Still, she had to ask. ''What about your kids? Don't you worry about dragging them all over the world?''

''My kids will see places most children won't,'' the brunette told her. ''And they'll be proud that their daddy served his country.'' Half turning to her friend, she said quietly, ''Come on, Sharon. We better get the kids home.''

The blonde smiled a goodbye, then started for their car. The brunette stayed a minute longer.

''My husband is a Staff Sergeant,'' she said. ''We've known Harding Casey off and on for years. They don't come any better than him.''

''I know,'' Elizabeth whispered and felt the truth of that statement down to her soul. If she could only be sure of his love. But she couldn't. If she surrendered to her own fears of being a single mother and married him now, she would never know if he had proposed because he loved her—or because of the baby.

The brunette stared at her for a long minute and apparently approved of what she saw. When she finally nodded, she smiled and said, "Good. If you know that much, any problem can be worked out." She stepped off the porch and onto the walk.

Elizabeth opened the door and called out, "Hey, I don't even know your name."

Stopping, the brunette turned around and grinned. "Sorry. I'm Tess Macguire." She jerked her head toward the car. "That's Sharon Trask." In a lower voice she added, "Her husband's still a corporal, but he's up for promotion."

"Thanks for stopping by," Elizabeth said automatically. Her manners were really excellent, she thought, as she realized she had just thanked two strangers for butting into her life.

The two women waved as their car pulled out from the curb. Before the sound of their engine had died away, a florist's van came to a stop in front of her house. As she watched, a young man leaped out of the van, walked around to the back and opened the doors. He reached inside and came back out with the biggest bouquet Elizabeth had ever seen.

Roses. Roses of every color and scent. Packed tightly together and tied with a pale blue ribbon attached to a mylar balloon that read Marry Me in bright red letters.

Dumbfounded, she took the flowers from the delivery boy, snatched a small white envelope from the cluster of blossoms and opened it. As the van drove off, her gaze scanned the brief message. "Elizabeth, I love you. Marry me. Harding."

She inhaled sharply, unwittingly drawing the mingled scents of the roses deep inside her lungs. Biting her lip, she clutched the bouquet tightly and stepped back inside the house. She hurriedly closed the door on the world, just in case a general happened by.

When the phone rang again, she wasn't even surprised.

It had to be Harding. Unwilling to set the flowers down, she held them to her chest and snatched up the cordless phone closest to her.

Before she could even say hello, she heard her mother's voice demand, ''Why didn't you tell us you were getting married?''

Twelve

She spent nearly a half hour soothing her mother and assuring her that she would be invited to the wedding—if there ever was one. Thank God Harding had had the sense not to mention the baby when he had made his call. But no sooner had she hung up with her mother than the phone rang again. Elizabeth spent the next hour fielding phone calls from everyone Harding Casey had ever known.

Finally, in desperation, she took the phone off the hook.

With her drapes drawn, door closed and locked, the phone beeping and metallically cursing at her, Elizabeth plopped down onto the couch. She felt like a prisoner in her own home. She was being outflanked by a professional soldier and didn't have the slightest idea how to fight back.

Turning her head, she glanced at the lead crystal vase, sitting in the center of the coffee table. She glared at the bouquet of roses and told herself she should throw them out or, better yet, send them back. But it was too late for the latter, and she couldn't quite bring herself to toss them into the trash.

She felt as though she was being bombarded from all sides. She couldn't think straight anymore. All she was sure of was that she couldn't afford to surrender to Harding's campaign. If she made a mistake, her baby would have to pay the price. And that, she wasn't willing to risk.

The doorbell rang, and her gaze shot to the closed door.

A moment later three brisk knocks sounded in the stillness. What now? she wondered. A parade? Groaning slightly, she pushed up from the couch and walked quietly to the door. There, she peered through the peephole and saw a thoroughly bored-looking teenage girl clutching a clipboard of all things. Looking past the gum-chewing redhead, Elizabeth studied her empty yard as if expecting an assault team to leap up from behind the rows of pansies and storm her house. A long minute passed before she decided the coast was clear.

She opened the door, faced the girl and asked, ''Yes?''

''You Elizabeth Stone?'' The redhead squinted at her.

Though she was beginning to seriously consider changing her name, she had to say, ''Yes, I am. What is it?''

The teenager held up the clipboard and gave it a wave. ''Got a telegram for you.'' She unhooked a small, yellow envelope, then held out the clipboard toward Elizabeth. ''Gotta sign for it.''

Sighing, Elizabeth edged the screen door open, scrawled her name across line nineteen, then took the envelope.

''You should get your phone checked, lady,'' the girl said. ''They tried to call the telegram in, but something's wrong with the line.''

''Thanks,'' she said, having no intention of putting that phone back on the hook. She reached for her purse, lying on the entry table. Grabbing for her wallet, she pulled a dollar bill free and handed it to the girl.

''Hey, thanks, lady,'' the teenager said with a grin.

Elizabeth nodded absently, then stepped back and closed the door. Leaning against it, she tore open the envelope and read the all-too-brief message inside. ''Six o'clock tonight. Be ready. We have to talk. Harding.''

Unbelievable.

She stared at the telegram a moment longer, then slowly, completely, crumpled it in one fist. He ignores her for two days, tells everyone he knows that they're engaged and sends them to plead his case for him, then has the nerve to order her around? Elizabeth pushed away from the door, stalked her way to the kitchen and unceremoniously tossed his precious telegram into the trash can. Who did he think he was, anyway? The man had even had the nerve to lie to *her* parents about them.

"Oh," she said with a tight smile, "I'll be ready, Harding Casey. I only hope you are."

Harding watched the limousine pull up and park. He tugged at the hem of his dress blue tunic and tried to ignore the rush of nerves sweeping through him. Hell, he'd been in battle. He'd crawled to safety under withering enemy fire.

Why was it that facing this one woman could bring him to his knees?

Because, he told himself, the object of war was to simply stay alive. To keep existing. The object of this crusade with Elizabeth was *life*. Not just existing. But really and truly living for the first time. If he lost this skirmish, he'd have nothing.

The limo driver opened the back door, and she stepped out. Just looking at her took his breath away. She straightened up, smoothed her black skirt and glanced around for a minute before she saw him. Then her eyes widened and her jaw dropped visibly.

Good. He'd gone to a lot of trouble to ensure just that reaction. As she looked around, he followed her gaze, seeing it through her eyes.

Alongside one of the fire rings set up for barbecues at the Huntington Beach pier, a small table was set up...with a white linen tablecloth, fine china and crystal glassware. A solitary candle burned brightly within the safe haven of a hurricane lamp. Standing a discreet distance away, a couple of Marines were stationed to keep other people from wandering in too close. For what he needed to say, he wanted privacy.

But he also had wanted the atmosphere of the

beach. He was hoping the memory of their walk on the sand that night they met would help his cause.

Bending slightly to one side, Harding punched a button on a nearly hidden tape recorder, and immediately the soft, delicate strains of Beethoven lifted into the cool, summer air.

He thought he saw a smile flit briefly across her face, but he couldn't be sure, because it vanished almost instantly. Then she was walking toward him, and it was all he could do to keep from going to her, drawing her close and kissing her senseless.

"What is going on, Harding?" she asked when she was within a few steps of him.

"Dinner," he said, and walked around to her side of the table. "And the chance to talk."

"You haven't been very interested in talking during the past couple of days," she said, her gaze locked on his.

It had about killed him to stay away from her. But he'd forced himself to. To give her a little time. To think. To realize that they belonged together.

Damn, why did he have to be shipping out now? Never once had being deployed bothered him. Not in the twenty years since he had signed up. Until now. Now, he couldn't bear the thought of leaving her. Of not being there to watch her body grow and swell with their child.

"Or maybe," she was saying, "you were too busy talking to everyone else to bother with talking to me directly."

He winced inwardly at her tone. All right, so he probably shouldn't have had his friends talk to her.

Obviously they hadn't accomplished what he had hoped they would.

"I'm sorry," he said softly, and reached for her unsuccessfully. She backed up, keeping a wary distance between them. "Maybe I shouldn't have, but you didn't leave me much choice, Elizabeth. I'm out of time. I had to try whatever ammunition I could come up with."

"You called my *parents!*"

"That, I'm not going to apologize for. I had to talk to your father, man to man. I'm in love with his daughter and I had to get his blessing on our marriage." That's how things were done. Couldn't she see that?

Elizabeth glared at him. "My mother called me and read me the riot act for a solid half hour because I hadn't confided in her about our 'engagement.'"

"Elizabeth—"

"I'm only surprised you didn't tell them about the—" she tossed a quick look at the two Marines, standing with their backs to them "—baby," she finished in a much quieter voice.

"I wouldn't do that without you." This was not working out as he had hoped. "Don't you get it? I *love* you."

"Stop it."

"I can't stop. And I wouldn't if I could."

She shook her head firmly. "You're only doing all of this because you're leaving. You're feeling guilty about leaving me alone and pregnant."

"You're damn right, I do!" He covered the steps separating them in two quick strides and grabbed both of her arms fiercely. "Can't you see what it's doing to me? Knowing I won't be here with you? Taking care of you?"

Her head fell back on her neck. "I told you, you don't have to worry. I'll be fine."

"But I won't." He stared into her eyes, feeling the same, swift punch to the gut he always felt when looking into their depths. "I'll be thousands of miles away from the one person I want more than my next breath."

Her features tightened, and she chewed at her bottom lip furiously. Indecision shone in her eyes, and he pressed his advantage ruthlessly.

"I want to marry you, Elizabeth. Now. Tonight. We can fly to Vegas and be back in the morning."

For one short, heart-stopping moment, he thought he had won. Then a shift of emotions clouded her eyes, and the moment was lost. Pulling away from him, she shook her head proudly.

"You can't bulldoze me into marriage, Harding."

"Elizabeth..."

"No. I won't be bullied into making such an important decision." Her heel caught in the sand, and she wobbled precariously for a minute. An ocean wind shot across the sand, lifting her hair into a wild, curly halo around her head. "You can't simply decide what's best for me and then steamroll me into agreeing with you. Marriage should be *our* decision, Harding. Not yours."

She headed for the limo. The chauffeur leaped out of the driver's seat and scurried for the back door.

Opening it just seconds before she arrived, he stood back while she slid inside.

Harding was just a step behind her. Jerking his head at the driver, he waited until the man moved off before looking down at the woman he loved and had to leave. Tears filled her eyes, but stubborn determination was stamped on her features.

Bracing both hands on the door frame, he leaned down and met her gaze squarely, silently daring her to look away. She didn't.

"Whether you believe me or not, Elizabeth. I do love you. Not just the baby. *You.*"

She didn't say a word, and he finally admitted to himself that he wasn't going to convince her. Not now. Not before he left. Pain stabbed at his heart until he thought he wouldn't be able to breathe. At last he finally understood what some of his married friends felt like when they were leaving behind all that they loved.

His fingers tightened helplessly on the cold metal. There was only one thing left to say.

"I want you to know," he said softly, "I've done what I can to protect you and the baby." He inhaled deeply, then told her, "I've named you my beneficiary and my next of kin. If anything should happen to me, you and the baby will be taken care of."

She gasped in surprise, then said, "You don't have to do that. I don't need financial help, Harding."

He scowled at her. She still didn't get it. "This isn't about money," he said firmly. "This is about honor. Love."

"I...don't know what to say." One tear spilled

from the corner of her eye and traced its way along her cheek.

"Say goodbye, Elizabeth. I leave tomorrow night."

"Tomorrow?" she said. "Already?"

He nodded. "Tell me you'll miss me. Even if it's a lie."

"Of course I'll miss you, Harding," she said as another tear traced its way down her cheek.

"Take care of yourself," he said softly.

She nodded jerkily. "You, too."

"This isn't the way I wanted to say goodbye to you, dammit," Harding growled, feeling a huge, black emptiness welling up within him. Time had run out on him. He had failed at the most important mission in his life. And now he would have to wait six long months before getting a second chance at winning her.

The months ahead stretched out in his mind, bleak and empty without her. He glanced at her trim figure and tried to imagine what she would look like, round with their child. Just the thought of all he would miss threatened to choke him. He had to go. Before he made a bigger mess than he had already.

But he couldn't leave without one last taste of her.

Bending down, he reached into the limo, cupped her face with his palms and pulled her head close. Planting his lips firmly on hers, he gave her all he had, pouring his love and concern and sorrow into a kiss that seared them both to their souls.

At last he released her and straightened away from the car. Staring down at her, he knew that this tear-streaked image of her was the one that would haunt him for six lonely months. He had had everything in the palm of his hand. How had it all disappeared so quickly?

"I love you, Elizabeth," he said, then closed the door and rapped his knuckles on the roof. The driver reacted to his signal instantly and keyed the ignition. With a muffled purr the long, white car drove away, taking Harding's world with it.

Elizabeth stared out the tinted back window until she couldn't see him anymore. Slowly she sank down into the plush seat and curled up in a corner. She'd made the right decision, she knew. A rushed marriage to a man shipping out immediately afterward wasn't the answer to a surprise pregnancy.

But if it was right…why did it suddenly feel so wrong?

Three weeks later, the first letter arrived.

Elizabeth plucked it from the stack of junk mail and tossed the circulars into the trash. Carrying the letter into the living room, she sat down in the corner of the couch and stared at the envelope in her hand. Lightly she dusted her fingertips across Harding's handwriting as if she was touching the man himself.

Lord, she missed him. More than she had imagined she would. And every day for the past three weeks, she had asked herself the same questions. Had she done the right thing in not marrying him? Or had she made the biggest mistake of her life?

Steeling herself, Elizabeth opened the envelope and slowly drew out the single sheet of paper. As slowly as a hungry man enjoying a fine meal, she devoured every word.

Dear Elizabeth,
I'm lying in my bunk wishing I was there, beside you. I know I made a mess of things before I left and I want you to know how sorry I am.

She sucked in a gulp of air and paused in her reading. Sorry? Sorry he had proposed?

You were right. I shouldn't have tried to bulldoze you into marriage. My only excuse is that I love you. And our baby. But during these weeks without you, I've realized that you need time to think about us. I want you to know I'll wait. My love won't change and it won't stop. Take care of both of you for me.

Yours, Harding

She let go of the letter, and the single page floated to her lap. Covering her mouth with one hand, she curled her legs up beneath her, laid her head on the sofa back and cried. For Harding. For herself. For lost chances.

Two months later Elizabeth reported for her first ultrasound. Her doctor had suggested the routine test as a "precaution." Uncomfortable after the seeming gallons of water she had had to drink, she stretched out on the examining table and stared at a blank TV screen.

A male technician, who looked about eighteen, with his long, pulled-back ponytail, entered the room and took a seat on the swivel stool beside her.

"All set?" he asked and readied his equipment.

"I guess so," she said, sighing.

His eyebrows rose slightly. "Well, you're the most unexcited mom I've had in here in a long time."

Mom. She shivered slightly. Even though she had broken the news to her family and everyone was now used to the idea of a baby coming, Elizabeth herself still sometimes had trouble believing it.

"So," the tech asked, "where's Dad? How come he's not here to catch the show?"

She swallowed heavily before answering. "He's overseas. In the Marines."

The teasing glint in his eyes softened a bit. "Sorry. Must be hard on him, missing all the fun."

"Yes," she muttered. "It is." She thought about the stack of letters she had received from Harding over the weeks. Almost every other day another one arrived. Lately she had found herself standing on the front porch, watching for the mailman's arrival. She tossed a glance at her purse, where all of those letters were safely tucked away. She kept them with her at all times. Somehow it made her feel closer to him. Less alone. Less afraid.

She couldn't help wondering if he felt the same about the letters she had mailed him.

"Well," the man said as he pulled back her gown and squirted cold jelly onto her abdomen, "I knew just from looking at you that you were the kind of woman whose man would be here if he could."

"You did?" She looked at him, watching him pick up the ultrasound scanner and position it above her belly.

"Sure," he said. "You see enough pregnant women, you get to know which ones are unhappy and which ones are, well, *loved.*"

Tears sprung up in her eyes. Elizabeth tried to blink them back, but the salty film was too much to be denied. She swiped at the tears on her cheeks, trying to hide them from the man beside her.

"Don't worry about it," he said, and patted her hand. "In my line of work, I see crying women every day." Nodding, he assured her, "It's just the hormones."

He went about his work, smoothing the scanner up and down across her flesh, the machine making a series of soft clicking sounds as it took pictures of her womb.

Elizabeth thought about what he had said. Hormones. No, it wasn't just the changes her body was going through. It was love. And misery. The younger man had been right about Harding. He would have been here if he could. Nothing would have kept him away. She and the baby were loved. *Really* loved. How foolish of her not to have believed it before. And how stupid of her to risk losing everything because of her own fears and doubts.

"There you go," the tech said. "He-e-e-re's junior!"

Elizabeth stared at the TV screen at the tiny spot of life she and Harding had created together. Her eyes filled again even as she felt a ridiculous grin spread across her face.

''Oh, Harding,'' she whispered in a broken voice, ''I wish you were here.''

Harding pulled the grainy eight-by-ten photo out of the envelope and studied it. What the hell? In bright red ink, someone had circled a small blob of *something* in the photo. Holding the picture in one hand, he picked up Elizabeth's letter and read it, hoping for a clue.

In seconds he had dropped the letter to his bunk and was holding the photograph under the desk lamp. A slow smile curved his lips as his gaze locked on the circled blob.

His baby.

Turning around quickly, he snatched at the letter and finished reading it. As he read the last paragraph, his smile faded and a worried frown creased his features.

> Harding, when you get back, I'd like for us to sit down together and talk about all of this. Surely after six months apart, we'll both be certain about what we want. And what we don't want. Take care of yourself. I miss you.
>
> Elizabeth

Damn. What did that mean? He winced inwardly. He knew just what it meant. Hadn't he lived through this before? Hadn't his ex-wife left him while he was deployed? Why should he expect Elizabeth—who hadn't even wanted to marry him—to be waiting for him with open arms?

He glanced at his child's first picture again and felt the first stirrings of fear thread through him.

Elizabeth stood near the back of the crowd. Hundreds of wives, mothers, husbands and children were stretched out along the edge of the Camp Pendleton parade deck. Signs dotted the eager crowd. Hand-painted with more love than style, they read Ooo-rah! and Get Some! the battalion's motto. There were other, more personal signs being waved high in the air by family members counting the minutes until their loved one arrived.

Elizabeth's fingers curled over her own sign as she clutched it tightly directly in front of her rounded belly. Maybe she shouldn't have come. Maybe she should have waited for him to call her. That's what she had planned to do. But at the last minute she had decided that the best way for her to know how Harding truly felt about her was to watch his expression when he unexpectedly caught sight of her.

She only hoped she would see what she wanted to see. Smiling at the families around her, she remembered other times, other bases. She recalled clearly, running into her father's arms as he came home from duty, and the all-encompassing sense of love that would wrap around her when he picked her up and swung her in the air.

Home wasn't a building. Home was love. The love that lived within the boundaries of a family.

That's what she wanted. That sense of belonging. With Harding.

"Here they come!" someone shouted, and Elizabeth looked up in time to see the first bus from March Air Force Base drive onto the asphalt.

She took a deep breath and watched, her heart in her throat. Within fifteen or twenty minutes the troops were assembled at attention on the parade grounds. After a brief welcome-home speech, the order, "Dismissed!" was shouted and pandemonium reigned.

Jostled as people streamed past her, Elizabeth laid one hand on her swollen stomach as if to comfort her child. Then she focused her gaze on the sea of soldiers, searching for the one face she had so longed to see.

Harding stayed near the back of the crowd. He had always been the last man off the tarmac. There had never been anyone waiting for him at the end of deployment. And this time would be no different. Elizabeth had already written him that she wouldn't be there to greet him. She would be waiting at home for his call.

He stopped dead as a young private darted in front of him, beelining toward a heavily pregnant, grinning woman. Harding watched their reunion for a moment, then continued on, slower than before. Better than being trampled in the rush of men running to their wives and kids. Slowly he walked across the tarmac, trying to ignore his friends' happiness. All around him new babies were being admired, and the kisses being shared were hot enough to melt the pavement.

He closed his eyes to everything, determined not

to torture himself unnecessarily. He didn't begrudge them their moments of joy. Blast it, he would have liked to be a part of it himself.

Shifting his duffel bag to his other shoulder, he continued to weave his way through the noisy crowd. In the distance he heard the base band strike up a tune, but he wasn't really listening. He slowed his steps, deliberately putting off the time when he would have to enter his empty quarters.

An aching loneliness settled in the pit of his stomach. What if he couldn't convince Elizabeth to marry him? What if he lost her and the child he already loved? He didn't know if he would be able to stand that kind of pain.

"Hey, Hard Case," someone close by shouted and he half turned to see Staff Sergeant Jack Macguire running up to him, hand outstretched. Grabbing Harding's right hand, Jack pumped it wildly for a minute before saying, "Congratulations, you old Devil Dog! Why didn't you tell me?"

"Tell you what?" Harding asked, but his question went unanswered as Jack spun around and raced back to his wife's impatient arms. He stared after his friend and mumbled, "Now what was that all about?"

Shaking his head, Harding started walking again. As he did, the crowd drifted away until he was looking directly at a lone woman standing at the edge of the tarmac. Her hair was longer than he remembered, but the lovely features, he recognized. Elizabeth. His gaze shifted to the sign she held in front of her. It read simply, "I love you."

Harding swallowed back a sudden, rushing tide of

hope inside him. Dodging around his fellow Marines, he kept his gaze locked with hers as he made his way toward her, desperately afraid that she would disappear before he reached her side.

She was here. Waiting for him. Surely that meant something. He felt a grin blossom on his face and didn't even bother trying to hide it. As he came closer, he dropped his duffel bag to the ground and stopped just inches away from her.

"You're here," he said softly, and wished all of the people, and most especially the blasted band, away.

"I had to be here," she whispered, meeting his gaze squarely. "I love you."

Something lodged in his throat, but he spoke around it. "I love you, Elizabeth. I always have."

"I know that now," she told him. "I can see it in your eyes. That's why I had to come."

He sucked in a gulp of air and risked everything he had ever wanted on one question. "Will you marry me?"

"Yes," she said quickly, tears spilling from her eyes and coursing unchecked down her cheeks.

"Ooo-rah!" Harding shouted and laughed all at once, feeling months of worry and fear fall from his shoulders like an unwanted blanket. He reached for her, but Elizabeth was still clutching that sign of hers and showed no intention of letting it drop. "Honey," he said with a smile, "to get the kind of kiss we both need, you're gonna have to let go of that so we can move in close."

Grimacing slightly, she lowered the posterboard to

reveal a very pregnant body. ''I'm afraid *close* is a relative term, Harding.''

Stunned, he stared at the mound of their child for a long minute before gently laying his palm atop it. She covered his hand with one of hers. The baby gave a solid kick, and Harding's eyes widened in disbelief. Finally, after too many years alone, he at last knew what it was to have a family.

''I'm fat,'' she whined with a half smile.

''Uh-uh, lady,'' he whispered as he bent to claim her lips, ''you're gorgeous.''

He tasted her tears and swallowed them, knowing them as the blessing they were. Love rose up around them as surely as the mounting applause from the surrounding soldiers and their families. Harding didn't care who was watching. Everything he had ever wanted was right there, held tight to his heart.

And he would never let them go.

Epilogue

Three months later.

"Ah, sweetheart," Harding whispered as he brushed her damp hair back off her forehead. "I swear to you, I'm going in for a vasectomy today."

Despite the pain, Elizabeth laughed and held his hand tightly. "Don't you dare," she told him. "I don't want junior to be an only child."

Eyes wild, he bent, kissed her forehead, then looked at her like she was crazy. "How can you even *think* about another baby now?"

The crushing pain ebbed slightly, and she lifted her gaze to her harried husband's worried features. God, how she loved him. Every day she gave thanks for whatever fates had brought them together.

''Don't worry so much, Harding,'' she said, then gasped as the next pain rushed at her, ''I'm not the first woman to have a baby.''

Whatever he might have said was lost as the doctor announced, ''All right, everybody, it's showtime! Harding, get behind your wife and prop her up.''

As he moved to follow orders, Harding brushed a kiss on the top of her head and whispered, ''I love you.''

''Me, too,'' she said, concentrating entirely on the task at hand.

''Here we go, Elizabeth, bear down.''

She did and in minutes, her son had entered the world, screaming his displeasure. Breathing deeply, Elizabeth lay back down and watched the doctor lift her baby so that she could get a good look at him before handing the newborn to his father.

Harding held the squirming infant confidently, as he did everything in his life. She smiled gently as she watched her bear of a Marine tenderly inspect his child with a loving touch and a soothing whisper of sound. At last he looked at her, his blue eyes brimming with unshed tears, his face touched with a smile of wonder.

''He's beautiful, Elizabeth,'' he said, and gently laid their son in the crook of his mother's arm. Bending protectively over them, he planted a quick, gentle kiss at the corner of her mouth. ''Thank you,'' he said in a tone meant only for her to hear. ''Thank you for bringing me to life.''

She reached up and caressed his cheek, wiping away a stray tear with her fingertips. Smiling up at him, she said, ‘‘I love you, Harding.’’ Then she winked and promised, ‘‘And don’t worry. I won’t tell your little Marine friends that their ‘Hard Case’ should really be called ‘Soft Touch.’’’

* * * * *

Look out for Maureen Child’s next book
The Marine & the Debutante *in March.*

Wife in the Mail

Marie Ferrarella

To
Dorothy Provine Day,
who first made me aware of Alaska
and gave me a goal to aspire to.
Thank you.

Chapter One

He wasn't here.

Sydney Elliot looked into the heart of the group of people gathered in front of the gate, welcoming the passengers disembarking Flight No. 17—*her* flight—and didn't see him. Didn't see the man she had flown more than two thousand miles to meet for the very first time.

The man whose proposal of marriage she had accepted only two weeks ago.

With effort, Sydney squelched the tiny bout of nervousness that threatened to grow into a full-scale, giant-size panic attack.

It was all right. He'd come. He'd promised he would be here and he would be. Time was just a relative thing; wasn't that something he'd written to her? That time up here in Alaska didn't mean the same thing it did in the other forty-nine states? It moved slower, more languidly, like a fish sunning itself in the stream after the first thaw.

All around Sydney people were being welcomed, hugged, kissed. Just in front of her, a woman was embraced by a huge, burly man while two children wiggled between them, eager to share in the homecoming, in the love that was so visibly there.

The scene warmed her. It was what she had come for. To find love again, or perhaps for the first time. To find a place for herself where she was needed.

What if he'd changed his mind?

What if he didn't come?

Trying to still the small, gnawing doubt within her that could, at any second, mushroom into something far less manageable, Sydney scanned the area, hoping to see a tall, broad-shouldered man hurrying through the doors in the rear of the terminal. Hurrying toward her.

There was no one like that.

Sydney shifted her carry-on luggage to her other hand. The strap was beginning to bite into her skin. There was no reason to panic. He'd obviously been delayed. After all, it wasn't as if he could just roll out his door to reach the airport. Ben Kerrigan lived some hundred miles away and, as he'd said in his last letter, at this time of year, even though it was fall, the road to Anchorage wouldn't be readily accessible by car. Ben had written that he'd have to fly his plane from Hades to get here.

Maybe he'd had to refuel first. Or maybe he'd gotten a late start. There were a hundred reasons why he wasn't here. She just had to pick one to focus on.

For a second Sydney shut her eyes to pull herself together. Panic wasn't her normal way of dealing with things. Ever since she was a little girl, she'd always been the levelheaded, practical one.

How levelheaded and practical had it been to uproot her entire life, pack it into a moving van and take off for the Alaskan terrain just because a man she had never met had asked her to marry him?

A smile curved her mouth as she recalled her best friend Marta's exact words on the subject. "Are you out of your mind?"

But she wasn't out of her mind, Sydney assured herself. She'd never been more serious, never been more sure of anything in her life than when she'd handed in her resignation to the principal of the elementary school where she taught, terminated her lease, sold most of her furniture and contracted Over The Hill Movers to move the most precious of her possessions not just over the hill, but halfway across the country.

Funny how fate managed to manipulate things. If she hadn't been in her dentist's office and picked up the magazine with the article about Alaska in it, she wouldn't be here. Ben had written the article and she had been completely captivated by his vitality. When he'd said that waking up in Alaska was like being reborn each morning, she knew she'd found her answer, her chance to turn things around for herself. She'd wanted to thank him for opening her eyes, so she'd written him a letter in care of the magazine. Less than a month later, there was a letter from him. After that, there were many letters, and over the course of eight months her future was finally forged.

Something had come to life in Sydney each time she'd read Ben's letters over the past eight months. Letters filled with the wonder of the place where he lived. Letters that made each moment in life seem like an adventure—fresh, exciting and precious out here in this pristine world. They reminded her of the letters that her Aunt Faye used to send to her father. Aunt Faye had made her life in Alaska. There was that same enthusiasm coming through. Ben's letters had also revealed his uncanny sensitivity for her feelings. A sensitivity that, in her time of need, had reached out to her. It was as if this man, living so far away in his icy domain, understood her. More than that, he understood what she needed. To be part of something, to be necessary, and to be loved.

The words in his letters made her feel that she could be all three. There was no question in her mind as she'd accepted his proposal that Dr. Ben Kerrigan was her soul mate.

There was also no question that he was still not here.

Sydney sighed as she struggled to ignore the strange, discomfiting premonition of dread, of something being wrong, that whispered insistently across her mind.

It was just prenuptial jitters, with a dash of jet lag thrown in, nothing more. She had to get hold of herself or else, when he did arrive, he'd take one look at her, turn on his heel and flee.

The group around her thinned. Very soon, there were no more passengers disembarking Flight No. 17. Except for the attendant closing the doors behind her, Sydney stood alone.

The look in the woman's eyes when she turned around told Sydney that there would be no stragglers coming off her plane. It was empty.

As empty as Sydney suddenly felt.

A genial, sympathetic look crossed the attendant's face as she approached Sydney. "May I help you?" The gently asked question resounded of kindness itself.

Sydney almost asked her if she knew Dr. Ben Kerrigan, but there was no earthly reason why the young woman should. He didn't practice here. Anchorage was large by Alaskan standards. It was Hades that was small.

Everyone there knew who Ben Kerrigan was. The doctor who, along with his brother, ran the only medical clinic in a hundred-mile radius.

Sydney merely shook her head.

"My ride's been delayed," she murmured. Until he finally arrived and found her, she had to get her things together. She licked a very dry lower lip and looked at the woman inquisitively. "Your baggage claim area is…?" With a comforting hand on Sydney's shoulder, the flight attendant turned her around and pointed to a huge white arrow suspended from the ceiling. Its sole function was to indicate the location of the down escalator.

"To your right as you get off the escalator. You can't miss it," she promised.

Sydney wasn't all that sure about that. She had a tendency to get lost very easily, even when things were clearly marked. That was another reason Marta had thought her coming out here insane.

"Give it up, Sydney. Nobody's a mail-order bride anymore, for crying out loud. Think," she'd all but begged two nights ago as she'd watched her pack. "You're going off into the wilderness, Sydney. You know what you're like. You'll get lost in the first damn snowdrift that crosses your path."

Sydney had laughed at the woman she'd known ever since her senior year in college. She'd taken no offense at the anger in Marta's voice, knowing that Marta only had her best interest at heart.

"Snowdrifts don't cross your path, Marta," she'd said, closing her last suitcase firmly and flipping the locks. "They're stationary."

"They have more sense than you do, then," Marta had moodily declared.

Maybe they did at that, Sydney thought now.

A moot point; she was here. This was going to be her new home. A fresh start. It was what she needed, what she wanted.

She focused on that.

Feeling somewhat better, Sydney shouldered her purse, shifted her carry-on back to her right hand and made her way to the escalator.

It's going to be all right, Sydney promised herself soothingly. *Ben's just late. Happens all the time here. Probably.*

People marked time differently in Alaska, that was all, she told herself again. Life had a more basic, less complicated purpose here. Wasn't that what had drawn her to Alaska to begin with? That, and Ben's letters. Or, more to the point, the man she'd discovered within the letters. An exciting, charming, intelligent man who made her feel alive again. The fact that the photos he'd sent showed him to be extremely good-looking was a bonus that fate had seen fit to throw in. If he'd lived anywhere but here, Sydney knew that Ben would have had his pick of anyone he wanted. But women were scarce in Hades, Alaska. And Ben had picked her.

At least she wouldn't have to worry about him running off just before the wedding and breaking her heart the way Ken had, she thought.

Gingerly, balancing her carry-on in front of her, offsetting it with the weight of her large, crammed purse, she stepped onto the escalator. As the metal stairs rhythmically made their way into the ground floor, she scrutinized the area, looking for any sign of him.

Dr. Ben Kerrigan was everything she had ever wanted in a man. Sydney'd known that a month into their correspondence, known from the way he wrote about his life out here with the unbridled joy of a child discovering everything for the first time. That, coupled with his dedication to his work, had made him perfect in her eyes.

So he was a little late, so what? In the grand scheme of things, that didn't mean anything. He'd be here soon enough.

Sydney was positive that Ben Kerrigan wasn't the type of man to go back on a promise. She had willingly bet her soul on it.

What was he doing here, looking for some woman who shouldn't even have been on the plane? If she'd had a single spark of sense in her head, this woman would have changed her mind, turned in her airline ticket, and stayed put.

He'd arrived late, almost not coming to the airport at all. And he didn't want to be here, he wanted to be at his clinic, working. Or even at home, awkwardly wrestling with the new role of fatherhood into which he'd suddenly been thrown.

Being a doctor in Alaska was a full-time job. There was no time for anything else. Which was why Barbara had left Alaska in the first place he reminded himself. Because he'd given too much of himself to his practice and not enough to her. Now that his ex-wife was dead, where the hell was he going to find the time to raise the two children she'd long ago stolen out of his life?

Not that he was any good at raising anyone. Look at the poor job he'd done of raising Ben after their parents had died. Ben had turned out to be all charm and little substance.

Shayne sighed, struggling with his anger.

How could Ben have done such a fool thing? Such a stupid, thoughtless thing? How could he have proposed to one woman—sight unseen—and then run off at the last minute because his ex-love Lila had come back into his life?

"I hope to hell you're enjoying yourself, Ben, because I'm sure not," he muttered under his breath as he made his way through the terminal.

The last place he wanted to be—the very last place—was the Anchorage Airport, looking for some woman who, if she did show up, probably didn't look a damn thing like the photograph he'd thought to take with him at the last minute. The one tucked away inside his pocket.

The photograph had to be a fake, taken of someone else, someone this "Sydney" woman knew. Nobody who looked that damn good would agree to marry a man she only knew on paper, a man she'd never met. More than that, nobody who looked that good would be willing leave civilization behind to come to what his late wife had referred to as "this godforsaken wilderness."

Shayne struggled to contain the impatience that mounted within him. Didn't he have enough to handle without this? He had two children in his life, children he barely knew. Children who looked at him with wary, distrustful eyes, probably because of all the things their mother had told them about him. Their divorce had been a bitter one. Bitter because he'd wanted her to remain, because he'd been so hurt that she could leave him so easily. Bitter because Barbara had taken off for New York and her affluent family without a backward glance, Sara and Mac in tow.

A court order, courtesy of an artful lawyer, had denied him visitation privileges. Her lawyer's justification: his visits, sporadic at best, would disrupt the flow of their young lives.

The one time he'd actually flown out to see his kids, Barbara had called the police. He hadn't even been able to broach the subject of having them come to visit him to Barbara, let alone the squadron of lawyers she'd employed to keep him away. Not wanting to pull the children into the center of the battlefield, and with no funds of his own to hire representation that even remotely approached the caliber of lawyers she had at her disposal, Shayne had retreated.

No, ''surrendered outright'' was more like it. But he'd never stopped loving them. His surrender had only had one term attached to it: that Barbara regularly send him photographs of the children. She'd reluctantly agreed.

The result: he had two children at home who didn't know him. Children he had to somehow incorporate into his life now that their mother was dead.

He didn't need to be out here, hunting for some woman who'd been foolish enough to believe Ben's silver-inked lies.

Didn't need to be out here, except that Ben had left him a note, asking him to do this ''one last favor'' for him. He supposed that he felt sorry for this woman and, in some remote way, responsible. Perhaps, if he had found a way to knock some sense of responsibility into Ben when they were growing up, instead of letting him slide, Ben wouldn't have done something this unpardonably thoughtless and cruel. Only three years older than Ben, Shayne had been no more prepared for the role of fatherhood at eighteen than he was now at thirty-four. But that was no excuse. He should have done a better job.

With an annoyed sigh, Shayne dragged a hand through his wayward black hair and looked around, feeling as if he was on a fool's errand.

People hurried by him. He looked at their faces, trying to make out features. He'd give this search half an hour, no more. There were far more pressing things waiting for him to tend to than looking for a woman who in all likelihood wasn't even here.

Part of him hoped she wasn't. He didn't relish having to explain this to her.

Shayne pulled out the photograph his brother had left with the note. Glancing at it again, Shayne shoved it back into his pocket, wrinkling it.

She wasn't here. He'd lay odds on it.

To be honest, Shayne had to admit a part of him had entertained the small hope that this woman Ben had been corresponding with would have a settling effect on his younger brother.

He should have known better.

There was no changing Ben. Not even medical school had tamed him. Why should a woman who was thousands of miles away make any difference to his brother?

But if that were the case, why had he asked her to marry him? What the hell had Ben been thinking?

That was just it. Ben hadn't been thinking. He'd just gone along with what had felt right at the moment. Running off with Lila had probably seemed right to him at the moment, too.

Ben's abrupt departure had squelched the last of Shayne's optimism. Not to mention removed the one buffer he'd had between him and his children. Ben had been the one highlight in their young lives since they'd been transplanted here two months ago. Mac and Sara both adored their uncle. He made them laugh and they could talk to him. Shayne didn't know what to say to them.

Shayne's mouth twisted into an ironic smile. When he and Ben were growing up, everyone had always depended on him, but it was Ben they had adored. Shayne had made his peace with that a long time ago.

So here he was, cleaning up another one of Ben's messes. The last one, if he was lucky.

Hers were the last two suitcases left on the carousel that displayed the disembarking passengers' luggage as it came off the conveyor belt. Instead of taking them, Sydney'd watched them go around and around as passenger after passenger subtracted pieces of luggage from the collection. It had given her an excuse to stay here, waiting in full view.

Her excuse was gone now. Everyone else had taken their luggage off. She couldn't just continue to stand beside the carousel, watching her suitcases move slowly around in a circle, only to appear time and again like the last two remaining wallflowers who hadn't been asked to dance.

Waiting until they reached her again, she took the suitcases off one at a time and debated what to do next. The logical thing was to remain in the airport until Ben appeared, or sent someone to get her. But she wasn't the type to stay put. She didn't like to wait, she liked to do, to move.

She thought of trying to locate a bush pilot who would be willing to fly her to Hades.

But what, if in doing that, she missed Ben? He could very well be on his way here right now. The idea of playing hide-and-seek between here and Hades was less than appealing.

They should have discussed an alternate plan, she thought. Too late now. Besides, it had never occurred to her that Ben wouldn't be here when she stepped off the plane. Everything he had ever written to her pointed to how reliable he was. Even the way he worried about his older brother, Shayne. He felt that Shayne had lost the ability to enjoy life, had allowed Alaska to deplete him rather than enhance him. It had begun early on, he'd written. Shayne had raised him after their parents had both died in an avalanche. His time to be young had abruptly ended. Ben's concern for Shayne was part of the reason she'd fallen in love with him. It just went to show her how large and caring a heart he had.

There had probably been an emergency for Ben to deal with, she finally decided. The clinic took up a great deal of his time and when he wasn't there, he was a bush pilot, flying supplies to people who lived and worked in even more out-of-the-way places than Hades. It would be just like him to put his own life on hold for someone else. In the short eight months that they'd corresponded, Sydney had felt that, with the exception of her late father and Marta, she had gotten to know Benjamin Kerrigan better than anyone she'd actually interacted face-to-face with.

It was time, she told herself, to do something before she grew roots in this airport terminal. Tucking her carry-on under her arm, and slinging her purse over her shoulder, she picked up her suitcases, ready to go in search of the information booth.

"Are you Sydney Elliot?"

The suitcases almost dropped from her fingers as her heart leaped to her throat.

Finally!

Sydney spun around in response to the gruffly voiced question, fully anticipating to see Ben standing behind her. As far as she knew, no one else here would know her name.

Her smile froze a little around the edges as a tinge of confusion took hold of her heart. The man standing in front of her resembled the man in the photograph she had in her purse, but in only the most cursory way. The man was a little older-looking, and... She supposed "harsher" would be the word she was looking for. His jaw appeared to be more chiseled than the one in the photograph, although that could be because of his expression.

The greatest difference was in the eyes. There was no laughter in this man's eyes. Instead of being the color of shamrocks in the morning, his emerald-green eyes were piercing, commanding. And troubled.

Something was very wrong here.

Sydney set her suitcases down, her eyes on the man's. "Yes?"

She wasn't as pretty as her photograph, Shayne realized. She was prettier, with hair like a golden sunset, eyes the color of the sky in the middle of summer, and skin the color of honey.

What was she doing here? he wondered again. Why would she want to live out her life in a place where most of the young inhabitants bailed out as soon as they reached the legal age of eighteen?

Sydney could feel his eyes boring into her, studying her dispassionately, as if she were an object rather than a person. The uneasiness within her grew a little greater.

She cleared her throat, hoping, too, to clear away her nervousness. "Did Ben send you?"

Even as she asked, she looked behind the man, praying that she'd see Ben walking toward her. But there was no one.

"Yes, he did." *Damn it, Ben, this was irresponsible, even for you.* The awkwardness of the situation chafed Shayne. There was no easy way to break this to her, and he'd never been much for talking. That, too, was Ben's gift, not his. "I didn't know how to reach you. By the time I found your address, you were already on your way here."

Her eyes narrowed as she tried to glean information from words that were just sailing past her without leaving an impression.

"I don't understand. Reach me about what?" She looked at him. "Who are you?"

"Shayne Kerrigan." As if in afterthought, he put out his hand. "Ben's brother."

The premonition she'd been sparring with scored a major hit and secured a huge toehold. Snatches of utterly opposing scenarios crowded her brain—Ben, taking the nearest dogsled out of Hades, escaping before her plane touched down. Ben, single-handedly fighting off some dreaded ebola virus. Ben—

She had to stop this. She couldn't keep speculating, not when there was a perfectly good way to access the information she sorely needed to calm her nerves.

"Why isn't Ben here?" She moved closer, searching Shayne's face. "Has something happened to him?"

Damn it, Shayne hated being put in this position. "Not exactly *to* him. But, yes, I'm afraid that something has happened."

The way he said that froze her heart. Iciness slipped completely over her, coating her skin with a thin layer of frost. Unwilling to let her imagination go any further, she placed her hand imploringly on his arm.

"What?" She wanted to know. "What's happened? Why isn't Ben here himself to tell me?"

Because he's a coward.

The words hovered on his lips, but Shayne didn't say them. He was loyal to the end, he supposed. Or maybe he was just stupid.

Shayne banked his annoyance. Ben wasn't bad, he just had this wild streak, a streak that refused to recognize that he was a grown man now and a grown man didn't propose to one woman, then run off with another. A grown man remained to sort things out and make them right.

When had Ben ever done that? The thought mocked Shayne. Ben had always relied on him to clean things up for him. Which then made this woman's dilemma his fault. If he'd instilled Ben with a better sense of responsibility—

But, damn it, no one had taught him that, Shayne thought. He just was.

Shayne looked at the woman in front of him, sympathy elbowing its way to the foreground. His tongue felt like a lead weight. ''Ben can't be here himself,'' he said again.

Why was he toying with her like this? Sydney wondered. ''Has he been detained?''

''No. Ben went to get married.''

She smiled at Shayne then. The man was pulling her leg. All right, she could enjoy a joke with the best of them. ''Yes, I know. Ben's getting married to me.''

But Shayne shook his head. ''Look, there's no polite, easy way to tell you this. Ben left a note for me early this morning.'' Shayne recited the essence of the note the way he would recite symptoms of frostbite to one of his patients. Quickly, dispassionately. ''His old fiancée returned to Hades to look him up. The long and the short of it is, they patched up their differences and they're getting married. Might already be married, for all I know. He asked me to tell you.''

Sydney could only stare at him in disbelief.

Chapter Two

Shayne faltered when he saw the look of abject distress enter her eyes. And then her eyes began to shimmer with welled-up tears.

She wasn't going to cry, was she? Shayne felt something twist in his gut as he cursed Ben's thoughtlessness again. He'd never known what to do when a woman cried. Ben was the one with a talent for making them smile again, not him.

Shayne's inclination was to turn around and walk out of the airport as fast as he could. But he knew he couldn't. Wouldn't. One irresponsible coward to a family was enough.

Feeling awkward as hell, Shayne mumbled, "I'm sorry," then mentally fumbled, knowing that wasn't enough. He really didn't feel like having her make a scene here, not with him in it. But more than that, though she was a stranger to him, he didn't relish being the cause of her pain.

He wasn't, he reminded himself. Ben was.

"Ben isn't the most reliable of people," Shayne added after a beat.

"No," Sydney agreed, the words leaving her lips slowly. "I guess not."

She felt as if she were in a dream. A horrible, suffocating, recurring dream where she was moving in slow motion through a thick haze, waiting for things to become clear again. Except they weren't. And they wouldn't, not after what Shayne Kerrigan had just told her.

First Ken, now Ben.

Sydney blinked, desperate to keep the tears back. Served her right for putting her heart on the line again, she chided herself. Hadn't she learned her lesson the first time?

Obviously not. Well, she certainly learned it this time.

Damn you, Ben, Shayne thought. *Why can't you do your own dirty work? And why can't you ever try to live up to expectations?*

Shayne dug into his front pocket and held out a handkerchief to the woman. The flash of a smile she offered in return seemed to pierce right through him. He thought of Ralph Teager. He'd treated the man for the flu last week. Maybe he'd picked up the bug himself. There was no other explanation for the sudden quickening of his heartbeat.

Shayne shifted, glancing around the airport. No one seemed to be paying any attention to them. He wanted to keep it that way. Shayne looked again at the woman in front of him.

She looked a great deal more stoic than he knew

Ben's Lila to be. Birds of a feather, Ben and Lila. Both wanting to drain all the fun out of something, then move on. He hated to think of the kinds of kids they'd raise, if they managed to stay together long enough to have any.

But then, how stable could this woman actually be, he asked himself, dropping everything to fly out here to marry a man she'd never met? That certainly didn't bode well in the common sense department as far as he was concerned.

Oh, damn, she *was* going to cry. Helplessness seared through him, skewered him.

Shayne winced inwardly at the tears glistening in her eyes. He could see the struggle she was waging to not let them fall. Admiration whispered through him, quelling the helpless feeling. He admired control. Seeing it affected him far more than vulnerability. It was easy to go to pieces, to hysterically throw up one's hands and give up, the way Barbara had with life in Alaska. It was a great deal harder not to.

The woman Ben had abandoned went up a notch in Shayne's regard. She shouldn't have to put up with this.

He wasn't impulsive by nature, yet Shayne found himself sliding his hands beneath his faded royal blue parka and digging a worn and cracked wallet out of his back jeans' pocket.

"Look, why don't I buy you a plane ticket back to..." Shayne paused, waiting for her to fill in the destination. All he knew about her was that she had come from one of the other states.

"Nebraska. Omaha." Even as she said it, the city felt a million miles away from here. She'd left it all behind her in more ways than just physically.

"Omaha." Shayne nodded.

A nice, sane place. The woman should have had more sense, coming from the heart of the country. It made him think of grounded people, people with their feet firmly planted and their heads a long way away from the clouds. It seemed to him that someone there should have talked to this woman.

Opening his wallet, Shayne took out all the money he had on him and realized that it wouldn't be enough to cover a ticket. Resigned, he took out a small, folded piece of beige paper tucked behind the bills. It was a blank check that he kept strictly for emergencies. Unfolding it carefully, he told himself he should have known he'd use it someday to take care of one of Ben's problems.

Shayne glanced at "Ben's problem" again and couldn't help but wonder if she had no family, no one with brains enough to insist that she stay where she belonged instead of flying off to a place that probably seemed as alien to her as the moon.

"Why don't I buy you a ticket back to Omaha," he offered, "and you can put this whole ugly thing behind you?"

It definitely seemed like a plan to him. And this way, his conscience would be clear. But when he turned to go, he realized that Ben's mail-ordered fiancée wasn't beside him. Turning, he looked back at her, raising a brow in a silent question. Now what?

He struggled to not sound impatient. He'd taken precious time off he couldn't afford to lose just to be here. "Aren't you coming?"

It was tempting—oh, so tempting, Sydney thought, to take this man up on his offer, cut her losses and run back to familiar surroundings. But even though she'd left her best friend behind, familiar surroundings weren't enough. They wouldn't do this time. What she needed was a fresh start in a fresh place. That didn't include Omaha.

Sydney shook her head. "No."

He blinked, certain he'd heard wrong. "Excuse me?"

She took a deep breath. It was easier this time. "I said no."

Shayne thought he understood what the problem was. She was probably suspicious of the offer. After what she'd been through, he supposed he couldn't blame her.

He held his position, waiting for her to come to him. "Maybe you don't understand." He held the blank check out to her. "I'm giving you your fare home. No strings attached. It's the least I can do after what Ben put you through."

It was also the most he could do because money was not something he had a great deal of. Enough for comfort, not enough for luxuries, and paying for a plane ticket for a strange woman came under the heading of luxuries.

Touched, Sydney crossed to him. She placed her hand over his and closed his fingers around the check. "Your offer is very kind, very generous, but I can't go back."

He didn't have time to argue. He'd promised to be back at the clinic by three. Removing her hand from his, Shayne tried to resolve the situation as quickly as possible.

"Look, if you're embarrassed to go home to your friends, I'm sure this kind of thing happens all the time." Although not to anyone he'd ever known, but Ben didn't have sole claim to being irresponsible. He couldn't have been the only one who had thoughtlessly left a woman twisting in the wind.

"More than you know," Sydney murmured. Even

though it had happened to her before with Ken, it wasn't embarrassment that was holding her back. ''But you don't understand. I quit my job, ended my lease, and packed up everything to come here. I thought I was starting a new life.''

So far, he didn't see the misunderstanding. ''I appreciate that, but—''

''And I intend to start that new life,'' she insisted, raising her voice so he'd hear her above his own.

Exasperation sliced through his patience. How many different ways did he have to say this? ''Didn't you hear me? Ben's gone. He eloped with someone and it wasn't you.''

Sydney refused to let the pain his words aroused get the better of her. Instead, she doggedly continued as if he hadn't said anything.

''That new life will just be a little different than I planned, that's all.'' Sydney fought to hold a tight rein on her emotions. It wasn't easy.

What were the odds, she wondered disparagingly, of picking two losers in a row? Two men, both charming, both intelligent and attractive in myriad ways, who'd promised her the Hope diamond in exchange for her heart and then left her holding a tiny rhinestone in its place? Talk about being a lousy judge of character...

All right, from now on, she promised herself, she was going to stick to what she knew. Children. She understood children, could look into their hearts and know what they were about. That intuitiveness failed her completely when it came to men.

She didn't understand men who said things they didn't mean.

Shayne took back everything he'd thought about this

woman. She was as scatterbrained as they came. ''And just what kind of life is that going to be?'' he demanded.

Because he'd tried to be kind, Sydney didn't take offense at his tone. He probably thought she was crazy. He didn't understand how much she needed to begin again. Why should he? He was a man, a breed that didn't have problems; they just caused them.

She squared her shoulders. Directly behind him was a large bay window. Beyond it was a wonderland filled with snow, the sun gleaming off the ageless, pristine peaks of the Chugach Mountains. It heartened her.

''Alaska's a big, beautiful state. There has to be a place for me here somewhere.''

''Oh, there're lots of places,'' he agreed. ''But you'll most likely freeze to death in most of them.'' He looked at her. At first appraisal, she'd seemed fragile. Definitely not tough enough to make it out here. ''Look, it takes a certain kind of person to move to Alaska.''

He wasn't going to talk her out of this. She'd never been very malleable once she'd made up her mind.

''Well, for all intents and purposes, I've already moved up here, so it's a moot point. My things are on their way to Hades.'' The moving van had left the day before she did. She'd spent her last night in Omaha on Marta's couch, counting the minutes until her flight.

''I can tell them to go back when they get here.''

And wouldn't the movers just love that? A round trip to Alaska, carting around her worldly goods. Her mouth curved mirthlessly. ''They're liable to dump everything on the nearest snowbank.''

''Alaska might be big, but there just aren't that many places for a woman to stay, not in a small town.''

Ben had written to her about Hades, but he hadn't covered everything. ''No hotels?''

Shayne laughed shortly. Hades was the very definition of small. Building a hotel was way down on the priority list. There were a few rooms over the Salty Saloon, but they weren't anything he'd recommend to a lady. "The town's not exactly a hot tourist attraction."

Sydney thought for a second, refusing to give up. "All right, what about Ben's place? You said he was gone." Pleased with her brainstorm, she picked up her suitcases. "I could stay there until I get my bearings."

And your brains, Shayne silently admonished. He took the suitcases from her and put them down again. "Ben doesn't have a place, he lives—lived—with me."

"I see." Sydney paused a moment, flagging, trying to regroup her thoughts. It seemed that there was an obstacle every way she turned.

As he waited, Shayne studied her face. Something in the set of her jaw softened him toward her. "You're determined to give this a try, aren't you?"

"Yes," she answered simply. "I have nothing left to lose now." She shrugged. Who knew? "Maybe I can still find that new life."

She had spirit, Shayne realized. It was coupled with stupidity, in his opinion, but it was spirit.

He refused to think over what he was about to say because if he did, he knew he wouldn't say it. As it was, he forced the words out of his mouth. "All right, you can stay with me."

Sydney had hoped he'd say that. But even as he did, she felt a little guilty. He clearly wasn't happy about the idea. "I can't put you out like that."

Picking up a suitcase in each hand, Shayne glared at her. The woman was turning out to be a handful. He really didn't need this. "Are you going to argue with me about everything?"

She didn't mean to sound as if she were arguing. ''No, but—''

The almighty ''but.'' Shayne turned on her, at the end of his patience. ''Look, lady—''

''Sydney,'' she corrected, siphoning the wind out of his sails.

Sydney, he snorted to himself. That wasn't a name for a woman. It belonged to a man. In a pinch, to a city. But not to a woman with hair the color of summer marigolds and eyes the color of robin's eggs in spring.

''Sydney,'' he echoed finally. ''If you want to stay in Hades, you don't have a whole lot of options open to you.'' He tightened his grip on the suitcase handles. ''You either stay with someone who'll make room for you or you build yourself an igloo in the middle of town and set up housekeeping there.''

She looked at him for a long moment, trying to read what was behind the stern expression. ''And you'll make room for me?''

''I have room,'' he corrected. There was no point in her getting the wrong idea that he was going any more out of his way for her than he actually was. ''Ben's room,'' he clarified. ''So, are you coming with me, or are you going to do the sensible thing and go back to Omaha?'' *Where you belong,* he added silently.

''I'm going ahead with my life,'' she answered. ''Not back.''

And with that, she turned toward the entrance of the airport, ready to face her somewhat altered destiny.

Already regretting his invitation, Shayne lengthened his stride to catch up with her.

They didn't have far to walk—Shayne had left his plane standing in the open field outside the terminal.

Sydney struggled somewhat to keep up because of the deep snow.

As she came closer to the airplane which looked small in comparison to the other planes around it, she could see that the diminutive Cessna had seen its share of travel. Sydney doubted that more than four people could fit into it comfortably. Maybe not even that.

She couldn't help but wonder if the old plane was safe.

Looking for something to say, she glanced at Shayne. He was behind her, tossing her luggage in under the rear seats.

"It's a nice plane."

"It gets me where I have to go," he said, not bothering to look at her.

Although, he admitted to himself, there were times when he hadn't been sure if it would. When he wasn't with patients, Shayne spent his time tinkering with the plane, trying to keep it running just a while longer until he had enough money to buy a new one. "Ben and I share it." A fond note entered his voice as he looked at the plane. They'd been through a lot together, he and the Cessna, and he tended to think of it in human terms. "I guess I should be grateful he didn't take this with him when he left."

Under the impression that Hades was only accessible by plane, Sydney had to ask. "How would he have—"

"There're a lot of ways to leave Hades if you really want to."

He'd seen her question coming. His guess was that Ben and Lila had prevailed on Jeb Kellogg. The general store owner's son was the only other person with a plane in the area. He could just picture Ben and Lila sharing space with ripened produce.

Abruptly, Shayne turned and slipped his hands around her waist to give her a boost up into the passenger seat. She felt even smaller than she looked, he realized, his fingers touching. The discovery almost made him lose the thread of the thought he was unraveling.

Leaning over her lap, he reached for her seat belt, then stopped. The less contact there was, the better. ''Buckle up,'' he said gruffly. ''This isn't going to be like the plane ride you just had.''

No, Sydney thought several minutes into the flight, it certainly wasn't like the plane ride she'd just had. That had been smooth and turbulent-free. Shayne's plane vibrated and groaned as it strained to become airborne and leave the ground behind. Every motion reverberated through her body. Sydney felt as if she were on a ride in an amusement park. A very old, rickety ride.

Shayne glanced to his right and saw that she was holding on to the armrest between them. There was a glove on her hand, but he had no doubt that the knuckles beneath it were white. He was so used to this, it never occurred to him that she'd be frightened.

But she wasn't whining or screaming, he noted, approval slipping through him. Barbara had screamed the first and only time he'd ever taken her up in the plane. It'd been brand-new then. At least, brand new to him, he amended. She'd been horrified over the experience and even more horrified that he had used all his life savings to pay for a second-hand plane. Born in the lap of luxury, her father a respected surgeon at a renowned hospital, she'd counted on enjoying more of the same by becoming a doctor's wife.

Shayne knew he'd disappointed her in so many ways during their four years of marriage, but never more than when he'd told her he wanted to come back home to practice. She'd resisted the move with every fiber of her being, but he'd managed to finally convince her to give it a try.

They'd spent more months arguing about it than she'd actually stayed. Less than six months after she'd accompanied him to Hades, holding Mac's hand and pressing their infant daughter to her breast, Barbara had boarded a plane out. Not just any plane, but a summoned friend's private Learjet. Barbara had always had style.

Or thought she did, he added silently.

The woman next to him had less style but far more courage and class. He noticed that she'd ceased all attempts at conversation ever since they'd taken off. A closer look showed him that she was positively pale.

"You all right?" The question was gruffly asked.

People certainly didn't come to him for his bedside manner, Sydney thought. She didn't turn her head toward him when he spoke. For the time being, she didn't trust herself to look anywhere but straight ahead. She had this feeling that if she took her eyes off the flight path, they'd plummet to their deaths.

It was the same as when she'd first learned to drive a car. She'd been afraid to look anywhere but several feet in front of her. Except now, she wasn't piloting the plane, thank God.

"Fine." The answer whooshed out of her breathlessly.

He almost smiled at her reply. He'd been a little nervous, too, his first time up. Nervous and exhilarated. He loved the freedom flying gave him. "Takes some getting used to."

Ever so slightly, she nodded her head. "That would be my guess."

Her hands were probably like ice, even with the gloves, Shayne thought. He placed one hand over hers, offering her warmth. "You know, you can breathe. There is oxygen in the cabin."

Sydney felt silly. She'd been holding her breath without realizing it. Slowly she released it. Released, too, the armrest that she'd been squeezing.

She flushed. He flew this plane all the time and probably thought she was being an idiot.

"I've never been in a small plane before." Sydney took in a long breath and forced herself to calm down. "Actually, until I flew here, I'd never been in a plane before, period."

Shayne spared her a glance. In this day and age of frequent flyer miles, it was hard to believe that there was anyone left under the age of seventy who hadn't flown. "Omaha that exciting?"

Excitement had nothing to do with it. A slight smile curved her lips. "No, I was just that busy."

"And now you're not?"

Sydney looked out to her right. There was only the slightest dusting of clouds, which looked like tiny bits of cotton pulled apart by eager, childish hands. She missed the kids she taught, she thought. A lot. She wasn't aware of the sigh that escaped as she murmured, "Not at the moment."

Seemed like a giant leap to come all the way here for a person who'd never flown before. "Why didn't you start out with something small, like a flight to Denver?"

She'd never wanted to go anywhere before. But after Ken had left her more than a year ago, she'd felt the need to get away, to find somewhere she could start her life over. Ben had offered her that chance. Or so she'd thought.

''Alaska seemed to have a lot more possibilities.'' She looked down, trying to envision the people who chose to make this land their home. ''Everything just seems so fresh here.''

''That's because it's refrigerated.''

The remark, so carelessly uttered, amused Sydney.

Her laughter, sparkling with delight, surrounded Shayne unexpectedly. As did the strange, small wave that washed over him in its wake. If he didn't know better, he would have mistaken it for pleasure.

But pleasure had absolutely nothing to do with the present situation.

Recovering, Sydney blew out a breath. ''After what you just told me in the airport, I didn't think I could laugh again.'' She turned to him, her eyes bright. ''Thank you.''

''I didn't mean it as a joke.''

The denial, roughly voiced, had Sydney wondering if he had a problem accepting gratitude. He seemed nothing like his brother—at least, the Ben she'd come to know on paper. And yet she suspected that there was something kind and good about Shayne Kerrigan. It just seemed to make him uncomfortable to have someone else notice.

She smiled warmly at his profile. ''Thanks just the same.''

He said nothing in response, pretending not to hear her.

Chapter Three

"How much of what Ben told me is true?"

Her question broke the silence that had existed between them for the past several minutes. Silence that had only been interrupted by the intermittent rattle of a plane that sporadically insisted on making its movements known.

It took Shayne a minute to absorb what she was asking. He felt like a man standing in front of a minefield. It wasn't a situation to relish. Lately there'd been a great many minefields in his life, but they couldn't be avoided. This one could have been.

The ever-mounting list of what his brother owed him grew a little longer.

Shayne glanced in the woman's direction. Who in their right mind would agree to being a mail-order bride these days? he wondered again. At least she didn't look as if she was going to cry anymore.

"I don't know, what did he tell you?"

As she tried to gather her thoughts together to form a succinct answer, Sydney stared out the small window. There was nothing but a blanket of white beneath them, occasionally fringed with clusters of small wooded areas. Evergreens. They made her think of Christmas, even though the holiday was almost two months away.

"That you and he were born here. That you're both doctors and that he flew medicine in when he wasn't running the clinic—"

"Ben never ran the clinic," Shayne interjected before she could continue. He'd never understand why Ben, given to embellishing whenever the whim moved him, always felt the need to dramatize the truth, or depart from it altogether. Just being Ben should have been more than enough for him.

"The clinic belongs to me," he stated flatly. He'd used his own money to build it and had driven in a good many of the nails himself. "Ben puts in—put in—" Shayne stopped, wondering if Ben ever meant to return to Hades. His brother hadn't mentioned it in the note he'd hastily dashed off, only that he intended to snap up happiness when it presented itself and it had presented itself in Lila.

"He put in hours at the clinic," Shayne finally said. "He flew the plane more to entertain himself than to deliver medicine." That sounded a little bitter, he realized, though he hadn't meant it to be. "Don't get me wrong, when the going got rough, Ben was right there by my side."

"And when it wasn't rough?" She had to know just how badly she'd been taken in by this man's brother. How much of a fool she'd been.

Shayne shrugged. ''He was somewhere else.'' And that, he had to admit, was most of the time.

In his letters, Sydney recalled, Ben had mentioned that he had a great many interests. She'd thought of him as a renaissance man. Now another image was beginning to form. Someone who enjoyed life and let his brother bear the lion's share of the responsibility.

''So he was a part-time doctor?''

That was one way to put it, but loyalty to his brother kept Shayne from agreeing.

''I don't think he ever really wanted to be one.'' Thinking out loud, he voiced a suspicion he'd kept locked up within him for a long time now. ''I think he became a doctor because he thought it would please me.'' In a way, Shayne supposed, that made him even more responsible for the way Ben behaved. ''And it did.''

He remembered how damn proud he'd been of Ben when his brother had come home with his degree a year ago. He'd felt that Ben had finally grown up and, with Ben at his side in the clinic, he wasn't going to be alone anymore. His brother was going to join his practice and between them, they could do so much good. He supposed that had been all hubris on his part.

Shayne sighed. ''Until I found out his heart wasn't in it.''

The feeling struck a chord within her. Sydney pressed her lips together. ''I guess his heart wasn't in a lot of things he did,'' she murmured more to herself than to Shayne. ''Or promised.''

He heard her. In an odd way, he realized that he empathized with Sydney. He knew how it felt to be abandoned. To feel so numb that you couldn't believe you were actually living through something so devastating, so appalling, or that you could go on living even when your heart had been ripped right out of your chest.

When he'd watched Barbara leave—even though he'd known that was what she intended to do—he hadn't been prepared for the emotional onslaught that followed in the wake of her departure. Hadn't been prepared for the horrid, gut-wrenching feelings that accompanied the realization that he hadn't meant enough to his wife for her to want to remain with him.

He moved the wheel, guiding the altimeter down a few degrees. ''You'll get over it.''

Sydney could feel her eyes growing moist. She couldn't let herself cry until she was alone. Gruff though this man next to her was, his kindness didn't deserve to be repaid with the tears of a sobbing woman.

She took a breath before she turned her head to look at him. ''Excuse me?''

Shayne wasn't given to being talkative and wasn't good at articulating his thoughts. But she was in pain and he was a doctor. It was his sworn duty to alleviate the pain if he could, even if it wasn't the kind of pain that was found in any medical book.

''That feeling you have now—the one that feels as if something just kicked you right in your gut...you'll get over it.''

He almost sounded gentle. She appreciated the effort. She had a feeling it probably didn't come easily to him. ''Is that your professional opinion?''

Shayne stared straight ahead at the cloud formation. It was a perfect day to fly. ''That's my personal opinion.''

Had someone hurt him? She knew she couldn't ask. The way he said it, the topic was now closed. He wasn't about to tell her any more.

Ever so slowly, Shayne set the pace for the plane's descent. The small airstrip he'd forged was located just ahead, very close to his home. He'd done this so many times, the movements came to him automatically, without any thought.

He prepared to lower the landing gear. "What is it that you do when you're not packing up and moving to Alaska?"

"I'm a teacher." It made her feel less rootless when she said that. She was connected to the world by her work, by the minds she'd touched. That meant a great deal to her.

"We don't have a school in Hades." Which was something that hadn't concerned him one way or another until the past few months.

So many things that hadn't concerned him a year ago were now pushing their way to the foreground. He was responsible for two small souls. A responsibility that didn't end when he wrote out a prescription or doled out a kind word. It continued, round-the-clock, twenty-four hours a day. Waking or sleeping.

It was humbling and unnerving at the same time.

"There's one in Snowshoe, though." He did a quick calculation. "That's about thirty minutes from Hades—shortest route," he added. He didn't bother mentioning that sometimes, during the winter, the shortest route was completely impassable.

Sydney supposed that it was worth looking into. Maybe tomorrow, once she pulled herself together, she'd try to hire someone to take her there. "Do you know if they need a teacher?"

"No, I don't." He would have thought she would have directed these questions to Ben in her letters.

He knew very little about the school there, other than

that it existed. Right now, he was leaving his children's education up to the wife of the general store owner. For now, Shirley Kellogg was doing a fair job of it. The woman had received accreditation in a home studies program to teach her own brood of seven. With all of them grown now, she taught children in the area. He'd begun his own schooling that way, in a tiny log cabin that seemed old even by Hades's standards. Miss Faye had been the teacher then, and he'd learned a great deal.

But looking into the school at Snowshoe was something he was going to have to do soon, though. Mac and Sara were eventually going to need more education than Shirley Kellogg could provide just as he and Ben had needed. They'd attended school in the once-thriving town of Shelbyville, but it was now just a ghost town.

"What was it you were planning on doing after you and my brother were married?" he finally asked. Too late, he realized he'd opened a very raw subject. "Sorry," he muttered. "I didn't mean for it to sound like that. I'm not the talker in the family, Ben is."

"It's all right."

Sydney thought of the long letters Ben had written to her, planning their future. He'd envisioned them working together side by side. It was hard to believe that the plans had all been lies. Maybe there'd been a grain of truth in them. Maybe, if this ex-love of his hadn't shown up, Ben would have been at the airport to meet her and they could have begun this life together.

Hashing all that over in her mind wasn't going to accomplish anything, Sydney knew. She had to face the future, whatever that held for her.

She looked at Shayne, a thought coming to her. Maybe he could still use her.

"Ben said I could work at the clinic."

This was the first he'd heard of it. "Oh, he did, did he?" Just when was Ben planning on springing that one on him? In Ben's defense, Shayne realized he hadn't been very receptive about Ben marrying some woman sight unseen when he'd told him about his plans last week. He'd tried to talk him out of marrying a virtual stranger. Ben probably thought it best not to mention having her work at the clinic until after she arrived.

Of course, all that was water under the bridge now. She wouldn't be marrying Ben and as soon as she experienced a hostile winter, she'd be on the first plane out of here.

Sydney didn't particularly like the tone in his voice. The decision for her to work at the clinic wasn't based on charity or a nebulous whim.

"I have some medical training. I was going to become a doctor."

It was that, in part, that had brought them together. Ben had mentioned in the article what it was like, being one of the only two doctors for miles. He'd sounded quietly heroic and selfless. She'd fallen in love with that image.

Just went to show her there were no white knights left.

"What happened?" Shayne didn't bother to erase the skepticism from his voice.

The plane was rattling. Hard. Sydney wrapped her fingers around the armrests again. Her breath felt like a solid entity, weighing heavily in her lungs as the plane approached the airstrip. Her nerves jangled, mimicking the rhythm of the plane. She couldn't imagine wanting to do this over and over again.

Sydney forced her mind back to the question he'd just asked.

"My father became ill. The money I had for medical school went to take care of him." She'd never regretted that decision. But she did, at times, regret not being able to become a doctor. "Becoming a teacher seemed the best compromise."

She'd left him behind with that leap in conversation. "I don't see the connection," he said, flipping a lever, preparing the plane for landing.

"I was going to be a pediatrician." She was trying her level best not to sound as afraid as she felt. "I love working with children."

The short, soft laugh was self-depreciating. "You're a braver man than I, Gunga Din."

That caught her attention, drawing it away from the swiftly approaching frozen ground. "Kipling?"

He shrugged one shoulder carelessly. "I do a lot of reading. Not much to do at night around here."

"What does being brave have to do with children?" He was the brave one, flying this shaky tin can on a regular basis.

He thought of his children, two small strangers he had yet to get to know, much less understand. Almost every word out of his mouth seemed to be the wrong one. "They're just difficult to deal with."

Was it her imagination, or was the shaking lessening? She certainly hoped so. "No more than anyone else."

"I have no idea how to talk to children," he readily admitted.

That there should be a difference had never occurred to Sydney. She dealt with everyone in the same manner—honestly and with compassion. She supposed that, in the case of men, that was her mistake.

"Just the way you'd talk to anyone else," she told him. She watched the ground as it continued to approach them quickly. ''Children surprise you. They're a great deal brighter than most adults give them credit for.'' The words dribbled out of her mouth as she braced herself for impact. ''The trick to communicating with them is to remember how you felt when you were their age.''

It seemed to Shayne that he had been born old. Childhood, if it had ever existed for him, was a million miles away. ''I don't remember being their age.''

His admission aroused her sympathy. ''That's a shame.''

He didn't deal well with pity. ''If you say so.'' Shayne braced as the wheels of the plane made contact with the ground.

Like a dentist's drill that had slipped and hit a nerve, the jolt went through her entire body. Recovering, she sucked in a long breath to steady herself before she hazarded a look at him. He seemed completely unfazed.

''Do you always land that way?''

''No.'' Pressing the button, he released his seat belt, then wiggled it out of the slot when it refused to budge. ''That was one of the smoother ones.''

She thought he was kidding until she looked at his face. The man was dead serious. ''Maybe you should get a bigger plane.''

He was already out and ducking under the wing to get to her side. ''I intend to. As soon as I can afford one.'' And from where he stood, that day wasn't going to be any time in the near future.

He held his arms out to her, waiting to help her down. She slid into them, realizing belatedly that her legs were shaky. When her feet touched the ground, they felt like limp dental floss. She sank as she tried to put her weight on them.

''Whoa.'' His arms tightened around her immediately, jerking her to him as he steadied her.

Something quick, sharp and elusive spiraled through her, discharging electricity like an eel that had been stepped on, the moment their bodies touched. Confusion creased her brow as she looked up at him.

The next second, the sensation was gone, vanishing as if it never existed. As if it were all in her mind.

Maybe it was, she thought. She'd been through a lot today and the day wasn't over.

Aware that he was holding her too close, Shayne loosened his grip. He peered at her face. ''Are you all right?''

She felt really foolish. ''Yes.'' With effort, she forced her legs to stiffen until they could support her. ''Just haven't got my sea legs yet—'' Sydney raised her eyes to his face. ''Or is the term 'air legs'?''

He wished she'd stop looking up at him like that. It made a man lose his train of thought. ''There is no term for it.'' He almost bit off the words. ''Can I let go now?''

To be on the safe side, Sydney kept a hand on his arm as she tested her legs before giving him an answer. Mercifully, they didn't buckle this time.

''They're steadier,'' she announced, then flashed a quick smile at him. ''Sorry, didn't mean to fall all over you like that.''

He'd had worse experiences. ''No harm done,'' he muttered.

But there had been harm, he thought. Holding her like that, however innocently, had only served to remind him just how long it had been since he'd held a woman in his arms. Up until this moment he'd talked himself into believing that it didn't matter. His practice kept him incredibly busy. And now, with his children here, he was *more* than busy. That was supposed to be enough.

It *had* been enough.

This wake-up call was far from welcome.

Abruptly, he turned from her and retrieved her luggage from behind the seats. He set the first suitcase on the ground, then leaned in to pull out the second one, setting it beside its mate as he secured the plane. Finished, he turned and picked up the suitcases. Snow clung to their bottoms as he grasped both handles in his hands.

Not accustomed to having someone else do for her, Sydney reached for the closest suitcase. But to her surprise, Shayne wouldn't release it.

"Here, let me take one." Sydney tried to reach for the handle again.

Shayne used the suitcase as a pointer, indicating the building in the distance. "Just walk," he instructed.

Since he couldn't be reasoned with, Sydney wrestled the suitcase out of his hand, then fell into step beside him. When he looked at her as if she'd just lost her mind, she asked pleasantly, "Were you in the army?"

Where had that come from? he wondered. "No, why?"

She grinned at him. "You sounded like a drill sergeant just then. I'm beginning to understand why you might have trouble talking to children."

There was no "might" about it. He had probably exchanged fewer than fifty sentences with Mac and Sara since they had come to live with him. And it was just getting harder, not easier, for him with each passing day.

Paying attention to what was in front of her, Sydney got her first clear view of the house where she would be staying. It looked exactly the way Ben had described it.

An old-styled, two-story Swiss chalet, all wood and stone perched on a tablecloth of pristine snow.

Sydney had a tremendous sense of homecoming, despite the extenuating circumstances.

"It's charming." Out of the corner of her eye, she saw the questioning look he gave her. "Your house," she explained.

Charming. Barbara hadn't thought so. She'd thought it hopelessly rustic and outdated. He'd promised to renovate it for her, but he hadn't found the time to get around to it. After six months, it ceased to be necessary.

As for himself, he'd never thought of the building in terms of adjectives. It was just home. It always had been.

"Thanks. Ben and I were born here," he heard himself unintentionally sharing with her, and shrugged it off to empathy.

"Really?" Ben had already told her that, but she pretended it was news. The house boasted four bedrooms and several fireplaces, she recalled. She'd thought it large for one man when Ben had described it. He'd promised that they'd fill it with children as soon as she was ready. The thought had thrilled her.

She couldn't believe that she'd been so easily taken in. With effort, she shook off the memory. "It looks so large. Were your parents wealthy?"

Only in terms of the love they bore one another, Shayne thought. Watching them, he'd grown up believing that husbands and wives adored each other and that marriage was forever. Finding out otherwise had been a rude revelation.

"No, my father was good with his hands," he explained matter-of-factly. "My mother wanted a large house. He wanted to please my mother."

''An admirable quality,'' she commented, shifting the suitcase to her other hand.

Shayne caught the motion out of the corner of his eye. Small wonder, he mused. It felt as if she'd packed rocks in both. Never breaking stride, he turned a hundred and eighty degrees, took the suitcase from her and then faced forward again. The expression on his face dared Sydney to offer any protest.

He noticed with satisfaction that she had enough sense to keep her mouth shut. They were at the front door quickly enough anyway.

Shayne nodded toward it. ''Get the door, will you?''

''Sure.'' She turned toward him. ''Where do you have the keys?'' There was no Welcome mat before the threshold and she doubted if he meant for her to rifle though the pockets of his parka.

His eyes indicated the doorknob. ''Just turn that, it's unlocked.''

She liked that, Sydney thought. Liked the idea of living somewhere where she could keep the doors unlocked. Where she felt safe. But she had to admit it was going to take some getting used to.

Turning the doorknob, she pushed open the door and heard a startled, shrilled yelp from the other side. She immediately pulled the door to her before looking around it.

There were two children, a boy and a girl, standing directly behind it.

Children. Shayne had children, she remembered belatedly. Ben had written all about his niece and nephew. The affection that had spilled out in his words was just another element that had tugged on her heart and sealed her fate.

She left the door standing open as she looked from

one child to the other. ''Oh, I'm sorry. Are you two all right?''

The boy, with his black hair and green eyes, looked like a miniature version of Shayne, right down to the scowl darkening his handsome face. His sister's features were far more delicate, her long, silky-blond hair unearthing the memory of a porcelain doll Sydney had once seen in a catalog.

''Yes.'' Huge blue eyes looked up at her as a shy smile made a hesitant appearance on the little girl's small lips.

There was no sign of a smile on the son's face. ''Who's she?'' he demanded of his father. It was obvious he was offended his father had brought someone into the house.

Instead of waiting for Shayne to make the introductions, Sydney put her hand out to the boy. ''Hi, I'm Sydney. What's your name?''

''Mac Kerrigan.'' He gave the information grudgingly, though Sydney had the impression that he liked her shaking his hand. The green eyes swept over her critically. ''Sydney's a funny name for a girl.''

''You think so, too, huh?'' Her agreement defused a little of his dark mood. ''It was my dad's name. He gave it to me because he liked it so much.'' And because he'd hoped for a son, she added silently. The bond that was forged between them over the years, though, had quickly made gender unimportant.

Mac loftily accepted the reason. He jerked a thumb at the little girl. ''This is Sara. She's my sister.''

''Pleased to meet you, Sara.'' The girl's hand felt slight and cold in hers. Sydney glanced over her shoulder. She'd already made enough mistakes today. For all she knew, Ben had lied about the children, too. "Are they yours?"

"We're ours," Mac contradicted defiantly.

The boy had been growing steadily more hostile since their arrival. While Shayne understood that his son had experienced a lot of changes in his life lately, it didn't excuse his rudeness toward Sydney. It certainly wasn't making this ordeal any easier.

"They're my son and daughter," he answered, setting her suitcases at the foot of the stairs.

There was enough tension in the room to fill a sports arena, she thought.

Sara ran to the door, peering outside. "Is Uncle Ben with you?" she wailed. She turned to look accusingly at her father. "He said he'd be back soon, but that was so long ago."

"I told you, he's not coming back," her brother said to her, his young face etched with anger. Sydney couldn't tell if he was angry at Sara for believing, or at Ben for violating that belief. Probably a little bit of both. "He left us, too."

Too. The word echoed in the room, hurtful and sharp. Tears sprang to Sara's eyes as she hugged her doll to her chest.

Sydney turned to look at Shayne. His lips were pressed together in a single, hard line. She was beginning to see what Shayne had meant about not knowing what to say to children.

There was a definite challenge here.

Chapter Four

The misery in the little girl's eyes cut through any awkward feelings or decorum. There was no way Sydney could bring herself to ignore an unhappy child. It never occurred to her to even try.

As Shayne watched, surprised, Sydney dropped down to her knees in front of his daughter. Very gently, she turned the little girl's face toward her. Making eye contact, she smiled.

''I don't think your uncle Ben was thinking about leaving you, Sara. He was just too excited about getting married to realize that he couldn't keep his promise to you.''

Sara's mouth formed a perfect *O*. ''Uncle Ben's getting married?'' She breathed the words in stunned disbelief.

''No, he's not,'' Mac insisted, elbowing his way between Sydney and his sister.

Sydney recognized it for what it was: Mac was being protective. For his own reasons, Mac was trying very hard to appear tough, but it was obvious that Sara was his weak spot.

"Oh, but he is," Sydney told him patiently. She looked from one child to the other, including them both. "To someone named Lila, wasn't it?"

She raised her eyes toward Shayne for confirmation. It cost her to talk about it so cavalierly, as if Ben were some stranger she didn't know instead of the man she'd come out to marry. But there was a great deal more at stake here than just her own feelings and wounded pride.

To be a child and feel abandoned had to be the worst of all possible worlds.

Shayne could only nod as he looked on. How could she look so detached, sharing something that he'd assumed was so painful and humiliating, for the sake of drying the tears of a child who meant nothing to her?

Maybe she wasn't nearly as upset about Ben jilting her as she'd earlier let on. In which case, he was being one hell of a fool, allowing himself to be suckered into letting her stay here because he felt guilty over what his brother had done.

He continued to watch Sydney in silence, trying to make up his mind about her.

Sara looked at Sydney uncertainly, vacillating between believing her and siding with her brother. "Uncle Ben was whistling when he left the house early this morning. I saw him," she volunteered, casting a side glance at Mac.

Sydney nodded. "That was because he was happy." She touched the little girl's cheek, affection already taking root. It didn't take long with her, she mused silently. She'd never met a child she didn't like. "He didn't mean to hurt you, Sara. Or you,'' she told Mac as she rose to her feet. She rested one hand on the boy's shoulder, but he shrugged it off. Sydney took it in stride. ''And he'll be back eventually, after his honeymoon.''

Sara stared at her, trying desperately to understand. ''What's a honeymoon?''

Something that she'd thought she'd be on very soon. Sydney blocked the thought. This wasn't about her, it was about two half-orphaned children not feeling as if everyone was leaving them emotionally stranded.

For their sake, Sydney forced herself to smile. ''That's something a man and woman go on right after they get married.''

Sara cocked her head, her brows drawing together. ''Like a vacation?''

Trust a child to cut to the heart of it. Sydney loved the way their minds were always working. ''Exactly like a vacation. A special kind of vacation for just the two of them.'' Sara's expression told her that, for the time being, the little girl was placated.

But the look on Mac's face indicated that he held everything suspect and was far from satisfied. Sydney had a feeling that he was probably more like his father than either one of them was aware of.

Turning toward Shayne, Sydney saw that he was looking at her as if he were working out a puzzle in his mind. Had she said something wrong, something to offend him?

But he didn't look angry, just…unreadable. And if body language was any indication of what he was feeling, he looked as though he was anxious to leave.

''Maybe you'd better show me where I'll be staying,'' she suggested.

Habit had him looking at his watch. Shayne frowned, letting his parka sleeve slip back down.

"Asia will have to do that." He'd used up more time than he'd realized. But that was because he hadn't expected to bring Sydney back with him. "I was due at the clinic fifteen minutes ago." He looked at Mac. "Where's Asia?"

Mac merely shrugged carelessly, a bored expression on his face. He didn't answer.

His insolence confounded and irritated Shayne, but before he could say anything to his son, Sara quickly volunteered. "She's in the kitchen."

In her own way, Sara was as protective of Mac as he was of her, Sydney noted.

"Asia." Shayne raised his voice to make it carry to the rear of the house.

Was that the housekeeper? Sydney wondered. It didn't matter, she didn't want to take the woman away from her work. The less waves she caused, the better she'd feel.

"That's all right," Sydney said, "if you just tell me which room it is—"

At that moment, a small, older woman walked into the room. She carried herself like a princess, her silver-gray hair falling in two long, perfect braids to her waist. As she approached, Sydney noted that her round face was the color of berries browned by the sun. The eyes belonged to a woman who had seen a great deal of life.

Her first real native Alaskan. The realization somehow made Sydney feel a little more familiar with her surroundings.

Eyes as black as midnight looked at Shayne, waiting.

"Asia, this is Miss Sydney." He gestured toward her.

"She'll be staying with us for a while. Show her to my brother's room, please."

Mac jumped on the words. "Then he's not coming back."

Sydney thought the triumph in his voice rang hollow. It couldn't be that Ben was the only one Mac had liked in this awful place he'd found himself transported to, could it? What about his own father?

"It's just temporary," Sydney put in quickly, sparing Shayne an explanation. "I'm kind of stranded right now and your father thought that until I figure out what I'm going to do, I could stay here. Since your uncle is away on his honeymoon, we didn't think that he'd mind my using the room."

Mac eyed her, uncertain as to whether or not he believed what she was saying. "When he comes back, you'll go?"

She heard the challenge in his voice. "I'll have to," Sydney answered simply. "There won't be any room for me here."

Maybe he *had* made a mistake, Shayne thought, upbraiding himself for his misguided invitation. She certainly didn't appear to be upset about being left at the proverbial altar. The woman sounded as removed from all this as if she were talking about an article she'd read in the newspaper.

Well, whether or not it was a mistake, he'd have to deal with it later. Right now, if past performance was any indication, he had a clinic full of patients waiting for him and no one to handle them.

He glanced at the housekeeper he'd been forced to engage with the children's arrival. Asia came from a village not far from Hades. He couldn't remember a time he hadn't seen her walking into town, trading goods at the general store. There'd always been several of her children in her wake. These days, the stragglers walking behind her were her grandchildren. She'd left their care to someone else to come work for him.

She wasn't a very good cook, and an even worse housekeeper, but at least there was someone here with Sara and Mac, which was what really counted.

"I'll be back after five, Asia."

Because their eyes met, entirely by accident on his part, Shayne nodded at Sydney as he crossed to the front door. A moment later the door closed behind him. He was gone.

She noted, uncomfortably, that Shayne hadn't said goodbye to either of his children and that they had made no effort to say anything to him, either. This was a family badly in need of mending.

"This way, please."

The softly spoken words roused her. Turning, Sydney saw that Asia was standing at the foot of the stairs, her expression completely impassive. She was waiting to take her to her new quarters, just as instructed.

Sydney picked up one of her suitcases and followed. "Coming." She forced herself to sound cheerful. It took a bit of doing.

Well, she thought as she followed the small woman up the stairs, she'd wanted a new life. This was certainly new. She was reminded of the adage that warned a person to be careful what they wished for.

"Have you been with Dr. Kerrigan long?" she asked.

Asia didn't bother turning around. "Not long."

"A month? A year?" she prodded, determined to at least get the woman to talk to her.

"Between." Asia went no further in pinpointing which it was.

She stopped at the second room on the right and gestured toward it. She made no effort to enter it, but merely stood back and waited for Sydney to open the door.

Why, was something going to spring out at her? At this point, Sydney decided she was braced for anything. Glancing at Asia, she reached for the knob, turned it, then opened the door.

Asia retreated a moment later, her mission accomplished.

Leaving the suitcase just inside the doorway, Sydney walked in. There was a stone fireplace on the far side and heavy wooden beams on the ceiling. The same kind of wood that made up the headboard and footboard of the large double bed. The room was as masculine as she would have expected it to be.

It was also in a state of complete chaos, as if its occupant had left in an extreme hurry.

As if its occupant had never bothered straightening things out to begin with, Sydney decided. She looked around slowly.

So, this belonged to the man she was to have married. Well, at least she wouldn't be faced with a lifetime of having to pick up after him.

The thought didn't do much to hearten her. Neither did knowing that, for whatever reason, she'd been made a fool of.

''Make lemonade, Syd, make lemonade,'' she muttered under her breath. It was something her father used to tell her whenever she felt as if she was faced with a horrible situation.

Sydney took a long, hard look around. She couldn't stay in a room that looked as though it had endured a lengthy visit from a passing tornado. Making up her mind, she blew out a breath and took off her parka.

The closet was as bad as the room, she discovered when she went to hang up her parka. What hangers were actually on the rod rather than on the closet floor were hopelessly tangled. Sydney looked around for somewhere to put the parka. Every available surface in the room was covered with clothing, books, papers.

How did the man ever find anything? She certainly hoped he was a better doctor than he was an organizer, otherwise she pitied his patients.

"It's messy."

The two-word sentence that came from behind her was hardly audible. Sydney turned to find Sara standing shyly in the doorway. The little girl was watching her every move.

Her first visitor. "It certainly is. But then, it's a boy's room and they tend to be messier than we are." The shared confidence brought a hint of a smile to Sara's mouth. Encouraged, Sydney ventured a little farther inside. "Would you like to come in? I think we can find a spot for you." To prove her point, Sydney quickly moved aside several thick sweaters from the foot of the unmade bed. She patted the cleared space, reinforcing her invitation. "There, how's that?"

Sara crossed to the bed. After a moment she hesitantly scooted onto it. Her legs dangled over the side. Sara clutched her doll to her, but she looked pleased by Sydney's attention. "Okay, I guess."

Sydney saw the way Sara looked around the room. There was loneliness in her eyes.

You're not the only one who misses him, Sara.

"There'll be more places for you to sit later after I clean up," she promised.

It was obvious that Sara was struggling to fit this newcomer into the scheme of things in this strange place she found herself. ''Are you going to be the maid?''

Sydney laughed softly. She thought about curbing her inclination to ruffle the little girl's hair, then gave in. The curls felt silky around her fingers as she tousled them.

''No, I'm just someone who likes things neat.''

Sara wiggled on the bed, settling in. She didn't seem to mind having Sydney touch her hair.

''We had a maid home.'' As soon as Sara mentioned home, the corners of her mouth drooped fornlornly. ''Her name was Alice. But that was before...before Mama died,'' she whispered, fighting back tears.

Sydney looked down at the hurting little soul perched on the bed. ''I'm very sorry about your mother, Sara.'' Sitting next to her, Sydney slipped her arm around the girl's shoulders. It warmed her when the child leaned into her. ''Do you know she's watching you right now?''

Sara raised her head, looking at her with huge, incredulous eyes. ''She is?''

Sydney nodded solemnly. ''Uh-huh. From heaven.'' She pointed toward the window. Outside the sky was a picturesque, crystal-clear blue. You couldn't beat the view here, she thought. ''She's looking down at you right now. And feeling very sad because you're feeling sad.'' The hope that entered Sara's eyes had Sydney going on. ''Do you know, if you shut your eyes real tight and stay very still, you can almost feel her arms around you, giving you a hug like she used to?''

Sara looked a little skeptical. She was her father's daughter, all right, Sydney thought, even if she didn't look a thing like him.

''How do you know that?'' Sara asked slowly.

''Because my dad's up there, too.''

The bond between her father and her had been a strong one. He'd been her mentor and her best friend while she was growing up. An only child, she'd devoted herself to him when he'd become ill even though he'd urged her to go on with her life. When he'd died almost three years ago, she'd been devastated. Sydney supposed that was why she'd been so eager to fall in love when Ken had come into her life. She missed having someone to talk to, someone to share things with.

But Ken had proven unequal to the position—and unworthy of her heart. As for Ben…

Well, they just didn't make men like her father anymore. Attributes such as honesty and kindness appeared to be in short supply these days.

But even if they were in abundance, she was off the market, this time for good.

"And sometimes, when I feel very lonely and really, really miss him, I shut my eyes and remember how safe I felt when he hugged me. And then I can feel him doing it. Why don't you try it?" Sydney urged. She knew that when a child believed hard enough, anything was possible. "It'll make you feel better."

Sara took a deep breath, still a little uncertain. "I don't know."

"Why are you lying to her?" Mac barged into the room, glaring at Sydney accusingly, his hands curled into fists at his sides. "Why are you making up stories? Who told you you could lie to my sister?"

The intense verbal attack, coming from someone so young, took Sydney by surprise. But she'd learned to bounce back quickly around children no matter what they said. It was important to not lose newly won ground.

Instead of answering Mac, she looked at Sara. "I see you have a white knight, Sara."

Sara looked around, expecting to see someone else in the room. "I do?"

"Yes." Sydney gestured toward the scowling boy. "White knights go around protecting ladies, and it looks like Mac is your white knight, ready to do anyone in who messes with his sister."

"I am not a white knight," he protested.

Sydney noted that his protest was not quite as vehemently voiced as it could have been. Apparently he didn't find the image nearly as reprehensible as he was pretending. She'd work with that.

"Oh, but I think you are, and it's very nice of you, to want to protect your sister like that." She rose from the bed. The room wasn't going to clean itself and she was going to need all the time and energy she could muster. "But you don't have to worry. I wasn't lying to her. Your mother is watching over her. And you."

His eyes grew dark again. The momentary truce was over.

"She's not watching over anyone. She didn't care about us," he insisted. "She left us. Left us so *he* could drag us out here, away from our friends, from our home. I hate it here," Mac told her angrily.

Her mother had died when she was a little younger than Mac. Sydney remembered how angry she'd been at her mother for dying. Almost as angry as Mac. But she'd had her father to help mitigate the pain. And she hadn't been required to make the kind of adjustments that Mac and Sara had.

She tried to slip her hand around the slim shoulders, but he shrugged her off, just as he had downstairs. She pretended not to notice. "It's hard to get used to something different, isn't it?"

The small, firm chin rose defiantly. "I don't want to get used to it. I want to go home."

She understood, probably more than she'd anticipated. There was a part of her that wanted to run home now, too. Except that there was no home. Not the one she'd known. The same was true for Mac and Sara. That gave them something in common.

"Sometimes," Sydney told them quietly, "things happen and we don't understand why. But we always have to make the best of them. Otherwise, we just stay unhappy and then nobody wins."

Sara was hanging on her every word, trying hard to understand. "Is it a game?"

Sydney smiled at her. There were a lot of times she'd thought of life as a game. A game with ever-changing rules. "In a way. The winner is the one who's the happiest with what he or she has."

Sara snuck a shy look at her brother. He bossed her around a lot, but she loved him more than anyone. More than Mama even. She didn't want to be a winner if he couldn't be one, too.

"Can there be two winners?"

She was a honey, this one, Sydney thought. Unable to resist, Sydney sat down next to her again and slid the little girl onto her lap. Flimsy barriers melted as Sara gave in to her natural inclination and cuddled up against her. Sydney lost her heart completely.

"Oh, there can be lots and lots of winners, sweetheart." She stroked Sara's head as her eyes met Mac's. "The only loser is the one who refuses to try to be happy."

She felt pretty confident that, despite the way his lips

curled in contempt, she'd given Mac something to think about.

As good as Sara felt in her arms, she had work to do. Very gently, she eased the little girl from her lap again and rose.

"Well, I'd better get busy if I want to get this cleaned up before tonight." That definitely cut her work out for her, she thought.

Sara wriggled off the bed. "Do you want some help?" The question was tendered with hope.

Sydney knew how badly an extra pair of small hands could interfere. It went without saying that she could make more headway alone. But she also knew that Sara needed to feel as if she were part of something, instead of just standing on the outside, looking in. Sara and Mac both did.

And maybe, just maybe, so did she.

Sydney grinned at her. "I would *love* some help, Sara. Thank you for asking." It warmed her to see Sara puff up her chest importantly.

One down. One to go.

Turning toward Mac, Sydney was in time to see him pivot on his heel and walk out, his hands shoved deep into his pockets. Taking a chance, she appealed to the protector in him.

"Mac, I need someone big and strong to bring up my other suitcase. Do you think you could help me?"

Mac never slowed his pace, nor did he answer her directly, although she heard him mumble something to himself under his breath. Probably calling her a variety of names, she guessed.

This was, she thought, going to take time. But that was all right. She suddenly found herself with plenty of it to spare.

''Cleaning this room is going to be a big project,'' she said, turning back to Sara. ''Why don't we start by picking up everything off the floor and putting it on the bed? That way, we can sort it out and maybe even get a glimpse of the floor.'' She looked around at the clutter. ''There *is* a floor under all this, isn't there?''

''I think so,'' Sara answered honestly. She'd never actually seen it herself.

One arm tucked around her doll, Sara mimicked Sydney. Methodically, she began to pick up everything in her path, one at a time. Each item necessitated a trip to the bed, where it was deposited. Little by little, a scarred wooden floor that had once been buffed to a golden-honey sheen began to emerge.

Sydney wondered if there was anything around she could use to restore the shine. She doubted if Shayne would be of any help. Pushing that thought aside, Sydney decided to see if she could somehow untangle the mess in the closet so she could hang up some of the clothing closest to her. Enmeshed in wire hangers that had mysteriously linked themselves together, she was unprepared for the loud thud she heard behind her.

Not certain what she expected to see, she swung around. Mac was standing in the doorway, her suitcase in front of him. From the looks of it, he'd dragged it up the stairs with both hands.

''I brought it up,'' he said as if he expected her to dispute the matter.

''So I see.'' Crossing to it, she picked up the suitcase and carried it into the room. ''Thank you.''

His shoulders rose and fell indifferently as Mac retreated again, his scowl intact.

Sydney smiled to herself. That noise she heard was the first chink in the armor opening up. Promising, she mused. Maybe befriending him wasn't going to take as much work as she'd initially thought.

"You have a nice brother, Sara." She purposely raised her voice so the boy belonging to the shadow that fell across the hallway floor could hear.

"Mac's okay," Sara said in the timeless voice of sisters everywhere.

"Yes, he certainly is."

The shadow in the hall remained for quite some time.

Chapter Five

The moment Shayne walked into his clinic with its reception area teeming with patients, all thoughts about his chaotic personal life vanished. There was too much else to occupy his mind.

Shayne had always had the ability to concentrate on his work, his patient, to the complete exclusion of everything else going on around him. That was part of what made him such a good doctor.

And that was also part, Barbara had told him, of what had driven her away from him. She'd vehemently objected to not being the center of his universe. Coupled with having to live in a "frozen wasteland," as she'd scathingly referred to the region, she found his ability to successfully tune her out while he was working more than she could possibly put up with.

It had been the last straw.

Shayne looked around the clinic. Without anyone to

help out, he'd had a difficult time today juggling all his patients. His last assistant had left over a month ago, desperate to move on. The last he'd heard, she was in New Mexico. So far, there'd been no new takers for the job. Hades didn't have an endless supply of people. With Ben no longer in the picture, Shayne was sure he was about to fall headfirst into hell.

He thought about what Sydney had said about Ben offering the position to Sydney, sight unseen, and he could almost understand Ben's logic. Why not? His brother'd offered himself to her under the same conditions.

Shayne couldn't help wondering, as he leaned over and switched off the lamp on his desk, if Ben would have really gone through with marrying Sydney had he remained here. As far as looks went, he could have done a lot worse.

A lot worse.

Tired, Shayne rose from his desk. He passed his hand over his forehead and rubbed at his temples. There was a tension headache building. Not from what he'd endured during the day, but in anticipation of what he was about to face at home. Maybe he'd be lucky and they would have all turned in early.

The last of the patients had left twenty minutes ago. Office hours had long since been over. There were no more traumas to occupy his thoughts, no continuing case to baffle him and lay claim to his concentration.

There was nothing to face but going home.

Home to a houseful of people who made him uncomfortable.

Didn't seem right, he thought, shrugging into his parka. A man shouldn't feel uncomfortable in his own home. Crisscrossing a woolen scarf at his chest, he tucked the ends in and zipped up his parka. Most of all, a man shouldn't feel uncomfortable with his own children. Raising the hood on his parka, he stepped outside and locked the door.

The cold air rubbed raw fingers over his face, stinging it as he got into his four-by-four and started the engine.

The wheel felt cold, even through his gloves. He'd never thought it would be this way. Whenever he'd envisioned his life, a century ago when he had dreams, he'd always thought there would be a wife, a family, by his side. A family who would give him all the warmth, all the support he had so sorely missed all those years he'd struggled to make a life for himself and his brother.

He exhaled and mist formed on the windshield. He rubbed it quickly away, shifted out of Park, and made his way down the familiar road.

Not that Ben and he hadn't been close. They were. But Ben...well, Ben was Ben. His brother had all the attributes he'd always wished he had. Ben had the outgoing manner that made people believe he cared about them. Shayne knew he cared just as much about his patients, maybe even more so, but for him, it had never been easy to show how he felt. Most people took that to mean that he was aloof, removed from them. After a while, it was just easier to let everyone believe what they wanted to believe. He busied himself in curing his patients, not keeping their demons away at night.

He supposed, Shayne conceded, it would have been easier to fall into that niche others saw him in and really not care. But he did. In his own fashion, he cared very much.

Cared, too, that his own children looked at him with either loathing or fear. He hadn't a clue how to cut through any of that. What the hell was he going to do now? he wondered as his snow-chained tires crunched through the newly fallen snow. Without Ben as a go-between, conversation with Mac and Sara would die altogether. There was no doubt in his mind that Mac somehow blamed him for Ben's absence, just as the boy seemed to blame him for his mother's death and for bringing him out here.

Maybe bringing them out here *had* been a mistake on his part. It was so hard to know how to do "the right thing." At the outset, it had seemed right. When he'd heard of Barbara's death, the first thing he'd thought of was his children. Of how they had to feel—scared, frightened, suddenly deprived of her love. Whatever else she had been with him, Shayne knew that Barbara had been a good mother to their children.

But now that they were here, in his home, he had absolutely no idea how to be their father.

High beams seared through the white world around him as he guided the vehicle toward his house. He tried to keep from thinking about how tired he felt. He knew from the accident victims he'd treated how easy it was to fall asleep behind the wheel, hypnotized by the sameness that existed out here. How easy it was to freeze to death.

The headlights from his vehicle bounced off his plane, standing regally in the field, poised to take off on its next run.

Almost home.

As he parked the four-by-four inside the detached garage he and Ben had built, he heard the roof groan under the weight of the snow as he closed the door. He'd have to see about clearing some of that off in the morning. If he remembered to get around to it.

Shayne looked toward the house. It was clear that the

children were unhappy here. Two months and they hadn't begun to adjust. Perhaps, for their own good, he should let his ex-in-laws take them. It wasn't something he wanted to do, but maybe it was for the best. The suggestion had been on the table when he'd flown to get Mac and Sara. To their credit, Barbara's parents hadn't pushed the matter.

Maybe they should have.

Standing on the front stoop, Shayne automatically stomped his feet. Bits of snow fell from the soles of his boots. Bracing himself, he opened the door.

The temperature change was a mild shock to his system. Pushing the door closed behind him, he heard the latch click into place as he opened his parka and looked around. At first, he saw no one in the room. A sigh of relief escaped his lips before he realized it.

Before he realized that he wasn't alone.

He saw her standing by the fireplace, the warm glow from the flames caressing her profile, getting lost in her hair. She'd undone it, he noticed. There was a great deal more of it than he'd first thought. It rained halfway down her back like a shimmering, pale gold shower.

His breath caught in his throat. The room was warmer than he remembered it.

When she looked in his direction, the smile that came to her lips in greeting went straight to his heart. He felt as if he'd just caught an electric eel, bare-handed. The tingling sensation raced up and down his body.

For one shining second, Shayne felt as if he'd stepped into someone else's life. Perhaps into his own life somewhere in that parallel universe where he was allowed to have the simple things that came so easily, so naturally, to other men. But not to him.

He shook himself.

Sydney had begun to think that they would have to go ahead with dinner without him. She'd already postponed it two hours and the children were getting hungry. There was just so long she could try to keep them entertained.

He looked so stunned, standing in front of the door, that she wondered if something was wrong. "I thought maybe an emergency took you away. It's been dark for a while." She'd heard him tell Asia he'd be home at five. Five had long since come and gone.

"It gets dark early here," he said matter-of-factly. "And sunrise is after ten."

About to remove his parka before he began to perspire, Shayne stopped to sniff the air. There was something tempting and delectable tantalizing his nose. Something quite apart from the light cologne he'd scented on her earlier.

He took in another whiff, still trying to place the aroma.

The puzzled expression on his face did a great deal to humanize him, Sydney decided as she stepped away from the fireplace. It almost made him look boyish, giving the hard, chiseled features more appeal.

She smiled in reply to the unspoken question in his eyes. "That's dinner."

"Not any dinner I've had in recent memory." Unless he and Ben went to the Salty Saloon, dinner usually consisted of whatever can he'd take it upon himself to open and heat. Asia had been put in charge of cooking when he'd brought the children to live here, but cooking was definitely not one of her strong points. Maybe Asia was picking up tips from her daughter-in-law.

"I took a few liberties with it. Asia looked like she needed help."

Because it seemed so natural to her, as she spoke she reached to take his parka from him, intending to hang it in the closet. She'd done this countless times before when her father had come home from work.

Except this time, she met with instant resistance.

Shayne held on to the parka. He hadn't brought her here to be a maid. "You don't have to wait on me."

"I wasn't aware that I was." To avoid arguing, she dropped her hands. "Although, in the strictest sense of the word, we all are."

He hung his parka on a hook, then turned to face her. What was she talking about? Who was "we"? "Excuse me?"

"We decided to wait with dinner until you arrived. It seemed only right," she added when he looked as if he didn't understand what she was saying.

Sara had told her that she and Mac usually ate in the kitchen by themselves. Sydney thought that was awful. Family meals were to be shared together whenever possible. So she'd talked them into waiting and entertained them as they waited. She read stories to Sara that Mac pretended to ignore.

Shayne looked at her suspiciously. Just what was she up to? "We, as in you and the children?"

She nodded. "Asia left shortly before five. One of her grandchildren came to get her." It had seemed like an emergency, and considering that the woman's idea of soup was warmed-over water with hunks of yellowed fat floating in it, Sydney thought they could definitely spare the housekeeper.

She saw anger crease his brow. Had she done something wrong in letting the woman go? There hadn't seemed to be much that she could do to prevent it. "I thought it would be all right since I was here with Mac and Sara.''

His eyes met hers. She was a stranger, Shayne thought. Where did she get off, letting Asia leave like that? He and Asia had an agreement. She was to remain with the children until he got home, no matter what that time was. He paid her accordingly.

''Making yourself at home, are you?''

Sydney wasn't sure if she was being challenged or not, and if she was, why. She struggled to keep her temper—something that had been badly frayed today—from flaring. ''Making myself useful.''

She was right. There was no reason for him to bite off her head like that. In all likelihood, she was just trying to help. He hung his scarf on top of the parka.

''Sorry, I'm not at my best at night.''

A smile curved the corners of her mouth as she cocked her head, studying him. ''Then that was your best I saw earlier, at the airport?''

He laughed shortly. She had him there. ''All right, this hasn't been my best day.''

Shayne glanced toward the alcove that doubled as a formal dining area on very rare occasions. The table his father had built with his own hands for his mother was set for four.

He didn't relish sitting across from accusing eyes. ''You could have had dinner without me.''

''I thought it might be better to have dinner with you.''

When he looked at her with another unspoken question in his eyes, she was ready for him. ''Your children are still adjusting to the change and to their loss. Any stability you can offer them will only help them with the transition.''

Terrific, Ben had proposed to someone who fancied herself a dime-store child psychologist. ''You obviously don't know my children.''

''No,'' she agreed, following him to the table. ''But I intend to. Sara and I had a long talk while she was helping me clean the bedroom.''

He stopped again, so abruptly that she walked right into him. He grabbed her shoulders to steady her. A second later, he dropped his hands, self-conscious at the unintended contact.

''Clean what bedroom?'' He wanted to know. When he'd brought her here, he hadn't thought in terms of her doing anything, just staying out of the way until she changed her mind and left. He certainly hadn't bargained on her rearranging things.

''Ben's room. Don't worry,'' she said quickly, ''I didn't throw anything out. I just sorted things and then stacked them out of the way. There's a lot more room to move around now.'' It hadn't been an easy feat, especially with the extra pair of small hands helping her. But she'd managed.

Wariness outweighed the sudden hunger that the warm aroma from the kitchen was creating within his belly. ''What else did you do?''

It sound like an accusation, but she did her best to ignore his tone. ''I already told you, I helped Asia with dinner. Actually, Sara and I did.'' She saw a little blond head peeking out from the kitchen. Smiling, Sydney held her hand out, urging Sara into the room. ''Sara salted the soup, didn't you, Sara?''

Shayne turned toward the kitchen in time to see his daughter coming into the alcove. Her eyes on Sydney for encouragement, Sara nodded. ''Yes.''

Looking from his daughter to Sydney, Shayne wasn't

quite sure what to make of all this, or how he felt about it. Sydney'd certainly made more headway with his daughter in the few hours they'd been together than he had in two months. He was beginning to see why Ben had been attracted to her. They obviously had the same outgoing nature.

"Well, then, I guess I'll have to give the soup a try since you went to all that trouble, Sara." Shayne was surprised to see that Sara was fairly beaming at him.

It was, Sydney thought, like being in the midst of an armed truce. The silence in the room pulsed and throbbed like the vital signs of a comatose entity, giving no indication that it was going to awaken anytime in the near future.

Was this what mealtime was like in this house? No wonder Shayne had seemed unhappy that they had held dinner for him, if this was all he had to look forward to. But it took at least two for a conversation and he was as much at fault as the children. More, since he knew better.

She thought of the conversations she and her father had always had around the table. Dinner was when they could touch base, exchange ideas, share experiences. It was her favorite part of the day.

Here it seemed like catered torture.

She'd kept quiet at the beginning because she thought it wasn't her place to intrude into their traditions, whatever they were. But it was now obvious that there were no traditions to intrude upon.

Were they going to go through the whole meal without saying a single word? Sydney cleared her throat as Shayne set aside his soup bowl.

He looked at her quizzically. She indicated the bowl

with her eyes, an expression on her face he couldn't quite understand.

This obviously had to be what leading a horse to water was all about, Sydney muttered silently. She looked at Sara. ''The soup was very good, Sara. I think the extra salt added just the right touch.''

Was that what she was trying to tell him? That she wanted him to comment on the soup? Seemed rather silly to him, but Shayne took his cue. ''Yes. It was very good, Sara.''

Sara fairly beamed. She wriggled in her chair, sitting up straighter. ''Mama let me help in the kitchen sometimes.''

Glaring, Mac pushed his bowl away from him. ''It's too salty.'' He looked at his father, daring him to dispute his declaration.

Sydney'd refereed enough playground disputes to recognize trouble before it exploded. ''It might have been the fish,'' she quickly interjected. ''You had that first,'' she told Mac, ''and I might have added too much pepper to the coating before I fried it.'' She knew she'd done no such thing, but felt the lie was justified if she could avert a problem in the making. Genially, Sydney flashed an apologetic smile at the boy. ''Sorry.''

His mouth closed, the biting words on the edge of his tongue disappearing, absorbed by surprise. He wasn't accustomed to adults apologizing to him. Or even bothering to take note of his opinion.

Magnanimously, Mac lifted one shoulder, then let it fall again. ''That's okay. The fish wasn't really that salty.'' His eyes shifted toward his sister. ''And I guess the soup's okay, too.''

Adoration gleamed in Sara's eyes. ''Really?''

''I said so, didn't I?'' Even at the tender age of nine,

Sydney could see that Mac was on his way to becoming a man, with a man's sense of the way things should be. Understated, of course, with little exposure of the emotions he entertained.

''Yes, you did,'' Sydney agreed before his tone could escalate and take the conversation off in another direction. She looked at Shayne. Other than the compliment she'd all but dragged out of his throat, he hadn't said anything. She gave it another try. ''So, how was your day?''

''My day?'' He looked surprised that she should ask.

''Yes. How was it?'' She tried to seem nonchalant.

Shayne had no idea what she was going after this time and he was too tired to try to accommodate her. He cut a piece of the fish and ate before answering. ''It was just another day.''

Was it really this difficult for him to make conversation, or was he just being stubborn? ''Did anything interesting happen at the clinic? Any patient stand out in your mind?''

He raised his eyes to hers. They held for a moment as he tried to figure out why she was asking him questions. Why should she care how his day went, or if his patients were interesting or not? They didn't even know each other. ''No.''

Pulling teeth was undoubtedly easier than this, Sydney thought. Doggedly, she kept at it. Ben had said his brother was a man of few words, but she hadn't thought it was this few. If ever a man had to be shown the way, it was Shayne Kerrigan. ''Did you operate on someone?''

Mac leaned forward in his chair. The word ''operate'' triggered a memory of a program he'd seen back home.

"Did someone come in with a big, old fishhook stuck in them?"

"No." It was the first time that Mac had asked him a question that wasn't couched in total hostility. Shayne saw that his answer disappointed the boy. "Not today. But I did have someone come in last week with one stuck in their finger."

For the first time in two months, Shayne saw that he had Mac's attention.

Sara shivered and squealed. "His finger? Did it hurt?"

Mac looked at her contemptuously. "Sure it hurt, stupid. You try having a fishhook in your finger and see if it don't hurt."

"Mac, don't call your sister stupid," Shayne said sharply. There was no excuse for name-calling.

The fragile thread of kinship broke instantly. The moment was gone. Mac pushed aside his dish. "I'm not hungry anymore." He turned a defiant face toward his father. "Can I go?"

Shayne's inclination was to make his son remain at the table, but he knew it was useless to try to talk to the boy, to make him understand. Silently, he waved him away.

Mac fairly stomped out of the room.

Upset, afraid, Sara stared down at her plate, rocking to and fro.

"You can go, too, if you want," Shayne told her. He tried his best to sound gentle, but knew Sara wouldn't hear the tone, only the words. She was gone within the moment.

Sydney waited until she felt the children were out of earshot. Then she looked at Shayne. His expression was unreadable again.

"You shouldn't chase them away," she said quietly.

Annoyed at his inability to communicate with his own children, Shayne lashed out at the only target in the room.

"I don't recall asking you for an opinion."

She couldn't remember the last time she'd been intimidated by a dark look. Only incensed by it. "No, but that doesn't mean you don't need it."

Shayne pushed back his chair, the legs scraping along the bare floor. "Lady, I took you in because my brother did you a dirty turn. Don't push your luck."

"I'm not trying to push my luck. I'm trying to help you."

Rising, he threw down his napkin. This was shaping up as one of the worst days he'd had in a long time. "When I want your help, I'll ask you for it."

She was on her feet, too. "No, you won't." She knew that much about him even without Ben's letters. She could see the stubbornness in his eyes. "I see three people hurting in this house and since you're the adult, you have to reach out to them—to make the hurting go away—for all of you."

Shayne had always been a private man. He didn't like anyone intruding into his life. "Ben didn't mention you were a philosopher."

It took more than sarcasm to make her back off when she thought she was right. "I'm not. I'm a human being—and an outsider, so maybe I can see things that you're too close to see."

"Don't trouble yourself."

She raised her chin, determined to make him understand. "No trouble at all."

Just who the hell did she think she was, spouting off solutions as if she somehow had turned to the last page of his life, where all the answers were supposed to be written?

Shayne blew out a breath, getting hold of himself. He hadn't meant to lose his temper like that. And maybe she had a point. God knew, he wasn't making any headway with Mac and Sara up until now. This tiny spate of conversation at the table tonight had been the longest one they'd enjoyed.

He eyed Sydney in pensive silence. She was obviously better at this sort of thing than he was. "You got Sara to help you?"

Sydney nodded. "Actually, she volunteered. Mac carried up my suitcase."

Shayne found that almost impossible to believe. Mac was like a brick wall. Even Ben had found it difficult to get the boy to open up.

"Mac?"

"Mac," she confirmed, a small smile of triumph playing on her lips.

"How about that," he murmured.

Maybe there was a place for minor miracles, after all. Shayne rubbed his neck, wondering if it had been just a fluke, or if all it took to open his son up was patience—and the right approach. An approach she seemed to have a lock on.

The antique mantel clock that had been passed down in his mother's family for generations chimed eight o'clock. Early by most standards. Late by the hours he kept. He looked at Sydney and thought she looked tired. She could probably use the rest after what she'd been through.

"It's been a long day. Why don't you call it a night and turn in?"

Sydney raised a brow, amused. ''Sending me to my room?''

She could go or stay, it was all the same to him. He had some reading to catch up on. ''Just making a suggestion.''

''And in this case, a good one.'' There were dishes on the table, but Sydney felt suddenly drained. Besides, he'd said he didn't want her waiting on him. That undoubtedly included clearing the table, as well. She'd leave that to him. ''I think I will go to bed.'' She turned to leave the room.

She heard the clink of dishes behind her. He was gathering them together. Sydney stopped. ''Want help with that?''

''No.''

''Why doesn't that surprise me?'' she said more to herself than to him. She was at the foot of the stairs when he called to her.

''Ms. Elliot.''

Pausing, she looked at him over her shoulder. ''Yes?''

Shayne kept his eyes on the dishes he was stacking. He'd been downright uncivil to her and he knew it. It wasn't her fault that she'd wandered into a demilitarized war zone. Under the circumstances, she was doing her best to get along.

''For what it's worth, I think Ben missed out.''

He probably had no idea how much she needed to hear something like that, Sydney thought. Or how good it sounded. She smiled her appreciation, even though it was to the top of his bent head.

''Thank you.''

Shayne didn't bother saying anything to her in response. As far as he was concerned, he'd already said too much.

Chapter Six

Sighing, Shayne closed his book. There was no point in sitting here, trying to make sense out of the words in front of him. He'd been on the same page for the past fifteen minutes, reading it over and over again. None of it was sinking in.

His mind just wasn't on Dumas or his novel about the prince history had chosen to hide. Rising from his chair, Shayne crossed to one of the two bookshelves that buffered the fireplace and returned the leather-bound volume to its place. Tonight it had failed to transport him beyond his four walls.

Normally, when the long night wrapped itself tightly around him, Shayne found he could loosen the day's tension by losing himself in the pages of the books he'd been collecting over the years.

But tonight was different. Tonight nothing could erase the unease he was feeling. Unease mingled with dissatisfaction and a restlessness that seemed to have no reason behind it, no identifying marks for him to trace with confidence to its source.

A restlessness that had begun the moment he'd walked into his house and seen Sydney standing by the fireplace. If he closed his eyes, he could still see her, looking every bit the embodiment of a dream he'd once deluded himself into having. A dream of hearth and home. And family.

He was far too much of a realist now to believe in dreams. That had belonged to the remnants of the child in him. A child who had long since grown up to face the world for what it was. A hard, exacting place that never allowed you to put your guard down.

The restlessness refused to recede.

Instead, it threatened to swallow him up. Maybe he was just reacting to Ben's latest escapade, an escapade that left him—however temporarily—not only without another pair of skilled hands at the clinic, but with a woman he hadn't the slightest idea what to do with.

The ratio out here being seven to one, he knew there would be a lot of men who'd offer very vocal suggestions as to what he *could* do with Sydney, but Shayne'd never been one for casual coupling. Which was why Barbara had hurt him as much as she had.

He supposed if he were a drinking man, he would have tried to lose himself inside a bottle tonight. But even if he were so inclined, he didn't have that luxury available to him. A doctor out here couldn't afford to drink and muddle his mind. Especially if he were the only doctor in a hundred-mile radius—and it looked like he was, at least for the time being.

So, he had no crutches to lean on, no quick fixes at

his disposal, other than his books, and they just weren't doing the trick tonight.

Sleep was the only solution left.

If he could sleep, he thought, agitation rippling through him like a freshly caught salmon thrown on the ground.

With careful movements, he banked the fire in the fireplace. Then, one by one, he switched off the lights until only the upstairs hallway light filtered down to him like a thin, winding golden thread.

He took the stairs slowly, his thoughts involuntarily straying to the woman whom he presumed was now fast asleep. How long was she going to stay here? God, he hoped not long. He had enough on his mind without having to put up with any of Ben's fallout.

He could hear the branches scraping against the upstairs hall window. The wind had been picking up steadily all evening and now mournfully strummed the branches of the surrounding trees. It only added to his restlessness.

Stopping at the landing, Shayne glanced toward the bedrooms opposite his own. Sara's and Mac's bedrooms. Every night, before he went to bed, he looked in on them, always when he was certain they were asleep.

At first, it had been out of pure amazement, to assure himself that, after all these years of separation, they were actually finally here in his house. Now it was a habit, something he did before closing the door to his own room. He wasn't even sure why he did it, only that he needed to, needed to see their faces, peaceful and devoid of any emotions directed against him, pressed softly against their pillows.

He eased open Mac's door first. The boy was on his stomach, his blanket a hopeless tangle at his feet. He slept like a spinning top. Very gently, Shayne freed enough of the blanket to spread over the wiry body. Mac slept like Ben, turning his bed into a huge battlefield as he sought out sleep. The thought made Shayne smile as he withdrew from the room.

Approaching Sara's room, Shayne thought he heard the soft murmur of a woman's voice. *Her* voice. Was he imagining it? He listened again. It sounded too real to be his imagination. Curious, he eased the door open.

Sara was in bed, her eyes shut, her hand curled around Sydney's. She looked sound asleep. What was Sydney doing in the room with her?

And then he saw that there was an open book on Sydney's lap. One of Sara's storybooks.

She'd heard him the moment he opened the door. Turning, she put her finger to her lips, afraid, he realized, that he would say something to wake Sara up. He watched as she looked at Sara again—apparently to satisfy herself that the little girl was still asleep—then, very slowly, eased her hand from Sara's.

It was like watching someone move in slow motion, he thought. Every movement was fluid, unhurried. A little like poetry on a soft summer's night. He found himself almost hypnotized, hardly breathing until, tiptoeing out of the room, she came to him.

Belatedly, Shayne backed up to give her room until they were both standing out in the hallway. Sydney closed the door quietly behind her, turning so that her body was a breath away from his.

And one breath too close.

Shayne didn't step back, not immediately, though he knew he should. Instead, in a hushed voice gauged not to wake either child, he asked, ''What were you doing in her room?''

Sydney thought it was obvious, but she explained anyway. ''Sara had a nightmare. I heard her whimpering in her sleep so I went in and woke her up. She was terrified, something to do with thunder and her mother dying.'' The little girl's eyes had looked haunted until she'd managed to calm Sara down. ''I didn't get it all. But whatever it was about, the nightmare was enough to make her afraid. I promised to stay with her until she fell asleep again. I figured the quickest way to make that happen was to read to her.'' Sydney grinned, tapping the book she held in her hand. ''Works every time.''

How many children had she read to sleep? Shayne wondered. And why didn't she have any of her own? Was there more to this woman than met the eye? He still couldn't get himself to believe that a woman as vibrant as Sydney Elliot had conducted a long-distance mail romance with a man she'd never met. Surely she'd have to have men in closer proximity in her life. Where were they?

''I didn't hear her,'' he confessed.

''It was a whimper, not a scream.'' Her words were swallowed by the rattle of the windows as they trembled before the wind. ''And that sounds pretty fierce.'' She nodded in the general direction of the windows on his side of the house. ''It would have blotted out even a loud whimper. Besides, my room's next to hers,'' Sydney added. ''I could hear her better than you could.''

Shayne knew he should be grateful to her for going to Sara, not subjecting her to the third degree. It was just that he wasn't accustomed to anyone helping him. He was always on the giving end, not the receiving one. ''Thank you for taking care of her.''

She smiled, erasing the tension of suspicion and inadvertently creating a whole different kind of tension in its wake.

It was obvious that words of thanks came hard to him, Sydney realized. "No hardship. As I said earlier, I like kids and I enjoy being in their company."

That settled, there seemed to be nothing more to say. Yet, he couldn't seem to make himself withdraw, not just yet. So he remained where he was, feeling awkward, like some bump in the rug, unable to move away. She wasn't helping, looking up at him like that, her eyes as warm as the sea in July.

Shayne cleared his throat, as if that would somehow help to clear his mind, as well. It felt muddled now. He couldn't seem to focus on a complete thought. Was he *that* tired?

"Have you given any thought to what you want to do? I mean, about finding work? If you're serious about staying, that is."

This wasn't coming out at all well. He'd never been particularly articulate in private, but if he continued in this backward evolutionary spiral, he was going to be reduced to a Neanderthal, making unintelligible sounds and grunts by morning.

It seemed to Sydney that they should have had this conversation earlier at the dinner table, when she'd tried to pry words out of his mouth. When she was fresher.

"I was hoping that maybe the job that Ben mentioned might still be open." Was that being presumptuous on her part? Shayne hadn't seemed very pleased when she'd mentioned earlier that Ben wanted her to work at the clinic.

Shayne thought of his day and how exhausted he'd become trying to do everything while patients poured into the clinic like the aftermath of a flash flood. He supposed he had nothing to lose by hiring her, at least on a trial basis. She certainly seemed willing enough to work and she was better than nothing.

His eyes drifted over the length of her. Sydney was wearing a silk robe that insisted on molding itself to her every movement like a second, shimmering peach skin.

Definitely better than nothing, he thought.

The restlessness within him intensified, blatantly hinting at its source.

Shayne banked the fire that leaped into his veins, just as he'd banked down the one in his den. It was late and he was tired. It was time to end this conversation.

"It's open, all right. I suppose we could give it a try for a few days, see how things work out. I usually go in at eight."

"Eight's fine," Sydney said quickly.

"Asia's here by seven. She sees to Mac and Sara while I'm gone." The words came out double-time, as if he were a military leader, snapping out orders. He had no idea why he was even bothering with the extra information. It wasn't necessary. She didn't need to know any of it. Yet he'd found himself elaborating.

"I don't mean to pry, but what about their education?"

He almost laughed. For a woman who didn't mean to pry, she certainly seemed very good at it. This wasn't any of her business.

"They're getting one," he assured her formally. "Asia takes them into town. Shirley Kellogg, the general store owner's wife, teaches the kids from the area for three hours a day."

"Three hours?" That didn't seem like very much, especially if the children were rowdy. In her experience, that meant most of the time would be spent refereeing.

How much could they really learn in that kind of atmosphere?

Shayne knew criticism in the offing when he heard it. "That's all that's needed, if it's done correctly."

Sydney had thoughts on that subject, but knew that, for the time being, if she wanted the job with Shayne, it was best to keep those thoughts to herself. "You may have a point," she conceded.

Taking advantage of the momentary break in conversation, Shayne turned on his heel before she could say anything else to keep him standing out here, entertaining thoughts that had no business existing. "I'll see you in the morning."

"In the morning," she echoed.

Eight wasn't fine, no matter what Sydney had said the night before, she groggily realized as the alarm went off. And if eight wasn't fine, that made six-thirty even less so.

When she'd agreed to the time, it had been from the comfortable side of an evening when she'd been wide awake and eager to get her life in gear and moving forward. It was a whole different matter now.

Despite her chosen vocation that required her to rise early, Sydney had never been a morning person. She faced it reluctantly, as a necessary evil to endure. An obstacle to overcome and vanquish—like a medieval dragon. Her absolute rock bottom requirement in facing such an early hour was that there be some semblance of daylight to make the passage from bed to bathroom acceptable and civilized.

There wasn't even any daylight. In fact, there was no light to speak of outside her window at all.

This had to be a mistake. The alarm clock had to have gone off by mistake, she thought groggily.

Her brain in a fog, Sydney groped for the alarm clock she'd brought with her, flirting with the idea of dropping it on the floor once she found it. As if in a desperate play for survival, the clock defied detection, continuing to ring, violently shredding the darkness that surrounded her.

The noise throbbed in her head like a headache in the making.

And then she heard the door to her room opening. Light from the hallway came spilling in, ushering with it a small, nightgown-shrouded form.

"Sydney? Are you up?"

Still more than half-asleep, Sydney raised her head from her pillow, focusing on the source of the voice. Slowly, the form solidified.

Sara.

It took almost superhuman effort, but Sydney managed to sit up and drag her hair, if not sleep, from her eyes. She released a long, shaky breath.

"I am now, sugar."

Sara peered nervously into the room. "What's that noise?" Hesitantly, she ventured into the room.

Focusing her eyes, Sydney finally zeroed in on the clock. Bracing one hand against the bed, she reached over and shut the alarm off. Finally!

Sydney settled back against the headboard. "That is something I bought to annoy myself."

It didn't make any sense to Sara, but she liked Sydney and she wanted to understand. "Why?"

"Long story." Sara's puzzled expression made her laugh softly. "It's an alarm clock, honey. I set it so it can wake me up." She sighed, knowing that there was no way she could go back to sleep now. "I have trouble waking up in the morning."

Sara thought the confession over for a moment. "I could come in and wake you up in the morning if you want me to." She rocked on her toes, eyeing Sydney to see how she liked her suggestion.

"And probably do a much nicer job than that old clock," Sydney agreed. She smiled at the girl. "That's very generous of you, Sara. Maybe I'll take you up on that."

Appearing pleased at the compliment, Sara asked, "Are you going to stay here with us today, too?"

The hope in the girl's voice touched Sydney. "No, I'm going in with your father and work at the clinic, but I'll be back tonight."

"You're going to work there like Uncle Ben?"

"Not exactly. I'm not a doctor." Sydney wasn't aware of the wistfulness in her voice until she heard it herself.

"I bet you could be if you wanted to."

Sydney couldn't resist. She pulled the girl to her and hugged her.

Sara squealed and giggled, purely delighted. Sydney hugged her harder, which only made Sara laugh louder.

Impulsively, Sara kissed her on the cheek.

Sydney completely lost her heart to the little girl. She brushed a kiss against the silky head. "Thank you, Sara. I needed that. I was running really low on hugs."

Sara scrambled up on her knees on the bed. "Do you need hugs?"

"Everybody needs hugs." Some people just didn't know it. Sydney had a feeling the good doctor fell into that category. "Don't you?"

Looking surprised at being found out, Sara nodded

vigorously, the ends of her hair bobbing up and down like tiny springs. ''Yes, but everybody doesn't need them. Mac says he doesn't. And my daddy doesn't.''

''Oh, I think you're wrong there. Mac and your daddy both need them. As a matter of fact, I think your daddy needs them most of all.'' She saw the doubt in Sara's eyes as she reached for her robe, not that it offered much protection from the cold. ''He just doesn't know how to ask. Tell you what—'' Sydney swung her legs over the side of the bed and rose ''—why don't you hug him when you go downstairs?'' She slipped the robe on over her arms and tied the sash. ''It'll be a nice surprise for him.''

Sara cocked her head, mulling the suggestion over. ''You think?''

Sydney ruffled her hair, laughing. ''I think.''

Shayne glanced at his watch, wondering if he should go and wake Sydney, or just leave when he said he would. It was almost seven-thirty. Sydney should have been down here by now if she was coming with him to the clinic. Probably sleeping in, he guessed. Morning without dawn took some getting used to. He had no doubt that her system was also thrown off by the time change she'd experienced, coming from Nebraska.

Just as well. The woman would probably only get in the way instead of help. The last thing he needed was someone getting in his way.

The bottom step squeaked. Hearing it, Shayne turned around. But instead of Sydney, he found himself looking down into his daughter's face. Mac was probably still upstairs—avoiding him, like most mornings.

''Good morning, Sara.''

''Good morning,'' she echoed, then tugged on his sleeve and beckoned him down to her level.

Not knowing what to expect, he knelt. ''Something wrong, Sara?''

She didn't answer. Instead she caught her lower lip between her teeth, worrying it a little. Then she put her small arms as far around him as she could and squeezed. Hard.

Startled, it took Shayne a moment before he responded. Had something happened? Was she afraid? But when he tilted Sara's head back slightly to look at her, none of that was evident in her face. She looked a little nervous, but that was all.

''What's this all about?''

Sara wondered if maybe she was doing it wrong. Did grown-ups hug different? ''I'm hugging you, Daddy.''

''Yes, I know, but why?''

This had come completely out of the blue. Sara hadn't hugged him when she'd first met him, and after that, there'd been no reason to. At least none that he could see. There still wasn't. For that matter, she hadn't called him Daddy before, either. The last time he'd seen her, she was six months old. To her, he was more of a stranger than ''Daddy.''

An impatient little frown creased her small mouth. Didn't he like being hugged? Was Sydney wrong? ''Because Sydney said you needed one.''

''Oh, she did, did she?'' Sydney took a lot upon herself, especially for a stranger, he thought. He had to admit, though, this once he couldn't find fault with that. ''I guess she's right.''

Like a man picking his way across a sheet of ice he knew was dangerously thin, Shayne lightly stroked his daughter's hair. Emotions too large and unwieldy to be captured and caged slammed through him, making holes, creating chasms. Leaving him stunned by their intensity. He had no idea just how much he'd missed having his children with him, missed having their love, until this very moment.

He held Sara to him, wondering how someone so small could be responsible for creating something so immense. Like a huge net, love spread completely over his heart, enmeshing it.

Wrapped up in this newly roused emotion, it took Shayne a few minutes to realize that he was no longer alone in the room with Sara. Raising his eyes, he saw Sydney in the doorway, a pleased smile on her lips as she watched them. He hadn't even heard the bottom step squeak.

Emotion quickened in his throat. He tried to clear it away. "I'm told I have you to thank for this."

Sydney raised one shoulder, letting it drop again. "The only one you have to thank is Sara." She looked toward the kitchen. There was no telltale aroma in the air. "Any breakfast ready? If not, I could whip up something."

He had no doubt that she could. And breakfast was only part of it. Surprised by the stray thought, he wondered where it had come from. "There's no need. Asia's taking care of it."

Asia. Sydney thought of last night's soup before she'd put her hand to it. Food for survival, not for enjoyment. She didn't think she was up to facing that this early. A sunless morning was difficult enough.

She began to edge her way out of the room. "I'll just go see if she needs any help."

He knew it was useless to tell her not to bother. She

didn't seem to be the type who listened to things she didn't want to hear. For now, he let it go.

Sara watched Sydney leave the room, then looked up at her father. "I like her," she pronounced. When he said nothing, she cocked her head, studying him. "Do you like Sydney?"

He knew she wanted him to say yes, but he wanted to be truthful with her at all times. That way, she'd never have cause to doubt him.

"I don't know yet." He looked down again at Sara's face.

She was smiling at him, her young eyes sparkling as if there were some delicious secret dancing inside of her. He had never seen them look so bright, so lively. He gave in to the feeling coursing through him and hugged Sara again. Sara nestled happily against him.

What he did know, he thought, was that this woman Ben had brought into their lives was apparently someone who knew what she wanted and went after it. As far as traits went, it wasn't a bad one to have.

As long as it didn't get in his way.

Chapter Seven

"And what's your problem?"

The question sounded a little short even to his own ear. But, as far as Shayne was concerned, there was a damn good reason for his being annoyed.

He looked at the man sitting on his examining table. Precariously perched was more like it.

Shayne and Klondyke LeBlanc had been best friends since childhood, back when their schooling had meant sitting on the floor of Faye Elliot's drafty little cabin, listening to her read aloud as the wind whistled through the cracks. "Ike," as he was affectionately known, was one of the few people in that group, along with Ben and Shayne, who hadn't fled Alaska for one of the lower forty-nine as soon as he was of legal age.

Ike had bought into the Salty Saloon as soon as he'd scraped together enough money. Eventually he'd taken over and now he and his cousin, Jean Luc, ran it.

Neither Ike nor Jean Luc had ever known a sick day in their lives. Which was why, as Ike sat before him now, as healthy as a prize-winning stallion, Shayne had reason to question his presence.

A sheepish grin tugged on Ike's wide mouth. He avoided looking into Shayne's eyes. He'd never been very good at lying, something some viewed as a shortcoming in his line of work.

"Well, it's this cough, Shayne."

Ike tapped his chest for emphasis, then coughed, rather dramatically. In the middle of his performance, his brown eyes slanted toward the waiting room, hoping to catch another glimpse of the woman who had ushered him in so nicely. The door separating the two areas had accidentally been left standing slightly ajar when she'd walked out.

Shayne crossed his arms in front of him, not buying into this third-rate performance. "My guess is that it would be your knee that's giving you trouble."

That caught Ike's attention. Arched dark eyebrows drew together over a surprisingly aristocratic nose. "My knee?"

"Yes." Shayne pointed to the leg dangling over the side of the table that was closest to the door. "The one you're going to land on after you fall off the table if you keeping leaning over like that." Walking over to the door, Shayne shut it. "Why are you really here?" As if he didn't know.

"I told you, it's this cough—" The sheepish grin broadened. Knowing when he was caught, Ike surrendered the lie amiably. After all, he and Shayne had shared a drink or three in their time. Nothing bonded two men together more than that. "And to check out the new talent," Ike confessed.

Ike began to button up his shirt, the expression on his face distracted. Since the reason for his visit was out, there was no longer any need to behave like a patient.

''Haven't seen a woman that handsome around here since...'' Slipping the ends of his shirt back into his jeans, he paused as he came to a realization. ''I don't recall *ever* seeing a woman that handsome before.'' For a muscular man he moved with a certain easy grace. He eased himself off the table. ''What's she doing here?''

''You tell me,'' Shayne suggested. ''I'm sure the rumor mill is already grinding.'' It had probably started as soon as she'd set foot in Hades.

''It's grinding, all right, but I figured you'd be the one to know, since she's here with you.''

Ike eyed him. ''You send for her?'' The fact would surprise him only because it was Shayne. Mail-order brides, or their modern equivalent, were not entirely unheard of in these parts. Ethan Parks had met his Emma that way and they seemed happy enough.

''No.''

Shayne removed the stethoscope from his neck. He supposed that, in the absolute sense, this was a pleasant change from his usual hectic pace. Today, so far, no one'd had so much as a hangnail. Just terminal nosiness.

He could see that Ike was still waiting for him to elaborate. ''Ben did.''

Ike whistled softly between his teeth. ''She's Ben's?'' And then he scratched the back of his head. It didn't add up. ''But he—''

''Ran off with Lila. Yes, I'm aware of that.'' Shayne thought of the note that was still in the pocket of his parka. ''Painfully aware of that.''

Ike's laugh, hearty and lusty, echoed in the office.

Shayne saw nothing funny in the situation. "Trust Ben to have two of them."

Shayne had no idea why that comment rankled him the way that it did. Or who he was taking offense for, Ben or Sydney. He just knew it annoyed him.

"He doesn't *have* two of them. He has Lila." Shayne nodded toward the outer office. "This one's just decided to stay on for a while, that's all."

That was good enough for Ike. He rubbed his hands together in anticipation. "Well, a while's all we're asking." He slipped on his fur-lined jacket, then set his black hat at a jaunty angle on his dark blond head. "What's her name, anyway?"

Shayne was surprised that wasn't common knowledge, too. "Sydney."

"Sydney?" Ike rolled the name around his tongue and made a face. "Damn silly name for a woman, especially a woman who looks like that, if you ask me."

"No one's asking you."

Hooded eyes scrutinized Shayne closely. "Hey, you're even testier than usual. Something bothering you?" A new light of understanding came into Ike's eyes. "You and her aren't—"

"No, we 'aren't,'" Shayne assured him quickly.

He had a pretty good idea he knew what Ike was implying. One hint, one ambiguous statement, and gossip would be off and running. In his experience, men were far worse than women.

"I just don't like having my time wasted by people who come here under false pretenses." He moved to the door and waited for Ike to join him. "The past three days, healthy, strapping men have been filing in here, mumbling things about bellyaches, flu, hair falling out—anything—just to come in and look her over."

If he was being admonished, Ike didn't seem to notice. "You get a box of candy delivered, Shayne, people are going to want to at least get a sniff of it." A wistful look came over his rugged face. "Chocolate's rare in these parts. Especially chocolate in a classy container."

Female companionship was always at a high premium in Hades. The mainstay of the town being the lumber mill, the workforce was almost all male. Except, of course, for the Widow Turner, who owned the mill and had buried three husbands. That made any woman who came into Hades fair and highly desirable game.

Shayne had often wondered, with such an eye for the ladies, why Ike hadn't left Alaska long ago. Or, if not Alaska, at least Hades.

He smiled tolerantly as he opened the door for Ike. "Try not to trip on your tongue on the way out."

Ike pretended to take offense, though he was too easygoing and good-natured to ever become annoyed.

"I'm not about to trip over anything—" And then an idea struck him. His eyes gleamed as he poked a finger into Shayne's chest. "Hey, you know what we should do?"

Shayne had no idea what Ike was thinking and even felt a little leery about asking. Not that he had to. Whether he asked or not, Ike would tell him.

"No, what?"

"Give her a party. A real big bash. Make her feel real welcome here." As soon as the words were out of his mouth, he started making plans. "Maybe then she'll stay permanently."

It was a bad notion all around. "I don't think—"

But Ike had already sold himself on the idea. He strode out into the waiting area and planted himself in front of Sydney's desk, his knuckles digging into the worn wood as he leaned toward her.

''Hey, darlin', how would you like to come to a party?''

She responded to both the wide grin on his face and the one in his voice. ''A party?''

''Yeah.'' Ike glanced over his shoulder at Shayne as if backup was coming from that direction. ''It's in your honor.''

That took Sydney a minute to absorb. She glanced at Shayne, but nothing coming from that quarter enlightened her. ''Mine?''

One of the men in the waiting room cheered his support of the idea.

Half the men in the room would have gladly supported any excuse for an extra round of beer, Shayne thought cynically. After a hard day at the mill, going to the Salty Saloon and knocking a few back with their friends was all some of the men had to look forward to.

''Sure. Hades is a real friendly place.'' Ike chuckled as he straightened. Man, but she smelled good. Someone should warn her about that. ''Time you met some of your neighbors and such. What do you say? Six o'clock tonight?''

''Tonight?'' When had all this been decided? Sydney wondered. Did Shayne have a hand in this? But looking at him, she knew without being told that he hadn't. He didn't seem like a man who fancied parties or noisy gatherings. ''Aren't you moving a little fast?''

''Have to in these parts in order to keep warm,'' Ike said. The chuckle deepened into a lusty laugh. He winked at her, the dark brown brow wriggling. ''Shayne knows the way, though he don't bend an elbow very much anymore,'' Ike imparted to her sorrowfully. ''And if he don't bring you, darlin'," Ike announced gallantly, knowing he had to get his marker in early, "I'll come get you myself."

About to leave, Ike stopped long enough to look around the waiting room. It was filled to capacity with men, all of whom he had served over his stained counter at one time or another. Most far more than once. "You're all invited."

Cheers met his announcement.

And that, Ike figured, took care of the invitations. Turning around again, he pointed an index finger at Sydney, simulating an old-fashioned six-shooter about to be fired. "See you tonight, darlin'."

"He's very friendly," she said to Shayne as the outer door closed behind Ike. She had to admit, the impromptu invitation really made her feel welcomed here.

Shayne watched Ike through the window as the man trudged away. "That's one way to put it."

Curious, Sydney looked at him. "And how would you put it?"

"You don't want to know."

Shayne scanned the waiting room, taking a long, hard look at the remaining men. The ones who hadn't been lucky enough to secure a chair leaned against the wall or sat on the floor. There wasn't much walking space to be had.

Time to clear the area.

"All right, everybody, this is Sydney Elliot—no relation to Faye Elliot," Shayne qualified. "She's going to be staying on for a while as my assistant until she realizes that it's too damn cold here and moves on. If you want to see her, do it on your own time, not mine." He walked over to the front door and opened it. Cold air rushed in, chilling him, but he held the door wide open, waiting. ''Now, I'd appreciate it if everyone who's not really sick leaves. I need the space for real patients.''

A low rumble of dissatisfaction undulated through the crowd as men of all ages rose to their feet beside their standing comrades. Slowly, they trickled out the door.

Several extended greetings to Sydney as they filed out, promising to see her later tonight at the Salty. She noticed that their words evoked an even darker frown from Shayne.

She waited until everyone had left and Shayne had closed the door again. The waiting room was empty. ''I know this is your clinic, but you could have worded that a little more politely.''

He didn't take criticism well, constructive or otherwise. Besides, where did she get off telling him how to behave around people he'd known far longer than he'd known her?

''I know those men. Being polite wouldn't have gotten me anywhere with them. You have to haul them out like mules.''

''If you say so.'' The image left something to be desired. ''By the way, you were wrong.''

Was she determined to argue about this? ''I already said there's only one way to—''

She shook her head, stopping him before he could continue. ''No, I mean about my not being related to Faye Elliot.''

That took him by surprise. As far as he knew, Faye Elliot had never mentioned anything about having a family, only her father, and Reverend Elliot had died long before Shayne had been born.

''You're related to Miss Faye?''

Sydney nodded. ''She was my father's aunt. He used to get postcards from her occasionally.'' She could remember how excited she'd get each time one arrived. The scenes depicted on them had looked so exotic to her. A fond smile curved her mouth. "I kept them all in a scrapbook. Sometimes there were letters." Long, voluminous letters—filled with details of daily life in a harsh, unforgiving land—that arrived sporadically, coming every few years just when it seemed that Aunt Faye had forgotten about them.

"I always envisioned her as this brave pioneer woman, carving out a life for herself after her father passed away."

In the tradition of a pioneer, Aunt Faye had come to Alaska with her father, an ordained minister, to do work among the Inuits. She'd often written that, rather than save their souls the way he'd intended, her father said that they had saved his by renewing his zest for life.

Shayne leaned a hip against the reception desk, looking at Sydney and trying to detect a resemblance between her and the small, stately woman who had taught him how to read and write and told long, beautiful stories about far-off, exotic places.

Maybe around the mouth, he thought. He could remember the way Miss Faye would set her mouth when she was attempting to coax a pupil into giving the right answer to a question. Pure determination. Rather like the way Sydney had looked at the airport.

"Folks said her father died trying to get to a sick child in the village." Bemused, amazed, Shayne shook his head, looking at Sydney again. "You're related to Miss Faye."

She smiled, amused at the expression on his face. He looked as if someone had just told him that the answer to two plus two was secretly five. "That's what I said."

"She was my teacher. My first teacher," he amended.

And one of the kindest people he had ever met. But he never recalled seeing her smile. She always struck him as a woman who lived with some deep sorrow.

"Small world."

And getting smaller all the time, he thought. "Listen, perhaps later you might like to—"

The front door banged open, blotting out whatever he was going to say and snaring their attention.

A towering man rushed in, a half-crazed look on his face. In his arms was a screaming child of no more than five. Blood smeared the man's face and clothing. It took Sydney a moment to pinpoint the source. The boy's left hand was wrapped in a towel—a very blood-soaked towel. Shayne moved from her side and took the boy into his arms.

The boy's pitiful cries of pain ricocheted around the room.

"Doctor, it's his hand, his finger." Hysteria built in the man's deep voice, matching the volume the child was achieving. "Oh God, I told him not to touch it."

Shayne raised his voice to be heard above both of them. "What happened?" he demanded.

"I don't know!" the man practically wailed, shadowing Shayne as he turned to enter the examining room. "One minute he was playing with his friends, showing them my fishing equipment, and then suddenly, I heard him screaming and there was blood everywhere."

Sydney positioned herself between the man and Shayne, placing her hands on the man's trembling, blood-stained arms. He would only get in Shayne's way.

"It's going to be all right," she said soothingly. "Just wait here, please." She blocked his access to the inner room. "You won't do him any good in here."

"But he's my son."

She met the angered look head-on. ''No one's disputing that. And if you want your son to get the best care as quickly as possible, you're going to have to stay out here.''

For a second she thought the man would toss her aside, out of his way. And then a hopeless look entered his eyes. Hopeless because he knew there was nothing he could do.

''But my boy...he needs me.'' The words were shrouded in despair.

''He needs to calm down more.'' She backstepped toward the door, watching, to make sure he wouldn't follow. ''We can handle this.'' It was a promise she had no authority to make.

Turning on her heel, she hurried into the room, shutting the door behind her. Quickly, she pulled out a fresh covering for the examining table.

''The instruments—'' Shayne began as he placed the boy on the table.

''Got 'em,'' she announced, sliding the tray parallel to the table.

The boy's screams rose in intensity as a new fear compounded his pain. He jerked upright the moment his back came in contact with the table. Sydney grasped the boy's right hand and wrapped her fingers around the small wrist.

''Look at me,'' she urged softly. His head tossing from side to side, Sidney knew they had to get him to lie still for the injection. She raised her eyes to Shayne. ''What's his name?''

''Joseph,'' Shayne answered as he tore open a fresh package of surgical gloves on the tray and pulled them on.

''Joseph. Look at me,'' she ordered, her voice soft,

commanding. When the boy didn't comply, she turned his head toward her with her free hand, forcing him to look in her direction. ''It's going to be all right. Do you hear me? Dr. Shayne is going to help you feel better. You're going to be all right. I promise.''

Her eyes met Shayne's. She could see admonishment in them.

''I promise,'' she repeated. The boy needed to hear that more than he needed to be apprised of the possibilities that faced him.

She could see Joseph's heart pounding in his chest as he cringed at the sight of the needle Shayne was preparing. ''No, no, don't hurt me. Please don't hurt me. It hurts. It hurts…it hurts,'' he sobbed.

Her own heart was in her mouth. She'd been around cuts and bruises, but nothing approaching the apparent severity of this young child's injury.

Releasing her grasp on his wrist, Sydney threaded her fingers through Joseph's and held on tight, trying to fuse courage into his small body. ''Of course it hurts. You had a very big accident.'' She talked quickly, hoping to distract him long enough for Shayne to administer the anesthetic.

''And there's going to be a great scar—something to impress your friends with. But first you have to stop screaming and let the doctor do his work.''

Huge tears rolled down Joseph's cheeks as he winced and tried to focus on her.

''Dr. Shayne's going to sew up your hand so you can play again. But he needs your help to do it, okay?''

His tears continued to flow, but slowly, the terror receded and he began to calm down. Within a few minutes, the anesthetic Shayne had given him began to take effect. Joseph's eyes drooped as he became drowsy.

Throughout it all, Sydney never stopped talking to him. She continued, touching on everything she could think of that might interest a boy, until the surgery was finally over.

Sydney didn't feel as if she released the breath she was holding until an eternity later when Shayne placed a groggy, bandaged Joseph into his father's outstretched arms.

He slipped a comforting arm around the man's shoulders. "There shouldn't be any permanent damage. You got him here in time."

Larry Elder hugged his son to him.

"I want you to give him two of these for the pain every four hours the first day." Shayne unlocked the small cabinet by his desk and doled out eight white pills into an envelope. Very carefully, he sealed it. "After that, it should be all right."

He tucked the pills into the man's shirt pocket, then tugged the open jacket back into place. "If not, I want to see him. Any sort of problem, I want to see him. Otherwise, bring him by in four days, I'll change the bandages and check on my handiwork." He walked over to the front door and opened it for them.

Larry Elder nodded his dark head at each instruction. "Right, absolutely. And thanks again." His dark eyes filled with tears. "Really."

Shayne spared them both. "That's what I'm here for. And next time, lock up your fishing equipment," he added.

He shut the door behind Elder. That was the last of the codeine pills, he thought. He would have to take a run down to the hospital pharmacy in Anchorage to get more.

When he turned around, Sydney was looking at him. ''Nice job.''

He shrugged off the compliment. He was a doctor, he was supposed to be equal to these kinds of situations. ''Thanks.'' Shayne nodded, realizing she hadn't lost her head the way his last assistant had. Whether by instinct or design, Sydney Elliot seemed to know her way around an emergency. Maybe that story about wanting to be a doctor had been on the level. ''I guess I could say the same to you.''

She wondered if he felt as reluctant as he sounded. ''If you want to.''

She knew how to draw things out of a person, Shayne thought grudgingly. ''All right, I want to. You did a good job, especially calming the boy down. You're right, kids do like you.''

She smiled. ''Most adults do, too.''

He thought of the men who had been in earlier. ''I noticed.'' He dragged a hand through his hair, feeling drained now that the crisis was over. ''So, I take it you want to go to that thing tonight at the Salty?''

Sydney was surprised he even had to ask. But then again, he would. ''Wouldn't be right not to, seeing as how I'm supposed to be the guest of honor.'' She peered at his face. ''Will you come with me?''

He shrugged again. ''I suppose I'll have to. The place is going to be full of men, falling all over each other just to get close to you. Someone has to protect you from that.''

So he was going to be her reluctant knight, was he? She rather liked the sound of that. But she didn't want him to think she was some helpless little female who needed looking after. It'd been a very long time since she'd been helpless.

"I can take care of myself."

He was beginning to believe that. Still, she was under his roof and his responsibility. "I'll come along anyway."

She smiled at him. "I'd like that."

She might, he mused, but the problem was, he wasn't too sure if he would.

Or worse, that he would.

Chapter Eight

Shayne didn't like the way Jean Luc was looking at Sydney. As if she were a rack of freshly roasted lamb and he was a timber wolf just coming off a fourteen-day hunger strike. Hell, if he were being honest with himself, Shayne'd have to say that he didn't particularly like the way any of the men crowding into the seventy-five-year-old saloon were looking at her.

One of the McGregor twins bumped into Shayne as he tried to forge his way into the thick of things. Into the huge misshapen circle of men weaving in and around Sydney. Every damn one of them wanted to get close to her. Like seals nudging each other out of the way for the best sunning place on the rock.

She was the only woman in the place. Not an unusual fact on its own, but a source of growing irritation for him right now.

Sydney looked as though she were enjoying all this

shallow attention she was receiving. She wasn't flirting the way he'd seen Ben's Lila do, but then, the last time he'd seen the woman who'd made his brother lose what little sense he had, it'd been several years ago. She'd been just a slip of a girl then, testing her powers, seeing how far they'd take her.

This was no mere girl at the opposite end of the Salty. Sydney was a woman full-blown and ripe. So ripe, she could make a grown man ache just by being there.

Shayne's fingers tightened around the handle of his mug. Sydney had no need to test any of her powers. He figured she knew what they were.

A jukebox, stocked with songs from a decade or two ago, was vainly trying to pierce the din of raised voices and laughter within the wide, wood-paneled building that had been painstakingly remodeled to resemble Juneau's Red Dog Saloon.

It hardly scratched the surface.

It seemed odd to Shayne, with all the noise that was ricocheting about in the Salty, that he could hear her laughter above everything else. It wasn't loud, or high, just haunting.

Like the scent she wore.

Like the look in her eyes.

He raised the mug to his lips, then put it down again, forgetting to drink as he watched Nils O'Hara whisper something in Sydney's ear. She laughed in response, the sound piercing him. Something stirred inside Shayne. He hadn't a clue as to what. The closest he could place it was the way it felt when he'd once gotten himself lost in the deserted mine for more than two days. His stomach was so empty and pinched so bad it felt as if it'd been stapled to his back.

It felt kind of like that. Only worse.

He frowned into his drink. It was none of his business, of course, what she did or didn't do. None at all. Still, he didn't have to like it.

And he didn't.

''Remind me to thank your brother the next time I see him.'' Shayne looked up to find Ike across from him at the bar.

Ike was wiping at an imaginary stain. Ike was always massaging the wood, polishing it when there was a lull in business, pampering it like an obsequious lover in between pouring drinks when business was booming. He loved this old place and it showed.

Leaning one elbow on the bar, Shayne looked down at the amber liquid in his glass mug. The overhead light grazed it, dancing along the surface like a fairy trying to pick her way over tiny stones in a rushing brook. He stared at it for a long moment before looking up again.

''What do you want to thank him for?'' It took an effort not to growl the question. He was having a hell of a time holding on to his temper tonight, something that usually gave him no trouble at all.

Ike laughed. ''Last time I remember business being this good, a blizzard trapped a quarter of the mill workers in here. They drank for the duration. Almost drank me dry.'' The till had overflowed that time, Ike recalled fondly. ''When the weather finally let up, they were feeling no pain.'' The look on his face was almost sentimental as he remembered. ''Jean Luc and I had to drive them all home, but hell, it was worth it. That's when I got the money to buy the jukebox and the satellite dish.''

Half the time the television set had as much snow on the screen as they had outside. Shayne looked at Ike's grinning face. ''Yeah, well, glad you're so happy.''

Jean Luc was busy tending the other end of the bar.

Ike figured he could pick up the overflow for a few minutes. He stopped rubbing the counter and leaned forward to peer at Shayne's face, growing serious.

"What's eating at you? Times tough without Ben?"

The last thing Shayne wanted to do was discuss his frame of mind. He didn't believe in baring his soul, not even to someone who'd known him for years. "You might say that."

"Heard from him, yet?"

"No, not yet."

Not that he expected to. It'd been less than a week since Ben and Lila had taken off. Ben was undoubtedly high on his newly achieved status as husband. Or fool. More than likely, knowing Ben, he'd be like that for some time to come. Once he came down, Ben might think to call him, but Shayne wasn't about to hold his breath until that happened.

"Look at it this way, you get to keep what he left behind." With a lift of a brow, he indicated where Sydney was standing with a nod of his head.

Ike had survived all that Alaska had to throw at a man, partially because he'd always been able to see the bright side of everything. His sense of hope was also what made him perfect for his chosen vocation.

Shayne looked at him sharply. "She's a woman, Ike, not a shirt."

Ike looked thoughtfully over toward where Sydney was holding court. He watched the way she held herself, the way she moved when she turned to look at someone. Made a man start thinking about giving up the high life and settling down.

"Sure wouldn't mind keeping her," Ike murmured, appreciation throbbing in his voice. And then he saw the look in Shayne's eyes. It was the kind of look that made a man step out of range. He'd seen that kind of look before. It had possession written all over it. Well, well, who would have thought it? ''You're going to have to make up your mind about this, Shayne.''

Shayne's expression darkened. What the hell was Ike going on about now? ''About what?''

Ike took no heed of the warning note in his friend's voice. He'd never been afraid to talk to Shayne, not even when Shayne's wife had picked up and left him. Everyone else in town had avoided the subject with Shayne because they were afraid of having their heads bitten off.

Ike looked Shayne in the eye. ''Either you don't want her, or you do.''

What the hell made Ike think he had the slightest interest in the woman? ''You've been sampling too much of your stock, Ike. I already said—''

''I know what you *said,*'' Ike stated flatly. ''How you look when you're saying it is a whole different matter.'' Because Shayne didn't immediately jump down his throat, Ike went a little further. ''I think she makes you remember that you're a flesh-and-blood man and not just the local witch doctor.''

That was so absurd, Shayne didn't know where to begin to refute Ike's observation. Exasperated, Shayne waved a disgusted hand at him. ''You don't know what you're talking about.''

Ike's broad shoulders rumbled beneath his shirt as they rose and fell, not in surrender but in momentary retreat. ''Have it your way.'' He looked at Shayne's mug, the contents of which had hardly changed since he'd first poured it. ''Are you going to drink that or just pray over it like you've been doing for the past two hours?''

From the corner of his eye, Shayne noticed a man

three stools over raise his hand, trying to get Ike's attention. Shayne pointed toward him. "Go peddle your spirits, Ike. Someone's buying. I'm doing fine just the way I am."

Shayne could have sworn he heard Ike mumble, "Your opinion," as he moved away to see what the man would have. Shayne wasn't about to ask Ike to repeat what he'd said. Ike just might tell him, and he was in no mood for more lectures.

Eyeing the contents of his mug, he finally raised it to his lips and took a long swallow. The beer tasted particularly bitter tonight.

He glanced toward Sydney again. There was a fresh circle of lechers around her.

Or maybe that was just the taste in his mouth and not the beer, he thought. No reason for the latter.

It didn't change anything, though.

Someone jostled against him, this time trying to get to the bathroom. Shayne was surprised there wasn't a huge line snaking its way out of the tiny accommodation. Ike had recently opened up a fresh keg, the third one tonight.

Ike was right, he mused. There was an inordinate amount of people in here. Far more than he ever remembered seeing. Hades's population hovered around five hundred souls at any given time. Right now, it felt as if two-thirds of them had shoehorned their way inside the 24 by 48 building.

The press of bodies was getting to be more than he could put up with. It was decidedly hot in here and growing more so. He'd removed his parka over an hour ago but that was no longer good enough. He needed to get some air, even if it was freezing outside. It'd be an improvement, if only for a few minutes.

Making up his mind, Shayne plucked his parka from one of the hooks that lined the back wall and began the slow journey toward the front door. He felt like a salmon trying to make it upstream. A salmon encountering a lot of other salmon swimming in the opposite direction.

He hadn't been out of her line of vision all evening, no matter who had been in front of her or what they'd been saying. Sydney thought of Shayne as her anchor. She saw him now, making his way to the door, despite the fact that she was carrying on a seven-way conversation with the Riley brothers and their cousins, a collection of men, mill workers all, ranging from the age of eighteen to seventy-one.

Shayne was leaving. The thought telegraphed itself through her brain. Was he going home without her? She wouldn't put it past him. Shayne was too accustomed to keeping his own counsel to probably even remember that he'd brought her here. There was no way she was about to be abandoned again. Twice in one week was twice too many.

"Excuse me," she murmured to the man directly in her path. She tried to move around him, but it wasn't as easy as she would have liked.

The youngest Riley, who fancied himself more of a ladies' man, was reluctant to let her get away. "Are you leaving?"

"Don't go yet," someone said from behind her. "It's still early."

She was already halfway to the door. Glancing over her shoulder, amusement played over her generous mouth. "How can you tell?"

The question was met with more than slightly inebriated laughter. The sound, swelling and lusty, followed her as the crowd obligingly parted the way it hadn't for Shayne.

The blast of cold air that met her as she walked out the front door of the Salty instantly stung her cheeks. It was like stepping into a cold shower, only far worse. The warm cocoon that had surrounded her only a moment ago cracked wide open and fell off.

Shivering, she pulled her parka closer to her, overlapping the two ends. In her haste to get out, she hadn't bothered to zip it up. Worse, she realized belatedly, she must have dropped her gloves inside somewhere. They weren't in her pockets.

Shayne turned when he heard the volley of voices crescendo then ebb as the door opened and closed. He raised a brow, surprised that she'd followed him.

"Had enough fawning?"

The choice of words confused her. "'Fawning'?"

"Fawning," he repeated. When she continued to look at him as if he were making things up, he elaborated. "Falling all over themselves to get close to you. Have you had enough of it?"

He looked angry. She had no doubt that somehow in his mind, it had to be her fault. Now what had she done?

"'Enough'? I wasn't aware that I was trying to get my fill." She shivered as the wind found its way under her parka. Why did he have to take such a dour view of things? He certainly wasn't a thing like his brother. But then, Ben was gone and Shayne was here. And he'd offered her a place to stay and a job. That counted for something. Her expression softened. "They were just being friendly."

Friendly, hell, Shayne muttered to himself. Was that what it was called these days? He laughed shortly. "Any friendlier and you'd all be bedding down together for the night.''

She stiffened and raised her chin, her eyes narrowing. She'd just about had her fill of the Doctors Kerrigan, present and absent. This one refused to react to kindness. ''Is there something you'd like to say to me in a straightforward manner, Shayne?''

He looked away. By his estimation, he'd already said too much. ''No.''

Sydney wasn't about to drop the subject that readily. ''I forgot, you don't like to say too much at all. But that doesn't stop you from thinking it, does it?''

His expression was mild when he looked at her again, his words carefully measured. Like the calculated steps involved in assembling a bomb. ''Last time I noticed, a man was still entitled to his own thoughts.''

She'd been having a good time, a harmless good time. She didn't think that was too much to ask, given what she'd been put through by the thoughtless actions of his brother. What was it that Shayne wanted from her? Why was he condemning her?

''Maybe, but when they're written all over your face, then I'd like to hear them.''

His eyes met hers. There was fire in them. A fire so intense, Shayne felt as if he could warm himself in them. Burn himself. ''If they're all over my face then you already know what they are.''

The man was insufferable and infuriating. ''Did you take a vow of semisilence or something?'' She could feel her temper flaring. ''You are the most difficult man to get a straight answer out of that I've ever met.''

Her eyes were beautiful, Shayne thought. Even in the dim light coming from the saloon. He could feel himself becoming hypnotized. He struggled to keep from going under.

"I give very straight answers, Sydney. And I don't lie. Be very sure you want to hear what I have to say before you ask."

He was putting her on notice. She wrapped her arms around herself, tucking her hands against her body. Her fingers were growing numb. "You don't like me very much, do you?"

Shayne didn't want it to sound personal. Personal carried implications with it that he wasn't ready to deal with. "I have nothing against you."

That, Sydney realized, left only one conclusion to be drawn. "Then it's the gender you don't care for?"

"I have no feelings for the 'gender' one way or another." At least, that was the way he was trying to keep it. But dealing with this particular member of the opposite sex threw a serious crimp into his resolve. "Unlike those men in there—" he nodded toward the building behind her "—I'm not in the market for anything—no night of hot love, no lifetime of companionship. I just don't like to see people make fools of themselves, that's all."

She didn't want to take that as an insult, but what else could he mean? And where did he get off, judging her? Sydney's eyes narrowed. "Are you referring to me or to the men?"

The heat that had assaulted him inside the saloon and had driven him out, seeking relief, had completely dissipated. If he was cold, Shayne thought, she had to be colder. She was standing with her parka unzipped and her hands had no gloves on them. Fool woman must have left her brains parked in there with those fawning jackasses. She was going to get sick and then he'd have one more patient to add to his roster. Just what he wanted.

"Both." Frowning a silent reprimand, Shayne stepped toward her, took the two ends of her parka and hooked one into the other. With a snap of his wrist, he moved the zipper all the way up. "Where are your gloves?"

He was talking to her as if she was younger than Sara. It killed her to admit that she didn't know. "I seem to have lost them."

Shaking his head, he stripped off his gloves and held them out to her. "Here."

They were far too big for her. "I can't take your gloves."

She'd hardly finished the protest before he was tugging the gloves on her hands himself. "If you're going to work for me, I don't want you starting out by taking sick time."

Sydney shook her head, amused and oddly disappointed at the same time. This could have been a very tender scene if he hadn't sounded like an irate employer. Still, her mouth curved at the humor of it. "You have a way of ruining a moment, you know that?"

Women definitely came from another planet. He hadn't the slightest idea what she was talking about. "We weren't having a 'moment.'"

But even as he said the words, that strange restlessness returned, a little stronger, a little more disorienting. Instead of moving to his car, he found himself just standing there, looking at her. Looking into her eyes.

She trapped him there, he realized too late. No matter how much he struggled, he couldn't seem to free himself. He just kept falling. Deeper. Losing his train of thought.

Losing himself.

''A word of advice,'' he said, striving to think rationally. ''Stop wearing that scent. Bears are attracted to perfume and cologne. Draws them out.''

''I'm not wearing perfume. Or cologne.''

Then that scent, he groaned, had to be her.

The restlessness gave way to an impulse that spun out of nowhere and refused to retreat. Doggedly, it ensnared him, taking hold and urging him on.

He hadn't had enough ale to inebriate a hamster, Shayne reasoned, so he couldn't blame his next move on what he'd consumed.

He blamed it on being male. There was nothing else left to buffer him from his actions. There had to be some reason, some explanation, why one minute he was shoving his gloves onto her hands and the next he was holding her. Holding her and on the verge of doing something he knew he would regret all through this long, lonely Alaskan night.

He did it anyway.

Pulses throbbing in his temples, he lowered his mouth and kissed her. Maybe to find out what it was like. Maybe just to still his curiosity.

Maybe because he'd finally lost his mind. A man had no business standing in near-freezing weather, kissing a woman when he had no gloves on.

This was the last thing she'd expected—and the first thing she'd wanted, Sydney realized with a start as everything that had gone into a deep freeze suddenly thawed within her. There were a thousand reasons why she might kiss someone.

And only one why she kissed him.

But right now Sydney wasn't thinking of reasons or explanations. She wasn't thinking at all. She wasn't doing anything except kissing—and feeling. And maybe hanging on for dear life as the bottom dropped out from beneath her feet.

Shayne's arms tightened around her as he pulled Sydney closer. He could feel the effect of her kiss throughout his whole body.

He'd been kicked by a mule once. The animal's hoof had just grazed his shoulder, but for weeks after, he'd imagined what the full impact might have felt like. He'd never have to wonder anymore. He knew.

But with a mule, he wouldn't have gone back for more. He did now. His mouth slanted over hers again and again. Each time, a little more forcefully. Each time, yielding a little piece of himself until it felt as if there was hardly anything left of him. Hardly anything to anchor him to the world.

The realization that he might plummet over the edge had him pulling up sharply.

Sydney, feeling more dazed than she had when she'd first woken up this morning, tried to focus on him. ''Was *that* a moment?''

''What?'' Shayne tried to make sense of the words, then remembered what she'd said earlier. ''Oh. Maybe.''

Why did she have to ask questions, questions that spawned questions within his own brain? He didn't want questions, he wanted answers. Such as the one addressing why he had just done that.

Backing away from her as if she'd suddenly turned into a live electrical wire, Shayne tried to collect his scattered thoughts. Only scraps came within reach.

''Are you ready to go home, yet?''

Sydney didn't know what she was ready for, only that she might have made one of the biggest blunders of her life. She knew she wasn't ready for this, wasn't ready to be with anyone. Wasn't ready to even be kissed by anyone, really. Except that she had been. And more than that, she'd kissed back.

Now what?

He was looking at her, waiting for an answer. She pressed her lips together.

"Sure." He took her arm, to lead her to his car. A light dusting of snow began to fall as she looked back at the saloon. "Shouldn't I say something to someone in there, let them know I'm leaving?" It didn't seem right just to pick up and go without a word.

Shayne had no intention of letting her go back inside. If she did, there was no telling how long it would take to get her out again.

"Don't worry, they'll figure it out on their own," he assured her.

The snow was coming down harder. There was always a chance the weather would turn ugly, and he wanted to make it home before that happened. He didn't like the idea of leaving his children alone for the night, even if Asia was there with them. It wasn't the same as being there with them himself.

"I've got to be up early tomorrow. But you can sleep in." Unlocking the car doors, he opened hers and then rounded the hood to his side.

She looked at him over the hood, blinking back snowflakes as they landed on her lashes. "Firing me already?"

From where he stood, she looked like someone out of an old-fashioned melodrama, flirting with him. He should have been laughing at the thought, not allowing it to curl through his belly like hot cereal on a cold morning. He squelched the desire to taste snowflakes as they melted along her eyelids.

Instead, he got into the vehicle. "No, I've got to fly

to Anchorage tomorrow morning to get more codeine pills.'' Weather permitting, he added silently. ''Joseph got the last of my supply.''

And Shayne hadn't charged his father for the medication, Sydney remembered. He was more the good doctor than he wanted to let on. ''Can I come with you?''

''Why?'' He glanced at her suspiciously as he turned on the ignition. ''I thought flying made you nervous.''

''That's why.'' Sydney could see he thought she was crazy. ''I don't want to be nervous,'' she explained. ''I want to be able to conquer every fear.'' She refused to be held a prisoner by feelings, *any* feelings. ''If I'm going to stay here, maybe I should learn how to fly a plane.''

I wouldn't want to be on that flight, Shayne quipped to himself as he pulled out of the parking lot. ''You can't do that from the passenger side.''

''No, but I can in the pilot's seat.'' She half turned in her seat, looking at him. Even sitting so close, she couldn't make out his expression. But she could guess. ''You could teach me.''

Shayne was glad there was nothing on the road ahead of him. The request wasn't one he'd been prepared for.

''I could also grow feathers and fly. Neither one is likely to happen in the foreseeable future.''

Like Mac, Sydney conceded, Shayne was going to require a lot of work. ''You don't make it easy for anyone to get along with you, do you?''

Shayne saw no reason to take exception to something he knew was true. In this case, he was trying not to be accommodating.

''Nope.''

He was going to be a *real* challenge. But not one, she

decided, running the tip of her tongue along her lower lip and tasting him, that she wasn't up to.

Turning her face toward him, she smiled serenely.

Though he couldn't pinpoint exactly why, Shayne had the uneasy feeling he'd silently been put on notice.

Chapter Nine

Shayne guided his plane past the only cloud formation around for miles. It was as white and pristine as the snow below.

The winds were with him for a change, and he was making good time. Not that he generally liked to hurry his flights. Flying was the only time he got to really relax. There were no demands on him here; no one who needed him immediately. Up here, with nothing but the sky wrapped around him and the earth below, he was able to let his mind occupy a timeless space where there were no problems for him to deal with.

Except this time, the problem had hitched a ride with him.

Again.

He glanced to his right. Sydney was sitting in the seat next to him, juwt the way she had on the half dozen or so other medical supply runs he'd made since she'd wangled her first flight with him several weeks ago. He still wasn't completely sure how she'd managed to talk him into it. Into coming along with him when he valued his privacy more than a miner valued his first panful of gold.

He'd kissed his privacy goodbye the first time he allowed her to step into his plane.

Even if she hadn't said a word, Shayne conceded, she would have filled the cockpit with just her presence. Just by being there, she seemed to disrupt the very air around her. Not to mention *him*.

"Disruptive" didn't begin to describe his train of thought, which derailed every time he came in contact with her.

But she wasn't not saying a word. She was saying a hell of a lot of them. No doubt about it, she'd come a long way since the first couple of flights when she'd sat quietly, obviously trying to regulate the pounding of her heart. Now, apparently having come to grips with her fear of flying in the small plane just the way she'd said she would, Sydney used their flight time to attempt to wear him down. She was as determined to get him to teach her how to fly as he was determined not to.

If the past few weeks was any indication, it was obvious she believed that if she talked long enough and hard enough, he would eventually give in.

As if he'd ever let her get her hands on his Cessna.

Still, it astounded Shayne that the woman just wouldn't give up, no matter how much he ignored her or turned her down. "Surrender" just wasn't in her vocabulary. Neither was quitting.

Sydney leaned forward to watch a flock of geese vanish into the horizon. It never ceased to astound her how each bird instinctively knew its position within the formation. She was still trying to find hers in the scheme of things. Although, she had a feeling, the move to Hades promised to bring her closer to that place.

She turned to look at Shayne's rigid profile. She certainly wasn't any closer to wearing him down. But that only made her more determined. There was only one other pilot in the area now that Ben wasn't around. But Jeb Kellogg was kept far too busy to take time to give her lessons. That left Shayne, who was as stubborn as a summer's day in Hades was long.

He'd only looked at her stonily when she'd offered to pay him for lessons. At the moment, he couldn't be cajoled or bought, but she intended to keep on trying one way or another until he agreed.

"I'm sure I'd be good at it if you just give me a chance."

Shayne should have known better than to think the lull in the conversation meant she'd given up. He kept his eyes straight ahead, even though he had to admit that she presented the more pleasing view.

"It's not like driving a car." How many ways and times had he said that already? She just couldn't seem to get it through her thick head. "You miscalculate here and there's no walking away from your mistake. It's a long first step down, Sydney."

The warning left her unfazed, just as all the other blatant warnings had. She was too positive a person to entertain the negative side of a situation for more than a moment.

"I won't be taking it." She stared at him, willing Shayne to look at her. "I'll have an excellent teacher who'll prepare me for any contingency."

He laughed to himself, shaking his head. Served him right for letting her come along with him. He'd known that this would be the topic of conversation. Why had he agreed?

The answer occurred to him, but he left it unexplored. It was better that way.

"Flattery isn't going to get you anywhere," he told her.

There was a pause before Sydney asked, "Then what will?"

It was an innocent enough question. Still, it seemed to almost pour along his skin, rousing a response that was formed completely against his will.

He kept the thought to himself. Thoughts like that could only lead to trouble for everyone, especially him. Once hinted at, there'd be no going back, and for now he didn't want to rock the boat. Against all his expectations, Sydney was working out surprisingly well at the clinic, not to mention the fact that she'd taken it upon herself to supplement whatever lessons Mrs. Kellogg taught the children. Even Mac seemed to look forward to doing homework at night. She certainly wasn't the liability he'd first thought she would be.

Not that, he amended quickly, her remaining involved at the clinic or with his children was by any means anything he was counting on permanently. But for now, it was going well.

If at times the sound of her voice as she read to Sara stirred him and led his mind onto paths best left untraveled, well, that was something he could deal with without letting anyone else know about it.

Least of all, the source of those fantasies.

He heard her draw a long breath. The woman was refueling. He knew he was in for another barrage of words. Sydney talked when he answered; she talked when he didn't. There didn't seem to be a way out for him, but he didn't want to continue going around and around about the lessons today.

In an effort to change the subject, Shayne pointed to a small dot on the pristine landscape that three snow-storms, one following on the heels of another, had recently created. He hadn't realized that they were this far south.

"That's Miss Faye's cabin down there, if you're interested." He knew that she would be. Sydney seemed to be interested in absolutely everything, no matter how trivial, and this, after all, had belonged to someone in her family. Or so she'd said.

Sydney immediately tried to see where he was pointing. She craned her neck for a better view. It was a single, lonely brown spot on the white terrain. One of the walls looked as if it was crumbling.

"That's where she lived?"

Shayne nodded. "For forty years, they say." He could only attest to the last eighteen of them.

The little cabin immediately captured her interest. She'd been meaning to ask if Aunt Faye's house was still standing, but so much else had been happening while she'd been trying to carve out a life here, she'd forgotten all about it.

"Is anyone living there now?" Sydney saw no signs of life in the area, but she'd learned that didn't mean anything up here. Still, it didn't appear as if there were any prints leading to or from the cabin. And if someone was living there, wouldn't they have fixed the wall?

In a moment, the cabin was far behind them.

"No, it's been deserted since she died." No one had been interested in appropriating the cabin. It was off the beaten path, even for out here.

It had looked so tiny, so fragile, from this vantage

point. A little, Shayne thought, like the photographs of Aunt Faye herself.

Sidney turned from the window. "Will you take me to see it?"

Habit had him starting to beg off, but then he shrugged. It might be interesting, at that, to see the old place again. He hadn't been within those four walls for almost fifteen years. He supposed a side trip might fit into his schedule somehow. Lately, he had a little more time on his hands than normal. That was Sydney's doing. She'd swiftly absorbed every aspect of running the clinic—except for the actual doctoring.

Not that she hadn't tried to do even that, a time or two. Just minor things, like chest colds and cuts, which she felt she was qualified to handle. The woman, given half a chance, was into everything.

Not for the first time, he thought that she would have been just what his brother needed to settle him into the stream of things.

His shrug was noncommittal. "When I get a chance."

She saw a chance to needle him a little and push her cause. "Of course, if I knew how to fly, I wouldn't have to bother you."

That made him laugh, really laugh. "Knowing you were up in the air with my plane would bother me a whole lot more than taking you would."

She rolled the sentence over in her mind. Amusement rose in her eyes as she asked, "Should I be flattered or insulted?"

That restlessness he was having such trouble shaking permanently was back, nibbling away at him. He knew it came with her presence. Which made his reasons for taking her with him a complete mystery.

"What you should be, is quiet," Shayne told her,

though his tone lacked conviction. ''But I don't suppose there's much chance of that happening, is there?''

Sydney merely smiled.

The door groaned in protest as it was opened and Sara shrank back, grasping Sydney's hand. Even with mittens in the way, holding on to Sydney comforted her. Her father and brother had come with them, but it was Sydney on whom she relied to chase away her uncertainties. Sydney who understood why she was afraid in the first place.

''It's just a cabin, sugar,'' Sydney whispered, sensing her unease. ''A tired, sad little cabin.''

Sidney looked around. There was dirt, debris, and what looked to be broken furniture scattered within the cabin. Half the stairs leading to a loft were missing and the wind whistled through the gaping opening where part of the wall had collapsed.

It was hard picturing her great-aunt living here. Her letters had been so articulate, so alive. The day-to-day existence Aunt Faye had known was now all but buried beneath layers of cobwebbed dust. Sydney hadn't thought of spiders being this far north. She moved around slowly, trying to recreate a time in her mind when all this had been new. Trying to see it as it had been for Aunt Faye.

Sydney paused to right an overturned chair, only to have it fall again because one of the legs had rotted clear through. When it collapsed, Sara stifled a scream.

''Baby,'' Mac jeered, then cast a sidelong glance at his father, waiting for the reprimand.

''I am not,'' Sara denied, though she was clinging to Sydney when she said it.

"No, of course you're not," Sydney said softly. "It's natural to be a little spooked in a place like this."

"Spooks?" It was Mac's turn to look around with wide, uncertain eyes.

"Poor choice of words," Sydney apologized.

"And you used to come here to learn stuff?" Sara asked in hushed disbelief, turning toward Shayne.

Shayne was standing in front of the dormant fireplace, remembering. This was where he'd sat, looking into the dancing flames while Miss Faye read to them, or told them about some distant land that might as well have been on the far side of the moon for all the difference it had made to him at the time.

But he'd loved listening to her voice, to the cadence in it.

The cabin had seemed so much larger then, Shayne thought. He was almost sorry that he'd come. Memories belonged in the past, untouched.

He turned from the fireplace. "Every day until I was old enough to go to school in Shelbyville."

Shayne glanced toward Mac, who was picking at something in the corner with a stick. Sydney'd been the one to suggest that bringing Mac and Sara along would make for a good family outing. He hadn't been convinced of the wisdom of it, but Sara had been eager. Mac, who had wanted no part of it, had ridden, silent and surly, in the back of the plane. He wasn't so surly now.

Shayne crossed to him. "What'd you find?"

Mac picked up a faded, torn photograph of a woman standing in front of the cabin. He held it up for his father's inspection. "Just this."

Taking it, Shayne brushed aside the thick layers of dust with his fingertips. As he did, he smiled. Curious,

Sara crossed to him and stood on her tiptoes to get a better look.

"Who's that?" she asked.

"That's Miss Faye." He held the photograph so that she could get a better look.

"Oh, let me see." Careful where she stepped, Sydney made her way over to him. She wondered if he was aware of the fond note in his voice. Had he had a crush on his first teacher? She found that incredibly sweet, especially in light of the brooding face he turned to the world now.

Sara looked from the photograph to Sydney and back again. "She doesn't look like you."

"Not there, no. But in the family album there're pictures of her when she was a girl," Sydney told her. "There's a family resemblance."

"What's a re-sem-ba-lance?" Sara drawled each syllable.

Sydney smiled. "It means I have her chin and her eyes."

"And her voice." Shayne hadn't realized it until just now, listening to Sydney explain things to Sara. Sydney had the same patient tone in her voice, the same lilt as Miss Faye when she had answered her pupils' never-ending questions.

Sydney looked at him in surprise. She'd never met Aunt Faye and her father had never mentioned the similarity. "I do?"

"Yeah." He looked away, feeling as if he'd left himself too open again. "Of course, you talk a lot faster most of the time."

She grinned. "These are faster times."

They were certainly moving too fast for him, he thought.

Crossing to the crumbling wall, he tripped over a pile of dark wood and caught himself at the last minute. "What the—"

Sydney was beside him in a minute, stunned. Moving aside some of the debris, she discovered half a keyboard. She knelt to examine it more closely.

"It's a piano." She looked at Shayne. "This is her piano. What's left of it, anyway."

Mac crowded between them, elbowing Sara aside. "What happened to it?"

"Looks like a bear sat on it," Shayne guessed. The remark elicited giggles from his children, which in turn tickled him, leaving behind a warm feeling.

"What a shame," Sydney murmured. Wiping her hands on the back pockets of her jeans, she rose again.

He tried not to watch her, but it was difficult looking at anything else when she prowled around like a sleek cat, studying everything. Restless, he wanted to get going. "Seen enough?"

"Yes." Moving in a complete circle, Sydney took one last long look around. Then she turned to face Shayne. "It's perfect."

He laughed shortly. This was far from perfect by any standards. "For what, a haunted house?"

"No, to live in." If she concentrated very hard, she could envision the cabin as it had been. As her aunt had described it in her letters.

Suspicion began to ripple through him. She couldn't mean what he thought she meant. "For whom?"

"For me." Why did he look so surprised? She couldn't continue living at his house. It wasn't right. Besides, it was obvious that he really didn't want her there. As soon as she'd walked into the cabin, she'd known she belonged here. ''If I'm going to remain here, I need a place to stay.''

The idea of not having her underfoot wasn't quite as pleasing to him as it should have been. He tried to justify his reaction to himself. Sure, he wanted her out, but not staying in a rundown shack. Didn't the woman have any common sense at all?

''It's out of the way,'' he noted pointedly.

''Everything here is out of the way,'' she countered. There, she decided, finding a spot. She'd put her sofa right there where it would get light from the window and the fireplace. When she had a sofa, she amended, smiling to herself.

What was she grinning about? Shayne frowned. ''It needs work.''

She paced off the length of the room, making plans. ''Nothing that can't be fixed with a little effort and some lumber.'' Shelves, she thought. She could put shelves in right beside the nook. Her books should be arriving soon. They were already overdue. ''Fortunately, I'm pretty handy. My dad loved to work with wood, and he didn't see anything wrong in passing on his tricks to me.''

The word caught Mac's attention despite his best efforts to tune everyone out. In an expression that mimicked his father's, his dark brows drew together. ''Your dad did tricks?''

She placed her hand on Mac's shoulder in a gesture that was pure camaraderie. With something akin to envy, Shayne noted that the boy didn't pull away. ''Sometimes, when it came to wood, he did magic.''

The list of her abilities, at least as seen through her own eyes, seemed endless, Shayne mused, his mouth curving in amused cynicism. ''A premed carpenter who teaches elementary school. Some would say you were becoming a very valuable asset here in Hades.''

''Some,'' she attested, looking at him over her shoulder. ''And what would you say?''

He wasn't about to comment on the effect of her presence in his life, on the town. ''I say you're biting off more than you can chew, taking this old cabin on.''

She never hesitated. ''All right, you can help me.''

She could whip things around faster than an old-fashioned turntable. ''That's not what I meant.''

''No, but it's what I meant.'' The wind's whistle was turning into a howl as it came through the large, gaping chinks in the walls. There was no doubt that the cabin was going to need a great deal of work. ''It'll go faster if there's two of us working on it.''

Sara cleared her throat. Looking down, Sydney laughed and caressed Sara's cheek. ''Three,'' she amended, then looked toward Mac. In a voice that would have done an auctioneer proud, she called out, ''Do I hear four?''

Mac looked down at his feet to hide the pleasure on his face at being included. Up until a second ago, he'd been feeling like an outsider. ''Yeah, maybe.''

She exchanged looks with Shayne. His amazement tickled her. ''I have a definite maybe. Far better than a firm no, I'd say.''

She would say, Shayne had come to realize, a lot of things. At any given moment.

''Just how in the hell did you manage all this?'' The question, directed at Sydney, was one Shayne had found himself asking—or thinking in one form or another—a lot these past few weeks.

All forms of the question revolved around Sydney.

This particular time came five days after she'd announced she wanted to move into the cabin. He wanted to know now how she had managed to rope in all the men swarming around to renovate Miss Faye's old cabin for her. Because she surely had roped them in. What had begun as a work party of four had multiplied until almost every available man, married or otherwise, had volunteered his services. Some of the men had brought along their wives, their families, and enough food to feed the whole town.

What they had here, Shayne realized, was an old-fashioned barn raising without the barn. And without electricity. The lines leading to the old cabin had long since gone down and fallen into disrepair. Several of the men had brought their own emergency generators to provide whatever power they absolutely couldn't do without.

Maybe someone should have thought of plugging the machines into Sydney, Shayne mused, because at the center of this whirlwind of activity, issuing orders in a velvety-soft voice, was Sydney who, he'd discovered, really did know her way around lumber and construction. She seemed completely tireless.

He was beginning to believe that she could do anything she claimed she could.

Sydney held a glass under the beer barrel's spigot and turned it. Beer foamed as it poured from the keg. ''I just asked Ike to spread the word that I was going to renovate Aunt Faye's cabin and that I needed help,'' she confessed, holding the glass out to him.

He thought of passing, then decided that there'd be no harm in having just one. He'd been at this since early morning and welcomed the break.

The beer felt good, going down.

Looking around, he saw Sara playing with Bill Hanson's little girl, Gem. Even Mac had stopped hanging back and was earnestly hammering in nails under the supervision of Tate Kellogg. He looked as though he was having a good time, too.

She saw where he was looking. ''Why don't you go over and help him?''

When was she going to stop interfering in his life? He hadn't asked her for advice. ''Mac's doing fine on his own.''

''Fine'' wasn't quite the word she would have used. ''A boy could always use some time with his father.''

Hadn't she been paying attention these past few weeks? ''Mac wants nothing to do with me.''

He was wrong there, Sidney thought. ''Mac wants nothing to do with the pain he's feeling inside, you just happen to be a handy target.''

She debated her next words. Maybe she was overstepping a boundary that the good doctor had drawn all around himself, but she couldn't let that stop her from saying what needed to be said. After all, if things had worked out differently, she'd be family by now. She'd been raised to believe that, in the name of love, family had a right to interfere.

''Mac won't know that you love him unless you let him know.''

There she went again, orchestrating his life. It was a damn good thing she was going to be moving out. ''If I let him know, it won't be with a crowd of people buzzing around.''

''It doesn't have to be in words,'' Sydney said. There were a great many ways to let someone know you cared. A touch, a nod, a thoughtful gesture. ''At least, not here.''

He finished his beer, then set down the mug. ''You just want more work out of me.''

She smiled. The man loved to grouse. It's what he hid behind, she thought. ''You've already done a great deal.''

How would she know that? There were men everywhere, getting in each other's way. ''Watching me?''

''Noticing things. I've always paid a great deal of attention to things around me.''

He had no doubts of that. Shayne wiped his hands on the back of his jeans. ''You know, when you said you were handy, I didn't realize you meant that in the Tom Sawyer sense of the word. He got those boys to whitewash the fence for him by pretending he liked doing the work himself.''

She knew exactly what he was driving at. ''I'm familiar with Tom Sawyer.'' She smiled. ''And Tom pretended. I'm not pretending. I really like the feeling of creating something out of rough materials. And I love the feel of wood in my hands.''

''Then, darlin','' Ike announced, coming up behind them, ''I'd say you came to the right place.'' He waved his hand in the general direction of the saw mill. ''Lots of wood to be had here. Of course,'' he added, taking a seat on the overturned crate, ''you could have picked a warmer time of year to do this. But then, just looking at you makes it suddenly seem plenty warm to me.'' Ike pretended to fan himself.

Sydney laughed. She'd grown to like Shayne's friend a great deal. ''You make a woman feel good, Ike.''

Ike raised and lowered his eyebrows, a full-blown leer on his lips as he looked her over. ''You don't know the half of it, darlin'.''

Shayne frowned. If she wanted to flirt with Ike, that

was her business, but he didn't have to stand around and watch. "I'll go see if Mac needs help."

She watched Shayne walk away. "I don't think he likes me very much." She wasn't accustomed to people not responding to her.

Ike helped himself to his own beer. "Funny, I was just thinking that he did."

"What gave him away, his biting off my head, or his growling at me?"

Ike laughed, giving her a chaste squeeze that left him wistful. "You're all right, darlin'."

He never addressed her by her name, Sydney noticed. "Why don't you call me Sydney?"

"Because no one with curves like yours should be called Sydney, darlin'. And as for our good doctor over there—" Ike nodded toward Shayne "—his late ex-wife did a real good number on him before she took off. And continued doing a number on him even after the divorce."

Ike knew how closed-mouth Shayne could be. While Shayne had shared a little of what had happened with him, although by no means all, he'd done a lot of reading between the lines. "He'd never been an outgoing person, so having his heart shredded by a bandsaw the one time he put himself on the line made him twice as leery of opening up." Ike studied Sydney's face, seeing more than possibly even she was aware of. "He's a good man, darlin', worth coaxing out of his shell."

Oh, no, not that tender trap. Sydney had been there twice already. "I'm really not interested in coaxing," she told him. "I've been seriously involved twice in my life and come up a loser both times. I'm not about to try for a third strike."

Ike had a feeling that this time it would be a home

run, but for now he kept that to himself. ''You've got that wrong, darlin'. You weren't the loser. The men who dropped out of your life were.'' He winked at her, then sighed as he looked toward the staircase that was being reconstructed. ''Better keep my cousin from nailing his fingers to the side of your new home. He won't be any use to me, then.'' He patted the side of the keg as he turned to walk away. ''You think on what I said.''

He left her doing exactly that.

Chapter Ten

Looking for paper, any paper, Sydney ventured into Shayne's den. He'd dropped her off at home and gone on to see a patient. Ever since renovations on the cabin had begun last week, he seemed to be trying to keep even more distance than usual between them. She knew that he wouldn't be very happy about her going through his desk drawer, but her goal was harmless enough. All she wanted was a piece of paper to make a list of things she still needed at the cabin. She had almost a houseful of furniture, thanks to donations from the people who had come to accept her as a citizen of their small town.

The cabin still needed a telephone line, and the electrical lines repaired, and the stairs still needed to be finished, but for the most part, it was almost renovated.

When she opened the first drawer, she found a jumble of papers, all with writing on them.

"You'd think a doctor would be more organized than

this,'' she murmured under her breath. But then, she'd seen his office before she'd taken over. Organization was not very high on his list of priorities.

Abandoning the middle drawer, she opened the side drawers one by one. Not a single pad was available. She'd almost given up when she discovered the box buried on the bottom of the double drawer. It was a battered box, the kind that might have once held a jacket. She opened it, though she thought she'd probably just find old medical journals or something equally as dry inside.

Instead, what was beneath the lid inside the sagging box were photographs. Dozens and dozens of well-handled photographs of all sizes. And all of the same two subjects. Mac and Sara.

She pulled out one photograph from the bottom. The date written on the back was six years old. Intrigued, Sydney flipped more photos over, pulling them out from various places within the box. He had an entire pictorial history of his children's past six years.

''Well, well, well. So you do have a sentimental bone in your body after all,'' she said smiling to herself.

''It's here, Sydney!'' Sara's boots thumped along the wooden floor as she ran into the house. The outer door banged against the wall, announcing her entrance before it sprang shut again.

Sydney's heart leaped into her throat. Quickly, she slid the lid back into place and replaced the box where she'd found it. She piled the other papers on top of it, hoping Shayne wouldn't notice the invasion of privacy. She knew he wouldn't appreciate her knowing that he had a softer side. He might not appreciate it, but she did.

Sydney looked out from the den, prepared for almost anything. Though she'd pretty much adjusted to Hades, and to her father, life was still one huge adventure for Sara.

She caught the little girl as she sailed by the den, obviously looking for her. "What's here, Sara?"

"The moving truck's here!"

The next moment Sydney found her hand firmly grasped within Sara's as the little girl dragged her to the front door.

"Van," Sydney corrected. She paused only long enough to snare her parka from the rack.

Glancing behind her, Sydney saw Mac hanging over the banister, drawn by the commotion, curious. Asia came trotting out of the kitchen, her interest piqued. Even the most minor thing became a major event in Hades, given half the chance. Boredom was as much an adversary out here as the cold, and nearly as deadly.

Sydney beckoned Mac forward. "Grab your parka and come out," she called.

There was, indeed, a large moving van parked in what amounted to Shayne's front yard. Pulling on her parka as she came out of the house, Sydney noted that the drivers were still sitting in the cab, eyeing the terrain, obviously reluctant to brave the cold.

To her it was invigorating.

Shoving her hands into her pockets, she approached the driver's side. "Where were you guys?" She'd almost given up hope of ever seeing her things again. "You were supposed to be here three weeks ago."

Resigned, braced, the driver pushed his door open, then got out. "Had some trouble with the rig. We got snowed in twice coming up the coast." It was obvious that he thought the only thing crazier than shipping possessions up here was electing to live here in the first place.

Rounding the back of the long vehicle, he hopped up on the rear platform and unlocked the double doors. The handle stuck and he wrestled with it in vain for a second before muttering a curse under his breath.

"Hey, Tom, get over here," he called to the front of the rig.

The other man, taller and broader than the driver, jumped down from the cab and made his way to the rear of the van. He gave the handle one good yank and the door opened.

The driver returned to the cab, took his clipboard from the front seat and, after glancing at the inventory that was listed, looked at Sydney. "It ain't none of my business, but you sure must want these things, considering what you paid to have them sent all the way up here."

She would have paid more. They were as much a part of her as her limbs. "I do."

"What'd they bring, Sydney?" Sara asked, hopping with excitement from one foot to the other beside her.

Sydney stepped out of the way, giving the men room. "Just some things that are very precious to me."

Boxed up within the van were her most necessary as well as her most prized possessions. Her books, her clothes, a computer, and a trunkful of photo albums that held irreplaceable photographs. Nothing that couldn't have been shipped by freight—except for one very large item that had been the deciding factor in how she would send the rest of her things.

"Let's get this over with, Tom," the driver grunted, beckoning his partner inside. "I want to get back to civilization before we run into any more bad weather."

Sara stood on her tiptoes, trying to see, but it was useless. "What've you got in there, Sydney? Tell me," she begged.

But Sydney merely grinned, knowing the value of drawing something like this out. ‘‘You’ll see. Let’s go inside and let these men do their job. Asia, can you get them some coffee?’’

Stopping what they were doing, the men looked at Sydney as if she were an answer to a prayer.

The boxes came first. To facilitate things, Sydney had the movers pile them in the hallway, out of the way. And then came the item she’d been waiting for. The singular item whose transport here meant that she was serious about permanently sinking her roots in Alaska.

Mac’s eyes grew larger than demitasse saucers. ‘‘A piano?’’ he cried, circling the upright’s perimeter as the larger of the two men angled the dolly underneath it. Mac’s mouth was all but hanging open. ‘‘You’ve got a real piano?’’

‘‘I’ve got a real piano.’’ Sydney tried not to laugh at Mac’s reaction. He’d been trying so hard to remain aloof until the movers had struggled out of the van with the piano.

Sydney greeted the sight of the honey-colored upright the way she would a long-lost friend who had finally arrived to offer her full comfort and support. It was all she could do to keep from running alongside it as the movers dollied it in. She winced as one of the corners came in contact with the wall.

‘‘Careful with it, please,’’ she begged.

The men didn’t want to be careful as much as they wanted to be finished.

‘‘Where do you want it?’’ the man called Tom huffed, struggling with his end.

Sara knew just the perfect place for it. ‘‘The living

room.'' As an afterthought, she pointed in the right direction.

It would look good there, Sydney thought. It was only temporary, of course, but even that would probably annoy Shayne. She looked toward the room uncertainly. ''Do you think your father'll mind?''

''Lady, please, I'm getting a hernia here,'' the driver begged impatiently.

''My father's a doctor,'' Sara announced with a tinge of pride.

They were coming along just fine, Sydney thought, glancing at Sara.

''Too bad he ain't a magician, then he could levitate this thing into position,'' the driver cracked.

''The living room'll be just fine,'' Sydney assured them. It was only going to stay here until she could move into her cabin.

Once in place, Mac continued to circle the piano as if he'd never seen one up close. He raised his eyes to Sydney. ''Can you play it?''

''Yes. I've been playing since I was five years old.'' Memories crowded through her head, memories of playing the piano, under duress at the time, on cold, snowy nights. Who knew she'd been preparing for her life out here all along?

He looked torn between admiration and suspicion. People said a lot of things that weren't true. Mac ran his hand across the wooden cover over the keys.

''Play something, Sydney.''

She didn't even bother pretending that she wanted to be coaxed. In a heartbeat, Sydney was standing beside him, playing. She only paused when the driver came in with the bench.

* * *

The run had taken longer than he'd anticipated. At one point, he thought he had ice forming on his wings, but it had just been the glare of the sun hitting a water spot. For five agonizing minutes, it had given him a hell of a scare, though. Left him wondering what these people, handfuls of men, women and children scattered like grain upon the wind, would do if something happened to his plane. And him.

Someone was going to have to learn to fly this thing if Ben never came back. Kellogg's son was too unreliable. He had that look about him. The look that said as soon as he was able, he'd be gone. That left only him.

The thought linked itself up to Sydney and her never-ending pleas for flying lessons. He'd made the run without her. When she'd offered to go, as she did each time he delivered medicine and supplies to someone, he'd given her some excuse. They both knew it didn't hold up, but for once she'd surprised him and backed off. Maybe she was finally losing interest.

In any event, it had been the first run he'd made without her since she'd turned up to burrow her way into his life.

He figured he should have enjoyed the solitude a whole lot more since it had become a rare event for him. It mystified him that he hadn't. Instead of relishing the quiet, allowing it to surround him the way it had before Sydney's initial intrusion, it had somehow seemed oddly out of place for him. The solitude wasn't as comforting, it had felt…almost lonely.

He wondered if the land was finally getting to him the way it had so many others out here. A man could only take so much before he was too full of emptiness to stand it.

That his restless dissatisfaction might have had its

source in something else was a possibility he didn't want to entertain.

Getting out of the plane's cockpit, he jumped down, frowning as the sight in the distance registered. There was a moving van in front of his house. He remembered a fragment of the conversation at the airport, something about Sydney's things being packed and on their way. He hadn't given it much thought then because he'd assumed she'd be turning around to go home. But now that she wasn't—

Damn it, the house was crammed enough as it was. If she thought she could jam her furniture into his life on top of jamming herself into it, then she was in for a big surprise. She was just going to have to make other arrangements.

Exhaustion vanished as he strode toward his house as quickly as he was able. Halfway there, Shayne could've sworn he heard the sound of a piano being played. And raised voices, singing along. It linked up to a memory, but he let the chain break.

He hurried his pace. The singing grew louder. Now what?

Sydney looked up when he opened the door, their eyes meeting instantly. The sight of her smile thawed the chill that had been forming in his bones. His reaction made him twice as irritable.

''Hi,'' Sydney said hesitantly. She couldn't help thinking he looked loaded for bear.

She sounded awfully innocent for a woman who kept insisting on turning his world upside down, Shayne thought, gesturing at the strangers and the piano they were all gathered around. ''What's this?''

''Oh, they're the movers.'' Sydney rose. ''Dr. Shayne Kerrigan, this is Boyd Hanes and Tom Kelly.''

"They brought Sydney's things," Sara chimed in needlessly.

He barely nodded in Sara's direction. His attention was riveted to the honey-colored object in the center of the living room. *His* living room. And she was leading a songfest. With movers, yet. "You didn't tell me you had a piano."

She lifted a delicate shoulder, letting it drop again. "It never worked its way into the conversation."

It was in the way of everything, couldn't she see that? No, of course not. She was in the way of everything and she couldn't seem to see that, either. Well, a man had to draw the line somewhere.

"It can't stay here."

To his surprise, she agreed. "It won't. Once Aunt Faye's cabin's finished, I'll take it there."

"How, strapped to your back?"

Sydney didn't like the edge in his voice, as if he was mocking her. When the time came, it would fall into place for her. She turned to look at him. Maybe Ike would help. "I'll find a way."

She would, too, even though he couldn't think of how offhand, Shayne knew. But somehow, he mused grudgingly, this damn stubborn woman would find a way—even if she wound up strapping Ike and Jean Luc, or any one of the dozen or so other men who came sniffing at her heels, to a sled and had them mush all the way there.

The driver looked uncomfortable at the confrontation. He picked up his jacket from the floor and shrugged into it. The other man followed suit in silence.

"Thanks for the coffee," Boyd told her. "And good luck to you." Nodding at the children, the men took their leave.

Sara and Mac ran outside to see them on their way. Shayne was surprised that Mac could be so animated.

He didn't realize that Sydney was behind him until he felt her hand on his arm. "Don't you like music?"

He turned to look at her, then felt something twist inside him. He almost came out and told her that he'd missed her today, but then thought better of it. If ever anyone could make a mile out of an inch, it was Sydney. "It has its place."

Sydney studied him for a moment, wishing she could understand him better. "But not in your life?" she guessed.

He was going to say no, that he didn't have time for such things, but then that same memory returned, stirring within him. The one that had whispered through him when he'd first heard the piano.

He merely shook his head as he walked away. "Not anymore."

Sydney crept down the stairs quietly. Mac and Sara were both asleep. She assumed Shayne was, too. It was almost eleven and his door was shut when she'd slipped out of her room just now. There was no noise, no line of light sneaking out from beneath his door. Everyone was asleep but her.

She couldn't seem to sleep tonight, though she was tired enough.

It probably had to do with having the piano arrive. She could remember playing it as a little girl, although then it had been a huge chore. She'd hated practice. The only thing that had made it bearable was the history behind the piano. It had once been her great-grandmother's, and she'd given performances on it. She and the man who was to become her husband traveled around from city to city, playing anywhere that would have them. It always made Sydney feel as if she were touching a piece of history.

She had an urge to touch it now, to reassure herself that it had really arrived safely and that she hadn't just been daydreaming.

When she came to the foot of the stairs, she was surprised to see a light coming from the living room. As far as she knew, Shayne had been the last one down here. It wasn't like him to forget to turn the lights off.

There was a reason why he hadn't turned it off, she discovered. He was still there. Shayne was sitting at her piano, his hands on the keyboard, his fingers poised. He was touching the keys, although not enough to make a sound.

She debated leaving him to his privacy. The debate was short-lived. Curiosity got the better of her. ''Did you ever play?''

Startled, he jerked his head up. Preoccupied, he hadn't heard her. Damn the woman, did she have to come skulking around into his every moment?

''No, not really.'' Embarrassed at being discovered, Shayne started to pull the cover down over the keys.

Sydney leaned over the bench and gently pushed the cover up again. ''Fakely, then?'' she teased.

He knew her by now, or at least this much about her: she was going to keep after him until he told her what she wanted to know. Shayne figured he'd spare himself a lot of grief by just telling her. It was no big deal, anyway.

''Miss Faye tried to teach me.''

Her mouth curved, remembering the parts of a piano they'd found in the debris at the cabin. Her father had told her that Aunt Faye loved to play. Sydney could just picture her aunt working with a very young Shayne, trying to make him feel the music in his soul. She must have thought he possessed some.

"Did she succeed?"

He shrugged. He'd never been really comfortable about talking about himself, even in a cursory manner. "I could pick out a tune or two, but that was a long time ago." He began to get up.

"Play something."

The softly voiced request lingered in the air between them, as if to draw something out of him that he felt wasn't there. She did that a lot, he realized. But this time, he was just going to walk away.

"I said it was a long time ago—"

Acting as if he hadn't said a word, Sydney stood behind him and placed her hands over his, coaxing them onto the keys.

"It's in there somewhere. Why don't you try?" Her eyes met his, her face far closer than he was happy about. "Everyone needs music in their lives."

That was what Miss Faye had said to him when she had talked him into taking lessons. She would have given them to him free, but he'd paid her back by doing chores. He had his pride. And he'd been proud, he remembered, playing for her.

The light touch of Sydney's hands over his generated a warmth through him he knew was unsafe. "I don't know about that," he muttered. Then, with a surrendering sigh, he nodded. "Remember, you asked for it."

"I'll remember," she promised, sitting beside him.

With stiff fingers, he picked out the song that inexplicably still existed in the recesses of his mind. He didn't remember the title, or even the words. It had something to do with a drunken soldier, or maybe it was a sailor. Searching for the notes, he struck the keys so slowly, it was almost impossible to string what emerged into a tune.

Or so he thought.

But as he stumbled through the song that hummed through his mind, Sydney began to mimic his movements, one complete scale higher. Grinning, she played with more assurance. A melody emerged.

''That's it.'' He wasn't aware that he sounded excited at the reunion.

His own fingers picked up the tempo, until they were playing a duet. Finished, pleased with himself, he sat back. Sydney's soft laughter mingled with the fading strains of the chords. It was obvious that she was delighted with his success.

''See, I told you you'd remember how to play. It's something that never leaves you, you just have to want it to come back.''

A little like the ability to love, a soft voice whispered in her mind.

The grin settled into a gentle smile as she looked into his eyes. There was a deep well of emotion there. Emotion she had a feeling he refused to take so much as a sip of. She placed her hand lightly on his arm, wishing she could coax that out of him, too.

He didn't like not being able to help himself. Because if he could help himself, Shayne knew he wouldn't be doing this, wouldn't be taking her into his arms, wouldn't be tilting her head back until their lips were touching. Wouldn't even be sitting at this damn piano, playing with memories when he had more important things to be doing.

Things that didn't include kissing her and losing his

way in the current of the sensation that raced over him, sweeping him away.

The instant his mouth touched hers with an urgency that took her breath away, Sydney felt alive again. Her pulse raced as she felt the kiss deepen, widen, dragging her in. She went willingly even though she knew it was a mistake to do so. Why did she think this time would be any different?

Yet she wanted this. Had wanted it from the moment she'd walked in to find him at the piano.

Wanted it longer than that.

He finally pulled back, afraid that if he didn't, he would give in to the demands pounding through him. Demands that urged him to sweep her into his arms and take her upstairs to his room.

To lose himself, just for the night, in the sweet softness of her body....

Shaken, Sydney strove for something to say that would lighten the moment. He couldn't be allowed to think that she meant anything by this. Men with the upper hand tended to press you into the ground.

"Wow," she finally said, trying to buy some time to pull herself together. She cleared her throat as she ran her hand through her hair. "It's a good thing we didn't play 'Flight of the Bumblebee.' I'm not sure where we would have wound up."

"Nowhere," he told her sternly. "We're not going to wind up anywhere."

Sydney straightened her shoulders against the sting of his words. Well, that put her in her place, she thought, rallying. Somehow, it felt like small comfort that he wasn't leading her on.

"Right." She rose. "Well, I'd better go upstairs and get some sleep." Not that she thought she could after he'd just lowered the boiling point of her blood. She bit her lip. There seemed to be only one way to save face here, to let him see that if the kiss meant nothing to him, it meant even less to her. "I thought maybe I'd move into the cabin before it's finished. Get out of your hair..."

It was a great proposition. He had no idea why he wasn't throwing his support behind it. All he knew was that the thought of her actually leaving annoyed him as much as the thought of her moving in had. Maybe more.

"It's not a good idea to go until they can run the lines for a telephone and get the electricity going." He didn't like the idea of her being cut off like that. What if she needed someone?

She shrugged. She'd obviously worn out the little welcome that there'd been. She wasn't about to remain where she wasn't wanted. "I can make do."

There she went again, thinking of herself as some sort of superwoman, about to charm small furry creatures with a single smile. "There're all sorts of things that could go wrong, Sydney. Don't be stupid."

Her eyes narrowed. She wasn't about to be browbeaten, which was exactly what he was doing. "I'll be stupid if I want to—" With that, she turned on her heel and marched toward the stairs.

He watched her go, knowing he was looking at the back of the most stubborn woman on the face of the earth. If he had any sense, he'd just agree and be done with it. But he didn't seem to have any sense, at least, none that he was using.

Shayne knew he was going to regret what he was about to say even before the words were out of his mouth. They came out, anyway.

"If you'll stay until the cabin's really inhabitable, I'll...teach you how to fly." He mumbled the last part.

She turned around slowly, not knowing if she'd heard him correctly, or just imagined it. "What?"

He didn't want to have to say it twice. Once was bad enough. "Are you losing your hearing?"

"Maybe." She took a step toward him. Then another and another, until she was at his side, eager, hopeful. "Probably, because then I wouldn't think I'd heard you saying—"

He exhaled. Everything about this woman was difficult. "I said, if you stay, I'll teach you how to fly. I don't want to have to come out and identify your frozen corpse just because you were too stubborn to listen to sense."

She nodded in agreement, although a smile had begun to creep back to her lips. "Can't have that."

Well, if she wasn't going to bed, he was. Before he swept her back into his arms. Because this time, it wasn't going to end in a kiss.

That scared the hell out of him.

Shayne strode to the stairs, muttering a careless, "Good night," as he passed her.

A third of the way up the stairs, he heard the strains of "Happy Days Are Here Again." They accompanied him the rest of the way.

The smile that came to his lips arrived there of its own accord.

Chapter Eleven

Sydney wondered when the clinic's front door had last been oiled. It needed it badly, though she had to admit that its high-pitched squeak was better than a doorbell when it came to announcing arrivals.

She looked up as the telltale creak seeped into her very bones.

A brisk wind pushed its way into the clinic, ushering in the cold, and a small, broad-shouldered woman as if in afterthought. Sydney smiled as recognition set in. She put down her pen.

"Nice to see you, Mrs. Hatcher."

The snow-white head bobbed back a greeting as the woman trudged heavily across the clinic's outer office to Sydney's reception desk, marking her path with bits of snow that had clung to her boots and were now gracing the floor.

Every one of Ursula Hatcher's sixty-three years was

etched into her face with a blunt-tipped chisel. She'd been Hades's postmistress for the past forty-one of those years and proud of it. It was her firm conviction that news, good or bad, didn't have a prayer of spreading without her aid.

People in the area knew better than to dispute that. Most figured she was right, anyway. Though no one had ever accused her of opening the mail, whose delivery she viewed as a sacred trust, there was little doubt that Ursula either knew, or divined, what was in those letters. And she was a great deal more colorful than the local newspaper.

Sydney had met Ursula during her first visit to the general store. Ursula had inspected her the way she might have inspected a package suspected of concealing a bomb. Obviously satisfied with what she'd seen, the woman had given Sydney her seal of approval.

''Got a letter for the doc. Thought I might as well bring these along, too.'' Digging into the weather-beaten pouch hanging off her shoulder, Ursula pulled out a bundle of letters gathered around a medical journal. She deposited everything on Sydney's desk.

Sydney raised a brow. Everyone went to Mrs. Hatcher's corner of the general store for their mail. It was rare that she made a delivery herself.

''Going in for the personal touch?'' Sydney looked her over, wondering for the reason behind the visit. ''Or did you want to see him professionally?''

Ursula's laugh bordered on a cackle and ended in an amused wheeze. Fisting her hand, she thudded her chest through the layers of clothing she wore.

''I ain't never been sick yet.'' Her blue eyes took on a sparkle. ''Wouldn't mind seeing the man personally, though.''

Sydney grinned. The woman had at least thirty years on Shayne, if not more. "Isn't he just a little young for you?"

Ursula could only shake her head at the naiveté that confronted her. "He's shaving, ain't he? That makes him the right age." She held up the top letter, waving it in front of Sydney. "Thought he might want to see this one right away. Might make a difference to him."

Dropping it back on top of the pile, she turned and walked out across the puddles of dissolving snow she'd brought in with her.

Curious, Sydney looked down at the envelope. And felt her heart stop for one long moment. She recognized the handwriting instantly. Why not? She'd spent enough time waiting for letters bearing it to arrive at her mailbox back in Omaha.

Gingerly picking the envelope up, she turned it slowly around, waiting for feelings to catch up to her surprise. When they finally did, they weren't nearly as intense as she'd expected them to be. Or as hurtful. Even though it had been only a month since she'd found herself figuratively stranded at the altar, the edge on the pain had been blunted considerably.

Because he was with a patient, Sydney waited to give Shayne the letter. She wouldn't have been human if she hadn't been curious about its contents. But that was the only thing she was feeling. It pleased her.

She glanced several times at her watch as she waited for Shayne to be finished, wondering if Ben had made any mention of her in his letter. Had he experienced any sort of regret for his behavior? At this point, she'd accepted the fact that she was supposed to have arrived here and he had been merely the catalyst that brought her. Grateful to him for having taken her out of the place where she'd been, Sydney realized that she had definitely moved on with her life.

A life she felt was slowly coming together for her.

It was another fifteen minutes before the door to the examining room opened and Rob Harris came out, muttering his thanks to Shayne.

''Put it on my account, will you, pretty lady?'' Harris put on his hat, covering a head that was as bald and as round as a perfect marble. ''I'll catch up with you the first of the month.''

The employees at the mill were paid twice a month. She'd already learned that the paycheck on the first was for bills, the one on the fifteenth for necessities and pleasure. It was then that the clientele at Salty's doubled.

Sydney made a careful entry in pen on Harris's ledger as he left the clinic. Though she'd offered Shayne the use of her computer for his office, he'd staunchly refused to be dragged into the twenty-first century. She supposed there was a certain kind of charm to that. The man was a traditionalist.

He was also stubborn as hell.

Closing the book, she took a deep breath, picked up the letter from Ben and walked into Shayne's office. She didn't quite know what sort of news she was the bearer of, but given human nature, she was braced for the worst.

Shayne was staring out the window. In the not-too-far distance he could see the forest, the one the government had strictly forbidden the loggers to touch. But he really wasn't thinking about the generations of trees there. His mind was elsewhere. In the next room, where it had no business straying.

The adage ''physician, heal thyself,'' ran through his mind. Except that in his case, he didn't know how to go about that. How to go about stemming this all-pervading restlessness that seemed to assail him every time she walked into the room. If asked, he wouldn't even be able to pinpoint exactly where this restlessness was coming from. Or where it was going to take him. He only knew what lay at the core. Or rather, who.

He didn't have to glance over his shoulder to know she was in the room. She wasn't saying anything. That was odd. "No more patients?"

Sydney walked in slowly, like a soldier picking her way through an area she suspected was heavily mined. "You seemed to have cured everyone, at least for now." There was no way to gracefully segue into what she had to give him. "This came for you while you were in with Mr. Harris." When he turned around, she held the letter out to him. "Mrs. Hatcher brought it."

"She delivered it?"

Surprise registered fleetingly in his eyes as he took the letter from her. And then he frowned when he saw the handwriting. Ben. If he was writing, that meant he wasn't coming back in person. At least not for now.

He raised his eyes to Sydney's, wondering if she knew who the letter was from.

"Yes." She answered the unspoken question. "I know it's from him."

He stared at it for a minute, debating about just tossing it on the desk and ignoring it until later. But later had a habit of becoming now and he'd never been a coward. Just some things he didn't want to know.

Because he wasn't the only one involved here, Shayne slit the envelope open.

Sydney wanted to remain in the room, to read the letter with him. It wasn't just curiosity, she had a feeling that maybe there was something in the letter that Shayne wouldn't want to read.

As if he needed her to shield him or offer comfort, Sydney mocked. She should know better by now. She turned and walked toward the door. Before she reached the sill, she heard the sound of paper being crumpled.

"He's not coming back."

Sydney turned around to look at Shayne. He was sitting on the edge of his desk, the letter a wadded scrap of paper in his hand.

"Ben's decided to open up a practice in Seattle. Says there're a great many more opportunities there for someone like him." The words echoed in his head. Shayne laughed quietly to himself. "I suppose there probably are." He looked up to see her watching him, waiting for more. For once, she wasn't asking or probing. Maybe because she wasn't, he volunteered, "In Seattle, Ben can specialize if he wants." Though he doubted Ben had the tenacity to go that route. "Or choose just to be a regular general practitioner without the constant threat of life and death hanging over him. He can just refer people to other doctors if he doesn't want to get any deeper into a treatment."

Doctoring in Alaska didn't give Shayne that luxury. Here he had to make up his mind quickly, and sometimes he was the difference between life and death.

Shayne saw that as important. Ben saw it as a heavy burden.

Something twisted inside Sydney. She wondered if he realized just how much of himself he'd given away just then. Probably not. She crossed to him slowly, her eyes on his face. "What are you going to do?"

He shrugged, throwing the letter into the wastepaper

basket. "Same as I did when Ben was in medical school. Go on alone."

Her heart twisted again. "But you're not, you know," she said softly. He raised his eyes to hers. "You're not alone. You have Sara and Mac. The town." She paused, then added, "And for what it's worth, me."

He stepped away from the implication. From the comfort. It was a tender trap, one he'd been in before. He had no desire to be in a position to have to gnaw off his own foot to survive. "I meant as a doctor."

She didn't back off. "I meant as a person."

The moment hung between them, filled with meaning, meaning he wasn't going to allow himself to explore. Because he'd been there before and, for him, there was no going back. He'd sworn that to himself, sworn that if he ever got over the pain of losing someone he loved to indifference, he would never allow himself to be in that kind of situation again. To willingly put himself there was idiotically foolhardy and he wasn't a fool.

He wasn't anything, except disillusioned.

He glanced around her, looking into the waiting room. "Any more patients out there?"

Despite the moment, she wanted to laugh at the hopeful note in his voice. "Not a one. You know, I've got just the thing to pull you out of your doldrums." His brow rose in a silent question. "How about giving me another flying lesson?"

"I don't have 'doldrums,' so there's no need to pull me out of them." And he hardly saw giving her flying lessons as a cure for anything, except maybe common sense. "You have a warped sense of humor, you know that?"

Her eyes were lit with amusement. If she couldn't offer him a shoulder to lean on or an ear to listen, she could at least give him a little diversion. And maybe, just maybe, a smile.

"Oh, I don't know. You have to admit, teaching me to fly puts all those other thoughts right out of your head, doesn't it?"

He couldn't argue with her there. She actually had a point.

But he wasn't about to capitulate without at least a semblance of a fight. "Any patients signed up for the afternoon?"

She shook her head. "Page is completely snow white."

He was out of excuses. With Sydney around, there wasn't even anything to catch up on. Accounts, records, inventory… She'd done it all for him.

Shayne sighed in resignation. He actually didn't mind the lessons as much as he said he did, but he'd be damned if he'd let her know that. She'd probably make something of it. Something she shouldn't. Something he didn't want her to.

"C'mon, then." He took his parka from the hook. "I guess I might as well teach you."

She followed him into the outer office. "You sound as if you're going to your own execution."

He glanced at her as he opened the door. "For all I know…"

The makeshift runway stretched before her like a huge canvas. On the ground were tire marks, all crisscrossing each other, evidence of all the times she'd traversed the same area in the past hour.

The cockpit felt almost claustrophobic compared to the wilderness that waited outside. Compared to the sky above, a sky she'd yet to take her virgin run in.

Sydney tightened her hands on the wheel. ''I've gotten fairly good at taxiing, wouldn't you say?''

Compliments weren't anything he gave freely, but Shayne had to admit she was doing a smooth job of it. ''Fairly good,'' he allowed offhandedly.

The man wouldn't recognize sarcasm if it bit him on the butt. She attacked the matter head-on. ''Don't you think it's time that I attempted to fly?''

The words came out slowly, as if he was weighing each one separately. ''You mean, with a plane?''

What else could she have meant, flapping her arms? Sydney thought. ''Yes.''

''No.'' The answer was firm, flat, leaving, he felt, no room for argument. Then to curb the disappointment he knew had to follow, he added, ''I'll let you know when it's time.''

She looked at him. ''No, I don't think you will. I think you're hoping that eventually, I'll get tired of asking you and give up.'' She pressed her lips together in that determined way of hers he'd come to recognize and expect. ''Well, I have news for you, I don't intend to give up.''

He pointed straight ahead, to get her eyes back on what she was doing. ''You're wrong.''

Did he think he knew everything? ''I should know my own mind—''

Shayne had to stop her before she got rolling, knowing he didn't stand a chance of getting a word in once she got under way. ''No, I meant that you're wrong that it's news to me. I've already figured out that you don't stop until you get your way.''

He said it as if it annoyed him, Sydney thought. It was people with her kind of determination that settled this state he loved so much. ''You know, some might find that an admirable quality.''

His eyes narrowed as he looked at her profile. ''And some might find it irritating.''

Sydney could feel his eyes on her. She baited him. ''Which 'some' are you?''

He couldn't lie any more than he could give voice to feelings. ''Somewhere in the middle.''

She considered that. ''Well, that's better than irritating, at any rate.'' She heard him laugh. The sound was pleasing, even if it was at her expense. ''What?'' she coaxed. ''Did I say something funny?''

''No, not exactly.'' Shayne settled back, beginning to relax. She really did have this down pat. ''It's just your attitude.''

He had her trained so that she expected a criticism behind every comment. ''What's wrong with my attitude?''

''Nothing, it's just that I'm not accustomed to anyone sounding so positive about things.'' Mostly, he was privy to people grumbling. About the weather, the harsh conditions, the lack of luxuries. Ben had been one of the few who had liked it here, and even Ben was gone. ''You really like it here, don't you?''

She smiled, her enthusiasm rising. ''Yes. Oh, I miss the malls occasionally, and having a restaurant close by if I feel like ordering out. But mostly, I like it.'' She spared him a glance. ''I like it very much.''

He thought of Barbara and how vehemently she'd despised everything about Hades, and Alaska. Even Anchorage hadn't seemed civilized enough to her. Nothing short of New York City would do. ''Why?''

Did he need reinforcement, or was he really curious about how she felt? ''It's big and wide and beautiful.'' She spared a hand to gesture at the view in front of her. ''And everything we take for granted back home is so new out here, so precious. Like telephones and electricity,'' she teased. ''It makes you take a fresh look at life and appreciate everything you have.'' She looked at him. ''And everything you might have.''

He was caught again, caught within the shimmer in her eyes. So much so that the very air had stopped moving for him.

But not the plane. At the last moment he realized that she'd ceased taxing in a circle and the plane was now heading in a direct path toward the shed.

''To the right,'' he ordered. ''To the right!''

Reflexes snapped into position. She jerked the wheel as far over to the right as she could. Sydney managed to divert the plane so that it missed the structure. But just barely.

Shayne exhaled the breath he'd been holding, grateful for the near miss. A collision would have devastated the shed, and it wouldn't have gone all that well for his plane, either.

He scowled at her, annoyed with himself. He should have his head examined for ever agreeing to this, much less suggesting it. When the plane came to a stop, Shayne took the keys away from her.

''You're not ready to fly yet.''

But Sydney seemed unfazed. ''Sure I am.''

He stared at her. Was she out of her mind? ''You almost hit the shed. How do you figure you're ready to fly?''

The answer was simple and she delivered it as if she was conducting a lesson in common sense for third graders. ''That's easy. If I'd been flying, I wouldn't have almost hit the shed. The shed's on the ground, I would have been in the air.''

At first, he looked at her, dumbfounded. Then he

started to laugh. Really laugh. Whether it was relief or tension that shed itself like skin off a snake, he had no idea. All he knew was that it felt damn good to really laugh again.

He shook his head as the laughter faded. ''God, but you are something else, Sydney.''

She smiled at him as if he'd just paid her a great compliment. ''Nice of you to notice.''

Shayne looked at her then, really looked at her. There were times he forgot how beautiful she was, and how attracted to her he was. But not for long. ''I notice, all right, but I just can't do anything about it.''

Sydney debated taking the compliment and letting the matter drop. She couldn't. She needed to know. ''Can't, or won't?''

He was honest with her. Maybe at one time he could have fallen for her. But not now. Besides, she'd been attracted to his brother, and he and Ben were as different as summer and winter. If she loved summer, the winter would only drive her away eventually.

''Both. I've been down that route, Sydney. Almost didn't find my way back.''

He could do anything he wanted to. *If* he wanted to. ''If you ask me, you still haven't.''

''No one's asking you.'' He knew that sounded too sharp. She didn't deserve that. Well, maybe she did, for delving too deep, but he was supposed to be civilized. That meant not jumping down her throat. ''Sorry.'' He thought of how devastated she'd looked that day at the airport. The day he'd had to tell her she'd been jilted. ''I suppose you have found your way back.''

Maybe not all the way, she allowed, but almost. ''To where I can laugh and live again, yes.''

''I was in love with my wife. Really in love, for the

first and only time in my life.'' Shayne had no idea why he was telling her this. Only that it felt good, finally letting it out. ''I grew up believing that love meant standing by someone, making it work, not giving up because things weren't going according to plan. But Barbara gave up. Gave up so easily, I felt she didn't care.''

The woman had been an idiot, Sydney thought. ''Did you fight for her, Shayne?''

For a second, the question didn't compute. ''What?''

Hampered by the seat belt, she unbuckled it and turned to face him. ''When she wanted to leave, did you fight for her? Did you try to make her stay?''

He remembered the last days, the heated words, the slammed doors. And he remembered Mac crying, frightened by the yelling and the discord. That had hurt him most of all, to hear his son crying.

Shayne banked the memories. There was no point in going over them again. ''I fought with her, if that's what you mean. But it didn't do any good. She'd made up her mind to go and she went.''

She reached out and covered his hand. ''Taking your heart with her.''

He pulled his hand away, but not immediately. Not before he felt the empathy in her gesture. ''That's far too romantic a notion. When she left, I grew up. I saw the world for what it was.''

No, he'd seen it for what he felt it had turned into for him. ''Haven't you heard, Shayne? Adults need love, too.''

She looked so sure of herself. So incredibly convinced that she was right. He could almost believe it, too. Except he knew different. ''You keep talking like that and—''

''And what?'' she whispered.

Damn, but he wanted her. It wasn't right—for either of them—but he did. "I don't want to have feelings for you, Sydney."

Her eyes held his. "No one's twisting your arm."

He framed her face in his hands. "Yeah, they are."

It wasn't easy kissing a would-be pilot while confined to the seat of a cockpit. But he managed.

Managed just fine, in her opinion.

Chapter Twelve

Sydney couldn't have felt dizzier than if the plane had suddenly gone into a tailspin, forming corkscrew patterns in the air. The impact of Shayne's lips was getting more and more lethal every time he kissed her. And it always left her wanting more of the same.

More of him.

With her fingers curling in his hair, she felt her body yearning for fulfillment. She wanted him. Wanted him to make love with her. Wanted him to want her the way she wanted him.

She knew she had more of a chance of the sun rising at six the next morning than getting her wish.

She struggled to ignore the wave of deprivation that washed over her as he pulled back. Very slowly, she opened her eyes and looked at him.

And knew she was in very deep trouble. It was happening. Completely without her consent, she was falling in love with him.

And he probably saw it all in her eyes. Catching her lower lip between her teeth, Sydney searched for a diversion. And then she looked over Shayne's shoulder, through the passenger window.

Relief blossomed into an amused smile. "What would people say if they saw their doctor necking in the front seat of his plane?"

He had to get better control over himself, Shayne upbraided himself. But every time he was around her, he found himself weakening just a little more.

"It's not a front seat, it's a cockpit, and no one saw. Besides, we weren't necking," he denied with feeling, "it was just a kiss."

Just a kiss. And the aurora borealis is just another mediocre scenic event. He could deny it all he wanted, but Sydney knew he had to be feeling at least part of what she was. There was too much emotion, too much protest on his part not to.

Right now, she was trying very hard not to laugh as she pointed behind him.

Feeling more than a little uneasy, Shayne turned to see Ike standing right outside the plane, a wide, wicked grin on his handsome face.

Ike tapped on the side window, beckoning for Shayne to open it.

"What?" Shayne demanded, pushing the door open. His only regret was that he hadn't managed to hit Ike's midsection with it.

"Nice to see you, too, Shayne." Ike couldn't wait to get back to the Salty with this. Making no effort to disguise his obvious pleasure at the turn of events, Ike looked at Sydney. "See you managed to finally thaw him out a little.'' He winked at her, a sense of camaraderie permeating the air. ''My money's been on you from the start, darlin'.''

Right now, Shayne hated being on the outside almost as much as he hated having attention drawn to him. ''Did you come all the way over here just to tell us about your betting propositions?''

''Hell, no.'' Ike held up the bag he'd brought with him. The item inside had to be special ordered and had just arrived at the general store. ''For your information, I came to give Sydney an early housewarming present.'' Ike thrust the bag at her. ''Didn't have time to wrap it,'' he confessed. ''But I thought you might like it right away.''

Curious, pleased, Sydney leaned over Shayne and took the bag from Ike. She looked inside. Within the bag was a box, a picture of a telephone stamped on either side.

''A telephone?'' she squealed.

Shayne glanced inside the bag. ''Looks that way,'' he muttered.

Ike's grin widened, pleased with her reaction. ''I just brought it straight from the general store. Came in an hour ago. Talk about timing.''

She realized what Ike was hinting at. Hope strummed through her. ''Does this mean the telephone lines have been strung up?''

It had been rough going, Ike reflected, but the weather had cooperated for the most part. Everything seemed to have become milder since she arrived.

''As of early this morning,'' he told her. ''Reed stopped by the Salty for some breakfast when he finished the installation. Said to tell you that you can now talk to anyone you want—weather permitting.''

One down. One to go. It was all falling into place. Sydney hugged the box to her. This was really becoming home for her. "And the electricity?" Mentally, she crossed her fingers.

Ike shook his head. "Not yet." He hated the disappointment that he saw in her eyes. "But I hear tell they're working on it. Hope to have the lines repaired before Christmas."

Christmas was less than three weeks away. In Alaskan time, that was less than a blink of an eye. "Doesn't matter. I have a phone." Her eyes moved from Ike to Shayne. "I'm invincible."

"Just don't try flying to test that theory," Shayne warned darkly, annoyed more with himself than with anyone else.

He hated this strange, possessive feeling that came over him every time someone paid attention to Sydney. She wasn't his to feel that way about; why couldn't he remember that?

"C'mere," she told Ike, who complied so quickly it elicited a harsh laugh from Shayne. Leaning over Shayne again, Sydney brushed her lips against Ike's cheek. "Thank you. It's wonderful."

Okay, he'd been a good guy long enough. Shayne cleared his throat, pointedly looking at his friend. "You two want to be alone?"

Ike took a step back, his hands raised as if he were on the wrong end of a bank robbery. "And be accused of trying to muscle in on your territory? Hell, no. I might need you someday, you quack. Just my luck you'd poison me instead of cure me."

"If I haven't done it yet, I'm not about to," Shayne growled. To point out that she wasn't his territory would have been unnecessarily embarrassing for him as well as for her. And useless on top of that, if he knew Ike. So he ignored his friend's assumption, hoping it would eventually die from lack of kindling to feed it.

Sydney had pried the box lid open and was looking at the pieces neatly tucked against one another inside a nest of packaging. "I can't wait to try this out." Impetuously, she looked up at Shayne. "Switch places with me."

He saw absolutely no reason for her to say that. "Why?"

Her mind was already three leagues ahead of her words. "Well, you won't let me fly, and flying's faster than driving."

Was he supposed to understand that? "Right on both accounts," he agreed slowly, as if he were talking to a three-year-old and choosing his words carefully. "But where are we supposed to be going?"

She held up the telephone. "I want to try it out."

He looked back toward his cabin. "You can plug it into the outlet at the house."

Holding the box against her, Sydney shook her head. "Not the same thing. I want to try it out at the cabin. My cabin." That had such a great ring to it, she thought.

Chuckling, Ike reached up and clapped Shayne on the back. "Humor the lady, Shayne."

Shayne glared down at Ike. "I've *been* humoring the lady ever since she came."

Ike's amusement only seemed to be multiplying. "Do tell."

What was the use? With both of them at him, he might as well give in or be pecked to death. Shayne got out and trudged around the nose of the plane, glaring at Ike. "Wipe the smirk off your face, Ike. It's not what you're thinking."

That only made Ike laugh again. ''You have no idea what I'm thinking, old friend.''

''Yeah, I do. And you're wrong.''

Ike struggled to mask his face in the soul of innocence. ''If you say so.''

The more he protested, the worse it became. Shayne gave up.

Instead of following suit and getting out, Sydney climbed over to the passenger seat. She was buckling up again when Shayne sat in the pilot's seat. Without bothering to say anything to Ike, and without a word to her, he turned on the ignition and began taxiing the short distance he needed for the plane to become airborne.

He didn't have to say anything. His actions spoke louder than any words. She was beginning to appreciate that. She supposed he reminded her of her father in that respect. Except her father had smiled a great deal more.

Sydney hugged the telephone box to her. ''Thank you.''

Shayne merely grumbled something unintelligible under his breath in response. He didn't want her thanks. He just wanted to be left alone.

At the time, he really believed that.

She looked like a kid at Christmas, Shayne thought. Or maybe Easter was the more appropriate holiday.

Yes, Easter. On an egg hunt. Stirring the fire he'd lit to warm the cabin, he glanced over his shoulder and watched Sydney as she went from baseboard to unfinished baseboard, looking for the telephone outlet.

A kid looking for colored Easter eggs, that's what she reminded him of.

''Found it,'' she announced triumphantly.

''Congratulations.''

"Sarcasm doesn't suit you, you know," she told him. Making herself comfortable on the scatter rug that had once been in Jean Luc's living room, Sydney sat cross-legged, taking the telephone pieces out of the box. With fingers flying, she quickly assembled it.

Sarcasm, he thought, was beginning to be his only line of defense against her. With the flames taking on a healthy size, he rose and crossed over to her. Amusement curved his mouth.

"You look like a woman desperate to make a call," he commented.

"I am," she confessed. Almost caressing the keys, she tapped in a number over the virgin keyboard. "This just makes me feel a little more in touch with everything."

He would have thought her manner would have taken care of that for her. He'd never met a woman more in touch with everyone around her than Sydney. Everywhere she went, people seemed to gravitate to her, to her smile, to her laugh. At the clinic, the Salty, the Championship games Hades had held at the end of last week, where everyone came out to compete in physical contests the rest of the country would only turn up their noses at. Whenever he looked into the heart of the thickest throng of people, he knew Sydney would be there.

She was a veritable people magnet.

Shayne perched on the arm of the overstuffed chair that Jaclyn Riley, the elder, had donated to help furnish Sydney's cabin.

"So who are you calling? Someone in Omaha?" A girlfriend? A past lover? The last thought teased his mind like a mosquito buzzing around his head during the wee hours of a summer's night.

Sydney merely shook her head in reply, absorbing the

sound of the telephone ringing on the other end as if she were listening to a symphony at Carnegie Hall.

The receiver on the other end was picked up, and she heard a childish voice say, ''Hello?'' Her smile bloomed in response.

''Hi, Sara, it's Sydney. Guess what I'm doing?'' She waited for the little girl to make several guesses, then said, ''I'm calling you on my new telephone. No, at the cabin, sweetheart. Yes, the one everyone was helping me fix up. It's almost ready now. Of course I'll let you use the phone when you come over here. Put Mac on, will you?'' She covered the receiver. ''You want to talk to him?'' When he shook his head, she wasn't surprised, just disappointed.

''Hi, Mac, just wanted you and your sister to be the first to get a phone call from me on my new phone. It's up at the cabin. No, I'm not moving in yet. Soon.'' She glanced at Shayne. ''Your dad says hi. Yes, really, he does. Okay, gotta go. We'll be home in a little while,'' she promised. ''Bye now.''

Replacing the receivery in the cradle, Sydney looked up to see Shayne watching her. She couldn't read his expression and it made her uneasy. The only time she was able to read it clearly was when he was angry about something. Usually her.

He wasn't angry now, at least she didn't think so, but she couldn't guess what was going on in his mind.

Brows drawn together, Shayne was trying to untangle the puzzle that was Sydney Elliot. He wasn't having much luck.

''With everyone you could have called back east, you called Sara and Mac, two children you talk to every day.'' It didn't make sense to him. ''Why?''

No big mystery. "I thought they'd get a kick out of being the first people I called. And I was right."

That still didn't explain it for him. The telephone was for communication, for spanning long distances, not for pleasing two kids. "You know, I don't understand you, Sydney."

He was delving too deep for an answer that was so close to the surface it almost floated. "I speak a fairly clear form of English." She smiled up at him. "What's not to understand?"

Something that had been nagging him ever since the beginning. "What I don't understand is what you're doing here."

She could have easily risen to her feet on her own. Instead, she put out her hand, waiting for him to help her up. "You know what I'm doing here. I came to marry your brother."

Taking her hand, he pulled her to her feet. "You could have turned around and gone home."

She shrugged a bit too carelessly in his estimation. "I wanted something new, remember?"

For once he wouldn't let a subject drop. This one time, he was determined to satisfy his curiosity. "Most women buy a pair of shoes when they feel like that, not a whole new way of life."

She shoved her hands into her back pockets, looking off. There were storm clouds gathering beyond the big bay window. She wished he'd stop pushing for an answer. "Maybe I needed that whole new way of life."

"Why?" he persisted. "I'm trying to understand why a woman who can obviously make friends wherever she goes would want to go into hiding."

Her chin jerked up. "It's not hiding, it's..." Oh, what did it matter? "My father died almost three years ago, and it devastated me. For the first time in my life, I felt as if I was adrift. And alone,'' she admitted. ''Very alone.'' She took a breath. Even now, it was painful to go over it. To touch upon her mistakes. ''Then I fell in love with the wrong man—''

''My brother.'' He meant it rhetorically. He didn't expect her to shake her head.

''No, this was someone before your brother.'' She could see that she'd surprised him. Well, he'd asked. ''Someone your brother helped me to forget with his letters.'' Letters that were so important to her, that had helped her out of the very difficult place she'd found herself in.

''What happened? With the other man, I mean.''

She shrugged. ''I wanted children, he wanted freedom. I thought we hit some sort of a compromise. He left me at the altar.'' She sighed. That was all behind her now. ''I thought that maybe things happened for a reason and I was meant to go through what I had in order for Ben to come into my life.'' She rocked back on her heels, looking back and feeling foolish. ''But I thought wrong.''

Twice, she'd been left at the altar, figuratively and literally. And yet she was still forging ahead. He wasn't sure whether to admire her, or call her a hopeless fool.

Raising her chin, she almost looked defiant to Shayne. ''My track record as far as making emotional choices is zero for two. So I've decided to stop looking for someone to share my life with and just live it instead.'' It seemed like a safe, sane way to go. ''So far, I think I'm doing pretty well.''

The firelight was playing on her hair, making it look as bright as the golden nuggets that had brought prospectors running in droves at the turn of the century. He would have been less than human if he could have resisted touching it. And he suddenly felt very human. He shifted a strand through his fingers, his eyes on hers.

"You know, sometimes they say when you stop looking so hard for something, you find it."

She felt as if her heart had gotten lodged in her throat. "What are you saying?"

Very slowly, he moved his head from side to side. "Damned if I know. Just like I don't know why I want to keep kissing you."

Her smile spread from her lips to her eyes. To him. "Don't they teach elementary biology to med students anymore?"

God, but he wanted her. Wanted her so badly, it almost hurt. "I slept through that class."

With less than a breath between them, she wound her arms around his neck.

"Oh, then let me give you a refresher course. It says that men and women are inherently attracted to each other." Her body leaned into his. "I think it has something to do with a theme and variation on that axiom about opposites attracting." *Kiss me, Shayne. Don't make me throw myself at you.*

He laughed softly, trying very hard not to give in to the heat he felt flaring through his body. "You might be on to something there. We're as opposite as two people can get."

"Absolutely." She took a breath, and then there was nothing between them, not even air. "You want to talk about the theory of relativity now, or are you going to kiss me?"

The resistance he thought he had against this sort of thing was melting faster than snow in July. "Physics was never my strong suit."

"Thank God."

She knew. Standing in this cabin where her great-aunt had once taught, Sydney knew. Knew as soon as he touched his lips to hers that this time it was going to be different. This time, short of an avalanche, there'd be no interruptions, no excuses to intrude and stop either one of them from the natural path they were on. Nothing could stop them, except perhaps common sense, and that was in pitifully poor supply on her end.

She didn't want to think about consequences, or the fact that kissing him, allowing her body to heat to the temperature of a roaring fire, was one of the most foolhardy things she'd ever done. Because right now, it wasn't foolhardy. Right now, it was wondrous and thrilling.

Shayne didn't know what it was about Sydney that made him lose his ability to think, to reason, to act rationally. All he knew was that if he couldn't have her, couldn't feel her soft body pliant and giving beneath his, he was going to go out of his mind.

He was going there anyway, but the route, he discovered, was a great deal sweeter than he'd ever anticipated.

Molding her to him, his mouth deepening the kiss with each pass, Shayne felt her tremble against him. In fear? The possibility throbbed in his brain.

Though it was the most difficult thing he'd ever done, he pulled his head away from hers and looked at her. Trying to find a clue. He couldn't just come out and ask her.

The ache within her was growing to proportions that were almost unmanageable. She drew a breath, trying to steady her rapidly beating pulse. It did no good.

Was something wrong? Had he suddenly changed his mind at the last minute? She searched his face. He wanted her. She could see it. So why had he stopped? ''Is justifiable homicide on the books in this state?''

It was the oddest question he could conceive at a time like this. ''I think so, why?''

''Because...'' she pressed her lips to his neck. ''If you stop kissing me now—'' spidery kisses circled his collarbone, tightening his gut, teasing his loins ''—I'm going to be forced to kill you.''

She was clouding his mind, heating his blood, breaking the last bands of his restraint. He struggled to hold off. ''Sydney, maybe we shouldn't.''

It was like a cold knife twisting in her gut. She raised her head and looked at him. Had she been wrong, after all? ''Do you want to stop?''

Shayne couldn't have lied even if salvation lay in the balance. ''No. Heaven help me, but no, I don't.''

She could have cried. ''Then don't. Don't stop,'' she whispered, the sound skimming along his skin. Signaling his doom.

And his victory.

Lowering his mouth to hers, Shayne kissed her as if his very soul was behind it. Because it was. He'd only just now discovered that he still had a soul and that it was alive and, if not well, possessed by needs.

What followed he would remember all the days of his life, no matter how many there would be. The urgency he experienced was almost overwhelming. Certainly overpowering. He didn't even try to resist.

They undressed one another in a synchronized symphony. Clothing instead of notes rained through the air, floating to the floor below.

Each newly exposed region he discovered on her body made him feel like an explorer, claiming a new territory for crown and country.

And for himself.

Shayne didn't delude himself into thinking he was her first and knew he wouldn't be her last. But for now, he was here with her and she was his and that was more than enough.

It was just right.

Her skin felt creamy beneath his hands as he skimmed first his fingers, then his palms over her smooth, naked flesh. She arched and moved in response to his every touch, silently urging him on. She was like a woman possessed. Shayne fanned the flames, kissing her over and over again, undoing her. Undoing himself.

He'd been married. Known, he thought, all the pleasures of the flesh that were to be had.

He knew nothing.

He learned everything, driven by the need to take his pleasure with her. To give her pleasure. He had no idea which gave him more satisfaction.

Laying her back on the rug, he followed each path he'd forged with his hands with his lips, thrilling at the sound of her moan, feeling suddenly empowered, reborn in the glisten of her skin as it caught the light from the fireplace.

The thrill he felt at touching her was more than matched by what he felt when she moved suddenly and switched positions. Now it was Sydney who was over him, Sydney who toyed, teased and suckled.

As her hands played over him, first lightly then more and more possessively, skimming his chest, his flat stomach, his thighs, he could feel everything within him tightening like the string stretched over the bridge of a guitar. Tightening and pulsing. Waiting for the grand moment when the final notes of the melody could be struck.

Wanting to hold them off forever.

Wanting to hear, to feel them now. Feel them vibrating through his body.

Knowing that if she continued what she was doing, her hands feathering along the muscles of his inner thighs, her fingertips possessing him, he wouldn't be able to hold back much longer, Shayne deftly moved so that she was beneath him again.

He made love to her with every fiber of his being, consumed with the desire to eliminate every other man from her mind. He caressed, possessed, nipped, kissed, and marked her indelibly as his.

She stored every sensation greedily within her, to be replayed and savored time and again, during future long nights when dawn seemed years away. He made her feel beautiful, wanted and happy. So exquisitely happy she thought she was going to burst.

To repay him, to revel in the sensations they shared, she found herself loving his body in ways she'd never dreamed. Because he made her want to do things, pleasuring things, just by the way he made love with her.

A twig snapped in the fire's greedy jaws as the first explosion Shayne created within her racked her body, exhausting her. Making her crave more.

And more again.

Shayne anticipated and provided, leaving her gasping. Leaving her dazed. Again and again he raised her to the highest plateau, taking her up and over. And then safely down, only to begin again.

She couldn't take any more. Not alone.

Sydney reached for him, blindly grasping his forearms and weakly dragging him to her. Anticipation danced through her as his body moved along the length of hers, into position.

With what seemed like her last ounce of strength, she smiled at him. "I know you can revive me if I pass out, but I want to be awake for this." She arched her hips, the invitation unmistakable.

He accepted it, sheathing himself in her and finding so much more than he had ever dreamed possible. It wasn't just the exquisite meeting of flesh to flesh, of needs to needs. Even the passion didn't explain it. It was the feeling that something far more momentous was happening that made this so wondrous.

Though he knew it was absurd to harbor the sensation, he couldn't shake the feeling that he was coming home, finally home. And for now, he didn't want to shake it. He wanted to savor it. Savor it the way he savored the sweetness of her mouth, the sensuality of her scent as it filled every part of him.

As it possessed him.

Together, the rhythm of their bodies growing frenzied, they found what they were each looking for.

For now.

Chapter Thirteen

A chill was beginning to creep into the room, slowly, like a cat checking out the premises for future habitation. Or maybe it'd already settled in and she was only just now noticing.

Sydney sighed, looking at the flames. "The fire's dying out."

He couldn't remember ever having been this exhausted. But feeling Sydney stir beside him, her breath lightly gliding along his skin as she spoke, was beginning to bring him around again.

"Give me a minute and I'll see what I can do about it."

Sydney raised herself up on her elbow, turning toward him. Her hair rained down on his chest, lightly skimming it with every movement like the soft flutter of an angel's wings.

Her mouth curved wickedly. "Promises, promises. I'd

say that what just happened now will warm me for a very long time to come.''

He felt like kissing her again. Like making love with her over and over the whole night long. He was too tired to realize that this was a first for him.

Shayne eyed the fireplace behind her. ''Which fire are we talking about?''

Her smile grew, taking him with it. ''Whichever one you want. Both, if you like.''

Duty and desire waged a quick battle within him. Duty won. But there was no winner, not in the real sense. ''What I'd like...''

She looked at him hopefully, not completely sure what it was she was hoping for. Only knowing that she needed to hear something positive from him, however small. ''Yes?''

For just a second longer, he tried to hold on to the sensation he'd felt making love with her. But it was already fading. ''What I'd like and what I have to do are two very different things.''

Sydney sat up, resigned. ''Not where I thought this conversation was going,'' she confessed with a sigh. She dragged a hand through her hair. ''But you're right, we have to get back to the children.'' She reached for her underwear and quickly wiggled into it, then began pulling on her jeans. ''I don't know if Asia can handle them both.''

He shouldn't be watching her get dressed, he should be getting dressed himself. His hands remained idle, his body heating. ''Not since you breathed life into them, at any rate.''

She cocked her head, scrutinizing him. ''Is that a compliment or a criticism?'' There was no clue in his voice, but she was getting used to that. With Shayne, you needed all your senses alert.

Getting up, he pulled on his jeans. He glanced over his shoulder in her direction. "Whichever one you like."

This time she heard the amusement in his voice. "Sorry, that quote's already been taken. Have to come up with one of your own, I'm afraid."

"And I'm afraid..." He turned just in time to see her slipping her sweater on over her head, her torso stretched. She'd neglected to put on her bra. His mouth turned to cotton.

Sydney yanked the sweater down so she could see again. "Yes?"

He let out the breath he was holding. His chest hurt, and the cause, he knew, was not rooted in anything remotely medical. "And I'm afraid that I can't seem to put two thoughts together anymore."

She saw how he looked at her and she smiled, pleased. Flattered. And wishing there was enough time to make love all over again. She stepped closer to him. "You're too young to be senile."

Urges, freshly satisfied, freshly tantalized, began to rise again for Shayne. Damn, but he could feel the heat of her body, even with space between them. "Is that your professional medical opinion?"

She laughed, splaying her hands over his chest. Leaning into him.

"Call it a gut feeling." Shifting, she moved against his side and he winced in reaction. The response occurred in less than a split second. Concern nudged her. "What's the matter?"

The pain came suddenly, sharply. Taken by surprise, Shayne concentrated on regulating his breathing. The pain began to fade. "Nothing."

It didn't look like "nothing" to her. He looked as if someone had just jabbed him with a cattle prod. "You winced."

He shrugged it off, wishing she wouldn't insist on making something out of everything. The pain was already a memory.

"A stitch," he insisted. "Nothing more."

And he wouldn't tell her even if it was, Sydney realized. No sense in her butting her head against this iron wall.

"You're the doctor, you should know." She refused to let anything mar what they'd just shared. The euphoria was still wrapped around her like a coat of airtight iron armor. Sydney raised her eyes to his. "I had a very nice time installing the telephone."

Even wanting, for simplicity's sake, to put what they'd just done behind him, Shayne couldn't help but laugh. "Is that what you call it now?"

She nodded, her eyes still on his. "From now on."

From now on. That had such a permanent ring to it.

But he knew there was no such thing as permanent. Barbara had shown him that, and so had Ben. And each had had a great deal more invested in his life than Sydney did. In comparison, he and Sydney were almost strangers.

Strangers who had made exquisite love together.

But still strangers.

Sydney frowned, looking up at him. Her euphoria began to slip away. "I know that face. It's your pessimistic face."

He frowned in response, then realized it was only reinforcing what she said. "I don't have a pessimistic face." Frustrated, he turned and began looking for his shirt. It had to be here somewhere.

Sydney followed him. ''Yes, you do. I would have said it was your regular face, except that I've seen you look differently, so I know you don't have to look like that if you don't want to.''

It took him a minute to untangle the words. He didn't know which was worse; that she rattled on, or that he could actually follow her with a little effort. ''I'm not a pessimist, I'm a realist.''

''You're a pessimist,'' she insisted, her tone mild. ''I'm an optimist. To me, the glass is half full and there's a waitress coming toward me with a pitcher, ready to fill it. Your glass is half empty and not only don't you see the waitress but you also think she's quit and taken the pitcher with her.''

She was right, he thought. But that still just made him a realist. He shrugged into his shirt. ''Are you through?''

Sydney began to close his buttons for him. ''For now.''

He moved her hands aside and finished the job. If he let her do it, he wouldn't be able to force himself to leave.

''One clings to small favors.'' He picked his parka up off the floor. ''Let's go before it gets too dark.''

Sydney slipped on her parka. ''I've got a feeling it already has.''

Shayne wasn't about to ask her what she was talking about. He didn't think he wanted to know.

With a sigh, Shayne closed the medical journal he'd been trying to read and massaged the bridge of his nose. He was having trouble concentrating.

It was all her fault.

In more ways than just one. The noise echoing outside his window—a noise Sydney had incited and for which she was directly responsible—made reading hard enough on its own. He could ignore that.

What he couldn't ignore was the way she lingered in his thoughts, how she'd burrowed into his life and set up residence like some Arctic hibernator. Burrowing in and giving him no peace.

She intruded on every facet of his life, physically and otherwise. Even here, in his den. The things the moving men had brought were being stored in this room until she made her final move into the cabin.

He could swear her perfume was on every one of the damn items. Even on the piano in the living room. Never mind that she'd said she didn't use any, it was here, haunting him. Reminding him of the one afternoon where discretion and his good judgment had left him. An afternoon more than a week in the past now.

Reminding him that, common sense not withstanding, he wanted her again.

He wished she'd moved out already. But that was his fault. She would have been living in Miss Faye's cabin by now if he hadn't bribed her into waiting with those flying lessons. But something inside him just couldn't ignore her.

What was the matter with him? She got underfoot, wedged herself into places she had no business being. Interfered with everything. He should have been glad for the opportunity to get rid of her.

And yet, he wasn't.

He didn't like the idea of her living out there all alone. Didn't like the idea of her leaving. And liked, even less, that it bothered him the way it did.

Damn it, he knew where such attachments led. Into gaping black holes. Why was he even thinking this way?

Because he couldn't help himself.

Yet.

But he would, by God, Shayne vowed silently. He would.

Shayne jumped at the sound of the sudden, unexpected "thud" that smacked against his window, rattling it. The next moment he saw Sydney peering in, her face reddened by the cold and the wind. Brightened with laughter he could only partially hear. She waved at him and mouthed an exaggerated, "Sorry." The remnants of the snowball she'd thrown clung to the pane. And then she disappeared.

Curious, Shayne opened the window to see where she'd gotten off to and inadvertently offered himself up as the perfect target. Another white missile flew through the air. This time, without the glass to stop it, it went crashing into his face.

Her laughter echoed loud and clear this time. Winding all through him. There was a chorus of childish laughter in its wake. Sara and Mac.

"C'mon out," Sydney crowed, beckoning to him. "The snow's fine!"

"The hell it is." He wiped the last of snowball from his face.

Shayne had no idea what possessed him. The last time he'd been in a snowball fight, he'd been ten, maybe eleven. After that, life had gotten too serious. But he hurried out now, grabbing his parka, determined to wash her face in snow and pay her back.

Sara was the first to see him. "Daddy, did you decide to play with us, after all?" She clapped together snow-covered mittens in excitement.

Shayne stopped long enough to pick up a handful of snow and mold it between his gloves. "Just for a few minutes. Just long enough to pay Sydney back."

Standing a good distance away, Sydney stuck out her chin, daring him to hit it. ''You probably throw like a girl.''

The next second, shrieking with laughter, she ducked out of range. He missed.

He didn't miss the second time. Or the third. Victorious, having done what he'd set out to do, he thought the battle over.

He thought wrong.

Sydney was more than ready for him with a cache of snowballs, waiting to be hurled, at her disposal. The wait was over the second Shayne's third snowball hit its target. Winding up, she began depleting her arsenal at an incredible speed.

Mac, his eyes bright with enthusiasm, rushed over to join Sydney. In less than a few minutes, the air was thick with snowballs.

Sizing up the situation, Sara threw her lot in with what she deemed in her young heart to be the underdog. Ducking her head, she scurried over to him. ''I'll help you, Daddy.''

''I appreciate it,'' Shayne told her, although he knew that Mac would be much better at snow warfare than his sister. Sara threw a malformed snowball that landed a foot away from her.

Just his luck, Shayne thought, but he smiled and said, ''Good try.''

Mac's snowball made the distance, squarely baptizing his sister in the face. She gasped and Shayne expected the confrontation to instantly break down into yelling and tears. Instead, he heard Sara laugh and rush to make another snowball.

His surprise cost him. Sydney hurled two snowballs

in quick succession, striking him with a one-two punch. Shayne held his hands up in front of his face.

"Uncle!"

"Aunt!" she yelled, hurling another one at him.

Shayne saw the arsenal that was still left. She was equipped to keep this up for half the afternoon. He saw no other avenue open to him. He could either stand and be pelted, or charge her.

He chose the latter and ran straight into Sydney, grabbing her by the waist and sending her crashing down into the snow. Perforce, he went with her. It was a small sacrifice to pay. And an enjoyable one, layers of clothing notwithstanding.

The next thing he knew, the children had piled themselves on top of both of them. The laughter and squeals fed into one another until it all formed one harmonious sound.

Music to his ears, he realized, pleasure spilling through him.

He struggled to his feet, succeeding on his second try, which necessitated untangling his body from his children. Shayne offered Sydney his hand. "I had no idea you were this bloodthirsty."

Sydney accepted his hand and found herself unceremoniously yanked upright. "A lot about me you don't know." Cheeks glowing, she paused to brush the snow out of her hair. She slanted a look at his face to see what he made of her comment. "The nights are long, maybe you'll learn."

"Maybe," he agreed. The remark was accompanied by a careless shrug.

His tone sounded ambiguous, but she supposed his answer was better than a silent reproof. In any case, Sydney let it be.

Dusting the snow off her legs and rear, Sydney looked around for Sara and Mac. Collectively, there was more snow on them than on the chalet roof. "Okay, who's for hot chocolate?"

Sara raised her hand excitedly. "I am."

It wasn't cool to be too excited. But Mac's eyes gave him away. "Me."

Shayne stared at her. "We have hot chocolate?" Since when? he wondered.

She looked at him, surprised that he thought she'd be careless enough to make promises, however small, without backup.

"Of course we have hot chocolate. What kind of a sadist would offer children hot chocolate if there wasn't any?" she teased. "Mr. Kellogg got in a whole case for me."

Of course he did, Shayne thought, surprised the general store owner hadn't ordered a private cow for her, as well. Everyone tried to be so damn accommodating to Sydney. "How much hot chocolate do you intend to drink?"

The smile on her face was enigmatic. "Nights get cold here."

He had no idea if she was mocking him or not.

The sound caught Sydney's attention. At first she dismissed it, thinking that it was just the wind winding its way through the trees. She'd learned to tell the difference now between the mournful sound of the wind and other things that were only close in timbre.

She listened again, harder. It was the sound of crying. Muffled crying.

One of the children was crying. Curious, moved, she crept softly into the hallway and listened, holding her breath so she could hear more clearly. There was nothing.

Her imagination was playing tricks on her. Turning away, she headed toward the stairs when the sound came again, escaping like a fugitive bound for freedom. It was coming from Mac's room.

Sydney tried Mac's door and found it wasn't locked. She debated, only for a second, giving him his privacy. But he was a little boy who needed comfort more than he needed a space to call his own. Pushing the door open slowly, she found Mac lying on his bed, his face buried in his pillow. The sobs escaped anyway.

She approached with caution, knowing that the Kerrigan men were a pride-laden lot, even the smallest one. "Mac, are you all right?"

Mac hunched his shoulders together, as if trying to sink further into his pillow. He refused to turn his head. "Go away."

She didn't budge. Instead, she placed her hand on his shoulder and felt it stiffen. He and his father had a great deal in common. "Mac, what's wrong?"

"I said go away." He sniffed, hard. Then the accusation came. "That's what you're going to do anyway, right? So go away now." He raised his head to look at her, tear tracks down both cheeks like war paint. "I mean it, go away."

Instead of leaving, Sydney sat on the edge of his bed. "I'm not going to go away. Not until I find out what's bothering you. And not even then."

He said nothing. And then, finally, struggling with his feelings, he looked at her again. "Then you're not moving out?"

So that was it. He thought she was abandoning him. She knew how hard it had been for him to reach out to her in the first place. She ran her hand along his hair, smoothing it. "Yes, I'm still moving out. But I'm not going away. I'll still be here in Hades. And I'll come see you and Sara every day if you want."

"How?" He stuck out his lower lip belligerently. "It's too far."

"It's not too far with a car."

"But you don't have a car."

"I will soon." She saw the surprise on his face. "I ordered one, and they're sending it all the way from Detroit."

It hadn't been an easy process. It wasn't like a large city, where she could have gone to a local dealer and pick out a car. She'd made her choice from a pamphlet, basing her decision on Shayne's judgment by ordering the same kind of vehicle he used. She'd bought the car on her own, without his knowledge. She'd figured it was one less thing to bother him about.

"Is that going to take time?"

She saw the hopeful look in Mac's eyes and it tugged on her heart. Why couldn't his father look at her that way? "Everything takes time here."

The answer satisfied him. Mac manfully brushed away the wet streaks his tears had left on his face. He looked at her sheepishly. "Pretty dumb, huh? Crying like a baby."

She couldn't help herself any longer. She hugged him to her. It touched her that he let her. "Babies aren't the only ones who cry, Mac. I cried when my dad died. A great deal. And men cry."

He shook his dark head. He knew better. "Men don't cry."

She crooked her finger beneath his chin and raised it

so that their eyes met. "Oh, yes, they do. They have feelings just like you do. Things hurt them."

Maybe some men, Mac allowed. But he knew of one who remained above all that. Above things like hurting and tears. And feeling scared.

"Not my dad. He doesn't have any feelings. Except maybe the hating kind." Mac pressed his lips together, wondering if he'd said too much.

Oh, God, was that what Mac thought? She took his face in her hands and said very carefully, "He doesn't hate you, Mac. He loves you and he loves Sara. Very, very much. He just doesn't know how to say it, that's all."

The big, dumb ape, she thought in silent frustration.

Sydney was just trying to be nice. He had proof that he was right and she was wrong. "He doesn't love me. He never came once to see me, not until after...after Mom died."

She gathered the boy to her, wishing there was some way she could shield him.

"He didn't come to see you because he couldn't. Your mother didn't want him to." It was a fine line she was walking and she knew it. Not wanting to upset any of Mac's memories of his mother, Sydney tried to remember what Ike had told her. "She did it because she thought it was best for you and your sister not to have your dad come in and out of your lives. Your dad thought you'd be okay if he did, and they argued about it. He decided not to try to see you because he didn't want the shouting to upset you." She caressed his hair. "They both loved you very much."

There were fresh tears forming. "I don't think so."

There had to be some way to convince him. And then she remembered. "If your dad didn't love you, he wouldn't have kept all those pictures of you in his desk.''

''He's got pictures of me?''

''Tons of them. Pictures of you and Sara. I'd say there were probably six years' worth.'' She saw his eyes light up. Bingo. ''I bet your dad spent a lot of nights just sitting in his chair, looking at those photographs over and over again. Missing you. Thinking he'd never get to see you again.''

A warm feeling came over Mac, like when Sydney tucked him into bed and made the blanket all snug around him when it was cold. ''How'd he get the pictures?''

He wasn't suspicious, she thought. He just wanted to know. ''When someone loves someone else, they find ways.''

Mac wanted to believe her, he really did. There was just one final question. ''How do you know my dad has pictures?''

''I saw them. I was looking for some paper one day and found them in a box in his bottom drawer,'' she confessed. She'd never said anything to Shayne. She knew he wouldn't have appreciated her going through his things, but even if he found out, the look she saw on Mac's face now, made the risk worth it for her. ''The deep one.''

He wriggled off the bed. ''Show me.''

The boy clearly had Missouri blood in him. This made discovery almost a sure thing. Sydney debated, but the hope in Mac's eyes cut the debate short.

''My pleasure.'' She took his hand and they headed for the door.

Chapter Fourteen

"What are you doing?"

Startled, Sydney looked up to see Shayne standing in the doorway. She hadn't heard him come into the house. Anticipating a scene, she moved from the desk where she and Mac had been looking at the photographs and placed her body between Shayne and his son.

"Mac didn't believe that you had photographs of Sara and him in your desk." She glanced at the pile in front of Mac. "I could put them into an album for you if you'd like."

Shayne had come home exhausted. The single patient he'd gone to see in the Inuit village had mushroomed to twelve. Though he hated admitting it, he'd sorely regretted not taking Sydney up on her offer to accompany him. Just having her around seemed to put people at ease. But he'd wanted to become less dependent on her, not more.

The light coming from his den had drawn him there instead of to the kitchen for food to placate his growling stomach. He hadn't expected to see her going through his things with his son.

"What I'd like, Sydney, is for my things to remain where I put them." Shayne frowned, looking at the contents scattered all over the top of his desk. "How did you know they were there?"

Sydney heard the accusation, sharp and cold in his voice. It wasn't a voice belonging to a man she'd made love with such a short while ago.

Served her right for thinking that anything had changed between them. Or that they had a future together.

Just her luck, she thought, to be doomed to give her heart to men who didn't want it. She stepped closer to him, lowering her voice. She didn't think she could be held responsible for what she'd do if he somehow ruined this for Mac. "That doesn't matter right now. What does, is that Mac knows you care about him."

What gave her the right to presume to know how to run his life? Why did she think she could just interfere in it anytime she felt like it? "He doesn't need to find photographs for that."

The look in her eyes cut him dead. "Everyone needs physical evidence of some sort."

Unaware of the storm brewing around him, Mac held up a photograph. "What does this say?" His question temporarily broke the tension.

Not trusting himself to say anything more to Sydney, Shayne crossed to his son and took the photograph from him. He looked at the back, then paused, reading the notation. It was in his own hand. Barbara had never bothered writing anything on the back. But as soon as he received them, he'd meticulously written dates and events on the back of every photograph she'd doled out to him so stringently.

"'Mac, first day of school.'" And then he read the date. Mac was smiling into the camera, his wide grin shy, one tooth in the front. He clutched a lunch box in one hand, a notebook in the other. Shayne remembered the pride he'd felt looking at that photograph. Pride mixed so strongly with resentment because he couldn't be there in person to witness it. Resentment because Barbara had barred him from his own children.

Mac took the photograph back and examined the writing. He shook his head. His dad must've flunked penmanship. "You've got funny handwriting."

The remark, so guilelessly tendered, made Shayne laugh. "I'm a doctor. I'm supposed to have funny handwriting."

Mac looked at the box. There were a great many photographs still in there, as well as the ones spread out all over the desk. The eyes he raised to his father forbade Shayne to lie.

"Why did you keep these?"

Shayne could feel Sydney looking at him, waiting for him to answer Mac. He didn't like explaining himself, but he knew his son's needs outweighed his own feelings in this case.

"Because I couldn't be there to see it happening firsthand." It cost him to bare his soul like this. "I asked your mother to send them to me. I wanted to see what you and Sara looked like while you were growing up."

Mac rolled every word over in his head, examining it carefully from all angles. He needed to be sure. "So you really did care?"

Shayne exchanged looks with Sydney. She was right,

damn her. Mac needed to hear this, needed to be told and shown that he mattered. It wasn't enough to assume that he understood.

Emotion filled him as he gathered his son to him, trying to make up for lost time. Knowing it wasn't possible. But at least he could try. "I did and I do."

Shayne heard the door close behind him. When he looked, he saw that Sydney had slipped out of the room. He'd underestimated her. She knew that some things required privacy.

Like a man getting reacquainted with his son.

Just when he thought he had the woman pegged.

Arms tightening around Mac, Shayne did his best to reassure the boy. Privacy or not, the words didn't come out any more easily. But he knew that they had to be said.

"Just because I wasn't there, Mac, didn't mean I didn't care. Didn't mean I wasn't thinking about you and your sister every minute of every day."

Mac looked up and studied him solemnly. Shayne could see that the boy really wanted to believe him. "Every minute?"

Shayne nodded, running his hand through the boy's hair. He couldn't help thinking how much Mac looked like Ben when Ben had been his age. "Every minute."

An almost imperceptible twinkle entered Mac's eyes. "Even when you were sleeping?"

Definitely Ben material. There'd been a great deal about his brother that had been lovable, Shayne remembered. "They're called dreams, then, wiseguy." Shayne laughed, tousling the boy's hair.

Mac grinned. "I dreamed about you, too. Lots of times."

Shayne doubted very much if Mac could have said

anything that would have meant more to him than what he'd just said.

Shayne spent a long time in the den with Mac, poring over photographs, talking. Discovering. The exhaustion he'd felt earlier when he'd arrived home peeled away from him like an outer covering that was no longer pertinent or in vogue.

He knew he had Sydney to thank for this. But how did he thank someone for invading his space, his privacy?

Nothing about the woman was simple.

Leaving Mac to return the photographs to the box, Shayne walked out of the den, looking for Sydney. He had to admit that it surprised him that she had left the two of them alone for so long. He'd half expected her to come in, ready to mediate or just place herself in the center of what was going on.

The woman was a complete enigma to him. He didn't know whether to shake her or hug her. Or both. No matter what he was doing, Sydney somehow managed to inspire such diametrically opposed emotions within him, it set his head spinning.

He wondered if she did that on purpose.

The strains of chords being slowly picked out on the piano came to him almost as soon as he opened the door. Shayne followed the sound to the living room.

Which was where he found her.

Sydney was sitting at the piano, sharing the bench with Sara. With a look of total concentration, Sara was trying to mimic Sydney's fingering on the keyboard.

Sydney looked up the moment he entered the room though he made no sound. It was as if she were somehow aware of his every movement. He wouldn't have been surprised if she were.

Sydney tried to read his expression. He didn't look annoyed. At least that was a good sign. "So, how did it go?"

"Well," he said slowly.

Maybe it was small of him, but he couldn't let her invasion pass lightly. If he did, he had a feeling that the incident would only repeat itself and mushroom to unmanageable proportions. And he didn't want her entrenched in his life any more than she already was.

As it was, she'd already upheaved the life he thought he'd made for himself.

Shayne crossed to the piano, to Sydney's side of the bench. He lowered his voice to keep from distracting Sara. "That still doesn't tell me what you were doing, going through my things."

The words stung, even though Sydney told herself it was just his way. It didn't have to be his way. He chose it to be.

"I wasn't going through your things," she replied tersely. "I was looking for paper."

He wanted to believe her, but Barbara had taught him that relationships were filled with lies. "Big difference between photographs and paper."

She knew what he was saying. That she should have just left the photographs alone when she'd seen them.

"I got curious," she admitted. Wasn't he human? Didn't he ever get curious about anything? About anyone? "I figured I wasn't intruding on national security, or your secret identity, so I looked."

Sara stopped playing. Her mouth fell open. "You have a secret identity?"

Shayne slanted an annoyed look at Sydney. Trust her to fuel a misunderstanding. ''No, I—''

Mac had walked in on his sister's question. He was clearly impressed. ''Like Batman?''

''No, not like Batman,'' Shayne denied patiently. ''And I don't have a secret identity. That's just Sydney talking.'' Sydney, he thought, was always talking.

Making use of the diversion, Sydney got up and indicated a corner of the room. ''I thought you could put the tree there.''

Maybe solitude had gotten the better of him, relegating his mind into a slower mode. Whatever the reason, he was having a really difficult time keeping up with her. As usual, he had no idea what she was talking about.

He followed her over to the corner. ''What tree?''

Sara was quick to join them. ''The Christmas tree, Daddy,'' she informed him. Sara gave him a pitying look, as if he'd just taken his first giant step into senility.

That, too, he figured, was Sydney's fault.

Most everything these days was Sydney's fault.

Sydney saw the look on his face and retreated a little. All right, so he didn't like her redecorating his house. She could understand that.

''Maybe I'm taking too much on myself…'' she began.

He didn't let her finish. Instead, he stared at her incredulously. ''Maybe?'' How could she possibly think otherwise? With every breath she took, she pushed further and further into his life, changing things, disorienting him.

She did not take offense at his tone. ''Okay, where do you usually put the tree?''

''I don't put it anywhere. I don't have a tree in the house.'' It wasn't until the words were out of his mouth that he realized how scroogelike that had to sound to his children.

Sara stared at him in alarm. ''Doesn't Christmas come here?''

Mac gave her a disgusted big brother look. Didn't she know anything? ''Sure it does. Christmas comes everywhere.'' He stole a glance at Sydney for confirmation. ''Doesn't it?''

''That it does,'' she agreed quickly before Shayne could say anything else to make things worse. ''And to prove it, your dad's going to put up the prettiest tree you ever saw. Right, 'Dad'?'' Sydney looked at him expectantly.

It felt really strange, hearing her address him that way. As if they were a family. Which they weren't. And couldn't be.

When he looked at his children, two sets of eyes were staring back at him with expectations and hopes he couldn't bring himself to dash.

''Right,'' he agreed as he took Sydney's arm. ''Could I have a word with you?''

''Always.'' With a fluid movement, she disengaged herself from him. ''But it's going to have to wait until I get a couple of kids off to bed.'' It was late and past their bedtime. She looked at Sara and Mac, a warm, coaxing smile on her lips. ''Right?''

Neither child looked very happy about the prospect of going off to bed Sydney thought, but they both reluctantly agreed and chorused a halfhearted, ''Right.'' Both seemed to know that it was far too close to Christmas to put up any sort of a real fuss.

With his chess piece in check on the board, Shayne had no choice but to wait until after his children were asleep before he could talk to Sydney. Maybe it was better that way. It'd give him time to pull his thoughts about her together.

As if there was that much time in the world.

"All right, you can yell at me now."

Coming into his room, Sydney eased the door closed behind her. She didn't want him waking up the children after she'd spent so much effort getting them to sleep.

Surprised, Shayne looked up from the book he was reading. Unable to collect his thoughts, he'd felt it appropriate to peruse the pages of Shakespeare's *Taming of the Shrew.* After a while, he'd given up waiting for her to get back to him and just lost himself in the play. He'd gained very little insight, but at least he'd been entertained.

Shayne sat up on the bed, swinging his legs over the side. The thick green cover joined the gold-edged pages, losing his place for him. "What makes you think I'm going to yell at you?"

He probably resented the image. "All right, not yell. Speak sternly," she amended, crossing to him. "Isn't that what you intended to do earlier? Put me in my place?"

He was no longer sure what he'd intended earlier. She could make him lose his train of thought faster than anything he'd ever known. "Maybe I would, if I knew where that was."

She looked down at him uncertainly. "Meaning?"

She would ask him to explain. "Meaning I know where I should put you, but I don't know if I want to put you there. And even if I wanted to, I don't know if I could." She was grinning broadly at him. He stopped talking. "What?"

"Don't look now, but you're beginning to sound like me." She thought it was adorable.

He sighed, dragging his hand through his hair. "Oh, God, it's worse than I thought."

"Is it?" Her grin melted into a soft smile. "Define 'worse.'"

That wasn't going to be easy, not where she was concerned. He rose from the bed to face her. "Look, after Barbara left, I finally made peace with the way my life was going to be."

Sydney doubted if peace was the word he was looking for. It was more as if he'd withdrawn from life altogether. But she let him talk. "And that was?"

"Solitary."

If that were true, he would have abandoned his practice and become a hermit. "Makes being a doctor difficult."

Shayne was determined to prove her wrong, at least about something. "Not really. You minister to their bodies and go on."

That's not the kind of doctor he was, no matter what he wanted to believe. She'd seen him with patients. Parts of him, of his compassion, came through in their care, no matter what he was trying to convince himself of.

"You're talking about assembling cars on a conveyor belt. People need more than that. People need to be comforted, to know that they're cared about as well as cared for." She saw that he was about to disagree, and retreated. It was enough that she'd made her point. "But I digress. You were talking about your life's plan. Go on."

For two cents, Shayne would wipe that smug look off her face. For less than that...

He felt himself getting stirred again. He tried to ignore the effect she had on him.

"Yeah, well, the plan I'd settled on was being alone. Then Barbara died and I got my kids back. Kids I didn't know what to do with."

Didn't he realize that he'd gone beyond that stage? "You're doing all right now."

He looked at her. Shayne was very aware of the debt he owed her. She'd been the one who'd turned Sara around. And Mac after that. Without her, who knew how long it would have taken them to come about, if at all? "That was your doing."

"Not really." She didn't want him to minimize his effect on the children. They loved him very much. "Sometimes you need a catalyst, that's all. I got elected."

A catalyst. What a strange way to think of herself. Had she affected everything around her—his life—without being affected herself? Was that what she was telling him? Damn, when did life get so complicated?

He knew when. The moment she'd stepped off the plane and into his life. "That's just my problem. I don't know what to make of my catalyst."

The smile on her lips curled right through him, going from his gut straight to his toes.

"Maybe you don't have to make something of her." She moved closer to him. Or was that him, moving toward her? He wasn't clear on that. Wasn't clear on very much, except that he wanted her. "Maybe you just have to let her be. As in exist, not as in alone," she clarified, lest he misunderstand.

He seized the word. "It'd be best if I could leave *her* alone." He threaded his arms around her waist, pulling her to him. Feeling the heat begin to flare. ''But I don't think I can.''

She settled against him. ''Are you coming on to me, Doctor?''

He wasn't sure he knew how to come on to a woman. That was something he'd never taken the time to pick up from Ben. ''Clumsily.''

Is that what he thought? Her eyes on his, Sydney moved her head from side to side. ''You underestimate yourself, Shayne. There isn't a single clumsy thing about you.''

Then why did he feel like a clumsy adolescent instead of a skilled physician who'd done more than his share of intricate surgery?

His hands were steady, his nerves were not. Shayne slowly began coaxing the first button of her blouse from its hole with the tips of his fingers when he stopped and looked toward the door.

She read his mind. ''They're sound asleep.'' But, she knew, children were known to wake up at the worst possible moments. ''And you have a lock.''

It was better to be safe than sorry. Shayne crossed to the door and flipped the lock into place, then returned to her. She could think clearly when he couldn't. ''You're always one step ahead of me.''

She sincerely doubted it. Right now, she just wanted to be in sync with him. ''I'll try to watch that,'' she promised softly.

His fingers occupied with the next button, Shayne pressed a kiss to her throat, sending the pulse there throbbing. He smiled to himself. ''I'd appreciate it.''

With his every touch, desire skittered along her body like tiny fireflies released from their prison and escaping toward freedom. He made her skin tingle and her pulse throb. Most of all, he made her want. Want with every fiber of her being that wondrous feeling that only came when he kissed her.

She shivered as he slowly removed the blouse from her shoulders, felt her loins tightening as the sleeves slid from her arms. The blouse fell to the floor as he toyed with the button on her jeans.

Heart pounding, she found his mouth and lost herself in his kiss.

Her moan served only to send Shayne over the brink that he'd been tottering on so precariously. He knew there was no use trying to hang on to his common sense; this time, he didn't waste the effort in trying. It was far more pleasurable using that energy in other ways.

In making love with her.

He hurried her out of the remainder of her clothes, his breath catching as she did the same. Each eager to find their way into the paradise they'd unwittingly stumbled into before.

Possessively, he skimmed his hands along her body, over and over again, until he could have recreated every curve, every nuance, that was Sydney with his eyes closed.

It wasn't enough.

He wanted more.

A starving man, he'd taken a morsel and found himself hopelessly craving more. Even if it meant his undoing.

Tumbling onto his bed, they feasted on one another, exploring not only each other's bodies, but the sensations that being together created. Sensations that were not entirely grounded in the physical act of lovemaking but in the feelings created by the act itself.

Lips sealed to hers, Shayne rolled over to gather her

closer to him. He caught his breath as a fresh, different heat flared from his side, rivaling the flame that was consuming him.

She felt his gasp play along her lips and pulled back, searching his face. He looked paler, stunned. ''What's the matter?''

The pain he'd felt had settled down, the way it had all the other times in the past few days. Shayne dismissed it instantly. His body looming over hers, he framed her face with his hands.

''The matter is—'' he grazed her mouth, once, twice and again ''—you talk too much.''

He was obliterating her thoughts. She struggled to protest. ''But—'

He wouldn't let her get the words out. He didn't want to discuss the strange pain that intermittently brandished his side like a hot sword.

Right now, all he wanted to do was make love with her. Everything else could be dealt with later. Much, much later.

Shayne kissed her protest away. Kissed away everything but the need she had to feel his body joined with hers.

Shayne made love to her with every part of his body. He melted her with his kisses, inflamed her with his caresses, and drove her to the edge of madness with hands that were far more skilled than any surgeon's.

He made love with her as if he were on fire. When she could still think, she wondered what had come over him, but the speed, the tempo, the mood he'd struck fed her own desire, her own passions. She forgot about the promises she'd made to herself in the wee hours of the night, when disappointment loomed large and happiness was something that seemed light-years removed.

Forgot everything but Shayne.

He was making her crazy and she knew that she had to have him, had to feel his hands on her body, his lips skimming lightly, teasingly, maddeningly over every part of her.

She was light and air, sea and sun. She was all things wondrous and pure, and he felt almost humbled with the gift she was giving him. Had he had just a little of his mind, he would have said the burden of that gift was far too great for him to bear. But those were the feelings of a thinking man, a man who'd loved and lost and sworn never to be hurt again.

He had no thoughts, only desires that gave him no peace with their demands. He had to have her, for she was his salvation. She was the light at the end of the lonely tunnel he'd been traveling in all these long, solitary years.

He wanted to tell her, wanted her to know what she meant to him, what she did for him. The words burned in his throat, on his lips, but somehow he couldn't release them. Even now, in the midst of the madness that seized him, something held him back.

So instead, he lost himself in the passion, in the throes of desire, and gave her a night that he prayed would be burned into her very soul.

Eyes on hers, he sheathed himself within her, feeling her breath on his face as she gasped his name. He laced his fingers with hers and began to move his hips slowly, then more and more intensely. He meant to watch her, meant to see her reaction as rapture came to claim them both. Meant to. But the feeling swept him up, as well.

Shayne could only hang on as it swallowed him up and took him for its own.

Chapter Fifteen

Sydney knew the moment Shayne withdrew from her. Even before he physically moved aside. Knew by the emptiness, chilling and distant, that encroached over her, seizing her in its grip.

She wanted to reach for him, to assure herself she was wrong, to banish the feeling from her that was so awful. Pride kept her still.

What was he thinking? Shayne upbraided himself. He wasn't Ben. He was supposed to keep a tight rein over his feelings, his yearnings.

Supposed to.

He rolled onto his back and stared at the ceiling. Wishing he didn't want her as much as he did. Wishing that having her didn't breed a desire to have her again and again. He knew what happened when he allowed himself to become dependent on someone.

Stoically, he stared ahead of him, resisting the desire

to slip his arm around her. To hold her and tell himself that this time, it would be different. This time, he'd found someone who would stay. How could she, when it was his brother she'd been attracted to? Ben, with his quick wit and his joy of life. Ben was all airy clouds and dreams. Shayne was the rocky ground below.

"We shouldn't have done that."

His words cut across her heart like a scalpel. "We, or you?"

He didn't want to get into an argument about it and seized the one excuse she could appreciate. "The children wouldn't understand."

She could feel tears stinging her eyes. It was small to hide behind defenseless children. "The children are asleep."

Unable to lay by her side like this and not take her into his arms, no matter what he was trying to convince himself of, Shayne sat up. The vague pain was back, distracting him, adding to his load. Frustrated, he ran his hands through his hair.

"They wake up, they go looking. You know that." He had to struggle to keep from snapping at her. Didn't she realize what he was going through? "I'm not up to explaining it to either of them."

The chill around her rivaled the cold outside. Sydney drew herself up, holding the sheet to her. "How about yourself? Are you up to explaining it to yourself?"

There was something in her tone that made him turn to look at her. "What?"

"Never mind." Angry, hurt, all she wanted to do was get out of the room and away from him before she broke down. In a frenzied daze, she picked up her clothes and quickly pulled them on. She must have been crazy, falling in love with him. He didn't even want her. ''Let me just go.''

But he wasn't about to let her charge out of the room, not without explaining her comment. ''What did you mean?'' he demanded.

He knew damn well what she meant, Sydney fumed. Why was he trying to make this seem as if it were her fault? Still hurrying into her clothes, she glared at him.

''I mean, when you're making love with me, you're one person. But as soon as the moment is over, you change. You become afraid of what you feel. Afraid that it'll blow up on you just like the last time.'' She shoved her arms through her sleeves and fastened the buttons quickly, hoping he wouldn't notice that her hands were trembling. ''Well, I have news for you. You're not alone in that lifeboat you're bobbing around in.''

If she cried now, she was never going to forgive herself. Closing the snap on her jeans, she tossed her head. ''Some of us in this relationship have the very same feelings and fears. Some of us have been cast adrift not once, but twice, and it's damn scary for us, too.''

Regret began to weave its way through his confusion. ''Sydney—''

Barefoot, holding her shoes in her hand, she was at the door. ''I'm going to my room.'' Sydney flipped the lock and opened the door. ''You stay nice and safe on your side of the world,'' she snapped as she stepped onto the hall. ''Let me know if your boat springs a leak.''

She shut the door behind her—not nearly as loud as she wanted to.

The night seemed endless. Sydney tossed and turned until she was sure she'd worn a hole in the mattress.

Sleep refused to relieve her. She wrestled with her thoughts, her feelings, for hours.

When morning arrived, leaving the sun to find its own way, Sydney had made up her mind. She couldn't take interacting with Shayne, knowing that he regretted making love with her. Maybe in time she could face him, but not right now. It hurt too much. She was going to move out. The cabin was nearly ready. They'd promised to have electricity restored by the end of the week.

As for the car, maybe it was foolish, but she wasn't going to wait for it to arrive. Ike had kiddingly told her that he'd be at her beck and call if she ever needed anything. She'd just have to take him up on that. Right after breakfast, she'd call Ike to see if he could help her move the rest of her things into the cabin. Especially the piano. If she had her piano with her, it wouldn't seem so lonely at night.

Or so she hoped.

And as for supplies, Sydney was certain she could prevail on Mr. Kellogg's son to bring them out to her. Someone would always be around to help. The rest of the citizens of Hades were a great deal friendlier toward her than Shayne was.

She intended to stop working at that clinic, too. He'd probably be a lot happier about that. There had to be something else she could do. Maybe she'd see about getting a teaching position, something she was more suited to doing. Anything so she didn't have to be near Shayne.

Boy, she thought, pulling on her boots, she could sure pick them. But this was it—really it. From now on, she was going to keep a firm lock on her heart. She wasn't going to love anything over the age of ten unless it had fur on it.

Her resolve in place, and determined to get things moving as quickly as possible, Sydney left her room. But as she passed Shayne's door, something—some tiny grain of residual affection—halted her in her tracks.

Stupid, stupid, stupid.

Calling herself names didn't seem to do any good. She couldn't get her feet to move.

So she knocked on his door, wanting to tell him she was going to be leaving. Wanting Shayne to tell her not to.

God, but she was an idiot.

There was no response to her knock. Listening at the door, she thought she heard him stirring. So now what? He was giving her the silent treatment, as well?

''Shayne?'' No response. She knocked again, harder this time. Still nothing. If she'd had any brains, she'd just walk away, Sydney told herself.

Maybe she didn't have brains, but what she did have was a great deal of hurt pride. And anger. Wanting to vent at least the latter, she abandoned all niceties and opened the door.

Shayne was sitting up in bed, his hands on either side of him, gripping the mattress. His knuckles were white and there was a sheen of perspiration on his forehead. He looked like a man trying to summon the strength to stand up.

Something was very wrong. Sydney took a step across the threshold, looking at him uncertainly. ''Shayne?''

He didn't answer. Instead, he raised his head and looked at her as if, until this moment, he hadn't realized she was in the room.

Newly formed plans crumbled instantly. Sydney crossed to the bed and looked at him more closely, almost afraid of what she'd see. There wasn't just a sheen of perspiration on his forehead, he was drenched.

Sydney dropped to her knees, feathering her hand across his forehead. It was hot. "What's the matter? Are you sick?"

Shayne shook his head, gritting his teeth. He pressed his fingers against his side, trying to press the pain away. It was the only way he could answer her. There were swords running through his side. "Just waiting for the pain to go away."

"Pain?" She looked him up and down quickly, as if pain had left a visible calling card. "What pain?" And then she noticed the way he was holding his right side. A single word came to mind. "Describe it to me."

Why couldn't she just go away and leave him in peace? Shayne groaned. He didn't need anyone badgering him right now. He hadn't the strength for it. Served him right for saying anything at all.

"I'm the doctor. I don't need to describe my pain to you."

Just because he was a doctor didn't mean he couldn't get sick. Only that he was too stubborn to admit it. Refusing to be intimidated by his attitude, she lightly pressed his side. His sharp intake of breath told her all she wanted to know.

"No, you need to admit you have appendicitis. Acute appendicitis from the looks of it."

It would pass. The pain had passed before. "I don't—"

She wasn't about to let him offer any feeble excuses or try to bully her away. Compassion mixed with her determination to help him, even if the man didn't want to be helped.

"I had it myself when I was sixteen. My cousin had

it at summer camp when she was twelve. I know the signs.'' She thought back to when they'd made love, and the way he'd winced for no apparent cause. ''This has been going on for a while now, hasn't it?''

It took effort to draw a breath. Shayne tried to think past the pain. He wasn't having a great deal of luck. ''Yes. Happy?''

She wished he was all right so she could slug him. ''What would make me happy is if you stopped being so damn stubborn and let me help you.''

He glared at her. It was hard to do when his eyelids insisted on drooping. Shayne fought to remain focused and not give in to the pain.

''Me stubborn? You're the most damn stubborn human being I've ever met.'' He tried to move her aside, but she stepped back, out of reach. Shayne found himself moving only air. ''Now if you'd give me a little privacy, I'd like to get dressed.'' A fresh wave of pain came, making gooseflesh out of the skin on his arms. He knew she noticed. There was no use in fighting this. She was right. ''All right, I'll stop being stubborn, as you put it, and fly myself to Anchorage.''

'''Anchorage'?'' she echoed.

''It's the nearest hospital—'' And he, he knew, was going to need surgery.

Before he could finish his sentence, Sydney had already gathered the clothes he'd left on the floor. She dumped them beside him on the bed. ''Stay right there, I'll dress you.''

''I—''

What he wanted to say was that he could dress himself. But he couldn't. He couldn't even argue with her about it. He was too weak and getting weaker by the minute. So he sat on the edge of the bed, feeling like a helpless child as Sydney quickly pulled a shirt over him, then coaxed his jeans over each leg.

"You can't fly that plane in your condition," she informed him tersely, her heart beating fast. Shayne looked awful, she thought. "I'm going to take you to Anchorage."

He was vaguely aware that she was pulling on his boots. "We can't drive there this time of year." The roads were impassable.

"I know." Even if they could, the trip would take too long and she wasn't sure just how long he had. She rose to her feet. "We'll go by plane."

Shayne stared at her. Was she saying what he thought she was saying? "You're going to fly?" Maybe he was hallucinating, after all.

Sydney did her best to look confident. "You're going to talk me through it."

He snorted, shaking his head. "The hell I am."

Sydney fixed him with the same look she'd give any third grader who acted up in her class.

"You have a choice. You either talk me through the flight, or talk me through your surgery, your choice. Because it's for damn sure that's not about to go away this time—" she nodded at his throbbing side "—and you're in no condition to fly on your own." Taking his arm, she helped him to his feet, then positioned herself so that she could place his arm over her shoulder. "Now lean on me so that we can get down the stairs in something under two hours."

Shayne did as she ordered. Every step hurt and felt as if he were taking it on legs that had been constructed out of gelatin. He could feel her struggling under his weight and hated the fact that he couldn't move on his own power. ''Aren't you going to carry me fireman-style?''

''Very funny.'' She got a better grip on his arm, wishing his bedroom had been downstairs. At least then she wouldn't have so far to walk. ''Next time.''

By the time they made it down the stairs, Sydney's legs were beginning to feel like rubber. She made it to the sofa, then eased him down as gently as she could.

''Stay here for a minute,'' she said, sucking air into her aching lungs. ''I've got to make a phone call''

He wanted to protest, to say he was going to fly himself and that was that. All he could do was sink onto the sofa.

Their passage hadn't gone unnoticed. Awakened by the noise, Mac and Sara had each ventured out of their rooms, curious. Mac was the first one down the stairs. He looked at his father, afraid of what he saw.

Mac turned to Sydney. ''Is Dad all right?''

Sydney glanced at the boy, hoping she looked and sounded more confident than she felt. ''He's going to be fine, honey.'' Quickly, she pressed the numbers on the telephone keypad, hoping that Ike was home and answering his phone.

Standing behind Mac, Sara began to cry. ''He's going to die, like Mama.''

Shayne reached for Sara, hardly having enough strength to stretch out his arm. She huddled against him. ''I'm not going to die, Sara.''

''Not if I have anything to say about it,'' Sydney promised all of them. She just prayed it wasn't an empty promise. And then, hearing the receiver being picked up, her attention was riveted to the man on the other end.

''Ike, it's Sydney.''

''How's Alaska's most beautiful woman?''

"Desperate." She hurried on before he could comment. "Listen carefully, Ike. I need you to come here and stay with the children." Asia wouldn't be coming until later, and Sydney had no way to reach her since the woman didn't have a phone. She needed someone here now. "I've got to get Shayne to the hospital at Anchorage." Because she saw fear in the children's eyes, she reworded what she was about to say. "I think his appendix is on the verge of going."

"Anchorage?" Ike sounded doubtful. "Is he up to flying the plane?"

She glanced at Shayne. He didn't look up to even walking. "No, I'm taking him."

"You're flying?" Ike asked, incredulous.

Sydney licked her lips. Was it too early to start praying? "I'm going to try."

"Darlin', you'd better do more than try." Ike thought a minute. "I'll call Tate and see if his son—no, damn, he said the kid was going to be gone until tomorrow." There was no one else to fly a plane. He fervently hoped her flying lessons had stuck. "I'll be right there."

She looked at Shayne. They were going to need every minute they could find. "I've got to leave with him now, Ike. Hurry. The kids are going to be alone until you get here."

"Already gone— And Sydney..."

She'd almost hung up. Quickly, she pressed the receiver to her ear again. "Yes?"

"Good luck."

She laughed, but there was no humor in the sound. "Thanks." She knew she was going to need it. By the bucketful.

Shayne was beginning to feel strange, light-headed. As if he were winking in and out of his head. How could he talk her through anything? ''Sydney, we could get a dogsled—''

She could just picture that. Sydney hurried to get their parkas. ''Right, and when the snow melts in the spring, they can find us huddled together.'' Quickly, carefully, she slipped his parka on Shayne, then shrugged into her own. ''Flying's our only option.'' She gave him the best confident grin she could muster. ''What's the matter, don't you trust yourself as a teacher?''

His teaching abilities had nothing to do with it. ''You've never gone up.''

And wasn't she acutely aware of that? Sydney shrugged cavalierly.

''Always a first time.'' She just prayed it wouldn't be her last. She was already at the front door. Her heart ached at the expression on the children's face. ''I'll taxi the plane as close to the house as I can, then come and get you.''

Adrenaline double-timing through every part of her body, she hurried out.

Somehow, with Mac doing his best to help, Sydney managed to get a much weakened Shayne into the cockpit. Hands trembling from the strain, she quickly secured his seat belt, then turned to look at the worried faces of the two children clustered around her.

Time was precious, but she shaved a little off to kneel between them. She placed a hand on either of their shoulders, making them a promise she knew they needed to hear.

''I'm not going to let anything happen to him, you hear? Nothing. Ike's coming to take care of you and I'll call as soon as I can. Mac, I want you to take your sister inside and take care of her until Ike gets here. Okay?''

He nodded, placing one arm around Sara's small shoulders. And then he looked at her with Shayne's eyes. "You promise you won't let anything happen to him?"

"I promise." She hugged them both quickly, then rose to her feet. It was all the time she could spare.

Sydney felt drenched as she climbed into the plane. Helping Shayne up to and then into the plane had been harder than she'd thought.

He turned his head and looked at her. She saw the uncertainty in his eyes.

"Don't worry, I'll get you there in one piece." She secured the door, trying not to shiver. Her clothes were sticking to her back. "And when you're on your feet again, you can treat me for pneumonia."

Lips dry as dust, Shayne struggled to hold on to consciousness. "Sydney—"

She didn't want him wasting his breath. "Save your strength. I'm going to need you to talk me through the rough patches."

Heart in her mouth, she turned the key, pumped gasoline through the lines, then pressed the button to engage the ignition. The engine came to life. As she began the short run to take off, Sydney could feel every pulse in her body throbbing.

Sometimes fear was a good thing, she told herself. Sometimes, it kept you alert.

Everything within her galvanized, Sydney concentrated on the controls, trying to remember everything Shayne had taught her.

The pain was getting unmanageable. Like some huge alien creature, it was sucking away his thoughts, leaving a void. It took him a moment, or maybe longer, to realize that there was nothing but sky around them. Perfect blue sky.

''We're airborne.''

He sounded as surprised as she felt. First part down, lots more to go, she told herself, trying to hang on to the confidence the takeoff had generated.

She let out the breath she'd been holding. ''Yes, and without our own personal set of wings, too.'' And, with just a little luck, she could keep it that way.

Smiling, she looked to her right. ''How are you doing?'' Not well, she could see that. Fear reared its head again, larger than before. She had to reach the hospital in time. She *had* to. ''Are you all right, Shayne?''

He struggled to stay conscious. ''As all right as I can be.'' Each word was an effort, but there were some he had to say. ''Sydney, if anything happens to me—''

She didn't want to go there. ''Nothing's going to happen.'' She was aware that the words strained through her teeth. ''You hear me? You're going to be fine. I can land this thing.''

Right, God? I can do this. Please, I'll never ask You for anything else again, just let me land this thing safely.

Shayne wasn't thinking about the landing. He knew she could do it, through sheer grit. But patients out here died before they received medical attention and he knew that he had waited too long.

''But if it does,'' he persisted. ''I want you to take care of Sara and Mac.''

''Don't worry about it.'' She didn't want him dwelling on the negative. He was going to be fine, just fine. She wasn't going to let him die. And then, because he needed to hear her promise, she said, ''I will.''

Shayne knew he could count on her. It was going to be all right. He could let go if he knew Sydney would be there for them. He should have put up more of a fight to have them in his life. And less of a fight to push Sydney out of it.

''And Sydney...''

''What?'' She realized she'd snapped the word. Her hands were rigid on the wheel. ''Sorry, just a little edgy. What do you want to tell me?''

''I love you.''

Only extreme concentration kept Sydney from dipping the plane. ''You really have to work on your timing, Shayne.'' He was delirious, she thought. He probably wouldn't even remember saying that to her once this was over. ''Hang on, we're almost there.'' When he didn't say anything, she glanced at him. He was slumped in his seat, his eyes shut. Her heart stopped. ''Shayne? Oh, God.'' Flipping on the autopilot switch, she felt his chest. It was moving. He was alive.

Sydney reclaimed control of the plane, then fumbled for the radio. ''Anchorage, I'm a small Cessna heading your way and I have a very big problem. Do you read me?''

After what felt like an eternity, she heard a crackling noise.

''Cessna, this is Anchorage. We read you loud and clear. What's your problem?''

The sound of another voice, a calm, competent resonant male voice, almost made her cry.

''I'm flying Dr. Shayne Kerrigan to the hospital. He has acute appendicitis and he's just passed out.'' It was going to be all right, she told herself. It was. Never mind that her whole body felt as if a squadron of ants was moving up and down it. ''And, Anchorage... I've never flown before. Talk me down, please.''

''Cessna, this is going to be smooth as silk,'' the voice promised.

She blinked back tears. ''I'm going to hold you to that.''

Her bones only turned to liquid afterward, as she stood in the hospital waiting area after what seemed like a thousand years later. The landing had been bumpy, but they'd made it. There was a medical helicopter waiting for them and she and Shayne had been whisked off to the hospital. She'd held Shayne's hand all the way there. He'd never regained consciousness.

She'd lived in terror for the entire two hours that the surgery had taken. Twice as long, she knew, as it should have. But that was because, she was told later, Shayne's appendix had burst on the operating table, making the surgery that much more complicated.

She'd kissed the surgeon when he'd come out of the operating room to tell her that Shayne was going to be all right.

Now, feeling oddly disembodied, she hit the numbers to Shayne's home. The phone was picked up on the first ring. She heard Ike's voice.

''Hello, Ike? It's Sydney.''

''Thank God. You made it then.'' He didn't begin to tell her the thoughts that had been going through his head as he'd tried to distract Shayne's children from the drama happening beyond their reach.

''No, they've installed phones in heaven.'' She laughed giddily, so grateful the ordeal was over. So grateful she'd made it just in time. ''Yes, we made it. They just finished operating on him. Doctor says he's going to be all right.'' She'd never let herself believe anything else. But now that it was over, now that she had said the words out loud, she realized how terrified she'd been. "Give me the kids, will you? Hold the receiver between them."

"Sure thing. They're right here, tugging on me."

She heard the sound of the receiver being moved. The next thing she knew, she heard both children shouting her name.

"Sydney, is he...?" Mac's voice trailed off.

"You dad's going to be fine, Mac. The doctor just came out and told me so."

"When can Daddy come home?" Sara wanted to know.

"In about three or four days." Sooner if he had anything to say about it, if she knew him. "I'll be home as soon as I can and tell you all about it."

She heard the receiver being transferred again and then Ike was on the line. "Hey, Earhart, why don't you stay there awhile until you're in shape to fly again? I can take care of the kids."

She wanted to get back, to reassure the children in person. Shayne would be asleep for most of the rest of the day. "I'm fine, Ike."

"You bet you are." He laughed.

As if she were handling something very fragile, Sydney carefully replaced the telephone receiver into its cradle. Then, with her back against the wall, she slid bonelessly to the floor and covered her face with both hands as relief flooded through her.

He was going to be all right.

Chapter Sixteen

Stepping away from the small Twin Otter, Sydney waved at Jeb Kellogg as he initiated takeoff. He'd just refused her invitation to come in for a cup of coffee and some pie. There was a load of fresh produce and dairy products waiting to be delivered to his father's store. The round trip to Anchorage to pick Shayne up from the hospital had taken longer than they had anticipated.

But that was because Shayne's doctor hadn't really wanted to release him. He'd wanted Shayne to remain one more day. Shayne had been very vocal about his thoughts on that matter.

Sydney had thought he should remain, too. But her opinion obviously counted for less than the doctor's, if Shayne's tone was any indication. Still, she wished he'd given in and agreed to stay the extra day. He looked thinner. It was the first thing that she really noticed coming into the hospital this morning, that he was thinner.

Not thin, just thinner. Four days had made a difference and he'd been through a lot, including peritonitis.

Shayne had waved it off, claiming the hospital food was responsible for his weight loss.

Knowing she wouldn't get anywhere arguing with him, Sydney had dropped the subject.

"C'mon, let's get you inside," Ike said, slinging Shayne's arm over his shoulder. They were almost the same height. The arrangement made for awkward progress at best.

Thinner or not, it was wonderful to see Shayne again, Sydney thought. She'd stayed away those four days, calling the hospital to see how he was doing. Sydney figured he needed the time away from her, and besides, she had Sara and Mac to care for, and the clinic to run. She'd rescheduled the patients with minor problems and rerouted the ones needing immediate attention to Anchorage. Jeb Kellogg had flown them there and back.

Leading the way into the house, Sydney looked over her shoulder at Shayne. "The nurses told me you were the worst patient they'd had in quite a while."

"Sounds about right," Ike agreed.

Shayne couldn't argue with the evaluation. "Occupational habit when you're a doctor. You don't like having anyone around, telling you they know what's best for you."

And that would be her, she thought. He was giving her a not-so-subtle message about their relationship. "So let me get this straight, that's why you became a doctor, to fit your personality? Because you wouldn't have liked anyone telling you they knew better than you even if you were a kayak salesman?"

God, but it was good to see her. All the way over from Anchorage, all Shayne could do was look at her. And realize over and over again how much he'd missed seeing her. "You could be right."

Sydney's hands flew to her chest, covering one another. "Wait, my heart. I don't think I can stand the strain of the all-knowing Shayne Kerrigan admitting someone else was right besides him."

She hadn't changed any. His mouth curved. "You saved my life, I'll let that pass."

Sydney turned from the front door. "I saved your life and you'll let a lot of things pass."

He exchanged looks with Ike. "Why do I get the feeling she'll hold me to that?"

"Because I will," she answered simply. Before opening the door, she stopped. He could do with a bit of coaching. "Now there are two small children in there who have lived in terror of your not coming back. I want you to give them the biggest, most reassuring grin you can muster."

Ike laughed. "Hell, then they won't know it's Shayne."

Shayne was growing impatient as well as weary. He hated feeling weak, it left him far too vulnerable. "You don't have to tell me how to behave with my kids."

She wasn't about to back down, not when it came to Sara and Mac. They were too impressionable. "Someone has to. Might as well be me. Ready?"

The sigh was more of a huff. "Just open the door, Sydney."

"Do as he says, darlin'," Ike begged. "This man's no featherweight."

The moment she opened the front door, Sara and Mac poured out onto the porch as if they'd been hovering behind the door all afternoon. Between them, they almost managed to knock Shayne down. If Ike hadn't been supporting him, they probably would have.

Sara buried her face in the bottom of his parka, her small arms unable to reach around him for the bear hug she so desperately wanted to give him. ''Daddy, you're back.''

He laid his hand on her head, stroking it. ''I said I would be.''

She raised her head to look up at him. ''We thought...''

He knew what she thought. What he'd thought, too. There was no purpose in going there. ''Never mind that now, I'm all right.''

Mac grinned, looking at Sydney. ''Just like Sydney said.''

''Yes, just like Sydney said,'' Shayne agreed.

''And now Sydney says, everybody get inside before you all get sick.'' Sydney shooed them all into the house. ''I'm not about to play Nancy Nurse to the lot of you.''

With a child on either side of him, Shayne entered the house he'd lived in all of his life. And thought how wonderful it was to be home again.

Sydney'd been busy in his absence, he noted. There was what looked to be at least a nine-foot tree standing in the corner, decked out in decorations he didn't recognize.

''See you put up a tree.''

She couldn't tell by his tone if he was annoyed at her presumption. That much hadn't changed about him, he still left her guessing. ''Had to do something to keep them occupied.''

Sara ran over to the sofa and hurried back with a small, rectangular box. Silver streamers protruded out of an opening, catching the light and gleaming. Sara offered the box to her father. ''We saved the tinsel for you.''

Sydney laid a restraining had on Sara's shoulder. ''Your dad's not up to throwing tinsel yet, Sara. Maybe tomorrow.''

But Shayne wanted to join in, to experience everything as if he'd been given a second chance to make up for all his shortcomings and all the time he'd lost.

"Sure I am." Gingerly, he picked several strands from the box and pitched them toward the tree. They fell almost a foot short.

"And that, ladies and gentlemen," Sydney murmured glibly, "is one of the main reasons why Alaska has no official baseball team. No local talent."

Mac quickly scrambled to pick up the strands, glossing over his father's failure.

"That's okay, Dad, you can do this later." He deposited the tinsel on the coffee table. "Christmas is still a couple of days off."

Christmas. The word finally sank in. Christmas was almost here and he had nothing to give either of them. He'd put off shopping and now it was too late.

"Might be longer than that," Shayne commented under his breath. How did he go about telling them that he didn't have anything for them? What kind of a father did that make him?

"Don't bet the clinic on it," Ike whispered in his ear. Shayne looked at him quizzically. Ike nodded toward Sydney who was hurrying up the stairs to get Shayne's bed ready. "She took care of things for you in that department." He should know. He helped her carry the things she'd bought at the general store to the four-by-four. Ike looked at Shayne significantly. "I'd say she takes damn good care of you in every department." And then he shrugged carelessly. "But then, that'd be just me talking."

"Something you do an awful lot of," Shayne agreed.

He owed her a great deal, Shayne thought. More, he was beginning to believe, than he could ever hope to pay back.

Ike shifted, getting a better grip around Shayne's

waist. He turned toward the stairs. ''And I'm going to do just a mite more talking while I get you up to your room. I don't have to tell you competition's stiff around here. You don't start acting like the smart man you are,'' he warned Shayne, ''one fine day you're going to find yourself real empty-handed.''

Shayne already knew that, but he'd just endured four days of poking and prodding. Not in the best of humors, he bristled at Ike's presumption. ''Is that supposed to mean something to me?''

Ike stopped at the landing, getting a second wind. He turned toward Shayne's room.

''Yeah, it is.'' A few more steps and Ike deposited Shayne onto the bed. He'd had lighter loads to maneuver. ''Okay, patient's all yours, darlin'. Not much to look at, but hell, we knew that already, didn't we?'' He grinned, backing out of the room. ''See you two around.''

Sydney walked him just to the doorway. ''Thanks for everything, Ike.'' And then she turned her attention to Shayne. He looked exhausted. Probably bite her head off if she mentioned it, though. ''Anything I can get you?''

When he shook his head, it didn't surprise her. ''No, you've already done plenty.''

Sydney laughed softly to herself. ''Well, that much hasn't changed. I still don't know if what you're saying is a compliment or a criticism.''

''It's neither. It's gratitude.''

Her surprise melted into something softer. ''That would explain why I didn't recognize it. You've never offered it before.''

There was so much he wanted to say to her, if he could only find the words. ''Maybe I should have.''

She smiled, seeing more in his eyes than she'd ever seen before. ''Don't strain yourself your first time out.''

Her smile widened. "I wouldn't want to have to fly you back to the hospital."

"I wouldn't want to have to go."

Again, she wasn't sure what he meant. Only what she wanted him to mean. "There's that quandary again." She moved toward the doorway. "I'll let you get some rest."

She was almost gone when she heard him call her name. "Sydney?"

Sydney ducked back inside the room. "Yes?"

"The tree looks nice."

She knew what it took for him to give out an actual compliment. Something a little shy of an act of Congress. She restrained the desire to fly back to his side and throw her arms around him. There was no way she could express how relieved she was that he was here, that he was alive.

"It'll look nicer with tinsel. Get your pitching arm in shape." And with that, she eased the door closed.

Shayne couldn't remember the last time Christmas had meant squeals, flying paper and joyous noise. Somewhere back in the early years of his childhood, probably. He sat on the sofa, absorbing it all. Thinking how much he enjoyed being in the center of this kind of chaos.

And he had Sidney to thank for it.

He had her to thank for a lot of things. Without Sydney, most of this wouldn't have happened. Hell, he probably wouldn't have been here to enjoy it, either. She'd given him back his life in more than one way.

"Wow, it's just what I wanted!" Mac cried. All smiles, he looked at Shayne as he clutched a box that contained the latest model of an electronic game system to his chest. "How did you know?"

There was a very simple explanation. He hadn't known. Hadn't been responsible for any of the myriad gifts that were scattered about, playing hide-and-seek with wrapping paper on his living room floor. It had all been Sydney's doing.

"Dads always know these kinds of things," Sydney told Mac, coming to Shayne's rescue.

She was always coming to his rescue, he thought, one way or another. She had from the very first.

"I just love my kitty," Sara said for the umpteenth time as she rubbed her face along the soft calico-colored fur.

"Be gentle with her," Sydney cautioned. "She's still a baby."

"I will," Sara promised solemnly.

Gingerly, Shayne stepped around the clutter to get to Sydney. It'd been two days since he'd come home and he was still feeling a little wobbly, but a great deal better than he had when he'd first walked through the door.

"Sydney, about what I said in the plane when you were taking me to the hospital..."

Wading through the sea of paper, she began picking it up. "You mean, when you asked me to take care of Sara and Mac if something—"

"No, after that."

Sydney turned away, picking up another flurry of paper, flattening it against the first pile. "You said something after that?"

With determination, he took the torn wrapping paper from her hands. She knew damn well he'd said something, something that desperation had prompted him to say. Something he meant. "I said I love you."

She looked at him, wondering what it was he wanted from her now. He'd already taken her heart and then walked over it. Wasn't that enough? What was this latest salvo he wanted to fire at her?

"You remember that?"

"Yes," he said quietly. This wasn't easy for him, but he owed it to her. Owed it to both of them.

She took a deep breath, shrugging off the feeling that was edging over her. "That's okay, I never hold a man to what he says just before he passes out. There's something in the Geneva convention about taking unfair advantage—"

Shayne knew what she was doing. She was throwing up a smoke screen. He wasn't about to let her. "What if the man wants to be held to it?" That, he saw, got her.

Sydney's mouth dropped open. "What?"

Before he could say anything more, Sara was tugging on her arm, pointing toward the tree behind her. "Sydney, there's a present for you."

She'd already opened up two boxes with handmade gifts from each of the children, gifts that warmed her heart. There'd even been a gift from Asia, gloves that the woman had made herself. There hadn't been one from Shayne, but then, realistically, she hadn't expected a gift. It was unrealistic that she'd cherished a tiny hope. Even she knew how foolish that was.

Sydney shook her head. Sara had to be mistaken. "I've already got my presents."

"No, there's one more," Mac insisted. "That little one right there." Both children were pointing toward the tree. Not under it but at the heart of it.

Confused, playing along, Sydney approached the Christmas tree. She didn't notice that Shayne was holding his breath, watching her every move.

And then she saw it. In the center of the profusely decorated Christmas tree was a tiny box suspended from a branch by a tiny, silver ribbon.

She could have sworn it wasn't there before.

Feeling suddenly very nervous, she plucked the box

from its perch. She took a deep breath. ''Are you sure it's for me?''

Mac stood on his toes and looked over her arm. But he already knew what he was going to see. His dad had shown him the box before he'd hung it. Sharing the secret made him feel very important.

''Got your name on it,'' Mac told her.

She looked at it, then glanced up at Shayne. She would have known that handwriting anywhere. ''So it does.''

Damn, thought Shayne, even his palms felt sweaty. She did everything fast, why had she suddenly slowed her pace to that of frozen molasses? She was putting him through hell.

''You going to stand there with it all day, or are you going to open it?''

What she was doing was trying to quell her nervousness. ''I like savoring things.''

Then, as she began to slip off the ribbon, he suddenly looked at Sara and Mac. He needed this time alone with Sydney. Just in case.

''Kids, why don't you see if Asia has breakfast ready yet?''

''Okay.'' Sara, a miniature woman in the making, took Mac's hand and pulled him along behind her.

When Shayne looked back at Sydney, she was still holding the box in her hand. It was unopened.

Shayne took a breath. ''Open it.'' Nerves danced all through him. He'd barely gotten the gift in time. He'd had to rely on Ike to select it and bring it to him. The complications had felt as if they were endless.

They'd all be worth it if she smiled.

Sydney could feel her hands shaking. They'd been steadier when she'd flown the plane to Anchorage. For some ridiculous reason, she was afraid that when she opened the gift, there wouldn't be anything there.

But there was. There was a black velvet box inside the paper. And ring inside of the box. A ring with a perfect small diamond mounted in the center of it.

Afraid to think, to let herself feel, she raised her eyes to his. ‘‘Shayne?’’

He couldn’t read her expression. Something twisted inside him. If she didn’t want it, he didn’t know what he was going to do.

Yes, he did. If he had to, he was going to beg her. This one time in his life, he’d humble himself and beg her to marry him. To stay in his life. Because he knew that life without her wasn’t life at all.

‘‘It’s an engagement ring.’’

She wanted to laugh. She wanted to cry. ‘‘I know what it is. Why are you giving it to me?’’

Was she rejecting him, after all? He took her hand. ‘‘Why do you think?’’

That was just it, she couldn’t think. Was afraid to think. ‘‘If this has anything to do with what you said to me in the plane, you don’t have to feel obligated, Shayne. I—’’

She was babbling. He placed a fingertip to her lips and stopped her words. ‘‘For once, will you please just let me talk?’’

She pressed her lips together. ‘‘Sorry.’’

He hadn’t meant to make that sound like an admonishment. This wasn’t starting out right, he thought in frustration. Not knowing what else to do, he pushed on.

‘‘I had a lot of time to think, lying awake in that hospital bed, listening to the intercom go off every few minutes.’’ He was digressing. Because he was afraid of the outcome. ‘‘Time to think about how you were always coming to my rescue. I don’t mean the plane flight—although I’d probably be dead by now if you hadn’t gotten me there in time. I mean, in my life. Taking down the wall between Sara, Mac and me. Making me realize that I was only half a man if I couldn't feel things.'' Without realizing it, he took hold of her shoulders to wage the argument of his life. ''You made me feel again, Sydney. You made me whole. Now make me happy, and say yes.''

She was afraid to breathe, afraid that if she did, she'd wake up and find that all this was just a lovely dream. ''You mean that?''

''I've never meant anything more in my life,'' Shayne swore.

Very slowly, she began to breathe. ''And you're not going to disappear?''

''Where would I go?'' He slipped his arms around her. ''Everything I love is right here, in this house, in this room. In my arms.''

Love. The word was so very precious to her. ''You love me?''

''I love you.'' Once the words were out, he couldn't help wondering why they had been so hard to say. They seemed so easy now. ''I've been afraid to say it, afraid to think it, but I do, Sydney. I really do, and I'll make you a good husband, I promise. If I don't, you can take me on another plane ride.'' He grinned, kissing her temple. ''One I'll stay conscious for.''

Her maiden run had been a bumpy one, but they had walked away alive and that was all that counted. ''It's a deal.''

Mouth stained with the remnants of the jelly doughnuts Sydney had stayed up late to make for them, Mac came running back into the room.

''What's a deal?'' he asked around a mouthful of jelly.

Shayne looked down at his son's face. How did one man deserve to have this much happiness? ''You're getting a new mom.''

Confused, Mac frowned. "I don't want a new mom. I want Sydney."

The boy had good taste, Shayne thought. "You're in luck. Two birds with one stone."

Sara came running into the room, chasing her new kitten. Catching it, she stared at her father. "We're getting a bird?" In her excitement, she squeezed the kitten, who mewed a protest and wriggled in her arms.

"No, I think Taffy would have something to say about that." Shayne scratched the kitten's head. "But you are getting a new mom."

Sara took the news in stride. "Can I pick her out?" She didn't wait for an answer. "Because if I can, I pick Sydney."

Apparently his kids were way ahead of him here. "Then I guess it's unanimous."

Sara scowled, trying to understand the new word. "What's u-nanny-mouse?"

"It means that we're all going to be happy." Shayne looked at Sydney. "Right?"

Sydney put her arms around his neck. "You bet 'right.'"

"Are you two going to kiss now, or do you need mistletoe?" Mac looked around the room, just in case.

"We don't need excuses anymore." Sydney smiled up into Shayne's face. "Do we?"

"Nope."

And to prove it, he kissed her.

* * * * *

Look out for Marie Ferrarella's next book in February—Lily and the Lawman.

GEN/38/RTL4V2

MATTERS
OF THE
HEART
ANN MAJOR
ANNETTE BROADRICK
PAMELA MORSI
It's more than a race to the altar in this Mother's Day Collection of three brand-new stories
SILHOUETTE®